Hewitt & Dorrington
Private Detectives

Hewitt & Dorrington Private Detectives

The Complete Casebooks

Arthur Morrison

LEONAUR

Hewitt & Dorrington
Private Detectives
The Complete Casebooks
by Arthur Morrison

FIRST EDITION

Leonaur is an imprint
of Oakpast Ltd

ISBN: 978-1-78282-541-8 (hardcover)
ISBN: 978-1-78282-542-5 (softcover)

http://www.leonaur.com

Contents

MARTIN HEWITT.

The Martin Hewitt Cases

The Lenton Croft Robberies

Those who retain any memory of the great law cases of fifteen or twenty years back will remember, at least, the title of that extraordinary will case, "Bartley *v.* Bartley and others," which occupied the Probate Court for some weeks on end, and caused an amount of public interest rarely accorded to any but the cases considered in the other division of the same court. The case itself was noted for the large quantity of remarkable and unusual evidence presented by the plaintiff's side—evidence that took the other party completely by surprise, and overthrew their case like a house of cards.

The affair will, perhaps, be more readily recalled as the occasion of the sudden rise to eminence in their profession of Messrs. Crellan, Hunt & Crellan, solicitors for the plaintiff—a result due entirely to the wonderful ability shown in this case of building up, apparently out of nothing, a smashing weight of irresistible evidence. That the firm has since maintained—indeed enhanced—the position it then won for itself need scarcely be said here; its name is familiar to everybody. But there are not many of the outside public who know that the credit of the whole performance was primarily due to a young clerk in the employ of Messrs. Crellan, who had been given charge of the seemingly desperate task of collecting evidence in the case.

This Mr. Martin Hewitt had, however, full credit and reward for his exploit from his firm and from their client, and more than one other firm of lawyers engaged in contentious work made good offers to entice Hewitt to change his employers. Instead of this, however, he determined to work independently for the future, having conceived the idea of making a regular business of doing, on behalf of such clients as might retain him, similar work to that he had just done with such conspicuous success for Messrs. Crellan, Hunt & Crellan. This was the beginning of the private detective business of Martin Hewitt, and his action at that time has been completely justified by the brilliant professional successes he has since achieved.

His business has always been conducted in the most private manner, and he has always declined the help of professional assistants, preferring to carry out himself such of the many investigations offered him as he could manage. He has always maintained that he has never lost by this policy, since the chance of his refusing a case begets competition for his services, and his fees rise by a natural process. At the same time, no man could know better how to employ casual assistance at the right time.

Some curiosity has been expressed as to Mr. Martin Hewitt's system, and, as he himself always consistently maintains that he has no system beyond a judicious use of ordinary faculties, I intend setting forth in detail a few of the more interesting of his cases in order that the public may judge for itself if I am right in estimating Mr. Hewitt's "ordinary faculties" as faculties very extraordinary indeed. He is not a man who has made many friendships (this, probably, for professional reasons), notwithstanding his genial and companionable manners. I myself first made his acquaintance as a result of an accident resulting in a fire at the old house in which Hewitt's office was situated, and in an upper floor of which I occupied bachelor chambers. I was able to help in saving a quantity of extremely important papers relating to his business, and, while repairs were being made, allowed him to lock them in an old wall-safe in one of my rooms which the fire had scarcely damaged.

The acquaintance thus begun has lasted many years, and has become a rather close friendship. I have even accompanied Hewitt on some of his expeditions, and, in a humble way, helped him. Such of the cases, however, as I personally saw nothing of I have put into narrative form from the particulars given me.

"I consider you, Brett," he said, addressing me, "the most remarkable journalist alive. Not because you're particularly clever, you know, because, between ourselves, I hope you'll admit you're not; but because you have known something of me and my doings for some years, and have never yet been guilty of giving away any of my little business secrets you may have become acquainted with. I'm afraid you're not so enterprising a journalist as some, Brett. But now, since you ask, you shall write something—if you think it worthwhile."

This he said, as he said most things, with a cheery, chaffing good-nature that would have been, perhaps, surprising to a stranger who thought of him only as a grim and mysterious discoverer of secrets and crimes. Indeed, the man had always as little of the aspect of the conventional detective as may be imagined. Nobody could appear more cordial or less observant in manner, although there was to be seen a certain sharpness of the eye—which might, after all, only be the twinkle of good humour.

I *did* think it worthwhile to write something of Martin Hewitt's investigations, and a description of one of his adventures follows.

★★★★★★

At the head of the first flight of a dingy staircase leading up from an ever-open portal in a street by the Strand stood a door, the dusty ground-glass upper panel of which carried in its centre the single word "Hewitt," while at its right-hand lower corner, in smaller letters, "Clerk's Office" appeared. On a morning when the clerks in the ground-floor offices had barely hung up their hats, a short, well-dressed young man, wearing spectacles, hastening to open the dusty door, ran into the arms of another man who suddenly issued from it.

"I beg pardon," the first said. "Is this Hewitt's Detective Agency Office?"

"Yes, I believe you will find it so," the other replied. He was a stoutish, clean-shaven man, of middle height, and of a cheerful, round countenance. "You'd better speak to the clerk."

In the little outer office, the visitor was met by a sharp lad with inky fingers, who presented him with a pen and a printed slip. The printed slip having been filled with the visitor's name and present business, and conveyed through an inner door, the lad reappeared with an invitation to the private office. There, behind a writing-table, sat the stoutish man himself, who had only just advised an appeal to the clerk.

"Good-morning, Mr. Lloyd—Mr. Vernon Lloyd," he said, affably, looking again at the slip. "You'll excuse my care to start even with my visitors—I must, you know. You come from Sir James Norris, I see."

"Yes; I am his secretary. I have only to ask you to go straight to Lenton Croft at once, if you can, on very important business. Sir James would have wired, but had not your precise address. Can you go by the next train? Eleven-thirty is the first available from Paddington."

"Quite possibly. Do you know anything of the business?"

"It is a case of a robbery in the house, or, rather, I fancy, of several robberies. Jewellery has been stolen from rooms occupied by visitors to the Croft. The first case occurred some months ago—nearly a year ago, in fact. Last night there was another. But I think you had better get the details on the spot. Sir James has told me to telegraph if you are coming, so that he may meet you himself at the station; and I must hurry, as his drive to the station will be rather a long one. Then I take it you will go, Mr. Hewitt? Twyford is the station."

"Yes, I shall come, and by the 11.30. Are you going by that train yourself?"

"No, I have several things to attend to now I am in town. Good-morning; I shall wire at once."

Mr. Martin Hewitt locked the drawer of his table and sent his clerk for a cab.

At Twyford Station Sir James Norris was waiting with a dog-cart. Sir James was a tall, florid man of fifty or thereabout, known away from home as something of a county historian, and nearer his own parts as a great supporter of the hunt, and a gentleman much troubled with poachers. As soon as he and Hewitt had found one another the baronet hurried the detective into his dog-cart. "We've something over seven miles to drive," he said, "and I can tell you all about this wretched business as we go. That is why I came for you myself, and alone."

Hewitt nodded.

"I have sent for you, as Lloyd probably told you, because of a rob-bery at my place last evening. It appears, as far as I can guess, to be one of three by the same hand, or by the same gang. Late yesterday afternoon——"

"Pardon me, Sir James," Hewitt interrupted, "but I think I must ask you to begin at the first robbery and tell me the whole tale in proper order. It makes things clearer, and sets them in their proper shape."

"Very well! Eleven months ago, or thereabout, I had rather a large party of visitors, and among them Colonel Heath and Mrs. Heath—the lady being a relative of my own late wife. Colonel Heath has not been long retired, you know—used to be political resident in an In-dian native state. Mrs. Heath had rather a good stock of jewellery of one sort and another, about the most valuable piece being a bracelet set with a particularly fine pearl—quite an exceptional pearl, in fact—that had been one of a heap of presents from the *maharajah* of his state when Heath left India.

"It was a very noticeable bracelet, the gold setting being a mere feather-weight piece of native filigree work—almost too fragile to trust on the wrist—and the pearl being, as I have said, of a size and

10

quality not often seen. Well, Heath and his wife arrived late one evening, and after lunch the following day, most of the men being off by themselves—shooting, I think—my daughter, my sister (who is very often down here), and Mrs. Heath took it into their heads to go walking—fern-hunting, and so on. My sister was rather long dressing, and, while they waited, my daughter went into Mrs. Heath's room, where Mrs. Heath turned over all her treasures to show her, as women do, you know. When my sister was at last ready, they came straight away, leaving the things littering about the room rather than stay longer to pack them up. The bracelet, with other things, was on the dressing-table then."

"One moment. As to the door?"

"They locked it. As they came away my daughter suggested turning the key, as we had one or two new servants about."

"And the window?"

"That they left open, as I was going to tell you. Well, they went on their walk and came back, with Lloyd (whom they had met somewhere) carrying their ferns for them. It was dusk and almost dinnertime. Mrs. Heath went straight to her room, and—the bracelet was gone."

"Was the room disturbed?"

"Not a bit. Everything was precisely where it had been left, except the bracelet. The door hadn't been tampered with, but of course the window was open, as I have told you."

"You called the police, of course?"

"Yes, and had a man from Scotland Yard down in the morning. He seemed a pretty smart fellow, and the first thing he noticed on the dressing-table, within an inch or two of where the bracelet had been, was a match, which had been lit and thrown down. Now nobody about the house had had occasion to use a match in that room that day, and, if they had, certainly wouldn't have thrown it on the cover of the dressing-table. So that, presuming the thief to have used that match, the robbery must have been committed when the room was getting dark—immediately before Mrs. Heath returned, in fact. The thief had evidently struck the match, passed it hurriedly over the various trinkets lying about, and taken the most valuable."

"Nothing else was even moved?"

"Nothing at all. Then the thief must have escaped by the window, although it was not quite clear how. The walking party approached the house with a full view of the window, but saw nothing, although the robbery must have been actually taking place a moment or two before they turned up.

"There was no water-pipe within any practicable distance of the window, but a ladder usually kept in the stable-yard was found lying along the edge of the lawn. The gardener explained, however, that he had put the ladder there after using it himself early in the afternoon."

"Of course it might easily have been used again after that and put back."

"Just what the Scotland Yard man said. He was pretty sharp, too, on the gardener, but very soon decided that he knew nothing of it. No stranger had been seen in the neighbourhood, nor had passed the lodge gates. Besides, as the detective said, it scarcely seemed the work of a stranger. A stranger could scarcely have known enough to go straight to the room where a lady—only arrived the day before—had left a valuable jewel, and away again without being seen. So all the people about the house were suspected in turn. The servants offered, in a body, to have their boxes searched, and this was done; everything was turned over, from the butler's to the new kitchen-maid's. I don't know that I should have had this carried quite so far if I had been the loser myself, but it was my guest, and I was in such a horrible position. Well, there's little more to be said about that, unfortunately. Nothing came of it all, and the thing's as great a mystery now as ever. I believe the Scotland Yard man got as far as suspecting *me* before he gave it up altogether, but give it up he did in the end. I think that's all I know about the first robbery. Is it clear?"

"Oh, yes; I shall probably want to ask a few questions when I have seen the place, but they can wait. What next?"

"Well," Sir James pursued, "the next was a very trumpery affair, that I should have forgotten all about, probably, if it hadn't been for one circumstance. Even now I hardly think it could have been the work of the same hand. Four months or thereabout after Mrs. Heath's disaster—in February of this year, in fact—Mrs. Armitage, a young widow, who had been a school-fellow of my daughter's, stayed with us for a week or so. The girls don't trouble about the London season, you know, and I have no town house, so they were glad to have their old friend here for a little in the dull time. Mrs. Armitage is a very active young lady, and was scarcely in the house half an hour before she arranged a drive in a pony-cart with Eva—my daughter—to look up old people in the village that she used to know before she was married. So they set off in the afternoon, and made such a round of it that they were late for dinner. Mrs. Armitage had a small plain gold brooch—not at all valuable, you know; two or three pounds, I suppose—which she used to pin up a cloak or anything of that sort. Before she went out she stuck this in the pin-cushion on her dressing-table, and left a ring—rather a good one, I believe—lying close by."

"This," asked Hewitt, "was not in the room that Mrs. Heath had occupied, I take it?"

"No; this was in another part of the building. Well, the brooch went—taken, evidently, by someone in a deuce of a hurry, for, when Mrs. Armitage got back to her room, there was the pin-cushion with a little tear in it, where the brooch had been simply snatched off. But the curious thing was that the ring—worth a dozen of the brooch—was left where it had been put. Mrs. Armitage didn't remember whether or not she had locked the door herself, although she found it locked when she returned; but my niece, who was indoors all the time, went and tried it once—because she remembered that a gas-fitter was at work on the landing nearby—and found it safely locked. The gas-fitter, whom we didn't know at the time, but who since seems to be quite an honest fellow, was ready to swear that nobody but my niece had been to the door while he was in sight of it—which was almost all the time. As to the window, the sash-line had broken that very morning, and Mrs. Armitage had propped open the bottom half about eight or ten inches with a brush; and, when she returned, that brush, sash, and all were exactly as she had left them. Now I scarcely need tell *you* what an awkward job it must have been for anybody to get noiselessly in at that unsupported window; and how unlikely he would have been to replace it, with the brush, exactly as he found it."

"Just so. I suppose the brooch, was really gone? I mean, there was no chance of Mrs. Armitage having mislaid it?"

"Oh, none at all! There was a most careful search."

"Then, as to getting in at the window, would it have been easy?"

"Well, yes," Sir James replied; "yes, perhaps it would. It was a first-floor window, and it looks over the roof and skylight of the billiard-room. I built the billiard-room myself—built it out from a smoking-room just at this corner. It would be easy enough to get at the window from the billiard-room roof. But, then," he added, "that couldn't have been the way. Somebody or other was in the billiard-room the whole time, and nobody could have got over the roof (which is nearly all skylight) without being seen and heard. I was there myself for an hour or two, taking a little practice."

"Well, was anything done?"

"Strict inquiry was made among the servants, of course, but nothing came of it. It was such a small matter that Mrs. Armitage wouldn't hear of my calling in the police or anything of that sort, although I felt pretty certain that there must be a dishonest servant about somewhere. A servant might take a plain brooch, you know, who would feel afraid of a valuable ring, the loss of which would be made a greater matter of."

"Well, yes, perhaps so, in the case of an inexperienced thief, who also would be likely to snatch up whatever she took in a hurry. But I'm doubtful. What made you connect these two robberies together?"

"Nothing whatever—for some months. They seemed quite of a different sort. But scarcely more than a month ago I met Mrs. Armitage at Brighton, and we talked, among other things, of the previous robbery—that of Mrs. Heath's bracelet. I described the circumstances pretty minutely, and, when I mentioned the match found on the table, she said: 'How strange! Why, *my* thief left a match on the dressing-table when he took my poor little brooch!'"

Hewitt nodded. "Yes," he said. "A spent match, of course?"

"Yes, of course, a spent match. She noticed it lying close by the pin-cushion, but threw it away without mentioning the circumstance. Still, it seemed rather curious to me that a match should be lit and dropped, in each case, on the dressing-cover an inch from where the article was taken. I mentioned it to Lloyd when I got back, and he agreed that it seemed significant."

"Scarcely," said Hewitt, shaking his head. "Scarcely, so far, to be called significant, although worth following up. Everybody uses matches in the dark, you know."

"Well, at any rate, the coincidence appealed to me so far that it struck me it might be worthwhile to describe the brooch to the police in order that they could trace it if it had been pawned. They had tried that, of course, over the bracelet without any result, but I fancied the shot might be worth making, and might possibly lead us on the track of the more serious robbery."

"Quite so. It was the right thing to do. Well?"

"Well, they found it. A woman had pawned it in London—at a shop in Chelsea. But that was some time before, and the pawnbroker had clean forgotten all about the woman's appearance. The name and address she gave were false. So that was the end of that business."

"Had any of the servants left you between the time the brooch was lost and the date of the pawn ticket?"

"No."

"Were all your servants at home on the day the brooch was pawned?"

"Oh, yes! I made that inquiry myself."

"Very good! What next?"

"Yesterday—and this is what made me send for you. My late wife's sister came here last Tuesday, and we gave her the room from which Mrs. Heath lost her bracelet. She had with her a very old-fashioned brooch, containing a miniature of her father, and set in front with three very fine brilliants and a few smaller stones. Here we are, though, at the Croft. I'll tell you the rest indoors."

Hewitt laid his hand on the baronet's arm. "Don't pull up, Sir James," he said. "Drive a little farther. I should like to have a general idea of the whole case before we go in."

"Very good!" Sir James Norris straightened the horse's head again and went on. "Late yesterday afternoon, as my sister-in-law was changing her dress, she left her room for a moment to speak to my daughter in her room, almost adjoining. She was gone no more than three minutes, or five at most, but on her return the brooch, which had been left on the table, had gone. Now the window was shut fast, and had not been tampered with. Of course the door was open, but so was my daughter's, and anybody walking near must have been heard. But the strangest circumstance, and one that almost makes me wonder whether I have been awake today or not, was that there lay *a used match* on the very spot, as nearly as possible, where the brooch had been—and it was broad daylight!"

Hewitt rubbed his nose and looked thoughtfully before him. "Um—curious, certainly," he said, "Anything else?"

"Nothing more than you shall see for yourself. I have had the room locked and watched till you could examine it. My sister-in-law had heard of your name, and suggested that you should be called in; so, of course, I did exactly as she wanted. That she should have lost that brooch, of all things, in my house is most unfortunate; you see, there was some small difference about the thing between my late wife and her sister when their mother died and left it. It's almost worse than the Heaths' bracelet business, and altogether I'm not pleased with things, I can assure you. See what a position it is for me! Here are three ladies, in the space of one year, robbed one after another in this mysterious fashion in my house, and I can't find the thief! It's horrible! People will be afraid to come near the place. And I can do nothing!"

"Ah, well, we'll see. Perhaps we had better turn back now. By-the-by, were you thinking of having any alterations or additions made to your house?"

"No. What makes you ask?"

"I think you might at least consider the question of painting and decorating, Sir James—or, say, putting up another coach-house, or something. Because I should like to be (to the servants) the architect—or the builder, if you please—come to look around. You haven't told any of them about this business?"

"Not a word. Nobody knows but my relatives and Lloyd. I took every precaution myself, at once. As to your little disguise, be the architect by all means, and do as you please. If you can only find this thief and put an end to this horrible state of affairs, you'll do me the greatest service I've ever asked for—and as to your fee, I'll gladly make it whatever is usual, and three hundred in addition."

Martin Hewitt bowed. "You're very generous, Sir James, and you may be sure I'll do what I can. As a professional man, of course, a good fee always stimulates my interest, although this case of yours certainly seems interesting enough by itself."

"Most extraordinary! Don't you think so? Here are three persons, all ladies, all in my house, two even in the same room, each successively robbed of a piece of jewellery, each from a dressing-table, and a used match left behind in every case. All in the most difficult—one would say impossible—circumstances for a thief, and yet there is no clue!"

"Well, we won't say that just yet, Sir James; we must see. And we must guard against any undue predisposition to consider the robberies in a lump. Here we are at the lodge gate again. Is that your gardener—the man who left the ladder by the lawn on the first occasion you spoke of?"

Mr. Hewitt nodded in the direction of a man who was clipping a box border.

"Yes; will you ask him anything?"

"No, no; at any rate, not now. Remember the building alterations. I think, if there is no objection, I will look first at the room that the lady—Mrs.——" Hewitt looked up, inquiringly.

"My sister-in-law? Mrs. Cazenove. Oh, yes! you shall come to her room at once."

"Thank you. And I think Mrs. Cazenove had better be there."

They alighted, and a boy from the lodge led the horse and dog-cart away.

Mrs. Cazenove was a thin and faded, but quick and energetic, lady of middle age. She bent her head very slightly on learning Martin Hewitt's name, and said: "I must thank you, Mr. Hewitt, for your very prompt attention. I need scarcely say that any help you can afford in tracing the thief who has my property—whoever it may be—will make me most grateful. My room is quite ready for you to examine."

The room was on the second floor—the top floor at that part of the building. Some slight confusion of small articles of dress was observable in parts of the room.

"This, I take it," inquired Hewitt, "is exactly as it was at the time the brooch was missed?"

"Precisely," Mrs. Cazenove answered. "I have used another room, and put myself to some other inconveniences, to avoid any disturbance."

Hewitt stood before the dressing-table. "Then this is the used match," he observed, "exactly where it was found?"

"Yes."

"Where was the brooch?"

"I should say almost on the very same spot. Certainly no more than a very few inches away."

Hewitt examined the match closely. "It is burned very little," he remarked. "It would appear to have gone out at once. Could you hear it struck?"

"I heard nothing whatever; absolutely nothing."

"If you will step into Miss Norris' room now for a moment," Hewitt suggested, "we will try an experiment. Tell me if you hear matches struck, and how many. Where is the match-stand?"

The match-stand proved to be empty, but matches were found in Miss Norris' room, and the test was made. Each striking could be heard distinctly, even with one of the doors pushed to.

"Both your own door and Miss Norris' were open, I understand; the window shut and fastened inside as it is now, and nothing but the brooch was disturbed?"

"Yes, that was so."

"Thank you, Mrs. Cazenove. I don't think I need trouble you any further just at present. I think, Sir James," Hewitt added, turning to the baronet, who was standing by the door, "I think we will see the other room and take a walk outside the house, if you please. I suppose, by the by, that there is no getting at the matches left behind on the first and second occasions?"

"No," Sir James answered. "Certainly not here. The Scotland Yard man may have kept his."

The room that Mrs. Armitage had occupied presented no peculiar feature. A few feet below the window the roof of the billiard-room was visible, consisting largely of skylight. Hewitt glanced casually about the walls, ascertained that the furniture and hangings had not been materially changed since the second robbery, and expressed his desire to see the windows from the outside. Before leaving the room, however, he wished to know the names of any persons who were known to have been about the house on the occasions of all three robberies.

"Just carry your mind back, Sir James," he said. "Begin with yourself, for instance. Where were you at these times?"

"When Mrs. Heath lost her bracelet, I was in Tagley Wood all the afternoon. When Mrs. Armitage was robbed, I believe I was somewhere about the place most of the time she was out. Yesterday I was down at the farm." Sir James' face broadened. "I don't know whether you call those suspicious movements," he added, and laughed.

"Not at all; I only asked you so that, remembering your own movements, you might the better recall those of the rest of the household. Was anybody, to your knowledge—*anybody*, mind—in the house on all three occasions?"

"Well, you know, it's quite impossible to answer for all the servants. You'll only get that by direct questioning—I can't possibly remember things of that sort. As to the family and visitors—why, you don't suspect any of them, do you?"

"I don't suspect a soul, Sir James," Hewitt answered, beaming genially, "not a soul. You see, I can't suspect people till I know something about where they were. It's quite possible there will be independent evidence enough as it is, but you must help me if you can. The visitors, now. Was there any visitor here each time—or even on the first and last occasions only?"

"No, not one. And my own sister, perhaps you will be pleased to know, was only there at the time of the first robbery."

"Just so! And your daughter, as I have gathered, was clearly absent from the spot each time—indeed, was in company with the party robbed. Your niece, now?"

"Why hang it all, Mr. Hewitt, I can't talk of my niece as a suspected criminal! The poor girl's under my protection, and I really can't al-

18

low——"

Hewitt raised his hand, and shook his head deprecatingly.

"My dear sir, haven't I said that I don't suspect a soul? *Do* let me know how the people were distributed, as nearly as possible. Let me see. It was your niece, I think, who found that Mrs. Armitage's door was locked—this door, in fact—on the day she lost her brooch?"

"Yes, it was."

"Just so—at the time when Mrs. Armitage herself had forgotten whether she locked it or not. And yesterday—was she out then?"

"No, I think not. Indeed, she goes out very little—her health is usually bad. She was indoors, too, at the time of the Heath robbery, since you ask. But come, now, I don't like this. It's ridiculous to suppose that *she* knows anything of it."

"I don't suppose it, as I have said. I am only asking for information. That is all your resident family, I take it, and you know nothing of anybody else's movements—except, perhaps, Mr. Lloyd's?"

"Lloyd? Well, you know yourself that he was out with the ladies when the first robbery took place. As to the others, I don't remember. Yesterday he was probably in his room, writing. I think that acquits *him*, eh?" Sir James looked quizzically into the broad face of the affable detective, who smiled and replied:

"Oh, of course nobody can be in two places at once, else what would become of the *alibi* as an institution? But, as I have said, I am only setting my facts in order. Now, you see, we get down to the servants—unless some stranger is the party wanted. Shall we go outside now?"

Lenton Croft was a large, desultory sort of house, nowhere more than three floors high, and mostly only two. It had been added to bit by bit, till it zigzagged about its site, as Sir James Norris expressed it, "like a game of dominoes." Hewitt scrutinized its external features carefully as they strolled around, and stopped some little while before the windows of the two bedrooms he had just seen from the inside. Presently they approached the stables and coach-house, where a groom was washing the wheels of the dog-cart.

"Do you mind my smoking?" Hewitt asked Sir James. "Perhaps you will take a cigar yourself—they are not so bad, I think. I will ask your man for a light."

Sir James felt for his own match-box, but Hewitt had gone, and was lighting his cigar with a match from a box handed him by the groom. A smart little terrier was trotting about by the coach-house, and Hewitt stooped to rub its head. Then he made some observation about the dog, which enlisted the groom's interest, and was soon absorbed in a chat with the man. Sir James, waiting a little way off, tapped the stones rather impatiently with his foot, and presently moved away.

For full a quarter of an hour Hewitt chatted with the groom, and, when at last he came away and overtook Sir James, that gentleman was about re-entering the house.

"I beg your pardon, Sir James," Hewitt said, "for leaving you in that unceremonious fashion to talk to your groom, but a dog, Sir James—a good dog—will draw me anywhere."

"Oh!" replied Sir James, shortly.

"There is one other thing," Hewitt went on, disregarding the other's curtness, "that I should like to know: There are two windows directly below that of the room occupied yesterday by Mrs. Cazenove—one on each floor. What rooms do they light?"

"That on the ground floor is the morning-room; the other is Mr. Lloyd's—my secretary. A sort of study or sitting-room."

"Now you will see at once, Sir James," Hewitt pursued, with an affable determination to win the baronet back to good-humour, "you will see at once that, if a ladder had been used in Mrs. Heath's case, anybody looking from either of these rooms would have seen it."

"Of course! The Scotland Yard man questioned everybody as to that, but nobody seemed to have been in either of the rooms when the thing occurred; at any rate, nobody saw anything."

"Still, I think I should like to look out of those windows myself; it will, at least, give me an idea of what *was* in view and what was not, if anybody had been there."

Sir James Norris led the way to the morning-room. As they reached the door a young lady, carrying a book and walking very languidly, came out. Hewitt stepped aside to let her pass, and afterward said interrogatively: "Miss Norris, your daughter, Sir James?"

"No, my niece. Do you want to ask her anything? Dora, my dear," Sir James added, following her in the corridor, "this is Mr. Hewitt, who is investigating these wretched robberies for me. I think he would like to hear if you remember anything happening at any of the three times."

The lady bowed slightly, and said in a plaintive drawl: "I, uncle? Really, I don't remember anything; nothing at all."

"You found Mrs. Armitage's door locked, I believe," asked Hewitt, "when you tried it, on the afternoon when she lost her brooch?"

"Oh, yes; I believe it was locked. Yes, it was."

"Had the key been left in?"

"The key? Oh, no! I think not; no."

"Do you remember anything out of the common happening—anything whatever, no matter how trivial—on the day Mrs. Heath lost her bracelet?"

"No, really, I don't. I can't remember at all."

"Nor yesterday?"

"No, nothing. I don't remember anything."

"Thank you," said Hewitt, hastily; "thank you. Now the morning-room, Sir James."

In the morning-room Hewitt stayed but a few seconds, doing little more than casually glance out of the windows. In the room above he took a little longer time. It was a comfortable room, but with rather effeminate indications about its contents. Little pieces of draped silk-work hung about the furniture, and Japanese silk fans decorated the mantel-piece. Near the window was a cage containing a grey parrot, and the writing-table was decorated with two vases of flowers.

"Lloyd makes himself pretty comfortable, eh?" Sir James observed. "But it isn't likely anybody would be here while he was out, at the time that bracelet went."

"No," replied Hewitt, meditatively. "No, I suppose not."

He stared thoughtfully out of the window, and then, still deep in thought, rattled at the wires of the cage with a quill toothpick and played a moment with the parrot. Then, looking up at the window again, he said: "That is Mr. Lloyd, isn't it, coming back in a fly?"

"Yes, I think so. Is there anything else you would care to see here?"

"No, thank you," Hewitt replied; "I don't think there is."

They went down to the smoking-room, and Sir James went away to speak to his secretary. When he returned, Hewitt said quietly: "I think, Sir James—I *think* that I shall be able to give you your thief presently."

"What! Have you a clue? Who do you think? I began to believe you were hopelessly stumped."

"Well, yes. I have rather a good clue, although I can't tell you much about it just yet. But it is so good a clue that I should like to know now whether you are determined to prosecute when you have the criminal?"

"Why, bless me, of course," Sir James replied, with surprise. "It doesn't rest with me; you know—the property belongs to my friends.

21

And even if they were disposed to let the thing slide, I shouldn't allow it—I couldn't, after they had been robbed in my house."

"Of course, of course! Then, if I can, I should like to send a message to Twyford by somebody perfectly trustworthy—not a servant. Could anybody go?"

"Well, there's Lloyd, although he's only just back from his journey. But, if it's important, he'll go."

"It is important. The fact is we must have a policeman or two here this evening, and I'd like Mr. Lloyd to fetch them without telling anybody else."

Sir James rang, and, in response to his message, Mr. Lloyd appeared. While Sir James gave his secretary his instructions, Hewitt strolled to the door of the smoking-room, and intercepted the latter as he came out.

"I'm sorry to give you this trouble, Mr. Lloyd," he said, "but I must stay here myself for a little, and somebody who can be trusted must go. Will you just bring back a police-constable with you? or rather two—two would be better. That is all that is wanted. You won't let the servants know, will you? Of course there will be a female searcher at the Twyford police-station? Ah—of course. Well, you needn't bring her, you know. That sort of thing is done at the station." And, chatting thus confidentially, Martin Hewitt saw him off.

When Hewitt returned to the smoking-room, Sir James said, suddenly: "Why, bless my soul, Mr. Hewitt, we haven't fed you! I'm awfully sorry. We came in rather late for lunch, you know, and this business has bothered me so I clean forgot everything else. There's no dinner till seven, so you'd better let me give you something now. I'm really sorry. Come along."

"Thank you, Sir James," Hewitt replied; "I won't take much. A few biscuits, perhaps, or something of that sort. And, by the by, if you don't mind, I rather think I should like to take it alone. The fact is I want to go over this case thoroughly by myself. Can you put me in a room?"

"Any room you like. Where will you go? The dining-room's rather large, but there's my study, that's pretty snug, or——"

"Perhaps I can go into Mr. Lloyd's room for half an hour or so; I don't think he'll mind, and it's pretty comfortable."

"Certainly, if you'd like. I'll tell them to send you whatever they've got."

"Thank you very much. Perhaps they'll also send me a lump of sugar and a walnut; it's—it's a little fad of mine."

"A—what? A lump of sugar and a walnut?" Sir James stopped for a moment, with his hand on the bell-rope. "Oh, certainly, if you'd like it; certainly," he added, and stared after this detective with curious tastes as he left the room.

When the vehicle, bringing back the secretary and the policeman, drew up on the drive, Martin Hewitt left the room on the first floor and proceeded downstairs. On the landing he met Sir James Norris and Mrs. Cazenove, who stared with astonishment on perceiving that the detective carried in his hand the parrot-cage.

"I think our business is about brought to a head now," Hewitt remarked, on the stairs. "Here are the police officers from Twyford." The men were standing in the hall with Mr. Lloyd, who, on catching sight of the cage in Hewitt's hand, paled suddenly.

"This is the person who will be charged, I think," Hewitt pursued, addressing the officers, and indicating Lloyd with his finger.

"What, Lloyd?" gasped Sir James, aghast. "No—not Lloyd—nonsense!"

"He doesn't seem to think it nonsense himself, does he?" Hewitt placidly observed. Lloyd had sunk on a chair, and, grey of face, was staring blindly at the man he had run against at the office door that morning. His lips moved in spasms, but there was no sound. The wilted flower fell from his button-hole to the floor, but he did not move.

"This is his accomplice," Hewitt went on, placing the parrot and cage on the hall table, "though I doubt whether there will be any use in charging *him*. Eh, Polly?"

The parrot put his head aside and chuckled. "Hullo, Polly!" it quietly gurgled. "Come along!"

Sir James Norris was hopelessly bewildered. "Lloyd—Lloyd," he said, under his breath. "Lloyd—and that!"

"This was his little messenger, his useful Mercury," Hewitt explained, tapping the cage complacently; "in fact, the actual lifter. Hold him up!"

The last remark referred to the wretched Lloyd, who had fallen forward with something between a sob and a loud sigh. The policemen took him by the arms and propped him in his chair.

★★★★★

"System?" said Hewitt, with a shrug of the shoulders, an hour or two after in Sir James' study. "I can't say I have a system. I call it nothing but common-sense and a sharp pair of eyes. Nobody using these could help taking the right road in this case. I began at the match, just as the Scotland Yard man did, but I had the advantage of taking a line through three cases. To begin with, it was plain that that match, being left there in daylight, in Mrs. Cazenove's room, could not have been used to light the table-top, in the full glare of the window; therefore, it had been used for some other purpose—*what* purpose I could not, at the moment, guess. Habitual thieves, you know, often have curious superstitions, and some will never take anything without leaving something behind—a pebble or a piece of coal, or something like that—in the premises they have been robbing. It seemed at first extremely likely that this was a case of that kind.

"The match had clearly been *brought in*—because, when I asked for matches, there were none in the stand, not even an empty box, and the room had not been disturbed. Also the match probably had not been struck there, nothing having been heard, although, of course, a mistake in this matter was just possible. This match, then, it was fair to assume, had been lit somewhere else and blown out immediately—I remarked at the time that it was very little burned. Plainly it could not have been treated thus for nothing, and the only possible object would have been to prevent it igniting accidentally. Following on this, it became obvious that the match was used, for whatever purpose, not *as* a match, but merely as a convenient splinter of wood.

"So far so good. But on examining the match very closely I observed, as you can see for yourself, certain rather sharp indentations in the wood. They are very small, you see, and scarcely visible, except upon narrow inspection; but there they are, and their positions are regular. See, there are two on each side, each opposite the corresponding mark of the other pair. The match, in fact, would seem to have been gripped in some fairly sharp instrument, holding it at two points above and two below—an instrument, as it may at once strike you, not unlike the beak of a bird.

"Now here was an idea. What living creature but a bird could possibly have entered Mrs. Heath's window without a ladder—supposing no ladder to have been used—or could have got into Mrs. Armitage's window without lifting the sash higher than the eight or ten inches it was already open? Plainly, nothing. Further, it is significant that only *one* article was stolen at a time, although others were about. A human being could have carried any reasonable number, but a bird could only take one at a time. But why should a bird carry a match in its beak? Certainly it must have been trained to do that for a purpose, and a little consideration made that purpose pretty clear. A noisy, chattering bird would probably betray itself at once. Therefore, it must be trained to keep quiet both while going for and coming away with its plunder. What readier or more probably effectual way than, while teaching it to carry without dropping, to teach it also to keep quiet while carrying? The one thing would practically cover the other.

"I thought at once, of course, of a jackdaw or a magpie—these birds' thievish reputations made the guess natural. But the marks on the match were much too wide apart to have been made by the beak of either. I conjectured, therefore, that it must be a raven. So that, when we arrived near the coach-house, I seized the opportunity of a little chat with your groom on the subject of dogs and pets in general, and ascertained that there was no tame raven in the place. I also, incidentally, by getting a light from the coach-house box of matches, ascertained that the match found was of the sort generally used about the establishment—the large, thick, red-topped English match. But I further found that Mr. Lloyd had a parrot which was a most intelligent pet, and had been trained into comparative quietness—for a parrot. Also, I learned that more than once the groom had met Mr. Lloyd carrying his parrot under his coat, it having, as its owner explained, learned the trick of opening its cage-door and escaping.

"I said nothing, of course, to you of all this, because I had as yet nothing but a train of argument and no results. I got to Lloyd's room as soon as possible. My chief object in going there was achieved when I played with the parrot, and induced it to bite a quill toothpick.

"When you left me in the smoking-room, I compared the quill and the match very carefully, and found that the marks corresponded exactly. After this I felt very little doubt indeed. The fact of Lloyd having met the ladies walking before dark on the day of the first robbery proved nothing, because, since it was clear that the match had *not* been used to procure a light, the robbery might as easily have taken place in daylight as not—must have so taken place, in fact, if my conjectures were right. That they were right I felt no doubt. There could be no other explanation.

"When Mrs. Heath left her window open and her door shut, anybody climbing upon the open sash of Lloyd's high window could have put the bird upon the sill above. The match placed in the bird's beak for the purpose I have indicated, and struck first, in case by accident it should ignite by rubbing against something and startle the bird—this match would, of course, be dropped just where the object to be removed was taken up; as you know, in every case the match was found almost upon the spot where the missing article had been left—scarcely a likely triple coincidence had the match been used by a human thief. This would have been done as soon after the ladies had left as possible, and there would then have been plenty of time for Lloyd to hurry out and meet them before dark—especially plenty of time to meet them *coming back*, as they must have been, since they were carrying their ferns. The match was an article well chosen for its purpose, as being a not altogether unlikely thing to find on a dressing-table, and, if noticed, likely to lead to the wrong conclusions adopted by the official detective.

"In Mrs. Armitage's case the taking of an inferior brooch and the leaving of a more valuable ring pointed clearly either to the operator being a fool or unable to distinguish values, and certainly, from other indications, the thief seemed no fool. The door was locked, and the gas-fitter, so to speak, on guard, and the window was only eight or ten inches open and propped with a brush. A human thief entering the window would have disturbed this arrangement, and would scarcely risk discovery by attempting to replace it, especially a thief in so great a hurry as to snatch the brooch up without unfastening the pin. The bird could pass through the opening as it was, and *would have* to tear the pin-cushion to pull the brooch off, probably holding the cushion down with its claw the while.

"Now in yesterday's case we had an alteration of conditions. The window was shut and fastened, but the door was open—but only left for a few minutes, during which time no sound was heard either of coming or going. Was it not possible, then, that the thief was *already* in the room, in hiding, while Mrs. Cazenove was there, and seized its first opportunity on her temporary absence? The room is full of draperies, hangings, and what not, allowing of plenty of concealment for a bird, and a bird could leave the place noiselessly and quickly. That the whole scheme was strange mattered not at all. Robberies presenting such unaccountable features must have been effected by strange means of one sort or another. There was no improbability. Consider how many hundreds of examples of infinitely higher degrees of bird-training are exhibited in the London streets every week for coppers.

"So that, on the whole, I felt pretty sure of my ground. But before taking any definite steps I resolved to see if Polly could not be persuaded to exhibit his accomplishments to an indulgent stranger. For that purpose, I contrived to send Lloyd away again and have a quiet hour alone with his bird. A piece of sugar, as everybody knows, is a good parrot bribe; but a walnut, split in half, is a better—especially if the bird be used to it; so I got you to furnish me with both. Polly was shy at first, but I generally get along very well with pets, and a little perseverance soon led to a complete private performance for my benefit. Polly would take the match, mute as wax, jump on the table, pick up the brightest thing he could see, in a great hurry, leave the match behind, and scuttle away round the room; but at first wouldn't give up the plunder to *me*.

"It was enough. I also took the liberty, as you know, of a general look round, and discovered that little collection of Brummagem rings and trinkets that you have just seen—used in Polly's education, no doubt. When we sent Lloyd away, it struck me that he might as well be usefully employed as not, so I got him to fetch the police, deluding him a little, I fear, by talking about the servants and a female searcher. There will be no trouble about evidence; he'll confess. Of that I'm sure. I know the sort of man. But I doubt if you'll get Mrs. Cazenove's brooch back. You see, he has been to London today, and by this time the swag is probably broken up."

Sir James listened to Hewitt's explanation with many expressions of assent and some of surprise. When it was over, he smoked a few whiffs and then said: "But Mrs. Armitage's brooch was pawned, and by a woman."

"Exactly. I expect our friend Lloyd was rather disgusted at his small luck—probably gave the brooch to some female connection in London, and she realized on it. Such persons don't always trouble to give a correct address."

The two smoked in silence for a few minutes, and then Hewitt continued: "I don't expect our friend has had an easy job altogether with that bird. His successes at most have only been three, and I suspect he had many failures and not a few anxious moments that we know nothing of. I should judge as much merely from what the groom told me of frequently meeting Lloyd with his parrot. But the plan was not a bad one—not at all. Even if the bird had been caught in the act, it would only have been 'That mischievous parrot!' you see. And his master would only have been looking for him."

THE LOSS OF SAMMY CROCKETT

It was, of course, always a part of Martin Hewitt's business to be thoroughly at home among any and every class of people, and to be able to interest himself intelligently, or to appear to do so, in their various pursuits. In one of the most important cases ever placed in his hands he could have gone but a short way toward success had he not displayed some knowledge of the more sordid aspects of professional sport, and a great interest in the undertakings of a certain dealer therein.

The great case itself had nothing to do with sport, and, indeed, from a narrative point of view, was somewhat uninteresting, but the man who alone held the one piece of information wanted was a keeper, backer, or "gaffer" of professional pedestrians, and it was through the medium of his pecuniary interest in such matters that Hewitt was enabled to strike a bargain with him.

The man was a publican on the outskirts of Padfield, a northern town, pretty famous for its sporting tastes, and to Padfield, therefore, Hewitt betook himself, and, arrayed in a way to indicate some inclination of his own toward sport, he began to frequent the bar of the Hare and Hounds. Kentish, the landlord, was a stout, bull-necked man, of no great communicativeness at first; but after a little acquaintance he opened out wonderfully, became quite a jolly (and rather intelligent) companion, and came out with innumerable anecdotes of his sporting adventures. He could put a very decent dinner on the table, too, at the Hare and Hounds, and Hewitt's frequent invitation to him to join therein and divide a bottle of the best in the cellar soon put the two on the very best of terms. Good terms with Mr. Kentish was Hewitt's great desire, for the information he wanted was of a sort that could never be extracted by casual questioning, but must be a matter of open communication by the publican, extracted in what way it might be.

"Look here," said Kentish one day, "I'll put you on to a good thing, my boy—a real good thing. Of course you know all about the Padfield 135 Yards Handicap being run off now?"

"Well, I haven't looked into it much," Hewitt replied. "Ran the first round of heats last Saturday and Monday, didn't they?"

"They did. Well"—Kentish spoke in a stage whisper as he leaned over and rapped the table—"I've got the final winner in this house." He nodded his head, took a puff at his cigar, and added, in his ordinary voice. "Don't say nothing."

"No, of course not. Got something on, of course?"

"Rather! What do you think? Got any price I liked. Been saving him up for this. Why, he's got twenty-one yards, and he can do even time all the way! Fact! Why, he could win runnin' back'ards. He won his heat on Monday like—like—like that!" The gaffer snapped his fingers, in default of a better illustration, and went on. "He might ha' took it a little easier, *I* think; it's shortened his price, of course, him jumpin' in by two yards. But you can get decent odds now, if you go about it right. You take my tip—back him for his heat next Saturday, in the second round, and for the final. You'll get a good price for the final, if you pop it down at once. But don't go makin' a song of it, will you, now? I'm givin' you a tip I wouldn't give anybody else."

"Thanks, very much; it's awfully good of you. I'll do what you advise. But isn't there a dark horse anywhere else?"

"Not dark to me, my boy, not dark to me. I know every man runnin' like a book. Old Taylor—him over at the Cop—he's got a very good lad at eighteen yards, a very good lad indeed; and he's a tryer this time, I know. But, bless you, my lad could give him ten, instead o' taking three, and beat him then! When I'm runnin' a real tryer, I'm generally runnin' something very near a winner, you bet; and this time, mind *this* time, I'm runnin' the certainest winner I *ever* run—and I don't often make a mistake. You back him."

"I shall, if you're as sure as that. But who is he?"

"Oh, Crockett's his name—Sammy Crockett. He's quite a new lad. I've got young Steggles looking after him—sticks to him like wax. Takes his little breathers in my bit o' ground at the back here. I've got a cinder-sprint path there, over behind the trees. I don't let him out o' sight much, I can tell you. He's a straight lad, and he knows it'll be worth his while to stick to me; but there's some 'ud poison him, if they thought he'd spoil their books."

Soon afterward the two strolled toward the taproom. "I expect Sammy'll be there," the landlord said, "with Steggles. I don't hide him too much—they'd think I'd got something extra on if I did."

In the tap-room sat a lean, wire-drawn-looking youth, with sloping shoulders and a thin face, and by his side was a rather short, thickset man, who had an odd air, no matter what he did, of proprietorship and surveillance of the lean youth. Several other men sat about, and there was loud laughter, under which the lean youth looked sheepishly angry.

"'Tarn't no good, Sammy, lad," someone was saying, "you a-makin' after Nancy Webb—she'll ha' nowt to do with 'ee."

"Don' like 'em so thread-papery," added another. "No, Sammy, you aren't the lad for she. I see her——"

"What about Nancy Webb?" asked Kentish, pushing open the door. "Sammy's all right, anyway. You keep fit, my lad, an' go on improving, and some day you'll have as good a house as me. Never mind the lasses. Had his glass o' beer, has he?" This to Raggy Steggles, who, answering in the affirmative, viewed his charge as though he were a post, and the beer a recent coat of paint.

"Has two glasses of mild a day," the landlord said to Hewitt. "Never puts on flesh, so he can stand it. Come out now." He nodded to Steggles, who rose and marched Sammy Crockett away for exercise.

★★★★★★

On the following afternoon (it was Thursday), as Hewitt and Kentish chatted in the landlord's own snuggery, Steggles burst into the room in a great state of agitation and spluttered out: "He—he's bolted; gone away!"

"What?"

"Sammy—gone! Hooked it! *I* can't find him."

The landlord stared blankly at the trainer, who stood with a sweater dangling from his hand and stared blankly back. "What d'ye mean?" Kentish said, at last. "Don't be a fool! He's in the place somewhere. Find him!"

But this Steggles defied anybody to do. He had looked already. He had left Crockett at the cinder-path behind the trees in his running-gear, with the addition of the long overcoat and cap he used in going between the path and the house to guard against chill. "I was goin' to give him a bust or two with the pistol," the trainer explained, "but, when we got over t'other side, 'Raggy,' ses he, 'it's blawin' a bit chilly. I think I'll ha' a sweater. There's one on my box, ain't there?' So in I coomes for the sweater, and it weren't on his box, and, when I found it and got back—he weren't there. They'd seen nowt o' him in t' house, and he weren't nowhere."

Hewitt and the landlord, now thoroughly startled, searched everywhere, but to no purpose. "What should he go off the place for?" asked Kentish, in a sweat of apprehension. "'Tain't chilly a bit—it's warm. He didn't want no sweater; never wore one before. It was a piece of kid to be able to clear out. Nice thing, this is. I stand to win two years' takings over him. Here—you'll have to find him."

"Ah, but how?" exclaimed the disconcerted trainer, dancing about distractedly. "I've got all I could scrape on him myself. Where can I look?"

Here was Hewitt's opportunity. He took Kentish aside and whispered. What he said startled the landlord considerably. "Yes, I'll tell you all about that," he said, "if that's all you want. It's no good or harm to

30

me whether I tell or no. But can you find him?"

"That I can't promise, of course. But you know who I am now, and what I'm here for. If you like to give me the information I want, I'll go into the case for you, and, of course, I shan't charge any fee. I may have luck, you know, but I can't promise, of course."

The landlord looked in Hewitt's face for a moment. Then he said: "Done! It's a deal."

"Very good," Hewitt replied; "get together the one or two papers you have, and we'll go into my business in the evening. As to Crockett, don't say a word to anybody. I'm afraid it must get out, since they all know about it in the house, but there's no use in making any unnecessary noise. Don't make hedging bets or do anything that will attract notice. Now we'll go over to the back and look at this cinder-path of yours."

Here Steggles, who was still standing near, was struck with an idea. "How about old Taylor, at the Cop, guv'nor, eh?" he said, meaningly. "His lad's good enough to win with Sammy out, and Taylor is backing him plenty. Think he knows anything o' this?"

"That's likely," Hewitt observed, before Kentish could reply. "Yes. Look here—suppose Steggles goes and keeps his eye on the Cop for an hour or two, in case there's anything to be heard of? Don't show yourself, of course."

Kentish agreed, and the trainer went. When Hewitt and Kentish arrived at the path behind the trees, Hewitt at once began examining the ground. One or two rather large holes in the cinders were made, as the publican explained, by Crockett, in practicing getting off his mark. Behind these were several fresh tracks of spiked shoes. The tracks led up to within a couple of yards of the high fence bounding the ground, and there stopped abruptly and entirely. In the fence, a little to the right of where the tracks stopped, there was a stout door. This Hewitt tried, and found ajar.

"That's always kept bolted," Kentish said. "He's gone out that way—he couldn't have gone any other without comin' through the house."

"But he isn't in the habit of making a step three yards long, is he?" Hewitt asked, pointing at the last footmark and then at the door, which was quite that distance away from it. "Besides," he added, opening the door, "there's no footprint here nor outside."

The door opened on a lane, with another fence and a thick plantation of trees at the other side. Kentish looked at the footmarks, then at the door, then down the lane, and finally back toward the house. "That's a licker!" he said.

"This is a quiet sort of lane," was Hewitt's next remark. "No houses in sight. Where does it lead?"

"That way it goes to the Old Kilns—disused. This way down to a turning off the Padfield and Catton road."

Hewitt returned to the cinder-path again, and once more examined the footmarks. He traced them back over the grass toward the house. "Certainly," he said, "he hasn't gone back to the house. Here is the double line of tracks, side by side, from the house—Steggles' ordinary boots with iron tips, and Crockett's running pumps; thus they came out. Here is Steggles' track in the opposite direction alone, made when he went back for the sweater. Crockett remained; you see various prints in those loose cinders at the end of the path where he moved this way and that, and then two or three paces toward the fence—not directly toward the door, you notice—and there they stop dead, and there are no more, either back or forward. Now, if he had wings, I should be tempted to the opinion that he flew straight away in the air from that spot—unless the earth swallowed him and closed again without leaving a wrinkle on its face."

Kentish stared gloomily at the tracks and said nothing.

"However," Hewitt resumed, "I think I'll take a little walk now and think over it. You go into the house and show yourself at the bar. If anybody wants to know how Crockett is, he's pretty well, thank you. By the by, can I get to the Cop—this place of Taylor's—by this back lane?"

"Yes, down to the end leading to the Catton road, turn to the left and then first on the right. Any one'll show you the Cop," and Kentish shut the door behind the detective, who straightway walked—toward the Old Kilns.

In little more than an hour he was back. It was now becoming dusk, and the landlord looked out papers from a box near the side window of his snuggery, for the sake of the extra light. "I've got these papers together for you," he said, as Hewitt entered. "Any news?"

"Nothing very great. Here's a bit of handwriting I want you to recognise, if you can. Get a light."

Kentish lit a lamp, and Hewitt laid upon the table half a dozen small pieces of torn paper, evidently fragments of a letter which had been torn up, here reproduced in facsimile:

The landlord turned the scraps over, regarding them dubiously. "These aren't much to recognise, anyhow. *I* don't know the writing. Where did you find 'em?"

"They were lying in the lane at the back, a little way down. Plainly they are pieces of a note addressed to someone called Sammy or something very like it. See the first piece, with its 'mmy'? That is clearly from the beginning of the note, because there is no line between it and the smooth, straight edge of the paper above; also, nothing follows on the same line. Someone writes to Crockett—presuming it to be a letter addressed to him, as I do for other reasons—as Sammy. It is a pity that there is no more of the letter to be found than these pieces. I expect the person who tore it up put the rest in his pocket and dropped these by accident."

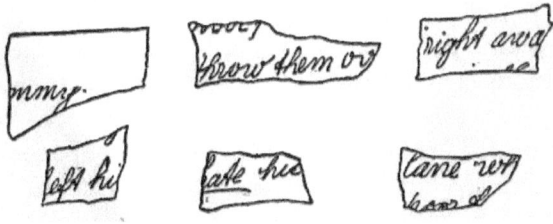

Kentish, who had been picking up and examining each piece in turn, now dolorously broke out:

"Oh, it's plain he's sold us—bolted and done us; me as took him out o' the gutter, too. Look here—'throw them over'; that's plain enough—can't mean anything else. Means throw *me* over, and my friends—me, after what I've done for him! Then 'right away'—go right away, I s'pose, as he has done. Then"—he was fiddling with the scraps and finally fitted two together—"why, look here, this one with 'lane' on it fits over the one about throwing over, and it says 'poor f' where its torn; that means 'poor fool,' I s'pose—*me*, or 'fathead,' or something like that. That's nice. Why, I'd twist his neck if I could get hold of him; and I will!"

Hewitt smiled. "Perhaps it's not quite so uncomplimentary, after all," he said. "If you can't recognise the writing, never mind. But, if he's gone away to sell you, it isn't much use finding him, is it? He won't win if he doesn't want to."

"Why, he wouldn't dare to rope under my very eyes. I'd—I'd——"

"Well, well; perhaps we'll get him to run, after all, and as well as he can. One thing is certain—he left this place of his own will. Further, I think he is in Padfield now; he went toward the town, I believe. And I don't think he means to sell you."

"Well, he shouldn't. I've made it worth his while to stick to me. I've put a fifty on for him out of my own pocket, and told him so; and, if he won, that would bring him a lump more than he'd probably get by going crooked, besides the prize money and anything I might give him over. But it seems to me he's putting me in the cart altogether."

"That we shall see. Meantime, don't mention anything I've told you to anyone—not even to Steggles. He can't help us, and he might blurt things out inadvertently. Don't say anything about these pieces of paper, which I shall keep myself. By-the-by, Steggles is indoors, isn't he? Very well, keep him in. Don't let him be seen hunting about this evening. I'll stay here tonight and we'll proceed with Crockett's business in the morning. And now we'll settle *my* business, please."

★★★★★★

In the morning Hewitt took his breakfast in the snuggery, carefully listening to any conversation that might take place at the bar. Soon after nine o'clock a fast dog-cart stopped outside, and a red-faced, loud-voiced man swaggered in, greeting Kentish with boisterous cordiality. He had a drink with the landlord, and said: "How's things? Fancy any of 'em for the sprint handicap? Got a lad o' your own in, haven't you?"

"Oh, yes," Kentish replied. "Crockett. Only a young un not got to his proper mark yet, I reckon. I think old Taylor's got No. 1 this time."

"Capital lad," the other replied, with a confidential nod. "Shouldn't wonder at all. Want to do anything yourself over it?"

"No, I don't think so. I'm not on at present. Might have a little flutter on the grounds just for fun; nothing else."

There were a few more casual remarks, and then the red-faced man drove away.

"Who was that?" asked Hewitt, who had watched the visitor through the snuggery window.

"That's Danby—bookmaker. Cute chap. He's been told Crockett's missing, I'll bet anything, and come here to pump me. No good, though. As a matter of fact, I've worked Sammy Crockett into his books for about half I'm in for altogether—through third parties, of course."

Hewitt reached for his hat. "I'm going out for half an hour now," he said. "If Steggles wants to go out before I come back, don't let him. Let him go and smooth over all those tracks on the cinder-path, very carefully. And, by the by, could you manage to have your son about the place today, in case I happen to want a little help out of doors?"

"Certainly; I'll get him to stay in. But what do you want the cinders smoothed for?"

Hewitt smiled, and patted his host's shoulder. "I'll explain all my tricks when the job's done," he said, and went out.

★★★★★★

On the lane from Padfield to Sedby village stood the Plough beer-house, wherein J. Webb was licensed to sell by retail beer to be consumed on the premises or off, as the thirsty list. Nancy Webb, with a very fine colour, a very curly fringe, and a wide smiling mouth revealing a fine set of teeth, came to the bar at the summons of a stoutish old gentleman in spectacles who walked with a stick.

The stoutish old gentleman had a glass of bitter beer, and then said in the peculiarly quiet voice of a very deaf man: "Can you tell me, if you please, the way into the main Catton road?"

"Down the lane, turn to the right at the cross-roads, then first to the left."

The old gentleman waited with his hand to his ear for some few seconds after she had finished speaking, and then resumed in his whispering voice: "I'm afraid I'm very deaf this morning." He fumbled in his pocket and produced a note-book and pencil. "May I trouble you to write it down? I'm so very deaf at times that I—Thank you."

The girl wrote the direction, and the old gentleman bade her good-morning and left. All down the lane he walked slowly with his stick. At the cross-roads he turned, put the stick under his arm, thrust his spectacles into his pocket, and strode away in the ordinary guise of Martin Hewitt. He pulled out his note-book, examined Miss Webb's direction very carefully, and then went off another way altogether, toward the Hare and Hounds.

Kentish lounged moodily in his bar. "Well, my boy," said Hewitt, "has Steggles wiped out the tracks?"

"Not yet; I haven't told him. But he's somewhere about; I'll tell him now."

"No, don't. I don't think we'll have that done, after all. I expect he'll want to go out soon—at any rate, sometime during the day. Let him go whenever he likes. I'll sit upstairs a bit in the club-room."

"Very well. But how do you know Steggles will be going out?"

"Well, he's pretty restless after his lost *protégé*, isn't he? I don't suppose he'll be able to remain idle long."

"And about Crockett. Do you give him up?"

"Oh, no! Don't you be impatient. I can't say I'm quite confident yet of laying hold of him—the time is so short you see—but I think I shall at least have news for you by the evening."

Hewitt sat in the club-room until the afternoon, taking his lunch there. At length he saw, through the front window, Raggy Steggles walking down the road. In an instant Hewitt was downstairs and at the door. The road bent eighty yards away, and as soon as Steggles passed the bend the detective hurried after him.

All the way to Padfield town and more than half through it Hewitt dogged the trainer. In the end Steggles stopped at a corner and gave a note to a small boy who was playing near. The boy ran with the note to a bright, well-kept house at the opposite corner. Martin Hewitt was interested to observe the legend, "H. Danby, Contractor," on a board over a gate in the side wall of the garden behind this house. In five minutes a door in the side gate opened, and the head and shoulders of the red-faced man emerged. Steggles immediately hurried across and disappeared through the gate.

This was both interesting and instructive. Hewitt took up a position in the side street and waited. In ten minutes the trainer reappeared and hurried off the way he had come, along the street Hewitt had considerately left clear for him. Then Hewitt strolled toward the smart house and took a good look at it. At one corner of the small piece of forecourt garden, near the railings, a small, baize-covered, glass-fronted notice-board stood on two posts. On its top edge appeared the words, "H. Danby. Houses to be Sold or Let." But the only notice pinned to the green baize within was an old and dusty one, inviting tenants for three shops, which were suitable for any business, and which would be fitted to suit tenants. Apply within.

Hewitt pushed open the front gate and rang the door-bell. "There are some shops to let, I see," he said, when a maid appeared. "I should like to see them, if you will let me have the key."

"Master's out, sir. You can't see the shops till Monday."

"Dear me, that's unfortunate, I'm afraid I can't wait till Monday. Didn't Mr. Danby leave any instructions, in case anybody should inquire?"

"Yes, sir—as I've told you. He said anybody who called about 'em must come again on Monday."

"Oh, very well, then; I suppose I must try. One of the shops is in High Street, isn't it?"

"No, sir; they're all in the new part—Granville Road."

"Ah, I'm afraid that will scarcely do. But I'll see. Good-day."

Martin Hewitt walked away a couple of streets' lengths before he inquired the way to Granville Road. When at last he found that thoroughfare, in a new and muddy suburb, crowded with brick-heaps and half-finished streets, he took a slow walk along its entire length. It was a melancholy example of baffled enterprise. A row of a dozen or more shops had been built before any population had arrived to demand goods. Would-be tradesmen had taken many of these shops, and failure and disappointment stared from the windows. Some were half covered by shutters, because the scanty stock scarce sufficed to fill the remaining half. Others were shut almost altogether, the inmates only keeping open the door for their own convenience, and, perhaps, keeping down a shutter for the sake of a little light. Others, again, had not yet fallen so low, but struggled bravely still to maintain a show of business and prosperity, with very little success. Opposite the shops there still remained a dusty, ill-treated hedge and a forlorn-looking field, which an old board offered on building leases. Altogether a most depressing spot.

There was little difficulty in identifying the three shops offered for letting by Mr. H. Danby. They were all together near the middle of the row, and were the only ones that appeared not yet to have been occupied. A dusty "To Let" bill hung in each window, with written directions to inquire of Mr. H. Danby or at No. 7. Now No. 7 was a melancholy baker's shop, with a stock of three loaves and a plate of stale buns. The disappointed baker assured Hewitt that he usually kept the keys of the shops, but that the landlord, Mr. Danby, had taken them away the day before to see how the ceilings were standing, and had not returned them. "But if you was thinking of taking a shop here," the poor baker added, with some hesitation, "I—I—if you'll excuse my advising you—I shouldn't recommend it. I've had a sickener of it myself."

Hewitt thanked the baker for his advice, wished him better luck in future, and left. To the Hare and Hounds his pace was brisk. "Come," he said, as he met Kentish's inquiring glance, "this has been a very good day, on the whole. I know where our man is now, and I think we can get him, by a little management."

"Where is he?"

"Oh, down in Padfield. As a matter of fact, he's being kept there against his will, we shall find. I see that your friend Mr. Danby is a builder as well as a bookmaker."

"Not a regular builder. He speculates in a street of new houses now and again, that's all. But is he in it?"

"He's as deep in it as anybody, I think. Now, don't fly into a passion. There are a few others in it as well, but you'll do harm if you don't keep quiet."

"But go and get the police; come and fetch him, if you know where they're keeping him. Why——"

"So we will, if we can't do it without them. But it's quite possible we can, and without all the disturbance and, perhaps, delay that calling in the police would involve. Consider, now, in reference to your own arrangements. Wouldn't it pay you better to get him back quietly, without a soul knowing—perhaps not even Danby knowing—till the heat is run tomorrow?"

"Well, yes, it would, of course."

"Very good, then, so be it. Remember what I have told you about keeping your mouth shut; say nothing to Steggles or anybody. Is there a cab or brougham your son and I can have for the evening?"

"There's an old hiring landau in the stables you can shut up into a cab, if that'll do."

"Excellent. We'll run down to the town in it as soon as it's ready. But, first, a word about Crockett. What sort of a lad is he? Likely to give them trouble, show fight, and make a disturbance?"

"No, I should say not. He's no plucked un, certainly; all his manhood's in his legs, I believe. You see, he ain't a big sort o' chap at best, and he'd be pretty easy put upon—at least, I guess so."

"Very good, so much the better, for then he won't have been damaged, and they will probably only have one man to guard him. Now the carriage, please."

Young Kentish was a six-foot sergeant of grenadiers home on furlough, and luxuriating in plain clothes. He and Hewitt walked a little way toward the town, allowing the landau to catch them up. They travelled in it to within a hundred yards of the empty shops and then alighted, bidding the driver wait.

"I shall show you three empty shops," Hewitt said, as he and young Kentish walked down Granville Road. "I am pretty sure that Sammy Crockett is in one of them, and I am pretty sure that that is the middle one. Take a look as we go past."

When the shops had been slowly passed, Hewitt resumed: "Now, did you see anything about those shops that told a tale of any sort?"

"No," Sergeant Kentish replied. "I can't say I noticed anything beyond the fact that they were empty—and likely to stay so, I should think."

"We'll stroll back, and look in at the windows, if nobody's watching us," Hewitt said. "You see, it's reasonable to suppose they've put him in the middle one, because that would suit their purpose best. The shops at each side of the three are occupied, and, if the prisoner struggled, or shouted, or made an uproar, he might be heard if he were in one of the shops next those inhabited. So that the middle shop is the most likely. Now, see there," he went on, as they stopped before the window of the shop in question, "over at the back there's a staircase not yet partitioned off. It goes down below and up above. On the stairs and on the floor near them there are muddy footmarks. These must have been made today, else they would not be muddy, but dry and dusty, since there hasn't been a shower for a week till today. Move on again. Then you noticed that there were no other such marks in the shop. Consequently, the man with the muddy feet did not come in by the front door, but by the back; otherwise he would have made a trail from the door. So we will go round to the back ourselves."

It was now growing dusk. The small pieces of ground behind the shops were bounded by a low fence, containing a door for each house.

"This door is bolted inside, of course," Hewitt said, "but there is no difficulty in climbing. I think we had better wait in the garden till dark. In the meantime, the jailer, whoever he is, may come out; in which case we shall pounce on him as soon as he opens the door. You have that few yards of cord in your pocket, I think? And my handkerchief, properly rolled, will make a very good gag. Now over."

They climbed the fence and quietly approached the house, placing themselves in the angle of an outhouse out of sight from the windows. There was no sound, and no light appeared. Just above the ground about a foot of window was visible, with a grating over it, apparently lighting a basement. Suddenly Hewitt touched his companion's arm and pointed toward the window. A faint rustling sound was perceptible, and, as nearly as could be discerned in the darkness, some white blind or covering was placed over the glass from the inside. Then came the sound of a striking match, and at the side edge of the window there was a faint streak of light.

"That's the place," Hewitt whispered. "Come, we'll make a push for it. You stand against the wall at one side of the door and I'll stand at the other, and we'll have him as he comes out. Quietly, now, and I'll startle them."

He took a stone from among the rubbish littering the garden and flung it crashing through the window. There was a loud exclamation from within, the blind fell, and somebody rushed to the back door and flung it open. Instantly Kentish let fly a heavy right-hander, and the man went over like a skittle. In a moment Hewitt was upon him and the gag in his mouth.

"Hold him," Hewitt whispered, hurriedly. "I'll see if there are others."

He peered down through the low window. Within Sammy Crockett, his bare legs dangling from beneath his long overcoat, sat on a packing-box, leaning with his head on his hand and his back toward the window. A guttering candle stood on the mantel-piece, and the newspaper which had been stretched across the window lay in scattered sheets on the floor. No other person besides Sammy was visible.

They led their prisoner indoors. Young Kentish recognised him as a public-house loafer and race-course ruffian, well known in the neighbourhood.

"So it's you, is it, Browdie?" he said. "I've caught you one hard clump, and I've half a mind to make it a score more. But you'll get it pretty warm one way or another before this job's forgotten."

Sammy Crockett was overjoyed at his rescue. He had not been ill-treated, he explained, but had been thoroughly cowed by Browdie, who had from time to time threatened him savagely with an iron bar by way of persuading him to quietness and submission. He had been fed, and had taken no worse harm than a slight stiffness from his adventure, due to his light under-attire of jersey and knee-shorts.

Sergeant Kentish tied Browdie's elbows firmly together behind, and carried the line round the ankles, bracing all up tight. Then he ran a knot from one wrist to the other over the back of the neck, and left the prisoner, trussed and helpless, on the heap of straw that had been Sammy's bed.

"You won't be very jolly, I expect," Kentish said, "for some time. You can't shout and you can't walk, and I know you can't untie yourself. You'll get a bit hungry, too, perhaps, but that'll give you an appetite. I don't suppose you'll be disturbed till sometime tomorrow, unless our friend Danby turns up in the meantime. But you can come along to jail instead, if you prefer it."

They left him where he lay, and took Sammy to the old landau. Sammy walked in slippers, carrying his spiked shoes, hanging by the lace, in his hand.

"Ah," said Hewitt, "I think I know the name of the young lady who gave you those slippers."

Crockett looked ashamed and indignant. "Yes," he said, "they've done me nicely between 'em. But I'll pay her—I'll——"

"Hush, hush!" Hewitt said; "you mustn't talk unkindly of a lady, you know. Get into this carriage, and we'll take you home. We'll see if I can tell you your adventures without making a mistake. First, you had a note from Miss Webb, telling you that you were mistaken in supposing she had slighted you, and that, as a matter of fact, she had quite done with somebody else—left him—of whom you were jealous. Isn't that so?"

"Well, yes," young Crockett answered, blushing deeply under the carriage-lamp; "but I don't see how you come to know that."

"Then she went on to ask you to get rid of Steggles on Thursday afternoon for a few minutes, and speak to her in the back lane. Now, your running pumps, with their thin soles, almost like paper, no heels and long spikes, hurt your feet horribly if you walk on hard ground, don't they?"

"Ay, that they do—enough to cripple you. I'd never go on much hard ground with 'em."

"They're not like cricket shoes, I see."

"Not a bit. Cricket shoes you can walk anywhere in!"

"Well, she knew this—I think I know who told her—and she promised to bring you a new pair of slippers, and to throw them over the fence for you to come out in."

"I s'pose she's been tellin' you all this?" Crockett said, mournfully. "You couldn't ha' seen the letter; I saw her tear it up and put the bits in her pocket. She asked me for it in the lane, in case Steggles saw it."

"Well, at any rate, you sent Steggles away, and the slippers did come over, and you went into the lane. You walked with her as far as the road at the end, and then you were seized and gagged, and put into a carriage."

"That was Browdie did that," said Crockett, "and another chap I don't know. But—why, this is Padfield High Street?" He looked through the window and regarded the familiar shops with astonishment.

"Of course it is. Where did you think it was?"

"Why, where was that place you found me in?"

"Granville Road, Padfield. I suppose they told you you were in another town?"

"Told me it was Newstead Hatch. They drove for about three or four hours, and kept me down on the floor between the seats so as I couldn't see where we was going."

"Done for two reasons," said Hewitt. "First, to mystify you, and prevent any discovery of the people directing the conspiracy; and second, to be able to put you indoors at night and unobserved. Well, I think I have told you all you know yourself now as far as the carriage.

"But there is the Hare and Hounds just in front. We'll pull up here, and I'll get out and see if the coast is clear. I fancy Mr. Kentish would rather you came in unnoticed."

In a few seconds Hewitt was back, and Crockett was conveyed indoors by a side entrance. Hewitt's instructions to the landlord were few, but emphatic. "Don't tell Steggles about it," he said; "make an excuse to get rid of him, and send him out of the house. Take Crockett into some other bedroom, not his own, and let your son look after him. Then come here, and I'll tell you all about it."

Sammy Crockett was undergoing a heavy grooming with white embrocation at the hands of Sergeant Kentish when the landlord returned to Hewitt. "Does Danby know you've got him?" he asked. "How did you do it?"

"Danby doesn't know yet, and with luck he won't know till he sees Crockett running tomorrow. The man who has sold you is Steggles."

"Steggles?"

"Steggles it is. At the very first, when Steggles rushed in to report Sammy Crockett missing, I suspected him. You didn't, I suppose?"

"No. He's always been considered a straight man, and he looked as startled as anybody."

"Yes, I must say he acted it very well. But there was something suspicious in his story. What did he say? Crockett had remarked a chilliness, and asked for a sweater, which Steggles went to fetch. Now, just think. You understand these things. Would any trainer who knew his business (as Steggles does) have gone to bring out a sweater for his man to change for his jersey in the open air, at the very time the man was complaining of chilliness? Of course not. He would have taken his man indoors again and let him change there under shelter. Then supposing Steggles had really been surprised at missing Crockett, wouldn't he have looked about, found the gate open, and *told* you it was open when he first came in? He said nothing of that—we found the gate open for ourselves. So that from the beginning I had a certain opinion of Steggles."

"What you say seems pretty plain now, although it didn't strike

42

me at the time. But, if Steggles was selling us, why couldn't he have drugged the lad? That would have been a deal simpler."

"Because Steggles is a good trainer, and has a certain reputation to keep up. It would have done him no good to have had a runner drugged while under his care; certainly it would have cooked his goose with *you*. It was much the safer thing to connive at kidnapping. That put all the active work into other hands, and left him safe, even if the trick failed. Now, you remember that we traced the prints of Crockett's spiked shoes to within a couple of yards from the fence, and that there they ceased suddenly?"

"Yes. You said it looked as though he had flown up into the air; and so it did."

"But I was sure that it was by that gate that Crockett had left, and by no other. He couldn't have got through the house without being seen, and there was no other way—let alone the evidence of the unbolted gate. Therefore, as the footprints ceased where they did, and were not repeated anywhere in the lane, I knew that he had taken his spiked shoes off—probably changed them for something else, because a runner anxious as to his chances would never risk walking on bare feet, with a chance of cutting them. Ordinary, broad, smooth-soled slippers would leave no impression on the coarse cinders bordering the track, and nothing short of spiked shoes would leave a mark on the hard path in the lane behind. The spike-tracks were leading, not directly toward the door, but in the direction of the fence, when they stopped; somebody had handed, or thrown, the slippers over the fence, and he had changed them on the spot. The enemy had calculated upon the spikes leaving a track in the lane that might lead us in our search, and had arranged accordingly.

"So far so good. I could see no footprints near the gate in the lane. You will remember that I sent Steggles off to watch at the Cop before I went out to the back—merely, of course, to get him out of the way. I went out into the lane, leaving you behind, and walked its whole length, first toward the Old Kilns and then back toward the road. I found nothing to help me except these small pieces of paper—which are here in my pocket-book, by the by. Of course this 'mmy' might have meant 'Jimmy' or 'Tommy' as possibly as 'Sammy,' but they were not to be rejected on that account. Certainly Crockett had been decoyed out of your ground, not taken by force, or there would have been marks of a scuffle in the cinders. And as his request for a sweater was probably an excuse—because it was not at all a cold afternoon—he must have previously designed going out. Inference, a letter received; and here were pieces of a letter.

"Now, in the light of what I have said, look at these pieces. First, there is the 'mmy'—that I have dealt with. Then see this 'throw them ov'—clearly a part of 'throw them over'; exactly what had probably been done with the slippers. Then the 'poor f,' coming just on the line before, and seen, by joining up with this other piece, might easily be a reference to 'poor feet.' These coincidences, one on the other, went far to establish the identity of the letter, and to confirm my previous impressions. But then there is something else. Two other pieces evidently mean 'left him,' and 'right away,' perhaps; but there is another, containing almost all of the words 'hate his,' with the word 'hate' underlined. Now, who writes 'hate' with the emphasis of underscoring—who but a woman? The writing is large and not very regular; it might easily be that of a half-educated woman. Here was something more—Sammy had been enticed away by a woman.

"Now, I remembered that, when we went into the tap-room on Wednesday, some of his companions were chaffing Crockett about a certain Nancy Webb, and the chaff went home, as was plain to see. The woman, then, who could most easily entice Sammy Crockett away was Nancy Webb. I resolved to find who Nancy Webb was and learn more of her.

"Meantime, I took a look at the road at the end of the lane. It was damper than the lane, being lower, and overhung by trees. There were many wheel-tracks, but only one set that turned in the road and went back the way it came, toward the town; and they were narrow wheels—carriage wheels. Crockett tells me now that they drove him about for a long time before shutting him up; probably the inconvenience of taking him straight to the hiding-place didn't strike them when they first drove off.

"A few inquiries soon set me in the direction of the Plough and Miss Nancy Webb. I had the curiosity to look around the place as I approached, and there, in the garden behind the house, were Steggles and the young lady in earnest confabulation!

"Every conjecture became a certainty. Steggles was the lover of whom Crockett was jealous, and he had employed the girl to bring Sammy out. I watched Steggles home, and gave you a hint to keep him there.

"But the thing that remained was to find Steggles' employer in this business. I was glad to be in when Danby called. He came, of course, to hear if you would blurt out anything, and to learn, if possible, what steps you were taking. He failed. By way of making assurance doubly sure I took a short walk this morning in the character of a deaf gentleman, and got Miss Webb to write me a direction that comprised three of the words on these scraps of paper—'left,' 'right,' and 'lane'; see, they correspond, the peculiar 'f's,' 't's,' and all.

"Now, I felt perfectly sure that Steggles would go for his pay today. In the first place, I knew that people mixed up with shady transactions in professional pedestrianism are not apt to trust one another far—they know better. Therefore, Steggles wouldn't have had his bribe first. But he would take care to get it before the Saturday heats were run, because once they were over the thing was done, and the principal conspirator might have refused to pay up, and Steggles couldn't have helped himself. Again I hinted he should not go out till I could follow him, and this afternoon, when he went, follow him I did. I saw him go into Danby's house by the side way and come away again. Danby it was, then, who had arranged the business; and nobody was more likely, considering his large pecuniary stake against Crockett's winning this race.

"But now how to find Crockett? I made up my mind he wouldn't be in Danby's own house. That would be a deal too risky, with servants about and so on. I saw that Danby was a builder, and had three shops to let—it was on a paper before his house. What more likely prison than an empty house? I knocked at Danby's door and asked for the keys of those shops. I couldn't have them. The servant told me Danby was out (a manifest lie, for I had just seen him), and that nobody could see the shops till Monday. But I got out of her the address of the shops, and that was all I wanted at the time.

"Now, why was nobody to see those shops till Monday? The interval was suspicious—just enough to enable Crockett to be sent away again and cast loose after the Saturday racing, supposing him to be kept in one of the empty buildings. I went off at once and looked at the shops, forming my conclusions as to which would be the most likely for Danby's purpose. Here I had another confirmation of my ideas. A poor, half-bankrupt baker in one of the shops had, by the bills, the custody of a set of keys; but he, too, told me I couldn't have them; Danby had taken them away—and on Thursday, the very day—with some trivial excuse, and hadn't brought them back. That was all I wanted or could expect in the way of guidance. The whole thing was plain. The rest you know all about."

"Well, you're certainly as smart as they give you credit for, I must say. But suppose Danby had taken down his 'To Let' notice, what would you have done, then?"

"We had our course, even then. We should have gone to Danby, astounded him by telling him all about his little games, terrorized him with threats of the law, and made him throw up his hand and send Crockett back. But, as it is, you see, he doesn't know at this moment—probably won't know till tomorrow afternoon—that the lad is safe and sound here. You will probably use the interval to make him pay for losing the game—by some of the ingenious financial devices you are no doubt familiar with."

"Ay, that I will. He'll give any price against Crockett now, so long as the bet don't come direct from me."

"But about Crockett, now," Hewitt went on. "Won't this confinement be likely to have damaged his speed for a day or two?"

"Ah, perhaps," the landlord replied; "but, bless ye, that won't matter. There's four more in his heat tomorrow. Two I know aren't tryers, and the other two I can hold in at a couple of quid apiece any day. The third round and final won't be till tomorrow week, and he'll be as fit as ever by then. It's as safe as ever it was. How much are you going to have on? I'll lump it on for you safe enough. This is a chance not to be missed; it's picking money up."

"Thank you; I don't think I'll have anything to do with it. This professional pedestrian business doesn't seem a pretty one at all. I don't call myself a moralist, but, if you'll excuse my saying so, the thing is scarcely the game I care to pick tap money at in any way."

"Oh, very well! if you think so, I won't persuade ye, though I don't think so much of your smartness as I did, after that. Still, we won't quarrel; you've done me a mighty good turn, that I must say, and I only feel I aren't level without doing something to pay the debt. Come, now, you've got your trade as I've got mine. Let me have the bill, and I'll pay it like a lord, and feel a deal more pleased than if you made a favour of it—not that I'm above a favour, of course. But I'd prefer paying, and that's a fact."

"My dear sir, you have paid," Hewitt said, with a smile. "You paid in advance. It was a bargain, wasn't it, that I should do your business if you would help me in mine? Very well; a bargain's a bargain, and we've both performed our parts. And you mustn't be offended at what I said just now."

"That I won't! But as to that Raggy Steggles, once those heats are over tomorrow, I'll—well——"

It was on the following Sunday week that Martin Hewitt, in his rooms in London, turned over his paper and read, under the head "Padfield Annual 135 Yards Handicap," this announcement:

Final heat: Crockett, first; Willis, second; Trewby, third; Owen, 0; Howell, 0. A runaway win by nearly three yards.

THE CASE OF MR. FOGGATT

Almost the only dogmatism that Martin Hewitt permitted himself in regard to his professional methods was one on the matter of accumulative probabilities. Often when I have remarked upon the apparently trivial nature of the clews by which he allowed himself to be guided—sometimes, to all seeming, in the very face of all likelihood—he has replied that two trivialities, pointing in the same direction, became at once, by their mere agreement, no trivialities at all, but enormously important considerations.

"If I were in search of a man," he would say, "of whom I knew nothing but that he squinted, bore a birthmark on his right hand, and limped, and I observed a man who answered to the first peculiarity, so far the clue would be trivial, because thousands of men squint. Now, if that man presently moved and exhibited a birthmark on his right hand, the value of that squint and that mark would increase at once a hundred or a thousand fold. Apart they are little; together much. The weight of evidence is not doubled merely; it would be only doubled if half the men who squinted had right-hand birthmarks; whereas the proportion, if it could be ascertained, would be, perhaps, more like one in ten thousand. The two trivialities, pointing in the same direction, become very strong evidence.

"And, when the man is seen to walk with a limp, that limp (another triviality), re-enforcing the others, brings the matter to the rank of a practical certainty. The Bertillon system of identification—what is it but a summary of trivialities? Thousands of men are of the same height, thousands of the same length of foot, thousands of the same girth of head—thousands correspond in any separate measurement you may name. It is when the measurements are taken *together* that you have your man identified forever. Just consider how few, if any, of your friends correspond exactly in any two personal peculiarities."

Hewitt's dogma received its illustration unexpectedly close at home.

The old house wherein my chambers and Hewitt's office were situated contained, besides my own, two or three more bachelors' dens, in addition to the offices on the ground and first and second floors. At the very top of all, at the back, a fat, middle-aged man, named Foggatt, occupied a set of four rooms. It was only after a long residence, by an accidental remark of the housekeeper's, that I learned the man's name, which was not painted on his door or displayed, with all the others, on the wall of the ground-floor porch.

Mr. Foggatt appeared to have few friends, but lived in something as nearly approaching luxury as an old bachelor living in chambers can live. An ascending case of champagne was a common phenomenon of the staircase, and I have more than once seen a picture, destined for the top floor, of a sort that went far to awaken green covetousness in the heart of a poor journalist.

The man himself was not altogether prepossessing. Fat as he was, he had a way of carrying his head forward on his extended neck and gazing widely about with a pair of the roundest and most prominent eyes I remember to have ever seen, except in a fish. On the whole, his appearance was rather vulgar, rather arrogant, and rather suspicious, without any very pronounced quality of any sort. But certainly he was not pretty. In the end, however, he was found shot dead in his sitting-room.

It was in this way: Hewitt and I had dined together at my club, and late in the evening had returned to my rooms to smoke and discuss whatever came uppermost. I had made a bargain that day with two speculative odd lots at a book sale, each of which contained a hidden prize. We sat talking and turning over these books while time went unperceived, when suddenly we were startled by a loud report. Clearly it was in the building. We listened for a moment, but heard nothing else, and then Hewitt expressed his opinion that the report was that of a gunshot. Gunshots in residential chambers are not common things, wherefore I got up and went to the landing, looking up the stairs and down.

At the top of the next flight I saw Mrs. Clayton, the housekeeper. She appeared to be frightened, and told me that the report came from Mr. Foggatt's room. She thought he might have had an accident with the pistol that usually lay on his mantel-piece. We went upstairs with her, and she knocked at Mr. Foggatt's door.

There was no reply. Through the ventilating fanlight over the door it could be seen that there were lights within, a sign, Mrs. Clayton maintained, that Mr. Foggatt was not out. We knocked again, much more loudly, and called, but still ineffectually. The door was locked, and an application of the housekeeper's key proved that the tenant's key had been left in the lock inside. Mrs. Clayton's conviction that "something had happened" became distressing, and in the end Hewitt pried open the door with a small poker.

Something *had* happened. In the sitting-room Mr. Foggatt sat with his head bowed over the table, quiet and still. The head was ill to look at, and by it lay a large revolver, of the full-sized army pattern. Mrs. Clayton ran back toward the landing with faint screams.

"Run, Brett!" said Hewitt; "a doctor and a policeman!"

I bounced down the stairs half a flight at a time. "First," I thought, "a doctor. He may not be dead." I could think of no doctor in the immediate neighbourhood, but ran up the street away from the Strand, as being the more likely direction for the doctor, although less so for the policeman. It took me a good five minutes to find the medico, after being led astray by a red lamp at a private hotel, and another five to get back, with a policeman.

Foggatt was dead, without a doubt. Probably had shot himself, the doctor thought, from the powder-blackening and other circumstances. Certainly nobody could have left the room by the door, or he must have passed my landing, while the fact of the door being found locked from the inside made the thing impossible. There were two windows to the room, both of which were shut, one being fastened by the catch, while the catch of the other was broken—an old fracture. Below these windows was a sheer drop of fifty feet or more, without a foot or hand-hold near. The windows in the other rooms were shut and fastened. Certainly it seemed suicide—unless it were one of those accidents that will occur to people who fiddle ignorantly with fire-arms. Soon the rooms were in possession of the police, and we were turned out.

We looked in at the housekeeper's kitchen, where her daughter was reviving and calming Mrs. Clayton with gin and water.

"You mustn't upset yourself, Mrs. Clayton," Hewitt said, "or what will become of us all? The doctor thinks it was an accident."

He took a small bottle of sewing-machine oil from his pocket and handed it to the daughter, thanking her for the loan.

★★★★★★

There was little evidence at the inquest. The shot had been heard, the body had been found—that was the practical sum of the matter.

No friends or relatives of the dead man came forward. The doctor gave his opinion as to the probability of suicide or an accident, and the police evidence tended in the same direction. Nothing had been found to indicate that any other person had been near the dead man's rooms on the night of the fatality. On the other hand, his papers, bankbook, etc., proved him to be a man of considerable substance, with no apparent motive for suicide. The police had been unable to trace any relatives, or, indeed, any nearer connections than casual acquaintances, fellow-clubmen, and so on. The jury found that Mr. Foggatt had died by accident.

"Well, Brett," Hewitt asked me afterward, "what do you think of the verdict?"

I said that it seemed to be the most reasonable one possible, and to square with the common-sense view of the case.

"Yes," he replied, "perhaps it does. From the point of view of the jury, and on their information, their verdict was quite reasonable. Nevertheless, Mr. Foggatt did not shoot himself. He was shot by a rather tall, active young man, perhaps a sailor, but certainly a gymnast—a young man whom I think I could identify if I saw him."

"But how do you know this?"

"By the simplest possible inferences, which you may easily guess, if you will but think."

"But, then, why didn't you say this at the inquest?"

"My dear fellow, they don't want any inferences and conjectures at an inquest; they only want evidence. If I had traced the murderer, of course then I should have communicated with the police. As a matter of fact, it is quite possible that the police have observed and know as much as I do—or more. They don't give everything away at an inquest, you know. It wouldn't do."

"But, if you are right, how did the man get away?"

"Come, we are near home now. Let us take a look at the back of the house. He *couldn't* have left by Foggatt's landing door, as we know; and as he *was* there (I am certain of that), and as the chimney is out of the question—for there was a good fire in the grate—he must have gone out by the window. Only one window is possible—that with the broken catch—for all the others were fastened inside. Out of that window, then, he went."

"But how? The window is fifty feet up."

"Of course it is. But why *will* you persist in assuming that the only way of escape by a window is downward? See, now, look up there.

The window is at the top floor, and it has a very broad sill. Over the window is nothing but the flat face of the gable-end; but to the right, and a foot or two above the level of the top of the window, an iron gutter ends. Observe, it is not of lead composition, but a strong iron gutter, supported, just at its end, by an iron bracket. If a tall man stood on the end of the window-sill, steadying himself by the left hand and leaning to the right, he could just touch the end of this gutter with his right hand. The full stretch, toe to finger, is seven feet three inches. I have measured it.

"An active gymnast, or a sailor, could catch the gutter with a slight spring, and by it draw himself upon the roof. You will say he would have to be *very* active, dexterous, and cool. So he would. And that very fact helps us, because it narrows the field of inquiry. We know the sort of man to look for. Because, being certain (as I am) that the man was in the room, I *know* that he left in the way I am telling you. He must have left in some way, and, all the other ways being impossible, this alone remains, difficult as the feat may seem. The fact of his shutting the window behind him further proves his coolness and address at so great a height from the ground."

All this was very plain, but the main point was still dark.

"You say you *know* that another man was in the room," I said; "how do you know that?"

"As I said, by an obvious inference. Come, now, you shall guess how I arrived at that inference. You often speak of your interest in my work, and the attention with which you follow it. This shall be a simple exercise for you. You saw everything in the room as plainly as I myself. Bring the scene back to your memory, and think over the various small objects littering about, and how they would affect the case. Quick observation is the first essential for my work. Did you see a newspaper, for instance?"

"Yes. There was an evening paper on the floor, but I didn't examine it."

"Anything else?"

"On the table there was a whisky decanter, taken from the Tantalus-stand on the sideboard, and one glass. That, by the by," I added, "looked as though only one person were present."

"So it did, perhaps, although the inference wouldn't be very strong. Go on!"

"There was a fruit-stand on the sideboard, with a plate beside it containing a few nutshells, a piece of apple, a pair of nut-crackers, and,

I think, some orange peel. There was, of course, all the ordinary furniture, but no chair pulled up to the table, except that used by Foggatt himself. That's all I noticed, I think. Stay—there was an ash-tray on the table, and a partly burned cigar near it—only one cigar, though."

"Excellent—excellent, indeed, as far as memory and simple observation go. You saw everything plainly, and you remember everything. Surely *now* you know how I found out that another man had just left?"

"No, I don't; unless there were different kinds of ash in the ash-tray."

"That is a fairly good suggestion, but there were not—there was only a single ash, corresponding in every way to that on the cigar. Don't you remember everything that I did as we went downstairs?"

"You returned a bottle of oil to the housekeeper's daughter, I think."

"I did. Doesn't that give you a hint? Come, you surely have it now?"

"I haven't."

"Then I sha'n't tell you; you don't deserve it. Think, and don't mention the subject again till you have at least one guess to make. The thing stares you in the face; you see it, you remember it, and yet you *won't* see it. I won't encourage your slovenliness of thought, my boy, by telling you what you can know for yourself if you like. Goodbye—I'm off now. There's a case in hand I can't neglect."

"Don't you propose to go further into this, then?"

Hewitt shrugged his shoulders. "I'm not a policeman," he said. "The case is in very good hands. Of course, if anybody comes to me to do it as a matter of business, I'll take it up. It's very interesting, but I can't neglect my regular work for it. Naturally, I shall keep my eyes open and my memory in order. Sometimes these things come into the hands by themselves, as it were; in that case, of course, I am a loyal citizen, and ready to help the law. *Au revoir!*"

★★★★★★

I am a busy man myself, and thought little more of Hewitt's conundrum for some time; indeed, when I did think, I saw no way to the answer. A week after the inquest I took a holiday (I had written my nightly leaders regularly every day for the past five years), and saw no more of Hewitt for six weeks. After my return, with still a few days of leave to run, one evening we together turned into Luzatti's, off Coventry Street, for dinner.

"I have been here several times lately," Hewitt said; "they feed you very well. No, not that table"—he seized my arm as I turned to an unoccupied corner—"I fancy it's draughty." He led the way to a longer table where a dark, lithe, and (as well as could be seen) tall young man already sat, and took chairs opposite him.

We had scarcely seated ourselves before Hewitt broke into a torrent of conversation on the subject of bicycling. As our previous conversation had been of a literary sort, and as I had never known Hewitt at any other time to show the slightest interest in bicycling, this rather surprised me. I had, however, such a general outsider's grasp of the subject as is usual in a journalist-of-all-work, and managed to keep the talk going from my side. As we went on I could see the face of the young man opposite brighten with interest. He was a rather fine-looking fellow, with a dark, though very clear skin, but had a hard, angry look of eye, a prominence of cheek-bone, and a squareness of jaw that gave him a rather uninviting aspect. As Hewitt rattled on, however, our neighbour's expression became one of pleasant interest merely.

"Of course," Hewitt said, "we've a number of very capital men just now, but I believe a deal in the forgotten riders of five, ten, and fifteen years back. Osmond, I believe, was better than any man riding now, and I think it would puzzle some of them to beat Furnivall as he was, at his best. But poor old Cortis—really, I believe he was as good as anybody. Nobody ever beat Cortis—except—let me see—I think somebody beat Cortis once—who was it now? I can't remember."

"Liles," said the young man opposite, looking up quickly.

"Ah, yes—Liles it was; Charley Liles. Wasn't it a championship?"

"Mile championship, 1880; Cortis won the other three, though."

"Yes, so he did. I saw Cortis when he first broke the old 2.46 mile record." And straightway Hewitt plunged into a whirl of talk of bicycles, tricycles, records, racing cyclists, Hillier, and Synyer and Noel Whiting, Taylerson and Appleyard—talk wherein the young man opposite bore an animated share, while I was left in the cold.

Our new friend, it seems, had himself been a prominent racing bicyclist a few years back, and was presently, at Hewitt's request, exhibiting a neat gold medal that hung at his watch-guard. That was won, he explained, in the old tall bicycle days, the days of bad tracks, when every racing cyclist carried cinder scars on his face from numerous accidents. He pointed to a blue mark on his forehead, which, he told us, was a track scar, and described a bad fall that had cost him two teeth, and broken others. The gaps among his teeth were plain to see as he smiled.

Presently the waiter brought dessert, and the young man opposite took an apple. Nut-crackers and a fruit-knife lay on our side of the stand, and Hewitt turned the stand to offer him the knife.

"No, thanks," he said; "I only polish a good apple, never peel it. It's a mistake, except with thick-skinned foreign ones."

And he began to munch the apple as only a boy or a healthy athlete can. Presently he turned his head to order coffee. The waiter's back was turned, and he had to be called twice. To my unutterable amazement Hewitt reached swiftly across the table, snatched the half-eaten apple from the young man's plate and pocketed it, gazing immediately, with an abstracted air, at a painted Cupid on the ceiling.

Our neighbour turned again, looked doubtfully at his plate and the table-cloth about it, and then shot a keen glance in the direction of Hewitt. He said nothing, however, but took his coffee and his bill, deliberately drank the former, gazing quietly at Hewitt as he did it, paid the latter, and left.

Immediately Hewitt was on his feet and, taking an umbrella, which stood near, followed. Just as he reached the door he met our late neighbour, who had turned suddenly back.

"Your umbrella, I think?" Hewitt asked, offering it.

"Yes, thanks." But the man's eye had more than its former hardness, and his jaw muscles tightened as I looked. He turned and went. Hewitt came back to me. "Pay the bill," he said, "and go back to your rooms; I will come on later. I must follow this man—it's the Foggatt case." As he went out I heard a cab rattle away, and immediately after it another.

I paid the bill and went home. It was ten o'clock before Hewitt turned up, calling in at his office below on his way up to me.

"Mr. Sidney Mason," he said, "is the gentleman the police will be wanting tomorrow, I expect, for the Foggatt murder. He is as smart a man as I remember ever meeting, and has done me rather neatly twice this evening."

"You mean the man we sat opposite at Luzatti's, of course?"

"Yes, I got his name, of course, from the reverse of that gold medal he was good enough to show me. But I fear he has bilked me over the address. He suspected me, that was plain, and left his umbrella by way of experiment to see if I were watching him sharply enough to notice the circumstance, and to avail myself of it to follow him. I was hasty and fell into the trap. He cabbed it away from Luzatti's, and I cabbed it after him. He has led me a pretty dance up and down London to-night, and two cabbies have made quite a stroke of business out of us. In the end he entered a house of which, of course, I have taken the address, but I expect he doesn't live there. He is too smart a man to lead me to his den; but the police can certainly find something of him at the house he went in at—and, I expect, left by the back way. By the way, you never guessed that simple little puzzle as to how I found that this *was* a murder, did you? You see it now, of course."

"Something to do with that apple you stole, I suppose?"

"Something to do with it? I should think so, you worthy innocent. Just ring your bell; we'll borrow Mrs. Clayton's sewing-machine oil again. On the night we broke into Foggatt's room you saw the nut-shells and the bitten remains of an apple on the sideboard, and you remembered it; and yet you couldn't see that in that piece of apple possibly lay an important piece of evidence. Of course I never ex-pected you to have arrived at any conclusion, as I had, because I had ten minutes in which to examine that apple, and to do what I did with it. But, at least, you should have seen the possibility of evidence in it.

"First, now, the apple was white. A bitten apple, as you must have observed, turns of a reddish brown colour if left to stand long. Differ-ent kinds of apples brown with different rapidities, and the browning always begins at the core. This is one of the twenty thousand tiny things that few people take the trouble to notice, but which it is useful for a man in my position to know. A russet will brown quite quickly. The apple on the sideboard was, as near as I could tell, a Newtown pippin or other apple of that kind, which will brown at the core in from twenty minutes to half an hour, and in other parts in a quarter of an hour more. When we saw it, it was white, with barely a tinge of brown about the exposed core. Inference, somebody had been eating it fifteen or twenty minutes before, perhaps a little longer—an infer-ence supported by the fact that it was only partly eaten.

"I examined that apple, and found it bore marks of very irregular teeth. While you were gone, I oiled it over, and, rushing down to my rooms, where I always have a little plaster of Paris handy for such work, took a mould of the part where the teeth had left the clearest marks. I then returned the apple to its place for the police to use if they thought fit. Looking at my mould, it was plain that the person who had bitten that apple had lost two teeth, one at top and one below, not exactly opposite, but nearly so. The other teeth, although they would appear to have been fairly sound, were irregular in size and line. Now, the dead man had, as I saw, a very excellent set of false teeth, regular and sharp, with none missing. Therefore, it was plain that somebody *else* had been eating that apple. Do I make myself clear?"

"Quite! Go on!"

"There were other inferences to be made—slighter, but all pointing the same way. For instance, a man of Foggatt's age does not, as a rule, munch an unpeeled apple like a school-boy. Inference, a young man, and healthy. Why I came to the conclusion that he was tall, active, a gymnast, and perhaps a sailor, I have already told you, when we examined the outside of Foggatt's window. It was also pretty clear that robbery was not the motive, since nothing was disturbed, and that a friendly conversation had preceded the murder—witness the drinking and the eating of the apple. Whether or not the police noticed these things I can't say. If they had had their best men on, they certainly would, I think; but the case, to a rough observer, looked so clearly one of accident or suicide that possibly they didn't.

"As I said, after the inquest I was unable to devote any immediate time to the case, but I resolved to keep my eyes open. The man to look for was tall, young, strong and active, with a very irregular set of teeth, a tooth missing from the lower jaw just to the left of the centre, and another from the upper jaw a little farther still toward the left. He might possibly be a person I had seen about the premises (I have a good memory for faces), or, of course, he possibly might not.

"Just before you returned from your holiday I noticed a young man at Luzatti's whom I remembered to have seen somewhere about the offices in this building. He was tall, young, and so on, but I had a client with me, and was unable to examine him more narrowly; indeed, as I was not exactly engaged on the case, and as there are several tall young men about, I took little trouble. But today, finding the same young man with a vacant seat opposite him, I took the opportunity of making a closer acquaintance."

"You certainly managed to draw him out."

"Oh, yes; the easiest person in the world to draw out is a cyclist. The easiest cyclist to draw out is, of course, the novice, but the next easiest is the veteran. When you see a healthy, well-trained-looking man, who, nevertheless, has a slight stoop in the shoulders, and, maybe, a medal on his watch-guard, it is always a safe card to try him first with a little cycle-racing talk. I soon brought Mr. Mason out of his shell, read his name on his medal, and had a chance of observing his teeth—indeed, he spoke of them himself. Now, as I observed just now, there are several tall, athletic young men about, and also there are several men who have lost teeth. But now I saw that this tall and athletic young man had lost exactly *two* teeth—one from the lower jaw, just to the left of the centre, and another from the upper jaw, farther still toward the left! Trivialities, pointing in the same direction, became important considerations. More, his teeth were irregular throughout, and, as nearly as I could remember it, looked remarkably like this little plaster mould of mine."

He produced from his pocket an irregular lump of plaster, about three inches long. On one side of this appeared in relief the likeness of two irregular rows of six or eight teeth, minus one in each row, where a deep gap was seen, in the position spoken of by my friend. He proceeded:

"This was enough at least to set me after this young man. But he gave me the greatest chance of all when he turned and left his apple (eaten unpeeled, remember!—another important triviality) on his plate. I'm afraid I wasn't at all polite, and I ran the risk of arousing his suspicions, but I couldn't resist the temptation to steal it. I did, as you saw, and here it is."

He brought the apple from his coat-pocket. One bitten side, placed against the upper half of the mould, fitted precisely, a projection of apple filling exactly the deep gap. The other side similarly fitted the lower half.

"There's no getting behind that, you see," Hewitt remarked. "Merely observing the man's teeth was a guide, to some extent, but this is as plain as his signature or his thumb impression. You'll never find two men *bite* exactly alike, no matter whether they leave distinct teeth-marks or not. Here, by the by, is Mrs. Clayton's oil. We'll take another mould from this apple, and compare *them*."

He oiled the apple, heaped a little plaster in a newspaper, took my water-jug, and rapidly pulled off a hard mould. The parts corresponding to the merely broken places in the apple were, of course, dissimilar; but as to the teeth-marks, the impressions were identical.

"That will do, I think," Hewitt said. "Tomorrow morning, Brett, I shall put up these things in a small parcel, and take them round to Bow Street."

"But are they sufficient evidence?"

"Quite sufficient for the police purpose. There is the man, and all the rest—his movements on the day and so forth—are simple matters of inquiry; at any rate, that is police business."

★★★★★★

I had scarcely sat down to my breakfast on the following morning when Hewitt came into the room and put a long letter before me.

"From our friend of last night," he said; "read it."

This letter began abruptly, and undated, and was as follows:

To Martin Hewitt, Esq.

Sir: I must compliment you on the adroitness you exhibited this evening in extracting from me my name. The address I was able to balk you of for the time being, although by the time you read this you will probably have found it through the *Law List*, as I am an admitted solicitor. That, however, will be of little use to you, for I am removing myself, I think, beyond the reach even of your abilities of search. I knew you well by sight, and was, perhaps, foolish to allow myself to be drawn as I did. Still, I had no idea that it would be dangerous, especially after seeing you, as a witness with very little to say, at the inquest upon the scoundrel I shot. Your somewhat discourteous seizure of my apple at first amazed me—indeed, I was a little doubtful as to whether you had really taken it—but it was my first warning that you might be playing a deep game against me, incomprehensible as the action was to my mind.

I subsequently reflected that I had been eating an apple, instead of taking the drink he first offered me, in the dead wretch's rooms on the night he came to his merited end. From this I assume that your design was in some way to compare what remained of the two apples—although I do not presume to fathom the depths of your detective system. Still, I have heard of many of your cases, and profoundly admire the keenness you exhibit. I am thought to be a keen man myself, but, although I was able, to some extent, to hold my own tonight, I admit that your acumen in this case alone is something beyond me.

I do not know by whom you are commissioned to hunt me, nor to what extent you may be acquainted with my connection with the creature I killed. I have sufficient respect for you, however, to wish that you should not regard me as a vicious criminal, and a couple of hours to spare in which to offer you an explanation that will convince you that such is not altogether the case. A hasty and violent temper I admit possessing; but

58

even now I cannot forget the one crime it has led me into—for it is, I suppose, strictly speaking, a crime. For it was the man Foggatt who made a felon of my father before the eyes of the world, and killed him with shame. It was he who murdered my mother, and none the less murdered her because she died of a broken heart. That he was also a thief and a hypocrite might have concerned me little but for that.

Of my father I remember very little. He must, I fear, have been a weak and incapable man in many respects. He had no business abilities—in fact, was quite unable to understand the complicated business matters in which he largely dealt. Foggatt was a consummate master of all those arts of financial jugglery that make so many fortunes, and ruin so many others, in matters of company promoting, stocks, and shares. He was unable to exercise them, however, because of a great financial disaster in which he had been mixed up a few years before, and which made his name one to be avoided in future. In these circumstances he made a sort of secret and informal partnership with my father, who, ostensibly alone in the business, acted throughout on the directions of Foggatt, understanding as little what he did, poor, simple man, as a schoolboy would have done. The transactions carried on went from small to large, and, unhappily from honourable to dishonourable.

My father relied on the superior abilities of Foggatt with an absolute trust, carrying out each day the directions given him privately the previous evening, buying, selling, printing prospectuses, signing whatever had to be signed, all with sole responsibility and as sole partner, while Foggatt, behind the scenes absorbed the larger share of the profits. In brief, my unhappy and foolish father was a mere tool in the hands of the cunning scoundrel who pulled all the wires of the business, himself unseen and irresponsible. At last three companies, for the promotion of which my father was responsible, came to grief in a heap. Fraud was written large over all their history, and, while Foggatt retired with his plunder, my father was left to meet ruin, disgrace, and imprisonment. From beginning to end he, and he only, was responsible. There was no shred of evidence to connect Foggatt with the matter, and no means of escape from the net drawn about my father. He lived through three years of imprisonment, and then, entirely abandoned by the man who had made use of his simplicity, he died—of nothing but shame and a broken heart.

Of this I knew nothing at the time. Again and again, as a small boy, I remember asking of my mother why I had no father at home, as other boys had—unconscious of the stab I thus inflicted on her gentle heart. Of her my earliest, as well as my latest, memory is that of a pale, weeping woman, who grudged to let me out of her sight.

Little by little I learned the whole cause of my mother's grief, for she had no other confidant, and I fear my character developed early, for my first coherent remembrance of the matter is that of a childish design to take a table-knife and kill the bad man who had made my father die in prison and caused my mother to cry.

One thing, however, I never knew—the name of that bad man. Again and again, as I grew older, I demanded to know, but my mother always withheld it from me, with a gentle reminder that vengeance was for a greater hand than mine.

I was seventeen years of age when my mother died. I believe that nothing but her strong attachment to myself and her desire to see me safely started in life kept her alive so long. Then I found that through all those years of narrowed means she had contrived to scrape and save a little money—sufficient, as it afterward proved, to see me through the examinations for entrance to my profession, with the generous assistance of my father's old legal advisers, who gave me my articles, and who have all along treated me with extreme kindness.

For most of the succeeding years my life does not concern the matter in hand. I was a lawyer's clerk in my benefactors' service, and afterward a qualified man among their assistants. All through the firm were careful, in pursuance of my poor mother's wishes, that I should not learn the name or whereabouts of the man who had wrecked her life and my father's. I first met the man himself at the Clifton Club, where I had gone with an acquaintance who was a member. It was not till afterward that I understood his curious awkwardness on that occasion. A week later I called (as I had frequently done) at the building in which your office is situated, on business with a solicitor who has an office on the floor above your own. On the stairs I almost ran against Mr. Foggatt. He started and turned pale, exhibiting signs of alarm that I could not understand, and asked me if I wished to see him.

'No,' I replied, 'I didn't know you lived here. I am after somebody else just now. Aren't you well?'

He looked at me rather doubtfully, and said he was *not* very well.

I met him twice or thrice after that, and on each occasion his manner grew more friendly, in a servile, flattering, and mean sort of way—a thing unpleasant enough in anybody, but doubly so in the intercourse of a man with another young enough to be his own son. Still, of course, I treated the man civilly enough. On one occasion he asked me into his rooms to look at a rather fine picture he had lately bought, and observed casually, lifting a large revolver from the mantel-piece:

'You see, I am prepared for any unwelcome visitors to my little den! He! He!' Conceiving him, of course, to refer to burglars, I could not help wondering at the forced and hollow character of his laugh. As we went down the stairs he said: 'I think we know one another pretty well now, Mr. Mason, eh? And if I could do anything to advance your professional prospects, I should be glad of the chance, of course. I understand the struggles of a young professional man—he! he!' It was the forced laugh again, and the man spoke nervously. 'I think,' he added, 'that if you will drop in tomorrow evening, perhaps I may have a little proposal to make. Will you?'

I assented, wondering what this proposal could be. Perhaps this eccentric old gentleman was a good fellow, after all, anxious to do me a good turn, and his awkwardness was nothing but a natural delicacy in breaking the ice. I was not so flush of good friends as to be willing to lose one. He might be desirous of putting business in my way.

I went, and was received with cordiality that even then seemed a little over-effusive. We sat and talked of one thing and another for a long while, and I began to wonder when Mr. Foggatt was coming to the point that most interested me. Several times he invited me to drink and smoke, but long usage to athletic training has given me a distaste for both practices, and I declined. At last he began to talk about myself. He was afraid that my professional prospects in this country were not great, but he had heard that in some of the colonies—South Africa, for example—young lawyers had brilliant opportunities.

'If you'd like to go there,' he said, 'I've no doubt, with a little capital, a clever man like you could get a grand practice together very soon. Or you might buy a share in some good established practice. I should be glad to let you have £500, or even a little more, if that wouldn't satisfy you, and——'

I stood aghast. Why should this man, almost a stranger, offer me £500, or even more, 'if that wouldn't satisfy' me? What claim had I on him? It was very generous of him, of course, but out of the question. I was, at least, a gentleman, and had a gentleman's self-respect. Meanwhile, he had gone maundering on, in a halting sort of way, and presently let slip a sentence that struck me like a blow between the eyes.

'I shouldn't like you to bear ill-will because of what has happened in the past,' he said. 'Your late—your late lamented mother—I'm afraid—she had unworthy suspicions—I'm sure—it was best for all parties—your father always appreciated——'

I set back my chair and stood erect before him. This grovelling wretch, forcing the words through his dry lips, was the thief who had made another of my father and had brought to miserable ends the lives of both my parents! Everything was clear. The creature went in fear of me, never imagining that I did not know him, and sought to buy me off—to buy me from the remembrance of my dead mother's broken heart for £500—£500 that he had made my father steal for him! I said not a word.

But the memory of all my mother's bitter years, and a savage sense of this crowning insult to myself, took a hold upon me, and I was a tiger. Even then I verily believe that one word of repentance, one tone of honest remorse, would have saved him. But he drooped his eyes, snuffled excuses, and stammered of 'unworthy suspicions' and 'no ill-will.' I let him stammer. Presently he looked up and saw my face; and fell back in his chair, sick with terror. I snatched the pistol from the mantel-piece, and, thrusting it in his face, shot him where he sat.

My subsequent coolness and quietness surprise me now. I took my hat and stepped toward the door. But there were voices on the stairs. The door was locked on the inside, and I left it so. I went back and quietly opened a window. Below was a clear drop into darkness, and above was plain wall; but away to one side, where the slope of the gable sprang from the roof, an iron gutter ended, supported by a strong bracket. It was the only way. I got upon the sill and carefully shut the window behind me, for people were already knocking at the lobby door.

From the end of the sill, holding on by the reveal of the window with one hand, leaning and stretching my utmost, I caught the gutter, swung myself clear, and scrambled on the roof. I climbed over many roofs before I found, in an adjoining street, a ladder lashed perpendicularly against the front of a house in course of repair. This, to me, was an easy opportunity of descent, notwithstanding the boards fastened over the face of the ladder, and I availed myself of it.

I have taken some time and trouble in order that you (so far as I am aware the only human being beside myself who knows me to be the author of Foggatt's death) shall have at least the means of appraising my crime at its just value of culpability. How much you already know of what I have told you I cannot guess. I am wrong, hardened, and flagitious, I make no doubt, but I speak of the facts as they are. You see the thing, of course, from your own point of view—I from mine. And I remember my mother!

Trusting that you will forgive the odd freak of a man—a criminal, let us say—who makes a confidant of the man set to hunt him down, I beg leave to be, sir, your obedient servant,

Sidney Mason.

I read the singular document through and handed it back to Hewitt.

"How does it strike you?" Hewitt asked.

"Mason would seem to be a man of very marked character," I said. "Certainly no fool. And, if his tale is true, Foggatt is no great loss to the world."

"Just so—if the tale is true. Personally I am disposed to believe it is."

"Where was the letter posted?"

"It wasn't posted. It was handed in with the others from the front-door letter-box this morning in an unstamped envelope. He must have dropped it in himself during the night. Paper," Hewitt proceeded, holding it up to the light, "Turkey mill, ruled foolscap. Envelope, blue, official shape, Pirie's watermark. Both quite ordinary and no special marks."

"Where do you suppose he's gone?"

"Impossible to guess. Some might think he meant suicide by the expression 'beyond the reach even of your abilities of search,' but I scarcely think he is the sort of man to do that. No, there is no telling. Something may be got by inquiring at his late address, of course; but, when such a man tells you he doesn't think you will find him, you may count upon its being a difficult job. His opinion is not to be despised."

"What shall you do?"

"Put the letter in the box with the casts for the police. *Fiat justitia*, you know, without any question of sentiment. As to the apple, I really think, if the police will let me, I'll make you a present of it. Keep it somewhere as a souvenir of your absolute deficiency in reflective observation in this case, and look at it whenever you feel yourself growing dangerously conceited. It should cure you."

★★★★★★

This is the history of the withered and almost petrified half apple that stands in my cabinet among a number of flint implements and one or two rather fine old Roman vessels. Of Mr. Sidney Mason we never heard another word. The police did their best, but he had left not a track behind him. His rooms were left almost undisturbed, and he had gone without anything in the way of elaborate preparation for his journey, and without leaving a trace of his intentions.

THE CASE OF THE DIXON TORPEDO

Hewitt was very apt, in conversation, to dwell upon the many curious chances and coincidences that he had observed, not only in connection with his own cases, but also in matters dealt with by the official police, with whom he was on terms of pretty regular, and, indeed, friendly, acquaintanceship. He has told me many an anecdote of singular happenings to Scotland Yard officials with whom he has exchanged experiences. Of Inspector Nettings, for instance, who spent many weary months in a search for a man wanted by the American Government, and in the end found, by the merest accident (a misdirected call), that the man had been lodging next door to himself the whole of the time; just as ignorant, of course, as was the inspector himself as to the enemy at the other side of the party-wall.

Also of another inspector, whose name I cannot recall, who, having been given rather meagre and insufficient details of a man whom he anticipated having great difficulty in finding, went straight down the stairs of the office where he had received instructions, and actually *fell over* the man near the door, where he had stooped down to tie his shoe-lace! There were cases, too, in which, when a great and notorious crime had been committed, and various persons had been arrested on suspicion, some were found among them who had long been badly wanted for some other crime altogether. Many criminals had met their deserts by venturing out of their own particular line of crime into another; often a man who got into trouble over something comparatively small found himself in for a startlingly larger trouble, the result of some previous misdeed that otherwise would have gone unpunished.

The *rouble* note-forger Mirsky might never have been handed over to the Russian authorities had he confined his genius to forgery alone. It was generally supposed at the time of his extradition that he had communicated with the Russian Embassy, with a view to giving himself up—a foolish proceeding on his part, it would seem, since his whereabouts, indeed even his identity as the forger, had not been suspected. He *had* communicated with the Russian Embassy, it is true, but for quite a different purpose, as Martin Hewitt well understood at the time. What that purpose was is now for the first time published.

★★★★★★

The time was half-past one in the afternoon, and Hewitt sat in his inner office examining and comparing the handwriting of two letters by the aid of a large lens. He put down the lens and glanced at the clock on the mantel-piece with a premonition of lunch; and as he did so his clerk quietly entered the room with one of those printed slips which were kept for the announcement of unknown visitors. It was filled up in a hasty and almost illegible hand, thus:

Name of visitor: *F. Graham Dixon.*
Address: *Chancery Lane.*
Business: *Private and urgent.*

"Show Mr. Dixon in," said Martin Hewitt.

Mr. Dixon was a gaunt, worn-looking man of fifty or so, well, although rather carelessly, dressed, and carrying in his strong, though drawn, face and dullish eyes the look that characterizes the life-long strenuous brain-worker. He leaned forward anxiously in the chair which Hewitt offered him, and told his story with a great deal of very natural agitation.

"You may possibly have heard, Mr. Hewitt—I know there are rumours—of the new locomotive torpedo which the government is about adopting; it is, in fact, the Dixon torpedo, my own invention, and in every respect—not merely in my own opinion, but in that of the government experts—by far the most efficient and certain yet produced. It will travel at least four hundred yards farther than any torpedo now made, with perfect accuracy of aim (a very great desideratum, let me tell you), and will carry an unprecedentedly heavy charge. There are other advantages—speed, simple discharge, and so forth—that I needn't bother you about.

"The machine is the result of many years of work and disappointment, and its design has only been arrived at by a careful balancing of principles and means, which are expressed on the only four existing sets of drawings. The whole thing, I need hardly tell you, is a profound secret, and you may judge of my present state of mind when I tell you that one set of drawings has been stolen."

"From your house?"

"From my office, in Chancery Lane, this morning. The four sets of drawings were distributed thus: Two were at the Admiralty Office, one being a finished set on thick paper, and the other a set of tracings therefrom; and the other two were at my own office, one being a pencilled set, uncoloured—a sort of finished draft, you understand—and the other a set of tracings similar to those at the Admiralty. It is this last set that has gone. The two sets were kept together in one drawer in my room. Both were there at ten this morning; of that I am sure, for I had to go to that very drawer for something else when I first arrived. But at twelve the tracings had vanished."

"You suspect somebody, probably?"

"I cannot. It is a most extraordinary thing. Nobody has left the office (except myself, and then only to come to you) since ten this morning, and there has been no visitor. And yet the drawings are gone!"

"But have you searched the place?"

"Of course I have! It was twelve o'clock when I first discovered my loss, and I have been turning the place upside down ever since—I and my assistants. Every drawer has been emptied, every desk and table turned over, the very carpet and linoleum have been taken up, but there is not a sign of the drawings. My men even insisted on turning all their pockets inside out, although I never for a moment suspected either of them, and it would take a pretty big pocket to hold the drawings, doubled up as small as they might be."

"You say your men—there are two, I understand—had neither left the office?"

"Neither; and they are both staying in now. Worsfold suggested that it would be more satisfactory if they did not leave till something was done toward clearing the mystery up, and, although, as I have said, I don't suspect either in the least, I acquiesced."

"Just so. Now—I am assuming that you wish me to undertake the recovery of these drawings?"

The engineer nodded hastily.

"Very good; I will go round to your office. But first perhaps you can tell me something about your assistants—something it might be awkward to tell me in their presence, you know. Mr. Worsfold, for instance?"

"He is my draughtsman—a very excellent and intelligent man, a very smart man, indeed, and, I feel sure, quite beyond suspicion. He has prepared many important drawings for me (he has been with me nearly ten years now), and I have always found him trustworthy. But, of course, the temptation in this case would be enormous. Still, I cannot suspect Worsfold. Indeed, how can I suspect anybody in the circumstances?"

"The other, now?"

"His name's Ritter. He is merely a tracer, not a fully skilled draughtsman. He is quite a decent young fellow, and I have had him two years. I don't consider him particularly smart, or he would have learned a little more of his business by this time. But I don't see the least reason to suspect him. As I said before, I can't reasonably suspect anybody."

"Very well; we will get to Chancery Lane now, if you please, and you can tell me more as we go."

"I have a cab waiting. What else can I tell you?"

"I understand the position to be succinctly this: The drawings were in the office when you arrived. Nobody came out, and nobody went in; and *yet* they vanished. Is that so?"

"That is so. When I say that absolutely nobody came in, of course I except the postman. He brought a couple of letters during the morning. I mean that absolutely nobody came past the barrier in the outer office—the usual thing, you know, like a counter, with a frame of ground glass over it."

"I quite understand that. But I think you said that the drawings were in a drawer in your *own* room—not the outer office, where the draughtsmen are, I presume?"

"That is the case. It is an inner room, or, rather, a room parallel with the other, and communicating with it; just as your own room is, which we have just left."

"But, then, you say you never left your office, and yet the drawings vanished—apparently by some unseen agency—while you were there in the room?"

"Let me explain more clearly." The cab was bowling smoothly along the Strand, and the engineer took out a pocket-book and pencil. "I fear," he proceeded, "that I am a little confused in my explanation—I am naturally rather agitated. As you will see presently, my offices consist of three rooms, two at one side of a corridor, and the other opposite—thus." He made a rapid pencil sketch.

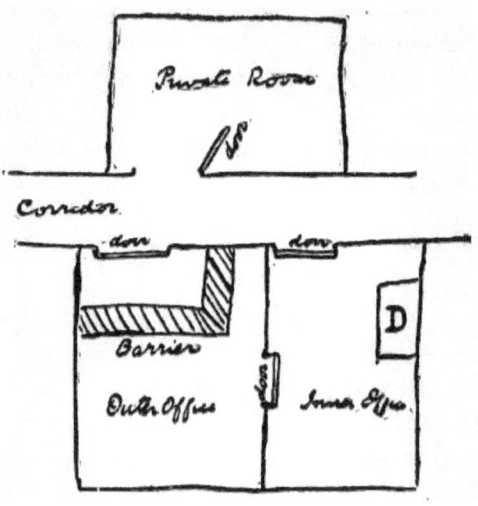

"In the outer office my men usually work. In the inner office I work myself. These rooms communicate, as you see, by a door. Our ordinary way in and out of the place is by the door of the outer office leading into the corridor, and we first pass through the usual lifting flap in the barrier. The door leading from the *inner* office to the corridor is always kept locked on the inside, and I don't suppose I unlock it once in three months. It has not been unlocked all the morning. The drawer in which the missing drawings were kept, and in which I saw them at ten o'clock this morning, is at the place marked D; it is a large chest of shallow drawers in which the plans lie flat."

"I quite understand. Then there is the private room opposite. What of that?"

"That is a sort of private sitting-room that I rarely use, except for business interviews of a very private nature. When I said I never left my office, I did not mean that I never stirred out of the inner office. I was about in one room and another, both the outer and the inner offices, and once I went into the private room for five minutes, but nobody came either in or out of any of the rooms at that time, for the door of the private room was wide open, and I was standing at the book-case (I had gone to consult a book), just inside the door, with a full view of the doors opposite. Indeed, Worsfold was at the door of the outer office most of the short time. He came to ask me a question."

"Well," Hewitt replied, "it all comes to the simple first statement. You know that nobody left the place or arrived, except the postman, who couldn't get near the drawings, and yet the drawings went. Is this your office?"

The cab had stopped before a large stone building. Mr. Dixon alighted and led the way to the first-floor. Hewitt took a casual glance round each of the three rooms. There was a sort of door in the frame of ground glass over the barrier to admit of speech with visitors. This door Hewitt pushed wide open, and left so.

He and the engineer went into the inner office. "Would you like to ask Worsfold and Ritter any questions?" Mr. Dixon inquired.

"Presently. Those are their coats, I take it, hanging just to the right of the outer office door, over the umbrella stand?"

"Yes, those are all their things—coats, hats, stick, and umbrella."

"And those coats were searched, you say?"

"Yes."

"And this is the drawer—thoroughly searched, of course?"

"Oh, certainly; every drawer was taken out and turned over."

"Well, of course I must assume you made no mistake in your hunt. Now tell me, did anybody know where these plans were, beyond yourself and your two men?"

"As far as I can tell, not a soul."

"You don't keep an office boy?"

"No. There would be nothing for him to do except to post a letter now and again, which Ritter does quite well for."

"As you are quite sure that the drawings were there at ten o'clock, perhaps the thing scarcely matters. But I may as well know if your men have keys of the office?"

"Neither. I have patent locks to each door and I keep all the keys myself. If Worsfold or Ritter arrive before me in the morning they have to wait to be let in; and I am always present myself when the rooms are cleaned. I have not neglected precautions, you see."

"No. I suppose the object of the theft—assuming it is a theft—is pretty plain: the thief would offer the drawings for sale to some foreign government?"

"Of course. They would probably command a great sum. I have been looking, as I need hardly tell you, to that invention to secure me a very large fortune, and I shall be ruined, indeed, if the design is taken abroad. I am under the strictest engagements to secrecy with the Admiralty, and not only should I lose all my labour, but I should lose all the confidence reposed in me at headquarters; should, in fact, be subject to penalties for breach of contract, and my career stopped forever. I cannot tell you what a serious business this is for me. If you cannot help me, the consequences will be terrible. Bad for the service of the country, too, of course."

"Of course. Now tell me this: It would, I take it, be necessary for the thief to *exhibit* these drawings to anybody anxious to buy the secret—I mean, he couldn't describe the invention by word of mouth."

"Oh, no, that would be impossible. The drawings are of the most complicated description, and full of figures upon which the whole thing depends. Indeed, one would have to be a skilled expert to properly appreciate the design at all. Various principles of hydrostatics, chemistry, electricity, and pneumatics are most delicately manipulated and adjusted, and the smallest error or omission in any part would upset the whole. No, the drawings are necessary to the thing, and they are gone."

At this moment the door of the outer office was heard to open and somebody entered. The door between the two offices was ajar, and Hewitt could see right through to the glass door left open over the barrier and into the space beyond. A well-dressed, dark, bushy-bearded man stood there carrying a handbag, which he placed on the ledge before him. Hewitt raised his hand to enjoin silence. The man spoke in a rather high-pitched voice and with a slight accent. "Is Mr. Dixon now within?" he asked.

"He is engaged," answered one of the draughtsmen; "very particularly engaged. I am afraid you won't be able to see him this afternoon. Can I give him any message?"

"This is two—the second time I have come today. Not two hours ago Mr. Dixon himself tells me to call again. I have a very important—

very excellent steam-packing to show him that is very cheap and the best of the market." The man tapped his bag. "I have just taken orders from the largest railway companies. Cannot I see him, for one second only? I will not detain him."

"Really, I'm sure you can't this afternoon; he isn't seeing anybody. But if you'll leave your name——"

"My name is Hunter; but what the good of that? He ask me to call a little later, and I come, and now he is engaged. It is a very great pity." And the man snatched up his bag and walking-stick, and stalked off, indignantly.

Hewitt stood still, gazing through the small aperture in the door-way.

"You'd scarcely expect a man with such a name as Hunter to talk with that accent, would you?" he observed, musingly. "It isn't a French accent, nor a German; but it seems foreign. You don't happen to know him I suppose?"

"No, I don't. He called here about half-past twelve, just while we were in the middle of our search and I was frantic over the loss of the drawings. I was in the outer office myself, and told him to call later. I have lots of such agents here, anxious to sell all sorts of engineering appliances. But what will you do now? Shall you see my men?"

"I think," said Hewitt, rising—"I think I'll get you to question them yourself."

"Myself?"

"Yes, I have a reason. Will you trust me with the 'key' of the private room opposite? I will go over there for a little, while you talk to your men in this room. Bring them in here and shut the door; I can look after the office from across the corridor, you know. Ask them each to detail his exact movements about the office this morning, and get them to recall each visitor who has been here from the beginning of the week. I'll let you know the reason of this later. Come across to me in a few minutes."

Hewitt took the key and passed through the outer office into the corridor.

Ten minutes later Mr. Dixon, having questioned his draughtsmen, followed him. He found Hewitt standing before the table in the private room, on which lay several drawings on tracing-paper.

"See here, Mr. Dixon," said Hewitt, "I think these are the drawings you are anxious about?"

The engineer sprang toward them with a cry of delight. "Why,

71

yes, yes," he exclaimed, turning them over, "every one of them! But where—how—they must have been in the place after all, then? What a fool I have been!"

Hewitt shook his head. "I'm afraid you're not quite so lucky as you think, Mr. Dixon," he said. "These drawings have most certainly been out of the house for a little while. Never mind how—we'll talk of that after. There is no time to lose. Tell me—how long would it take a good draughtsman to copy them?"

"They couldn't possibly be traced over properly in less than two or two and a half long days of very hard work," Dixon replied with eagerness.

"Ah! then it is as I feared. These tracings have been photographed, Mr. Dixon, and our task is one of every possible difficulty. If they had been copied in the ordinary way, one might hope to get hold of the copy. But photography upsets everything. Copies can be multiplied with such amazing facility that, once the thief gets a decent start, it is almost hopeless to checkmate him. The only chance is to get at the negatives before copies are taken. I must act at once; and I fear, be-tween ourselves, it may be necessary for me to step very distinctly over the line of the law in the matter. You see, to get at those negatives may involve something very like house-breaking. There must be no delay, no waiting for legal procedure, or the mischief is done. Indeed, I very much question whether you have any legal remedy, strictly speaking."

"Mr. Hewitt, I implore you, do what you can. I need not say that all I have is at your disposal. I will guarantee to hold you harmless for anything that may happen. But do, I entreat you, do everything pos-sible. Think of what the consequences may be!"

"Well, yes, so I do," Hewitt remarked, with a smile. "The con-sequences to me, if I were charged with house-breaking, might be something that no amount of guarantee could mitigate. However, I will do what I can, if only from patriotic motives. Now, I must see your tracer, Ritter. He is the traitor in the camp."

"Ritter? But how?"

"Never mind that now. You are upset and agitated, and had better not know more than is necessary for a little while, in case you say or do something unguarded. With Ritter I must take a deep course; what I don't know I must appear to know, and that will seem more likely to him if I disclaim acquaintance with what I do know. But first put these tracings safely away out of sight."

Dixon slipped them behind his bookcase.

"Now," Hewitt pursued, "call Mr. Worsfold and give him something to do that will keep him in the inner office across the way, and tell him to send Ritter here."

Mr. Dixon called his chief draughtsman and requested him to put in order the drawings in the drawers of the inner room that had been disarranged by the search, and to send Ritter, as Hewitt had suggested.

Ritter walked into the private room with an air of respectful attention. He was a puffy-faced, unhealthy-looking young man, with very small eyes and a loose, mobile mouth.

"Sit down, Mr. Ritter," Hewitt said, in a stern voice. "Your recent transactions with your friend Mr. Hunter are well known both to Mr. Dixon and myself."

Ritter, who had at first leaned easily back in his chair, started forward at this, and paled.

"You are surprised I observe; but you should be more careful in your movements out of doors if you do not wish your acquaintances to be known. Mr. Hunter, I believe, has the drawings which Mr. Dixon has lost, and, if so, I am certain that you have given them to him. That, you know, is theft, for which the law provides a severe penalty."

Ritter broke down completely and turned appealingly to Mr. Dixon.

"Oh, sir," he pleaded, "it isn't so bad, I assure you. I was tempted, I confess, and hid the drawings; but they are still in the office, and I can give them to you—really, I can."

"Indeed?" Hewitt went on. "Then, in that case, perhaps you'd better get them at once. Just go and fetch them in; we won't trouble to observe your hiding-place. I'll only keep this door open, to be sure you don't lose your way, you know—down the stairs, for instance."

The wretched Ritter, with hanging head, slunk into the office opposite. Presently he reappeared, looking, if possible, ghastlier than before. He looked irresolutely down the corridor, as if meditating a run for it, but Hewitt stepped toward him and motioned him back to the private room.

"You mustn't try any more of that sort of humbug," Hewitt said with increased severity. "The drawings are gone, and you have stolen them; you know that well enough. Now attend to me. If you received your deserts, Mr. Dixon would send for a policeman this moment, and have you hauled off to the jail that is your proper place. But, unfortunately, your accomplice, who calls himself Hunter—but who has other names besides that—as I happen to know—has the drawings, and it is absolutely necessary that these should be recovered. I am afraid that it will be necessary, therefore, to come to some arrangement with this scoundrel—to square him, in fact. Now, just take that pen and paper, and write to your confederate as I dictate. You know the alternative if you cause any difficulty."

Ritter reached tremblingly for the pen.

"Address him in your usual way," Hewitt proceeded. "Say this: 'There has been an alteration in the plans.' Have you got that? 'There has been an alteration in the plans. I shall be alone here at six o'clock. Please come, without fail.' Have you got it? Very well; sign it, and address the envelope. He must come here, and then we may arrange matters. In the meantime, you will remain in the inner office opposite."

The note was written, and Martin Hewitt, without glancing at the address, thrust it into his pocket. When Ritter was safely in the inner office, however, he drew it out and read the address. "I see," he observed, "he uses the same name, Hunter; 27 Little Carton Street, Westminster, is the address, and there I shall go at once with the note. If the man comes here, I think you had better lock him in with Ritter, and send for a policeman—it may at least frighten him. My object is, of course, to get the man away, and then, if possible, to invade his house, in some way or another, and steal or smash his negatives if they are there and to be found. Stay here, in any case, till I return. And don't forget to lock up those tracings."

★★★★★★

It was about six o'clock when Hewitt returned, alone, but with a smiling face that told of good fortune at first sight.

"First, Mr. Dixon," he said, as he dropped into an easy chair in the private room, "let me ease your mind by the information that I have been most extraordinarily lucky; in fact, I think you have no further cause for anxiety. Here are the negatives. They were not all quite dry when I—well, what?—stole them, I suppose I must say; so that they have stuck together a bit, and probably the films are damaged. But you don't mind that, I suppose?"

He laid a small parcel, wrapped in a newspaper, on the table. The engineer hastily tore away the paper and took up five or six glass photographic negatives, of a half-plate size, which were damp, and stuck together by the gelatine films in couples. He held them, one after another, up to the light of the window, and glanced through them. Then, with a great sigh of relief, he placed them on the hearth and pounded them to dust and fragments with the poker.

For a few seconds neither spoke. Then Dixon, flinging himself into a chair, said:

"Mr. Hewitt, I can't express my obligation to you. What would have happened if you had failed, I prefer not to think of. But what shall we do with Ritter now? The other man hasn't been here yet, by the by."

"No; the fact is I didn't deliver the letter. The worthy gentleman saved me a world of trouble by taking himself out of the way." Hewitt laughed. "I'm afraid he has rather got himself into a mess by trying two kinds of theft at once, and you may not be sorry to hear that his attempt on your torpedo plans is likely to bring him a dose of penal servitude for something else. I'll tell you what has happened.

"Little Carton Street, Westminster, I found to be a seedy sort of place—one of those old streets that have seen much better days. A good many people seem to live in each house—they are fairly large houses, by the way—and there is quite a company of bell-handles on each doorpost, all down the side like organ-stops. A barber had possession of the ground floor front of No. 27 for trade purposes, so to him I went. 'Can you tell me,' I said, 'where in this house I can find Mr. Hunter?' He looked doubtful, so I went on: 'His friend will do, you know—I can't think of his name; foreign gentleman, dark, with a bushy beard.'

"The barber understood at once. 'Oh, that's Mirsky, I expect,' he said. 'Now, I come to think of it, he has had letters addressed to Hunter once or twice; I've took 'em in. Top floor back.'

"This was good so far. I had got at 'Mr. Hunter's' other *alias*. So, by way of possessing him with the idea that I knew all about him, I determined to ask for him as Mirsky before handing over the letter addressed to him as Hunter. A little bluff of that sort is invaluable at the right time. At the top floor back I stopped at the door and tried to open it at once, but it was locked. I could hear somebody scuttling about within, as though carrying things about, and I knocked again. In a little while the door opened about a foot, and there stood Mr. Hunter—or Mirsky, as you like—the man who, in the character of a traveller in steam-packing, came here twice today. He was in his shirtsleeves, and cuddled something under his arm, hastily covered with a spotted pocket-handkerchief.

"'I have called to see M. Mirsky,' I said, 'with a confidential letter——'

"'Oh, yas, yas,' he answered hastily; 'I know—I know. Excuse me

75

one minute.' And he rushed off down-stairs with his parcel.

"Here was a noble chance. For a moment I thought of following him, in case there might be something interesting in the parcel. But I had to decide in a moment, and I decided on trying the room. I slipped inside the door, and, finding the key on the inside, locked it. It was a confused sort of room, with a little iron bedstead in one corner and a sort of rough boarded enclosure in another. This I rightly conjectured to be the photographic dark-room, and made for it at once.

"There was plenty of light within when the door was left open, and I made at once for the drying-rack that was fastened over the sink. There were a number of negatives in it, and I began hastily examining them one after another. In the middle of this our friend Mirsky returned and tried the door. He rattled violently at the handle and pushed. Then he called.

"At this moment I had come upon the first of the negatives you have just smashed. The fixing and washing had evidently only lately been completed, and the negative was drying on the rack. I seized it, of course, and the others which stood by it.

"'Who are you, there, inside?' Mirsky shouted indignantly from the landing. 'Why for you go in my room like that? Open this door at once, or I call the police!'

"I took no notice. I had got the full number of negatives, one for each drawing, but I was not by any means sure that he had not taken an extra set; so I went on hunting down the rack. There were no more, so I set to work to turn out all the undeveloped plates. It was quite possible, you see, that the other set, if it existed, had not yet been developed.

"Mirsky changed his tune. After a little more banging and shouting I could hear him kneel down and try the key-hole. I had left the key there, so that he could see nothing. But he began talking softly and rapidly through the hole in a foreign language. I did not know it in the least, but I believe it was Russian. What had led him to believe I understood Russian I could not at the time imagine, though I have a notion now. I went on ruining his stock of plates. I found several boxes, apparently of new plates, but, as there was no means of telling whether they were really unused or were merely undeveloped, but with the chemical impress of your drawings on them, I dragged every one ruthlessly from its hiding-place and laid it out in the full glare of the sunlight—destroying it thereby, of course, whether it was unused or not.

"Mirsky left off talking, and I heard him quietly sneaking off. Perhaps his conscience was not sufficiently clear to warrant an appeal to the police, but it seemed to me rather probable at the time that that was what he was going for. So I hurried on with my work. I found three dark slides—the parts that carried the plates in the back of the camera, you know—one of them fixed in the camera itself. These I opened, and exposed the plates to ruination as before. I suppose nobody ever did so much devastation in a photographic studio in ten minutes as I managed.

"I had spoiled every plate I could find, and had the developed negatives safely in my pocket, when I happened to glance at a porcelain washing-well under the sink. There was one negative in that, and I took it up. It was *not* a negative of a drawing of yours, but of a Russian twenty-rouble note!"

This *was* a discovery. The only possible reason any man could have for photographing a bank-note was the manufacture of an etched plate for the production of forged copies. I was almost as pleased as I had been at the discovery of *your* negatives. He might bring the police now as soon as he liked; I could turn the tables on him completely. I began to hunt about for anything else relating to this negative.

"I found an inking-roller, some old pieces of blanket (used in printing from plates), and in a corner on the floor, heaped over with newspapers and rubbish, a small copying-press. There was also a dish of acid, but not an etched plate or a printed note to be seen. I was looking at the press, with the negative in one hand and the inking-roller in the other, when I became conscious of a shadow across the window. I looked up quickly, and there was Mirsky hanging over from some ledge or projection to the side of the window, and staring straight at me, with a look of unmistakable terror and apprehension.

"The face vanished immediately. I had to move a table to get at the window, and by the time I had opened it there was no sign or sound of the rightful tenant of the room. I had no doubt now of his reason for carrying a parcel downstairs. He probably mistook me for another visitor he was expecting, and, knowing he must take this visitor into his room, threw the papers and rubbish over the press, and put up his plates and papers in a bundle and secreted them somewhere downstairs, lest his occupation should be observed.

"Plainly, my duty now was to communicate with the police. So, by the help of my friend the barber downstairs, a messenger was found and a note sent over to Scotland Yard. I awaited, of course, for the arrival of the police, and occupied the interval in another look round—finding nothing important, however. When the official detective arrived, he recognised at once the importance of the case. A large number of forged Russian notes have been put into circulation on the Continent lately, it seems, and it was suspected that they came from London. The Russian Government have been sending urgent messages to the police here on the subject.

"Of course I said nothing about your business; but, while I was talking with the Scotland Yard man, a letter was left by a messenger, addressed to Mirsky. The letter will be examined, of course, by the proper authorities, but I was not a little interested to perceive that the envelope bore the Russian imperial arms above the words 'Russian Embassy.' Now, why should Mirsky communicate with the Russian Embassy? Certainly not to let the officials know that he was carrying on a very extensive and lucrative business in the manufacture of spurious Russian notes. I think it is rather more than possible that he wrote—probably before he actually got your drawings—to say that he could sell information of the highest importance, and that this letter was a reply. Further, I think it quite possible that, when I asked for him by his Russian name and spoke of 'a confidential letter,' he at once concluded that *I* had come from the embassy in answer to his letter.

"That would account for his addressing me in Russian through the key-hole; and, of course, an official from the Russian Embassy would be the very last person in the world whom he would like to observe any indications of his little etching experiments. But, anyhow, be that as it may," Hewitt concluded, "your drawings are safe now, and if once Mirsky is caught, and I think it likely, for a man in his shirt-sleeves, with scarcely any start, and, perhaps, no money about him, hasn't a great chance to get away—if he is caught, I say, he will probably get something handsome at St. Petersburg in the way of imprisonment, or Siberia, or what not; so that you will be amply avenged."

"Yes, but I don't at all understand this business of the drawings even now. How in the world were they taken out of the place, and how in the world did you find it out?"

"Nothing could be simpler; and yet the plan was rather ingenious. I'll tell you exactly how the thing revealed itself to me. From your original description of the case many people would consider that an impossibility had been performed. Nobody had gone out and nobody had come in, and yet the drawings had been taken away. But an impossibility is an impossibility, after all, and as drawings don't run away of themselves, plainly somebody had taken them, unaccountable as it might seem. Now, as they were in your inner office, the only people who could have got at them besides yourself were your assistants, so that it was pretty clear that one of them, at least, had something to do with the business. You told me that Worsfold was an excellent and intelligent draughtsman.

"Well, if such a man as that meditated treachery, he would probably be able to carry away the design in his head—at any rate, a little at a time—and would be under no necessity to run the risk of stealing a set of the drawings. But Ritter, you remarked, was an inferior sort of man. 'Not particularly smart,' I think, were your words—only a mechanical sort of tracer. *He* would be unlikely to be able to carry in his head the complicated details of such designs as yours, and, being in a subordinate position, and continually overlooked, he would find it impossible to make copies of the plans in the office. So that, to begin with, I thought I saw the most probable path to start on.

"When I looked round the rooms, I pushed open the glass door of the barrier and left the door to the inner office ajar, in order to be able to see anything that *might* happen in any part of the place, without actually expecting any definite development. While we were talking, as it happened, our friend Mirsky (or Hunter—as you please) came into the outer office, and my attention was instantly called to him by the first thing he did. Did you notice anything peculiar yourself?"

"No, really, I can't say I did. He seemed to behave much as any traveller or agent might."

"Well, what I noticed was the fact that as soon as he entered the place he put his walking-stick into the umbrella-stand over there by the door, close by where he stood, a most unusual thing for a casual caller to do, before even knowing whether you were in. This made me watch him closely. I perceived with increased interest that the stick was exactly of the same kind and pattern as one already standing there, also a curious thing. I kept my eyes carefully on those sticks, and was all the more interested and edified to see, when he left, that he took the *other* stick—not the one he came with—from the stand, and carried it away, leaving his own behind. I might have followed him, but I decided that more could be learned by staying, as, in fact, proved to be the case. This, by the by, is the stick he carried away with him. I took the liberty of fetching it back from Westminster, because I conceive it to be Ritter's property."

Hewitt produced the stick. It was an ordinary, thick Malacca cane, with a buck-horn handle and a silver band. Hewitt bent it across his knee and laid it on the table.

"Yes," Dixon answered, "that is Ritter's stick. I think I have often seen it in the stand. But what in the world——"

"One moment; I'll just fetch the stick Mirsky left behind." And Hewitt stepped across the corridor.

He returned with another stick, apparently an exact facsimile of the other, and placed it by the side of the other.

"When your assistants went into the inner room, I carried this stick off for a minute or two. I knew it was not Worsfold's, because there was an umbrella there with his initial on the handle. Look at this."

Martin Hewitt gave the handle a twist and rapidly unscrewed it from the top. Then it was seen that the stick was a mere tube of very thin metal, painted to appear like a Malacca cane.

"It was plain at once that this was no Malacca cane—it wouldn't bend. Inside it I found your tracings, rolled up tightly. You can get a marvellous quantity of thin tracing-paper into a small compass by tight rolling."

"And this—this was the way they were brought back!" the engineer exclaimed. "I see that clearly. But how did they get away? That's as mysterious as ever."

"Not a bit of it! See here. Mirsky gets hold of Ritter, and they agree to get your drawings and photograph them. Ritter is to let his confederate have the drawings, and Mirsky is to bring them back as soon as possible, so that they sha'n't be missed for a moment. Ritter habitually carries this Malacca cane, and the cunning of Mirsky at once suggests that this tube should be made in outward facsimile. This morning Mirsky keeps the actual stick, and Ritter comes to the office with the tube. He seizes the first opportunity—probably when you were in this private room, and Worsfold was talking to you from the corridor—to get at the tracings, roll them up tightly, and put them in the tube, putting the tube back into the umbrella-stand. At half-past twelve, or whenever it was, Mirsky turns up for the first time with the actual stick and exchanges them, just as he afterward did when he brought the drawings back."

"Yes, but Mirsky came half an hour after they were—Oh, yes, I see. What a fool I was! I was forgetting. Of course, when I first missed the tracings, they were in this walking-stick, safe enough, and I was tearing my hair out within arm's reach of them!"

"Precisely. And Mirsky took them away before your very eyes. I expect Ritter was in a rare funk when he found that the drawings were missed. He calculated, no doubt, on your not wanting them for the hour or two they would be out of the office."

"How lucky that it struck me to jot a pencil-note on one of them! I might easily have made my note somewhere else, and then I should never have known that they had been away."

"Yes, they didn't give you any too much time to miss them. Well, I think the rest pretty clear. I brought the tracings in here, screwed up the sham stick and put it back. You identified the tracings and found none missing, and then my course was pretty clear, though it looked difficult. I knew you would be very naturally indignant with Ritter, so, as I wanted to manage him myself, I told you nothing of what he had actually done, for fear that, in your agitated state, you might burst out with something that would spoil my game. To Ritter I pretended to know nothing of the return of the drawings or *how* they had been stolen—the only things I did know with certainty. But I *did* pretend to know all about Mirsky—or Hunter—when, as a matter of fact, I knew nothing at all, except that he probably went under more than one name. That put Ritter into my hands completely.

"When he found the game was up, he began with a lying confession. Believing that the tracings were still in the stick and that we knew nothing of their return, he said that they had not been away, and that he would fetch them—as I had expected he would. I let him go for them alone, and, when he returned, utterly broken up by the discovery that they were not there, I had him altogether at my mercy. You see, if he had known that the drawings were all the time behind your book-case, he might have brazened it out, sworn that the drawings had been there all the time, and we could have done nothing with him. We couldn't have sufficiently frightened him by a threat of prosecution for theft, because there the things were in your possession, to his knowledge.

"As it was he answered the helm capitally: gave us Mirsky's address on the envelope, and wrote the letter that was to have got him out of the way while I committed burglary, if that disgraceful expedient had not been rendered unnecessary. On the whole, the case has gone very well."

"It has gone marvellously well, thanks to yourself. But what shall I do with Ritter?"

"Here's his stick—knock him downstairs with it, if you like. I should keep the tube, if I were you, as a memento. I don't suppose the respectable Mirsky will ever call to ask for it. But I should certainly kick Ritter out of doors—or out of window, if you like—without delay."

Mirsky was caught, and, after two remands at the police-court, was extradited on the charge of forging Russian notes. It came out that he had written to the embassy, as Hewitt had surmised, stating that he had certain valuable information to offer, and the letter which Hewitt had seen delivered was an acknowledgment, and a request for more definite particulars. This was what gave rise to the impression that Mirsky had himself informed the Russian authorities of his forgeries. His real intent was very different, but was never guessed.

★★★★★★

"I wonder," Hewitt has once or twice observed, "whether, after all, it would not have paid the Russian authorities better on the whole if I had never investigated Mirsky's little note factory. The Dixon torpedo was worth a good many twenty-*rouble* notes."

The Quinton Jewel Affair

It was comparatively rarely that Hewitt came into contact with members of the regular criminal class—those, I mean, who are thieves, of one sort or another, by exclusive profession. Still, nobody could have been better prepared than Hewitt for encountering this class when it became necessary. By some means, which I never quite understood, he managed to keep abreast of the very latest fashions in the ever-changing slang dialect of the fraternity, and he was a perfect master of the more modern and debased form of Romany. So much so that frequently a gypsy who began (as they always do) by pretending that he understood nothing, and never heard of a gypsy language, ended by confessing that Hewitt could *rocker* better than most Romany *chals* themselves.

By this acquaintance with their habits and talk Hewitt was sometimes able to render efficient service in cases of especial importance. In the Quinton jewel affair Hewitt came into contact with a very accomplished thief.

The case will probably be very well remembered. Sir Valentine Quinton, before he married, had been as poor as only a man of rank with an old country establishment to keep up can be. His marriage, however, with the daughter of a wealthy financier had changed all that, and now the Quinton establishment was carried on on as lavish a scale as might be; and, indeed, the extravagant habits of Lady Quinton herself rendered it an extremely lucky thing that she had brought a fortune with her.

Among other things her jewels made quite a collection, and chief among them was the great ruby, one of the very few that were sent to this country to be sold (at an average price of somewhere about twenty thousand pounds apiece, I believe) by the Burmese king before the annexation of his country. Let but a ruby be of a great size and colour, and no equally fine diamond can approach its value. Well, this great ruby (which was set in a pendant, by the by), together with a necklace, brooches, bracelets, ear-rings—indeed, the greater part of Lady Quinton's collection—were stolen. The robbery was effected at the usual time and in the usual way in cases of carefully planned jewellery robberies. The time was early evening—dinner-time, in fact—and an entrance had been made by the window to Lady Quinton's dressing-room, the door screwed up on the inside, and wires artfully stretched about the grounds below to overset anybody who might observe and pursue the thieves.

On an investigation by London detectives, however, a feature of singularity was brought to light. There had plainly been only one thief at work at Radcot Hall, and no other had been inside the grounds. Alone he had planted the wires, opened the window, screwed the door, and picked the lock of the safe. Clearly this was a thief of the most accomplished description.

Some few days passed, and, although the police had made various arrests, they appeared to be all mistakes, and the suspected persons were released one after another. I was talking of the robbery with Hewitt at lunch, and asked him if he had received any commission to hunt for the missing jewels.

"No," Hewitt replied, "I haven't been commissioned. They are offering an immense reward however—a very pleasant sum, indeed. I have had a short note from Radcot Hall informing me of the amount, and that's all. Probably they fancy that I may take the case up as a speculation, but that is a great mistake. I'm not a beginner, and I must be commissioned in a regular manner, hit or miss, if I am to deal with the case. I've quite enough commissions going now, and no time to waste hunting for a problematical reward."

But we were nearer a clue to the Quinton jewels than we then supposed.

We talked of other things, and presently rose and left the restaurant, strolling quietly toward home. Some little distance from the Strand, and near our own door, we passed an excited Irishman—without doubt an Irishman by appearance and talk—who was pouring a torrent of angry complaints in the ears of a policeman. The policeman obviously thought little of the man's grievances, and with an amused smile appeared to be advising him to go home quietly and think no more about it. We passed on and mounted our stairs. Something interesting in our conversation made me stop for a little while at Hewitt's office door on my way up, and, while I stood there, the Irishman we had seen in the street mounted the stairs. He was a poorly dressed but sturdy-looking fellow, apparently a labourer, in a badly-worn best suit of clothes. His agitation still held him, and without a pause he immediately burst out:

"Which of ye jintlemen will be Misther Hewitt, sor?"

"This is Mr. Hewitt," I said. "Do you want him?"

"It's protecshin I want, sor—protecshin! I spake to the polis, an' they laff at me, begob. Foive days have I lived in London, an' 'tis nothin' but battle, murdher, an' suddhen death for me here all day an' ivery day! An' the polis say I'm dhrunk!"

He gesticulated wildly, and to me it seemed just possible that the police might be right.

"They say I'm drunk, sor," he continued, "but, begob, I b'lieve they think I'm mad. An' me being thracked an' folleyed an' dogged an' waylaid an' poisoned an' blandandhered an' kidnapped an' murdhered, an' for why I do not know!"

"And who's doing all this?"

"Sthrangers, sor—sthrangers. 'Tis a sthranger here I am mesilf, an' fwy they do it bates me, onless I do be so like the Prince av Wales or other crowned head they thry to slaughter me. They're layin' for me in the sthreet now, I misdoubt not, and fwat they may thry next I can tell no more than the Lord Mayor. An' the polis won't listen to me!"

This, I thought, must be one of the very common cases of mental hallucination which one hears of every day—the belief of the sufferer that he is surrounded by enemies and followed by spies. It is probably the most usual delusion of the harmless lunatic.

"But what have these people done?" Hewitt asked, looking rather interested, although amused. "What actual assaults have they committed, and when? And who told you to come here?"

"Who towld me, is ut? Who but the payler outside—in the street below! I explained to 'um, an' sez he: 'Ah, you go an' take a slape,' sez he; 'you go an' take a good slape, an' they'll be all gone whin ye wake up.' 'But they'll murdher me,' sez I. 'Oh, no!' sez he, smilin' behind av his ugly face. 'Oh, no, they won't; you take ut aisy, me frind, an' go home!' 'Take it aisy, is ut, an' go home!' sez I; 'why, that's just where they've been last, a-ruinationin' an' a-turnin' av the place upside down, an' me strook on the head onsensible a mile away. Take ut aisy, is ut, ye say, whin all the demons in this unholy place is jumpin' on me every minut in places promiscuous till I can't tell where to turn, descendin' an' vanishin' marvelious an' onaccountable? Take ut aisy, is ut?' sez I. 'Well, me frind,' sez he, 'I can't help ye; that's the marvelious an' onaccountable departmint up the stairs forninst ye. Misther Hewitt ut is,' sez he, 'that attinds to the onaccountable departmint, him as wint by a minut ago. You go an' bother him.' That's how I was towld, sor."

Hewitt smiled.

"Very good," he said; "and now what are these extraordinary troubles of yours? Don't declaim," he added, as the Irishman raised his hand and opened his mouth, preparatory to another torrent of complaint; "just say in ten words, if you can, what they've done to you."

"I will, sor. Wan day had I been in London, sor—wan day only, an' a low scutt thried to poison me dhrink; next day some udther thief av sin shoved me off av a railway platform undher a train, malicious and purposeful; glory be, he didn't kill me! but the very docther that felt me bones thried to pick me pockut, I du b'lieve. Sunday night I was grabbed outrageous in a darrk turnin', rowled on the groun', half strangled, an' me pockuts nigh ripped out av me trousies. An' this very blessed mornin' av light I was strook onsensible an' left a livin' corpse, an' my lodgin's penethrated an' all the thruck mishandled an' bruk up behind me back. Is that a panjandhery for the polis to laff at, sor?"

Had Hewitt not been there I think I should have done my best to quiet the poor fellow with a few soothing words and to persuade him to go home to his friends. His excited and rather confused manner, his fantastic story of a sort of general conspiracy to kill him, and the absurd reference to the doctor who tried to pick his pocket seemed to me plainly to confirm my first impression that he was insane. But Hewitt appeared strangely interested.

"Did they steal anything?" he asked.

"Divil a shtick but me door-key, an' that they tuk home an' lift in the door."

Hewitt opened his office door.

"Come in," he said, "and tell me all about this. You come, too,

Brett."

The Irishman and I followed him into the inner office, where, shutting the door, Hewitt suddenly turned on the Irishman and exclaimed sharply: "*Then you've still got it?*"

He looked keenly in the man's eyes, but the only expression there was one of surprise.

"Got ut?" said the Irishman. "Got fwhat, sor? Is ut you're thinkin' I've got the horrors, as well as the polis?"

Hewitt's gaze relaxed. "Sit down, sit down!" he said. "You've still got your watch and money, I suppose, since you weren't robbed?"

"Oh, that? Glory be, I have ut still! though for how long—or me own head, for that matter—in this state of besiegement, I cannot say."

"Now," said Hewitt, "I want a full, true, and particular account of yourself and your doings for the last week. First, your name?"

"Leamy's my name, sor—Michael Leamy."

"Lately from Ireland?"

"Over from Dublin this last blessed Wednesday, and a crooil bad poundherin' tit was in the boat, too—shpakin'av that same."

"Looking for work?"

"That is my purshuit at prisint, sor."

"Did anything noticeable happen before these troubles of yours began—anything here in London or on the journey?"

"Sure," the Irishman smiled, "part av the way I thraveled first-class by favor av the gyard, an' I got a small job before I lift the train."

"How was that? Why did you travel first-class part of the way?"

"There was a station fwhere we shtopped afther a long run, an' I got down to take the cramp out av me joints, an' take a taste av dhrink. I over-shtayed somehow, an', whin I got to the train, begob, it was on the move. There was a first-class carr'ge door opin right forninst me, an' into that the gyard crams me holus-bolus. There was a juce of a foine jintleman sittin' there, an' he stares at me umbrageous, but I was not dishcommoded, bein' onbashful by natur'. We thravelled along a heap av miles more, till we came near London. Afther we had shtopped at a station where they tuk tickets we wint ahead again, an' prisintly, as we rips through some udther station, up jumps the jintleman opposite, swearin' hard undher his tongue, an' looks out at the windy. 'I thought this train shtopped here,' sez he."

"Chalk Farm," observed Hewitt, with a nod.

"The name I do not know, sor, but that's fwhat he said. Then he looks at me onaisy for a little, an' at last he sez: 'Wud ye loike a small job, me good man, well paid?'

"'Faith,' sez I, ''tis that will suit me well.'

"'Then, see here,' sez he, 'I should have got out at that station, havin' particular business; havin' missed, I must sen' a telegrammer from Euston. Now, here's a bag,' sez he, 'a bag full of imporrtant papers for my solicitor—imporrtant to me, ye ondershtand, not worth the shine av a brass farden to a sowl else—an' I want 'em tuk on to him. Take you this bag,' he sez, 'an' go you straight out wid it at Euston an' get a cab. I shall stay in the station a bit to see to the telegrammer. Dhrive out av the station, across the road outside, an' wait there five minuts by the clock. Ye ondershtand? Wait five minuts, an, maybe I'll come an' join ye. If I don't 'twill be bekase I'm detained onexpected, an' then ye'll dhrive to my solicitor straight. Here's his address, if ye can read writin',' an' he put ut on a piece av paper. He gave me half-a-crown for the cab, an' I tuk his bag."

"One moment—have you the paper with the address now?"

"I have not, sor. I missed ut afther the blayguards overset me yesterday; but the solicitor's name was Hollams, an' a liberal jintleman wid his money he was, too, by that same token."

"What was his address?"

"'Twas in Chelsea, and 'twas Gold or Golden something, which I know by the good token av fwhat he gave me; but the number I misremember."

Hewitt turned to his directory. "Gold Street is the place, probably," he said, "and it seems to be a street chiefly of private houses. You would be able to point out the house if you were taken there, I suppose?"

"I should that, sor; indade, I was thinkin' av goin' there an' tellin' Misther Hollams all my throubles, him havin' been so kind."

"Now tell me exactly what instructions the man in the train gave you, and what happened?"

"He sez: 'You ask for Misther Hollams, an' see nobody else. Tell him ye've brought the sparks from Misther W.'"

I fancied I could see a sudden twinkle in Hewitt's eye, but he made no other sign, and the Irishman proceeded.

"'Sparks?' sez I. 'Yes, sparks,' sez he. 'Misther Hollams will know; 'tis our jokin' word for 'em; sometimes papers is sparks when they set a lawsuit ablaze,' and he laffed. 'But be sure ye say the *sparks from Misther W.*,' he sez again, 'bekase then he'll know ye're jinuine an' he'll pay ye han'some. Say Misther W. sez you're to have your reg'lars, if ye like.

D'ye mind that?'

"'Ay,' sez I, 'that I'm to have my reg'lars.'

"Well, sor, I tuk the bag and wint out of the station, tuk the cab, an' did all as he towld me. I waited the foive minuts, but he niver came, so off I druv to Misther Hollams, and he threated me han'some, sor."

"Yes, but tell me exactly all he did."

"'Misther Hollams, sor?' sez I. 'Who are ye?' sez he. 'Mick Leamy, sor,' sez I, 'from Misther W. wid the sparks.' 'Oh,' sez he, 'thin come in.' I wint in. 'They're in here, are they?' sez he, takin' the bag. 'They are, sor,' sez I, 'an' Misther W. sez I'm to have me reg'lars.' 'You shall,' sez he. 'What shall we say, now—afinnip?' 'Fwhat's that, sor?' sez I. 'Oh,' sez he, 'I s'pose ye're a new hand; five quid—ondershtand that?'"

"Begob, I did ondershtand it, an' moighty plazed I was to have come to a place where they pay five-pun' notes for carryin' bags. So whin he asked me was I new to London an' shud I kape in the same line av business, I towld him I shud for certin, or any thin' else payin' like it. 'Right,' sez he; 'let me know whin ye've got any thin'—ye'll find me all right.' An' he winked frindly. 'Faith, that I know I shall, sor,' sez I, wid the money safe in me pockut; an' I winked him back, conjanial. 'I've a smart family about me,' sez he, 'an' I treat 'em all fair an' liberal.' An', saints, I thought it likely his family 'ud have all they wanted, seein' he was so free-handed wid a stranger. Thin he asked me where I was a livin' in London, and, when I towld him nowhere, he towld me av a room in Musson Street, here by Drury Lane, that was to let, in a house his fam'ly knew very well, an' I wint straight there an' tuk ut, an' there I do be stayin' still, sor."

I hadn't understood at first why Hewitt took so much interest in the Irishman's narrative, but the latter part of it opened my eyes a little. It seemed likely that Leamy had, in his innocence, been made a conveyer of stolen property. I knew enough of thieves' slang to know that "sparks" meant diamonds or other jewels; that "regulars" was the term used for a payment made to a brother thief who gave assistance in some small way, such as carrying the booty; and that the "family" was the time-honoured expression for a gang of thieves.

"This was all on Wednesday, I understand," said Hewitt. "Now tell me what happened on Thursday—the poisoning, or drugging, you know?"

"Well, sor, I was walking out, an' toward the evenin' I lost me-silf. Up comes a man, seemin'ly a sthranger, and shmacks me on the showldher. 'Why, Mick!' sez he; 'it's Mick Leamy, I du b'lieve!'

"'I am that,' sez I, 'but you I do not know.'

"'Not know me?' sez he. 'Why, I wint to school wid ye.' An' wid that he hauls me off to a bar, blarneyin' and minowdherin', an' orders dhrinks.

"Can ye rache me a poipe-loight?' sez he, an' I turned to get ut, but, lookin' back suddent, there was that onblushin' thief av the warl' tippin' a paperful of phowder stuff into me glass."

"What did you do?" Hewitt asked.

"I knocked the dhirty face av him, sor, an' can ye blame me? A mane scutt, thryin' for to poison a well-manin' sthranger. I knocked the face av him, an' got away home."

"Now the next misfortune?"

"Faith, that was av a sort likely to turn out the last of all misfortunes. I wint that day to the Crystial Palace, bein' dishposed for a little sphort, seein' as I was new to London. Comin' home at night, there was a juce av a crowd on the station platform, consekins of a late thrain. Sthandin' by the edge av the platform at the fore end, just as thrain came in, some onvisible murdherer gives me a stupenjus drive in the back, and over I wint on the line, mid-betwixt the rails. The engine came up an' wint half over me widout givin' me a scratch, bekase av my centraleous situation, an' then the porther-men pulled me out, nigh sick wid fright, sor, as ye may guess. A jintleman in the crowd sings out: 'I'm a medical man!' an' they tuk me in the waitin'-room, an' he investigated me, havin' turned everybody else out av the room. There wuz no bones bruk, glory be! and the docthor-man he was tellin' me so, after feelin' me over, whin I felt his hand in me waistcoat pockut.

"'An' fwhat's this, sor?' sez I. 'Do you be lookin' for your fee that thief's way?'

"He laffed, and said: 'I want no fee from ye, me man, an' I did but feel your ribs,' though on me conscience he had done that undher me waistcoat already. An' so I came home."

"What did they do to you on Saturday?"

"Saturday, sor, they gave me a whole holiday, and I began to think less of things; but on Saturday night, in a dark place, two blayguards tuk me throat from behind, nigh choked me, flung me down, an' wint through all me pockuts in about a quarter av a minut."

"And they took nothing, you say?"

"Nothing, sor. But this mornin' I got my worst dose. I was trapesing along distreshful an' moighty sore, in a street just away off the

Strand here, when I observed the docthor-man that was at the Crystal Palace station a-smilin' an' beckonin' at me from a door.

"'How are ye now?' sez he. 'Well,' sez I, 'I'm moighty sore an' sad bruised,' sez I. 'Is that so?' sez he. 'Sthep in here.' So I sthepped in, an' before I could wink there dhropped a crack on the back av me head that sent me off as unknowledgable as a corrpse. I knew no more for a while, sor, whether half an hour or an hour, an' thin I got up in a room av the place, marked 'To Let.' 'Twas a house full av offices, by the same token, like this. There was a sore bad lump on me head—see ut, sor?—an' the whole warl' was shpinnin' roun' rampageous. The things out av me pockuts were lyin' on the flure by me—all barrin' the key av me room. So that the demons had been through me posseshins again, bad luck to 'em.'"

"You are quite sure, are you, that everything was there except the key?" Hewitt asked.

"Certin, sor? Well, I got along to me room, sick an' sorry enough, an' doubtsome whether I might get in wid no key. But there was the key in the open door, an', by this an' that, all the shtuff in the room—chair, table, bed, an' all—was shtandin' on their heads twisty-ways, an' the bedclothes an' every thin' else; such a disgraceful stramash av conglomerated thruck as ye niver dhreamt av. The chist av drawers was lyin' on uts face, wid all the dhrawers out an' emptied on the flure. 'Twas as though an arrmy had been lootin', sor!"

"But still nothing was gone?"

"Nothin', so far as I investigated, sor. But I didn't shtay. I came out to spake to the polis, an' two av them laffed at me—wan afther another!"

"It has certainly been no laughing matter for you. Now, tell me—have you anything in your possession—documents, or valuables, or anything—that any other person, to your knowledge, is anxious to get hold of?"

"I have not, sor—divil a document! As to valuables, thim an' me is the cowldest av sthrangers."

"Just call to mind, now, the face of the man who tried to put powder in your drink, and that of the doctor who attended to you in the railway station. Were they at all alike, or was either like anybody you have seen before?"

Leamy puckered his forehead and thought.

"Faith," he said presently, "they were a bit alike, though one had a beard an' the udther whiskers only."

"Neither happened to look like Mr. Hollams, for instance?"

Leamy started. "Begob, but they did! They'd ha' been mortal like him if they'd been shaved." Then, after a pause, he suddenly added: "Holy saints! is ut the fam'ly he talked av?"

Hewitt laughed. "Perhaps it is," he said. "Now, as to the man who sent you with the bag. Was it an old bag?"

"Bran' cracklin' new—a brown leather bag."

"Locked?"

"That I niver thried, sor. It was not my consarn."

"True. Now, as to this Mr. W. himself." Hewitt had been rummaging for some few minutes in a portfolio, and finally produced a photograph, and held it before the Irishman's eye. "Is that like him?" he asked.

"Shure it's the man himself! Is he a friend av yours, sor?"

"No, he's not exactly a friend of mine," Hewitt answered, with a grim chuckle. "I fancy he's one of that very respectable *family* you heard about at Mr. Hollams'. Come along with me now to Chelsea, and see if you can point out that house in Gold Street. I'll send for a cab."

He made for the outer office, and I went with him.

"What is all this, Hewitt?" I asked. "A gang of thieves with stolen property?"

IS THAT LIKE HIM?"

Hewitt looked in my face and replied: "*It's the Quinton ruby!*"

"What! The ruby? Shall you take the case up, then?"

"I shall. It is no longer a speculation."

"Then do you expect to find it at Hollams' house in Chelsea?" I asked.

"No, I don't, because it isn't there—else why are they trying to get it from this unlucky Irishman? There has been bad faith in Hollams' gang, I expect, and Hollams has missed the ruby and suspects Leamy of having taken it from the bag."

"Then who is this Mr. W. whose portrait you have in your possession?"

"See here!" Hewitt turned over a small pile of recent newspapers and selected one, pointing at a particular paragraph. "I kept that in my mind, because to me it seemed to be the most likely arrest of the lot," he said.

It was an evening paper of the previous Thursday, and the paragraph was a very short one, thus:

"The man Wilks, who was arrested at Euston Station yesterday, in connection with the robbery of Lady Quinton's jewels, has been released, nothing being found to incriminate him."

"How does that strike you?" asked Hewitt. "Wilks is a man well known to the police—one of the most accomplished burglars in this country, in fact. I have had no dealings with him as yet, but I found means, some time ago, to add his portrait to my little collection, in case I might want it, and today it has been quite useful."

The thing was plain now. Wilks must have been bringing his booty to town, and calculated on getting out at Chalk Farm and thus eluding the watch which he doubtless felt pretty sure would be kept (by telegraphic instruction) at Euston for suspicious characters arriving from the direction of Radcot. His transaction with Leamy was his only possible expedient to save himself from being hopelessly taken with the swag in his possession. The paragraph told me why Leamy had waited in vain for "Mr. W." in the cab.

"What shall you do now?" I asked.

"I shall go to the Gold Street house and find out what I can as soon as this cab turns up."

There seemed a possibility of some excitement in the adventure, so I asked: "Will you want any help?"

Hewitt smiled. "I *think* I can get through it alone," he said.

"Then may I come to look on?" I said. "Of course I don't want to be in your way, and the result of the business, whatever it is, will be to your credit alone. But I am curious."

"Come, then, by all means. The cab will be a four-wheeler, and there will be plenty of room."

******

Gold Street was a short street of private houses of very fair size and of a half-vanished pretension to gentility. We drove slowly through, and Leamy had no difficulty in pointing out the house wherein he had been paid five pounds for carrying a bag. At the end the cab turned the corner and stopped, while Hewitt wrote a short note to an official of Scotland Yard.

"Take this note," he instructed Leamy, "to Scotland Yard in the cab, and then go home. I will pay the cabman now."

"I will, sor. An' will I be protected?"

"Oh, yes! Stay at home for the rest of the day, and I expect you'll be left alone in future. Perhaps I shall have something to tell you in a day or two; if I do, I'll send. Goodbye."

The cab rolled off, and Hewitt and I strolled back along Gold Street. "I think," Hewitt said, "we will drop in on Mr. Hollams for a few minutes while we can. In a few hours I expect the police will have him, and his house, too, if they attend promptly to my note."

"Have you ever seen him?"

"Not to my knowledge, though I may know him by some other name. Wilks I know by sight, though he doesn't know me."

"What shall we say?"

"That will depend on circumstances. I may not get my cue till the door opens, or even till later. At worst, I can easily apply for a reference as to Leamy, who, you remember, is looking for work."

But we were destined not to make Mr. Hollams' acquaintance, after all. As we approached the house a great uproar was heard from the lower part giving on to the area, and suddenly a man, hatless, and with a sleeve of his coat nearly torn away burst through the door and up the area steps, pursued by two others. I had barely time to observe that one of the pursuers carried a revolver, and that both hesitated and retired on seeing that several people were about the street, when Hewitt, gripping my arm and exclaiming: "That's our man!" started at a run after the fugitive.

We turned the next corner and saw the man thirty yards before us, walking, and pulling up his sleeve at the shoulder, so as to conceal the rent. Plainly he felt safe from further molestation.

"That's Sim Wilks," Hewitt explained, as we followed, "the 'juce of a foine jintleman' who got Leamy to carry his bag, and the man who knows where the Quinton ruby is, unless I am more than usually mistaken. Don't stare after him, in case he looks round. Presently, when we get into the busier streets, I shall have a little chat with him."

But for some time the man kept to the back streets. In time, however, he emerged into the Buckingham Palace Road, and we saw him stop and look at a hat-shop. But after a general look over the window and a glance in at the door he went on.

"Good sign!" observed Hewitt; "got no money with him—makes it easier for us."

In a little while Wilks approached a small crowd gathered about a woman fiddler. Hewitt touched my arm, and a few quick steps took us past our man and to the opposite side of the crowd. When Wilks emerged, he met us coming in the opposite direction.

"What, Sim!" burst out Hewitt with apparent delight. "I haven't piped your mug, (seen your face), for a stretch; (a year), I thought you'd fell, (been imprisoned). Where's your cady (hat)?"

Wilks looked astonished and suspicious. "I don't know you," he said. "You've made a mistake."

Hewitt laughed. "I'm glad you don't know me," he said. "If you don't, I'm pretty sure the reelers, (police), won't. I think I've faked my mug pretty well, and my clobber, (clothes), too. Look here: I'll stand you a new cady. Strange blokes don't do that, eh?"

Wilks was still suspicious. "I don't know what you mean," he said. Then, after a pause, he added: "Who are you, then?"

Hewitt winked and screwed his face genially aside. "Hooky!" he said. "I've had a lucky touch, (robbery), and I'm Mr. Smith till I've melted the pieces, (spent the money). You come and damp it."

"I'm off," Wilks replied. "Unless you're pal enough to lend me a quid," he added, laughing.

"I am that," responded Hewitt, plunging his hand in his pocket. "I'm flush, my boy, flush, and I've been wetting it pretty well today. I feel pretty jolly now, and I shouldn't wonder if I went home cannon, (drunk). Only a quid? Have two, if you want 'em—or three; there's plenty more, and you'll do the same for me some day. Here y'are."

Hewitt had, of a sudden, assumed the whole appearance, manners, and bearing of a slightly elevated rowdy. Now he pulled his hand from his pocket and extended it, full of silver, with five or six sovereigns interspersed, toward Wilks.

"I'll have three quid," Wilks said, with decision, taking the money; "but I'm blowed if I remember you. Who's your pal?"

Hewitt jerked his hand in my direction, winked, and said, in a low voice: "He's all right. Having a rest. Can't stand Manchester," and winked again.

Wilks laughed and nodded, and I understood from that that Hewitt had very flatteringly given me credit for being "wanted" by the Manchester police.

We lurched into a public house, and drank a very little very bad whisky and water. Wilks still regarded us curiously, and I could see him again and again glancing doubtfully in Hewitt's face. But the loan of three pounds had largely reassured him. Presently Hewitt said:

"How about our old pal down in Gold Street? Do anything with him now? Seen him lately?"

Wilks looked up at the ceiling and shook his head.

"That's a good job. It 'ud be awkward if you were about there to-day, I can tell you."

"Why?"

"Never mind, so long as you're not there. I know something, if I *have* been away. I'm glad I haven't had any truck with Gold Street lately, that's all."

"D'you mean the reelers are on it?"

Hewitt looked cautiously over his shoulder, leaned toward Wilks, and said: "Look here: this is the straight tip. I know this—I got it from the very nark, (police spy), that's given the show away: By six o'clock No. 8 Gold Street will be turned inside out, like an old glove, and everyone in the place will be——" He finished the sentence by crossing his wrists like a handcuffed man. "What's more," he went on, "they know all about what's gone on there lately, and everybody that's been in or out for the last two moons, months), will be wanted particular—and will be found, I'm told." Hewitt concluded with a confidential frown, a nod, and a wink, and took another mouthful of whisky. Then he added, as an after-thought: "So I'm glad you haven't been there lately."

Wilks looked in Hewitt's face and asked: "Is that straight?"

"*Is* it?" replied Hewitt with emphasis. "You go and have a look, if you ain't afraid of being smugged yourself. Only *I* shan't go near No. 8 just yet—I know that."

Wilks fidgeted, finished his drink, and expressed his intention of going. "Very well, if you *won't* have another——" replied Hewitt. But he had gone.

"Good!" said Hewitt, moving toward the door; "he has suddenly developed a hurry. I shall keep him in sight, but you had better take a cab and go straight to Euston. Take tickets to the nearest station to Radcot—Kedderby, I think it is—and look up the train arrangements. Don't show yourself too much, and keep an eye on the entrance. Unless I am mistaken, Wilks will be there pretty soon, and I shall be on his heels. If I *am* wrong, then you won't see the end of the fun, that's all."

Hewitt hurried after Wilks, and I took the cab and did as he wished. There was an hour and a few minutes, I found, to wait for the next train, and that time I occupied as best I might, keeping a sharp lookout across the quadrangle. Barely five minutes before the train was to leave, and just as I was beginning to think about the time of the next, a cab dashed up and Hewitt alighted. He hurried in, found me, and drew me aside into a recess, just as another cab arrived.

"Here he is," Hewitt said. "I followed him as far as Euston Road and then got my cabby to spurt up and pass him. He had had his moustache shaved off, and I feared you mightn't recognise him, and so let him see you."

From our retreat we could see Wilks hurry into the booking-office. We watched him through to the platform and followed. He wasted no time, but made the best of his way to a third-class carriage at the extreme fore end of the train.

"We have three minutes," Hewitt said, "and everything depends on his not seeing us get into this train. Take this cap. Fortunately, we're both in tweed suits."

He had bought a couple of tweed cricket caps, and these we assumed, sending our "bowler" hats to the cloak-room. Hewitt also put on a pair of blue spectacles, and then walked boldly up the platform and entered a first-class carriage. I followed close on his heels, in such a manner that a person looking from the fore end of the train would be able to see but very little of me.

"So far so good," said Hewitt, when we were seated and the train began to move off. "I must keep a lookout at each station, in case our friend goes off unexpectedly."

"I waited some time," I said; "where did you both go to?"

"First he went and bought that hat he is wearing. Then he walked some distance, dodging the main thoroughfares and keeping to the back streets in a way that made following difficult, till he came to a little tailor's shop. There he entered and came out in a quarter of an hour with his coat mended. This was in a street in Westminster. Presently he worked his way up to Tothill Street, and there he plunged into a barber's shop. I took a cautious peep at the window, saw two or three other customers also waiting, and took the opportunity to rush over to a 'notion' shop and buy these blue spectacles, and to a hatter's for these caps—of which I regret to observe that yours is too big. He was rather a long while in the barber's, and finally came out, as you saw him, with no moustache. This was a good indication. It made it plainer than ever that he had believed my warning as to the police descent on the house in Gold Street and its frequenters; which was right and proper, for what I told him was quite true. The rest you know. He cabbed to the station, and so did I."

"And now perhaps," I said, "after giving me the character of a thief wanted by the Manchester police, forcibly depriving me of my hat in exchange for this all-too-large cap, and rushing me off out of London without any definite idea of when I'm coming back, perhaps you'll tell me what we're after?"

Hewitt laughed. "You wanted to join in, you know," he said, "and you must take your luck as it comes. As a matter of fact, there is scarcely anything in my profession so uninteresting and so difficult as this watching and following business. Often it lasts for weeks. When we alight, we shall have to follow Wilks again, under the most difficult possible conditions, in the country. There it is often quite impossible to follow a man unobserved. It is only because it is the only way that I am undertaking it now. As to what we're after, you know that as well as I—the Quinton ruby. Wilks has hidden it, and without his help it would be impossible to find it. We are following him so that he will find it for us."

"He must have hidden it, I suppose, to avoid sharing with Hollams?"

"Of course, and availed himself of the fact of Leamy having carried the bag to direct Hollams's suspicion to him. Hollams found out by his repeated searches of Leamy and his lodgings, that this was wrong, and this morning evidently tried to persuade the ruby out of Wilks' possession with a revolver. We saw the upshot of that."

Kedderby Station was about forty miles out. At each intermediate stopping station Hewitt watched earnestly, but Wilks remained in the train. "What I fear," Hewitt observed, "is that at Kedderby he may take a fly. To stalk a man on foot in the country is difficult enough; but you *can't* follow one vehicle in another without being spotted. But if

he's so smart as I think, he won't do it. A man traveling in a fly is noticed and remembered in these places."

He did *not* take a fly. At Kedderby we saw him jump out quickly
and hasten from the station. The train stood for a few minutes, and
he was out of the station before we alighted. Through the railings
behind the platform we could see him walking briskly away to the
right. From the ticket collector we ascertained that Radcot lay in that
direction, three miles off.

To my dying day I shall never forget that three miles. They seemed
three hundred. In the still country almost every footfall seemed audible for any distance, and in the long stretches of road one could see
half a mile behind or before. Hewitt was cool and patient, but I got
into a fever of worry, excitement, want of breath, and backache. At
first, for a little, the road zig-zagged, and then the chase was comparatively easy. We waited behind one bend till Wilks had passed the next,
and then hurried in his trail, treading in the dustiest parts of the road
or on the side grass, when there was any, to deaden the sound of our
steps.

At the last of these short bends we looked ahead and saw a long,
white stretch of road with the dark form of Wilks a couple of hundred
yards in front. It would never do to let him get to the end of this great
stretch before following, as he might turn off at some branch road out
of sight and be lost. So we jumped the hedge and scuttled along as we
best might on the other side, with backs bent, and our feet often many
inches deep in wet clay. We had to make continual stoppages to listen
and peep out, and on one occasion, happening, incautiously, to stand
erect, looking after him, I was much startled to see Wilks, with his face
toward me, gazing down the road.

I ducked like lightning, and, fortunately, he seemed not to have observed me, but went on as before. He had probably heard some slight
noise, but looked straight along the road for its explanation, instead of
over the hedge. At hilly parts of the road there was extreme difficulty;
indeed, on approaching a rise it was usually necessary to lie down
under the hedge till Wilks had passed the top, since from the higher
ground he could have seen us easily. This improved neither my clothes,
my comfort, nor my temper. Luckily we never encountered the difficulty of a long and high wall, but once we were nearly betrayed by a
man who shouted to order us off his field.

At last we saw, just ahead, the square tower of an old church, set
about with thick trees. Opposite this Wilks paused, looked irresolutely

up and down the road, and then went on. We crossed the road, availed ourselves of the opposite hedge, and followed. The village was to be seen some three or four hundred yards farther along the road, and toward it Wilks sauntered slowly. Before he actually reached the houses he stopped and turned back.

"The churchyard!" exclaimed Hewitt, under his breath. "Lie close and let him pass."

Wilks reached the churchyard gate, and again looked irresolutely about him. At that moment a party of children, who had been playing among the graves, came chattering and laughing toward and out of the gate, and Wilks walked hastily away again, this time in the opposite direction.

"That's the place, clearly," Hewitt said. "We must slip across quietly, as soon as he's far enough down the road. Now!"

We hurried stealthily across, through the gate, and into the churchyard, where Hewitt threw his blue spectacles away. It was now nearly eight in the evening, and the sun was setting. Once again Wilks approached the gate, and did not enter, because a labourer passed at the time. Then he came back and slipped through.

The grass about the graves was long, and under the trees it was already twilight. Hewitt and I, two or three yards apart, to avoid falling over one another in case of sudden movement, watched from behind gravestones. The form of Wilks stood out large and black against the fading light in the west as he stealthily approached through the long grass. A light cart came clattering along the road, and Wilks dropped at once and crouched on his knees till it had passed. Then, staring warily about him, he made straight for the stone behind which Hewitt waited.

I saw Hewitt's dark form swing noiselessly round to the other side of the stone. Wilks passed on and dropped on his knee beside a large, weather-worn slab that rested on a brick under-structure a foot or so high. The long grass largely hid the bricks, and among it Wilks plunged his hand, feeling along the brick surface. Presently he drew out a loose brick, and laid it on the slab. He felt again in the place, and brought forth a small dark object. I saw Hewitt rise erect in the gathering dusk, and with extended arm step noiselessly toward the stooping man. Wilks made a motion to place the dark object in his pocket, but checked himself, and opened what appeared to be a lid, as though to make sure of the safety of the contents. The last light, straggling under the trees, fell on a brilliantly sparkling object within, and like a flash Hewitt's hand shot over Wilks' shoulder and snatched the jewel.

The man actually screamed—one of those curious sharp little screams that one may hear from a woman very suddenly alarmed. But he sprang at Hewitt like a cat, only to meet a straight drive of the fist that stretched him on his back across the slab. I sprang from behind my stone, and helped Hewitt to secure his wrists with a pocket-handkerchief. Then we marched him, struggling and swearing, to the village.

When, in the lights of the village, he recognised us, he had a perfect fit of rage, but afterward he calmed down, and admitted that it was a "very clean cop." There was some difficulty in finding the village constable, and Sir Valentine Quinton was dining out and did not arrive for at least an hour. In the interval Wilks grew communicative.

"How much d'ye think I'll get?" he asked.

"Can't guess," Hewitt replied. "And as we shall probably have to give evidence, you'll be giving yourself away if you talk too much."

"Oh, I don't care; that'll make no difference. It's a fair cop, and I'm in for it. You got at me nicely, lending me three quid. I never knew a reeler do that before. That blinded me. But was it kid about Gold Street?"

"No, it wasn't. Mr. Hollams is safely shut up by this time, I expect, and you are avenged for your little trouble with him this afternoon."

"What did you know about that? Well, you've got it up nicely for me, I must say. S'pose you've been following me all the time?"

"Well, yes; I haven't been far off. I guessed you'd want to clear out of town if Hollams was taken, and I knew this"—Hewitt tapped his breast pocket—"was what you'd take care to get hold of first. You hid it, of course, because you knew that Hollams would probably have you searched for it if he got suspicious?"

"Yes, he did, too. Two blokes went over my pockets one night, and somebody got into my room. But I expected that, Hollams is such a greedy pig. Once he's got you under his thumb he don't give you half your makings, and, if you kick, he'll have you smugged. So that I wasn't going to give him *that* if I could help it. I s'pose it ain't any good asking how you got put on to our mob?"

"No," said Hewitt, "it isn't."

★★★★★★

We didn't get back till the next day, staying for the night, despite an inconvenient want of requisites, at the Hall. There were, in fact, no late trains. We told Sir Valentine the story of the Irishman, much to his amusement.

"Leamy's tale sounded unlikely, of course," Hewitt said, "but it was noticeable that every one of his misfortunes pointed in the same direction—that certain persons were tremendously anxious to get at something they supposed he had. When he spoke of his adventure with the bag, I at once remembered Wilks' arrest and subsequent release. It was a curious coincidence, to say the least, that this should happen at the very station to which the proceeds of this robbery must come, if they came to London at all, and on the day following the robbery itself. Kedderby is one of the few stations on this line where no trains would stop after the time of the robbery, so that the thief would have to wait till the next day to get back. Leamy's recognition of Wilks' portrait made me feel pretty certain. Plainly, he had carried stolen property; the poor, innocent fellow's conversation with Hollams showed that, as, in fact, did the sum, five pounds, paid to him by way of 'regulars,' or customary toll, from the plunder of services of carriage. Hollams obviously took Leamy for a criminal friend of Wilks', because of his use of the thieves' expressions 'sparks' and 'regulars,' and suggested, in terms which Leamy misunderstood, that he should sell any plunder he might obtain to himself, Hollams. Altogether it would have been very curious if the plunder were *not* that from Radcot Hall, especially as no other robbery had been reported at the time.

"Now, among the jewels taken, only one was of a very pre-eminent value—the famous ruby. It was scarcely likely that Hollams would go to so much trouble and risk, attempting to drug, injuring, waylaying, and burgling the rooms of the unfortunate Leamy, for a jewel of small value—for any jewel, in fact, but the ruby. So that I felt a pretty strong presumption, at all events, that it was the ruby Hollams was after. Leamy had not had it, I was convinced, from his tale and his manner, and from what I judged of the man himself.

"The only other person was Wilks, and certainly he had a temptation to keep this to himself, and avoid, if possible, sharing with his London director, or principal; while the carriage of the bag by the Irishman gave him a capital opportunity to put suspicion on him, with the results seen. The most daring of Hollams' attacks on Leamy was doubtless the attempted maiming or killing at the railway station, so as to be able, in the character of a medical man, to search his pockets. He was probably desperate at the time, having, I have no doubt, been following Leamy about all day at the Crystal Palace without finding an opportunity to get at his pockets.

"The struggle and flight of Wilks from Hollams' confirmed my previous impressions. Hollams, finally satisfied that very morning that Leamy certainly had not the jewel, either on his person or at his lodging, and knowing, from having so closely watched him, that he had been nowhere where it could be disposed of, concluded that Wilks was cheating him, and attempted to extort the ruby from him by the aid of another ruffian and a pistol. The rest of my way was plain. Wilks, I knew, would seize the opportunity of Hollams' being safely locked up to get at and dispose of the ruby. I supplied him with funds and left him to lead us to his hiding-place. He did it, and I think that's all."

"He must have walked straight away from my house to the churchyard," Sir Valentine remarked, "to hide that pendant. That was fairly cool."

"Only a cool hand could carry out such a robbery single-handed," Hewitt answered. "I expect his tools were in the bag that Leamy carried, as well as the jewels. They must have been a small and neat set."

They were. We ascertained on our return to town the next day that the bag, with all its contents intact, including the tools, had been taken by the police at their surprise visit to No. 8 Gold Street, as well as much other stolen property.

Hollams and Wilks each got very wholesome doses of penal servitude, to the intense delight of Mick Leamy. Leamy himself, by the by, is still to be seen, clad in a noble uniform, guarding the door of a well-known London restaurant. He has not had any more five-pound notes for carrying bags, but knows London too well now to expect it.

THE STANWAY CAMEO MYSTERY

It is now a fair number of years back since the loss of the famous Stanway Cameo made its sensation, and the only person who had the least interest in keeping the real facts of the case secret has now been dead for some time, leaving neither relatives nor other representatives. Therefore, no harm will be done in making the inner history of the case public; on the contrary, it will afford an opportunity of vindicating the professional reputation of Hewitt, who is supposed to have completely failed to make anything of the mystery surrounding the case. At the present time connoisseurs in ancient objects of art are often heard regretfully to wonder whether the wonderful cameo, so suddenly discovered and so quickly stolen, will ever again be visible to the public eye. Now this question need be asked no longer.

The cameo, as may be remembered from the many descriptions published at the time, was said to be absolutely the finest extant. It was a sardonyx of three *strata*—one of those rare sardonyx cameos in which it has been possible for the artist to avail himself of three different colours of superimposed stone—the lowest for the ground and the two others for the middle and high relief of the design. In size it was, for a cameo, immense, measuring seven and a half inches by nearly six. In subject it was similar to the renowned Gonzaga Cameo—now the property of the Czar of Russia—a male and a female head with imperial insignia; but in this case supposed to represent Tiberius Claudius and Messalina. Experts considered it probably to be the work of Athenion, a famous gem-cutter of the first Christian century, whose most notable other work now extant is a smaller cameo, with a mythological subject, preserved in the Vatican.

The Stanway Cameo had been discovered in an obscure Italian village by one of those traveling agents who scour all Europe for valuable antiquities and objects of art. This man had hurried immediately to London with his prize, and sold it to Mr. Claridge of St. James Street, eminent as a dealer in such objects. Mr. Claridge, recognising the importance and value of the article, lost no opportunity of making its existence known, and very soon the Claudius Cameo, as it was at first usually called, was as famous as any in the world. Many experts in ancient art examined it, and several large bids were made for its purchase.

In the end it was bought by the Marquis of Stanway for five thousand pounds for the purpose of presentation to the British Museum. The marquis kept the cameo at his town house for a few days, showing it to his friends, and then returned it to Mr. Claridge to be finally and carefully cleaned before passing into the national collection. Two nights after Mr. Claridge's premises were broken into and the cameo stolen.

Such, in outline, was the generally known history of the Stanway Cameo. The circumstances of the burglary in detail were these: Mr. Claridge had himself been the last to leave the premises at about eight in the evening, at dusk, and had locked the small side door as usual. His assistant, Mr. Cutler, had left an hour and a half earlier. When Mr. Claridge left, everything was in order, and the policeman on fixed-point duty just opposite, who bade Mr. Claridge good-evening as he left, saw nothing suspicious during the rest of his term of duty, nor did his successors at the point throughout the night.

In the morning, however, Mr. Cutler, the assistant, who arrived first, soon after nine o'clock, at once perceived that something unlooked-for had happened. The door, of which he had a key, was still fastened, and had not been touched; but in the room behind the shop Mr. Claridge's private desk had been broken open, and the contents turned out in confusion. The door leading on to the staircase had also been forced. Proceeding up the stairs, Mr. Cutler found another door open, leading from the top landing to a small room; this door had been opened by the simple expedient of unscrewing and taking off the lock, which had been on the inside. In the ceiling of this room was a trap-door, and this was six or eight inches open, the edge resting on the half-wrenched-off bolt, which had been torn away when the trap was levered open from the outside.

Plainly, then, this was the path of the thief or thieves. Entrance had been made through the trap-door, two more doors had been opened, and then the desk had been ransacked. Mr. Cutler afterward explained that at this time he had no precise idea what had been stolen, and did not know where the cameo had been left on the previous evening. Mr. Claridge had himself undertaken the cleaning, and had been engaged on it, the assistant said, when he left.

There was no doubt, however, after Mr. Claridge's arrival at ten o'clock—the cameo was gone. Mr. Claridge, utterly confounded at his loss, explained incoherently, and with curses on his own carelessness, that he had locked the precious article in his desk on relinquishing work on it the previous evening, feeling rather tired, and not taking the trouble to carry it as far as the safe in another part of the house.

The police were sent for at once, of course, and every investigation made, Mr. Claridge offering a reward of five hundred pounds for the recovery of the cameo. The affair was scribbled off at large in the earliest editions of the evening papers, and by noon all the world was aware of the extraordinary theft of the Stanway Cameo, and many people were discussing the probabilities of the case, with very indistinct ideas of what a sardonyx cameo precisely was.

It was in the afternoon of this day that Lord Stanway called on Martin Hewitt. The marquis was a tall, upstanding man of spare figure and active habits, well known as a member of learned societies and a great patron of art. He hurried into Hewitt's private room as soon as his name had been announced, and, as soon as Hewitt had given him a chair, plunged into business.

"Probably you already guess my business with you, Mr. Hewitt—you have seen the early evening papers? Just so; then I needn't tell you again what you already know. My cameo is gone, and I badly want it back. Of course the police are hard at work at Claridge's, but I'm not quite satisfied. I have been there myself for two or three hours, and can't see that they know any more about it than I do myself. Then, of course, the police, naturally and properly enough from their point of view, look first to find the criminal, regarding the recovery of the property almost as a secondary consideration. Now, from *my* point of view, the chief consideration is the property. Of course I want the thief caught, if possible, and properly punished; but still more I want the cameo."

"Certainly it is a considerable loss. Five thousand pounds——"

"Ah, but don't misunderstand me! It isn't the monetary value of the thing that I regret. As a matter of fact, I am indemnified for that already. Claridge has behaved most honourably—more than honourably. Indeed, the first intimation I had of the loss was a cheque from him for five thousand pounds, with a letter assuring me that the restoration to me of the amount I had paid was the least he could do to repair the result of what he called his unpardonable carelessness. Legally, I'm not sure that I could demand anything of him, unless I could prove very flagrant neglect indeed to guard against theft."

"Then I take it, Lord Stanway," Hewitt observed, "that you much prefer the cameo to the money?"

"Certainly. Else I should never have been willing to pay the money for the cameo. It was an enormous price—perhaps much above the market value, even for such a valuable thing—but I was particularly anxious that it should not go out of the country. Our public collections here are not so fortunate as they should be in the possession of the very finest examples of that class of work. In short, I had determined on the cameo, and, fortunately, happen to be able to carry out determinations of that sort without regarding an extra thousand pounds or so as an obstacle. So that, you see, what I want is not the value, but the thing itself. Indeed, I don't think I can possibly keep the money Claridge has sent me; the affair is more his misfortune than his fault. But I shall say nothing about returning it for a little while; it may possibly have the effect of sharpening everybody in the search."

"Just so. Do I understand that you would like me to look into the case independently, on your behalf?"

"Exactly. I want you, if you can, to approach the matter entirely from my point of view—your sole object being to find the cameo. Of course, if you happen on the thief as well, so much the better. Perhaps, after all, looking for the one is the same thing as looking for the other?"

"Not always; but usually it is, or course; even if they are not to-gether, they certainly *have* been at one time, and to have one is a very long step toward having the other. Now, to begin with, is anybody suspected?"

"Well, the police are reserved, but I believe the fact is they've noth-ing to say. Claridge won't admit that he suspects any one, though he believes that whoever it was must have watched him yesterday eve-ning through the back window of his room, and must have seen him put the cameo away in his desk; because the thief would seem to have gone straight to the place. But I half fancy that, in his inner mind, he is inclined to suspect one of two people. You see, a robbery of this sort is different from others. That cameo would never be stolen, I imagine, with the view of its being sold—it is much too famous a thing; a man might as well walk about offering to sell the Tower of London. There are only a very few people who buy such things, and every one of them knows all about it. No dealer would touch it; he could never even show it, much less sell it, without being called to account. So that it really seems more likely that it has been taken by somebody who wishes to keep it for mere love of the thing—a collector, in fact—who would then have to keep it secretly at home, and never let a soul besides himself see it, living in the consciousness that at his death it must be found and this theft known; unless, indeed, an ordinary vulgar burglar has taken it without knowing its value."

"That isn't likely," Hewitt replied. "An ordinary burglar, ignorant of its value, wouldn't have gone straight to the cameo and have taken it in preference to many other things of more apparent worth, which must be lying near in such a place as Claridge's."

"True—I suppose he wouldn't. Although the police seem to think that the breaking in is clearly the work of a regular criminal—from the jimmy-marks, you know, and so on."

"Well, but what of the two people you think Mr. Claridge sus-pects?"

"Of course I can't say that he does suspect them—I only fancied from his tone that it might be possible; he himself insists that he can't, in justice, suspect anybody. One of these men is Hahn, the traveling agent who sold him the cameo. This man's character does not ap-pear to be absolutely irreproachable; no dealer trusts him very far. Of course Claridge doesn't say what he paid him for the cameo; these dealers are very reticent about their profits, which I believe are as of-ten something like five hundred *per cent* as not. But it seems Hahn bargained to have something extra, depending on the amount Claridge could sell the carving for. According to the appointment he should have turned up this morning, but he hasn't been seen, and nobody seems to know exactly where he is."

"Yes; and the other person?"

"Well, I scarcely like mentioning him, because he is certainly a gentleman, and I believe, in the ordinary way, quite incapable of anything in the least degree dishonourable; although, of course, they say a collector has no conscience in the matter of his own particular hobby, and certainly Mr. Woollett is as keen a collector as any man alive. He lives in chambers in the next turning past Claridge's premises—can, in fact, look into Claridge's back windows if he likes. He examined the cameo several times before I bought it, and made several high offers—appeared, in fact, very anxious indeed to get it. After I had bought it he made, I understand, some rather strong remarks about people like myself 'spoiling the market' by paying extravagant prices, and altogether cut up 'crusty,' as they say, at losing the specimen." Lord Stanway paused a few seconds, and then went on: "I'm not sure that I ought to mention Mr. Woollett's name for a moment in connection with such a matter; I am personally perfectly certain that he is as incapable of anything like theft as myself. But I am telling you all I know."

"Precisely. I can't know too much in a case like this. It can do no harm if I know all about fifty innocent people, and may save me from the risk of knowing nothing about the thief. Now, let me see: Mr. Woollett's rooms, you say, are near Mr. Claridge's place of business? Is there any means of communication between the roofs?"

"Yes, I am told that it is perfectly possible to get from one place to the other by walking along the leads."

"Very good! Then, unless you can think of any other information that may help me, I think, Lord Stanway, I will go at once and look at the place."

"Do, by all means. I think I'll come back with you. Somehow, I don't like to feel idle in the matter, though I suppose I can't do much. As to more information, I don't think there is any."

"In regard to Mr. Claridge's assistant, now: Do you know anything of him?"

"Only that he has always seemed a very civil and decent sort of man. Honest, I should say, or Claridge wouldn't have kept him so many years—there are a good many valuable things about at Claridge's. Besides, the man has keys of the place himself, and, even if he

107

were a thief, he wouldn't need to go breaking in through the roof."

"So that," said Hewitt, "we have, directly connected with this cameo, besides yourself, these people: Mr. Claridge, the dealer; Mr. Cutler, the assistant in Mr. Claridge's business; Hahn, who sold the article to Claridge, and Mr. Woollett, who made bids for it. These are all?"

"All that I know of. Other gentlemen made bids, I believe, but I don't know them."

"Take these people in their order. Mr. Claridge is out of the question, as a dealer with a reputation to keep up would be, even if he hadn't immediately sent you this five thousand pounds—more than the market value, I understand, of the cameo. The assistant is a reputable man, against whom nothing is known, who would never need to break in, and who must understand his business well enough to know that he could never attempt to sell the missing stone without instant detection. Hahn is a man of shady antecedents, probably clever enough to know as well as anybody how to dispose of such plunder—if it be possible to dispose of it at all; also, Hahn hasn't been to Claridge's today, although he had an appointment to take money. Lastly, Mr. Woollett is a gentleman of the most honourable record, but a perfectly rabid collector, who had made every effort to secure the cameo before you bought it; who, moreover, could have seen Mr. Claridge working in his back room, and who has perfectly easy access to Mr. Claridge's roof. If we find it can't be none of these, then we must look where circumstances indicate."

There was unwonted excitement at Mr. Claridge's place when Hewitt and his client arrived. It was a dull old building, and in the windows there was never more show than an odd blue china vase or two, or, mayhap, a few old silver shoe-buckles and a curious small sword. Nine men out of ten would have passed it without a glance; but the tenth at least would probably know it for a place famous through the world for the number and value of the old and curious objects of art that had passed through it.

On this day two or three loiterers, having heard of the robbery, extracted what gratification they might from staring at nothing between the railings guarding the windows. Within, Mr. Claridge, a brisk, stout, little old man, was talking earnestly to a burly police-inspector in uniform, and Mr. Cutler, who had seized the opportunity to attempt amateur detective work on his own account, was grovelling perseveringly about the floor, among old porcelain and loose pieces of armour, in the futile hope of finding any clue that the thieves might have considerately dropped.

Mr. Claridge came forward eagerly.

"The leather case has been found, I am pleased to be able to tell you, Lord Stanway, since you left."

"Empty, of course?"

"Unfortunately, yes. It had evidently been thrown away by the thief behind a chimney-stack a roof or two away, where the police have found it. But it is a clue, of course."

"Ah, then this gentleman will give me his opinion of it," Lord Stanway said, turning to Hewitt. "This, Mr. Claridge, is Mr. Martin Hewitt, who has been kind enough to come with me here at a moment's notice. With the police on the one hand and Mr. Hewitt on the other we shall certainly recover that cameo, if it is to be recovered, I think."

Mr. Claridge bowed, and beamed on Hewitt through his spectacles. "I'm very glad Mr. Hewitt has come," he said. "Indeed, I had already decided to give the police till this time tomorrow, and then, if they had found nothing, to call in Mr. Hewitt myself."

Hewitt bowed in his turn, and then asked: "Will you let me see the various breakages? I hope they have not been disturbed."

"Nothing whatever has been disturbed. Do exactly as seems best. I need scarcely say that everything here is perfectly at your disposal. You know all the circumstances, of course?"

"In general, yes. I suppose I am right in the belief that you have no resident housekeeper?"

"No," Claridge replied, "I haven't. I had one housekeeper who sometimes pawned my property in the evening, and then another who used to break my most valuable china, till I could never sleep or take a moment's ease at home for fear my stock was being ruined here. So I gave up resident housekeepers. I felt some confidence in doing it because of the policeman who is always on duty opposite."

"Can I see the broken desk?"

Mr. Claridge led the way into the room behind the shop. The desk was really a sort of work-table, with a lifting top and a lock. The top had been forced roughly open by some instrument which had been pushed in below it and used as a lever, so that the catch of the lock was torn away. Hewitt examined the damaged parts and the marks of the lever, and then looked out at the back window.

"There are several windows about here," he remarked, "from which it might be possible to see into this room. Do you know any of the people who live behind them?"

"Two or three I know," Mr. Claridge answered, "but there are two windows—the pair almost immediately before us—belonging to a room or office which is to let. Any stranger might get in there and watch."

"Do the roofs above any of those windows communicate in any way with yours?"

"None of those directly opposite. Those at the left do; you may walk all the way along the leads."

"And whose windows are they?"

Mr. Claridge hesitated. "Well," he said, "they're Mr. Woollett's, an excellent customer of mine. But he's a gentleman, and—well, I really think it's absurd to suspect him."

"In a case like this," Hewitt answered, "one must disregard nothing but the impossible. Somebody—whether Mr. Woollett himself or another person—could possibly have seen into this room from those windows, and equally possibly could have reached this room from that one. Therefore, we must not forget Mr. Woollett. Have any of your neighbours been burgled during the night? I mean that strangers anxious to get at your trap-door would probably have to begin by getting into some other house close by, so as to reach your roof."

"No," Mr. Claridge replied; "there has been nothing of that sort. It was the first thing the police ascertained."

Hewitt examined the broken door and then made his way up the stairs with the others. The unscrewed lock of the door of the top back-room required little examination. In the room below the trap-door was a dusty table on which stood a chair, and at the other side of the table sat Detective-Inspector Plummer, whom Hewitt knew very well, and who bade him "good-day" and then went on with his docket.

"This chair and table were found as they are now, I take it?" Hewitt asked.

"Yes," said Mr. Claridge; "the thieves, I should think, dropped in through the trap-door, after breaking it open, and had to place this chair where it is to be able to climb back."

Hewitt scrambled up through the trap-way and examined it from the top. The door was hung on long external barn-door hinges, and had been forced open in a similar manner to that practiced on the desk. A jimmy had been pushed between the frame and the door near the bolt, and the door had been pried open, the bolt being torn away from the screws in the operation.

Presently Inspector Plummer, having finished his docket, climbed up to the roof after Hewitt, and the two together went to the spot, close under a chimney-stack on the next roof but one, where the case had been found. Plummer produced the case, which he had in his coat-tail pocket, for Hewitt's inspection.

"I don't see anything particular about it; do you?" he said. "It shows us the way they went, though, being found just here."

"Well, yes," Hewitt said; "if we kept on in this direction, we should be going toward Mr. Woollett's house, and *his* trap-door, shouldn't we!"

The inspector pursed his lips, smiled, and shrugged his shoulders. "Of course we haven't waited till now to find that out," he said.

"No, of course. And, as you say, I didn't think there is much to be learned from this leather case. It is almost new, and there isn't a mark on it." And Hewitt handed it back to the inspector.

"Well," said Plummer, as he returned the case to his pocket, "what's your opinion?"

"It's rather an awkward case."

"Yes, it is. Between ourselves—I don't mind telling you—I'm having a sharp lookout kept over there"—Plummer jerked his head in the direction of Mr. Woollett's chambers—"because the robbery's an unusual one. There's only two possible motives—the sale of the cameo or the keeping of it. The sale's out of the question, as you know; the thing's only saleable to those who would collar the thief at once, and who wouldn't have the thing in their places now for anything. So that it must be taken to keep, and that's a thing nobody but the maddest of collectors would do, just such persons as—" and the inspector nodded again toward Mr. Woollett's quarters. "Take that with the other circumstances," he added, "and I think you'll agree it's worthwhile looking a little farther that way. Of course some of the work—taking off the lock and so on—looks rather like a regular burglar, but it's just possible that any one badly wanting the cameo would like to hire a man who was up to the work."

"Yes, it's possible."

"Do you know anything of Hahn, the agent?" Plummer asked, a moment later.

"No, I don't. Have you found him yet?"

"I haven't yet, but I'm after him. I've found he was at Charing Cross a day or two ago, booking a ticket for the Continent. That and his failing to turn up today seem to make it worthwhile not to miss *him* if we can help it. He isn't the sort of man that lets a chance of drawing a bit of money go for nothing."

They returned to the room. "Well," said Lord Stanway, "what's the result of the consultation? We've been waiting here very patiently, while you two clever men have been discussing the matter on the roof."

On the wall just beneath the trap-door a very dusty old tall hat hung on a peg. This Hewitt took down and examined very closely, smearing his fingers with the dust from the inside lining. "Is this one of your valuable and crusted old antiques?" he asked, with a smile, of Mr. Claridge.

"That's only an old hat that I used to keep here for use in bad weather," Mr. Claridge said, with some surprise at the question. "I haven't touched it for a year or more."

"Oh, then it couldn't have been left here by your last night's visitor," Hewitt replied, carelessly replacing it on the hook. "You left here at eight last night, I think?"

"Eight exactly—or within a minute or two."

"Just so. I think I'll look at the room on the opposite side of the landing, if you'll let me."

"Certainly, if you'd like to," Claridge replied; "but they haven't been there—it is exactly as it was left. Only a lumber-room, you see," he concluded, flinging the door open.

A number of partly broken-up packing-cases littered about this room, with much other rubbish. Hewitt took the lid of one of the newest-looking packing-cases, and glanced at the address label. Then he turned to a rusty old iron box that stood against a wall. "I should like to see behind this," he said, tugging at it with his hands. "It is heavy and dirty. Is there a small crowbar about the house, or some similar lever?"

Mr. Claridge shook his head. "Haven't such a thing in the place," he said.

"Never mind," Hewitt replied, "another time will do to shift that old box, and perhaps, after all, there's little reason for moving it. I will just walk round to the police-station, I think, and speak to the constables who were on duty opposite during the night. I think, Lord Stanway, I have seen all that is necessary here."

"I suppose," asked Mr. Claridge, "it is too soon yet to ask if you have formed any theory in the matter?"

"Well—yes, it is," Hewitt answered. "But perhaps I may be able to surprise you in an hour or two; but that I don't promise. By the by," he added suddenly, "I suppose you're sure the trap-door was bolted last night?"

"Certainly," Mr. Claridge answered, smiling. "Else how could the bolt have been broken? As a matter of fact, I believe the trap hasn't been opened for months. Mr. Cutler, do you remember when the trap-door was last opened?"

Mr. Cutler shook his head. "Certainly not for six months," he said.

"Ah, very well; it's not very important," Hewitt replied.

As they reached the front shop a fiery-faced old gentleman bounced in at the street door, stumbling over an umbrella that stood in a dark corner, and kicking it three yards away.

"What the deuce do you mean," he roared at Mr. Claridge, "by sending these police people smelling about my rooms and asking questions of my servants? What do you mean, sir, by treating me as a thief? Can't a gentleman come into this place to look at an article without being suspected of stealing it, when it disappears through your wretched carelessness? I'll ask my solicitor, sir, if there isn't a remedy for this sort of thing. And if I catch another of your spy fellows on my staircase, or crawling about my roof, I'll—I'll shoot him!"

"Really, Mr. Woollett——" began Mr. Claridge, somewhat abashed, but the angry old man would hear nothing.

"Don't talk to me, sir; you shall talk to my solicitor. And am I to understand, my lord"—turning to Lord Stanway—"that these things are being done with your approval?"

"Whatever is being done," Lord Stanway answered, "is being done by the police on their own responsibility, and entirely without prompting, I believe, by Mr. Claridge—certainly without a suggestion of any sort from myself. I think that the personal opinion of Mr. Claridge—certainly my own—is that anything like a suspicion of your position in this wretched matter is ridiculous. And if you will only consider the matter calmly——"

"Consider it calmly? Imagine yourself considering such a thing calmly, Lord Stanway. I *won't* consider it calmly. I'll—I'll—I won't have it. And if I find another man on my roof, I'll pitch him off!" And Mr. Woollett bounced into the street again.

"Mr. Woollett is annoyed," Hewitt observed, with a smile. "I'm afraid Plummer has a clumsy assistant somewhere."

Mr. Claridge said nothing, but looked rather glum, for Mr. Woollett was a most excellent customer.

Lord Stanwood and Hewitt walked slowly down the street, Hewitt staring at the pavement in profound thought. Once or twice Lord Stanway glanced at his face, but refrained from disturbing him. Presently, however, he observed: "You seem, at least, Mr. Hewitt, to have noticed something that has set you thinking. Does it look like a clue?"

Hewitt came out of his cogitation at once. "A clue?" he said; "the case bristles with clues. The extraordinary thing to me is that Plummer, usually a smart man, doesn't seem to have seen one of them. He must be out of sorts, I'm afraid. But the case is decidedly a most remarkable one."

"Remarkable in what particular way?"

"In regard to motive. Now it would seem, as Plummer was saying to me just now on the roof, that there were only two possible motives for such a robbery. Either the man who took all this trouble and risk to break into Claridge's place must have desired to sell the cameo at a good price, or he must have desired to keep it for himself, being a lover of such things. But neither of these has been the actual motive."

"Perhaps he thinks he can extort a good sum from me by way of ransom?"

"No, it isn't that. Nor is it jealousy, nor spite, nor anything of that kind. I know the motive, I *think*—but I wish we could get hold of Hahn. I will shut myself up alone and turn it over in my mind for half an hour presently."

"Meanwhile, what I want to know is, apart from all your professional subtleties—which I confess I can't understand—can you get back the cameo?"

"That," said Hewitt, stopping at the corner of the street, "I am rather afraid I cannot—nor anybody else. But I am pretty sure I know the thief."

"Then surely that will lead you to the cameo?"

"It *may*, of course; but, then, it is just possible that by this evening you may not want to have it back, after all."

Lord Stanway stared in amazement.

"Not want to have it back!" he exclaimed. "Why, of course I shall want to have it back. I don't understand you in the least; you talk in conundrums. Who is the thief you speak of?"

"I think, Lord Stanway," Hewitt said, "that perhaps I had better not say until I have quite finished my inquiries, in case of mistakes. The case is quite an extraordinary one, and of quite a different character from what one would at first naturally imagine, and I must be very careful to guard against the possibility of error. I have very little fear of a mistake, however, and I hope I may wait on you in a few hours at Piccadilly with news. I have only to see the policemen."

"Certainly, come whenever you please. But why see the policemen? They have already most positively stated that they saw nothing whatever suspicious in the house or near it."

"I shall not ask them anything at all about the house," Hewitt responded. "I shall just have a little chat with them—about the weather." And with a smiling bow he turned away, while Lord Stanway stood and gazed after him, with an expression that implied a suspicion that his special detective was making a fool of him.

★★★★★★

In rather more than an hour Hewitt was back in Mr. Claridge's shop. "Mr. Claridge," he said, "I think I must ask you one or two questions in private. May I see you in your own room?"

They went there at once, and Hewitt, pulling a chair before the window, sat down with his back to the light. The dealer shut the door, and sat opposite him, with the light full in his face.

"Mr. Claridge," Hewitt proceeded slowly, "*when did you first find that Lord Stanway's cameo was a forgery?*"

Claridge literally bounced in his chair. His face paled, but he managed to stammer sharply: "What—what—what d'you mean? Forgery? Do you mean to say I sell forgeries? Forgery? It wasn't a forgery!"

"Then," continued Hewitt in the same deliberate tone, watching the other's face the while, "if it wasn't a forgery, *why did you destroy it and burst your trap-door and desk to imitate a burglary?*"

The sweat stood thick on the dealer's face, and he gasped. But he struggled hard to keep his faculties together, and ejaculated hoarsely: "Destroy it? What—what—I didn't—didn't destroy it!"

"Threw it into the river, then—don't prevaricate about details."

"No—no—it's a lie! Who says that? Go away! You're insulting me!" Claridge almost screamed.

"Come, come, Mr. Claridge," Hewitt said more placably, for he had gained his point; "don't distress yourself, and don't attempt to deceive me—you can't, I assure you. I know everything you did before you left here last night—everything."

Claridge's face worked painfully. Once or twice he appeared to be on the point of returning an indignant reply, but hesitated, and finally broke down altogether.

"Don't expose me, Mr. Hewitt!" he pleaded; "I beg you won't ex-

115

pose me! I haven't harmed a soul but myself. I've paid Lord Stanway every penny back, and I never knew the thing was a forgery till I began to clean it. I'm an old man, Mr. Hewitt, and my professional reputation has been spotless until now. I beg you won't expose me."

Hewitt's voice softened. "Don't make an unnecessary trouble of it," he said. "I see a decanter on your sideboard—let me give you a little brandy and water. Come, there's nothing criminal, I believe, in a man's breaking open his own desk, or his own trap-door, for that matter. Of course I'm acting for Lord Stanway in this affair, and I must, in duty, report to him without reserve. But Lord Stanway is a gentleman, and I'll undertake he'll do nothing inconsiderate of your feelings, if you're disposed to be frank. Let us talk the affair over; tell me about it."

"It was that swindler Hahn who deceived me in the beginning," Claridge said. "I have never made a mistake with a cameo before, and I never thought so close an imitation was possible. I examined it most carefully, and was perfectly satisfied, and many experts examined it afterward, and were all equally deceived. I felt as sure as I possibly could feel that I had bought one of the finest, if not actually the finest, cameos known to exist. It was not until after it had come back from Lord Stanway's, and I was cleaning it the evening before last, that in course of my work it became apparent that the thing was nothing but a consummately clever forgery. It was made of three layers of moulded glass, nothing more nor less. But the glass was treated in a way I had never before known of, and the surface had been cunningly worked on till it defied any ordinary examination. Some of the glass imitation cameos made in the latter part of the last century, I may tell you, are regarded as marvellous pieces of work, and, indeed, command very fair prices, but this was something quite beyond any of those.

"I was amazed and horrified. I put the thing away and went home. All that night I lay awake in a state of distraction, quite unable to decide what to do. To let the cameo go out of my possession was impossible. Sooner or later the forgery would be discovered, and my reputation—the highest in these matters in this country, I may safely claim, and the growth of nearly fifty years of honest application and good judgment—this reputation would be gone forever. But without considering this, there was the fact that I had taken five thousand pounds of Lord Stanway's money for a mere piece of glass, and that money I must, in mere common honesty as well as for my own sake, return. But how? The name of the Stanway Cameo had become a household word, and to confess that the whole thing was a sham would ruin my reputation and destroy all confidence—past, present, and future—in me and in my transactions.

"Either way spelled ruin. Even if I confided in Lord Stanway privately, returned his money, and destroyed the cameo, what then? The sudden disappearance of an article so famous would excite remark at once. It had been presented to the British Museum, and if it never appeared in that collection, and no news were to be got of it, people would guess at the truth at once. To make it known that I myself had been deceived would have availed nothing. It is my business *not* to be deceived; and to have it known that my most expensive specimens might be forgeries would equally mean ruin, whether I sold them cunningly as a rogue or ignorantly as a fool. Indeed, my pride, my reputation as a connoisseur, is a thing near to my heart, and it would be an unspeakable humiliation to me to have it known that I had been imposed on by such a forgery. What could I do? Every expedient seemed useless but one—the one I adopted.

"It was not straightforward, I admit; but, oh! Mr. Hewitt, consider the temptation—and remember that it couldn't do a soul any harm. No matter who might be suspected, I knew there could not possibly be evidence to make them suffer. All the next day—yesterday—I was anxiously worrying out the thing in my mind and carefully devising the—the trick, I'm afraid you'll call it, that you by some extraordinary means have seen through. It seemed the only thing—what else was there? More I needn't tell you; you know it. I have only now to beg that you will use your best influence with Lord Stanway to save me from public derision and exposure. I will do anything—pay anything—anything but exposure, at my age, and with my position."

"Well, you see," Hewitt replied thoughtfully, "I've no doubt Lord Stanway will show you every consideration, and certainly I will do what I can to save you in the circumstances; though you must remember that you *have* done some harm—you have caused suspicions to rest on at least one honest man. But as to reputation, I've a professional reputation of my own. If I help to conceal your professional failure, I shall appear to have failed in *my* part of the business."

"But the cases are different, Mr. Hewitt. Consider. You are not expected—it would be impossible—to succeed invariably; and there are only two or three who know you have looked into the case. Then your other conspicuous successes——"

"Well, well, we shall see. One thing I don't know, though—whether you climbed out of a window to break open the trap-door, or whether you got up through the trap-door itself and pulled the bolt with a string through the jamb, so as to bolt it after you."

"There was no available window. I used the string, as you say. My poor little cunning must seem very transparent to you, I fear. I spent hours of thought over the question of the trap-door—how to break it open so as to leave a genuine appearance, and especially how to bolt it inside after I had reached the roof. I thought I had succeeded beyond the possibility of suspicion; how you penetrated the device surpasses my comprehension. How, to begin with, could you possibly know that the cameo was a forgery? Did you ever see it?"

"Never. And, if I had seen it, I fear I should never have been able to express an opinion on it; I'm not a connoisseur. As a matter of fact, I *didn't* know that the thing was a forgery in the first place; what I knew in the first place was that it was *you* who had broken into the house. It was from that that I arrived at the conclusion, after a certain amount of thought, that the cameo must have been forged. Gain was out of the question. You, beyond all men, could never sell the Stanway Cameo again, and, besides, you had paid back Lord Stanway's money. I knew enough of your reputation to know that you would never incur the scandal of a great theft at your place for the sake of getting the cameo for yourself, when you might have kept it in the beginning, with no trouble and mystery. Consequently, I had to look for another motive, and at first another motive seemed an impossibility. Why should you wish to take all this trouble to lose five thousand pounds? You had nothing to gain; perhaps you had something to save—your professional reputation, for instance. Looking at it so, it was plain that you were *suppressing* the cameo—burking it; since, once taken as you had taken it, it could never come to light again. That suggested the solution of the mystery at once—you had discovered, after the sale, that the cameo was not genuine."

"Yes, yes—I see; but you say you began with the knowledge that I broke into the place myself. How did you know that? I cannot imagine a trace——"

"My dear sir, you left traces everywhere. In the first place, it struck me as curious, before I came here, that you had sent off that cheque for five thousand pounds to Lord Stanway an hour or so after the robbery was discovered; it looked so much as though you were sure of the cameo never coming back, and were in a hurry to avert suspicion. Of course I understood that, so far as I then knew the case, you were the most unlikely person in the world, and that your eagerness to repay

Lord Stanway might be the most creditable thing possible. But the point was worth remembering, and I remembered it.

"When I came here, I saw suspicious indications in many directions, but the conclusive piece of evidence was that old hat hanging below the trap-door."

"But I never touched it; I assure you, Mr. Hewitt, I never touched the hat; haven't touched it for months——"

"Of course. If you *had* touched it, I might never have got the clue. But we'll deal with the hat presently; that wasn't what struck me at first. The trap-door first took my attention. Consider, now: Here was a trap-door, most insecurely hung on *external* hinges; the burglar had a screwdriver, for he took off the door-lock below with it. Why, then, didn't he take this trap off by the hinges, instead of making a noise and taking longer time and trouble to burst the bolt from its fastenings? And why, if he were a stranger, was he able to plant his jimmy from the outside just exactly opposite the interior bolt? There was only one mark on the frame, and that precisely in the proper place.

"After that I saw the leather case. It had not been thrown away, or some corner would have shown signs of the fall. It had been put down carefully where it was found. These things, however, were of small importance compared with the hat. The hat, as you know, was exceedingly thick with dust—the accumulation of months. But, on the top side, presented toward the trap-door, were a score or so of *raindrop marks*. That was all. They were new marks, for there was no dust over them; they had merely had time to dry and cake the dust they had fallen on. *Now, there had been no rain since a sharp shower just after seven o'clock last night.*

"At that time, you, by your own statement, were in the place. You left at eight, and the rain was all over at ten minutes or a quarter past seven. The trap-door, you also told me, had not been opened for months. The thing was plain. You, or somebody who was here when you were, had opened that trap-door during, or just before, that shower. I said little then, but went, as soon as I had left, to the police-station. There I made perfectly certain that there had been no rain during the night by questioning the policemen who were on duty outside all the time. There had been none. I knew everything.

"The only other evidence there was pointed with all the rest. There were no rain-marks on the leather case; it had been put on the roof as an after-thought when there was no rain. A very poor after-thought, let me tell you, for no thief would throw away a useful case that concealed his booty and protected it from breakage, and throw it away just so as to leave a clue as to what direction he had gone in. I also saw, in the lumber-room, a number of packing-cases—one with a label dated two days back—which had been opened with an iron lever; and yet, when I made an excuse to ask for it, you said there was no such thing in the place. Inference, you didn't want me to compare it with the marks on the desks and doors. That is all, I think."

Mr. Claridge looked dolorously down at the floor. "I'm afraid," he said, "that I took an unsuitable role when I undertook to rely on my wits to deceive men like you. I thought there wasn't a single vulnerable spot in my defence, but you walk calmly through it at the first attempt. Why did I never think of those raindrops?"

"Come," said Hewitt, with a smile, "that sounds unrepentant. I am going, now, to Lord Stanway's. If I were you, I think I should apologize to Mr. Woollett in some way."

Lord Stanway, who, in the hour or two of reflection left him after parting with Hewitt, had come to the belief that he had employed a man whose mind was not always in order, received Hewitt's story with natural astonishment. For some time, he was in doubt as to whether he would be doing right in acquiescing in anything but a straightforward public statement of the facts connected with the disappearance of the cameo, but in the end was persuaded to let the affair drop, on receiving an assurance from Mr. Woollett that he unreservedly accepted the apology offered him by Mr. Claridge.

As for the latter, he was at least sufficiently punished in loss of money and personal humiliation for his escapade. But the bitterest and last blow he sustained when the unblushing Hahn walked smilingly into his office two days later to demand the extra payment agreed on in consideration of the sale. He had been called suddenly away, he exclaimed, on the day he should have come, and hoped his missing the appointment had occasioned no inconvenience. As to the robbery of the cameo, of course he was very sorry, but "pishness was pishness," and he would be glad of a cheque for the sum agreed on. And the unhappy Claridge was obliged to pay it, knowing that the man had swindled him, but unable to open his mouth to say so.

The reward remained on offer for a long time; indeed, it was never publicly withdrawn, I believe, even at the time of Claridge's death. And several intelligent newspapers enlarged upon the fact that an ordinary burglar had completely baffled and defeated the boasted acumen of Mr. Martin Hewitt, the well-known private detective.

Very often Hewitt was tempted, by the fascination of some particularly odd case, to neglect his other affairs to follow up a matter that
from a business point of view was of little or no value to him. As a rule,
he had a sufficient regard for his own interests to resist such tempta-
tions, but in one curious case, at least, I believe he allowed it largely to
influence him. It was certainly an extremely odd case—one of those
affairs that, coming to light at intervals, but more often remaining
unheard of by the general public, convince one that, after all, there is
very little extravagance about Mr. R.L. Stevenson's bizarre imaginings
of doings in London in his *New Arabian Nights.* "There is nothing in
this world that is at all possible," I have often heard Martin Hewitt say,
"that has not happened or is not happening in London." Certainly he
had opportunities of knowing.

The case I have referred to occurred sometime before my own
acquaintance with him began—in 1878, in fact. He had called one
Monday morning at an office in regard to something connected
with one of those uninteresting, though often difficult, cases which
formed, perhaps, the bulk of his practice, when he was informed of
a most mysterious murder that had taken place in another part of
the same building on the previous Saturday afternoon. Owing to the
circumstances of the case, only the vaguest account had appeared in
the morning papers, and even this, as it chanced, Hewitt had not read.

The building was one of a new row in a partly rebuilt street near
the National Gallery. The whole row had been built by a speculator
for the purpose of letting out in flats, suites of chambers, and in one or
two cases, on the ground floors, offices. The rooms had let very well,
and to desirable tenants, as a rule. The least satisfactory tenant, the pro-
prietor reluctantly admitted, was a Mr. Rameau, a negro gentleman,
single, who had three rooms on the top floor but one of the particular
building that Hewitt was visiting. His rent was paid regularly, but his
behaviour had produced complaints from other tenants. He got up-
roariously drunk, and screamed and howled in unknown tongues. He
fell asleep on the staircase, and ladies were afraid to pass. He bawled
rough chaff down the stairs and along the corridors at butcher-boys
and messengers, and played on errand-boys brutal practical jokes that
ended in police-court summonses. He once had a way of sliding down
the balusters, shouting: "Ho! ho! ho! yah!" as he went, but as he was
a big, heavy man, and the balusters had been built for different treatment, he had very soon and very firmly been requested to stop it. He

had plenty of money, and spent it freely; but it was generally felt that there was too much of the light-hearted savage about him to fit him to live among quiet people.

How much longer the landlord would have stood this sort of thing, Hewitt's informant said, was a matter of conjecture, for on the Saturday afternoon in question the tenancy had come to a startling full-stop. Rameau had been murdered in his room, and the body had, in the most unaccountable fashion, been secretly removed from the premises.

The strongest possible suspicion pointed to a man who had been employed in shovelling and carrying coals, cleaning windows, and chopping wood for several of the buildings, and who had left that very Saturday. The crime had, in fact, been committed with this man's chopper, and the man himself had been heard, again and again, to threaten Rameau, who, in his brutal fashion, had made a butt of him. This man was a Frenchman, Victor Goujon by name, who had lost his employment as a watchmaker by reason of an injury to his right hand, which destroyed its steadiness, and so he had fallen upon evil days and odd jobs.

He was a little man of no great strength, but extraordinarily excitable, and the coarse gibes and horse-play of the big negro drove him almost to madness. Rameau would often, after some more than ordinarily outrageous attack, contemptuously fling Goujon a shilling, which the little Frenchman, although wanting a shilling badly enough, would hurl back in his face, almost weeping with impotent rage. "Pig! *Canaille!*" he would scream. "Dirty pig of Africa! Take your sheelin' to vere you 'ave stole it! *Voleur!* Pig!"

There was a tortoise living in the basement, of which Goujon had made rather a pet, and the negro would sometimes use this animal as a missile, flinging it at the little Frenchman's head. On one such occasion the tortoise struck the wall so forcibly as to break its shell, and then Goujon seized a shovel and rushed at his tormentor with such blind fury that the latter made a bolt of it. These were but a few of the passages between Rameau and the fuel-porter, but they illustrate the state of feeling between them.

Goujon, after correspondence with a relative in France who offered him work, gave notice to leave, which expired on the day of the crime. At about three that afternoon a housemaid, proceeding toward Rameau's rooms, met Goujon as he was going away. Goujon bade her goodbye, and, pointing in the direction of Rameau's rooms, said exultantly: "Dere shall be no more of the black pig for me; vit 'im I 'ave done for. Zut! I mock me of 'im! 'E vill never *tracasser* me no more." And he went away.

The girl went to the outer door of Rameau's rooms, knocked, and got no reply. Concluding that the tenant was out, she was about to use her keys, when she found that the door was unlocked. She passed through the lobby and into the sitting-room, and there fell in a dead faint at the sight that met her eyes. Rameau lay with his back across the sofa and his head—drooping within an inch of the ground. On the head was a fearful gash, and below it was a pool of blood.

The girl must have lain unconscious for about ten minutes. When she came to her senses, she dragged herself, terrified, from the room and up to the housekeeper's apartments, where, being an excitable and nervous creature, she only screamed "Murder!" and immediately fell in a fit of hysterics that lasted three-quarters of an hour. When at last she came to herself, she told her story, and, the hall-porter having been summoned, Rameau's rooms were again approached.

The blood still lay on the floor, and the chopper, with which the crime had evidently been committed, rested against the fender; but the body had vanished! A search was at once made, but no trace of it could be seen anywhere. It seemed impossible that it could have been carried out of the building, for the hall-porter must at once have noticed anybody leaving with so bulky a burden. Still, in the building it was not to be found.

When Hewitt was informed of these things on Monday, the police were, of course, still in possession of Rameau's rooms. Inspector Nettings, Hewitt was told, was in charge of the case, and as the inspector was an acquaintance of his, and was then in the rooms upstairs, Hewitt went up to see him.

Nettings was pleased to see Hewitt, and invited him to look around the rooms. "Perhaps you can spot something we have overlooked," he said. "Though it's not a case there can be much doubt about."

"You think it's Goujon, don't you?"

"Think? Well, rather! Look here! As soon as we got here on Saturday, we found this piece of paper and pin on the floor. We showed it to the housemaid, and then she remembered—she was too much upset to think of it before—that when she was in the room the paper was laying on the dead man's chest—pinned there, evidently. It must have dropped off when they removed the body. It's a case of half-mad revenge on Goujon's part, plainly. See it; you read French, don't you?"

The paper was a plain, large half-sheet of note-paper, on which a sentence in French was scrawled in red ink in a large, clumsy hand, thus:

puni par un vengeur de la tortue.

"*Puni par un vengeur de la tortue*," Hewitt repeated musingly. "'Punished by an avenger of the tortoise,' That seems odd."

"Well, rather odd. But you understand the reference, of course. Have they told you about Rameau's treatment of Goujon's pet tortoise?"

"I think it was mentioned among his other pranks. But this is an extreme revenge for a thing of that sort, and a queer way of announcing it."

"Oh, he's mad—mad with Rameau's continual ragging and baiting," Nettings answered. "Anyway, this is a plain indication—plain as though he'd left his own signature. Besides, it's in his own language—French. And there's his chopper, too."

"Speaking of signatures," Hewitt remarked, "perhaps you have already compared this with other specimens of Goujon's writing?"

"I did think of it, but they don't seem to have a specimen to hand, and, anyway, it doesn't seem very important. There's 'avenger of the tortoise' plain enough, in the man's own language, and that tells everything. Besides, handwritings are easily disguised."

"Have you got Goujon?"

"Well, no; we haven't. There seems to be some little difficulty about that. But I expect to have him by this time tomorrow. Here comes Mr. Styles, the landlord."

Mr. Styles was a thin, querulous, and withered-looking little man, who twitched his eyebrows as he spoke, and spoke in short, jerky phrases.

"No news, eh, inspector, eh? eh? Found out nothing else, eh? Terrible thing for my property—terrible! Who's your friend?"

Nettings introduced Hewitt.

"Shocking thing this, eh, Mr. Hewitt? Terrible! Comes of having anything to do with these blood-thirsty foreigners, eh? New buildings and all—character ruined. No one come to live here now, eh? Tenants—noisy niggers—murdered by my own servants—terrible! *You* formed any opinion, eh?"

"I dare say I might if I went into the case."

"Yes, yes—same opinion as inspector's, eh? I mean an opinion of your own?" The old man scrutinized Hewitt's face sharply.

"If you'd like me to look into the matter——" Hewitt began.

"Eh? Oh, look into it! Well, I can't commission you, you know—matter for the police. Mischief's done. Police doing very well, I think—must be Goujon. But look about the place, certainly, if you like. If you see anything likely to serve *my* interests, tell me, and—and—perhaps I'll employ you, eh, eh? Good-afternoon."

The landlord vanished, and the inspector laughed. "Likes to see what he's buying, does Mr. Styles," he said.

Hewitt's first impulse was to walk out of the place at once. But his interest in the case had been roused, and he determined, at any rate, to examine the rooms, and this he did very minutely. By the side of the lobby was a bathroom, and in this was fitted a tip-up wash-basin, which Hewitt inspected with particular attention. Then he called the housekeeper, and made inquiries about Rameau's clothes and linen. The housekeeper could give no idea of how many overcoats or how much linen he had had.

He had all a negro's love of display, and was continually buying new clothes, which, indeed, were lying, hanging, littering, and choking up the bedroom in all directions. The housekeeper, however, on Hewitt's inquiring after such a garment in particular, did remember one heavy black ulster, which Rameau had very rarely worn—only in the coldest weather.

"After the body was discovered," Hewitt asked the housekeeper, "was any stranger observed about the place—whether carrying anything or not?"

"No, sir," the housekeeper replied. "There's been particular inquiries about that. Of course, after we knew what was wrong and the body was gone, nobody was seen, or he'd have been stopped. But the hall-porter says he's certain no stranger came or went for half an hour or more before that—the time about when the housemaid saw the body and fainted."

At this moment a clerk from the landlord's office arrived and handed Nettings a paper. "Here you are," said Nettings to Hewitt; "they've found a specimen of Goujon's handwriting at last, if you'd like to see it. I don't want it; I'm not a graphologist, and the case is clear enough for me anyway."

Hewitt took the paper. "This" he said, "is a different sort of handwriting from that on the paper. The red-ink note about the avenger of the tortoise is in a crude, large, clumsy, untaught style of writing. This is small, neat, and well formed—except that it is a trifle shaky, probably because of the hand injury."

"That's nothing," contended Nettings. "handwriting clues are worse than useless, as a rule. It's so easy to disguise and imitate writing; and besides, if Goujon is such a good penman as you seem to say, why, he could all the easier alter his style. Say now yourself, can any fiddling question of handwriting get over this thing about 'avenging the tortoise'—practically a written confession—to say nothing of the chopper, and what he said to the housemaid as he left?"

"Well," said Hewitt, "perhaps not; but we'll see. Meantime"—turning to the landlord's clerk—"possibly you will be good enough to tell me one or two things. First, what was Goujon's character?"

"Excellent, as far as we know. We never had a complaint about him except for little matters of carelessness—leaving coal-scuttles on the staircases for people to fall over, losing shovels, and so on. He was certainly a bit careless, but, as far as we could see, quite a decent little fellow. One would never have thought him capable of committing murder for the sake of a tortoise, though he was rather fond of the animal."

"The tortoise is dead now, I understand?"

"Yes."

"Have you a lift in this building?"

"Only for coals and heavy parcels. Goujon used to work it, sometimes going up and down in it himself with coals, and so on; it goes into the basement."

"And are the coals kept under this building?"

"No. The store for the whole row is under the next two houses—the basements communicate."

"Do you know Rameau's other name?"

"César Rameau he signed in our agreement."

"Did he ever mention his relations?"

"No. That is to say, he did say something one day when he was very drunk; but, of course, it was all rot. Someone told him not to make such a row—he was a beastly tenant—and he said he was the best man in the place, and his brother was Prime Minister, and all sorts of things. Mere drunken rant! I never heard of his saying anything sensible about relations. We know nothing of his connections; he came here on a banker's reference."

"Thanks. I think that's all I want to ask. You notice," Hewitt proceeded, turning to Nettings, "the only ink in this place is scented and violet, and the only paper is tinted and scented, too, with a mono-gram—characteristic of a negro with money. The paper that was pinned on Rameau's breast is in red ink on common and rather grub-by paper, therefore it was written somewhere else and brought here. Inference, premeditation."

"Yes, yes. But are you an inch nearer with all these speculations? Can you get nearer than I am now without them?"

"Well, perhaps not," Hewitt replied. "I don't profess at this mo-ment to know the criminal; you do. I'll concede you that point for the present. But you don't offer an opinion as to who removed Rameau's body—which I think I know."

"Who was it, then?"

"Come, try and guess that yourself. It wasn't Goujon; I don't mind letting you know that. But it was a person quite within your knowl-edge of the case. You've mentioned the person's name more than once."

Nettings stared blankly. "I don't understand you in the least," he said. "But, of course, you mean that this mysterious person you speak of as having moved the body committed the murder?"

"No, I don't. Nobody could have been more innocent of that."

"Well," Nettings concluded with resignation, "I'm afraid one of us is rather thick-headed. What will you do?"

"Interview the person who took away the body," Hewitt replied, with a smile.

"But, man alive, why? Why bother about the person if it isn't the criminal?"

"Never mind—never mind; probably the person will be a most valuable witness."

"Do you mean you think this person—whoever it is—saw the crime?"

"I think it very probable indeed."

"Well, I won't ask you any more. I shall get hold of Goujon; that's simple and direct enough for me. I prefer to deal with the heart of the case—the murder itself—when there's such clear evidence as I have."

"I shall look a little into that, too, perhaps," Hewitt said, "and, if you like, I'll tell you the first thing I shall do."

"What's that?"

"I shall have a good look at a map of the West Indies, and I advise you to do the same. Good-morning."

Nettings stared down the corridor after Hewitt, and continued staring for nearly two minutes after he had disappeared. Then he said to the clerk, who had remained: "What was he talking about?"

"Don't know," replied the clerk. "Couldn't make head nor tail of it."

"I don't believe there *is* a head to it," declared Nettings; "nor a tail either. He's kidding us."

✶✶✶✶✶✶

Nettings was better than his word, for within two hours of his conversation with Hewitt, Goujon was captured and safe in a cab bound for Bow Street. He had been stopped at Newhaven in the morning on his way to Dieppe, and was brought back to London. But now Nettings met a check.

Late that afternoon he called on Hewitt to explain matters. "We've got Goujon," he said, gloomily, "but there's a difficulty. He's got two friends who can swear an *alibi*. Rameau was seen alive at half-past one on Saturday, and the girl found him dead about three. Now, Goujon's two friends, it seems, were with him from one o'clock till four in the afternoon, with the exception of five minutes when the girl saw him, and then he left them to take a key or something to the housekeeper before finally leaving. They were waiting on the landing below when Goujon spoke to the housemaid, heard him speaking, and had seen him go all the way up to the housekeeper's room and back, as they looked up the wide well of the staircase. They are men employed near the place, and seem to have good characters. But perhaps we shall find something unfavourable about them. They were drinking with Goujon, it seems, by way of 'seeing him off.'"

"Well," Hewitt said, "I scarcely think you need trouble to damage these men's characters. They are probably telling the truth. Come, now, be plain. You've come here to get a hint as to whether my theory of the case helps you, haven't you?"

"Well, if you can give me a friendly hint, although, of course, I may be right, after all. Still, I wish you'd explain a bit as to what you meant by looking at a map and all that mystery. Nice thing for me to be taking a lesson in my own business after all these years! But perhaps I deserve it."

"See, now," quoth Hewitt, "you remember what map I told you to look at?"

"The West Indies."

"Right! Well, here you are." Hewitt reached an atlas from his bookshelf. "Now, look here: the biggest island of the lot on this map, barring Cuba, is Hayti. You know as well as I do that the western part of that island is peopled by the black republic of Hayti, and that the country is in a degenerate state of almost unexampled savagery, with a ridiculous show of civilization. There are revolutions all the time; the South American republics are peaceful and prosperous compared to Hayti. The state of the country is simply awful—read Sir Spenser St. John's book on it. President after president of the vilest sort forces his way to power and commits the most horrible and bloodthirsty excesses, murdering his opponents by the hundred and seizing their property for himself and his satellites, who are usually as bad, if not worse, than the president himself.

"Whole families—men, women, and children—are murdered at the instance of these ruffians, and, as a consequence, the most deadly feuds spring up, and the presidents and their followers are always themselves in danger of reprisals from others. Perhaps the very worst of these presidents in recent times has been the notorious Domingue, who was overthrown by an insurrection, as they all are sooner or later, and compelled to fly the country. Domingue and his nephews, one of whom was Chief Minister, while in power committed the cruellest bloodshed, and many members of the opposite party sought refuge in a small island lying just to the north of Hayti, but were sought out there and almost exterminated. Now, I will show you that island on the map. What is its name?"

"Tortuga."

"It is. 'Tortuga,' however, is only the old Spanish name; the Haytians speak French—Creole French. Here is a French atlas: now see the name of that island."

"La Tortue!"

"La Tortue it is—the tortoise. Tortuga means the same thing in Spanish. But that island is always spoken of in Hayti as La Tortue. Now, do you see the drift of that paper pinned to Rameau's breast?"

"Punished by an avenger of—or from—the tortoise or La Tortue—clear enough. It would seem that the dead man had something to do with the massacre there, and somebody from the island is avenging it. The thing's most extraordinary."

"And now listen. The name of Domingue's nephew, who was Chief Minister, was *Septimus Rameau.*"

"And this was César Rameau—his brother, probably. I see. Well, this *is* a case."

"I think the relationship probable. Now you understand why I was inclined to doubt that Goujon was the man you wanted."

"Of course, of course! And now I suppose I must try to get a nigger—the chap who wrote that paper. I wish he hadn't been such an ignorant nigger. If he'd only have put the capitals to the words 'La Tortue,' I might have thought a little more about them, instead of taking it for granted that they meant that wretched tortoise in the basement of the house. Well, I've made a fool of a start, but I'll be after that nigger now."

"And I, as I said before," said Hewitt, "shall be after the person that carried off Rameau's body. I have had something else to do this afternoon, or I should have begun already."

"You said you thought he saw the crime. How did you judge that?"

Hewitt smiled. "I think I'll keep that little secret to myself for the present," he said. "You shall know soon."

"Very well," Nettings replied, with resignation. "I suppose I mustn't grumble if you don't tell me everything. I feel too great a fool altogether over this case to see any farther than you show me." And Inspector Nettings left on his search; while Martin Hewitt, as soon as he was alone, laughed joyously and slapped his thigh.

★★★★★★

There was a cab-rank and shelter at the end of the street where Mr. Styles' building stood, and early that evening a man approached it and hailed the cabmen and the waterman. Anyone would have known the newcomer at once for a cabman taking a holiday. The brim of the hat, the bird's-eye neckerchief, the immense coat-buttons, and, more than all, the rolling walk and the wrinkled trousers, marked him out distinctly.

"Watcheer!" he exclaimed, affably, with the self-possessed nod only possible to cabbies and 'busmen. "I'm a-lookin' for a bilker. I'm told one o' the blokes off this rank carried 'im last Saturday, and I want to know where he went. I ain't 'ad a chance o' gettin' 'is address yet. Took a cab just as it got dark, I'm told. Tallish chap, muffled up a lot, in a long black overcoat. Any of ye seen 'im?"

The cabbies looked at one another and shook their heads; it chanced that none of them had been on that particular rank at that time. But the waterman said: "'Old on—I bet 'e's the bloke wot old Bill Stammers took. Yorkey was fust on the rank, but the bloke wouldn't 'ave a 'ansom—wanted a four-wheeler, so old Bill took 'im. Biggish chap in a long black coat, collar up an' muffled thick; soft wide-awake 'at, pulled over 'is eyes; and he was in a 'urry, too. Jumped

130

in sharp as a weasel."

"Didn't see 'is face, did ye?"

"No—not an inch of it; too much muffled. Couldn't tell if he 'ad a face."

"Was his arm in a sling?"

"Ay, it looked so. Had it stuffed through the breast of his coat, like as though there might be a sling inside."

"That's 'im. Any of ye tell me where I might run across old Bill Stammers? He'll tell me where my precious bilker went to."

As to this there was plenty of information, and in five minutes Martin Hewitt, who had become an unoccupied cabman for the occasion, was on his way to find old Bill Stammers. That respectable old man gave him full particulars as to the place in the East End where he had driven his muffled fare on Saturday, and Hewitt then begun an eighteen, or twenty hours' search beyond Whitechapel.

★★★★★★

At about three on Tuesday afternoon, as Nettings was in the act of leaving Bow Street Police Station, Hewitt drove up in a four-wheeler. Some prisoner appeared to be crouching low in the vehicle, but, leaving him to take care of himself, Hewitt hurried into the station and shook Nettings by the hand. "Well," he said, "have you got the murderer of Rameau yet?"

"No," Nettings growled. "Unless—well, Goujon's under remand still, and, after all, I've been thinking that he may know something——"

"Pooh, nonsense!" Hewitt answered. "You'd better let him go. Now, I *have* got somebody." Hewitt laughed and slapped the inspector's shoulder. "I've got the man who carried Rameau's body away!"

"The deuce you have! Where? Bring him in. We must have him—"

"All right, don't be in a hurry; he won't bolt." And Hewitt stepped out to the cab and produced his prisoner, who, pulling his hat farther over his eyes, hurried furtively into the station. One hand was stowed in the breast of his long coat, and below the wide brim of his hat a small piece of white bandage could be seen; and, as he lifted his face, it was seen to be that of a negro.

"Inspector Nettings," Hewitt said ceremoniously, "allow me to introduce Mr. César Rameau!"

Netting's gasped.

"What!" he at length ejaculated. "What! You—you're Rameau?"

The negro looked round nervously, and shrank farther from the door.

"Yes," he said; "but please not so loud—please not loud. Zey may be near, and I'm 'fraid."

"You will certify, will you not," asked Hewitt, with malicious glee, "not only that you were not murdered last Saturday by Victor Goujon, but that, in fact, you were not murdered at all? Also, that you carried your own body away in the usual fashion, on your own legs."

"Yes, yes," responded Rameau, looking haggardly about; "but is not zis—zis room *publique?* I should not be seen."

"Nonsense!" replied Hewitt rather testily; "you exaggerate your danger and your own importance, and your enemies' abilities as well. You're safe enough."

"I suppose, then," Nettings remarked slowly, like a man on whose mind something vast was beginning to dawn, "I suppose—why, hang it, you must have just got up while that fool of a girl was screaming and fainting upstairs, and walked out. They say there's nothing so hard as a nigger's skull, and yours has certainly made a fool of me. But, then, *somebody* must have chopped you over the head; who was it?"

"My enemies—my great enemies—enemies *politique*. I am a great man"—this with a faint revival of vanity amid his fear—"a great man in my countree. Zey have great secret club-sieties to kill me—me and my fren's; and one enemy coming in my rooms does zis—one, two"— he indicated wrist and head—"wiz a choppa."

Rameau made the case plain to Nettings, so far as the actual circumstances of the assault on himself were concerned. A negro whom he had noticed near the place more than once during the previous day or two had attacked him suddenly in his rooms, dealing him two savage blows with a chopper. The first he had caught on his wrist, which was seriously damaged, as well as excruciatingly painful, but the second had taken effect on his head.

His assailant had evidently gone away then, leaving him for dead; but, as a matter of fact, he was only stunned by the shock, and had, thanks to the adamantine thickness of the negro skull and the ill-direction of the chopper, only a very bad scalp-wound, the bone being no more than grazed. He had lain insensible for some time, and must have come to his senses soon after the housemaid had left the room. Terrified at the knowledge that his enemies had found him out, his only thought was to get away and hide himself. He hastily washed and tied up his head, enveloped himself in the biggest coat he could find, and let himself down into the basement by the coal-lift, for fear of observation.

He waited in the basement of one of the adjoining buildings till dark and then got away in a cab, with the idea of hiding himself in the East End. He had had very little money with him on his flight, and it was by reason of this circumstance that Hewitt, when he found him, had prevailed on him to leave his hiding-place, since it would be impossible for him to touch any of the large sums of money in the keeping of his bank so long as he was supposed to be dead. With much difficulty, and the promise of ample police protection, he was at last convinced that it would be safe to declare himself and get his property, and then run away and hide wherever he pleased.

Nettings and Hewitt strolled off together for a few minutes and chatted, leaving the wretched Rameau to cower in a corner among several policemen.

"Well, Mr. Hewitt," Nettings said, "this case has certainly been a shocking beating for me. I must have been as blind as a bat when I started on it. And yet I don't see that you had a deal to go on, even now. What struck you first?"

"Well, in the beginning it seemed rather odd to me that the body should have been taken away, as I had been told it was, after the written paper had been pinned on it. Why should the murderer pin a label on the body of his victim if he meant carrying that body away? Who would read the label and learn of the nature of the revenge gratified? Plainly, that indicated that the person who had carried away the body was *not* the person who had committed the murder. But as soon as I began to examine the place I saw the probability that there was no murder, after all. There were any number of indications of this fact, and I can't understand your not observing them. First, although there was a good deal of blood on the floor just below where the housemaid had seen Rameau lying, there was none between that place and the door.

Now, if the body had been dragged, or even carried, to the door, blood must have become smeared about the floor, or at least there would have been drops, but there were none, and this seemed to hint that the corpse might have come to itself, sat up on the sofa, stanched the wound, and walked out. I reflected at once that Rameau was a full-blooded negro, and that a negro's head is very nearly invulnerable to anything short of bullets. Then, if the body had been dragged out—as such a heavy body must have been—almost of necessity the carpet and rugs would show signs of the fact, but there were no such signs. But beyond these there was the fact that no long black over-

133

coat was left with the other clothes, although the housekeeper distinctly remembered Rameau's possession of such a garment. I judged he would use some such thing to assist his disguise, which was why I asked her. *Why* he would want to disguise was plain, as you shall see presently. There were no towels left in the bath-room; inference, used for bandages.

Everything seemed to show that the only person responsible for Rameau's removal was Rameau himself. Why, then, had he gone away secretly and hurriedly, without making complaint, and why had he stayed away? What reason would he have for doing this if it had been Goujon that had attacked him? None. Goujon was going to France. Clearly, Rameau was afraid of another attack from some implacable enemy whom he was anxious to avoid—one against whom he feared legal complaint or defence would be useless. This brought me at once to the paper found on the floor. If this were the work of Goujon and an open reference to his tortoise, why should he be at such pains to disguise his handwriting? He would have been already pointing himself out by the mere mention of the tortoise. And, if he could not avoid a shake in his natural, small handwriting, how could he have avoided it in a large, clumsy, slowly drawn, assumed hand? No, the paper was not Goujon's."

"As to the writing on the paper," Nettings interposed, "I've told you how I made that mistake. I took the readiest explanation of the words, since they seemed so pat, and I wouldn't let anything else outweigh that. As to the other things—the evidences of Rameau's having gone off by himself—well, I don't usually miss such obvious things; but I never thought of the possibility of the *victim* going away on the quiet and not coming back, as though *he'd* done something wrong. Comes of starting with a set of fixed notions."

"Well," answered Hewitt, "I fancy you must have been rather 'out of form,' as they say; everybody has his stupid days, and you can't keep up to concert pitch forever. To return to the case. The evidence of the chopper was very untrustworthy, especially when I had heard of Goujon's careless habits—losing shovels and leaving coal-scuttles on stairs. Nothing more likely than for the chopper to be left lying about, and a criminal who had calculated his chances would know the advantage to himself of using a weapon that belonged to the place, and leaving it behind to divert suspicion. It is quite possible, by the way, that the man who attacked Rameau got away down the coal-lift and out by an adjoining basement, just as did Rameau himself; this, however, is mere conjecture.

"The would-be murderer had plainly prepared for the crime: witness the previous preparation of the paper declaring his revenge, an indication of his pride at having run his enemy to earth at such a distant place as this—although I expect he was only in England by chance, for Haytians are not a persistently energetic race. In regard to the use of small instead of capital letters in the words 'La Tortue' on the paper, I observed, in the beginning, that the first letter of the whole sentence—the 'p' in '*puni*'—was a small one. Clearly, the writer was an illiterate man, and it was at once plain that he may have made the same mistake with ensuing words.

"On the whole, it was plain that everybody had begun with a too ready disposition to assume that Goujon was guilty. Everybody insisted, too, that the body had been carried away—which was true, of course, although not in the sense intended—so I didn't trouble to contradict, or to say more than that I guessed who *had* carried the body off. And, to tell you the truth, I was a little piqued at Mr. Styles' manner, and indisposed, interested in the case as I was, to give away my theories too freely.

"The rest of the job was not very difficult. I found out the cabman who had taken Rameau away—you can always get readier help from cabbies if you go as one of themselves, especially if you are after a bilker—and from him got a sufficiently near East End direction to find Rameau after inquiries. I ventured, by the way, on a rather long shot. I described my man to the cabman as having an injured arm or wrist—and it turned out a correct guess. You see, a man making an attack with a chopper is pretty certain to make more than a single blow, and as there appeared to have been only a single wound on the head, it seemed probable that another had fallen somewhere else—almost certainly on the arm, as it would be raised to defend the head. At Limehouse I found he had had his head and wrist attended to at a local, and a big nigger in a fright, with a long black coat, a broken head, and a lame hand, is not so difficult to find in a small area. How I persuaded him up here you know already; I think I frightened him a little, too, by explaining how easily I had tracked him, and giving him a hint that others might do the same. He is in a great funk. He seems to have quite lost faith in England as a safe asylum."

The police failed to catch Rameau's assailant—chiefly because Rameau could not be got to give a proper description of him, nor to do anything except get out of the country in a hurry. In truth, he was glad to be quit of the matter with nothing worse than his broken head. Little Goujon made a wild storm about his arrest, and before he did go to France managed to extract twenty pounds from Rameau by way of compensation, in spite of the absence of any strictly legal claim against his old tormentor. So that, on the whole, Goujon was about the only person who derived any particular profit from the tortoise mystery.

THE IVY COTTAGE MYSTERY

I had been working double tides for a month: at night on my morning paper, as usual; and in the morning on an evening paper as *locum tenens* for another man who was taking a holiday. This was an exhausting plan of work, although it only actually involved some six hours' attendance a day, or less, at the two offices. I turned up at the headquarters of my own paper at ten in the evening, and by the time I had seen the editor, selected a subject, written my leader, corrected the slips, chatted, smoked, and so on, and cleared off, it was very usually one o'clock. This meant bed at two, or even three, after supper at the club.

This was all very well at ordinary periods, when any time in the morning would do for rising, but when I had to be up again soon after seven, and round at the evening paper office by eight, I naturally felt a little worn and disgusted with things by midday, after a sharp couple of hours' leaderette scribbling and paragraphing, with attendant sundries.

But the strain was over, and on the first day of comparative comfort I indulged in a midday breakfast and the first undisgusted glance at a morning paper for a month. I felt rather interested in an inquest, begun the day before, on the body of a man whom I had known very slightly before I took to living in chambers.

His name was Gavin Kingscote, and he was an artist of a casual and desultory sort, having, I believe, some small private means of his own. As a matter of fact, he had boarded in the same house in which I had lodged myself for a while, but as I was at the time a late homer and a fairly early riser, taking no regular board in the house, we never became much acquainted. He had since, I understood, made some judicious Stock Exchange speculations, and had set up house in Finchley.

Now the news was that he had been found one morning murdered in his smoking-room, while the room itself, with others, was in a state of confusion. His pockets had been rifled, and his watch and chain were gone, with one or two other small articles of value. On the night of the tragedy a friend had sat smoking with him in the room where the murder took place, and he had been the last person to see Mr. Kingscote alive. A jobbing gardener, who kept the garden in order by casual work from time to time, had been arrested in consequence of footprints exactly corresponding with his boots, having been found on the garden beds near the French window of the smoking-room.

I finished my breakfast and my paper, and Mrs. Clayton, the house-keeper, came to clear my table. She was sister of my late landlady of the house where Kingscote had lodged, and it was by this connection that I had found my chambers. I had not seen the housekeeper since the crime was first reported, so I now said:

"This is shocking news of Mr. Kingscote, Mrs. Clayton. Did you know him yourself?"

She had apparently only been waiting for some such remark to burst out with whatever information she possessed.

"Yes, sir," she exclaimed: "shocking indeed. Pore young feller! I see him often when I was at my sister's, and he was always a nice, quiet gentleman, so different from some. My sister, she's awful cut up, sir, I assure you. And what d'you think 'appened, sir, only last Tuesday? You remember Mr. Kingscote's room where he painted the wood-work so beautiful with gold flowers, and blue, and pink? He used to tell my sister she'd always have something to remember him by. Well, two young fellers, gentlemen I can't call them, come and took that room (it being to let), and went and scratched off all the paint in mere wicked mischief, and then chopped up all the panels into sticks and bits! Nice sort o' gentlemen them! And then they bolted in the morn-ing, being afraid, I s'pose, of being made to pay after treating a pore widder's property like that. That was only Tuesday, and the very next day the pore young gentleman himself's dead, murdered in his own 'ouse, and him going to be married an' all! Dear, dear! I remember once he said——"

Mrs. Clayton was a good soul, but once she began to talk some-one else had to stop her. I let her run on for a reasonable time, and then rose and prepared to go out. I remembered very well the panels that had been so mischievously destroyed. They made the room the show-room of the house, which was an old one. They were indeed less than half finished when I came away, and Mrs. Lamb, the landlady, had shown them to me one day when Kingscote was out. All the walls of the room were panelled and painted white, and Kingscote had put upon them an eccentric but charming decoration, obviously suggested by some of the work of Mr. Whistler. Tendrils, flowers, and butterflies in a quaint convention wandered thinly from panel to panel, giving the otherwise rather uninteresting room an unwonted atmosphere of richness and elegance. The lamentable jackasses who had destroyed this had certainly selected the best feature of the room whereon to inflict their senseless mischief.

I strolled idly downstairs, with no particular plan for the afternoon in my mind, and looked in at Hewitt's offices. Hewitt was reading a note, and after a little chat he informed me that it had been left an hour ago, in his absence, by the brother of the man I had just been speaking of.

"He isn't quite satisfied," Hewitt said, "with the way the police are investigating the case, and asks me to run down to Finchley and look round. Yesterday I should have refused, because I have five cases in progress already, but today I find that circumstances have given me a day or two. Didn't you say you knew the man?"

"Scarcely more than by sight. He was a boarder in the house at Chelsea where I stayed before I started chambers."

"Ah, well; I think I shall look into the thing. Do you feel particularly interested in the case? I mean, if you've nothing better to do, would you come with me?"

"I shall be very glad," I said. "I was in some doubt what to do with myself. Shall you start at once?"

"I think so. Kerrett, just call a cab. By the way, Brett, which paper has the fullest report of the inquest yesterday? I'll run over it as we go down."

As I had only seen one paper that morning, I could not answer Hewitt's question. So we bought various papers as we went along in the cab, and I found the reports while Martin Hewitt studied them. Summarised, this was the evidence given—

Sarah Dodson, general servant, deposed that she had been in service at Ivy Cottage, the residence of the deceased, for five months, the only other regular servant being the housekeeper and cook. On the evening of the previous Tuesday both servants retired a little before eleven, leaving Mr. Kingscote with a friend in the smoking or sitting room. She never saw her master again alive. On coming downstairs, the following morning and going to open the smoking-room windows, she was horrified to discover the body of Mr. Kingscote lying on the floor of the room with blood about the head. She at once raised an alarm, and, on the instructions of the housekeeper, fetched a doctor, and gave information to the police. In answer to questions, witness stated she had heard no noise of any sort during the night, nor had anything suspicious occurred.

Hannah Carr, housekeeper and cook, deposed that she had been in the late Mr. Kingscote's service since he had first taken Ivy Cottage—a period of rather more than a year. She had last seen the deceased alive on the evening of the previous Tuesday, at half-past ten, when she knocked at the door of the smoking-room, where Mr. Kingscote was sitting with a friend, to ask if he would require anything more. Nothing was required, so witness shortly after went to bed. In the morning she was called by the previous witness, who had just gone downstairs, and found the body of deceased lying as described. Deceased's watch and chain were gone, as also was a ring he usually wore, and his pockets appeared to have been turned out.

All the ground floor of the house was in confusion, and a bureau, a writing-table, and various drawers were open—a bunch of keys usually carried by deceased being left hanging at one keyhole. Deceased had drawn some money from the bank on the Tuesday, for current expenses; how much she did not know. She had not heard or seen anything suspicious during the night. Besides Dodson and herself, there were no regular servants; there was a charwoman, who came occasionally, and a jobbing gardener, living near, who was called in as required.

Mr. James Vidler, surgeon, had been called by the first witness between seven and eight on Wednesday morning. He found the deceased lying on his face on the floor of the smoking-room, his feet being about eighteen inches from the window, and his head lying in the direction of the fireplace. He found three large contused wounds on the head, any one of which would probably have caused death. The wounds had all been inflicted, apparently, with the same blunt instrument—probably a club or life preserver, or other similar weapon. They could not have been done with the poker. Death was due to concussion of the brain, and deceased had probably been dead seven or eight hours when witness saw him. He had since examined the body more closely, but found no marks at all indicative of a struggle having taken place; indeed, from the position of the wounds and their severity, he should judge that the deceased had been attacked unawares from behind, and had died at once. The body appeared to be perfectly healthy.

Then there was police evidence, which showed that all the doors and windows were found shut and completely fastened, except the front door, which, although shut, was not bolted. There were shutters behind the French windows in the smoking-room, and these were found fastened. No money was found in the bureau, nor in any of the opened drawers, so that if any had been there, it had been stolen. The pockets were entirely empty, except for a small pair of nail scissors, and there was no watch upon the body, nor a ring. Certain footprints were found on the garden beds, which had led the police to take certain steps. No footprints were to be seen on the garden path, which was hard gravel.

Mr. Alexander Campbell, stockbroker, stated that he had known deceased for some few years, and had done business for him. He and Mr. Kingscote frequently called on one another, and on Tuesday evening they dined together at Ivy Cottage. They sat smoking and chatting till nearly twelve o'clock, when Mr. Kingscote himself let him out, the servants having gone to bed. Here the witness proceeded rather excitedly: "That is all I know of this horrible business, and I can say nothing else. What the police mean by following and watching me——"

The Coroner. "Pray be calm, Mr. Campbell. The police must do what seems best to them in a case of this sort. I am sure you would not have them neglect any means of getting at the truth."

Witness: "Certainly not. But if they suspect me, why don't they say so? It is intolerable that I should be——"

The Coroner. "Order, order, Mr. Campbell. You are here to give evidence."

The witness then, in answer to questions, stated that the French windows of the smoking-room had been left open during the evening, the weather being very warm. He could not recollect whether or not deceased closed them before he left, but he certainly did not close the shutters. Witness saw nobody near the house when he left.

Mr. Douglas Kingscote, architect, said deceased was his brother. He had not seen him for some months, living as he did in another part of the country. He believed his brother was fairly well off, and he knew that he had made a good amount by speculation in the last year or two. Knew of no person who would be likely to owe his brother a grudge, and could suggest no motive for the crime except ordinary robbery. His brother was to have been married in a few weeks. Questioned further on this point, witness said that the marriage was to have taken place a year ago, and it was with that view that Ivy Cottage, deceased's residence, was taken. The lady, however, sustained a domestic bereavement, and afterwards went abroad with her family: she was, witness believed, shortly expected back to England.

William Bates, jobbing gardener, who was brought up in custody, was cautioned, but elected to give evidence. Witness, who appeared to be much agitated, admitted having been in the garden of Ivy Cottage at four in the morning, but said that he had only gone to attend to certain plants, and knew absolutely nothing of the murder. He however admitted that he had no order for work beyond what he had done the day before. Being further pressed, witness made various contradictory statements, and finally said that he had gone to take certain plants away.

The inquest was then adjourned.

This was the case as it stood—apparently not a case presenting any very striking feature, although there seemed to me to be doubtful peculiarities in many parts of it. I asked Hewitt what he thought.

"Quite impossible to think anything, my boy, just yet; wait till we see the place. There are any number of possibilities. Kingscote's friend, Campbell, may have come in again, you know, by way of the window—or he may not. Campbell may have owed him money or something—or he may not. The anticipated wedding may have something to do with it—or, again, *that* may not. There is no limit to the possibilities, as far as we can see from this report—a mere dry husk of the affair. When we get closer we shall examine the possibilities by the light of more detailed information. One *probability* is that the wretched gardener is innocent. It seems to me that his was only a comparatively blameless manoeuvre not unheard of at other times in his trade. He came at four in the morning to steal away the flowers he had planted the day before, and felt rather bashful when questioned on the point. Why should he trample on the beds, else? I wonder if the police thought to examine the beds for traces of rooting up, or questioned the housekeeper as to any plants being missing? But we shall see."

We chatted at random as the train drew near Finchley, and I mentioned *inter alia* the wanton piece of destruction perpetrated at Kingscote's late lodgings. Hewitt was interested.

"That was curious," he said, "very curious. Was anything else damaged? Furniture and so forth?"

"I don't know. Mrs. Clayton said nothing of it, and I didn't ask her. But it was quite bad enough as it was. The decoration was really good, and I can't conceive a meaner piece of tomfoolery than such an attack on a decent woman's property."

Then Hewitt talked of other cases of similar stupid damage by creatures inspired by a defective sense of humour, or mere love of mischief. He had several curious and sometimes funny anecdotes of such affairs at museums and picture exhibitions, where the damage had been so great as to induce the authorities to call him in to discover the offender. The work was not always easy, chiefly from the mere absence of intelligible motive; nor, indeed, always successful. One of the anecdotes related to a case of malicious damage to a picture—the outcome of blind artistic jealousy—a case which had been hushed up by a large expenditure in compensation. It would considerably startle most people, could it be printed here, with the actual names of the parties concerned.

Ivy Cottage, Finchley, was a compact little house, standing in a compact little square of garden, little more than a third of an acre, or perhaps no more at all. The front door was but a dozen yards or so back from the road, but the intervening space was well treed and shrubbed. Mr. Douglas Kingscote had not yet returned from town, but the housekeeper, an intelligent, matronly woman, who knew of his intention to call in Martin Hewitt, was ready to show us the house.

"*First*," Hewitt said, when we stood in the smoking-room, "I observe that somebody has shut the drawers and the bureau. That is unfortunate. Also, the floor has been washed and the carpet taken up, which is much worse. That, I suppose, was because the police had finished their examination, but it doesn't help me to make one at all. Has *anything*—anything *at all*—been left as it was on Tuesday morning?"

"Well, sir, you see everything was in such a muddle," the housekeeper began, "and when the police had done——"

"Just so. I know. You 'set it to rights,' eh? Oh, that setting to rights! It has lost me a fortune at one time and another. As to the other rooms, now, have they been set to rights?"

"Such as was disturbed have been put right, sir, of course."

"Which were disturbed? Let me see them. But wait a moment."

He opened the French windows, and closely examined the catch and bolts. He knelt and inspected the holes whereinto the bolts fell, and then glanced casually at the folding shutters. He opened a drawer or two, and tried the working of the locks with the keys the house-

142

keeper carried. They were, the housekeeper explained, Mr. Kingscote's own keys. All through the lower floors Hewitt examined some things attentively and closely, and others with scarcely a glance, on a system unaccountable to me. Presently, he asked to be shown Mr. Kingscote's bedroom, which had not been disturbed, "set to rights," or slept in since the crime. Here, the housekeeper said, all drawers were kept unlocked but two—one in the wardrobe and one in the dressing-table, which Mr. Kingscote had always been careful to keep locked. Hewitt immediately pulled both drawers open without difficulty. Within, in addition to a few odds and ends, were papers. All the contents of these drawers had been turned over confusedly, while those of the unlocked drawers were in perfect order.

"The police," Hewitt remarked, "may not have observed these matters. Any more than such an ordinary thing as *this*," he added, picking up a bent nail lying at the edge of a rug.

The housekeeper doubtless took the remark as a reference to the entire unimportance of a bent nail, but I noticed that Hewitt dropped the article quietly into his pocket.

We came away. At the front gate we met Mr. Douglas Kingscote, who had just returned from town. He introduced himself, and expressed surprise at our promptitude both of coming and going.

"You can't have got anything like a clue in this short time, Mr. Hewitt?" he asked.

"Well, no," Hewitt replied, with a certain dryness, "perhaps not. But I doubt whether a month's visit would have helped me to get anything very striking out of a washed floor and a houseful of carefully cleaned-up and 'set-to-rights' rooms. Candidly, I don't think you can reasonably expect much of me. The police have a much better chance—they had the scene of the crime to examine. I have seen just such a few rooms as any one might see in the first well-furnished house he might enter. The trail of the housemaid has overlaid all the others."

"I'm very sorry for that; the fact was, I expected rather more of the police; and, indeed, I wasn't here in time entirely to prevent the clearing up. But still, I thought your well-known powers——"

"My dear sir, my 'well-known powers' are nothing but common sense assiduously applied and made quick by habit. That won't enable me to see the invisible."

"But can't we have the rooms put back into something of the state they were in? The cook will remember——"

"No, no. That would be worse and worse; that would only be the housemaid's trail in turn overlaid by the cook's. You must leave things with me for a little, I think."

"Then you don't give the case up?" Mr. Kingscote asked anxiously.

"Oh, no! I don't give it up just yet. Do you know anything of your brother's private papers—as they were before his death?"

"I never knew anything till after that. I have gone over them, but they are all very ordinary letters. Do you suspect a theft of papers?"

Martin Hewitt, with his hands on his stick behind him, looked sharply at the other, and shook his head. "No," he said, "I can't quite say that."

We bade Mr. Douglas Kingscote good-day, and walked towards the station. "Great nuisance, that setting to rights," Hewitt observed, on the way. "If the place had been left alone, the job might have been settled one way or another by this time. As it is, we shall have to run over to your old lodgings."

"My old lodgings?" I repeated, amazed. "Why my old lodgings?"

Hewitt turned to me with a chuckle and a wide smile. "Because we can't see the broken panel-work anywhere else," he said. "Let's see—Chelsea, isn't it?"

"Yes, Chelsea. But why—you don't suppose the people who defaced the panels also murdered the man who painted them?"

"Well," Hewitt replied, with another smile, "that would be carrying a practical joke rather far, wouldn't it? Even for the ordinary picture damager."

"You mean you *don't* think they did it, then? But what *do* you mean?"

"My dear fellow, I don't mean anything but what I say. Come now, this is rather an interesting case despite appearances, and it *has* interested me: so much, in fact, that I really think I forgot to offer Mr. Douglas Kingscote my condolence on his bereavement. You see a problem is a problem, whether of theft, assassination, intrigue, or anything else, and I only think of it as one. The work very often makes me forget merely human sympathies. Now, you have often been good enough to express a very flattering interest in my work, and you shall have an opportunity of exercising your own common sense in the way I am always having to exercise mine. You shall see all my evidence (if I'm lucky enough to get any) as I collect it, and you shall make your own inferences. That will be a little exercise for you; the sort of exercise I should give a pupil if I had one. But I will give you what information I have, and you shall start fairly from this moment. You know the inquest evidence, such as it was, and you saw everything I did in Ivy Cottage?"

"Yes; I think so. But I'm not much the wiser."

"Very well. Now I will tell you. What does the whole case look like? How would you class the crime?"

"I suppose as the police do. An ordinary case of murder with the object of robbery."

"It is *not* an ordinary case. If it were, I shouldn't know as much as I do, little as that is; the ordinary cases are always difficult. The assailant did not come to commit a burglary, although he was a skilled burglar, or one of them was, if more than one were concerned. The affair has, I think, nothing to do with the expected wedding, nor had Mr. Campbell anything to do in it—at any rate, personally—nor the gardener. The criminal (or one of them) was known personally to the dead man, and was well-dressed: he (or again one of them, and I think there were two) even had a chat with Mr. Kingscote before the murder took place. He came to ask for something which Mr. Kingscote was unwilling to part with,—perhaps hadn't got. It was not a bulky thing. Now you have all my materials before you."

"But all this doesn't look like the result of the blind spite that would ruin a man's work first and attack him bodily afterwards."

"Spite isn't always blind, and there are other blind things besides spite; people with good eyes in their heads are blind sometimes, even detectives."

"But where did you get all this information? What makes you suppose that this was a burglar who didn't want to burgle, and a well-dressed man, and so on?"

Hewitt chuckled and smiled again.

"I saw it—saw it, my boy, that's all," he said. "But here comes the train."

On the way back to town, after I had rather minutely described Kingscote's work on the boarding-house panels, Hewitt asked me for the names and professions of such fellow lodgers in that house as I might remember. "When did you leave yourself?" he ended.

"Three years ago, or rather more. I can remember Kingscote himself; Turner, a medical student—James Turner, I think; Harvey Challitt, diamond merchant's articled pupil—he was a bad egg entirely, he's doing five years for forgery now; by the bye he had the room we are going to see till he was marched off, and Kingscote took it—a year before I left; there was Norton—don't know what he was; 'something in the City,' I think; and Carter Paget, in the Admiralty Office. I don't remember any more at this moment; there were pretty frequent changes. But you can get it all from Mrs. Lamb, of course."

"Of course; and Mrs. Lamb's exact address is—what?"

I gave him the address, and the conversation became disjointed. At Farringdon station, where we alighted, Hewitt called two hansoms. Preparing to enter one, he motioned me to the other, saying, "You get straight away to Mrs. Lamb's at once. She may be going to burn that splintered wood, or to set things to rights, after the manner of her kind, and you can stop her. I must make one or two small inquiries, but I shall be there half an hour after you."

"Shall I tell her our object?"

"Only that I may be able to catch her mischievous lodgers—nothing else yet." He jumped into the hansom and was gone.

I found Mrs. Lamb still in a state of indignant perturbation over the trick served her four days before. Fortunately, she had left everything in the panelled room exactly as she had found it, with an idea of the being better able to demand or enforce reparation should her lodgers return.

"The room's theirs, you see, sir," she said, "till the end of the week, since they paid in advance, and they may come back and offer to make amends, although I doubt it. As pleasant-spoken a young chap as you might wish, he seemed, him as come to take the rooms. 'My cousin,' says he, 'is rather an invalid, havin' only just got over congestion of the lungs, and he won't be in London till this evening late. He's comin' up from Birmingham,' he ses, 'and I hope he won't catch a fresh cold on the way, although of course we've got him muffled up plenty.' He took the rooms, sir, like a gentleman, and mentioned several gentlemen's names I knew well, as had lodged here before; and then he put down on that there very table, sir."

Mrs. Lamb indicated the exact spot with her hand, as though that made the whole thing much more wonderful. "He put down on that very table a week's rent in advance, and ses, 'That's always the best sort of reference, Mrs. Lamb, I think,' as kind-mannered as anything—and never 'aggled about the amount nor nothing. He only had a little black bag, but he said his cousin had all the luggage coming in the train, and as there was so much p'r'aps they wouldn't get it here till next day. Then he went out and came in with his cousin at eleven that night—Sarah let 'em in her own self—and in the morning they was gone—and this!" Poor Mrs. Lamb, plaintively indignant, stretched her arm towards the wrecked panels.

"If the gentleman as you say is comin' on, sir," she pursued, "can do anything to find 'em, I'll prosecute 'em, that I will, if it costs me ten pound. I spoke to the constable on the beat, but he only looked like a fool, and said if I knew where they were I might charge 'em with wilful damage, or county court 'em. Of course I know I can do that if I knew where they were, but how can I find 'em? Mr. Jones he said his name was; but how many Joneses is there in London, sir?"

I couldn't imagine any answer to a question like this, but I condoled with Mrs. Lamb as well as I could. She afterwards went on to express herself much as her sister had done with regard to Kingscote's death, only as the destruction of her panels loomed larger in her mind, she dwelt primarily on that. "It might almost seem," she said, "that somebody had a deadly spite on the pore young gentleman, and went breakin' up his paintin' one night, and murderin' him the next!"

I examined the broken panels with some care having half a notion to attempt to deduce something from them myself, if possible. But I could deduce nothing. The beading had been taken out, and the panels, which were thick in the centre but bevelled at the edges, had been removed and split up literally into thin firewood, which lay in a tumbled heap on the hearth and about the floor. Every panel in the room had been treated in the same way, and the result was a pretty large heap of sticks, with nothing whatever about them to distinguish them from other sticks, except the paint on one face, which I observed in many cases had been scratched and scraped away. The rug was drawn half across the hearth, and had evidently been used to deaden the sound of chopping. But mischief—wanton and stupid mischief—was all I could deduce from it all.

Mr. Jones's cousin, it seemed, only Sarah had seen, as she admitted him in the evening, and then he was so heavily muffled that she could not distinguish his features, and would never be able to identify him. But as for the other one, Mrs. Lamb was ready to swear to him anywhere.

Hewitt was long in coming, and internal symptoms of the approach of dinner-time (we had had no lunch) had made themselves felt before a sharp ring at the door-bell foretold his arrival. "I have had to wait for answers to a telegram," he said in explanation, "but at any rate I have the information I wanted. And these are the mysterious panels, are they?"

147

Mrs. Lamb's true opinion of Martin Hewitt's behaviour as it proceeded would have been amusing to know. She watched in amazement the antics of a man who purposed finding out who had been splitting sticks by dint of picking up each separate stick and staring at it. In the end he collected a small handful of sticks by themselves and handed them to me, saying, "Just put these together on the table, Brett, and see what you make of them."

I turned the pieces painted side up, and fitted them together into a complete panel, joining up the painted design accurately. "It is an entire panel," I said.

"Good. Now look at the sticks a little more closely, and tell me if you notice anything peculiar about them—any particular in which they differ from all the others."

I looked. "Two adjoining sticks," I said, "have each a small semicircular cavity stuffed with what seems to be putty. Put together it would mean a small circular hole, perhaps a knot-hole, half an inch or so in diameter, in the panel, filled in with putty, or whatever it is."

"A *knot-hole?*" Hewitt asked, with particular emphasis.

"Well, no, not a knot-hole, of course, because that would go right through, and this doesn't. It is probably less than half an inch deep from the front surface."

"Anything else? Look at the whole appearance of the wood itself. Colour, for instance."

"It is certainly darker than the rest."

"So it is." He took the two pieces carrying the puttied hole, threw the rest on the heap, and addressed the landlady. "The Mr. Harvey Challitt who occupied this room before Mr. Kingscote, and who got into trouble for forgery, was the Mr. Harvey Challitt who was himself robbed of diamonds a few months before on a staircase, wasn't he?"

"Yes, sir," Mrs. Lamb replied in some bewilderment. "He certainly was that, on his own office stairs, chloroformed."

"Just so, and when they marched him away because of the forgery, Mr. Kingscote changed into his rooms?"

"Yes, and very glad I was. It was bad enough to have the disgrace brought into the house, without the trouble of trying to get people to take his very rooms, and I thought——"

"Yes, yes, very awkward, very awkward!" Hewitt interrupted rather impatiently. "The man who took the rooms on Monday, now—you'd never seen him before, had you?"

"No, sir."

"Then is *that* anything like him?" Hewitt held a cabinet photograph before her.

"Why—why—law, yes, that's *him!*"

Hewitt dropped the photograph back into his breast pocket with a contented "Um," and picked up his hat. "I think we may soon be able to find that young gentleman for you, Mrs. Lamb. He is not a very respectable young gentleman, and perhaps you are well rid of him, even as it is. Come, Brett," he added, "the day hasn't been wasted, after all."

We made towards the nearest telegraph office. On the way I said, "That puttied-up hole in the piece of wood seems to have influenced you. Is it an important link?"

"Well—yes," Hewitt answered, "it is. But all those other pieces are important, too."

"But why?"

"Because there are no holes in them." He looked quizzically at my wondering face, and laughed aloud. "Come," he said, "I won't puzzle you much longer. Here is the post-office. I'll send my wire, and then we'll go and dine at Luzatti's."

He sent his telegram, and we cabbed it to Luzatti's. Among actors, journalists, and others who know town and like a good dinner, Luzatti's is well known. We went upstairs for the sake of quietness, and took a table standing alone in a recess just inside the door. We ordered our dinner, and then Hewitt began:

"Now tell me what *your* conclusion is in this matter of the Ivy Cottage murder."

"Mine? I haven't one. I'm sorry I'm so very dull, but I really haven't."

"Come, I'll give you a point. Here is the newspaper account (torn sacrilegiously from my scrap-book for your benefit) of the robbery perpetrated on Harvey Challitt a few months before his forgery. Read it."

"Oh, but I remember the circumstances very well. He was carrying two packets of diamonds belonging to his firm downstairs to the office of another firm of diamond merchants on the ground-floor. It was a quiet time in the day, and half-way down he was seized on a dark landing, made insensible by chloroform, and robbed of the diamonds—five or six thousand pounds' worth altogether, of stones of various smallish individual values up to thirty pounds or so. He lay unconscious on the landing till one of the partners, noticing that he had been rather long gone, followed and found him. That's all, I think."

"Yes, that's all. Well, what do you make of it?"

"I'm afraid I don't quite see the connection with this case."

"Well, then, I'll give you another point. The telegram I've just sent releases information to the police, in consequence of which they will probably apprehend Harvey Challitt and his confederate, Henry Gillard, *alias* Jones, for the murder of Gavin Kingscote. Now, then."

"Challitt! But he's in gaol already."

"Tut, tut, consider. Five years' penal was his dose, although for the first offence, because the forgery was of an extremely dangerous sort. You left Chelsea over three years ago yourself, and you told me that his difficulty occurred a year before. That makes four years, at least. Good conduct in prison brings a man out of a five years' sentence in that time or a little less, and, as a matter of fact, Challitt was released rather more than a week ago."

"Still, I'm afraid I don't see what you are driving at."

"Whose story is this about the diamond robbery from Harvey Challitt?"

"His own."

"Exactly. His own. Does his subsequent record make him look like a person whose stories are to be accepted without doubt or question?"

"Why, no. I think I see—no, I don't. You mean he stole them himself? I've a sort of dim perception of your drift now, but still I can't fix it. The whole thing's too complicated."

"It is a little complicated for a first effort, I admit, so I will tell you. This is the story. Harvey Challitt is an artful young man, and decides on a theft of his firm's diamonds. He first prepares a hiding-place somewhere near the stairs of his office, and when the opportunity arrives he puts the stones away, spills his chloroform, and makes a smell—possibly sniffs some, and actually goes off on the stairs, and the whole thing's done. He is carried into the office—the diamonds are gone. He tells of the attack on the stairs, as we have heard, and he is believed. At a suitable opportunity he takes his plunder from the hiding-place, and goes home to his lodgings. What is he to do with those diamonds? He can't sell them yet, because the robbery is publicly notorious, and all the regular jewel buyers know him.

"Being a criminal novice, he doesn't know any regular receiver of stolen goods, and if he did would prefer to wait and get full value by an ordinary sale. There will always be a danger of detection so long as the stones are not securely hidden, so he proceeds to hide them. He knows that if any suspicion were aroused his rooms would be searched in every likely place, so he looks for an unlikely place. Of course, he thinks of taking out a panel and hiding them behind that. But the idea is so obvious that it won't do; the police would certainly take those panels out to look behind them. Therefore, he determines to hide them *in* the panels. See here—he took the two pieces of wood with the filled hole from his tail pocket and opened his penknife—the putty near the surface is softer than that near the bottom of the hole; two different lots of putty, differently mixed, perhaps, have been used, therefore, presumably, at different times."

"But to return to Challitt. He makes holes with a centre-bit in different places on the panels, and in each hole he places a diamond, embedding it carefully in putty. He smooths the surface carefully flush with the wood, and then very carefully paints the place over, shading off the paint at the edges so as to leave no signs of a patch. He doesn't do the whole job at once, creating a noise and a smell of paint, but keeps on steadily, a few holes at a time, till in a little while the whole wainscoting is set with hidden diamonds, and every panel is apparently sound and whole."

"But, then—there was only one such hole in the whole lot."

"Just so, and that very circumstance tells us the whole truth. Let me tell the story first—I'll explain the clue after. The diamonds lie hidden for a few months—he grows impatient. He wants the money, and he can't see a way of getting it. At last he determines to make a bolt and go abroad to sell his plunder. He knows he will want money for expenses, and that he may not be able to get rid of his diamonds at once. He also expects that his suddenly going abroad while the robbery is still in people's minds will bring suspicion on him in any case, so, in for a penny in for a pound, he commits a bold forgery, which, had it been successful, would have put him in funds and enabled him to leave the country with the stones. But the forgery is detected, and he is haled to prison, leaving the diamonds in their wainscot setting.

"Now we come to Gavin Kingscote. He must have been a shrewd fellow—the sort of man that good detectives are made of. Also he must have been pretty unscrupulous. He had his suspicions about the genuineness of the diamond robbery, and kept his eyes open. What indications he had to guide him we don't know, but living in the same house a sharp fellow on the look-out would probably see enough. At any rate, they led him to the belief that the diamonds were in the thief's rooms, but not among his movables, or they would have been found after the arrest. Here was his chance. Challitt was out of the way for years, and there was plenty of time to take the house to pieces if it were necessary. So he changed into Challitt's rooms.

"How long it took him to find the stones we shall never know. He probably tried many other places first, and, I expect, found the diamonds at last by pricking over the panels with a needle. Then came the problem of getting them out without attracting attention. He decided not to trust to the needle, which might possibly leave a stone or two undiscovered, but to split up each panel carefully into splinters so as to leave no part unexamined. Therefore, he took measurements, and had a number of panels made by a joiner of the exact size and pattern of those in the room, and announced to his landlady his intention of painting her panels with a pretty design. This to account for the wet paint, and even for the fact of a panel being out of the wall, should she chance to bounce into the room at an awkward moment. All very clever, eh?"

"Very."

"Ah, he was a smart man, no doubt. Well, he went to work, taking out a panel, substituting a new one, painting it over, and chopping up the old one on the quiet, getting rid of the splinters out of doors when the booty had been extracted. The decoration progressed and the little heap of diamonds grew. Finally, he came to the last panel, but found that he had used all his new panels and hadn't one left for a substitute. It must have been at some time when it was difficult to get hold of the joiner—Bank Holiday, perhaps, or Sunday, and he was impatient. So he scraped the paint off, and went carefully over every part of the surface—experience had taught him by this that all the holes were of the same sort—and found one diamond. He took it out, refilled the hole with putty, painted the old panel and put it back. *These* are pieces of that old panel—the only old one of the lot.

"Nine men out of ten would have got out of the house as soon as possible after the thing was done, but he was a cool hand and stayed. That made the whole thing look a deal more genuine than if he had unaccountably cleared out as soon as he had got his room nicely decorated. I expect the original capital for those Stock Exchange operations we heard of came out of those diamonds. He stayed as long as suited him, and left when he set up housekeeping with a view to his wedding. The rest of the story is pretty plain. You guess it, of course?"

"Yes," I said, "I think I can guess the rest, in a general sort of way—except as to one or two points."

"It's all plain—perfectly. See here! Challitt, in gaol, determines to get those diamonds when he comes out. To do that without being suspected it will be necessary to hire the room. But he knows that he won't be able to do that himself, because the landlady, of course, knows him, and won't have an ex-convict in the house. There is no help for it; he must have a confederate, and share the spoil. So he makes the acquaintance of another convict, who seems a likely man for the job, and whose sentence expires about the same time as his own. When they come out, he arranges the matter with this confederate, who is a well-mannered (and pretty well-known) housebreaker, and the latter calls at Mrs. Lamb's house to look for rooms. The very room itself happens to be to let, and of course it is taken, and Challitt (who is the invalid cousin) comes in at night muffled and unrecognisable.

"The decoration on the panel does not alarm them, because, of course, they suppose it to have been done on the old panels and over the old paint. Challitt tries the spots where diamonds were left—there are none—there is no putty even. Perhaps, think they, the panels have been shifted and interchanged in the painting, so they set to work and split them all up as we have seen, getting more desperate as they go on. Finally, they realise that they are done, and clear out, leaving Mrs. Lamb to mourn over their mischief.

"They know that Kingscote is the man who has forestalled them, because Gillard (or Jones), in his chat with the landlady, has heard all about him and his painting of the panels. So the next night they set off for Finchley. They get into Kingscote's garden and watch him let Campbell out. While he is gone, Challitt quietly steps through the French window into the smoking-room, and waits for him, Gillard remaining outside.

"Kingscote returns, and Challitt accuses him of taking the stones. Kingscote is contemptuous—doesn't care for Challitt, because he knows he is powerless, being the original thief himself; besides, knows there is no evidence, since the diamonds are sold and dispersed long ago. Challitt offers to divide the plunder with him—Kingscote laughs and tells him to go; probably threatens to throw him out, Challitt being the smaller man. Gillard, at the open window, hears this, steps in behind, and quietly knocks him on the head. The rest follows as a matter of course. They fasten the window and shutters, to exclude observation; turn over all the drawers, etc., in case the jewels are there; go to the best bedroom and try there, and so on. Failing (and possibly being disturbed after a few hours' search by the noise of the acquisitive gardener), Gillard, with the instinct of an old thief, determines they shan't go away with nothing, so empties Kingscote's pockets and takes his watch and chain and so on. They go out by the front door and shut it after them. *Voilà tout.*"

I was filled with wonder at the prompt ingenuity of the man who in these few hours of hurried inquiry could piece together so accurately all the materials of an intricate and mysterious affair such as this; but more, I wondered where and how he had collected those materials.

"There is no doubt, Hewitt," I said, "that the accurate and minute application of what you are pleased to call your common sense has become something very like an instinct with you. What did you deduce from? You told me your conclusions from the examination of Ivy Cottage, but not how you arrived at them."

"They didn't leave me much material downstairs, did they? But in the bedroom, the two drawers which the thieves found locked were ransacked—opened probably with keys taken from the dead man. On the floor I saw a bent French nail; here it is. You see, it is twice bent at right angles, near the head and near the point, and there is the faint mark of the pliers that were used to bend it. It is a very usual burglars' tool, and handy in experienced hands to open ordinary drawer locks. Therefore, I knew that a professional burglar had been at work. He had probably fiddled at the drawers with the nail first, and then had thrown it down to try the dead man's keys.

"But I knew this professional burglar didn't come for a burglary, from several indications. There was no attempt to take plate, the first thing a burglar looks for. Valuable clocks were left on mantelpieces, and other things that usually go in an ordinary burglary were not disturbed. Notably, it was to be observed that no doors or windows were broken, or had been forcibly opened; therefore, it was plain that the thieves had come in by the French window of the smoking-room, the only entrance left open at the last thing. *Therefore*, they came in, or one did, knowing that Mr. Kingscote was up, and being quite willing—presumably anxious—to see him. Ordinary burglars would have waited till he had retired, and then could have got through the closed French window as easily almost as if it were open, notwithstanding the thin wooden shutters, which would never stop a burglar for more than five minutes. Being anxious to see him, they—or again, *one of* them—presumably knew him.

"That they had come to *get* something was plain, from the ransacking. As, in the end, they *did* steal his money, and watch, but did *not* take larger valuables, it was plain that they had no bag with them—which proves not only that they had not come to burgle, for every burglar takes his bag, but that the thing they came to get was not bulky. Still, they could easily have removed plate or clocks by rolling them up in a table-cover or other wrapper, but such a bundle, carried by well-dressed men, would attract attention—therefore it was probable that they were well dressed. Do I make it clear?"

"Quite—nothing seems simpler now it is explained—that's the way with difficult puzzles."

"There was nothing more to be got at the house. I had already in my mind the curious coincidence that the panels at Chelsea had been broken the very night before that of the murder, and determined to look at them in any case. I got from you the name of the man who had lived in the panelled room before Kingscote, and at once remembered it (although I said nothing about it) as that of the young man who had been chloroformed for his employer's diamonds. I keep things of that sort in my mind, you see—and, indeed, in my scrap-book. You told me yourself about his imprisonment, and there I was with what seemed now a hopeful case getting into a promising shape.

"You went on to prevent any setting to rights at Chelsea, and I made enquiries as to Challitt. I found he had been released only a few days before all this trouble arose, and I also found the name of another man who was released from the same establishment only a few days earlier. I knew this man (Gillard) well, and knew that nobody was a more likely rascal for such a crime as that at Finchley. On my way to Chelsea I called at my office, gave my clerk certain instructions, and looked up my scrap-book. I found the newspaper account of the chloroform business, and also a photograph of Gillard—I keep as many of these things as I can collect. What I did at Chelsea you know. I saw that one panel was of old wood and the rest new. I saw the hole in the old panel, and I asked one or two questions. The case was complete."

We proceeded with our dinner. Presently I said: "It all rests with the police now, of course?"

"Of course. I should think it very probable that Challitt and Gillard will be caught. Gillard, at any rate, is pretty well known. It will be rather hard on the surviving Kingscote, after engaging me, to have his dead brother's diamond transactions publicly exposed as a result, won't it? But it can't be helped. *Fiat justitia*, of course."

"How will the police feel over this?" I asked. "You've rather cut them out, eh?"

"Oh, the police are all right. They had not the information I had, you see; they knew nothing of the panel business. If Mrs. Lamb had gone to Scotland Yard instead of to the policeman on the beat, perhaps I should never have been sent for."

The same quality that caused Martin Hewitt to rank as mere "common-sense" his extraordinary power of almost instinctive deduction, kept his respect for the abilities of the police at perhaps a higher level than some might have considered justified.

We sat some little while over our dessert, talking as we sat, when there occurred one of those curious conjunctions of circumstances that we notice again and again in ordinary life, and forget as often, unless the importance of the occasion fixes the matter in the memory. A young man had entered the dining-room, and had taken his seat at a corner table near the back window. He had been sitting there for some little time before I particularly observed him. At last he happened to turn his thin, pale face in my direction, and our eyes met. It was Challitt—the man we had been talking of!

I sprang to my feet in some excitement.

"That's the man!" I cried. "Challitt!"

Hewitt rose at my words, and at first attempted to pull me back. Challitt, in guilty terror, saw that we were between him and the door, and turning, leaped upon the sill of the open window, and dropped out. There was a fearful crash of broken glass below, and everybody rushed to the window.

Hewitt drew me through the door, and we ran downstairs. "Pity you let out like that," he said, as he went. "If you'd kept quiet we could have sent out for the police with no trouble. Never mind—can't help it."

Below, Challitt was lying in a broken heap in the midst of a crowd of waiters. He had crashed through a thick glass skylight and fallen, back downward, across the back of a lounge. He was taken away on a stretcher unconscious, and, in fact, died in a week in hospital from injuries to the spine.

During his periods of consciousness, he made a detailed statement, bearing out the conclusions of Martin Hewitt with the most surprising exactness, down to the smallest particulars. He and Gillard had parted immediately after the crime, judging it safer not to be seen together. He had, he affirmed, endured agonies of fear and remorse in the few days since the fatal night at Finchley, and had even once or twice thought of giving himself up. When I so excitedly pointed him out, he knew at once that the game was up, and took the one desperate chance of escape that offered. But to the end he persistently denied that he had himself committed the murder, or had even thought of it till he saw it accomplished. That had been wholly the work of Gillard, who, listening at the window and perceiving the drift of the conversation, suddenly beat down Kingscote from behind with a life-preserver. And so Harvey Challitt ended his life at the age of twenty-six.

Gillard was never taken. He doubtless left the country, and has probably since that time become "known to the police" under another name abroad. Perhaps he has even been hanged, and if he has been, there was no miscarriage of justice, no matter what the charge against him may have been.

THE *NICOBAR* BULLION CASE

1.

The whole voyage was an unpleasant one, and Captain Mackrie, of the Anglo-Malay Company's steamship *Nicobar*, had at last some excuse for the ill-temper that had made him notorious and unpopular in the company's marine staff. Although the fourth and fifth mates in the seclusion of their berth ventured deeper in their search for motives, and opined that the "old man" had made a deal less out of this voyage than usual, the company having lately taken to providing its own stores; so that "makings" were gone clean and "cumshaw" (which means commission in the trading lingo of the China seas) had shrunk small indeed. In confirmation they adduced the uncommonly long face of the steward (the only man in the ship satisfied with the skipper), whom the new regulations hit with the same blow.

But indeed the steward's dolor might well be credited to the short passenger list, and the unpromising aspect of the few passengers in the eyes of a man accustomed to gauge one's tip-yielding capacity a month in advance. For the steward it was altogether the wrong time of year, the wrong sort of voyage, and certainly the wrong sort of passengers. So that doubtless the confidential talk of the fourth and fifth officers was mere youthful scandal. At any rate, the captain had prospect of a good deal in private trade home, for he had been taking curiosities and Japanese oddments aboard (plainly for sale in London) in a way that a third steward would have been ashamed of, and which, for a captain, was a scandal and an ignominy; and he had taken pains to insure well for the lot. These things the fourth and fifth mates often spoke of, and more than once made a winking allusion to, in the presence of the third mate and the chief engineer, who laughed and winked too, and sometimes said as much to the second mate, who winked without laughing; for of such is the tittle-tattle of shipboard.

The *Nicobar* was bound home with few passengers, as I have said, a small general cargo, and gold bullion to the value of £200,000—the bullion to be landed at Plymouth, as usual. The presence of this bullion was a source of much conspicuous worry on the part of the second officer, who had charge of the bullion-room. For this was his first voyage on his promotion from third officer, and the charge of £200,000 worth of gold bars was a thing he had not been accustomed to. The placid first officer pointed out to him that this wasn't the first shipment of bullion the world had ever known, by a long way, nor the largest.

Also that every usual precaution was taken, and the keys were in the captain's cabin; so that he might reasonably be as easy in his mind as the few thousand other second officers who had had charge of hatches and special cargo since the world began. But this did not comfort Brasyer. He fidgeted about when off watch, considering and puzzling out the various means by which the bullion-room might be got at, and fidgeted more when on watch, lest somebody might be at that moment putting into practice the ingenious dodges he had thought of. And he didn't keep his fears and speculations to himself. He bothered the first officer with them, and when the first officer escaped he explained the whole thing at length to the third officer.

"Can't think what the company's about," he said on one such occasion to the first mate, "calling a tin-pot bunker like that a bullion-room."

"Skittles!" responded the first mate, and went on smoking.

"Oh, that's all very well for you who aren't responsible," Brasyer went on, "but I'm pretty sure something will happen some day; if not on this voyage on some other. Talk about a strong room! Why, what's it made of?"

"Three-eighths boiler plate."

"Yes, three-eighths boiler plate—about as good as a sixpenny tin money box. Why, I'd get through that with my grandmother's scissors!"

"All right; borrow 'em and get through. *I* would if I had a grandmother."

"There it is down below there out of sight and hearing, nice and handy for anybody who likes to put in a quiet hour at plate cutting from the coal bunker next door—always empty, because it's only a seven-ton bunker, not worth trimming. And the other side's against the steward's pantry. What's to prevent a man shipping as steward, getting quietly through while he's supposed to be bucketing about among his slops and his crockery, and strolling away with the plunder at the next port? And then there's the carpenter. *He's* always messing about somewhere below, with a bag full of tools. Nothing easier than for him to make a job in a quiet corner, and get through the plates."

"But then what's he to do with the stuff when he's got it? You can't take gold ashore by the hundredweight in your boots."

"Do with it. Why, dump it, of course. Dump it overboard in a quiet port and mark the spot. Come to that, he could desert clean at Port Said—what easier place?—and take all he wanted. You know what Port Said's like. Then there are the firemen—oh, *anybody* can do it!" And Brasyer moved off to take another peep under the hatchway.

The door of the bullion-room was fastened by one central patent lock and two padlocks, one above and one below the other lock. A day or two after the conversation recorded above, Brasyer was carefully examining and trying the lower of the padlocks with a key, when a voice immediately behind him asked sharply, "Well, sir, and what are you up to with that padlock?"

Brasyer started violently and looked round. It was Captain Mackrie.

"There's—that is—I'm afraid these are the same sort of padlocks as those in the carpenter's stores," the second mate replied, in a hurry of explanation. "I—I was just trying, that's all; I'm afraid the keys fit."

"Just you let the carpenter take care of his own stores, will you, Mr. Brasyer? There's a Chubb's lock there as well as the padlocks, and the key of that's in my cabin, and I'll take care doesn't go out of it without my knowledge. So perhaps you'd best leave off experiments till you're asked to make 'em, for your own sake. That's enough now," the captain added, as Brasyer appeared to be ready to reply; and he turned on his heel and made for the steward's quarters.

Brasyer stared after him ragefully. "Wonder what *you* want down here," he muttered under his breath. "Seems to me one doesn't often see a skipper as thick with the steward as that." And he turned off growling towards the deck above.

"Hanged if I like that steward's pantry stuck against the side of the bullion-room," he said later in the day to the first officer. "And what does a steward want with a lot of boiler-maker's tools aboard? You know he's got them."

"In the name of the prophet, rats!" answered the first mate, who was of a less fussy disposition. "What a fatiguing creature you are, Brasyer! Don't you know the man's a boiler-maker by regular trade, and has only taken to stewardship for the last year or two? That sort of man doesn't like parting with his tools, and as he's a widower, with no home ashore, of course he has to carry all his traps aboard. Do shut up, and take your proper rest like a Christian. Here, I'll give you a cigar; it's all right—Burman; stick it in your mouth, and keep your jaw tight on it."

But there was no soothing the second officer. Still he prowled about the after orlop deck, and talked at large of his anxiety for the contents of the bullion-room. Once again, a few days later, as he approached the iron door, he was startled by the appearance of the captain coming, this time, *from* the steward's pantry. He fancied he had heard tapping, Brasyer explained, and had come to investigate. But the captain turned him back with even less ceremony than before, swearing he would give charge of the bullion-room to another officer if Brasyer persisted in his eccentricities. On the first deck the second officer was met by the carpenter, a quiet, sleek, soft-spoken man, who asked him for the padlock and key he had borrowed from the stores during the week. But Brasyer put him off, promising to send it back later. And the carpenter trotted away to a job he happened to have, singularly enough, in the hold, just under the after orlop deck, and below the floor of the bullion-room.

As I have said, the voyage was in no way a pleasant one. Everywhere the weather was at its worst, and scarce was Gibraltar passed before the Lascars were shivering in their cotton trousers, and the Seedee boys were buttoning tight such old tweed jackets as they might muster from their scanty kits. It was January. In the Bay the weather was tremendous, and the *Nicobar* banged and shook and pitched distractedly across in a howling world of thunderous green sea, washed within and without, above and below. Then, in the Chops, as night fell, something went, and there was no more steerage-way, nor, indeed, anything else but an aimless wallowing. The screw had broken.

The high sea had abated in some degree, but it was still bad. Such sail as the steamer carried, inadequate enough, was set, and shift was made somehow to worry along to Plymouth—or to Falmouth if occasion better served—by that means. And so the *Nicobar* beat across the Channel on a rather better, though anything but smooth, sea, in a black night, made thicker by a storm of sleet, which turned gradually to snow as the hours advanced.

The ship laboured slowly ahead, through a universal blackness that seemed to stifle. Nothing but a black void above, below, and around, and the sound of wind and sea; so that one coming before a deck-light was startled by the quiet advent of the large snowflakes that came like moths as it seemed from nowhere. At four bells—two in the morning—a foggy light appeared away on the starboard bow—it was the Eddystone light—and an hour or two later, the exact whereabouts of the ship being a thing of much uncertainty, it was judged best to lay her to till daylight. No order had yet been given, however, when suddenly there were dim lights over the port quarter, with a more solid blackness beneath them. Then a shout and a thunderous crash, and the whole ship shuddered, and in ten seconds had belched up every living soul from below. The *Nicobar's* voyage was over—it was a collision.

The stranger backed off into the dark, and the two vessels drifted apart, though not till some from the *Nicobar* had jumped aboard the other. Captain Mackrie's presence of mind was wonderful, and never for a moment did he lose absolute command of every soul on board. The ship had already begun to settle down by the stern and list to port. Life-belts were served out promptly. Fortunately, there were but two women among the passengers, and no children. The boats were lowered without a mishap, and presently two strange boats came as near as they dare from the ship (a large coasting steamer, it afterwards appeared) that had cut into the *Nicobar*. The last of the passengers were being got off safely, when Brasyer, running anxiously to the captain, said:—

"Can't do anything with that bullion, can we, sir? Perhaps a box or two——"

"Oh, damn the bullion!" shouted Captain Mackrie. "Look after the boat, sir, and get the passengers off. The insurance companies can find the bullion for themselves."

But Brasyer had vanished at the skipper's first sentence. The skipper turned aside to the steward as the crew and engine-room staff made for the remaining boats, and the two spoke quietly together. Presently the steward turned away as if to execute an order, and the skipper continued in a louder tone:—

"They're the likeliest stuff, and we can but drop 'em, at worst. But be slippy—she won't last ten minutes."

She lasted nearly a quarter of an hour. By that time, however, everybody was clear of her, and the captain in the last boat was only just near enough to see the last of her lights as she went down.

2.

The day broke in a sulky grey, and there lay the *Nicobar*, in ten fathoms, not a mile from the shore, her topmasts forlornly visible above the boisterous water. The sea was rough all that day, but the snow had ceased, and during the night the weather calmed considerably. Next day Lloyd's agent was steaming about in a launch from Plymouth, and soon a salvage company's tug came up and lay to by the emerging masts. There was every chance of raising the ship as far as could be seen, and a diver went down from the salvage tug to measure the breach made in the *Nicobar's* side, in order that the necessary oak planking or sheeting might be got ready for covering the hole, preparatory to pumping and raising. This was done in a very short time, and the necessary telegrams having been sent, the tug remained in its place through the night, and prepared for the sending down of several divers on the morrow to get out the bullion as a commencement.

Just at this time Martin Hewitt happened to be engaged on a case of some importance and delicacy on behalf of Lloyd's Committee, and was staying for a few days at Plymouth. He heard the story of the wreck, of course, and speaking casually with Lloyd's agent as to the salvage work just beginning, he was told the name of the salvage company's representative on the tug, Mr. Percy Merrick—a name he immediately recognised as that of an old acquaintance of his own. So that on the day when the divers were at work in the bullion-room of the sunken *Nicobar*, Hewitt gave himself a holiday, and went aboard the tug about noon.

Here he found Merrick, a big, pleasant man of thirty-eight or so. He was very glad to see Hewitt, but was a great deal puzzled as to the results of the morning's work on the wreck. Two cases of gold bars were missing.

"There was £200,000 worth of bullion on board," he said, "that's plain and certain. It was packed in forty cases, each of £5,000 value. But now there are only thirty-eight cases! Two are gone clearly. I wonder what's happened?"

"I suppose your men don't know anything about it?" asked Hewitt.

"No, they're all right. You see, it's impossible for them to bring anything up without its being observed, especially as they have to be unscrewed from their diving-dresses here on deck. Besides, bless you, I was down with them."

"Oh! Do you dive yourself, then?"

"Well, I put the dress on sometimes, you know, for any such special occasion as this. I went down this morning. There was no difficulty in getting about on the vessel below, and I found the keys of the bullion-room just where the captain said I would, in his cabin. But the locks were useless, of course, after being a couple of days in salt water. So we just burgled the door with crowbars, and then we saw that we might have done it a bit more easily from outside. For that coasting-steamer cut clean into the bunker next the bullion-room, and ripped open the sheet of boiler-plate dividing them."

"The two missing cases couldn't have dropped out that way, of course?"

"Oh, no. We looked, of course, but it would have been impossible. The vessel has a list the other way—to starboard—and the piled cases didn't reach as high as the torn part. Well, as I said, we burgled the door, and there they were, thirty-eight sealed bullion cases, neither more nor less, and they're down below in the after-cabin at this moment. Come and see."

Thirty-eight they were; pine cases bound with hoop-iron and sealed at every joint, each case about eighteen inches by a foot, and six inches deep. They were corded together, two and two, apparently for convenience of transport.

"Did you cord them like this yourself?" asked Hewitt.

"No, that's how we found 'em. We just hooked 'em on a block and tackle, the pair at a time, and they hauled 'em up here aboard the tug."

"What have you done about the missing two—anything?"

"Wired off to headquarters, of course, at once. And I've sent for Captain Mackrie—he's still in the neighbourhood, I believe—and Brasyer, the second officer, who had charge of the bullion-room. They may possibly know something. Anyway, *one* thing's plain. There were forty cases at the beginning of the voyage, and now there are only thirty-eight."

There was a pause; and then Merrick added, "By the bye, Hewitt, this is rather your line, isn't it? You ought to look up these two cases."

Hewitt laughed. "All right," he said; "I'll begin this minute if you'll commission me."

"Well," Merrick replied slowly, "of course I can't do that without authority from headquarters. But if you've nothing to do for an hour or so there is no harm in putting on your considering cap, is there? Although, of course, there's nothing to go upon as yet. But you might listen to what Mackrie and Brasyer have to say. Of course I don't know, but as it's a £10,000 question probably it might pay you, and if you *do* see your way to anything I'd wire and get you commissioned at once."

There was a tap at the door and Captain Mackrie entered. "Mr. Merrick?" he said interrogatively, looking from one to another.

"That's myself, sir," answered Merrick.

"I'm Captain Mackrie, of the *Nicobar*. You sent for me, I believe. Something wrong with the bullion I'm told, isn't it?"

Merrick explained matters fully. "I thought perhaps you might be able to help us, Captain Mackrie. Perhaps I have been wrongly informed as to the number of cases that should have been there?"

"No; there were forty right enough. I think though—perhaps I might be able to give you a sort of hint."—and Captain Mackrie looked hard at Hewitt.

"This is Mr. Hewitt, Captain Mackrie," Merrick interposed. "You may speak as freely as you please before him. In fact, he's sort of working on the business, so to speak."

"Well," Mackrie said, "if that's so, speaking between ourselves, I should advise you to turn your attention to Brasyer. He was my second officer, you know, and had charge of the stuff."

"Do you mean," Hewitt asked, "that Mr. Brasyer might give us some useful information?"

Mackrie gave an ugly grin. "Very likely he might," he said, "if he were fool enough. But I don't think you'd get much out of him direct. I meant you might watch him."

"What, do you suppose he was concerned in any way with the disappearance of this gold?"

"I should think—speaking, as I said before, in confidence and between ourselves—that it's very likely indeed. I didn't like his manner all through the voyage."

"Why?"

"Well, he was so eternally cracking on about his responsibility, and pretending to suspect the stokers and the carpenter, and one person and another, of trying to get at the bullion cases—that that alone was almost enough to make one suspicious. He protested so much, you see. He was so conscientious and diligent himself, and all the rest of it, and everybody else was such a desperate thief, and he was so sure there would be some of that bullion missing some day that—that—well, I don't know if I express his manner clearly, but I tell you I didn't like it a bit. But there was something more than that. He was eternally smelling about the place, and peeping in at the steward's pantry—which adjoins the bullion-room on one side, you know—and nosing about in the bunker on the other side. And once I actually caught him fitting keys to the padlocks—keys he'd borrowed from the carpenter's stores. And every time his excuse was that he fancied he heard somebody else trying to get in to the gold, or something of that sort; every time I caught him below on the orlop deck that was his excuse—happened to have heard something or suspected something or somebody every time. Whether or not I succeed in conveying my impressions to you, gentlemen, I can assure you that I regarded his whole manner and actions as very suspicious throughout the voyage, and I made up my mind I wouldn't forget it if by chance anything *did* turn out wrong. Well, it has, and now I've told you what I've observed. It's for you to see if it will lead you anywhere."

"Just so," Hewitt answered. "But let me fully understand, Captain Mackrie. You say that Mr. Brasyer had charge of the bullion-room, but that he was trying keys on it from the carpenter's stores. Where were the legitimate keys then?"

"In my cabin. They were only handed out when I knew what they were wanted for. There was a Chubb's lock between the two padlocks, but a duplicate wouldn't have been hard for Brasyer to get. He could easily have taken a wax impression of my key when he used it at the port where we took the bullion aboard."

"Well, and suppose he had taken these boxes, where do you think he would keep them?"

Mackrie shrugged his shoulders and smiled. "Impossible to say," he replied. "He might have hidden 'em somewhere on board, though I don't think that's likely. He'd have had a deuce of a job to land them at Plymouth, and would have had to leave them somewhere while he came on to London. Bullion is always landed at Plymouth, you know, and if any were found to be missing, then the ship would be overhauled at once, every inch of her; so that he'd have to get his plunder ashore somehow before the rest of the gold was unloaded—almost impossible. Of course, if he's done that it's somewhere below there now, but that isn't likely. He'd be much more likely to have 'dumped' it—dropped it overboard at some well-known spot in a foreign port, where he could go later on and get it. So that you've a deal of scope for search, you see. Anywhere under water from here to Yokohama;" and Captain Mackrie laughed.

Soon afterward he left, and as he was leaving a man knocked at the cabin door and looked in to say that Mr. Brasyer was on board. "You'll be able to have a go at him now," said the captain. "Good-day."

"There's the steward of the *Nicobar* there too, sir," said the man after the captain had gone, "and the carpenter."

"Very well, we'll see Mr. Brasyer first," said Merrick, and the man vanished. "It seems to have got about a bit," Merrick went on to Hewitt. "I only sent for Brasyer, but as these others have come, perhaps they've got something to tell us."

Brasyer made his appearance, overflowing with information. He required little assurance to encourage him to speak openly before Hewitt, and he said again all he had so often said before on board the *Nicobar*. The bullion-room was a mere tin box, the whole thing was as easy to get at as anything could be, he didn't wonder in the least at the loss—he had prophesied it all along.

The men whose movements should be carefully watched, he said, were the captain and the steward. "Nobody ever heard of a captain and a steward being so thick together before," he said. "The steward's pantry was next against the bullion-room, you know, with nothing but that wretched bit of three-eighths boiler plate between. You wouldn't often expect to find the captain down in the steward's pantry, would you, thick as they might be. Well, that's where I used to find him, time and again. And the steward kept boiler-makers' tools there! That I can swear to. And he's been a boiler-maker, so that, likely as not, he could open a joint somewhere and patch it up again neatly so that it wouldn't be noticed. He was always messing about down there in his pantry, and once I distinctly heard knocking there, and when I went down to see, whom should I meet?

"Why, the skipper, coming away from the place himself, and he bullyragged me for being there and sent me on deck. But before that he bullyragged me because I had found out that there were other keys knocking about the place that fitted the padlocks on the bullion-room door. Why should he slang and threaten me for looking after these things and keeping my eye on the bullion-room, as was my duty? But that was the very thing that he didn't like. It was enough for him to see me anxious about the gold to make him furious. Of course his character for meanness and greed is known all through the company's service—he'll do anything to make a bit."

"But have you any positive idea as to what has become of the gold?"

"Well," Brasyer replied, with a rather knowing air, "I don't think they've dumped it."

"Do you mean you think it's still in the vessel—hidden somewhere?"

"No, I don't. I believe the captain and the steward took it ashore, one case each, when we came off in the boats."

"But wouldn't that be noticed?"

"It needn't be, on a black night like that. You see, the parcels are not so big—look at them, a foot by a foot and a half by six inches or so, roughly. Easily slipped under a big coat or covered up with anything. Of course they're a bit heavy—eighty or ninety pounds apiece altogether—but that's not much for a strong man to carry—especially in such a handy parcel, on a black night, with no end of confusion on. Now you just look here—I'll tell you something. The skipper went ashore last in a boat that was sent out by the coasting steamer that ran into us. That ship's put into dock for repairs and her crew are mostly having an easy time ashore. Now I haven't been asleep this last day or two, and I had a sort of notion there might be some game of this sort on, because when I left the ship that night I thought we might save a little at least of the stuff, but the skipper wouldn't let me go near the bullion-room, and that seemed odd.

"So I got hold of one of the boat's crew that fetched the skipper ashore, and questioned him quietly—pumped him, you know—and he assures me that the skipper *did* have a rather small, heavy sort of parcel with him. What do you think of that? Of course, in the circumstances, the man couldn't remember any very distinct particulars, but he thought it was a sort of square wooden case about the size I've mentioned. But there's something more." Brasyer lifted his fore-finger and then brought it down on the table before him—"something more. I've made inquiries at the railway station and I find that two heavy parcels were sent off yesterday to London—deal boxes wrapped in brown paper, of just about the right size. And the paper got torn before the things were sent off, and the clerk could see that the boxes inside were fastened with hoop-iron—like those!" and the second officer pointed triumphantly to the boxes piled at one side of the cabin.

"Well done!" said Hewitt. "You're quite a smart detective. Did you find out who brought the parcels, and who they were addressed to?"

"No, I couldn't get quite as far as that. Of course the clerk didn't know the names of the senders, and not knowing me, wouldn't tell me exactly where the parcels were going. But I got quite chummy with him after a bit, and I'm going to meet him presently—he has the afternoon off, and we're going for a stroll. I'll find something more, I'll bet you!"

"Certainly," replied Hewitt, "find all you can—it may be very important. If you get any valuable information you'll let us know at once, of course. Anything else, now?"

"No, I don't think so; but I think what I've told you is pretty well enough for the present, eh? I'll let you know some more soon."

Brasyer went, and Norton, the steward of the old ship, was brought into the cabin. He was a sharp-eyed, rather cadaverous-looking man, and he spoke with sepulchral hollowness. He had heard, he said, that there was something wrong with the chests of bullion, and came on board to give any information he could. It wasn't much, he went on to say, but the smallest thing might help. If he might speak strictly confidentially he would suggest that observation be kept on Wickens, the carpenter. He (Norton) didn't want to be uncharitable, but his pantry happened to be next the bullion-room, and he had heard Wickens at work for a very long time just below—on the underside of the floor of the bullion-room, it seemed to him, although, of course, he *might* have been mistaken.

Still, it was very odd that the carpenter always seemed to have a job just at that spot. More, it had been said—and he (Norton) believed it to be true—that Wickens, the carpenter, had in his possession, and kept among his stores, keys that fitted the padlocks on the bullion-room door. That, it seemed to him, was a very suspicious circumstance. He didn't know anything more definite, but offered his ideas for what they were worth, and if his suspicions proved unfounded nobody would be more pleased than himself. But—but—and the steward shook his head doubtfully.

"Thank you, Mr. Norton," said Merrick, with a twinkle in his eye; "we won't forget what you say. Of course, if the stuff is found in consequence of any of your information, you won't lose by it."

The steward said he hoped not, and he wouldn't fail to keep his eye on the carpenter. He had noticed Wickens was in the tug, and he trusted that if they were going to question him they would do it cautiously, so as not to put him on his guard. Merrick promised they would.

"By the bye, Mr. Norton," asked Hewitt, "supposing your suspicions to be justified, what do you suppose the carpenter would do with the bullion?"

"Well, sir," replied Norton, "I don't think he'd keep it on the ship. He'd probably dump it somewhere."

The steward left, and Merrick lay back in his chair and guffawed aloud. "This grows farcical," he said, "simply farcical. What a happy family they must have been aboard the *Nicobar*! And now here's the captain watching the second officer, and the second officer watching the captain and the steward, and the steward watching the carpenter! It's immense. And now we're going to see the carpenter. Wonder whom *he* suspects?"

Hewitt said nothing, but his eyes twinkled with intense merriment, and presently the carpenter was brought into the cabin.

"Good-day to you, gentlemen," said the carpenter in a soft and deferential voice, looking from one to the other. "Might I 'ave the honour of addressin' the salvage gentlemen?"

"That's right," Merrick answered, motioning him to a seat. "This is the salvage shop, Mr. Wickens. What can we do for you?"

The carpenter coughed gently behind his hand. "I took the liberty of comin', gentlemen, consekins o' 'earin' as there was some bullion missin'. P'raps I'm wrong."

"Not at all. We haven't found as much as we expected, and I suppose by this time nearly everybody knows it. There are two cases wanting. You can't tell us where they are, I suppose?"

"Well, sir, as to that—no. I fear I can't exactly go as far as that. But if I am able to give vallable information as may lead to recovery of same, I presoom I may without offence look for some reasonable small recognition of my services?"

"Oh, yes," answered Merrick, "that'll be all right, I promise you. The company will do the handsome thing, of course, and no doubt so will the underwriters."

"Presoomin' I may take that as a promise—among gentlemen"— this with an emphasis—"I'm willing to tell something."

"It's a promise, at any rate as far as the company's concerned," returned Merrick. "I'll see it's made worth your while—of course, providing it leads to anything."

"Purvidin' that, sir, o' course. Well, gentlemen, my story ain't a long one. All I've to say was what I 'eard on board, just before she went down. The passengers was off, and the crew was gettin' into the other boats when the skipper turns to the steward an' speaks to him quiet-like, not observin', gentlemen, as I was agin 'is elbow, so for to say. "'Ere, Norton,' 'e sez, or words to that effeck, 'why shouldn't we try gettin' them things ashore with us—you know, the cases—eh? I've a notion we're pretty close inshore,' 'e sez, 'and there's nothink of a sea now. You take one, anyway, and I'll try the other,' 'e says, 'but don't make a flourish.' Then he sez, louder, 'cos o' the steward goin' off, 'They're the likeliest stuff, and at worst we can but drop 'em. But look sharp,' 'e says. So then I gets into the nearest boat, and that's all I 'eard."

"That was all?" asked Hewitt, watching the man's face sharply.

"All?" the carpenter answered with some surprise. "Yes, that was all; but I think it's pretty well enough, don't you? It's plain enough what was meant—him and the steward was to take two cases, one apiece, on the quiet, and they was the likeliest stuff aboard, as he said himself. And now there's two cases o' bullion missin'. Ain't that enough?"

The carpenter was not satisfied till an exact note had been made of the captain's words. Then after Merrick's promise on behalf of the company had been renewed, Wickens took himself off.

"Well," said Merrick, grinning across the table at Hewitt, "this is a queer go, isn't it? What that man says makes the skipper's case look pretty fishy, doesn't it? What he says, and what Brasyer says, taken together, makes a pretty strong case—I should say makes the thing a certainty. But what a business! It's likely to be a bit serious for someone, but it's a rare joke in a way. Wonder if Brasyer will find out anything more? Pity the skipper and steward didn't agree as to whom they should pretend to suspect. *That's* a mistake on their part."

"Not at all," Hewitt replied. "*If* they are conspiring, and know what they're about, they will avoid seeming to be both in a tale. The bullion is in bars, I understand?"

"Yes, five bars in each case; weight, I believe, sixteen pounds to a bar."

"Let me see," Hewitt went on, as he looked at his watch; "it is now nearly two o'clock. I must think over these things if I am to do anything in the case. In the meantime, if it could be managed, I should like enormously to have a turn under water in a diving-dress. I have always had a curiosity to see under the sea. Could it be managed now?"

"Well," Merrick responded, "there's not much fun in it, I can assure you; and it's none the pleasanter in this weather. You'd better have a try later in the year if you really want to—unless you think you can learn anything about this business by smelling about on the *Nicobar* down below?"

Hewitt raised his eyebrows and pursed his lips.

"I *might* spot something," he said; "one never knows. And if I do anything in a case I always make it a rule to see and hear everything that can possibly be seen or heard, important or not. Clues lie where least expected. But beyond that, probably I may never have another chance of a little experience in a diving-dress. So if it can be managed I'd be glad."

"Very well, you shall go, if you say so. And since it's your first venture, I'll come down with you myself. The men are all ashore, I think, or most of them. Come along."

Hewitt was put in woollens and then in india-rubbers. A leaden-soled boot of twenty pounds' weight was strapped on each foot, and weights were hung on his back and chest.

"That's the dress that Gullen usually has," Merrick remarked. "He's a very smart fellow; we usually send him first to make measurements and so on. An excellent man, but a bit too fond of the diver's lotion."

"What's that?" asked Hewitt.

"Oh, you shall try some if you like, afterwards. It's a bit too heavy for me; rum and gin mixed, I think."

A red nightcap was placed on Martin Hewitt's head, and after that a copper helmet, secured by a short turn in the segmental screw joint at the neck. In the end he felt a vast difficulty in moving at all. Merrick had been meantime invested with a similar rig-out, and then each was provided with a communication cord and an incandescent electric lamp. Finally, the front window was screwed on each helmet, and all was ready.

Merrick went first over the ladder at the side, and Hewitt with much difficulty followed. As the water closed over his head, his sensations altered considerably. There was less weight to carry; his arms in particular felt light, though slow in motion. Down, down they went slowly, and all round about it was fairly light, but once on the sunken vessel and among the lower decks, the electric lamps were necessary enough. Once or twice Merrick spoke, laying his helmet against Hewitt's for the purpose, and instructing him to keep his air-pipe, life-line, and lamp connection from fouling something at every step. Here and there shadowy swimming shapes came out of the gloom, attracted by their lamps, to dart into obscurity again with a twist of the tail. The fishes were exploring the *Nicobar*. The hatchway of the lower deck was open, and down this they passed to the orlop deck. A little way along this they came to a door standing open, with a broken lock hanging to it. It was the door of the bullion-room, which had been forced by the divers in the morning.

Merrick indicated by signs how the cases had been found piled on the floor. One of the sides of the room of thin steel was torn and thrust in the length of its whole upper half, and when they backed out of the room and passed the open door they stood in the great breach made by the bow of the strange coasting vessel. Steel, iron, wood, and everything stood in rents and splinters, and through the great gap they looked out into the immeasurable ocean. Hewitt put up his hand and felt the edge of the bullion-room partition where it had been torn. It was just such a tear as might have been made in cardboard.

They regained the upper deck, and Hewitt, placing his helmet against his companion's, told him that he meant to have a short walk on the ocean bed. He took to the ladder again, where it lay over the side, and Merrick followed him.

The bottom was of that tough, slimy sort of clay-rock that is found in many places about our coasts, and was dotted here and there with lumps of harder rock and clumps of curious weed. The two divers turned at the bottom of the ladder, walked a few steps, and looked up at the great hole in the *Nicobar's* side. Seen from here it was a fearful chasm, laying open hold, orlop, and lower deck.

Hewitt turned away, and began walking about. Once or twice he stood and looked thoughtfully at the ground he stood on, which was fairly flat. He turned over with his foot a whitish, clean-looking stone about as large as a loaf. Then he wandered on slowly, once or twice stopping to examine the rock beneath him, and presently stooped to look at another stone nearly as large as the other, weedy on one side only, standing on the edge of a cavity in the claystone. He pushed the stone into the hole, which it filled, and then he stood up.

Merrick put his helmet against Hewitt's, and shouted—

"Satisfied now? Seen enough of the bottom?"

"In a moment!" Hewitt shouted back; and he straightway began striding out in the direction of the ship. Arrived at the bows, he turned back to the point he started from, striding off again from there to the white stone he had kicked over, and from there to the vessel's side again. Merrick watched him in intense amazement, and hurried, as well as he might, after the light of Hewitt's lamp. Arrived for the second time at the bows of the ship, Hewitt turned and made his way along the side to the ladder, and forthwith ascended, followed by

Merrick. There was no halt at the deck this time, and the two made their way up and up into the lighter water above, and so to the world of air.

On the tug, as the men were unscrewing them from there water-proof prisons, Merrick asked Hewitt—

"Will you try the 'lotion' now?"

"No," Hewitt replied, "I won't go quite so far as that. But I *will* have a little whisky, if you've any in the cabin. And give me a pencil and a piece of paper."

These things were brought, and on the paper Martin Hewitt immediately wrote a few figures and kept it in his hand.

"I might easily forget those figures," he observed.

Merrick wondered, but said nothing.

Once more comfortably in the cabin, and clad in his usual garments, Hewitt asked if Merrick could produce a chart of the parts thereabout.

"Here you are," was the reply, "coast and all. Big enough, isn't it? I've already marked the position of the wreck on it in pencil. She lies pointing north by east as nearly exact as anything."

"As you've begun it," said Hewitt, "I shall take the liberty of making a few more pencil marks on this." And with that he spread out the crumpled note of figures, and began much ciphering and measuring. Presently he marked certain points on a spare piece of paper, and drew through them two lines forming an angle. This angle he transferred to the chart, and, placing a ruler over one leg of the angle, lengthened it out till it met the coast-line.

"There we are," he said musingly. "And the nearest village to that is Lostella—indeed, the only coast village in that neighbourhood." He rose. "Bring me the sharpest-eyed person on board," he said; "that is, if he were here all day yesterday."

"But what's up? What's all this mathematical business over? Going to find that bullion by rule of three?"

Hewitt laughed. "Yes, perhaps," he said, "but where's your sharp look-out? I want somebody who can tell me everything that was visible from the deck of this tug all day yesterday."

"Well, really I believe the very sharpest chap is the boy. He's most annoyingly observant sometimes. I'll send for him."

He came—a bright, snub-nosed, impudent-looking young ruffian.

"See here, my boy," said Merrick, "polish up your wits and tell this gentleman what he asks."

"Yesterday," said Hewitt, "no doubt you saw various pieces of wreckage floating about?"

"Yessir."

"What were they?"

"Hatch-gratings mostly—nothin' much else. There's some knockin' about now."

"I saw them. Now, remember. Did you see a hatch-grating floating yesterday that was different from the others? A painted one, for instance—those out there now are not painted, you know."

"Yessir, I see a little white 'un painted, bobbin' about away beyond the foremast of the *Nicobar*."

"You're sure of that?"

"Certain sure, sir—it was the only painted thing floatin'. And today it's washed away somewheres."

"So I noticed. You're a smart lad. Here's a shilling for you—keep your eyes open and perhaps you'll find a good many more shillings before you're an old man. That's all."

The boy disappeared, and Hewitt turned to Merrick and said, "I think you may as well send that wire you spoke of. If I get the commission, I think I may recover that bullion. It may take some little time, or, on the other hand, it may not. If you'll write the telegram at once, I'll go in the same boat as the messenger. I'm going to take a walk down to Lostella now—it's only two or three miles along the coast, but it will soon be getting dark."

"But what sort of a clue have you got? I didn't——"

"Never mind," replied Hewitt, with a chuckle. "Officially, you know, I've no right to a clue just yet—I'm not commissioned. When I am I'll tell you everything."

Hewitt was scarcely ashore when he was seized by the excited Brasyer. "Here you are," he said. "I was coming aboard the tug again. I've got more news. You remember I said I was going out with that railway clerk this afternoon, and meant pumping him? Well, I've done it and rushed away—don't know what he'll think's up. As we were going along we saw Norton, the steward, on the other side of the way, and the clerk recognised him as one of the men who brought the cases to be sent off; the other was the skipper, I've no doubt, from his description. I played him artfully, you know, and then he let out that both the cases were addressed to Mackrie at his address in London! He looked up the entry, he said, after I left when I first questioned him, feeling curious. That's about enough, I think, eh? I'm off to London now—I believe

Mackrie's going tonight. I'll have him! Keep it dark!" And the zealous second officer dashed off without waiting for a reply. Hewitt looked after him with an amused smile, and turned off towards Lostella.

3

It was about eleven the next morning when Merrick received the following note, brought by a boatman:—

Dear Merrick,—Am I commissioned? If not, don't trouble, but if I am, be just outside Lostella, at the turning before you come to the Smack Inn, at two o'clock. Bring with you a light cart, a policeman—or two perhaps will be better—and a man with a spade. There will probably be a little cabbage-digging. Are you fond of the sport?—Yours,

Martin Hewitt.

P.S.—*Keep all your men aboard*; bring the spade artist from the town.

Merrick was off in a boat at once. His principals had replied to his telegram after Hewitt's departure the day before, giving him a free hand to do whatever seemed best. With some little difficulty he got the policemen, and with none at all he got a light cart and a jobbing man with a spade. Together they drove off to the meeting-place.

It was before the time, but Martin Hewitt was there, waiting. "You're quick," he said, "but the sooner the better. I gave you the earliest appointment I thought you could keep, considering what you had to do."

"Have you got the stuff, then?" Merrick asked anxiously.

"No, not exactly yet. But I've got this," and Hewitt held up the point of his walking-stick. Protruding half an inch or so from it was the sharp end of a small gimlet, and in the groove thereof was a little white wood, such as commonly remains after a gimlet has been used.

"Why, what's that?"

"Never mind. Let us move along—I'll walk. I think we're about at the end of the job—it's been a fairly lucky one, and quite simple. But I'll explain after."

Just beyond the Smack Inn, Hewitt halted the cart, and all got down. They looped the horse's reins round a hedge-stake and proceeded the small remaining distance on foot, with the policemen behind, to avoid a premature scare. They turned up a lane behind a few small and rather dirty cottages facing the sea, each with its patch of kitchen garden behind. Hewitt led the way to the second garden, pushed open the small wicket gate and walked boldly in, followed by the others.

Cabbages covered most of the patch, and seemed pretty healthy in their situation, with the exception of half a dozen—singularly enough, all together in a group. These were drooping, yellow, and wilted, and towards these Hewitt straightway walked. "Dig up those wilted cabbages," he said to the jobbing man. "They're really useless now. You'll probably find something else six inches down or so."

The man struck his spade into the soft earth, wherein it stopped suddenly with a thud. But at this moment a gaunt, slatternly woman, with a black eye, a handkerchief over her head, and her skirt pinned up in front, observing the invasion from the back door of the cottage, rushed out like a maniac and attacked the party valiantly with a broom. She upset the jobbing man over his spade, knocked off one policeman's helmet, lunged into the other's face with her broom, and was making her second attempt to hit Hewitt (who had dodged), when Merrick caught her firmly by the elbows from behind, pressed them together, and held her. She screamed, and people came from other cottages and looked on. "Peter! Peter!" the woman screamed, "come 'ee, come 'ee here! Davey! They're come!"

A grimy child came to the cottage door, and seeing the woman thus held, and strangers in the garden, set up a piteous howl. Meantime the digger had uncovered two wooden boxes, each eighteen inches long or so, bound with hoop-iron and sealed. One had been torn partly open at the top, and the broken wood roughly replaced. When this was lifted, bars of yellow metal were visible within.

The woman still screamed vehemently, and struggled. The grimy child retreated, and then there appeared at the door, staggering hazily and rubbing his eyes, a shaggy, unkempt man, in shirt and trousers. He looked stupidly at the scene before him, and his jaw dropped.

"Take that man," cried Hewitt. "He's one!" And the policeman promptly took him, so that he had handcuffs on his wrists before he had collected his faculties sufficiently to begin swearing.

Hewitt and the other policeman entered the cottage. In the lower two rooms there was nobody. They climbed the few narrow stairs, and in the front room above they found another man, younger, and fast asleep. "He's the other," said Hewitt. "Take *him*." And this one was handcuffed before he woke.

Then the recovered gold was put into the cart, and with the help of the village constable, who brought his own handcuffs for the benefit and adornment of the lady with the broom, such a procession marched out of Lostella as had never been dreamed of by the oldest inhabitant in his worst nightmare, nor recorded in the whole history of Cornwall.

"Now," said Hewitt, turning to Merrick, "we must have that fellow of yours—what's his name—Gullen, isn't it? The one that went down to measure the hole in the ship. You've kept him aboard, of course?"

"What, Gullen?" exclaimed Merrick. "Gullen? Well, as a matter of fact he went ashore last night and hasn't come back. But you don't mean to say——"

"I *do*," replied Hewitt. "And now you've lost him."

4

"But tell me all about it now we've a little time to ourselves," asked Merrick an hour or two later, as they sat and smoked in the after-cabin of the salvage tug. "We've got the stuff, thanks to you, but I don't in the least see how *they* got it, nor how you found it out."

"Well, there didn't seem to be a great deal either way in the tales told by the men from the *Nicobar*. They cancelled one another out, so to speak, though it seemed likely that there might be something in them in one or two respects. Brasyer, I could see, tried to prove too much. If the captain and the steward were conspiring to rob the bullion-room, why should the steward trouble to cut through the boiler-plate walls when the captain kept the keys in his cabin? And if the captain had been stealing the bullion, why should he stop at two cases when he had all the voyage to operate in and forty cases to help himself to? Of course the evidence of the carpenter gave some colour to the theory, but I think I can imagine a very reasonable explanation of that.

"You told me, of course, that you were down with the men yourself when they opened the bullion-room door and got out the cases, so that there could be no suspicion of *them*. But at the same time you told me that the breach in the *Nicobar's* side had laid open the bullion-room partition, and that you might more easily have got the cases out that way. You told me, of course, that the cases couldn't have *fallen* out that way because of the list of the vessel, the position of the rent in the boiler-plate, and so on. But I reflected that the day before a diver had been down alone—in fact, that his business had been with the very hole that extended partly to the bullion-room: he had to measure it. That diver might easily have got at the cases through the breach. But then, as you told me, a diver can't bring things up from below unobserved. This diver would know this, and might therefore hide the booty below. So that I made up my mind to have a look under water before I jumped to any conclusion.

"I didn't think it likely that he had hidden the cases, mind you. Because he would have had to dive again to get them, and would have been just as awkwardly placed in fetching them to the light of day then as ever. Besides, he couldn't come diving here again in the company's dress without some explanation. So what more likely than that he would make some ingenious arrangement with an accomplice, whereby he might make the gold in some way accessible to him?

"We went under water. I kept my eyes open, and observed, among other things, that the vessel was one of those well-kept 'swell' ones on which all the hatch gratings and so on are in plain oak or teak, kept holystoned. This (with the other things) I put by in my mind in case it should be useful. When we went over the side and looked at the great gap, I saw that it would have been quite easy to get at the broken bullion-room partition from outside."

"Yes," remarked Merrick, "it would be no trouble at all. The ladder goes down just by the side of the breach, and anyone descending by that might just step off at one side on to the jagged plating at the level of the after orlop, and reach over into the bullion safe."

"Just so. Well, next I turned my attention to the sea-bed, which I was extremely pleased to see was of soft, slimy claystone. I walked about a little, getting farther and farther away from the vessel as I went, till I came across that clean stone which I turned over with my foot. Do you remember?"

"Yes."

"Well, that was noticeable. It was the only clean, bare stone to be seen. Every other was covered with a green growth, and to most clumps of weed clung. The obvious explanation of this was that the stone was a newcomer—lately brought from dry land—from the shingle on the sea-shore, probably, since it was washed so clean. Such a stone could not have come a mile out to sea by itself. Somebody had brought it in a boat and thrown it over, and whoever did it didn't take all that trouble for nothing. Then its shape told a tale; it was something of the form, rather exaggerated, of a loaf—the sort that is called a 'cottage'—the most convenient possible shape for attaching to a line and lowering. But the line had gone, so somebody must have been down there to detach it.

"Also it wasn't unreasonable to suppose that there might have been a hook on the end of that line. This, then, was a theory. Your man had gone down alone to take his measurement, had stepped into the broken side, as you have explained he could, reached into the bullion-room, and lifted the two cases. Probably he unfastened the cord, and brought them out one at a time for convenience in carrying. Then he carried the cases, one at a time, as I have said, over to that white stone which lay there sunk with the hook and line attached by previous arrangement with some confederate. He detached the rope from the stone—it was probably fixed by an attached piece of cord, tightened round the stone with what you call a timber-hitch, easily loosened—replaced the cord round the two cases, passed the hook under the cord, and left it to be pulled up from above. But then it could not have been pulled up there in broad daylight, under your very noses. The confederates would wait till night. That meant that the other end of the rope was attached to some floating object, so that it might be readily recovered. The whole arrangement was set one night to be carried away the next."

"But why didn't Gullen take more than two cases?"

"He couldn't afford to waste the time, in the first place. Each case removed meant another journey to and from the vessel, and you were waiting above for his measurements. Then he was probably doubtful as to weight. Too much at once wouldn't easily be drawn up, and might upset a small boat.

"Well, so much for the white stone. But there was more; close by the stone I noticed (although I think you didn't) a mark in the clay-stone. It was a triangular depression or pit, sharp at the bottom—just the hole that would be made by the sharp impact of the square corner of a heavy box, if shod with iron, as the bullion cases are. This was one important thing. It seemed to indicate that the boxes had not been lifted directly up from the sea-bed, but had been dragged sideways—at all events at first—so that a sharp corner had turned over and dug into the claystone! I walked a little farther and found more indications—slight scratches, small stones displaced, and so on, that convinced me of this, and also pointed out the direction in which the cases had been dragged. I followed the direction, and presently arrived at another stone, rather smaller than the clean one.

"The cases had evidently caught against this, and it had been dis-placed by their momentum, and perhaps by a possible wrench from above. The green growth covered the part which had been exposed to the water, and the rest of the stone fitted the hole beside it, from which it had been pulled. Clearly these things were done recently, or the sea would have wiped out all the traces in the soft claystone. The rest of what I did under water of course you understood."

"I suppose so: you took the bearings of the two stones in relation to the ship by pacing the distances."

"That is so. I kept the figures in my head till I could make a note of them, as you saw, on paper. The rest was mere calculation. What I judged had happened was this. Gullen had arranged with somebody, identity unknown, but certainly somebody with a boat at his disposal, to lay the line, and take it up the following night. Now anything larger than a rowing boat could not have got up quite so close to you in the night (although your tug was at the other end of the wreck) without a risk of being seen. *But* no rowing boat could have *dragged* those cases forcibly along the bottom; they would act as an anchor to it.

"Therefore, this was what had happened. The thieves had come in a large boat—a fishing smack, lugger, or something of that sort—with a small boat in tow. The sailing boat had lain to at a convenient distance, *in the direction in which it was afterwards to go*, so as to save time if observed, and a man had put off quietly in the small boat to pick up the float, whatever it was. There must have been a lot of slack line on this for the purpose, as also for the purpose of allowing the float to drift about fairly freely, and not attract attention by remaining in one place. The man pulled off to the sailing boat, and took the float and line aboard. Then the sailing boat swung off in the direction of home, and the line was hauled in with the plunder at the end of it."

"One would think you had seen it all—or done it," Merrick remarked, with a laugh.

"Nothing else could have happened, you see. That chain of events is the only one that will explain the circumstances. A rapid grasp of the whole circumstances and a perfect appreciation of each is more than half the battle in such work as this. Well, you know I got the exact bearings of the wreck on the chart, worked out from that the lay of the two stones with the scratch marks between, and then it was obvious that a straight line drawn through these and carried ahead would indicate, approximately, at any rate, the direction the thieves' vessel had taken. The line fell on the coast close by the village of Lostella—indeed that was the only village for some few miles either way. The indication was not certain, but it was likely, and the only one available, therefore it must be followed up."

"And what about the painted hatch? How did you guess that?"

"Well, I saw there were hatch-gratings belonging to the *Nicobar* floating about, and it seemed probable that the thieves would use for a float something similar to the other wreckage in the vicinity, so as not to attract attention. Nothing would be more likely than a hatch-grating. But then, in small vessels, such as fishing-luggers and so on, fittings are almost always painted—they can't afford to be such holy-stoning swells as those on the *Nicobar*. So I judged the grating might be painted, and this would possibly have been noticed by some sharp person. I made the shot, and hit. The boy remembered the white grating, which had gone—'washed away,' as he thought. That was useful to me, as you shall see.

"I made off toward Lostella. The tide was low and it was getting dusk when I arrived. A number of boats and smacks were lying anchored on the beach, but there were few people to be seen. I began looking out for smacks with white-painted fittings in them. There are not so many of these among fishing vessels—brown or red is more likely, or sheer colourless dirt over paint unrecognisable. There were only two that I saw last night. The first *might* have been the one I wanted, but there was nothing to show it. The second *was* the one. She was half-decked and had a small white-painted hatch. I shifted the hatch and found a long line, attached to the grating at one end and carrying a hook at the other! They had neglected to unfasten their apparatus—perhaps had an idea that there might be a chance of using it again in a few days. I went to the transom and read the inscription, '*Rebecca*. Peter and David Garthew, Lostella.' Then my business was to find the Garthews.

"I wandered about the village for some little time, and presently got hold of a boy. I made a simple excuse for asking about the Garthews—wanted to go for a sail tomorrow. The boy, with many grins, confided to me that both of the Garthews were 'on the booze.' I should find them at the Smack Inn, where they had been all day, drunk as fiddlers. This seemed a likely sort of thing after the haul they had made. I went to the Smack Inn, determined to claim old friendship with the Garthews, although I didn't know Peter from David. There they were—one sleepy drunk, and the other loving and crying drunk. I got as friendly as possible with them under the circumstances, and at closing time stood another gallon of beer and carried it home for them, while they carried each other. I took care to have a good look round in the cottage. I even helped Peter's 'old woman'—the lady with the broom—to carry them up to bed. But nowhere could I see anything that looked like a bullion-case or a hiding-place for one.

So I came away, determined to renew my acquaintance in the morning, and to carry it on as long as might be necessary; also to look at the garden in the daylight for signs of burying. With that view I fixed that little gimlet in my walking-stick, as you saw.

"This morning I was at Lostella before ten, and took a look at the Garthews' cabbages. It seemed odd that half a dozen, all in a clump together, looked withered and limp, as though they had been dug up hastily, the roots broken, perhaps, and then replanted. And altogether these particular cabbages had a dissipated, leaning-different-ways look, as though *they* had been on the loose with the Garthews. So, seeing a grubby child near the back door of the cottage, I went towards him, walking rather unsteadily, so as, if I were observed, to favour the delusion that I was not yet quite got over last night's diversions. 'Hullo, my b-boy,' I said, 'hullo, li'l b-boy, look here,' and I plunged my hand into my trousers' pocket and brought it out full of small change.

"Then, making a great business of selecting him a penny, I managed to spill it all over the dissipated cabbages. It was easy then, in stooping to pick up the change, to lean heavily on my stick and drive it through the loose earth. As I had expected, there was a box below. So I gouged away with my walking-stick while I collected my coppers, and finally swaggered off, after a few civil words with the 'old woman,' carrying with me evident proof that it was white wood recently buried there. The rest you saw for yourself. I think you and I may congratulate each other on having dodged that broom. It hit all the others."

"What I'm wild about," said Merrick, "is having let that scoundrel Gullen get off. He's an artful chap, without a doubt. He saw us go over the side, you know, and after you had gone he came into the cabin for some instructions. Your pencil notes and the chart were on the table, and no doubt he put two and two together (which was more than I could, not knowing what had happened), and concluded to make himself safe for a bit. He had no leave that night—he just pulled away on the quiet. Why didn't you give me the tip to keep him?"

"That wouldn't have done. In the first place, there was no legal evidence to warrant his arrest, and ordering him to keep aboard would have aroused his suspicions. I didn't know at the time how many days, or weeks, it would take me to find the bullion, if I ever found it, and in that time Gullen might have communicated in some way with his accomplices, and so spoilt the whole thing. Yes, certainly he seems to have been fairly smart in his way. He knew he would probably be sent down first, as usual, alone to make measurements, and conceived his plan and made his arrangements forthwith."

"But now what I want to know is what about all those *Nicobar* people watching and suspecting one another? More especially what about the cases the captain and the steward are said to have fetched ashore?"

Hewitt laughed. "Well," he said, "as to that, the presence of the bullion seems to have bred all sorts of mutual suspicion on board the ship. Brasyer was over-fussy, and his continual chatter started it probably, so that it spread like an infection. As to the captain and the steward, of course I don't know anything but that their rescued cases were not bullion cases. Probably they were doing a little private trading—it's generally the case when captain and steward seem unduly friendly for their relative positions—and perhaps the cases contained something specially valuable: vases or bronzes from Japan, for instance; possibly the most valuable things of the size they had aboard. Then, if they had insured their things, Captain Mackrie (who has the reputation of a sharp and not very scrupulous man) might possibly think it rather a stroke of business to get the goods and the insurance money too, which would lead him to keep his parcels as quiet as possible. But that's as it may be."

The case was much as Hewitt had surmised. The zealous Brasyer, posting to London in hot haste after Mackrie, spent some days in watching him. At last the captain and the steward with their two boxes took a cab and went to Bond Street, with Brasyer in another cab behind them. The two entered a shop, the window of which was set out with rare curiosities and much old silver and gold. Brasyer could restrain himself no longer. He grabbed a passing policeman, and rushed with him into the shop. There they found the captain and the steward with two small packing cases opened before them, trying to sell—a couple of very ancient-looking Japanese bronze figures, of that curious old workmanship and varied colour of metal that in genuine examples mean nowadays high money value.

Brasyer vanished: there was too much chaff for him to live through in the British mercantile marine after this adventure. The fact was, the steward had come across the bargain, but had not sufficient spare cash to buy, so he called in the aid of the captain, and they speculated in the bronzes as partners. There was much anxious inspection of the prizes on the way home, and much discussion as to the proper price to ask. Finally, it was said, they got three hundred pounds for the pair.

Now and again Hewitt meets Merrick still. Sometimes Merrick says, "Now, I wonder after all whether or not some of those *Nicobar* men who were continually dodging suspiciously about that bullion-room *did* mean having a dash at the gold if there were a chance?" And Hewitt replies, "I wonder."

THE HOLFORD WILL CASE

At one time, in common, perhaps, with most people, I took a sort of languid, amateur interest in questions of psychology, and was impelled there-by to plunge into the pages of the many curious and rather abstruse books which attempt to deal with phenomena of mind, soul and sense. Three things of the real nature of which, I am convinced, no man will ever learn more than we know at present—which is nothing.

From these I strayed into the many volumes of *Transactions* of the Psychical Research Society, with an occasional by-excursion into mental telepathy and theosophy; the last, a thing whereof my Philistine intelligence obstinately refused to make head or tail.

It was while these things were occupying part of my attention that I chanced to ask Hewitt whether, in the course of his divers odd and out-of-the-way experiences, he had met with any such weird adventures as were detailed in such profusion in the books of "authenticated" spooks, doppelgangers, poltergeists, clairvoyance, and so forth.

"Well," Hewitt answered, with reflection, "I haven't been such a wallower in the uncanny as some of the worthy people who talk at large in those books of yours, and, as a matter of fact, my little adventures, curious as some of them may seem, have been on the whole of the most solid and matter-of-fact description. One or two things have happened that perhaps your 'psychical' people might be interested in, but they've mostly been found to be capable of a disappointingly simple explanation. One case of some genuine psychological interest, however, I have had; although there's nothing even in that which isn't a matter of well-known scientific possibility." And he proceeded to tell me the story that I have set down here, as well as I can, from recollection.

I think I have already said, in another place, that Hewitt's professional start as a private investigator dated from his connection with the famous will case of Bartley *v.* Bartley and others, in which his then principals, Messrs. Crellan, Hunt & Crellan, chiefly through his exertions established their extremely high reputation as solicitors. It was ten years or so after this case that Mr. Crellan senior—the head of the firm—retired into private life, and by an odd chance Hewitt's first meeting with him after that event was occasioned by another will difficulty.

These were the terms of the telegram that brought Hewitt again into personal relations with his old principal:—

Can you run down at once on a matter of private business? I will be at Guildford to meet eleven thirty-five from Waterloo. If later or prevented please wire. Crellan.

The day and the state of Hewitt's engagements suited, and there was full half an hour to catch the train. Taking, therefore, the small travelling-bag that always stood ready packed in case of any sudden excursion that presented the possibility of a night from home, he got early to Waterloo, and by half-past twelve was alighting at Guildford Station. Mr. Crellan, a hale, white-haired old gentleman, wearing gold-rimmed spectacles, was waiting with a covered carriage.

"How d'ye do, Mr. Hewitt, how d'ye do?" the old gentleman exclaimed as soon as they met, grasping Hewitt's hand, and hurrying him toward the carriage. "I'm glad you've come, very glad. It isn't raining, and you might have preferred something more open, but I brought the brougham because I want to talk privately. I've been vegetating to such an extent for the last few years down here that any little occurrence out of the ordinary excites me, and I'm sure I couldn't have kept quiet till we had got indoors. It's been bad enough, keeping the thing to myself, already."

The door shut, and the brougham started. Mr. Crellan laid his hand on Hewitt's knee, "I hope," he said, "I haven't dragged you away from any important business?"

"No," Hewitt replied, "you have chosen a most excellent time. Indeed, I did think of making a small holiday today, but your telegram——"

"Yes, yes. Do you know, I was almost ashamed of having sent it after it had gone. Because, after all, the matter is, probably, really a very simple sort of affair that you can't possibly help me in. A few years ago I should have thought nothing of it, nothing at all. But as I have told you, I've got into such a dull, vegetable state of mind since I retired and have nothing to do that a little thing upsets me, and I haven't mental energy enough to make up my mind to go to dinner sometimes. But you're an old friend, and I'm sure you'll forgive my dragging you all down here on a matter that will, perhaps, seem ridiculously simple to you, a man in the thick of active business. If I hadn't known you so well I wouldn't have had the impudence to bother you. But never mind all that. I'll tell you.

"Do you ever remember my speaking of an intimate friend, a Mr. Holford? No. Well, it's a long time ago, and perhaps I never happened to mention him. He was a most excellent man—old fellow, like me, you know; two or three years older, as a matter of fact. We were chums many years ago; in fact, we lodged in the same house when I was an articled clerk and he was a student at Guy's. He retired from the medical profession early, having come into a fortune, and came down here to live at the house we're going to; as a matter of fact, Wedbury Hall.

"When I retired I came down and took up my quarters not far off, and we were a very excellent pair of old chums till last Monday—the day before yesterday—when my poor old friend died. He was pretty well in years—seventy-three—and a man can't live for ever. But I assure you it has upset me terribly, made a greater fool of me than ever, in fact, just when I ought to have my wits about me.

"The reason I particularly want my wits just now, and the reason I have requisitioned yours, is this: that I can't find poor old Holford's will. I drew it up for him years ago, and by it I was appointed his sole executor. I am perfectly convinced that he cannot have destroyed it, because he told me everything concerning his affairs. I have always been his only adviser, in fact, and I'm sure he would have consulted me as to any change in his testamentary intentions before he made it. Moreover, there are reasons why I know he could not have wished to die intestate."

"Which are——?" queried Hewitt as Mr. Crellan paused in his statement.

"Which are these: Holford was a widower, with no children of his own. His wife, who has been dead nearly fifteen years now, was a most excellent woman, a model wife, and would have been a model mother if she had been one at all. As it was she adopted a little girl, a poor little soul who was left an orphan at two years of age. The child's father, an unsuccessful man of business of the name of Garth, maddened by a sudden and ruinous loss, committed suicide, and his wife died of the shock occasioned by the calamity.

"The child, as I have said, was taken by Mrs. Holford and made a daughter of, and my old friend's daughter she has been ever since, practically speaking. The poor old fellow couldn't possibly have been more attached to a daughter of his own, and on her part she couldn't possibly have been a better daughter than she was. She stuck by him night and day during his last illness, until she became rather ill herself, although of course there was a regular nurse always in attendance.

"Now, in his will, Mr. Holford bequeathed rather more than half of his very large property to this Miss Garth; that is to say, as residuary legatee, her interest in the will came to about that. The rest was distributed in various ways. Holford had largely spent the leisure of his retirement in scientific pursuits. So there were a few legacies to learned societies; all his servants were remembered; he left me a certain number of his books; and there was a very fair sum of money for his nephew, Mr. Cranley Mellis, the only near relation of Mr. Holford's still living. So that you see what the loss of this will may mean. Miss Garth, who was to have taken the greater part of her adoptive father's property, will not have one shilling's worth of claim on the estate and will be turned out into the world without a cent. One or two very old servants will be very awkwardly placed, too, with nothing to live on, and very little prospect of doing more work."

"Everything will go to this nephew," said Hewitt, "of course?"

"Of course. That is unless I attempt to prove a rough copy of the will which I may possibly have by me. But even if I have such a thing and find it, long and costly litigation would be called for, and the result would probably be all against us."

"You say you feel sure Mr. Holford did not destroy the will himself?"

"I am quite sure he would never have done so without telling me of it; indeed, I am sure he would have consulted me first. Moreover, it can never have been his intention to leave Miss Garth utterly unprovided for; it would be the same thing as disinheriting his only daughter."

"Did you see him frequently?"

"There's scarcely been a day when I haven't seen him since I have lived down here. During his illness—it lasted a month—I saw him every day."

"And he said nothing of destroying his will?"

"Nothing at all. On the contrary, soon after his first seizure—indeed, on the first visit at which I found him in bed—he said, after telling me how he felt, 'Everything's as I want it, you know, in case I go under.' That seemed to me to mean his will was still as he desired it to be."

"Well, yes, it would seem so. But counsel on the other side (supposing there were another side) might quite as plausibly argue that he meant to die intestate, and had destroyed his will so that everything should be as he wanted it, in that sense. But what do you want me to do—find the will?"

"Certainly, if you can. It seemed to me that you, with your clever head, might be able to form a better judgment than I as to what has happened and who is responsible for it. Because if the will *has* been taken away, someone has taken it."

"It seems probable. Have you told anyone of your difficulty?"

"Not a soul. I came over as soon as I could after Mr. Holford's death, and Miss Garth gave me all the keys, because, as executor, the case being a peculiar one, I wished to see that all was in order, and, as you know, the estate is legally vested in the executor from the death of the testator, so that I was responsible for everything; although, of course, if there is no will I'm not executor. But I thought it best to keep the difficulty to myself till I saw you."

"Quite right. Is this Wedbury Hall?"

The brougham had passed a lodge gate, and approached, by a wide drive, a fine old red brick mansion carrying the heavy stone dressings and copings distinctive of early eighteenth century domestic architecture.

"Yes," said Mr. Crellan, "this is the place. We will go straight to the study, I think, and then I can explain details."

The study told the tale of the late Mr. Holford's habits and interests. It was half a library, half a scientific laboratory—pathological curiosities in spirits, a retort or two, test tubes on the writing-table, and a fossilized lizard mounted in a case, balanced the many shelves and cases of books disposed about the walls. In a recess between two book-cases stood a heavy, old-fashioned mahogany bureau.

"Now it was in that bureau," Mr. Crellan explained, indicating it with his finger, "that Mr. Holford kept every document that was in the smallest degree important or valuable. I have seen him at it a hundred times, and he always maintained it was as secure as any iron safe. That may not have been altogether the fact, but the bureau is certainly a tremendously heavy and strong one. Feel it."

Hewitt took down the front and pulled out a drawer that Mr. Crellan unlocked for the purpose.

"Solid Spanish mahogany an inch thick," was his verdict, "heavy, hard, and seasoned; not the sort of thing you can buy nowadays. Locks, Chubb's patent, early pattern, but not easily to be picked by anything short of a blast of gunpowder. If there are no marks on this bureau it hasn't been tampered with."

"Well," Mr. Crellan pursued, "as I say, *that* was where Mr. Holford kept his will. I have often seen it when we have been here together, and this was the drawer, the top on the right, that he kept it in. The will was a mere single sheet of foolscap, and was kept, folded of course, in a blue envelope."

"When did you yourself last actually see the will?"

"I saw it in my friend's hand two days before he took to his bed. He merely lifted it in his hand to get at something else in the drawer, replaced it, and locked the drawer again."

"Of course there are other drawers, bureaux, and so on, about the place. You have examined them carefully, I take it?"

"I've turned out ever possible receptacle for that will in the house, I positively assure you, and there isn't a trace of it."

"You've thought of secret drawers, I suppose?"

"Yes. There are two in the bureau which I always knew of. Here they are." Mr. Crellan pressed his thumb against a partition of the pigeon-holes at the back of the bureau and a strip of mahogany flew out from below, revealing two shallow drawers with small ivory catches in lieu of knobs. "Nothing there at all. And this other, as I have said, was the drawer where the will was kept. The other papers kept in the same drawer are here as usual."

"Did anybody else know where Mr. Holford kept his will?"

"Everybody in the house, I should think. He was a frank, above-board sort of man. His adopted daughter knew, and the butler knew, and there was absolutely no reason why all the other servants shouldn't know; probably they did."

"First," said Hewitt, "we will make quite sure there are no more secret drawers about this bureau. Lock the door in case anybody comes."

Hewitt took out every drawer of the bureau, and examined every part of each before he laid it aside. Then he produced a small pair of silver callipers and an ivory pocket-rule and went over every inch of the heavy framework, measuring, comparing, tapping, adding, and subtracting dimensions. In the end he rose to his feet satisfied. "There is most certainly nothing concealed there," he said.

The drawers were put back, and Mr. Crellan suggested lunch. At Hewitt's suggestion it was brought to the study.

"So far," Hewitt said, "we arrive at this: either Mr. Holford has destroyed his will, or he has most effectually concealed it, or somebody has stolen it. The first of these possibilities you don't favour."

"I don't believe it is a possibility for a moment. I have told you why; and I knew Holford so well, you know. For the same reasons I am sure he never concealed it."

"Very well, then. Somebody has stolen it. The question is, who?"

"That is so."

"It seems to me that everyone in this house had a direct and personal interest in preserving that will. The servants have all something left them, you say, and without the will that goes, of course. Miss Garth has the greatest possible interest in the will. The only person I have heard of as yet who would benefit by its loss or destruction would be the nephew, Mr. Mellis. There are no other relatives, you say, who would benefit by intestacy?"

"Not one."

"Well, what do you think yourself, now? Have you any suspicions?"

Mr. Crellan shrugged his shoulders. "I've no more right to suspicions than you have, I suppose," he said. "Of course, if there are to be suspicions they can only point one way. Mr. Mellis is the only person who can gain by the disappearance of this will."

"Just so, Now, what do you know of him?"

"I don't know much of the young man," Mr. Crellan said slowly. "I must say I never particularly took to him. He is rather a clever fellow, I believe. He was called to the bar some time ago, and afterwards studied medicine, I believe, with the idea of priming himself for a practice in medical jurisprudence. He took a good deal of interest in my old friend's researches, I am told—at any rate he *said* he did; he may have been thinking of his uncle's fortune. But they had a small tiff on some medical question. I don't know exactly what it was, but Mr. Holford objected to something—a method of research or something of that kind—as being dangerous and unprofessional. There was no actual rupture between them, you understand, but Mellis's visits slacked off, and there was a coolness."

"Where is Mr. Mellis now?"

"In London, I believe."

"Has he been in this house between the day you last saw the will in that drawer and yesterday, when you failed to find it?"

"Only once. He came to see his uncle two days before his death—last Saturday, in fact. He didn't stay long."

"Did you see him?"

"Yes."

"What did he do?"

"Merely came into the room for a few minutes—visitors weren't

190

allowed to stay long—spoke a little to his uncle, and went back to town."

"Did he do nothing else, or see anybody else?"

"Miss Garth went out of the room with him as he left, and I should think they talked for a little before he went away, to judge by the time she was gone; but I don't know."

"You are sure he went then?"

"I saw him in the drive as I looked from the window."

"Miss Garth, you say, has kept all the keys since the beginning of Mr. Holford's illness?"

"Yes, until she gave them up to me yesterday. Indeed, the nurse, who is rather a peppery customer, and was jealous of Miss Garth's presence in the sick room all along, made several difficulties about having to go to her for everything."

"And there is no doubt of the bureau having been kept locked all the time?"

"None at all. I have asked Miss Garth that—and, indeed, a good many other things—without saying why I wanted the information."

"How are Mr. Mellis and Miss Garth affected toward one another—are they friendly?"

"Oh, yes. Indeed, some while ago I rather fancied that Mellis was disposed to pay serious addresses in that quarter. He may have had a fancy that way, or he may have been attracted by the young lady's expectations. At any rate, nothing definite seems to have come of it as yet. But I must say—between ourselves, of course—I have more than once noticed a decided air of agitation, shyness perhaps, in Miss Garth when Mr. Mellis has been present. But, at any rate, that scarcely matters. She is twenty-four years of age now, and can do as she likes. Although, if I had anything to say in the matter—well, never mind."

"You, I take it, have known Miss Garth a long time?"

"Bless you, yes. Danced her on my knee twenty years ago. I've been her 'Uncle Leonard' all her life."

"Well, I think we must at least let Miss Garth know of the loss of the will. Perhaps, when they have cleared away these plates, she will come here for a few minutes."

"I'll go and ask her," Mr. Crellan answered, and having rung the bell, proceeded to find Miss Garth.

Presently he returned with the lady. She was a slight, very pale young woman; no doubt rather pretty in ordinary, but now not looking her best. She was evidently worn and nervous from anxiety and want of sleep, and her eyes were sadly inflamed. As the wind slammed a loose casement behind her she started nervously, and placed her hand to her head.

"Sit down at once, my dear," Mr. Crellan said; "sit down. This is Mr. Martin Hewitt, whom I have taken the liberty of inviting down here to help me in a very important matter. The fact is, my dear," Mr. Crellan added gravely, "I can't find your poor father's will."

Miss Garth was not surprised. "I thought so," she said mildly, "when you asked me about the bureau yesterday."

"Of course I need not say, my dear, what a serious thing it may be for you if that will cannot be found. So I hope you'll try and tell Mr. Hewitt here anything he wants to know as well as you can, without forgetting a single thing. I'm pretty sure that he will find it for us if it is to be found."

"I understand, Miss Garth," Hewitt asked, "that the keys of that bureau never left your possession during the whole time of Mr. Holford's last illness, and that the bureau was kept locked?"

"Yes, that is so."

"Did you ever have occasion to go to the bureau yourself?"

"No, I have not touched it."

"Then you can answer for it, I presume, that the bureau was never unlocked by *anyone* from the time Mr. Holford placed the keys in your hands till you gave them to Mr. Crellan?"

"Yes, I am sure of that."

"Very good. Now is there any place on the whole premises that you can suggest where this will may possibly be hidden?"

"There is no place that Mr. Crellan doesn't know of, I'm sure."

"It is an old house, I observe," Hewitt pursued. "Do you know of any place of concealment in the structure—any secret doors, I mean, you know, or sliding panels, or hollow door frames, and so forth?"

Miss Garth shook her head. "There is not a single place of the sort you speak of in the whole building, so far as I know," she said, "and I have lived here almost all my life."

"You knew the purport of Mr. Holford's will, I take it, and understand what its loss may mean to yourself?"

"Perfectly."

"Now I must ask you to consider carefully. Take your mind back to two or three days before Mr. Holford's illness began, and tell me if you can remember any single fact, occurrence, word, or hint from that day to this in any way bearing on the will or anything connected with it?"

192

Miss Garth shook her head thoughtfully. "I can't remember the thing being mentioned by anybody, except perhaps by the nurse, who is rather a touchy sort of woman, and once or twice took it upon herself to hint that my recent anxiety was chiefly about my poor father's money. And that once, when I had done some small thing for him, my father—I have always called him father, you know—said that he wouldn't forget it, or that I should be rewarded, or something of that sort. Nothing else that I can remember in the remotest degree concerned the will."

"Mr. Mellis said nothing about it, then?"

Miss Garth changed colour slightly, but answered, "No, I only saw him to the door."

"Thank you, Miss Garth, I won't trouble you any further just now. But if you *can* remember anything more in the course of the next few hours it may turn out to be of great service."

Miss Garth bowed and withdrew. Mr. Crellan shut the door behind her and returned to Hewitt. "*That* doesn't carry us much further," he said. "The more certain it seems that the will cannot have been got at, the more difficult our position is from a legal point of view. What shall we do now?"

"Is the nurse still about the place?"

"Yes, I believe so."

"Then I'll speak to her."

The nurse came in response to Mr. Crellan's summons: a sharp-featured, pragmatical woman of forty-five. She took the seat offered her, and waited for Hewitt's questions.

"You were in attendance on Mr. Holford, I believe, Mrs. Turton, since the beginning of his last illness?"

"Since October 24th."

"Were you present when Mr. Mellis came to see his uncle last Saturday?"

"Yes."

"Can you tell me what took place?"

"As to what the gentleman said to Mr. Holford," the nurse replied, bridling slightly, "of course I don't know anything, it not being my business and not intended for my ears. Mr. Crellan was there, and knows as much as I do, and so does Miss Garth. I only know that Mr. Mellis stayed for a few minutes and then went out of the room with Miss Garth."

"How long was Miss Garth gone?"

"I don't know, ten minutes or a quarter of an hour, perhaps."

"Now Mrs. Turton, I want you to tell me in confidence—it is very important—whether you, at any time, heard Mr. Holford during his illness say anything of his wishes as to how his property was to be left in case of his death?"

The nurse started and looked keenly from Hewitt to Mr. Crellan and back again.

"Is it the will you mean?" she asked sharply.

"Yes. Did he mention it?"

"You mean you can't find the will, isn't that it?"

"Well, suppose it is, what then?"

"Suppose won't do," the nurse answered shortly; "I *do* know something about the will, and I believe you can't find it."

"I'm sure, Mrs. Turton, that if you know anything about the will you will tell Mr. Crellan in the interests of right and justice."

"And who's to protect me against the spite of those I shall offend if I tell you?"

Mr. Crellan interposed.

"Whatever you tell us, Mrs. Turton," he said, "will be held in the strictest confidence, and the source of our information shall not be divulged. For that I give you my word of honour. And, I need scarcely add, I will see that you come to no harm by anything you may say."

"Then the will *is* lost. I may understand that?"

Hewitt's features were impassive and impenetrable. But in Mr. Crellan's disturbed face the nurse saw a plain answer in the affirmative.

"Yes," she said, "I see that's the trouble. Well, I know who took it."

"Then who was it?"

"*Miss Garth!*"

"Miss Garth! Nonsense!" cried Mr. Crellan, starting upright. "Nonsense!"

"It may be nonsense," the nurse replied slowly, with a monotonous emphasis on each word. "It may be nonsense, but it's a fact. I saw her take it."

Mr. Crellan simply gasped. Hewitt drew his chair a little nearer.

"If you saw her take it," he said gently, closely watching the woman's face the while, "then, of course, there's no doubt."

"I tell you I saw her take it," the nurse repeated. "What was in it, and what her game was in taking it, I don't know. But it was in that bureau, wasn't it?"

"Yes—probably."

"In the right hand top drawer?"

"Yes."

"A white paper in a blue envelope?"

"Yes."

"Then I saw her take it, as I said before. She unlocked that drawer before my eyes, took it out, and locked the drawer again."

Mr. Crellan turned blankly to Hewitt, but Hewitt kept his eyes on the nurse's face.

"When did this occur?" he asked, "and how?"

"It was on Saturday night, rather late. Everybody was in bed but Miss Garth and myself, and she had been down to the dining-room for something. Mr. Holford was asleep, so as I wanted to re-fill the water-bottle, I took it up and went. As I was passing the door of this room that we are in now, I heard a noise, and looked in at the door, which was open. There was a candle on the table which had been left there earlier in the evening. Miss Garth was opening the top right hand drawer of *that* bureau"—Mrs. Turton stabbed her finger spitefully toward the piece of furniture, as though she owed it a personal grudge—"and I saw he take out a blue foolscap envelope, and as the flap was open, I could see the enclosed paper was white. She shut the drawer, locked it, and came out of the room with the envelope in her hand."

"And what did you do?"

"I hurried on, and she came away without seeing me, and went in the opposite direction—toward the small staircase."

"Perhaps," Mr. Crellan ventured at a blurt, "perhaps she was walking in her sleep?"

"That she wasn't!" the nurse replied, "for she came back to Mr. Holford's room almost as soon as I returned there, and asked some questions about the medicine—which was nothing new, for I must say she was very fond of interfering in things that were part of my business."

"That is quite certain, I suppose," Hewitt remarked—"that she could not have been asleep?"

"Quite certain. She talked for about a quarter of an hour, and wanted to kiss Mr. Holford, which might have wakened him, before she went to bed. In fact, I may say we had a disagreement."

Hewitt did not take his steady gaze from the nurse's face for some seconds after she had finished speaking. Then he only said, "Thank you, Mrs. Turton. I need scarcely assure you, after what Mr. Crellan has said, that your confidence shall not be betrayed. I think that is all, unless you have more to tell us."

Mrs. Turton bowed and rose. "There is nothing more," she said, and left the room.

As soon as she had gone, "Is Mrs. Turton at all interested in the will," Hewitt asked.

"No, there is nothing for her. She is a newcomer, you see. Perhaps," Mr. Crellan went on, struck by an idea, "she may be jealous, or something. She seems a spiteful woman—and really, I can't believe her story for a moment."

"Why?"

"Well, you see, it's absurd. Why should Miss Garth go to all this secret trouble to do herself an injury—to make a beggar of herself? And besides, she's not in the habit of telling barefaced lies. She distinctly assured us, you remember, that she had never been to the bureau for any purpose whatever."

"But the nurse has an honest character, hasn't she?"

"Yes, her character is excellent. Indeed, from all accounts, she is a very excellent woman, except for a desire to govern everybody, and a habit of spite if she is thwarted. But, of course, that sort of thing sometimes leads people rather far."

"So it does," Hewitt replied. "But consider now. Is it not possible that Miss Garth, completely infatuated with Mr. Mellis, thinks she is doing a noble thing for him by destroying the will and giving up her whole claim to his uncle's property? Devoted women do just such things, you know."

Mr. Crellan stared, bent his head to his hand, and considered. "So they do, so they do," he said. "Insane foolery. Really, it's the sort of thing I can imagine her doing—she's honour and generosity itself. But then those lies," he resumed, sitting up and slapping his leg; "I can't believe she'd tell such tremendous lies as that for anybody. And with such a calm face, too—I'm sure she couldn't."

"Well, that's as it may be. You can scarcely set a limit to the lengths a woman will go on behalf of a man she loves. I suppose, by the bye, Miss Garth is not exactly what you would call a 'strong-minded' woman?"

"No, she's not that. She'd never get on in the world by herself. She's a good little soul, but nervous—very; and her month of anxiety, grief, and want of sleep seems to have broken her up."

"Mr. Mellis knows of the death, I suppose?"

"I telegraphed to him at his chambers in London the first thing yesterday—Tuesday—morning, as soon as the telegraph office was open. He came here (as I've forgotten to tell you as yet) the first thing this morning—before I was over here myself, in fact. He had been staying not far off—at Ockham, I think—and the telegram had been sent on. He saw Miss Garth, but couldn't stay, having to get back to London. I met him going away as I came, about eleven o'clock. Of course I said nothing about the fact that I couldn't find the will, but he will probably be down again soon, and may ask questions."

"Yes," Hewitt replied. "And speaking of that matter, you can no doubt talk with Miss Garth on very intimate and familiar terms?"

"Oh yes—yes; I've told you what old friends we are."

"I wish you could manage, at some favourable opportunity today, to speak to her alone, and without referring to the will in any way, get to know, as circumspectly and delicately as you can, how she stands in regard to Mr. Mellis. Whether he is an accepted lover, or likely to be one, you know. Whatever answer you may get, you may judge, I expect, by her manner how things really are."

"Very good—I'll seize the first chance. Meanwhile what to do?"

"Nothing, I'm afraid, except perhaps to examine other pieces of furniture as closely as we have examined this bureau."

Other bureaux, desks, tables, and chests were examined fruitlessly. It was not until after dinner that Mr. Crellan saw a favourable opportunity of sounding Miss Garth as he had promised. Half an hour later he came to Hewitt in the study, more puzzled than ever.

"There's no engagement between them," he reported, "secret or open, nor ever has been. It seems, from what I can make out, going to work as diplomatically as possible, that Mellis *did* propose to her, or something very near it, a time ago, and was point-blank refused. Altogether, Miss Garth's sentiment for him appears to be rather dislike than otherwise."

"That rather knocks a hole in the theory of self-sacrifice, doesn't it?" Hewitt remarked. "I shall have to think over this, and sleep on it. It's possible that it may be necessary tomorrow for you to tax Miss Garth, point-blank, with having taken away the will. Still, I hope not."

"I hope not, too," Mr. Crellan said, rather dubious as to the result of such an experiment. "She has been quite upset enough already. And, by the bye, she didn't seem any the better or more composed after Mellis' visit this morning."

"Still, *then* the will was gone."

"Yes."

And so Hewitt and Mr. Crellan talked on late into the evening, turning over every apparent possibility and finding reason in none. The household went to bed at ten, and, soon after, Miss Garth came to bid Mr. Crellan goodnight. It had been settled that both Martin Hewitt and Mr. Crellan should stay the night at Wedbury Hall.

Soon all was still, and the ticking of the tall clock in the hall below could be heard as distinctly as though it were in the study, while the rain without dropped from eaves and sills in regular splashes. Twelve o'clock struck, and Mr. Crellan was about to suggest retirement, when the sound of a light footstep startled Hewitt's alert ear. He raised his hand to enjoin silence, and stepped to the door of the room, Mr. Crellan following him.

There was a light over the staircase, seven or eight yards away, and down the stairs came Miss Garth in dressing gown and slippers; she turned at the landing and vanished in a passage leading to the right.

"Where does that lead to?" Hewitt whispered hurriedly.

"Toward the small staircase—other end of house," Mr. Crellan replied in the same tones.

"Come quietly," said Hewitt, and stepped lightly after Miss Garth, Mr. Crellan at his heels.

She was nearing the opposite end of the passage, walking at a fair pace and looking neither to right nor left. There was another light over the smaller staircase at the end. Without hesitation Miss Garth turned down the stairs till about half down the flight, and then stopped and pressed her hand against the oak wainscot.

Immediately the vertical piece of framing against which she had placed her hand turned on central pivots top and bottom, revealing a small recess, three feet high and little more than six inches wide. Miss Garth stooped and felt about at the bottom of this recess for several seconds. Then with every sign of extreme agitation and horror she withdrew her hand empty, and sank on the stairs. Her head rolled from side to side on her shoulders, and beads of perspiration stood on her forehead. Hewitt with difficulty restrained Mr. Crellan from going to her assistance.

Presently, with a sort of shuddering sigh, Miss Garth rose, and after standing irresolute for a moment, descended the flight of stairs to the bottom. There she stopped again, and pressing her hand to her forehead, turned and began to re-ascend the stairs.

Hewitt touched his companion's arm, and the two hastily but

noiselessly made their way back along the passage to the study. Miss Garth left the open framing as it was, reached the top of the landing, and without stopping proceeded along the passage and turned up the main staircase, while Hewitt and Mr. Crellan still watched her from the study door.

At the top of the flight she turned to the right, and up three or four more steps toward her own room. There she stopped, and leaned thoughtfully on the handrail.

"Go up," whispered Hewitt to Mr. Crellan, "as though you were going to bed. Appear surprised to see her; ask if she isn't well, and, if you can, manage to repeat that question of mine about secret hiding-places in the house."

Mr. Crellan nodded and started quickly up the stairs. Half-way up he turned his head, and, as he went on, "Why, Nelly, my dear," he said, "what's the matter? Aren't you well?"

Mr. Crellan acted his part well, and waiting below, Hewitt heard this dialogue:

"No, uncle, I don't feel very well, but it's nothing. I think my room seems close. I can scarcely breathe."

"Oh, it isn't close tonight. You'll be catching cold, my dear. Go and have a good sleep; you mustn't worry that wise little head of yours, you know. Mr. Hewitt and I have been making quite a night of it, but I'm off to bed now."

"I hope they've made you both quite comfortable, uncle?"

"Oh, yes; capital, capital. We've been talking over business, and, no doubt, we shall put that matter all in order soon. By the bye, I suppose since you saw Mr. Hewitt you haven't happened to remember anything more to tell him?"

"No."

"You still can't remember any hiding-places or panels, or that sort of thing in the wainscot or anywhere?"

"No, I'm sure I don't know of any, and I don't believe for a moment that any exist."

"Quite sure of that, I suppose?"

"Oh yes."

"All right. Now go to bed. You'll catch *such* a cold in these draughty landings. Come, I won't move a step till I see your door shut behind you. Goodnight."

"Goodnight, uncle."

Mr. Crellan came downstairs again with a face of blank puzzlement.

"I wouldn't have believed it," he assured Martin Hewitt; "positively I wouldn't have believed she'd have told such a lie, and with such confidence, too. There's something deep and horrible here, I'm afraid. What does it mean?"

"We'll talk of that afterwards," Hewitt replied. "Come now and take a look at that recess."

They went, quietly still, to the small staircase, and there, with a candle, closely examined the recess. It was a mere box, three feet high, a foot or a little more deep, and six or seven inches wide. The piece of oak framing, pivoted to the stair at the bottom and to a horizontal piece of framing at the top, stood edge forward, dividing the opening down the centre. There was nothing whatever in the recess.

Hewitt ascertained that there was no catch, the plank simply remaining shut by virtue of fitting tightly, so that nothing but pressure on the proper part was requisite to open it. He had closed the plank and turned to speak to Mr. Crellan, when another interruption occurred.

On each floor the two staircases were joined by passages, and the ground-floor passage, from the foot of the flight they were on, led to the entrance hall. Distinct amid the loud clicking of the hall clock, Hewitt now heard a sound, as of a person's foot shifting on a stone step.

Mr. Crellan heard it too, and each glanced at the other. Then Hewitt, shading the candle with his hand, led the way to the hall. There they listened for several seconds—almost an hour—it seemed—and then the noise was repeated. There was no doubt of it. It was at the other side of the front door.

In answer to Hewitt's hurried whispers, Mr. Crellan assured him that there was no window from which, in the dark, a view could be got of a person standing outside the door. Also that any other way out would be equally noisy, and would entail the circuit of the house. The front door was fastened by three heavy bolts, an immense old-fashioned lock, and a bar. It would take nearly a minute to open at least, even if everything went easily. But, as there was no other way, Hewitt determined to try it. Handing the candle to his companion, he first lifted the bar, conceiving that it might be done with the least noise. It went easily, and, handling it carefully, Hewitt let it hang from its rivet without a sound.

Just then, glancing at Mr. Crellan, he saw that he was forgetting to shade the candle, whose rays extended through the fanlight above the door, and probably through the wide crack under it. But it was too late. At the same moment the light was evidently perceived from outside; there was a hurried jump from the steps, and for an instant a sound of running on gravel. Hewitt tore back the bolts, flung the door open, and dashed out into the darkness, leaving Mr. Crellan on the doorstep with the candle.

Hewitt was gone, perhaps, five or ten minutes, although to Mr. Crellan—standing there at the open door in a state of high nervous tension, and with no notion of what was happening or what it all meant—the time seemed an eternity. When at last Hewitt reached the door again, "What was it?" asked Mr. Crellan, much agitated. "Did you see? Have you caught them?"

Hewitt shook his head.

"I hadn't a chance," he said. "The wall is low over there, and there's a plantation of trees at the other side. But I think—yes, I begin to think—that I may possibly be able to see my way through this business in a little while. See this?"

On the top step in the sheltered porch there remained the wet prints of two feet. Hewitt took a letter from his pocket, opened it out, spread it carefully over the more perfect of the two marks, pressed it lightly and lifted it. Then, when the door was shut, he produced his pocket scissors, and with great care cut away the paper round the wet part, leaving a piece, of course, the shape of a boot sole.

"Come," said Hewitt, "we may get at something after all. Don't ask me to tell you anything now; I don't know anything, as a matter of fact. I hope this is the end of the night's entertainment, but I'm afraid the case is rather an unpleasant business. There is nothing for us to do now but to go to bed, I think. I suppose there's a handy man kept about the place?"

"Yes, he's gardener and carpenter and carpet-beater, and so on."

"Good! Where's his sanctum? Where does he keep his shovels and carpet sticks?"

"In the shed by the coach house, I believe. I think it's generally unlocked."

"Very good. We've earned a night's rest, and now we'll have it."

The next morning, after breakfast, Hewitt took Mr. Crellan into the study.

"Can you manage," he said, "to send Miss Garth out for a walk this morning—with somebody?"

"I can send her out for a ride with the groom—unless she thinks it wouldn't be the thing to go riding so soon after her bereavement."

"Never mind, that will do. Send her at once, and see that she goes. Call it doctor's orders; say she must go for her health's sake—anything."

Mr. Crellan departed, used his influence, and in half an hour Miss Garth had gone.

"I was up pretty early this morning," Hewitt remarked on Mr. Crellan's return to the study, "and, among other things, I sent a telegram to London. Unless my eyes deceive me, a boy with a peaked cap—a telegraph boy, in fact—is coming up the drive this moment. Yes, he is. It is probably my answer."

In a few minutes a telegram was brought in. Hewitt read it and then asked,—

"Your friend Mr. Mellis, I understand, was going straight to town yesterday morning?"

"Yes."

"Read that, then."

Mr. Crellan took the telegram and read:

Mellis did not sleep at chambers last night. Been out of town for some days past. Kerrett.

Mr. Crellan looked up.

"Who's Kerrett?" he asked.

"Lad in my office; sharp fellow. You see, Mellis didn't go to town after all. As a matter of fact, I believe he was nearer this place than we thought. You said he had a disagreement with his uncle because of scientific practices which the old gentleman considered 'dangerous and unprofessional,' I think?"

"Yes, that was the case."

"Ah, then the key to all the mystery of the will is in this room."

"Where?"

"There." Hewitt pointed to the book-cases. "Read Bernheim's *Suggestive Therapeutics*, and one or two books of Heidenhain's and Björnström's and you'll see the thing more clearly than you can without them; but that would be rather a long sort of job, so——but why, who's this? Somebody coming up the drive in a fly, isn't it?"

"Yes," Mr. Crellan replied, looking out of the window. Presently he added, "It's Cranley Mellis."

"Ah," said Hewitt, "he won't trouble us for a little. I'll bet you a

202

penny cake he goes first by himself to the small staircase and tries that secret recess. If you get a little way along the passage you will be able to see him; but that will scarcely matter—I can see you don't guess now what I am driving at."

"I don't in the least."

"I told you the names of the books in which you could read the matter up; but that would be too long for the present purpose. The thing is fairly well summarised, I see, in that encyclopaedia there in the corner. I have put a marker in volume seven. Do you mind opening it at that place and seeing for yourself?"

Mr. Crellan, doubtful and bewildered, reached the volume. It opened readily, and in the place where it opened lay a blue foolscap envelope. The old gentleman took the envelope, drew from it a white paper, stared first at the paper, then at Hewitt, then at the paper again, let the volume slide from his lap, and gasped,—

"Why—why—it's the will!"

"Ah, so I thought," said Hewitt, catching the book as it fell. "But don't lose this place in the encyclopaedia. Read the name of the article. What is it?"

Mr. Crellan looked absent-mindedly at the title, holding the will before him all the time. Then, mechanically, he read aloud the word, "*Hypnotism.*"

"Hypnotism it is," Hewitt answered. "A dangerous and terrible power in the hands of an unscrupulous man."

"But—but how? I don't understand it. This—this is the real will, I suppose?"

"Look at it; you know best."

Mr. Crellan looked.

"Yes," he said, "this certainly is the will. But where did it come from? It hasn't been in this book all the time, has it?"

"No. Didn't I tell you I put it there myself as a marker? But come, you'll understand my explanation better if I first read you a few lines from this article. See here now:—

Although hypnotism has power for good when properly used by medical men, it is an exceedingly dangerous weapon in the hands of the unskilful or unscrupulous. Crimes have been committed by persons who have been hypnotised. Just as a person when hypnotised is rendered extremely impressionable, and therefore capable of receiving beneficial suggestions, so he is

203

nearly as liable to receive suggestions for evil; and it is quite possible for an hypnotic subject, while under hypnotic influence, to be impressed with the belief that he is to commit some act after the influence is removed, and that act he is safe to commit, acting at the time as an automaton. Suggestions may be thus made of which the subject, in his subsequent uninfluenced moments, has no idea, but which he will proceed to carry out automatically at the time appointed. In the case of a complete state of hypnotism the subject has subsequently no recollection whatever of what has happened. Persons whose will or nerve power has been weakened by fear or other similar causes can be hypnotised without consent on their part.

". . . .there now, what do you make of that?"

"Why, do you mean that Miss Garth has been hypnotised by—by—Cranley Mellis?"

"I think that is the case; indeed, I am pretty sure of it. Notice, on the occasion of each of his last two visits, he was alone with Miss Garth for some little time. On the evening following each of those visits she does something which she afterwards knows nothing about—something connected with the disappearance of this will, the only thing standing between Mr. Mellis and the whole of his uncle's property. Who could have been in a weaker nervous state than Miss Garth has been lately? Remember, too, on the visit of last Saturday, while Miss Garth says she only showed Mellis to the door, both you and the nurse speak of their being gone some little time. Miss Garth must have forgotten what took place then, when Mellis hypnotised her, and impressed on her the suggestion that she should take Mr. Holford's will that night, long after he—Mellis—had gone, and when he could not be suspected of knowing anything of it. Further, that she should, at that time when her movements would be less likely to be observed, secrete that will in a place of hiding known only to himself."

"Dear, dear, what a rascal! Do you really think he did that?"

"Not only that, but I believe he came here yesterday morning while you were out to get the will from the recess. The recess, by the bye, I expect he discovered by accident on one of his visits (he has been here pretty often, I suppose, altogether), and kept the secret in case it might be useful. Yesterday, not finding the will there, he hypnotised Miss Garth once again, and conveyed the suggestion that, at midnight last night, she should take the will from wherever she had put it and pass it to him under the front door."

"What, do you mean it was he you chased across the grounds last night?"

"That is a thing I am pretty certain of. If we had Mr. Mellis's boot here we could make sure by comparing it with the piece of paper I cut out, as you will remember, in the entrance hall. As we have the will, though, that will scarcely be necessary. What he will do now, I expect, will be to go to the recess again on the vague chance of the will being there now, after all, assuming that his second dose of mesmerism has somehow miscarried. If Miss Garth were here he might try his tricks again, and that is why I got you to send her out."

"And where did you find the will?"

"Now you come to practical details. You will remember that I asked about the handyman's tool-house? Well, I paid it a visit at six o'clock this morning, and found therein some very excellent carpenter's tools in a chest. I took a selection of them to the small staircase, and took out the tread of a stair—the one that the pivoted framing-plank rested on."

"And you found the will there?"

"The will, as I rather expected when I examined the recess last night, had slipped down a rather wide crack at the end of the stair timber, which, you know, formed, so to speak, the floor of the recess. The fact was, the stair-tread didn't quite reach as far as the back of the recess. The opening wasn't very distinct to see, but I soon felt it with my fingers. When Miss Garth, in her hypnotic condition on Saturday night, dropped the will into the recess, it shot straight to the back corner and fell down the slit. That was why Mellis found it empty, and why Miss Garth also found it empty on returning there last night under hypnotic influence. You observed her terrible state of nervous agitation when she failed to carry out the command that haunted her. It was frightful. Something like what happens to a suddenly awakened somnambulist, perhaps. Anyway, that is all over. I found the will under the end of the stair-tread, and here it is. If you will come to the small staircase now you shall see where the paper slipped out of sight. Perhaps we shall meet Mr. Mellis."

"He's a scoundrel," said Mr. Crellan. "It's a pity we can't punish him."

"That's impossible, of course. Where's your proof? And if you had any I'm not sure that a hypnotist is responsible at law for what his subject does. Even if he were, moving a will from one part of the house to another is scarcely a legal crime. The explanation I have given you accounts entirely for the disturbed manner of Miss Garth in the presence of Mellis. She merely felt an indefinite sense of his power over her. Indeed, there is all the possibility that, finding her an easy subject, he had already practised his influence by way of experiment. A hypnotist, as you will see in the books, has always an easier task with a person he has hypnotised before."

As Hewitt had guessed, in the corridor they met Mr. Mellis. He was a thin, dark man of about thirty-five, with large, bony features, and a slight stoop. Mr. Crellan glared at him ferociously.

"Well, sir, and what do you want?" he asked.

Mr. Mellis looked surprised. "Really, that's a very extraordinary remark, Mr. Crellan," he said. "This is my late uncle's house. I might, with at least as much reason, ask you what you want."

"I'm here, sir, as Mr. Holford's executor."

"Appointed by will?"

"Yes."

"And is the will in existence?"

"Well—the fact is—we couldn't find it——"

"Then, what do you mean, sir, by calling yourself an executor with no will to warrant you?" interrupted Mellis. "Get out of this house. If there's no will, I administrate."

"But there *is* a will," roared Mr. Crellan, shaking it in his face. "There is a will. I didn't say we hadn't found it yet, did I? There *is* a will, and here it is in spite of all your diabolical tricks, with your scoundrelly hypnotism and secret holes, and the rest of it! Get out of this place, sir, or I'll have you thrown out of the window!"

Mr. Mellis shrugged his shoulders with an appearance of perfect indifference. "If you've a will appointing you executor it's all right, I suppose, although I shall take care to hold you responsible for any irregularities. As I don't in the least understand your conduct, unless it is due to drink, I'll leave you." And with that he went.

Mr. Crellan boiled with indignation for a minute, and then turning to Hewitt, "I say, I hope it's all right," he said, "connecting him with all this queer business?"

"We shall soon see," replied Hewitt, "if you'll come and look at the pivoted plank."

They went to the small staircase, and Hewitt once again opened the recess. Within lay a blue foolscap envelope, which Hewitt picked up. "See," he said, "it is torn at the corner. He has been here and opened it. It's a fresh envelope, and I left it for him this morning, with the corner gummed down a little so that he would have to tear it in opening. This is what was inside," Hewitt added, and laughed aloud as he drew forth a rather crumpled piece of white paper. "It was only a childish trick after all," he concluded, "but I always liked a small practical joke on occasion." He held out the crumpled paper, on which was inscribed in large capital letters the single word—"SOLD."

THE CASE OF THE MISSING HAND

I think I have recorded in another place Hewitt's frequent aphorism that "there is nothing in this world that is at all possible that has not happened or is not happening in London." But there are many strange happenings in this matter-of-fact country and in these matter-of-fact times that occur far enough from London. Fantastic crimes, savage revenges, medieval superstitions, horrible cruelty, though less in sight, have been no more extinguished by the advent of the nineteenth century than have the ancient races who practised them in the dark ages. Some of the races have become civilized, and some of the savageries are heard of no more. But there are survivals in both cases. I say these things having in my mind a particular case that came under the personal notice of both Hewitt and myself—an affair that brought one up standing with a gasp and a doubt of one's era.

My good uncle, the Colonel, was not in the habit of gathering large house parties at his place at Ratherby, partly because the place was not a great one, and partly because the Colonel's gout was. But there was an excellent bit of shooting for two or three guns, and even when he was unable to leave the house himself, my uncle was always pleased if some good friend were enjoying a good day's sport in his territory. As to myself, the good old soul was in a perpetual state of offence because I visited him so seldom, though whenever my scant holidays fell in a convenient time of the year I was never insensible to the attractions of the Ratherby stubble.

More than once had I sat by the old gentleman when his foot was exceptionally troublesome, amusing him with accounts of some of the doings of Martin Hewitt, and more than once had my uncle expressed his desire to meet Hewitt himself, and commissioned me with an invitation to be presented to Hewitt at the first likely opportunity, for a joint excursion to Ratherby. At length I persuaded Hewitt to take a fortnight's rest, coincident with a little vacation of my own, and we got down to Ratherby within a few days past September the 1st, and before a gun had been fired at the Colonel's bit of shooting. The Colonel himself we found confined to the house with his foot on the familiar rest, and though ourselves were the only guests, we managed to do pretty well together. It was during this short holiday that the case I have mentioned arose.

When first I began to record some of the more interesting of Hewitt's operations, I think I explained that such cases as I myself had not witnessed I should set down in impersonal narrative form, without intruding myself. The present case, so far as Hewitt's work was concerned, I saw, but there were circumstances which led up to it that we only fully learned afterwards. These circumstances, however, I shall put in their proper place—at the beginning.

The Fosters were a fairly old Ratherby family, of whom Mr. John Foster had died by an accident at the age of about forty, leaving a wife twelve years younger than himself and three children, two boys and one girl, who was the youngest. The boys grew up strong, healthy, out-of-door young ruffians, with all the tastes of sportsmen, and all the qualities, good and bad, natural to lads of fairly well-disposed character allowed a great deal too much of their own way from the beginning.

Their only real bad quality was an unfortunate knack of bearing malice, and a certain savage vindictiveness towards such persons as they chose to consider their enemies. With the louts of the village they were at unceasing war, and, indeed, once got into serious trouble for peppering the butcher's son (who certainly was a great blackguard) with sparrow-shot. At the usual time they went to Oxford together, and were fraternally sent down together in their second year, after enjoying a spell of rustication in their first. The offence was never specifically mentioned about Ratherby, but was rumoured of as something particularly outrageous.

It was at this time, sixteen years or thereabout after the death of their father, that Henry and Robert Foster first saw and disliked Mr. Jonas Sneathy, a director of penny banks and small insurance offices. He visited Ranworth (the Fosters' home) a great deal more than the brothers thought necessary, and, indeed, it was not for lack of rudeness on their part that Mr. Sneathy failed to understand, as far as they were concerned, his room was preferred to his company.

But their mother welcomed him, and in the end it was announced that Mrs. Foster was to marry again, and that after that her name would be Mrs. Sneathy.

Hereupon there were violent scenes at Ranworth. Henry and

Robert Foster denounced their prospective father-in-law as a fortune-hunter, a snuffler, a hypocrite. They did not stop at broad hints as to the honesty of his penny banks and insurance offices, and the house straightway became a house of bitter strife. The marriage took place, and it was not long before Mr. Sneathy's real character became generally obvious. For months he was a model, if somewhat sanctimonious husband, and his influence over his wife was complete. Then he discovered that her property had been strictly secured by her first husband's will, and that, willing as she might be, she was unable to raise money for her new husband's benefit, and was quite powerless to pass to him any of her property by deed of gift. Hereupon the man's nature showed itself.

Foolish woman as Mrs. Sneathy might be, she was a loving, indeed, an infatuated wife; but Sneathy repaid her devotion by vulgar derision, never hesitating to state plainly that he had married her for his own profit, and that he considered himself swindled in the result. More, he even proceeded to blows and other practical brutality of a sort only devisable by a mean and ugly nature. This treatment, at first secret, became open, and in the midst of it Mr. Sneathy's penny banks and insurance offices came to a grievous smash all at once, and everybody wondered how Mr. Sneathy kept out of gaol.

Keep out of gaol he did, however, for he had taken care to remain on the safe side of the law, though some of his co-directors learnt the taste of penal servitude. But he was beggared, and lived, as it were, a mere pensioner in his wife's house. Here his brutality increased to a frightful extent, till his wife, already broken in health in consequence, went in constant fear of her life, and Miss Foster passed a life of weeping misery. All her friends' entreaties, however, could not persuade Mrs. Sneathy to obtain a legal separation from her husband. She clung to him with the excuse—for it was no more—that she hoped to win him to kindness by submission, and with a pathetic infatuation that seemed to increase as her bodily strength diminished.

Henry and Robert, as may be supposed, were anything but silent in these circumstances. Indeed, they broke out violently again and again, and more than once went near permanently injuring their worthy father-in-law. Once especially, when Sneathy, absolutely without provocation, made a motion to strike his wife in their presence, there was a fearful scene. The two sprang at him like wild beasts, knocked him down and dragged him to the balcony with the intention of throwing him out of the window. But Mrs. Sneathy impeded them, hysterically imploring them to desist.

"If you lift your hand to my mother," roared Henry, gripping Sneathy by the throat till his fat face turned blue, and banging his head against the wall, "if you lift your hand to my mother again I'll chop it off—I will! I'll chop it off and drive it down your throat!"

"We'll do worse," said Robert, white and frantic with passion, "we'll hang you—hang you to the door! You're a proved liar and thief, and you're worse than a common murderer. I'd hang you to the front door for twopence!"

For a few days Sneathy was comparatively quiet, cowed by their violence. Then he took to venting redoubled spite on his unfortunate wife, always in the absence of her sons, well aware that she would never inform them. On their part, finding him apparently better behaved in consequence of their attack, they thought to maintain his wholesome terror, and scarcely passed him without a menace, taking a fiendish delight in repeating the threats they had used during the scene, by way of keeping it present to his mind.

"Take care of your hands, sir," they would say. "Keep them to yourself, or, by George, we'll take 'em off with a billhook!"

But his revenge for all this Sneathy took unobserved on their mother. Truly a miserable household.

Soon, however, the brothers left home, and went to London by way of looking for a profession. Henry began a belated study of medicine, and Robert made a pretence of reading for the bar. Indeed, their departure was as much as anything a consequence of the earnest entreaty of their sister, who saw that their presence at home was an exasperation to Sneathy, and aggravated her mother's secret sufferings. They went, therefore; but at Ranworth things became worse.

Little was allowed to be known outside the house, but it was broadly said that Mr. Sneathy's behaviour had now become outrageous beyond description. Servants left faster than new ones could be found, and gave their late employer the character of a raving maniac. Once, indeed, he committed himself in the village, attacking with his walking-stick an inoffensive tradesman who had accidentally brushed against him, and immediately running home. This assault had to be compounded for by a payment of fifty pounds. And then Henry and Robert Foster received a most urgent letter from their sister requesting their immediate presence at home.

They went at once, of course, and the servants' account of what occurred was this. When the brothers arrived Mr. Sneathy had just left the house. The brothers were shut up with their mother and sister for about a quarter of an hour, and then left them and came out to the stable yard together. The coachman (he was a new man, who had only arrived the day before) overheard a little of their talk as they stood by the door.

Mr. Henry said that "the thing must be done, and at once. There are two of us, so that it ought to be easy enough." And afterwards Mr. Robert said, "You'll know best how to go about it, as a doctor." After which Mr. Henry came towards the coachman and asked in what direction Mr. Sneathy had gone. The coachman replied that it was in the direction of Ratherby Wood, by the winding footpath that led through it. But as he spoke he distinctly with the corner of his eye saw the other brother take a halter from a hook by the stable door and put it into his coat pocket.

So far for the earlier events, whereof I learned later bit by bit. It was on the day of the arrival of the brothers Foster at their old home, and, indeed, little more than two hours after the incident last set down, that news of Mr. Sneathy came to Colonel Brett's place, where Hewitt and I were sitting and chatting with the Colonel. The news was that Mr. Sneathy had committed suicide—had been found hanging, in fact, to a tree in Ratherby Wood, just by the side of the footpath.

Hewitt and I had of course at this time never heard of Sneathy, and the Colonel told us what little he knew. He had never spoken to the man, he said—indeed, nobody in the place outside Ranworth would have anything to do with him. "He's certainly been an unholy scoundrel over those poor people's banks," said my uncle, "and if what they say's true, he's been about as bad as possible to his wretched wife. He must have been pretty miserable, too, with all his scoundrelism, for he was a completely ruined man, without a chance of retrieving his position, and detested by everybody. Indeed, some of his recent doings, if what I have heard is to be relied on, have been very much those of a madman. So that, on the whole, I'm not much surprised. Suicide's about the only crime, I suppose, that he has never experimented with till now, and, indeed, it's rather a service to the world at large—his only service, I expect."

The Colonel sent a man to make further inquiries, and presently this man returned with the news that now it was said that Mr. Sneathy had not committed suicide, but had been murdered. And hard on the man's heels came Mr. Hardwick, a neighbour of my uncle's and a fellow J. P. He had had the case reported to him, it seemed, as soon as the body had been found, and had at once gone to the spot. He had found the body hanging—*and with the right hand cut off.*

"It's a murder, Brett," he said, "without doubt—a most horrible case of murder and mutilation. The hand is cut off and taken away, but whether the atrocity was committed before or after the hanging of course I can't say. But the missing hand makes it plainly a case of murder, and not suicide. I've come to consult you about issuing a warrant, for I think there's no doubt as to the identity of the murderers."

"That's a good job," said the Colonel, "else we should have had some work for Mr. Martin Hewitt here, which wouldn't be fair, as he's taking a rest. Whom do you think of having arrested?"

"The two young Fosters. It's plain as it can be—and a most revolting crime too, bad as Sneathy may have been. They came down from London today and went out deliberately to it, it's clear. They were heard talking of it, asked as to the direction in which he had gone, and followed him—and with a rope."

"Isn't that rather an unusual form of murder—hanging?" Hewitt remarked.

"Perhaps it is," Mr. Hardwick replied; "but it's the case here plain enough. It seems, in fact, that they had a way of threatening to hang him and even to cut off his hand if he used it to strike their mother. So that they appear to have carried out what might have seemed mere idle threats in a diabolically savage way. Of course they *may* have strangled him first and hanged him after, by way of carrying out their threat and venting their spite on the mutilated body. But that they did it is plain enough for me. I've spent an hour or two over it, and feel I am certainly more than justified in ordering their apprehension. Indeed, they were with him at the time, as I have found by their tracks on the footpath through the wood."

The Colonel turned to Martin Hewitt. "Mr. Hardwick, you must know," he said, "is by way of being an amateur in your particular line—and a very good amateur, too, I should say, judging by a case or two I have known in this county."

Hewitt bowed, and laughingly expressed a fear lest Mr. Hardwick should come to London and supplant him altogether. "This seems a curious case," he added. "If you don't mind, I think I should like to take a glance at the tracks and whatever other traces there may be, just by way of keeping my hand in."

"Certainly," Mr. Hardwick replied, brightening. "I should of all things like to have Mr. Hewitt's opinions on the observations I have made—just for my own gratification. As to his opinion—there can be no room for doubt; the thing is plain."

With many promises not to be late for dinner, we left my uncle and walked with Mr. Hardwick in the direction of Ratherby Wood. It was an unfrequented part, he told us, and by particular care he had managed, he hoped, to prevent the rumour spreading to the village yet, so that we might hope to find the trails not yet overlaid. It was a man of his own, he said, who, making a short cut through the wood, had come upon the body hanging, and had run immediately to inform him. With this man he had gone back, cut down the body, and made his observations. He had followed the trail backward to Ranworth, and there had found the new coachman, who had once been in his own service. From him he had learned the doings of the brothers Foster as they left the place, and from him he had ascertained that they had not then returned. Then, leaving his man by the body, he had come straight to my uncle's.

Presently we came on the footpath leading from Ranworth across the field to Ratherby Wood. It was a mere trail of bare earth worn by successive feet amid the grass. It was damp, and we all stooped and examined the footmarks that were to be seen on it. They all pointed one way—towards the wood in the distance.

"Fortunately it's not a greatly frequented path," Mr. Hardwick said. "You see, there are the marks of three pairs of feet only, and as first Sneathy and then both of the brothers came this way, these footmarks must be theirs. Which are Sneathy's is plain—they are these large flat ones. If you notice, they are all distinctly visible in the centre of the track, showing plainly that they belong to the man who walked alone, which was Sneathy. Of the others, the marks of the *outside* feet—the left on the left side and the right on the right—are often not visible. Clearly they belong to two men walking side by side, and more often than not treading, with their outer feet, on the grass at the side. And where these happen to drop on the same spot as the marks in the middle they cover them. Plainly they are the footmarks of Henry and Robert Foster, made as they followed Sneathy. Don't you agree with me Mr. Hewitt?"

"Oh yes, that's very plain. You have a better pair of eyes than most people, Mr. Hardwick, and a good idea of using them, too. We will go into the wood now. As a matter of fact, I can pretty clearly distinguish most of the other footmarks—those on the grass; but that's a matter of much training."

We followed the footpath, keeping on the grass at its side, in case it should be desirable to refer again to the foot-tracks. For some little distance into the wood the tracks continued as before, those of the brothers overlaying those of Sneathy. Then there was a difference. The path here was broader and muddy, because of the proximity of trees, and suddenly the outer footprints separated, and no more overlay the larger ones in the centre, but proceeded at an equal distance on either side of them.

"See there," cried Mr. Hardwick, pointing triumphantly to the spot, "this is where they over took him, and walked on either side. The body was found only a little farther on—you could see the place now if the path didn't zigzag about so."

Hewitt said nothing, but stooped and examined the tracks at the sides with great care and evident thought, spanning the distances between them comparatively with his arms. Then he rose and stepped lightly from one mark to another, taking care not to tread on the mark itself. "Very good," he said shortly on finishing his examination. "We'll go on."

We went on, and presently came to the place where the body lay. Here the ground sloped from the left down towards the right, and a tiny streamlet, a mere trickle of a foot or two wide, ran across the path. In rainy seasons it was probably wider, for all the earth and clay had been washed away for some feet on each side, leaving flat, bare and very coarse gravel, on which the trail was lost. Just beyond this, and to the left, the body lay on a grassy knoll under the limb of a tree, from which still depended a part of the cut rope. It was not a pleasant sight. The man was a soft, fleshy creature, probably rather under than over the medium height, and he lay there, with his stretched neck and protruding tongue, a revolting object. His right arm lay by his side, and the stump of the wrist was clotted with black blood. Mr. Hardwick's man was still in charge, seemingly little pleased with his job, and a few yards off stood a couple of countrymen looking on.

Hewitt asked from which direction these men had come, and having ascertained and noticed their footmarks, he asked them to stay exactly where they were, to avoid confusing such other tracks as might be seen. Then he addressed himself to his examination. "*First*," he said, glancing up at the branch, that was scarce a yard above his head, "this rope has been here for some time."

"Yes," Mr. Hardwick replied, "it's an old swing rope. Some children used it in the summer, but it got partly cut away, and the odd couple of yards has been hanging since."

"Ah," said Hewitt, "then if the Fosters did this they were saved some trouble by the chance, and were able to take their halter back with them—and so avoid *one* chance of detection." He very closely scrutinised the top of a tree stump, probably the relic of a tree that had been cut down long before, and then addressed himself to the body.

"When you cut it down," he said, "did it fall in a heap?"

"No, my man eased it down to some extent."

"Not on to its face?"

"Oh no. On to its back, just as it is now." Mr. Hardwick saw that Hewitt was looking at muddy marks on each of the corpse's knees, to one of which a small leaf clung, and at one or two other marks of the same sort on the fore part of the dress. "That seems to show pretty plainly," he said, "that he must have struggled with them and was thrown forward, doesn't it?"

Hewitt did not reply, but gingerly lifted the right arm by its sleeve. "Is either of the brothers Foster left-handed?" he asked.

"No, I think not. Here, Bennett, you have seen plenty of their doings—cricket, shooting, and so on—do you remember if either is left-handed?"

"Nayther, sir," Mr. Hardwick's man answered. "Both on 'em's right-handed."

Hewitt lifted the lapel of the coat and attentively regarded a small rent in it. The dead man's hat lay near, and after a few glances at that, Hewitt dropped it and turned his attention to the hair. This was coarse and dark and long, and brushed straight back with no parting.

"This doesn't look very symmetrical, does it?" Hewitt remarked, pointing to the locks over the right ear. They were shorter just there than on the other side, and apparently very clumsily cut, whereas in every other part the hair appeared to be rather well and carefully trimmed. Mr. Hardwick said nothing, but fidgeted a little, as though he considered that valuable time was being wasted over irrelevant trivialities.

Presently, however, he spoke. "There's very little to be learned from the body, is there?" he said. "I think I'm quite justified in ordering their arrest, eh?—indeed, I've wasted too much time already."

Hewitt was groping about among some bushes behind the tree from which the corpse had been taken. When he answered, he said, "I don't think I should do anything of the sort just now, Mr. Hardwick. As a matter of fact, I *fancy*"—this word with an emphasis—"that the brothers Foster may not have seen this man Sneathy at all today."

"Not seen him? Why, my dear sir, there's no question of it. It's certain, absolutely. The evidence is positive. The fact of the threats and of the body being found treated so is pretty well enough, I should think. But that's nothing—look at those footmarks. They've walked along with him, one each side, without a possible doubt; plainly they were the last people with him, in any case. And you don't mean to ask anybody to believe that the dead man, even if he hanged himself, cut off his own hand first. Even if you do, where's the hand? And even putting aside all these considerations, each a complete case in itself, the Fosters *must* at least have seen the body as they came past, and yet nothing has been heard of them yet. Why didn't they spread the alarm? They went straight away in the opposite direction from home—there are their footmarks, which you've not seen yet, beyond the gravel."

Hewitt stepped over to where the patch of clean gravel ceased, at the opposite side to that from which we had approached the brook, and there, sure enough, were the now familiar footmarks of the brothers leading away from the scene of Sneathy's end. "Yes," Hewitt said, "I see them. Of course, Mr. Hardwick, you'll do what seems right in your own eyes, and in any case not much harm will be done by the arrest beyond a terrible fright for that unfortunate family. Nevertheless, if you care for my impression, it is, as I have said, that the Fosters have not seen Sneathy today."

"But what about the hand?"

"As to that I have a conjecture, but as yet it is only a conjecture, and if I told it you would probably call it absurd—certainly you'd disregard it, and perhaps quite excusably. The case is a complicated one, and, if there is anything at all in my conjecture, one of the most remarkable I have ever had to do with. It interests me intensely, and I shall devote a little time now to following up the theory I have formed. You have, I suppose, already communicated with the police?"

"I wired to Shopperton at once, as soon as I heard of the matter. It's a twelve miles' drive, but I wonder the police have not arrived yet. They can't be long; I don't know where the village constable has got to, but in any case *he* wouldn't be much good. But as to your idea that the Fosters can't be suspected—well, nobody could respect your opinion, Mr. Hewitt, more than myself, but really, just think. The notion's impossible—fiftyfold impossible. As soon as the police arrive I shall have that trail followed and the Fosters apprehended. I should be a fool if I didn't."

"Very well, Mr. Hardwick," Hewitt replied; "you'll do what you consider your duty, of course, and quite properly, though I *would* recommend you to take another glance at those three trails in the path. I shall take a look in this direction." And he turned up by the side of the streamlet, keeping on the gravel at its side.

I followed. We climbed the rising ground, and presently, among the trees, came to the place where the little rill emerged from the broken ground in the highest part of the wood. Here the clean ground ceased, and there was a large patch of wet clayey earth. Several marks left by the feet of cattle were there, and one or two human footmarks. Two of these (a pair), the newest and the most distinct, Hewitt studied carefully, and measured each direction.

"Notice these marks," he said. "They may be of importance or they may not—that we shall see. Fortunately, they are very distinctive—the right boot is a badly worn one, and a small tag of leather, where the soul is damaged, is doubled over and trodden into the soft earth. Nothing could be luckier. Clearly they are the most recent footsteps in this direction—from the main road, which lies right ahead, through the rest of the wood."

"Then you think somebody else has been on the scene of the tragedy, beside the victim and the brothers?" I said.

"Yes, I do. But hark; there is a vehicle in the road. Can you see between the trees? Yes, it is the police cart. We shall be able to report its arrival to Mr. Hardwick as we go down."

We turned and walked rapidly down the incline to where we had come from. Mr. Hardwick and his man were still there, and another rustic had arrived to gape. We told Mr. Hardwick that he might expect the police presently, and proceeded along the gravel skirting the stream, toward the lower part of the wood.

Here Hewitt proceeded very cautiously, keeping a sharp look-out on either side for footprints on the neighbouring soft ground. There were none, however, for the gravel margin of the stream made a sort of footpath of itself, and the trees and undergrowth were close and thick on each side. At the bottom we emerged from the wood on a small piece of open ground skirting a lane, and here, just by the side of the lane, where the stream fell into a trench, Hewitt suddenly pounced on another footmark. He was unusually excited.

"See," he said, "here it is—the right foot with its broken leather, and the corresponding left foot on the damp edge of the lane itself. He—the man with the broken shoe—has walked on the hard gravel all the way down from the source of the stream, and his is the only trail unaccounted for near the body. Come, Brett, we've an adventure on foot. Do you care to let your uncle's dinner go by the board, and follow?"

"Can't we go back and tell him?"

"No—there's no time to lose; we must follow up this man—or at least I must. You go or stay, of course, as you think best."

I hesitated a moment, picturing to myself the excellent Colonel as he would appear after waiting dinner an hour or two for us, but decided to go. "At any rate," I said, "if the way lies along the roads we shall probably meet somebody going in the direction of Ratherby who will take a message. But what is your theory? I don't understand at all. I must say everything Hardwick said seemed to me to be beyond question. There were the tracks to prove that the three had walked together to the spot, and that the brothers had gone on alone; and every other circumstance pointed the same way. Then, what possible motive could anybody else about here have for such a crime? Unless, indeed, it was one of the people defrauded by Sneathy's late companies."

"The motive," said Hewitt, "is, I fancy, a most extraordinary—indeed, a weird one. A thing as of centuries ago. Ask me no questions—I think you will be a little surprised before very long. But come, we must move." And we mended our pace along the lane.

The lane, by the bye, was hard and firm, with scarcely a spot where a track might be left, except in places at the sides; and at these places Hewitt never gave a glance. At the end the lane turned into a by-road, and at the turning Hewitt stopped and scrutinised the ground closely. There was nothing like a recognisable footmark to be seen; but almost immediately Hewitt turned off to the right, and we continued our brisk march without a glance at the road.

"How did you judge which way to turn then?" I asked.

"Didn't you see?" replied Hewitt; "I'll show you at the next turning."

Half a mile farther on the road forked, and here Hewitt stooped and pointed silently to a couple of small twigs, placed crosswise, with the longer twig of the two pointing down the branch of the road to the left. We took the branch to the left, and went on.

"Our man's making a mistake," Hewitt observed. "He leaves his friends' messages lying about for his enemies to read."

We hurried forward with scarcely a word. I was almost too bewildered by what Hewitt had said and done to formulate anything like a reasonable guess as to what our expedition tended, or even to make an effective inquiry—though, after what Hewitt had said, I knew that would be useless. Who was this mysterious man with the broken shoe? what had he to do with the murder of Sneathy? what did the mutilation mean? and who were his friends who left him signs and messages by means of crossed twigs?

We met a man, by whom I sent a short note to my uncle, and soon after we turned into a main road. Here again, at the corner, was the curious message of twigs. A cart-wheel had passed over and crushed them, but it had not so far displaced them as to cause any doubt that the direction to take was to the right. At an inn a little farther along we entered, and Hewitt bought a pint of Irish whisky and a flat bottle to hold it in, as well as a loaf of bread and some cheese, which we carried away wrapped in paper.

"This will have to do for our dinner," Hewitt said as we emerged.

"But we're not going to drink a pint of common whisky between us?" I asked in some astonishment.

"Never mind," Hewitt answered with a smile. "Perhaps we'll find somebody to help us—somebody not so fastidious as yourself as to quality."

Now we hurried—hurried more than ever, for it was beginning to get dusk, and Hewitt feared a difficulty in finding and reading the twig signs in the dark. Two more turnings we made, each with its silent direction—the crossed twigs. To me there was something almost weird and creepy in this curious hunt for the invisible and incomprehensible, guided faithfully and persistently at every turn by this now unmistakable signal. After the second turning we broke into a trot along a long, winding lane, but presently Hewitt's hand fell on my shoulder, and we stopped. He pointed ahead, where some large object, round a bend of the hedge was illuminated as though by a light from below.

"We will walk now," Hewitt said. "Remember that we are on a walking tour, and have come along here entirely by accident."

We proceeded at a swinging walk, Hewitt whistling gaily. Soon we turned the bend, and saw that the large object was a travelling van drawn up with two others on a space of grass by the side of the lane. It was a gipsy encampment, the caravan having apparently only lately stopped, for a man was still engaged in tugging at the rope of a tent that stood near the vans. Two or three sullen-looking ruffians lay about a fire which burned in the space left in the middle of the encampment. A woman stood at the door of one van with a large kettle in her hand, and at the foot of the steps below her a more pleasant-looking old man sat on an inverted pail. Hewitt swung towards the fire from the road, and with an indescribable mixture of slouch, bow, and smile addressed the company generally with "*Kooshto bock, pals!*" ("Good luck, brothers!")

The men on the ground took no notice, but continued to stare doggedly before them. The man working at the tent looked round quickly for a moment, and the old man on the bucket looked up and nodded.

Quick to see the most likely friend, Hewitt at once went up to the old man, extending his hand, "*Sarshin, daddo?*" he said; "*Dell mandy tooty's varst.*" ("How do you do, father? Give me your hand.")

The old man smiled and shook hands, though without speaking. Then Hewitt proceeded, producing the flat bottle of whisky, "*Tatty for pawny, chals. Dell mandy the pawny, and lell posh the tatty.*" (Spirits for water, lads. Give me the water and take your share of the spirits.")

The whisky did it. We were Romany ryes in twenty minutes or less, and had already been taking tea with the gipsies for half the time. The two or three we had found about the fire were still reserved, but these, I found, were only half-gipsies, and understood very little Romany. One or two others, however, including the old man, were of purer breed, and talked freely, as did one of the women. They were Lees, they said, and expected to be on Wirksby racecourse in three days' time. We, too, were *pirimengroes*, or travellers, Hewitt explained, and might look to see them on the course.

Then he fell to telling gipsy stories, and they to telling others back, to my intense mystification. Hewitt explained afterwards that they were mostly stories of poaching, with now and again a horse-coping anecdote thrown in. Since then I have learned enough of Romany to take my part in such a conversation, but at the time a word or two here and there was all I could understand. In all this talk the man we had first noticed stretching the tent-rope took very little interest, but lay, with his head away from the fire, smoking his pipe. He was a much darker man than any other present—had, in fact, the appearance of a man of even a swarthier race than that of the others about us.

Presently, in the middle of a long and, of course, to me unintelligible story by the old man, I caught Hewitt's eye. He lifted one eyebrow almost imperceptibly, and glanced for a single moment at his walking-stick. Then I saw that it was pointed toward the feet of the very dark man, who had not yet spoken. One leg was thrown over the others as he lay, with the soles of his shoes presented toward the fire, and in its glare I saw—that the right sole was worn and broken, and that a small triangular tag of leather was doubled over beneath in just the place we knew of from the prints in Ratherby Wood.

I could not take my eyes off that man with his broken shoe. There lay the secret, the whole mystery of the fantastic crime in Ratherby Wood centred in that shabby ruffian. What was it?

But Hewitt went on, talking and joking furiously. The men who were not speaking mostly smoked gloomily, but whenever one spoke, he became animated and lively. I had attempted once or twice to join in, though my efforts were not particularly successful, except in inducing one man to offer me tobacco from his box—tobacco that almost made me giddy in the smell. He tried some of mine in exchange, and though he praised it with native politeness, and smoked the pipe through, I could see that my Hignett mixture was poor stuff in his estimation, compared with the awful tobacco in his own box.

Presently the man with the broken shoe got up, slouched over to his tent, and disappeared. Then said Hewitt (I translate):

"You're not all Lees here, I see?"

"Yes, *pal*, all Lees."

"But *he's* not a Lee?" and Hewitt jerked his head towards the tent.

"Why not a Lee, *pal*? We be Lees, and he is with us. Thus he is a Lee."

"Oh yes, of course. But I know he is from over the *pawny*. Come, I'll guess the *tem, (country)*, he comes from—it's from Roumania, eh? Perhaps the Wallachian part?"

The men looked at one another, and then the old Lee said:

"You're right, pal. You're cleverer than we took you for. That is what they calls his *tem*. He is a *petulengro*, (smith), and he comes with us to shoe the *gries, (horses)*, and mend the *vardoes*, (vans). But he is with us, and so he is a Lee."

The talk and the smoke went on, and presently the man with the broken shoe returned, and lay down again. Then, when the whisky had all gone, and Hewitt, with some excuse that I did not understand, had begged a piece of cord from one of the men, we left in a chorus of *kooshto rardies*, (goodnight).

By this time, it was nearly ten o'clock. We walked briskly till we came back again to the inn where we had bought the whisky. Here Hewitt, after some little trouble, succeeded in hiring a village cart, and while the driver was harnessing the horse, cut a couple of short sticks from the hedge. These, being each divided into two, made four short, stout pieces of something less than six inches long apiece. Then Hewitt joined them together in pairs, each pair being connected from centre to centre by about nine or ten inches of the cord he had brought from the gipsies' camp. These done, he handed one pair to me. "Handcuffs," he explained, "and no bad ones either. See—you use them so." And he passed the cord round my wrist, gripping the two handles, and giving them a slight twist that sufficiently convinced me of the excruciating pain that might be inflicted by a vigorous turn, and the utter helplessness of a prisoner thus secured in the hands of captors prepared to use their instruments.

"Whom are these for?" I asked. "The man with the broken shoe?" Hewitt nodded.

"Yes," he said. "I expect we shall find him out alone about midnight. You know how to use these now."

It was fully eleven before the cart was ready and we started. A quarter of a mile or so from the gipsy encampment Hewitt stopped the cart and gave the driver instructions to wait. We got through the hedge, and made our way on the soft ground behind it in the direction of the vans and the tent.

"Roll up your handkerchief," Hewitt whispered, "into a tight pad. The moment I grab him, ram it into his mouth—*well* in, mind, so that it doesn't easily fall out. Probably he will be stooping—that will make it easier; we can pull him suddenly backward. Now be quiet."

We kept on till nothing but the hedge divided us from the space whereon stood the encampment. It was now nearer twelve o'clock than eleven, but the time we waited seemed endless. But time is not eternity after all, and at last we heard a move in the tent. A minute after, the man we sought was standing before us. He made straight for a gap in the hedge which we had passed on our way, and we crouched low and waited. He emerged on our side of the hedge with his back towards us, and began walking, as we had walked, behind the hedge, but in the opposite direction. We followed.

He carried something in his hand that looked like a large bundle of sticks and twigs, and he appeared to be as anxious to be secret as we ourselves. From time to time he stopped and listened; fortunately, there was no moon, or in turning about, as he did once or twice, he would probably have observed us. The field sloped downward just before us, and there was another hedge at right angles, leading down to a slight hollow. To this hollow the man made his way, and in the shade of the new hedge we followed. Presently he stopped suddenly, stooped, and deposited his bundle on the ground before him. Crouching before it, he produced matches from his pocket, struck one, and in a moment had a fire of twigs and small branches, that sent up a heavy white smoke. What all this portended I could not imagine, but a sense of the weirdness of the whole adventure came upon me unchecked. The horrible corpse in the wood, with its severed wrist, Hewitt's enigmatical forebodings, the mysterious tracking of the man with the broken shoe, the scene round the gipsies' fire, and now the strange behaviour of this man, whose connection with the tragedy was so intimate and yet so inexplicable—all these things contributed to make up a tale of but a few hours' duration, but of an inscrutable impressiveness that I began to feel in my nerves.

The man bent a thin stick double, and using it as a pair of tongs, held some indistinguishable object over the flames before him. Excited as I was, I could not help noticing that he bent and held the stick with his left hand. We crept stealthily nearer, and as I stood scarcely three yards behind him and looked over his shoulder, the form of the object stood out clear and black against the dull red of the flame. It was a *human hand*.

I suppose I may have somehow betrayed my amazement and horror to my companion's sharp eyes, for suddenly I felt his hand tightly grip my arm just above the elbow. I turned, and found his face close by mine and his finger raised warningly. Then I saw him produce his wrist-grip and make a motion with his palm toward his mouth, which I understood to be intended to remind me of the gag. We stepped forward.

The man turned his horrible cookery over and over above the crackling sticks, as though to smoke and dry it in every part. I saw Hewitt's hand reach out toward him, and in a flash we had pulled him back over his heels and I had driven the gag between his teeth as he opened his mouth. We seized his wrists in the cords at once, and I shall never forget the man's look of ghastly, frantic terror as he lay on the ground. When I knew more I understood the reason of this.

Hewitt took both wrist-holds in one hand and drove the gag entirely into the man's mouth, so that he almost choked. A piece of sacking lay near the fire, and by Hewitt's request I dropped that awful hand from the wooden twigs upon it and rolled it up in a parcel—it was, no doubt, what the sacking had been brought for. Then we lifted the man to his feet and hurried him in the direction of the cart. The whole capture could not have occupied thirty seconds, and as I stumbled over the rough field at the man's left elbow I could only think of the thing as one thinks of a dream that one knows all the time *is* a dream.

But presently the man, who had been walking quietly, though gasping, sniffing and choking because of the tightly rolled handkerchief in his mouth—presently he made a sudden dive, thinking doubtless to get his wrists free by surprise. But Hewitt was alert, and gave them a twist that made him roll his head with a dismal, stifled yell, and with the opening of his mouth, by some chance the gag fell away. Immediately the man roared aloud for help.

"Quick," said Hewitt, "drag him along—they'll hear in the vans. Bring the hand!"

I seized the fallen handkerchief and crammed it over the man's mouth as well as I might, and together we made as much of a trot as we could, dragging the man between us, while Hewitt checked any reluctance on his part by a timely wrench of the wrist-holds. It was a hard two hundred and fifty yards to the lane even for us—for the gipsy it must have been a bad minute and a half indeed. Once more as we went over the uneven ground he managed to get out a shout, and we thought we heard a distinct reply from somewhere in the direction of the encampment.

We pulled him over a stile in a tangle; and dragged and pushed him through a small hedge-gap all in a heap. Here we were but a short distance from the cart, and into that we flung him without wasting time or tenderness, to the intense consternation of the driver, who, I believe, very nearly set up a cry for help on his own account. Once in the cart, however, I seized the reins and the whip myself and, leaving Hewitt to take care of the prisoner, put the turn-out along toward Ratherby at as near ten miles an hour as it could go.

We made first for Mr. Hardwick's, but he, we found, was with my uncle, so we followed him. The arrest of the Fosters had been effected, we learned, not very long after we had left the wood, as they returned by another route to Ranworth. We brought our prisoner into the Colonel's library, where he and Mr. Hardwick were sitting.

"I'm not quite sure what we can charge him with unless it's anatomical robbery," Hewitt remarked, "but here's the criminal."

The man only looked down, with a sulkily impenetrable countenance. Hewitt spoke to him once or twice, and at last he said, in a strange accent, something that sounded like "*kekin jin-navvy,*"

"*Keck jin?*" ("Not understand?"),)asked Hewitt, in the loud, clear tone one instinctively adopts in talking to a foreigner, "*Keckeno jinny?*"

The man understood and shook his head, but not another word would he say or another question answer.

"He's a foreign gipsy," Hewitt explained, "just as I thought—a Wallachian, in fact. Theirs is an older and purer dialect than that of the English gipsies, and only some of the root-words are alike. But I think we can make him explain tomorrow that the Fosters at least had nothing to do with, at any rate, cutting off Sneathy's hand. Here it is, I think." And he gingerly lifted the folds of sacking from the ghastly object as it lay on the table, and then covered it up again.

"But what—what does it all mean?" Mr. Hardwick said in bewildered astonishment. "Do you mean this man was an accomplice?"

"Not at all—the case was one of suicide, as I think you'll agree, when I've explained. This man simply found the body hanging and stole the hand."

"But what in the world for?"

"For the Hand of Glory. Eh?" He turned to the gipsy and pointed to the hand on the table: "*Yag-varst*, (fire-hand), eh?"

There was a quick gleam of intelligence in the man's eye, but he said nothing. As for myself I was more than astounded. Could it be possible that the old superstition of the Hand of Glory remained alive in a practical shape at this day?

"You know the superstition, of course," Hewitt said. "It did exist in this country in the last century, when there were plenty of dead men hanging at cross-roads, and so on. On the Continent, in some places, it has survived later. Among the Wallachian gipsies it has always been a great article of belief, and the superstition is quite active still. The belief is that the right hand of a hanged man, cut off and dried over the smoke of certain wood and herbs, and then provided with wicks at each finger made of the dead man's hair, becomes, when lighted at each wick (the wicks are greased, of course), a charm, whereby a thief may walk without hindrance where he pleases in a strange house, push open all doors and take what he likes. Nobody can stop him, for everybody the Hand of Glory approaches is made helpless, and can neither move nor speak. You may remember there was some talk of 'thieves' candles' in connection with the horrible series of Whitechapel murders not long ago. That is only one form of the cult of the Hand of Glory."

"Yes," my uncle said, "I remember reading so. There is a story about it in the Ingoldsby Legends, too, I believe."

"There is—it is called 'The Hand of Glory,' in fact. You remember the spell, 'Open lock to the dead man's knock,' and so on. But I think you'd better have the constable up and get this man into safe quarters for the night. He should be searched, of course. I expect they will find on him the hair I noticed to have been cut from Sneathy's head."

The village constable arrived with his iron handcuffs in substitution for those of cord which had so sorely vexed the wrists of our prisoner, and marched him away to the little lock-up on the green.

Then my uncle and Mr. Hardwick turned on Martin Hewitt with doubts and many questions:

"Why do you call it suicide?" Mr. Hardwick asked. "It is plain the Fosters were with him at the time from the tracks. Do you mean to say that they stood there and watched Sneathy hang himself without interfering?"

"No, I don't," Hewitt replied, lighting a cigar. "I think I told you that they never saw Sneathy."

"Yes, you did, and of course that's what they said themselves when they were arrested. But the thing's impossible. Look at the tracks!"

"The tracks are exactly what revealed to me that it was *not* impossible," Hewitt returned. "I'll tell you how the case unfolded itself to me from the beginning. As to the information you gathered from the Ranworth coachman, to begin with. The conversation between the Fosters which he overheard might well mean something less serious than murder. What did they say? They had been sent for in a hurry and had just had a short consultation with their mother and sister. Henry said that 'the thing must be done at once'; also that as there were two of them it should be easy. Robert said that Henry, as a doctor, would know best what to do.

"Now you, Colonel Brett, had been saying—before we learned these things from Mr. Hardwick—that Sneathy's behaviour of late had become so bad as to seem that of a madman. Then there was the story of his sudden attack on a tradesman in the village, and equally sudden running away—exactly the sort of impulsive, wild thing that madmen do. Why then might it not be reasonable to suppose that Sneathy *had* become mad—more especially considering all the circumstances of the case, his commercial ruin and disgrace and his horrible life with his wife and her family?—had become suddenly much worse and quite uncontrollable, so that the two wretched women left alone with him were driven to send in haste for Henry and Robert to help them? That would account for all.

"The brothers arrive just after Sneathy had gone out. They are told in a hurried interview how affairs stand, and it is decided that Sneathy must be at once secured and confined in an asylum before something serious happens. He has just gone out—something terrible may be happening at this moment. The brothers determine to follow at once and secure him wherever he may be. Then the meaning of their conversation is plain. The thing that 'must be done, and at once,' is the capture of Sneathy and his confinement in an asylum. Henry, as a doctor, would 'know what to do' in regard to the necessary formalities. And they took a halter in case a struggle should ensue and it were found necessary to bind him. Very likely, wasn't it?"

"Well, yes," Mr. Hardwick replied, "it certainly is. It never struck me in that light at all."

"That was because you believed, to begin with, that a murder had been committed, and looked at the preliminary circumstances which you learned after in the light of your conviction. But now, to come to my actual observations. I saw the footmarks across the fields, and agreed with you (it was indeed obvious) that Sneathy had gone that way first, and that the brothers had followed, walking over his tracks. This state of the tracks continued until well into the wood, when suddenly the tracks of the brothers opened out and proceeded on each side of Sneathy's. The simple inference would seem to be, of course, the one you made—that the Fosters had here overtaken Sneathy, and walked one at each side of him.

"But of this I felt by no means certain. Another very simple explanation was available, which might chance to be the true one. It was just at the spot where the brothers' tracks separated that the path became suddenly much muddier, because of the closer overhanging of the trees at the spot. The path was, as was to be expected, wettest in the middle. It would be the most natural thing in the world for two well-dressed young men, on arriving here, to separate so as to walk one on each side of the mud in the middle.

"On the other hand, a man in Sneathy's state (assuming him, for the moment, to be mad and contemplating suicide) would walk straight along the centre of the path, taking no note of mud or anything else. I examined all the tracks very carefully, and my theory was confirmed. The feet of the brothers had everywhere alighted in the driest spots, and the steps were of irregular lengths—which meant, of course, that they were picking their way; while Sneathy's footmarks had never turned aside even for the dirtiest puddle. Here, then, were the rudiments of a theory.

"At the watercourse, of course, the footmarks ceased, because of the hard gravel. The body lay on a knoll at the left—a knoll covered with grass. On this the signs of footmarks were almost undiscoverable, although I am often able to discover tracks in grass that are invisible to others. Here, however, it was almost useless to spend much time in examination, for you and your man had been there, and what slight marks there might be would be indistinguishable one from another.

"Under the branch from which the man had hung there was an old tree stump, with a flat top, where the tree had been sawn off. I examined this, and it became fairly apparent that Sneathy had stood on it when the rope was about his neck—his muddy footprint was plain to see; the mud was not smeared about, you see, as it probably would have been if he had been stood there forcibly and pushed off. It was a simple, clear footprint—another hint at suicide.

"But then arose the objection that you mentioned yourself. Plainly the brothers Foster were following Sneathy, and came this way. Therefore, if he hanged himself before they arrived, it would seem that they must have come across the body. But now I examined the body itself. There was mud on the knees, and clinging to one knee was a small leaf. It was a leaf corresponding to those on the bush behind the tree, and it was not a dead leaf, so must have been just detached.

"After my examination of the body I went to the bush, and there, in the thick of it, were, for me, sufficiently distinct knee-marks, in one of which the knee had crushed a spray of the bush against the ground, and from that spray a leaf was missing. Behind the knee-marks were the indentations of boot-toes in the soft, bare earth under the bush, and thus the thing was plain. The poor lunatic had come in sight of the dangling rope, and the temptation to suicide was irresistible. To people in a deranged state of mind the mere sight of the means of self-destruction is often a temptation impossible to withstand. But at that moment he must have heard the steps—probably the voices—of the brothers behind him on the winding path. He immediately hid in the bush till they had passed. It is probable that seeing who the men were, and conjecturing that they were following him—thinking also, perhaps, of things that had occurred between them and himself—his inclination to self-destruction became completely ungovernable, with the result that you saw.

"But before I inspected the bush I noticed one or two more things about the body. You remember I inquired if either of the brothers

Foster was left-handed, and was assured that neither was. But clearly the hand had been cut off by a left-handed man, with a large, sharply pointed knife. For well away to the *right* of where the wrist had hung the knife-point had made a tiny triangular rent in the coat, so that the hand must have been held in the mutilator's right hand, while he used the knife with his left—clearly a left-handed man.

"But most important of all about the body was the jagged hair over the right ear. Everywhere else the hair was well cut and orderly—here it seemed as though a good piece had been, so to speak, *sawn* off. What could anybody want with a dead man's right hand and certain locks of his hair? Then it struck me suddenly—the man was hanged; it was the Hand of Glory!

"Then you will remember I went, at your request, to see the footprints of the Fosters on the part of the path *past* the watercourse. Here again it was muddy in the middle, and the two brothers had walked as far apart as before, although nobody had walked between them. A final proof, if one were needed, of my theory as to the three lines of footprints.

"Now I was to consider how to get at the man who had taken his hand. He should be punished for the mutilation, but beyond that he would be required as a witness. Now all the foot-tracks in the vicinity had been accounted for. There were those of the brothers and of Sneathy, which we have been speaking of; those of the rustics looking on, which, however, stopped a little way off, and did not interfere with our sphere of observation; those of your man, who had cut straight through the wood when he first saw the body, and had come back the same way with you; and our own, which we had been careful to keep away from the others. Consequently, there was *no* track of the man who had cut off the hand; therefore, it was certain that he must have come along the hard gravel by the watercourse, for that was the only possible path which would not tell the tale. Indeed, it seemed quite a likely path through the wood for a passenger to take, coming from the high ground by the Shopperton road.

"Brett and I left you and traversed the watercourse, both up and down. We found a footprint at the top, left lately by a man with a broken shoe. Right down to the bottom of the watercourse where it emerged from the wood there was no sign on either side of this man having left the gravel. (Where the body was, as you will remember, he would simply have stepped off the gravel on to the grass, which I thought it useless to examine, as I have explained.) But at the bottom, by the lane, the footprint appeared again.

"This then was the direction in which I was to search for a left-handed man with a broken-soled shoe, probably a gipsy—and most probably a foreign gipsy—because a foreign gipsy would be the most likely still to hold the belief in the Hand of Glory. I conjectured the man to be a straggler from a band of gipsies—one who probably had got behind the caravan and had made a short cut across the wood after it; so at the end of the lane I looked for a *patrin*. This is a sign that gipsies leave to guide stragglers following up. Sometimes it is a heap of dead leaves, sometimes a few stones, sometimes a mark on the ground, but more usually a couple of twigs crossed, with the longer twig pointing the road.

"Guided by these *patrins* we came in the end on the gipsy camp just as it was settling down for the night. We made ourselves agreeable (as Brett will probably describe to you better than I can), we left them, and after they had got to sleep we came back and watched for the gentleman who is now in the lock-up. He would, of course, seize the first opportunity of treating his ghastly trophy in the prescribed way, and I guessed he would choose midnight, for that is the time the superstition teaches that the hand should be prepared. We made a few small preparations, collared him, and now you've got him. And I should think the sooner you let the brothers Foster go the better."

"But why didn't you tell me all the conclusions you had arrived at at the time?" asked Mr. Hardwick.

"Well, really," Hewitt replied, with a quiet smile, "you were so positive, and some of the traces I relied on were so small, that it would probably have meant a long argument and a loss of time. But more than that, confess, if I had told you bluntly that Sneathy's hand had been taken away to make a medieval charm to enable a thief to pass through a locked door and steal plate calmly under the owner's nose, what *would* you have said?"

"Well, well, perhaps I *should* have been a little sceptical. Appearances combined so completely to point to the Fosters as murderers that any other explanation almost would have seemed unlikely to me, and *that*—well no, I confess, I shouldn't have believed in it. But it is a startling thing to find such superstitions alive now-a-days."

"Yes, perhaps it is. Yet we find survivals of the sort very frequently. The Wallachians, however, are horribly superstitious still—the gipsies among them are, of course, worse. Don't you remember the case reported a few months ago, in which a child was drowned as a sacrifice in Wallachia in order to bring rain? And that was not done by gipsies either. Even in England, as late as 1865, a poor paralysed Frenchman was killed by being 'swum' for witchcraft—that was in Essex. And less atrocious cases of belief in wizardry occur again and again even now."

Then Mr. Hardwick and my uncle fell into a discussion as to how the gipsy in the lock-up could be legally punished. Mr. Hardwick thought it should be treated as a theft of a portion of a dead body, but my uncle fancied there was a penalty for mutilation of a dead body *per se*, though he could not point to the statute. As it happened, however, they were saved the trouble of arriving at a decision, for in the morning he was discovered to have escaped. He had been left, of course, with free hands, and had occupied the night in wrenching out the bars at the top of the back wall of the little prison-shed (it had stood on the green for a hundred and fifty years) and climbing out. He was not found again, and a month or two later the Foster family left the district entirely.

THE CASE OF LAKER, ABSCONDED

There were several of the larger London banks and insurance offices from which Hewitt held a sort of general retainer as detective adviser, in fulfilment of which he was regularly consulted as to the measures to be taken in different cases of fraud, forgery, theft, and so forth, which it might be the misfortune of the particular firms to encounter. The more important and intricate of these cases were placed in his hands entirely, with separate commissions, in the usual way. One of the most important companies of the sort was the General Guarantee Society, an insurance corporation which, among other risks, took those of the integrity of secretaries, clerks, and cashiers. In the case of a cash-box elopement on the part of any person guaranteed by the society, the directors were naturally anxious for a speedy capture of the culprit, and more especially of the booty, before too much of it was spent, in order to lighten the claim upon their funds, and in work of this sort Hewitt was a times engaged, either in general advice and direction, or in the actual pursuit of the plunder and the plunderer.

Arriving at his office a little later than usual one morning, Hewitt found an urgent message awaiting him from the General Guarantee Society, requesting his attention to a robbery which had taken place on the previous day. He had gleaned some hint of the case from the morning paper, wherein appeared a short paragraph, which ran thus:—

"Serious Bank Robbery.—In the course of yesterday a clerk employed by Messrs. Liddle, Neal & Liddle, the well-known bankers, disappeared, having in his possession a large sum of money, the property of his employers—a sum reported to be rather over £15,000. It would seem that he had been entrusted to collect the money in his capacity of "walk-clerk" from various other banks and trading concerns during the morning, but failed to return at the usual time. A large number of the notes which he received had been cashed at the Bank of England before suspicion was aroused. We understand that Detective-Inspector Plummer, of Scotland Yard, has the case in hand."

The clerk, whose name was Charles William Laker, had, it appeared from the message, been guaranteed in the usual way by the General Guarantee Society, and Hewitt's presence at the office was at once desired, in order that steps might quickly be taken for the man's apprehension, and in the recovery, at any rate, of as much of the booty as possible.

A smart hansom brought Hewitt to Threadneedle Street in a bare quarter of an hour, and there a few minutes' talk with the manager, Mr. Lyster, put him in possession of the main facts of the case, which appeared to be simple. Charles William Laker was twenty-five years of age, and had been in the employ of Messrs. Liddle, Neal & Liddle for something more than seven years—since he left school, in fact—and until the previous day there had been nothing in his conduct to complain of. His duties as walk-clerk consisted in making a certain round, beginning at about half-past ten each morning.

There were a certain number of the more important banks between which and Messrs. Liddle, Neal & Liddle there were daily transactions, and a few smaller semi-private banks and merchant firms acting as financial agents, with whom there was business intercourse of less importance and regularity; and each of these, as necessary, he visited in turn, collecting cash due on bills and other instruments of a like nature. He carried a wallet, fastened securely to his person by a chain, and this wallet contained the bills and the cash. Usually at the end of his round, when all his bills had been converted into cash, the wallet held very large sums. His work and responsibilities, in fine, were those common to walk-clerks in all banks.

On the day of the robbery he had started out as usual—possibly a little earlier than was customary—and the bills and other securities in his possession represented considerably more than £15,000. It had been ascertained that he had called in the usual way at each establishment on the round, and had transacted his business at the last place by about a quarter-past one, being then, without doubt, in possession of cash to the full value of the bills negotiated. After that, Mr. Lyster said, yesterday's report was that nothing more had been heard of him. But this morning there had been a message to the effect that he had been traced out of the country—to Calais, at least, it was thought. The directors of the society wished Hewitt to take the case in hand personally and at once, with a view of recovering what was possible from the plunder by way of salvage; also, of course, of finding Laker, for it is an important moral gain to guarantee societies, as an example, if a thief is caught and punished. Therefore, Hewitt and Mr. Lyster, as soon as might be, made for Messrs. Liddle, Neal & Liddle's, that the investigation might be begun.

The bank premises were quite near—in Leadenhall Street. Having arrived there, Hewitt and Mr. Lyster made their way to the firm's private rooms. As they were passing an outer waiting-room, Hewitt noticed two women. One, the elder, in widow's weeds, was sitting with her head bowed in her hand over a small writing-table. Her face was not visible, but her whole attitude was that of a person overcome with unbearable grief; and she sobbed quietly. The other was a young woman of twenty-two or twenty-three. Her thick black veil revealed no more than that her features were small and regular, and that her face was pale and drawn. She stood with a hand on the elder woman's shoulder, and she quickly turned her head away as the two men entered.

Mr. Neal, one of the partners, received them in his own room. "Good-morning, Mr. Hewitt," he said, when Mr. Lyster had introduced the detective. "This is a serious business—very. I think I am sorrier for Laker himself than for anybody else, ourselves included—or, at any rate, I am sorrier for his mother. She is waiting now to see Mr. Liddle, as soon as he arrives—Mr. Liddle has known the family for a long time. Miss Shaw is with her, too, poor girl. She is a governess, or something of that sort, and I believe she and Laker were engaged to be married. It's all very sad."

"Inspector Plummer, I understand," Hewitt remarked, "has the affair in hand, on behalf of the police?"

"Yes," Mr. Neal replied; "in fact, he's here now, going through the contents of Laker's desk, and so forth; he thinks it possible Laker may have had accomplices. Will you see him?"

"Presently. Inspector Plummer and I are old friends. We met last, I think, in the case of the Stanway cameo, some months ago. But, first, will you tell me how long Laker has been a walk-clerk?"

"Barely four months, although he has been with us altogether seven years. He was promoted to the walk soon after the beginning of the year."

"Do you know anything of his habits—what he used to do in his spare time, and so forth?"

"Not a great deal. He went in for boating, I believe, though I have heard it whispered that he had one or two more expensive tastes—expensive, that is, for a young man in his position," Mr. Neal explained, with a dignified wave of the hand that he peculiarly affected. He was a stout old gentleman, and the gesture suited him.

"You have had no reason to suspect him of dishonesty before, I take it?"

"Oh, no. He made a wrong return once, I believe, that went for some time undetected, but it turned out, after all, to be a clerical error—a mere clerical error."

"Do you know anything of his associates out of the office?"

"No, how should I? I believe Inspector Plummer has been making inquiries as to that, however, of the other clerks. Here he is, by the bye, I expect. Come in!"

It was Plummer who had knocked, and he came in at Mr. Neal's call. He was a middle-sized, small-eyed, impenetrable-looking man, as yet of no great reputation in the force. Some of my readers may remember his connection with that case, so long a public mystery, that I have elsewhere fully set forth and explained under the title of "The Stanway Cameo Mystery." Plummer carried his billy-cock hat in one hand and a few papers in the other. He gave Hewitt good-morning, placed his hat on a chair, and spread the papers on the table.

"There's not a great deal here," he said, "but one thing's plain—Laker had been betting. See here, and here, and here"—he took a few letters from the bundle in his hand—"two letters from a bookmaker about settling—wonder he trusted a clerk—several telegrams from tipsters, and a letter from some friend—only signed by initials—asking Laker to put a sovereign on a horse for the friend 'with his own.' I'll keep these, I think. It may be worthwhile to see that friend, if we can find him. Ah, we often find it's betting, don't we, Mr. Hewitt? Meanwhile, there's no news from France yet."

"You are sure that is where he is gone?" asked Hewitt.

"Well, I'll tell you what we've done as yet. First, of course, I went round to all the banks. There was nothing to be got from that. The cashiers all knew him by sight, and one was a personal friend of his. He had called as usual, said nothing in particular, cashed his bills in the ordinary way, and finished up at the Eastern Consolidated Bank at about a quarter-past one. So far there was nothing whatever. But I had started two or three men meanwhile making inquiries at the railway stations, and so on. I had scarcely left the Eastern Consolidated when one of them came after me with news. He had tried Palmer's Tourist Office, although that seemed an unlikely place, and there struck the track."

"Had he been there?"

"Not only had he been there, but he had taken a tourist ticket for France. It was quite a smart move, in a way. You see it was the sort of ticket that lets you do pretty well what you like; you have the choice of two or three different routes to begin with, and you can break your journey where you please, and make all sorts of variations. So that a man with a ticket like that, and a few hours' start, could twist about on some remote branch route, and strike off in another direction altogether, with a new ticket, from some out-of-the-way place, while we were carefully sorting out and inquiring along the different routes he *might* have taken.

"Not half a bad move for a new hand; but he made one bad mistake, as new hands always do—as old hands do, in fact, very often. He was fool enough to give his own name, C. Laker! Although that didn't matter much, as the description was enough to fix him. There he was, wallet and all, just as he had come from the Eastern Consolidated Bank. He went straight from there to Palmer's, by the bye, and probably in a cab. We judge that by the time. He left the Eastern Consolidated at a quarter-past one, and was at Palmer's by twenty-five-past—ten minutes. The clerk at Palmer's remembered the time because he was anxious to get out to his lunch, and kept looking at the clock, expecting another clerk in to relieve him. Laker didn't take much in the way of luggage, I fancy.

"We inquired carefully at the stations, and got the porters to remember the passengers for whom they had been carrying luggage, but none appeared to have had any dealings with our man. That, of course, is as one would expect. He'd take as little as possible with him, and buy what he wanted on the way, or when he'd reached his hiding-place. Of course, I wired to Calais (it was a Dover to Calais route ticket) and sent a couple of smart men off by the 8.15 mail from Charing Cross.

I expect we shall hear from them in the course of the day. I am being kept in London in view of something expected at headquarters, or I should have been off myself."

"That is all, then, up to the present? Have you anything else in view?"

"That's all I've absolutely ascertained at present. As for what I'm going to do"—a slight smile curled Plummer's lip—"well, I shall see. I've a thing or two in my mind."

Hewitt smiled slightly himself; he recognised Plummer's touch of professional jealousy. "Very well," he said, rising, "I'll make an inquiry or two for myself at once. Perhaps, Mr. Neal, you'll allow one of your clerks to show me the banks, in their regular order, at which Laker called yesterday. I think I'll begin at the beginning."

Mr. Neal offered to place at Hewitt's disposal anything or anybody the bank contained, and the conference broke up. As Hewitt, with the clerk, came through the rooms separating Mr. Neal's sanctum from the outer office, he fancied he saw the two veiled women leaving by a side door.

The first bank was quite close to Liddle, Neal & Liddle's. There the cashier who had dealt with Laker the day before remembered nothing in particular about the interview. Many other walk-clerks had called during the morning, as they did every morning, and the only circumstances of the visit that he could say anything definite about were those recorded in figures in the books. He did not know Laker's name till Plummer had mentioned it in making inquiries on the previous afternoon. As far as he could remember, Laker behaved much as usual, though really he did not notice much; he looked chiefly at the bills. He described Laker in a way that corresponded with the photograph that Hewitt had borrowed from the bank; a young man with a brown moustache and ordinary-looking, fairly regular face, dressing much as other clerks dressed—tall hat, black cutaway coat, and so on. The numbers of the notes handed over had already been given to Inspector Plummer, and these Hewitt did not trouble about.

The next bank was in Cornhill, and here the cashier was a personal friend of Laker's—at any rate, an acquaintance—and he remembered a little more. Laker's manner had been quite as usual, he said; certainly he did not seem preoccupied or excited in his manner. He spoke for a moment or two—of being on the river on Sunday, and so on—and left in his usual way.

"Can you remember *everything* he said?" Hewitt asked. "If you can tell me, I should like to know exactly what he did and said to the smallest particular."

"Well, he saw me a little distance off—I was behind there, at one of the desks—and raised his hand to me, and said, 'How d'ye do?' I came across and took his bills, and dealt with them in the usual way. He had a new umbrella lying on the counter—rather a handsome umbrella—and I made a remark about the handle. He took it up to show me, and told me it was a present he had just received from a friend. It was a gorse-root handle, with two silver bands, one with his monogram C.W.L. I said it was a very nice handle, and asked him whether it was fine in his district on Sunday. He said he had been up the river, and it was very fine there. And I think that was all."

"Thank you. Now about this umbrella. Did he carry it rolled? Can you describe it in detail?"

"Well, I've told you about the handle, and the rest was much as usual, I think; it wasn't rolled—just flapping loosely, you know. It was rather an odd-shaped handle, though. I'll try and sketch it, if you like, as well as I can remember." He did so, and Hewitt saw in the result rough indications of a gnarled crook, with one silver band near the end, and another, with the monogram, a few inches down the handle. Hewitt put the sketch in his pocket, and bade the cashier good-day.

At the next bank the story was the same as at the first—there was nothing remembered but the usual routine. Hewitt and the clerk turned down a narrow paved court, and through into Lombard Street for the next visit. The bank—that of Buller, Clayton, Ladds & Co.—was just at the corner at the end of the court, and the imposing stone entrance-porch was being made larger and more imposing still, the way being almost blocked by ladders and scaffold-poles. Here there was only the usual tale, and so on through the whole walk. The cashiers knew Laker only by sight, and that not always very distinctly. The calls of walk-clerks were such matters of routine that little note was taken of the persons of the clerks themselves, who were called by the names of their firms, if they were called by any names at all. Laker had behaved much as usual, so far as the cashiers could remember, and when finally, the Eastern Consolidated was left behind, nothing more had been learnt than the chat about Laker's new umbrella.

Hewitt had taken leave of Mr. Neal's clerk, and was stepping into a hansom, when he noticed a veiled woman in widow's weeds hailing another hansom a little way behind. He recognised the figure again, and said to the driver, "Drive fast to Palmer's Tourist Office, but keep your eye on that cab behind, and tell me presently if it is following us."

The cabman drove off, and after passing one or two turnings, opened the lid above Hewitt's head, and said, "That there other keb *is* a-follerin' us, sir, an' keepin' about even distance all along."

"All right; that's what I wanted to know. Palmer's now."

At Palmer's the clerk who had attended to Laker remembered him very well, and described him. He also remembered the wallet, *thought* he remembered the umbrella—was practically sure of it, in fact, upon reflection. He had no record of the name given, but remembered it distinctly to be Laker. As a matter of fact, names were never asked in such a transaction, but in this case Laker appeared to be ignorant of the usual procedure, as well as in a great hurry, and asked for the ticket and gave his name all in one breath, probably assuming that the name would be required.

Hewitt got back to his cab, and started for Charing Cross. The cabman once more lifted the lid and informed him that the hansom with the veiled woman in it was again following, having waited while Hewitt had visited Palmer's. At Charing Cross Hewitt discharged his cab and walked straight to the lost property office. The man in charge knew him very well, for his business had carried him there frequently before.

"I fancy an umbrella was lost in the station yesterday," Hewitt said. "It was a new umbrella, silk, with a gnarled gorse-root handle and two silver bands, something like this sketch. There was a monogram on the lower band—'C. W. L.' were the letters. Has it been brought here?"

"There was two or three yesterday," the man said; "let's see." He took the sketch and retired to a corner of his room. "Oh, yes—here it is, I think; isn't this it? Do you claim it?"

"Well, not exactly that, but I think I'll take a look at it, if you'll let me. By the way, I see it's rolled up. Was it found like that?"

"No; the chap rolled it up what found it—porter he was. It's a fad of his, rolling up umbrellas close and neat, and he's rather proud of it. He often looks as though he'd like to take a man's umbrella away and roll it up for him when it's a bit clumsy done. Rum fad, eh?"

"Yes; everybody has his little fad, though. Where was this found—close by here?"

"Yes, sir; just there, almost opposite this window, in the little corner."

"About two o'clock?"

"Ah, about that time, more or less."

Hewitt took the umbrella up, unfastened the band, and shook the silk out loose. Then he opened it, and as he did so a small scrap of paper fell from inside it. Hewitt pounced on it like lightning. Then, after examining the umbrella thoroughly, inside and out, he handed it back to the man, who had not observed the incident of the scrap of paper.

"That will do, thanks," he said. "I only wanted to take a peep at it—just a small matter connected with a little case of mine. Good-morning."

He turned suddenly and saw, gazing at him with a terrified expression from a door behind, the face of the woman who had followed him in the cab. The veil was lifted, and he caught but a mere glance of the face ere it was suddenly withdrawn. He stood for a moment to allow the woman time to retreat, and then left the station and walked toward his office, close by.

Scarcely thirty yards along the Strand he met Plummer.

"I'm going to make some much closer inquiries all down the line as far as Dover," Plummer said. "They wire from Calais that they have no clue as yet, and I mean to make quite sure, if I can, that Laker hasn't quietly slipped off the line somewhere between here and Dover. There's one very peculiar thing," Plummer added confidentially. "Did you see the two women who were waiting to see a member of the firm at Liddle, Neal & Liddle's?"

"Yes. Laker's mother and his *fiancée*, I was told."

"That's right. Well, do you know that girl—Shaw her name is—has been shadowing me ever since I left the bank. Of course I spotted it from the beginning—these amateurs don't know how to follow anybody—and, as a matter of fact, she's just inside that jeweller's shop door behind me now, pretending to look at the things in the window. But it's odd, isn't it?"

"Well," Hewitt replied, "of course it's not a thing to be neglected. If you'll look very carefully at the corner of Villiers Street, without appearing to stare, I think you will possibly observe some signs of Laker's mother. She's shadowing *me*."

Plummer looked casually in the direction indicated, and then immediately turned his eyes in another direction.

"I see her," he said; "she's just taking a look round the corner. That's a thing not to be ignored. Of course, the Lakers' house is being watched—we set a man on it at once, yesterday. But I'll put someone on now to watch Miss Shaw's place, too. I'll telephone through to Liddle's—probably they'll be able to say where it is. And the women themselves must be watched, too. As a matter of fact, I had a notion that Laker wasn't alone in it. And it's just possible, you know, that he has sent an accomplice off with his tourist ticket to lead us a dance while he looks after himself in another direction. Have you done anything?"

"Well," Hewitt replied, with a faint reproduction of the secretive smile with which Plummer had met an inquiry of his earlier in the morning, "I've been to the station here, and I've found Laker's umbrella in the lost property office."

"Oh! Then probably he *has* gone. I'll bear that in mind, and perhaps have a word with the lost property man."

Plummer made for the station and Hewitt for his office. He mounted the stairs and reached his door just as I myself, who had been disappointed in not finding him in, was leaving. I had called with the idea of taking Hewitt to lunch with me at my club, but he declined lunch. "I have an important case in hand," he said. "Look here, Brett. See this scrap of paper. You know the types of the different newspapers—which is this?"

He handed me a small piece of paper. It was part of a cutting containing an advertisement, which had been torn in half.

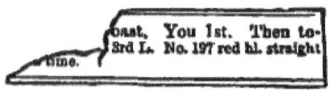

"I *think*," I said, "this is from the *Daily Chronicle*, judging by the paper. It is plainly from the 'agony column,' but all the papers use pretty much the same type for these advertisements, except the *Times*. If it were not torn I could tell you at once, because the *Chronicle* columns are rather narrow."

"Never mind—I'll send for them all." He rang, and sent Kerrett for a copy of each morning paper of the previous day. Then he took from a large wardrobe cupboard a decent but well-worn and rather roughened tall hat. Also a coat a little worn and shiny on the collar. He exchanged these for his own hat and coat, and then substituted an old necktie for his own clean white one, and encased his legs in mud-spotted leggings. This done, he produced a very large and thick pocket-book, fastened by a broad elastic band, and said, "Well, what do you think of this? Will it do for Queen's taxes, or sanitary inspection, or the gas, or the water-supply?"

"Very well indeed, I should say," I replied. "What's the case?"

"Oh, I'll tell you all about that when it's over—no time now. Oh, here you are, Kerrett. By the bye, Kerrett, I'm going out presently by the back way. Wait for about ten minutes or a quarter of an hour after I am gone, and then just go across the road and speak to that lady in black, with the veil, who is waiting in that little foot-passage opposite. Say Mr. Martin Hewitt sends his compliments, and he advises her not to wait, as he has already left his office by another door, and has been gone some little time. That's all; it would be a pity to keep the poor woman waiting all day for nothing. Now the papers. *Daily News, Standard, Telegraph, Chronicle*—yes, here it is, in the *Chronicle*."

The whole advertisement read thus:—

YOB.—H.R. Shop roast. You 1st. Then tonight. 02. 2nd top 3rd L. No. 197 red bl.
straight mon. One at a time.

"What's this," I asked, "a cryptogram?"

"I'll see," Hewitt answered. "But I won't tell you anything about it till afterwards, so you get your lunch. Kerrett, bring the directory."

This was all I actually saw of this case myself, and I have written the rest in its proper order from Hewitt's information, as I have written some other cases entirely.

To resume at the point where, for the time I lost sight of the matter. Hewitt left by the back way and stopped an empty cab as it passed. "Abney Park Cemetery" was his direction to the driver. In little more than twenty minutes the cab was branching off down the Essex Road on its way to Stoke Newington, and in twenty minutes more Hewitt stopped it in Church Street, Stoke Newington. He walked through a street or two, and then down another, the houses of which he scanned carefully as he passed. Opposite one which stood by itself he stopped, and, making a pretence of consulting and arranging his large pocket-book, he took a good look at the house. It was rather larger, neater, and more pretentious than the others in the street, and it had a natty little coach-house just visible up the side entrance. There were red blinds hung with heavy lace in the front windows, and behind one of these blinds Hewitt was able to catch the glint of a heavy gas chandelier.

He stepped briskly up the front steps and knocked sharply at the door. "Mr. Merston?" he asked, pocket-book in hand, when a neat parlour-maid opened the door.

"Yes."

"Ah!" Hewitt stepped into the hall and pulled off his hat; "it's only

241

the meter. There's been a deal of gas running away somewhere here, and I'm just looking to see if the meters are right. Where is it?"

The girl hesitated. "I'll—I'll ask master," she said.

"Very well. I don't want to take it away, you know—only to give it a tap or two, and so on."

The girl retired to the back of the hall, and without taking her eyes off Martin Hewitt, gave his message to some invisible person in a back room, whence came a growling reply of "All right."

Hewitt followed the girl to the basement, apparently looking straight before him, but in reality taking in every detail of the place. The gas meter was in a very large lumber cupboard under the kitchen stairs. The girl opened the door and lit a candle. The meter stood on the floor, which was littered with hampers and boxes and odd sheets of brown paper. But a thing that at once arrested Hewitt's attention was a garment of some sort of bright blue cloth, with large brass buttons, which was lying in a tumbled heap in a corner, and appeared to be the only thing in the place that was not covered with dust. Nevertheless, Hewitt took no apparent notice of it, but stooped down and solemnly tapped the meter three times with his pencil, and listened with great gravity, placing his ear to the top. Then he shook his head and tapped again. At length he said:—

"It's a bit doubtful. I'll just get you to light the gas in the kitchen a moment. Keep your hand to the burner, and when I call out shut it off *at once*; see?"

The girl turned and entered the kitchen, and Hewitt immediately seized the blue coat—for a coat it was. It had a dull red piping in the seams, and was of the swallow-tail pattern—a livery coat, in fact. He held it for a moment before him, examining its pattern and colour, and then rolled it up and flung it again into the corner.

"Right!" he called to the servant. "Shut off!"

The girl emerged from the kitchen as he left the cupboard.

"Well," she asked, "are you satisfied now?"

"Quite satisfied, thank you," Hewitt replied.

"Is it all right?" she continued, jerking her hand toward the cupboard.

"Well, no, it isn't; there's something wrong there, and I'm glad I came. You can tell Mr. Merston, if you like, that I expect his gas bill will be a good deal less next quarter." And there was a suspicion of a chuckle in Hewitt's voice as he crossed the hall to leave. For a gas inspector is pleased when he finds at length what he has been searching for.

Things had fallen out better than Hewitt had dared to expect. He saw the key of the whole mystery in that blue coat; for it was the uniform coat of the hall porters at one of the banks that he had visited in the morning, though which one he could not for the moment remember. He entered the nearest post-office and despatched a telegram to Plummer, giving certain directions and asking the inspector to meet him; then he hailed the first available cab and hurried toward the City.

At Lombard Street he alighted, and looked in at the door of each bank till he came to Buller, Clayton, Ladds & Co.'s. This was the bank he wanted. In the other banks the hall porters wore mulberry coats, brick-dust coats, brown coats, and what not, but here, behind the ladders and scaffold poles which obscured the entrance, he could see a man in a blue coat, with dull red piping and brass buttons. He sprang up the steps, pushed open the inner swing door, and finally satisfied himself by a closer view of the coat, to the wearer's astonishment. Then he regained the pavement and walked the whole length of the bank premises in front, afterwards turning up the paved passage at the side, deep in thought. The bank had no windows or doors on the side next the court, and the two adjoining houses were old and supported in places by wooden shores. Both were empty, and a great board announced that tenders would be received in a month's time for the purchase of the old materials of which they were constructed; also that some part of the site would be let on a long building lease.

Hewitt looked up at the grimy fronts of the old buildings. The windows were crusted thick with dirt—all except the bottom window of the house nearer the bank, which was fairly clean, and seemed to have been quite lately washed. The door, too, of this house was cleaner than that of the other, though the paint was worn. Hewitt reached and fingered a hook driven into the left-hand doorpost about six feet from the ground. It was new, and not at all rusted; also a tiny splinter had been displaced when the hook was driven in, and clean wood showed at the spot.

Having observed these things, Hewitt stepped back and read at the bottom of the big board the name, "Winsor & Weekes, Surveyors and Auctioneers, Abchurch Lane." Then he stepped into Lombard Street.

Two hansoms pulled up near the post-office, and out of the first stepped Inspector Plummer and another man. This man and the two who alighted from the second hansom were unmistakably plain-clothes constables—their air, gait, and boots proclaimed it.

"What's all this?" demanded Plummer, as Hewitt approached.

"You'll soon see, I think. But, first, have you put the watch on No. 197, Hackworth Road?"

"Yes; nobody will get away from there alone."

"Very good. I am going into Abchurch Lane for a few minutes. Leave your men out here, but just go round into the court by Buller, Clayton & Ladds's, and keep your eye on the first door on the left. I think we'll find something soon. Did you get rid of Miss Shaw?"

"No, she's behind now, and Mrs. Laker's with her. They met in the Strand, and came after us in another cab. Rare fun, eh! They think we're pretty green! It's quite handy, too. So long as they keep behind me it saves all trouble of watching *them*." And Inspector Plummer chuckled and winked.

"Very good. You don't mind keeping your eye on that door, do you? I'll be back very soon," and with that Hewitt turned off into Abchurch Lane.

At Winsor & Weekes's information was not difficult to obtain. The houses were destined to come down very shortly, but a week or so ago an office and a cellar in one of them was let temporarily to a Mr. Westley. He brought no references; indeed, as he paid a fortnight's rent in advance, he was not asked for any, considering the circumstances of the case. He was opening a London branch for a large firm of cider merchants, he said, and just wanted a rough office and a cool cellar to store samples in for a few weeks till the permanent premises were ready. There was another key, and no doubt the premises might be entered if there were any special need for such a course. Martin Hewitt gave such excellent reasons that Winsor & Weekes's managing clerk immediately produced the key and accompanied Hewitt to the spot.

"I think you'd better have your men handy," Hewitt remarked to Plummer when they reached the door, and a whistle quickly brought the men over.

The key was inserted in the lock and turned, but the door would not open; the bolt was fastened at the bottom. Hewitt stooped and looked under the door.

"It's a drop bolt," he said. "Probably the man who left last let it fall loose, and then banged the door, so that it fell into its place. I must try my best with a wire or a piece of string."

A wire was brought, and with some manoeuvring Hewitt contrived to pass it round the bolt, and lift it little by little, steadying it with the blade of a pocket-knife. When at length the bolt was raised out of the hole, the knife-blade was slipped under it, and the door swung open.

They entered. The door of the little office just inside stood open, but in the office there was nothing, except a board a couple of feet long in a corner. Hewitt stepped across and lifted this, turning its downward face toward Plummer. On it, in fresh white paint on a black ground, were painted the words—

Buller, Clayton, Ladds & Co.,
Temporary Entrance.

Hewitt turned to Winsor & Weekes's clerk and asked, "The man who took this room called himself Westley, didn't he?"

"Yes."

"Youngish man, clean-shaven, and well-dressed?"

"Yes, he was."

"I fancy," Hewitt said, turning to Plummer, "I *fancy* an old friend of yours is in this—Mr. Sam Gunter."

"What, the 'Hoxton Yob'?"

"I think it's possible he's been Mr. Westley for a bit, and somebody else for another bit. But let's come to the cellar."

Winsor & Weekes's clerk led the way down a steep flight of steps into a dark underground corridor, wherein they lighted their way with many successive matches. Soon the corridor made a turn to the right, and as the party passed the turn, there came from the end of the passage before them a fearful yell.

"Help! help! Open the door! I'm going mad—mad! O my God!"

And there was a sound of desperate beating from the inside of the cellar door at the extreme end. The men stopped, startled.

"Come," said Hewitt, "more matches!" and he rushed to the door. It was fastened with a bar and padlock.

"Let me out, for God's sake!" came the voice, sick and hoarse, from the inside. "Let me out!"

"All right!" Hewitt shouted. "We have come for you. Wait a moment."

The voice sank into a sort of sobbing croon, and Hewitt tried several keys from his own bunch on the padlock. None fitted. He drew from his pocket the wire he had used for the bolt of the front door, straightened it out, and made a sharp bend at the end.

"Hold a match close," he ordered shortly, and one of the men obeyed. Three or four attempts were necessary, and several different bendings of the wire were effected, but in the end Hewitt picked the lock, and flung open the door.

From within a ghastly figure fell forward among them fainting, and knocked out the matches.

"Hullo!" cried Plummer. "Hold up! Who are you?"

"Let's get him up into the open," said Hewitt. "He can't tell you who he is for a bit, but I believe he's Laker."

"Laker! What, here?"

"I think so. Steady up the steps. Don't bump him. He's pretty sore already, I expect."

Truly the man was a pitiable sight. His hair and face were caked in dust and blood, and his finger-nails were torn and bleeding. Water was sent for at once, and brandy.

"Well," said Plummer hazily, looking first at the unconscious prisoner and then at Hewitt, "but what about the swag?"

"You'll have to find that yourself," Hewitt replied. "I think my share of the case is about finished. I only act for the Guarantee Society, you know, and if Laker's proved innocent——"

"Innocent! How?"

"Well, this is what took place, as near as I can figure it. You'd better undo his collar, I think"—this to the men. "What I believe has happened is this. There has been a very clever and carefully prepared conspiracy here, and Laker has not been the criminal, but the victim."

"Been robbed himself, you mean? But how? Where?"

"Yesterday morning, before he had been to more than three banks—here, in fact."

"But then how? You're all wrong. We *know* he made the whole round, and did all the collection. And then Palmer's office, and all, and the umbrella; why——"

The man lay still unconscious. "Don't raise his head," Hewitt said. "And one of you had best fetch a doctor. He's had a terrible shock." Then turning to Plummer he went on, "As to *how* they managed the job I'll tell you what I think. First it struck some very clever person that a deal of money might be got by robbing a walk-clerk from a bank. This clever person was one of a clever gang of thieves—perhaps the Hoxton Row gang, as I think I hinted. Now you know quite as well as I do that such a gang will spend any amount of time over a job that promises a big haul, and that for such a job they can always command the necessary capital. There are many most respectable persons living in good style in the suburbs whose chief business lies in financing such ventures, and taking the chief share of the proceeds. Well, this is their plan, carefully and intelligently carried out.

"They watch Laker, observe the round he takes, and his habits. They find that there is only one of the clerks with whom he does business that he is much acquainted with, and that this clerk is in a bank which is commonly second in Laker's round. The sharpest man among them—and I don't think there's a man in London could do this as well as young Sam Gunter—studies Laker's dress and habits just as an actor studies a character. They take this office and cellar, as we have seen, *because it is next door to a bank whose front entrance is being altered*—a fact which Laker must know from his daily visits. The smart man—Gunter, let us say, and I have other reasons for believing it to be he—makes up precisely like Laker, false moustache, dress, and everything, and waits here with the rest of the gang. One of the gang is dressed in a blue coat with brass buttons, like a hall-porter in Buller's bank. Do you see?"

"Yes, I think so. It's pretty clear now."

"A confederate watches at the top of the court, and the moment Laker turns in from Cornhill—having already been, mind, at the only bank where he was so well known that the disguised thief would not have passed muster—as soon as he turns in from Cornhill, I say, a signal is given, and that board"—pointing to that with the white letters—"is hung on the hook in the doorpost. The sham porter stands beside it, and as Laker approaches says, 'This way in, sir, this morning. The front way's shut for the alterations.' Laker, suspecting nothing, and supposing that the firm have made a temporary entrance through the empty house, enters. He is seized when well along the corridor, the board is taken down and the door shut. Probably he is stunned by a blow on the head—see the blood now. They take his wallet and all the cash he has already collected.

"Gunter takes the wallet and also the umbrella, since it has Laker's initials, and is therefore distinctive. He simply completes the walk in the character of Laker, beginning with Buller, Clayton & Ladds's just round the corner. It is nothing but routine work, which is quickly done, and nobody notices him particularly—it is the bills they examine. Meanwhile this unfortunate fellow is locked up in the cellar here, right at the end of the underground corridor, where he can never make himself heard in the street, and where next him are only the empty cellars of the deserted house next door. The thieves shut the front door and vanish. The rest is plain. Gunter, having completed the round, and bagged some £15,000 or more, spends a few pounds in a tourist ticket at Palmer's as a blind, being careful to give Laker's name. He leaves the umbrella at Charing Cross in a conspicuous place right opposite the lost property office, where it is sure to be seen, and so completes his false trail."

"Then who are the people at 197, Hackworth Road?"

"The capitalist lives there—the financier, and probably the directing spirit of the whole thing. Merston's the name he goes by there, and I've no doubt he cuts a very imposing figure in chapel every Sunday. He'll be worth picking up—this isn't the first thing he's been in, I'll warrant."

"But—but what about Laker's mother and Miss Shaw?"

"Well, what? The poor women are nearly out of their minds with terror and shame, that's all, but though they may think Laker a criminal, they'll never desert him. They've been following us about with a feeble, vague sort of hope of being able to baffle us in some way or help him if we caught him, or something, poor things. Did you ever hear of a real woman who'd desert a son or a lover merely because he was a criminal? But here's the doctor. When he's attended to him will you let your men take Laker home? I must hurry and report to the Guarantee Society, I think."

"But," said the perplexed Plummer, "where did you get your clue? You must have had a tip from someone, you know—you can't have done it by clairvoyance. What gave you the tip?"

"The *Daily Chronicle*."

"The *what?*"

"The *Daily Chronicle*. Just take a look at the 'agony column' in yesterday morning's issue, and read the message to 'Yob'—to Gunter, in fact. That's all."

By this time a cab was waiting in Lombard Street, and two of Plummer's men, under the doctor's directions, carried Laker to it. No sooner, however, were they in the court than the two watching women threw themselves hysterically upon Laker, and it was long before they could be persuaded that he was not being taken to gaol. The mother shrieked aloud, "My boy—my boy! Don't take him! Oh, don't take him! They've killed my boy! Look at his head—oh, his head!" and wrestled desperately with the men, while Hewitt attempted to soothe her, and promised to allow her to go in the cab with her son if she would only be quiet. The younger woman made no noise, but she held one of Laker's limp hands in both hers.

Hewitt and I dined together that evening, and he gave me a full account of the occurrences which I have here set down. Still, when he was finished I was not able to see clearly by what process of reasoning he had arrived at the conclusions that gave him the key to the mystery, nor did I understand the "agony column" message, and I said so.

"In the beginning," Hewitt explained, "the thing that struck me as curious was the fact that Laker was said to have given his own name at Palmer's in buying his ticket. Now, the first thing the greenest and newest criminal thinks of is changing his name, so that the giving of his own name seemed unlikely to begin with. Still, he *might* have made such a mistake, as Plummer suggested when he said that criminals usually make a mistake somewhere—as they do, in fact. Still, it was the least likely mistake I could think of—especially as he actually didn't wait to be asked for his name, but blurted it out when it wasn't really wanted. And it was conjoined with another rather curious mistake, or what would have been a mistake if the thief were Laker. Why should he conspicuously display his wallet—such a distinctive article—for the clerk to see and note? Why rather had he not got rid of it before showing himself? Suppose it should be somebody personating Laker? In any case I determined not to be prejudiced by what I had heard of Laker's betting. A man may bet without being a thief.

"But, again, supposing it *were* Laker? Might he not have given his name, and displayed his wallet, and so on, while buying a ticket for France, in order to draw pursuit after himself in that direction while he made off in another, in another name, and disguised? Each supposition was plausible. And, in either case, it might happen that whoever was laying this trail would probably lay it a little farther. Charing Cross was the next point, and there I went. I already had it from Plummer that Laker had not been recognised there. Perhaps the trail had been laid in some other manner. Something left behind with Laker's name on it, perhaps? I at once thought of the umbrella with his monogram, and, making a long shot, asked for it at the lost property office, as you know.

"The guess was lucky. In the umbrella, as you know, I found that scrap of paper. That, I judged, had fallen in from the hand of the man carrying the umbrella. He had torn the paper in half in order to fling it away, and one piece had fallen into the loosely flapping umbrella. It is a thing that will often happen with an omnibus ticket, as you may have noticed. Also, it was proved that the umbrella *was* unrolled when found, and rolled immediately after. So here was a piece of paper dropped by the person who had brought the umbrella to Charing Cross and left it. I got the whole advertisement, as you remember, and I studied it. 'Yob' is back-slang for 'boy,' and it is often used in nicknames to denote a young smooth-faced thief. Gunter, the man I suspect, as a matter of fact, is known as the 'Hoxton Yob.' The message, then, was addressed to someone known by such a nickname.

"Next, 'H.R. shop roast.' Now, in thieves' slang, to 'roast' a thing or a person is to watch it or him. They call any place a shop—notably, a thieves' den. So that this meant that some resort—perhaps the 'Hoxton Row shop'—was watched. 'You 1st then tonight' would be clearer, perhaps, when the rest was understood. I thought a little over the rest, and it struck me that it must be a direction to some other house, since one was warned of as being watched. Besides, there was the number, 197, and 'red bl.,' which would be extremely likely to mean 'red blinds,' by way of clearly distinguishing the house. And then the plan of the thing was plain. You have noticed, probably, that the map of London which accompanies the Post Office Directory is divided, for convenience of reference, into numbered squares?"

"Yes. The squares are denoted by letters along the top margin and figures down the side. So that if you consult the directory, and find a place marked as being in D 5, for instance, you find vertical divisions D, and run your finger down it till it intersects horizontal division 5, and there you are."

"Precisely. I got my Post Office Directory, and looked for 'O 2.' It was in North London, and took in parts of Abney Park Cemetery and Clissold Park; '2nd top' was the next sign. Very well, I counted the second street intersecting the top of the square—counting, in the usual way, from the left. That was Lordship Road. Then, '3rd L.' From the point where Lordship Road crossed the top of the square, I ran my finger down the road till it came to '3rd L,' or, in other words, the third turning on the left—Hackworth Road. So there we were, unless my guesses were altogether wrong. 'Straight mon' probably meant 'straight moniker'—that is to say, the proper name, a thief's *real* name, in contradistinction to that he may assume.

"I turned over the directory till I found Hackworth Road, and found that No. 197 was inhabited by a Mr. Merston. From the whole thing I judged this. There was to have been a meeting at the 'H.R. shop,' but that was found, at the last moment, to be watched by the police for some purpose, so that another appointment was made for this house in the suburbs. 'You 1st. Then tonight'—the person addressed was to come first, and the others in the evening. They were to ask for the householder's 'straight moniker'—Mr. Merston. And they were to come one at a time.

"Now, then, what was this? What theory would fit it? Suppose this were a robbery, directed from afar by the advertiser. Suppose, on the day before the robbery, it was found that the place fixed for division of spoils were watched. Suppose that the principal thereupon advertised (as had already been agreed in case of emergency) in these terms. The principal in the actual robbery—the 'Yob' addressed—was to go first with the booty. The others were to come after, one at a time. Anyway, the thing was good enough to follow a little further, and I determined to try No. 197, Hackworth Road. I have told you what I found there, and how it opened my eyes. I went, of course, merely on chance, to see what I might chance to see. But luck favoured, and I happened on that coat—brought back rolled up, on the evening after the robbery, doubtless by the thief who had used it, and flung carelessly into the handiest cupboard. *That* was this gang's mistake."

"Well, I congratulate you," I said. "I hope they'll catch the rascals."

"I rather think they will, now they know where to look. They can scarcely miss Merston, anyway. There has been very little to go upon in this case, but I stuck to the thread, however slight, and it brought me through. The rest of the case, of course, is Plummer's. It was a peculiarity of my commission that I could equally well fulfil it by catching the man with all the plunder, or by proving him innocent. Having done the latter, my work was at an end, but I left it where Plummer will be able to finish the job handsomely."

Plummer did. Sam Gunter, Merston, and one accomplice were taken—the first and last were well known to the police—and were identified by Laker. Merston, as Hewitt had suspected, had kept the lion's share for himself, so that altogether, with what was recovered from him and the other two, nearly £11,000 was saved for Messrs. Liddle, Neal & Liddle. Merston, when taken, was in the act of packing up to take a holiday abroad, and there cash his notes, which were found, neatly packed in separate thousands, in his portmanteau. As Hewitt had predicted, his gas bill *was* considerably less next quarter, for less than half-way through it he began a term in gaol.

As for Laker, he was reinstated, of course, with an increase of salary by way of compensation for his broken head. He had passed a terrible twenty-six hours in the cellar, unfed and unheard. Several times he had become insensible, and again and again he had thrown himself madly against the door, shouting and tearing at it, till he fell back exhausted, with broken nails and bleeding fingers.

For some hours before the arrival of his rescuers he had been sitting in a sort of stupor, from which he was suddenly aroused by the sound of voices and footsteps. He was in bed for a week, and required a rest of a month in addition before he could resume his duties. Then he was quietly lectured by Mr. Neal as to betting, and, I believe, dropped that practice in consequence. I am told that he is "at the counter" now—a considerable promotion.

The Case of the Lost Foreigner

I have already said in more than one place that Hewitt's personal relations with the members of the London police force were of a cordial character. In the course of his work it has frequently been Hewitt's hap to learn of matters on which the police were glad of information, and that information was always passed on at once; and so long as no infringement of regulations or damage to public service were involved, Hewitt could always rely on a return in kind.

It was with a message of a useful sort that Hewitt one day dropped into Vine Street police-station and asked for a particular inspector, who was not in. Hewitt sat and wrote a note, and by way of making conversation said to the inspector on duty, "Anything very startling this way today?"

"Nothing *very* startling, perhaps, as yet," the inspector replied. "But one of our chaps picked up rather an odd customer a little while ago. Lunatic of some sort, I should think—in fact, I've sent for the doctor to see him. He's a foreigner—a Frenchman, I believe. He seemed horribly weak and faint; but the oddest thing occurred when one of the men, thinking he might be hungry, brought in some bread. He went into fits of terror at the sight of it, and wouldn't be pacified till they took it away again."

"That was strange."

"Odd, wasn't it? And he *was* hungry too. They brought him some more a little while after, and he didn't funk it a bit,—pitched into it, in fact, like anything, and ate it all with some cold beef. It's the way with some lunatics—never the same five minutes together. He keeps crying like a baby, and saying things we can't understand. As it happens, there's nobody in just now who speaks French."

"I speak French," Hewitt replied. "Shall I try him?"

"Certainly, if you will. He's in the men's room below. They've been making him as comfortable as possible by the fire until the doctor comes. He's a long time. I expect he's got a case on."

Hewitt found his way to the large mess-room, where three or four policemen in their shirt-sleeves were curiously regarding a young man of very disordered appearance who sat on a chair by the fire. He was pale, and exhibited marks of bruises on his face, while over one eye was a scarcely healed cut. His figure was small and slight, his coat was torn, and he sat with a certain indefinite air of shivering suffering. He started and looked round apprehensively as Hewitt entered. Hewitt bowed smilingly, wished him good-day, speaking in French, and asked him if he spoke the language.

The man looked up with a dull expression, and after an effort or two, as of one who stutters, burst out with, "*Je le nie!*"

"That's strange," Hewitt observed to the men. "I ask him if he speaks French, and he says he denies it—speaking *in* French."

"He's been saying that very often, sir," one of the men answered, "as well as other things we can't make anything of."

Hewitt placed his hand kindly on the man's shoulder and asked his name. The reply was for a little while an inarticulate gurgle, presently merging into a meaningless medley of words and syllables—"*Qu'est ce qu'—il n'a*—Leystar Squarr—*sacré nom*—not spik it—*quel chemin*—sank you ver' mosh—*je le nie! je le nie!*" He paused, stared, and then, as though realizing his helplessness, he burst into tears.

"He's been a-cryin' two or three times," said the man who had spoken before. "He was a-cryin' when we found him."

Several more attempts Hewitt made to communicate with the man, but though he seemed to comprehend what was meant, he replied with nothing but meaningless gibber, and finally gave up the attempt, and, leaning against the side of the fireplace, buried his head in the bend of his arm.

Then the doctor arrived and made *his* examination. While it was in progress Hewitt took aside the policeman who had been speaking before and questioned him further. He had himself found the Frenchman in a dull back street by Golden Square, where the man was standing helpless and trembling, apparently quite bewildered and very weak. He had brought him in, without having been able to learn anything about him. One or two shopkeepers in the street where he was found were asked, but knew nothing of him—indeed, had never seen him before.

"But the curiousest thing," the policeman proceeded, "was in this 'ere room, when I brought him a loaf to give him a bit of a snack, seein' he looked so weak an' 'ungry. You'd 'a thought we was a-goin' to poison 'im. He fair screamed at the very sight o' the bread, an' he scrouged hisself up in that corner an' put his hands in front of his face. I couldn't make out what was up at first—didn't tumble to it's bein' the bread he was frightened of, seein' as he looked like a man as 'ud be frightened at anything else afore *that*. But the nearer I came with it the more he yelled, so I took it away an' left it outside, an' then he calmed down. An' s'elp me, when I cut some bits off that there very loaf an' brought 'em in, with a bit o' beef, he just went for 'em like one o'clock. *He* wasn't frightened o' no bread then, you bet. Rum thing, how the fancies takes 'em when they're a bit touched, ain't it? All one way one minute, all the other the next."

"Yes, it is. By the way, have you another uncut loaf in the place?"

"Yes, sir. Half a dozen if you like."

"One will be enough. I am going over to speak to the doctor. Wait awhile until he seems very quiet and fairly comfortable; then bring a loaf in quietly and put it on the table, not far from his elbow. Don't attract his attention to what you are doing."

The doctor stood looking thoughtfully down on the Frenchman, who, for his part, stared gloomily, but tranquilly, at the fireplace. Hewitt stepped quietly over to the doctor and, without disturbing the man by the fire, said interrogatively, "Aphasia?"

The doctor tightened his lips, frowned, and nodded significantly. "Motor," he murmured, just loudly enough for Hewitt to hear; "and there's a general nervous break-down as well, I should say. By the way, perhaps there's no agraphia. Have you tried him with pen and paper?"

Pen and paper were brought and set before the man. He was told, slowly and distinctly, that he was among friends, whose only object was to restore him to his proper health. Would he write his name and address, and any other information he might care to give about himself, on the paper before him?

The Frenchman took the pen and stared at the paper; then slowly, and with much hesitation, he traced these marks:—

The man paused after the last of these futile characters, and his pen stabbed into the paper with a blot, as he dazedly regarded his work. Then with a groan he dropped it, and his face sank again into the bend of his arm.

The doctor took the paper and handed it to Hewitt. "Complete agraphia, you see," he said. "He can't write a word. He begins to write '*Monsieur*' from sheer habit in beginning letters thus; but the word tails off into a scrawl. Then his attempts become mere scribble, with just a trace of some familiar word here and there—but quite meaningless all."

Although he had never before chanced to come across a case of aphasia (happily a rare disease), Hewitt was acquainted with its general nature. He knew that it might arise either from some physical injury to the brain, or from a break-down consequent on some terrible nervous strain. He knew that in the case of motor aphasia the sufferer, though fully conscious of all that goes on about him, and though quite understanding what is said to him is entirely powerless to put his own thoughts into spoken words—has lost, in fact, the connection between words and their spoken symbols. Also that in most bad cases agraphia—the loss of ability to write words with any reference to their meaning—is commonly an accompaniment.

"You will have him taken to the infirmary, I suppose?" Hewitt asked.

"Yes," the doctor replied. "I shall go and see about it at once."

The man looked up again as they spoke. The policeman had, in accordance with Hewitt's request, placed a loaf of bread on the table near him, and now as he looked up he caught sight of it. He started visibly and paled, but gave no such signs of abject terror as the policeman had previously observed. He appeared nervous and uneasy, however, and presently reached stealthily toward the loaf. Hewitt continued to talk to the doctor, while closely watching the Frenchman's behaviour from the corner of his eye.

The loaf was what is called a "plain cottage," of solid and regular shape. The man reached it and immediately turned it bottom up on the table. Then he sank back in his chair with a more contented expression, though his gaze was still directed toward the loaf. The policeman grinned silently at this curious manoeuvre.

The doctor left, and Hewitt accompanied him to the door of the room. "He will not be moved just yet, I take it?" Hewitt asked as they parted.

"It may take an hour or two," the doctor replied. "Are you anxious to keep him here?"

"Not for long; but I think there's a curious inside to the case, and I may perhaps learn something of it by a little watching. But I can't spare very long."

At a sign from Hewitt the loaf was removed. Then Hewitt pulled the small table closer to the Frenchman and pushed the pen and sheets of paper toward him. The manoeuvre had its result. The man looked up and down the room vacantly once or twice and then began to turn the papers over. From that he went to dipping the pen in the inkpot, and presently he was scribbling at random on the loose sheets. Hewitt affected to leave him entirely alone, and seemed to be absorbed in a contemplation of a photograph of a police-division brass band that hung on the wall, but he saw every scratch the man made.

At first there was nothing but meaningless scrawls and attempted words. Then rough sketches appeared, of a man's head, a chair or what not. On the mantelpiece stood a small clock—apparently a sort of humble presentation piece, the body of the clock being set in a horse-shoe frame, with crossed whips behind it. After a time, the Frenchman's eyes fell on this, and he began a crude sketch of it. That he relinquished, and went on with other random sketches and scribblings on the same piece of paper, sketching and scribbling over the sketches in a half-mechanical sort of way, as of one who trifles with a pen during a brown study. Beginning at the top left-hand corner of the paper, he travelled all round it till he arrived at the left-hand bottom corner. Then dashing his pen hastily across his last sketch he dropped it, and with a great shudder turned away again and hid his face by the fireplace.

Hewitt turned at once and seized the papers on the table. He stuffed them all into his coat-pocket, with the exception of the last which the man had been engaged on, and this, a facsimile of which is

subjoined, he studied earnestly for several minutes.

Hewitt wished the men good-day, and made his way to the inspector.

"Well," the inspector said, "not much to be got out of him, is there? The doctor will be sending for him presently."

"I fancy," said Hewitt, "that this may turn out a very important case. Possibly—quite possibly—I may not have guessed correctly, and so I won't tell you anything of it till I know a little more. But what I want now is a messenger. Can I send somebody at once in a cab to my friend Brett at his chambers?"

"Certainly. I'll find somebody. Want to write a note?"

Hewitt wrote and despatched a note, which reached me in less than ten minutes. Then he asked the inspector, "Have you searched the Frenchman?"

"Oh, yes. We went all over him, when we found he couldn't explain himself, to see if we could trace his friends or his address. He didn't seem to mind. But there wasn't a single thing in his pocket—not a single thing, barring a rag of a pocket-handkerchief with no marking on it."

"You noticed that somebody had stolen his watch, I suppose?"

"Well, he hadn't got one."

"But he had one of those little vertical button-holes in his waistcoat, used to fasten a watch-guard to, and it was much worn and frayed, so that he must be in the habit of carrying a watch; and it is gone."

"Yes, and everything else too, eh? Looks like robbery. He's had a knock or two in the face—notice that?"

"I saw the bruises and the cut, of course; and his collar has been broken away, with the back button; somebody has taken him by the collar or throat. Was he wearing a hat when he was found?"

"No."

"That would imply that he had only just left a house. What street was he found in?"

"Henry Street—a little off Golden Square. Low street, you know."

"Did the constable notice a door open nearby?"

The inspector shook his head. "Half the doors in the street are open," he said, "pretty nearly all day."

"Ah, then there's nothing in that. I don't think he lives there, by the bye. I fancy he comes from more in the Seven Dials or Drury Lane direction. Did you notice anything about the man that gave you a clue to his occupation—or at any rate to his habits?"

"Can't say I did."

"Well, just take a look at the back of his coat before he goes away—just over the loins. Good-day."

As I have said, Hewitt's messenger was quick. I happened to be in—having lately returned from a latish lunch—when he arrived with this note:—

My dear B.,—I meant to have lunched with you today, but have been kept. I expect you are idle this afternoon, and I have a case that will interest you—perhaps be useful to you from a journalistic point of view. If you care to see anything of it, cab away *at once* to Fitzroy Square, south side, where I'll meet you. I will wait no later than 3.30. Yours, M. H.

I had scarce a quarter of an hour, so I seized my hat and left my chambers at once. As it happened, my cab and Hewitt's burst into Fitzroy Square from opposite sides almost at the same moment, so that we lost no time.

"Come," said Hewitt, taking my arm and marching me off, "we are going to look for some stabling. Try to feel as though you'd just set up a brougham and had come out to look for a place to put it in. I fear we may have to delude some person with that belief presently."

"Why—what do you want stables for? And why make me your excuse?"

"As to what I want the stables for—really I'm not altogether sure myself. As to making you an excuse—well, even the humblest excuse is better than none. But come, here are some stables. Not good enough, though, even if any of them were empty. Come on."

We had stopped for an instant at the entrance to a small alley of rather dirty stables, and Hewitt, paying apparently but small attention to the stables themselves, had looked sharply about him with his gaze in the air.

"I know this part of London pretty well," Hewitt observed, "and I can only remember one other range of stabling nearby; we must try that. As a matter of fact, I'm coming here on little more than conjecture, though I shall be surprised if there isn't something in it. Do you know anything of aphasia?"

"I have heard of it, of course, though I can't say I remember ever knowing a case."

"I've seen one today—very curious case. The man's a Frenchman, discovered helpless in the street by a policeman. The only thing he can say that has any meaning in it at all is '*je le nie*,' and that he says mechanically, without in the least knowing what he is saying. And he can't write. But he got sketching and scrawling various things on some paper, and his scrawls—together with another thing or two—have given me an idea. We're following it up now. When we are less busy, and in a quiet place, I'll show you the sketches and explain things generally; there's no time now, and I *may* want your help for a bit, in which case ignorance may prevent you spoiling things, you clumsy ruffian. Hullo! here we are, I think!"

We had stopped at the end of another stable-yard, rather dirtier than the first. The stables were sound but inelegant sheds, and one or two appeared to be devoted to other purposes, having low chimneys, on one of which an old basket was rakishly set by way of cowl. Beside the entrance a worn-out old board was nailed, with the legend, "Stabling to Let," in letters formerly white on a ground formerly black.

"Come," said Hewitt, "we'll explore."

We picked our way over the greasy cobble-stones and looked about us. On the left was the wall enclosing certain back-yards, and on the right the stables. Two doors in the middle of these were open, and a butcher's young man, who with his shiny bullet head would have been known for a butcher's young man anywhere, was wiping over the new-washed wheel of a smart butcher's cart.

"Good-day," Hewitt said pleasantly to the young man. "I notice there's some stabling to let here. Now, where should I inquire about it?"

"Jones, Whitfield Street," the young man answered, giving the wheel a final spin. "But there's only one little place to let now, I think, and it ain't very grand."

"Oh, which is that?"

"Next but one to the street there. A chap 'ad it for wood-choppin', but 'e chucked it. There ain't room for more'n a donkey an' a barrow."

"Ah, that's a pity. We're not particular, but want something big enough, and we don't mind paying a fair price. Perhaps we might make an arrangement with somebody here who has a stable?"

The young man shook his head.

"I shouldn't think so," he said doubtfully; "they're mostly shop-people as wants all the room theirselves. My guv'nor couldn't do no-think, I know. These 'ere two stables ain't scarcely enough for all 'e wants as it is. Then there's Barkett the greengrocer 'ere next door. *That* ain't no good. Then, next to that, there's the little place as is to let, and at the end there's Griffith's at the butter-shop."

"And those the other way?"

"Well, this 'ere first one's Curtis's, Euston Road—that's a butter-shop, too, an' 'e 'as the next after that. The last one, up at the end—I dunno quite whose that is. It ain't been long took, but I b'lieve it's some foreign baker's. I ain't ever see anythink come out of it, though; but there's a 'orse there, I know—I seen the feed took in."

Hewitt turned thoughtfully away.

"Thanks," he said. "I suppose we can't manage it, then. Good-day."

We walked to the street as the butcher's young man wheeled in his cart and flung away his pail of water.

"Will you just hang about here, Brett," he asked, "while I hurry round to the nearest iron-monger's? I shan't be gone long. We're going to work a little burglary. Take note if anybody comes to that stable at the farther end."

He hurried away and I waited. In a few moments the butcher's young man shut his doors and went whistling down the street, and in a few moments more Hewitt appeared.

"Come," he said, "there's nobody about now; we'll lose no time. I've bought a pair of pliers and a few nails."

We re-entered the yard at the door of the last stable. Hewitt stooped and examined the padlock. Taking a nail in his pliers he bent it carefully against the brick wall. Then using the nail as a key, still held by the pliers, and working the padlock gently in his left hand, in an astonishingly few seconds he had released the hasp and taken off the padlock. "I'm not altogether a bad burglar," he remarked. "Not so bad, really."

The padlock fastened a bar which, when removed, allowed the door to be opened. Opening it, Hewitt immediately seized a candle stuck in a bottle which stood on a shelf, pulled me in, and closed the door behind us.

"We'll do this by candle-light," he said, as he struck a match. "If the door were left open it would be seen from the street. Keep your ears open in case anybody comes down the yard."

The part of the shed that we stood in was used as a coach-house, and was occupied by a rather shabby tradesman's cart, the shafts of which rested on the ground. From the stall adjoining came the sound of the shuffling and trampling of an impatient horse.

We turned to the cart. On the name-board at the side were painted in worn letters the words, "Schuyler, Baker." The address, which had been below, was painted out.

Hewitt took out the pins and let down the tail board. Within the cart was a new bed-mattress which covered the whole surface at the bottom. I felt it, pressed it from the top, and saw that it was an ordinary spring mattress—perhaps rather unusually soft in the springs. It seemed a curious thing to keep in a baker's cart.

Hewitt, who had set the candle on a convenient shelf, plunged his arm into the farthermost recesses of the cart and brought forth a very long French loaf, and then another. Diving again he produced certain loaves of the sort known as the "plain cottage"—two sets of four each, each set baked together in a row. "Feel this bread," said Hewitt, and I felt it. It was stale—almost as hard as wood.

Hewitt produced a large pocket-knife, and with what seemed to me to be superfluous care and elaboration, cut into the top of one of the cottage loaves. Then he inserted his fingers in the gap he had made and firmly but slowly tore the hard bread into two pieces. He pulled away the crumb from within till there was nothing left but a rather thick outer shell.

"No," he said, rather to himself than to me, "there's nothing in *that*." He lifted one of the very long French loaves and measured it against the interior of the cart. It had before been propped diagonally, and now it was noticeable that it was just a shade longer than the inside of the cart was wide. Jammed in, in fact, it held firmly. Hewitt produced his knife again, and divided this long loaf in the centre; there was nothing but bread in *that*. The horse in the stall fidgeted more than ever.

"That horse hasn't been fed lately, I fancy," Hewitt said. "We'll give the poor chap a bit of this hay in the corner."

"But," I said, "what about this bread? What did you expect to find in it? I can't see what you're driving at."

"I'll tell you," Hewitt replied, "I'm driving after something I expect to find, and close at hand here, too. How are your nerves today—pretty steady? The thing may try them."

Before I could reply there was a sound of footsteps in the yard outside, approaching. Hewitt lifted his finger instantly for silence and whispered hurriedly, "There's only one. If he comes *here*, we grab him."

The steps came nearer and stopped outside the door. There was a pause, and then a slight drawing in of breath, as of a person suddenly surprised. At that moment the door was slightly shifted ajar and an eye peeped in.

"Catch him!" said Hewitt aloud, as we sprang to the door. "He mustn't get away!"

I had been nearer the doorway, and was first through it. The stranger ran down the yard at his best, but my legs were the longer, and halfway to the street I caught him by the shoulder and swung him round. Like lightning he whipped out a knife, and I flung in my left instantly on the chance of flooring him. It barely checked him, however, and the knife swung short of my chest by no more than two inches; but Hewitt had him by the wrist and tripped him forward on his face. He struggled like a wild beast, and Hewitt had to stand on his forearm and force up his wrist till the bones were near breaking before he dropped his knife. But throughout the struggle the man never shouted, called for help, nor, indeed, made the slightest sound, and we on our part were equally silent. It was quickly over, of course, for he was on his face, and we were two. We dragged our prisoner into the stable and closed the door behind us. So far as we had seen, nobody had witnessed the capture from the street, though, of course, we had been too busy to be certain.

"There's a set of harness hanging over at the back," said Hewitt; "I think we'll tie him up with the traces and reins—nothing like leather. We don't need a gag; I know he won't shout."

While I got the straps Hewitt held the prisoner by a peculiar neck-and-wrist grip that forbade him to move except at the peril of a snapped arm. He had probably never been a person of pleasant aspect, being short, strongly and squatly built, large and ugly of feature, and wild and dirty of hair and beard. And now, his face flushed with struggling and smeared with mud from the stable-yard, his nose bleeding and his forehead exhibiting a growing bump, he looked particularly repellent. We strapped his elbows together behind, and as he sullenly ignored a demand for the contents of his pockets Hewitt unceremoniously turned them out. Helpless as he was, the man struggled to prevent this, though, of course, ineffectually. There were papers, tobacco, a bunch of keys, and various odds and ends. Hewitt was glancing hastily at the papers when, suddenly dropping them, he caught the prisoner by the shoulder and pulled him away from a partly-consumed hay-truss which stood in a corner, and toward which he had quietly sidled.

"Keep him still," said Hewitt; "we haven't examined this place yet." And he commenced to pull away the hay from the corner.

Presently a large piece of sackcloth was revealed, and this being lifted left visible below it another batch of loaves of the same sort as we had seen in the cart. There were a dozen of them in one square batch, and the only thing about them that differed them from those in the cart was their position, for the batch lay bottom side up.

"That's enough, I think," Hewitt said. "Don't touch them, for Heaven's sake!" He picked up the papers he had dropped. "That has saved us a little search," he continued. "See here, Brett; I was in the act of telling you my suspicions when this little affair interrupted me. If you care to look at one or two of these letters, you'll see what I should have told you. It's Anarchism and bombs, of course. I'm about as certain as I can be that there's a reversible dynamite bomb inside each of those innocent loaves, though I assure you I don't mean meddling with them now. But see here. Will you go and bring in a four-wheeler? Bring it right down the yard. There's more to do, and we mustn't attract attention."

I hurried away and found the cab. The meaning of the loaves, the cart, and the spring-mattress was now plain. There was an Anarchist plot to carry out a number of explosions probably simultaneously, in different parts of the city. I had, of course, heard much of the terrible "reversing" bombs—those bombs which, containing a tube of acid plugged by wadding, required no fuse, and only needed to be inverted to be set going to explode in a few minutes. The loaves containing these bombs would form an effectual "blind," and they were to be distributed, probably in broad daylight, in the most natural manner possible, in a baker's cart. A man would be waiting near the scene of each contemplated explosion. He would be given a loaf taken from the inverted batch. He would take it—perhaps wrapped in paper, but still inverted, and apparently the most innocent object possible—to the spot selected, deposit it, right side up—which would reverse the inner tube and set up the action—in some quiet corner, behind a door or what not, and make his own escape, while the explosion tore down walls and—if the experiment were lucky—scattered the flesh and bones of unsuspecting people.

The infernal loaves were made and kept reversed, to begin with, in order to stand more firmly, and—if observed—more naturally, when turned over to explode. Even if a child picked up the loaf and carried it off, that child at least would be blown to atoms, which at any rate would have been something for the conspirators to congratulate themselves upon. The spring-mattress, of course, was to ease the jolting to the bombs, and obviate any random jerking loose of the acid, which might have had the deplorable result of sacrificing the valuable life of the conspirator who drove the cart. The other loaves, too, with no explosive contents, had their use. The two long ones, which fitted across the inside of the cart, would be jammed across so as to hold the bombs in the centre, and the others would be used to pack the batch on the other sides and prevent any dangerous slipping about. The thing seemed pretty plain, except that as yet I had no idea of how Hewitt learned anything of the business.

I brought the four-wheeler up to the door of the stable and we thrust the man into it, and Hewitt locked the stable door with its proper key. Then we drove off to Tottenham Court Road police-station, and, by Hewitt's order, straight into the yard.

In less than ten minutes from our departure from the stable our prisoner was finally secured, and Hewitt was deep in consultation with police officials. Messengers were sent and telegrams despatched, and presently Hewitt came to me with information.

"The name of the helpless Frenchman the police found this morning," he said, "appears to be Gérard—at least I am almost certain of it. Among the papers found on the prisoner—whose full name doesn't appear, but who seems to be spoken of as Luigi (he is Italian)—among the papers, I say, is a sort of notice convening a meeting for this evening to decide as to the 'final punishment' to be awarded the 'traitor Gérard, now in charge of comrade Pingard.'

"The place of meeting is not mentioned, but it seems more than probable that it will be at the Bakunin Club, not five minutes' walk from this place. The police have all these places under quiet observation, of course, and that is the club at which apparently important Anarchist meetings have been held lately. It is the only club that has never been raided as yet, and, it would seem, the only one they would feel at all safe in using for anything important.

"Moreover, Luigi just now simply declined to open his mouth when asked where the meeting was to be, and said nothing when the names of several other places were suggested, but suddenly found his tongue at the mention of the Bakunin Club, and denied vehemently that the meeting was to be there—it was the only thing he uttered. So that it seems pretty safe to assume that it *is* to be there. Now, of course, the matter's very serious. Men have been despatched to take charge of the stable very quietly, and the club is to be taken possession of at once—also very quietly. It must be done without a moment's delay, and as there is a chance that the only detective officers within reach at the moment may be known by sight, I have undertaken to get in first. Perhaps you'll come? We may have to take the door with a rush."

Of course I meant to miss nothing if I could help it, and said so.

"Very well," replied Hewitt, "we'll get ourselves up a bit." He began taking off his collar and tie. "It is getting dusk," he proceeded, "and we shan't want old clothes to make ourselves look sufficiently shabby. We're both wearing bowler hats, which is lucky. Make a dent in yours—if you can do so without permanently damaging it."

We got rid of our collars and made chokers of our ties. We turned our coat-collars up at one side only, and then, with dented hats worn raffishly, and our hands in our pockets, we looked disreputable enough for all practical purposes in twilight. A cordon of plain-clothes police had already been forming round the club, we were told, and so we sallied forth. We turned into Windmill Street, crossed Whitfield Street, and in a turning or two we came to the Bakunin Club. I could see no sign of anything like a ring of policemen, and said so. Hewitt chuckled. "Of course not," he said; "they don't go about a job of this sort with drums beating and flags flying. But they are all there, and some are watching us. There is the house. I'll negotiate."

The house was one of the very shabby *passé* sort that abound in that quarter. The very narrow area was railed over, and almost choked with rubbish. Visible above it were three floors, the lowest indicated by the door and one window, and the other two by two windows each— mean and dirty all. A faint light appeared in the top floor, and another from somewhere behind the refuse-heaped area. Everywhere else was in darkness. Hewitt looked intently into the area, but it was impossible to discern anything behind the sole grimy patch of window that was visible. Then we stepped lightly up the three or four steps to the door and rang the bell.

We could hear slippered feet mounting a stair and approaching. A latch was shifted, a door opened six inches, an indistinct face appeared, and a female voice asked, "*Qui est là?*"

"*Deux camarades,*" Hewitt grunted testily. "*Ouvrez vite.*"

I had noticed that the door was kept from opening further by a short chain. This chain the woman unhooked from the door, but still kept the latter merely ajar, as though intending to assure herself still further. But Hewitt immediately pushed the door back, planted his foot against it, and entered, asking carelessly as he did so, "*Où se trouve Luigi?*"

I followed on his heels, and in the dark could just distinguish that

Hewitt pushed the woman instantly against the wall and clapped his hand to her mouth. At the same moment a file of quiet men were suddenly visible ascending the steps at my heels. They were the police.

The door was closed behind us almost noiselessly, and a match was struck. Two men stood at the bottom of the stairs, and the others searched the house. Only two men were found—both in a top room. They were secured and brought down.

The woman was now ungagged, and she used her tongue at a great rate. One of the men was a small, meek-looking slip of a fellow, and he appeared to be the woman's husband. "Eh, *messieurs le police*," she exclaimed vehemently, "it ees not of'im, *mon pauvre* Pierre, zat you sall rrun in. 'Im and me—we are not of the clob—we work only—we housekeep."

Hewitt whispered to an officer, and the two men were taken below. Then Hewitt spoke to the woman, whose protests had not ceased. "You say you are not of the club," he said, "but what is there to prove that? If you are but housekeepers, as you say, you have nothing to fear. But you can only prove it by giving the police information. For instance, now, about Gérard. What have they done with him?"

"Jean Pingard—'im you 'ave take downstairs—'e 'ave lose 'im. Jean Pingard get last night all a-boosa—all dronk like zis"—she rolled her head and shoulders to express intoxication—"and he sleep too much today, when Émile go out, and Gérard, he go too, and nobody know. I will tell you anysing. We are not of the clob—we housekeep, me and Pierre."

"But what did they do to Gérard before he went away?"

The woman was ready and anxious to tell anything. Gérard had been selected to do something—what it was exactly she did not know, but there was a horse and cart, and he was to drive it. Where the horse and cart was also she did not know, but Gérard had driven a cart before in his work for a baker, and he was to drive one in connection with some scheme among the members of the club. But *le pauvre Gérard* at the last minute disliked to drive the cart; he had fear. He did not say he had fear, but he prepared a letter—a letter that was not signed. The letter was to be sent to the police, and it told them the whereabouts of the horse and cart, so that the police might seize these things, and then there would be nothing for Gérard, who had fear, to do in the way of driving. No, he did not betray the names of the comrades, but he told the place of the horse and the cart.

Nevertheless, the letter was never sent. There was suspicion, and the letter was found in a pocket and read. Then there was a meeting, and Gérard was confronted with his letter. He could say nothing but "*Je le nie!*"—found no explanation but that. There was much noise, and she had observed from a staircase, from which one might see through a ventilating hole, Gérard had much fear—very much fear. His face was white, and it moved; he prayed for mercy, and they talked of killing him. It was discussed how he should be killed, and the poor Gérard was more terrified. He was made to take off his collar, and a razor was drawn across his throat, though without cutting him, till he fainted.

Then water was flung over him, and he was struck in the face till he revived. He again repeated, "*Je le nie! je le nie!*" and nothing more. Then one struck him with a bottle, and another with a stick; the point of a knife was put against his throat and held there, but this time he did not faint, but cried softly, as a man who is drunk, "*Je le nie! je le nie!*" So they tied a handkerchief about his neck, and twisted it till his face grew purple and black, and his eyes were round and terrible, and then they struck his face, and he fainted again. But they took away the handkerchief, having fear that they could not easily get rid of the body if he were killed, for there was no preparation. So they decided to meet again and discuss when there would be preparation. Wherefore they took him away to the rooms of Jean Pingard—of Jean and Émile Pingard—in Henry Street, Golden Square. But Émile Pingard had gone out, and Jean was drunk and slept, and they lost him. Jean Pingard was he downstairs—the taller of the two; the other was but *le pauvre Pierre*, who, with herself, was not of the club. They worked only; they were the keepers of the house. There was nothing for which they should be arrested, and she would give the police any information they might ask.

"As I thought, you see," Hewitt said to me, "the man's nerves have broken down under the terror and the strain, and aphasia is the result. I think I told you that the only articulate thing he could say was '*Je le nie!*' and now we know how those words were impressed on him till he now pronounces them mechanically, with no idea of their meaning. Come, we can do no more here now. But wait a moment."

There were footsteps outside. The light was removed, and a policeman went to the door and opened it as soon as the bell rang. Three men stepped in one after another, and the door was immediately shut behind them—they were prisoners.

We left quietly, and although we, of course, expected it, it was not till the next morning that we learned absolutely that the largest arrest of Anarchists ever made in this country was made at the Bakunin Club that night. Each man as he came was admitted—and collared.

★★★★★★

We made our way to Luzatti's, and it was over our dinner that Hewitt put me in full possession of the earlier facts of this case, which I have set down as impersonal narrative in their proper place at the beginning.

"But," I said, "what of that aimless scribble you spoke of that Gérard made in the police station? Can I see it?"

Hewitt turned to where his coat hung behind him and took a handful of papers from his pocket.

"Most of these," he said, "mean nothing at all. *That* is what he wrote at first," and he handed me the first of the two papers which were presented in facsimile in the earlier part of this narrative.

"You see," he said, "he has begun mechanically from long use to write '*monsieur*'—the usual beginning of a letter. But he scarcely makes three letters before tailing off into sheer scribble. He tries again and again, and although once there is something very like '*que*,' and once something like a word preceded by a negative 'n,' the whole thing is meaningless.

"This" (he handed me the other paper which has been printed in facsimile) "*does* mean something, though Gérard never intended it. Can you spot the meaning? Really, I think it's pretty plain—especially now that you know as much as I about the day's adventures. The thing at the top left-hand corner, I may tell you, Gérard intended for a sketch of a clock on the mantelpiece in the police-station."

I stared hard at the paper, but could make nothing whatever of it. "I only see the horse-shoe clock," I said, "and a sort of second, unsuccessful attempt to draw it again. Then there is a horse-shoe dotted, but scribbled over, and then a sort of kite or balloon on a string, a Highlander, and—well, I don't understand it, I confess. Tell me."

"I'll explain what I learned from that," Hewitt said, "and also what led me to look for it. From what the inspector told me, I judged the man to be in a very curious state, and I took a fancy to see him. Most I was curious to know why he should have a terror of bread at one moment and eat it ravenously at another. When I saw him I felt pretty sure that he was not mad, in the common sense of the term. As far as I could judge it seemed to be a case of aphasia.

"Then when the doctor came I had a chat (as I have already told you) with the policeman who found the man. He told me about the incident of the bread with rather more detail than I had had from the inspector. Thus it was plain that the man was terrified at the bread only when it was in the form of a loaf, and ate it eagerly when it was cut into pieces. That was *one* thing to bear in mind. He was not afraid of *bread*, but only of a *loaf.*

"Very well. I asked the policeman to find another uncut loaf, and to put it near the man when his attention was diverted. Meantime the doctor reported that my suspicion as to aphasia was right. The man grew more comfortable, and was assured that he was among friends and had nothing to fear, so that when at length he found the loaf near his elbow he was not so violently terrified, only very uneasy. I watched him and saw him turn it bottom up—a very curious thing to do; he immediately became less uneasy—the turning over of the loaf seemed to have set his mind at rest in some way. This was more curious still. I thought for some little while before accepting the bomb theory as the most probable.

"The doctor left, and I determined to give the man another chance with pen and paper. I felt pretty certain that if he were allowed to scribble and sketch as he pleased, sooner or later he would do something that would give me some sort of a hint. I left him entirely alone and let him do as he pleased, but I watched.

"After all the futile scribble which you have seen, he began to sketch, first a man's head, then a chair—just what he might happen to see in the room. Presently he took to the piece of paper you have before you. He observed that clock and began to sketch it, then went on to other things, such as you see, scribbling idly over most of them when finished. When he had made the last of the sketches he made a hasty scrawl of his pen over it and broke down. It had brought his terror to his mind again somehow.

"I seized the paper and examined it closely. Now just see. Ignore the clock, which was merely a sketch of a thing before him, and look at the three things following. What are they? A horse-shoe, a captive balloon, and a Highlander. Now, can't you think of something those three things in that order suggest?"

I could think of nothing whatever, and I confessed as much.

"Think, now. Tottenham Court Road!"

I started. "Of course," I said. "That never struck me. There's the Horse-shoe Hotel, with the sign outside, there's the large toy and fancy shop halfway up, where they have a captive balloon moored to the roof as an advertisement, and there's the tobacco and snuff shop on the left, toward the other end, where they have a life-size wooden Highlander at the door—an uncommon thing, indeed, nowadays."

"You are right. The curious conjunction struck me at once. There they are, all three, and just in the order in which one meets them going up from Oxford Street. Also, as if to confirm the conjecture, note the *dotted* horse-shoe. Don't you remember that at night the Horse-shoe Hotel sign is illuminated by two rows of gas lights?

"Now here was my clue at last. Plainly, this man, in his mechanical sketching, was following a regular train of thought, and unconsciously illustrating it as he went along. Many people in perfect health and mental soundness do the same thing if a pen and a piece of waste paper be near. The man's train of thought led him, in memory, up Tottenham Court Road, and further, to where some disagreeable recollection upset him. It was my business to trace this train of thought. Do you remember the feat of Dupin in Poe's story, *The Murders in the Rue Morgue*—how he walks by his friend's side in silence for some distance, and then suddenly breaks out with a divination of his thoughts, having silently traced them from a fruiterer with a basket, through paving-stones, Epicurus, Dr. Nichols, the constellation Orion, and a Latin poem, to a cobbler lately turned actor?

"Well, it was some such task as this (but infinitely simpler, as a matter of fact) that was set me. This man begins by drawing the horse-shoe clock. Having done with that, and with the horse-shoe still in his mind, he starts to draw a horse-shoe simply. It is a failure, and he scribbles it out. His mind at once turns to the Horse-shoe Hotel, which he knows from frequently passing it, and its sign of gas-jets. He sketches *that*, making dots for the gas lights. Once started in Tottenham Court Road, his mind naturally follows his usual route along it. He remembers the advertising captive balloon half-way up, and down *that* goes on his paper. In imagination he crosses the road, and keeps on till he comes to the very noticeable Highlander outside the tobacconist's. *That* is sketched. Thus it is plain that a familiar route with him was from New Oxford Street up Tottenham Court Road.

"At the police-station I ventured to guess from this that he lived somewhere near Seven Dials. Perhaps before long we shall know if this was right. But to return to the sketches. After the Highlander there is something at first not very distinct. A little examination, however, shows it to be intended for a chimney-pot partly covered with a basket. Now an old basket, stuck sideways on a chimney by way of cowl, is not an uncommon thing in parts of the country, but it is very unusual in London. Probably, then, it would be in some by-street or alley. Next and last, there is a horse's head, and it was at this that the man's trouble returned to him.

"Now, when one goes to a place and finds a horse there, that place is not uncommonly a stable; and, as a matter of fact, the basket-cowl would be much more likely to be found in use in a range of back stabling than anywhere else. Suppose, then, that after taking the direction indicated in the sketches—the direction of Fitzroy Square, in fact—one were to find a range of stabling with a basket-cowl visible about it? I know my London pretty well, as you are aware, and I could remember but two likely stable-yards in that particular part—the two we looked at, in the second of which you may possibly have noticed just such a basket-cowl as I have been speaking of.

"Well, what we did you know, and that we found confirmation of my conjecture about the loaves you also know. It was the recollection of the horse and cart, and what they were to transport, and what the end of it all had been, that upset Gérard as he drew the horse's head. You will notice that the sketches have not been done in separate rows, left to right—they have simply followed one another all round the paper, which means preoccupation and unconsciousness on the part of the man who made them."

"But," I asked, "supposing those loaves to contain bombs, how were the bombs put there? Baking the bread round them would have been risky, wouldn't it?"

"Certainly. What they did was to cut the loaves, each row, down the centre. Then most of the crumb was scooped out, the explosive inserted, and the sides joined up and glued. I thought you had spotted the joins, though they certainly were neat."

"No, I didn't examine closely. Luigi, of course, had been told off for a daily visit to feed the horse, and that is how we caught him."

"One supposes so. They hadn't rearranged their plans as to going on with the outrages after Gérard's defection. By the way, I noticed that he was accustomed to driving when I first saw him. There was an unmistakable mark on his coat, just at the small of the back, that drivers get who lean against a rail in a cart."

The loaves were examined by official experts, and, as everybody now knows, were found to contain, as Hewitt had supposed, large charges of dynamite. What became of some half-dozen of the men captured is also well known: their sentences were exemplary.

It has struck me that many of my readers may wonder that, although I have set down in detail a number of interesting cases wherein Hewitt figured with success, I have scarcely as much as alluded to his failures. For failures he had, and of a fair number. More than once he has found his search met, perhaps at the beginning, perhaps after some little while, by an impenetrable wall of darkness through which no clue led. At other times he has lost time on a false trail while his quarry escaped. At others still the stupidity or inaccuracy of some person upon whom he has depended for information has set his plans to naught.

The reason why none of these cases have been embodied in the present papers is simply this; that a problem with no answer, a puzzle with no explanation, an incident with no satisfactory end, as a rule lends itself but poorly to purposes of popular narrative, and it is often difficult to make understood and appreciated any degree of skill and acumen unless it produces a clear and intelligible result. That such results attended Hewitt's efforts in an extraordinary degree those who have followed my narratives so far will need no assurance; but withal impossibilities still remain impossibilities, for Hewitt as for the dullest creature alive. On some other occasion I may perhaps set out at length a case in which Martin Hewitt achieved nothing more than unqualified failure; for the present I shall content myself with a case which, although it was completely cleared up in the end, yet for some while baffled Hewitt because of some of the reasons I have alluded to.

On the ground floor of the building wherein Hewitt kept his office, and in which I myself had my chambers, were the offices of Messrs. Streatley and Raikes, an old-fashioned firm of family solicitors. Messrs. Streatley and Raikes's junior clerk appeared in Hewitt's outer office one morning with the query, "Is your guv'nor in?"

Kerrett admitted the fact.

"Will you tell him Mr. Raikes sends his compliments and will be obliged if he can step downstairs for a few minutes? It's a client of ours—a lady—and she's in a great state about losing her baby or something. Say Mr. Raikes would bring her up only she seems too ill to get up the stairs."

This was the purport of the message which Kerrett brought into the inner room, and in three minutes Hewitt was in Streatley and Raikes's office.

"I thought the only useful thing possible would be to send for you, Mr Hewitt," Mr. Raikes explained; "indeed, if my client had been better acquainted with London no doubt she would have come to you direct. She is in a bad state in the inner office. Her name is Mrs. Seton; her husband is a recent client of ours. Quite young, and rather wealthy people, so far as I know. Made a fortune early, I believe, in South Africa, and came here to live. Their child—their only child, a little toddler of two years or thereabout—disappeared yesterday in a most mysterious way, and all efforts to find it seem to have failed as yet. The police have been set going everywhere, but there is no news as yet.

"Mrs. Seton seems to have passed a dreadful night, and could think of nothing better to do this morning than to come to us. She has her maid with her, and looks to be breaking down entirely. I believe she's lying on the sofa in my private room now. Will you see her? I think you might hear what she has to say, whether you take the case in hand or not; something may strike you, and in any case it will comfort her to get your opinion. I told her all about you, you know, and she clutched at the chance eagerly. Shall I see if we may go in?"

Mr. Raikes knocked at the door of his inner sanctum and waited; then he knocked again and set the door ajar. There was a quiet "Come in," and pushing open the door the lawyer motioned Hewitt to follow him.

On the sofa facing the door sat a lady, very pale, and exhibiting plain signs of grief and physical weariness. A heavy veil was thrown back over her bonnet, and her maid stood at her side holding a bottle of salts. As she saw Hewitt she made as if to rise, but he stepped quickly forward and laid his hand on her shoulder. "Pray don't disturb yourself, Mrs. Seton," he said; "Mr. Raikes has told me something of your trouble, and perhaps when I know a little more I shall be able to offer you some advice. But remember that it will be very important for you to maintain your strength and spirits as much as possible."

"This is Mr. Martin Hewitt, you know," Mr. Raikes here put in— "of whom I was speaking."

Mrs. Seton inclined her head and with a very obvious effort began.

"It is my child, you know, Mr. Hewitt—my little boy Charley; we can't find him."

"Mr. Raikes has told me so. When did you see the child last?"

"Yesterday morning. His nurse left him sitting on the floor in a room we call the small morning-room, where we sometimes allowed him to play when nurse was out, because the nursery was out of hear-

On the sofa facing the door sat a lady,
very pale, and exhibiting plain signs of grief.

ing, except from the bedrooms. I myself was in the large morning-room, and as he seemed to be very quiet I went to look, and found he was not there."

"You looked elsewhere, of course?"

"Yes; but he was nowhere in the house, and none of the servants had seen him. At first I supposed that his nurse had gone back to the small morning-room and taken him with her—I had sent her on an errand—but when she returned I found that was not the case."

"Can he walk?"

"Oh, yes, he can walk quite well. But he could scarcely have come out from the room without my hearing him. The two rooms, the morning-room and the small sitting-room, are on opposite sides of the same passage."

"Do the doors face each other?"

"No; the door of the small room is farther up the passage than the other. But in any case he was nowhere in the house."

"But if he left the room he must have got out somehow. Is there no other door?"

"Yes, there is a French window, with the lower panels of wood, in the room; it gives on to a few steps leading down into the garden; but that was closed and bolted on the inside."

"You found no trace whatever of him, I take it, on the whole premises?"

"Not a trace of any sort, nor had anybody about the place seen him."

"Did you yourself actually see him in this room, or have you merely the nurse's word for it?"

"I saw her put him there. She left him playing with a box of toys. When I went to look for him the toys were there, scattered on the floor, but he had gone." Mrs. Seton sank on the arms of her maid and her breast heaved.

"I'm sure," Hewitt said, "You'll keep your nerves as steady as you can, Mrs. Seton; much may depend on it. If you have nothing else to tell me now I think I will come to your house at once, look at it, and question your servants myself. Meantime what has been done?"

"The police have been notified everywhere, of course," Mr. Raikes said, handing Hewitt a printed bill, damp from the press; "and here is a bill containing a description of the child and offering a reward, which is being circulated now."

Hewitt glanced at the bill and nodded. "That is quite right," he said, "so far as I can tell at present. But I must see the place. Do you feel strong enough to come home now, Mrs. Seton?"

Hewitt's business-like decision and confidence of manner gave the lady fresh strength. "The brougham is here," she said, "and we can drive home at once. We live at Cricklewood."

A fine pair of horses stood before the brougham, though they still bore signs of hard work; and indeed they had been kept at their best pace all that morning. All the way to Cricklewood Hewitt kept Mrs. Seton in conversation, never for a moment leaving her attention disengaged. The missing child, he learned, was the only one, and the family had only been in England for something less than a year. Mr. Seton had become possessed of real property in South Africa, had sold it in London, and had determined to settle here.

A little way past Shoot-up Hill the coachman swung his pair off to the left, and presently entering a gate pulled up before a large old-fashioned house.

Here Hewitt immediately began a complete examination of the

premises. The possible exits from the grounds, he found, were four in number. The two wide front gates giving on to the carriage-drive, the kitchen and stable entrance, and a side gate in a fence—always locked, however. Inside the house, from the central hall, a passage to the right led to another wherein was the door of the small morning-room. This was a very ordinary room, 15 feet square or so, lighted by the glass in the French window, the bottom panes of which, however, had been filled in with wood. The contents of a box of toys lay scattered on the floor, and the box itself lay near.

"Have these toys been moved," Hewitt asked, "since the child was missed?"

"No, we haven't allowed anything to be disturbed. The disappearance seemed so wholly unaccountable that we thought the police might wish to examine the place exactly as it was. They did not seem to think it necessary, however."

Hewitt knelt and examined the toys without disturbing them. They were of very good quality, and represented a farmyard, with horses, carts, ducks, geese and cows complete. One of the carts had had a string attached so that it might be pulled along the floor.

"Now," Hewitt said rising, "you think, Mrs. Seton, that the child could not have toddled through the passage, and so into some other part of the house, without you hearing him?"

"Well," Mrs. Seton answered with indecision, "I thought so at first, but I begin to doubt. Because he *must* have done so, I suppose."

They went into the passage. The door of the large morning-room was four or five yards further toward the passage leading to the hall, and on the opposite side. "The floor in this passage," Hewitt observed, "is rather thickly carpeted. See here, I can walk on it at a good pace without noise."

Mrs. Seton assented. "Of course," she said, "if he got past here he might have got anywhere about the house, and so into the grounds. There is a veranda outside the drawing-room, and doors in various places.'

"Of course the grounds have been completely examined?"

"Oh, yes, every inch."

"The weather has been very dry, unfortunately," Hewitt said, "and it would be useless for me to look for footprints on your hard gravel, especially of so small a child. Let us come back to the room. Is the French window fastened as you found it?"

"Yes; nothing has been changed."

The French window was, as is usual, one of two casements joining in the centre and fastened by bolts top and bottom. "It is not your habit, I see," Hewitt observed, "to open both halves of the window."

"No; one side is always fastened, the other we secure by the bottom bolt because the catch of the handle doesn't always act properly."

"And you found that bolt fastened as I see it now?"

"Yes."

Hewitt lifted the bolt and opened the door. Four or five steps led parallel with the face of the wall to a sort of path which ran the whole length of the house on this side, and was only separated from a quiet public lane by a low fence and a thin hedge. Almost opposite a small, light gate stood in the fence, firmly padlocked.

"I see," Hewitt remarked, "your house is placed close against one side of the grounds. Is that the side gate which you always keep locked?"

Mrs. Seton replied in the affirmative, and Hewitt laid his hand on the gate in question. "Still," he said, "if security is the object I should recommend hinges a little less rural in pattern; see here," and he gave the gate a jerk upward, lifting the hinge-pins from their sockets and opening the gate from that side, the padlock acting as hinge. "Those hinges," he added, "were meant for a heavier gate than that," and he replaced the gate.

"Yes," Mrs. Seton replied; "I am obliged to you; but that doesn't concern us now. The French window was bolted on the inside. Would you like to see the servants?"

The servants were produced, and Hewitt questioned each in turn, but not one would admit having seen anything of Master Charles Seton after he had been left in the small morning-room. A rather stupid groom fancied he had seen Master Charles on the side lawn, but then remembered that that must have been the day before. The cook, an uncommonly thin, sharp-featured woman for one of her trade, was especially positive that she had not seen him all that day. "And she would be sure to have remembered if she had seen him leaving the house," she said, "because she was the more particular since he was lost the last time."

This was news to Hewitt. "Lost the last time?" he asked; "why, what is this, Mrs. Seton? Was he lost once before?"

"Oh, yes," Mrs. Seton answered, "six or seven weeks ago. But that was quite different. He strayed out at the front gate and was brought back from the police station in the evening."

"Those hinges were meant for a heavier gate than that."

"But this may be most important," Hewitt said. "You should certainly have told me. Tell me now exactly what happened on this first occasion."

"But it was really quite an ordinary sort of accident. He was left alone and got out through an open gate. Of course we were very anxious; but we had him back the same evening. Need we waste time in talking about that?"

"But it will be no waste of time, I assure you. What was it that happened, exactly?"

"Nurse was about to take him for a short walk just before lunch. On the front lawn he suddenly remembered a whip which had been left in the nursery and insisted on taking it with him. She left him and went back for it, taking however some little time to find it. When she returned he was nowhere to be seen; but one of the gates was a couple of feet or more open—it had caught on a loose stone in swinging to—and no doubt he had wandered off that way. A lady found him some distance away and, not knowing to whom he belonged, took him that evening to a police station, and as messages had been sent to the police stations, we had him back soon after he was left there."

"Do you know who the lady was?"

"Her name was Mrs. Clark. She left her name and address at the police station, and of course I wrote to thank her. But there was some mistake in taking it down, I suppose, for the letter was returned marked not known.'"

"Then you never saw this lady yourself?"

"No."

"I think I will make a note of the exact description of the child and then visit the police station to which this lady took him six weeks ago. Fair, curly hair, I think, and blue eyes? Age two years and three months; walks and runs well, and speaks fairly plainly. Dress?"

"Pale blue llama frock with lace, white under-linen, linen overall, pale blue silk socks and tan shoes. Everything good as new except the shoes, which were badly worn at the backs through a habit he has of kicking back and downward with his heels when sitting. They were rather old shoes, and only used indoors."

"If I remember aright nothing was said of those shoes in the print-ed bill?"

"Was that so? No, I believe not. I have been so worried."

"Yes, Mrs. Seton, of course. It is most creditable in you to have kept up so well while I have been making my inquiries. Go now and take a good rest while I do what is possible. By the way, where was Mr. Seton yesterday morning when you missed the boy?"

"In the City. He has some important business in hand just now."

"And today?"

"He has gone to the City again. Of course he is sadly worried; but he saw that everything possible was done, and his business was very important."

"Just so. Mr. Seton was not married before, I presume—if I may?"

"No, certainly not; why do you ask?"

"I beg your pardon, but I have a habit of asking almost every question I can think of; I can't know too much of a case, you know, and most unlikely pieces of information sometimes turn out useful. Thank you for your patience; I will try another plan now."

Mrs. Seton had kept up remarkably well during Hewitt's examination, but she was plainly by no means a strong woman, and her maid came again to her assistance as Hewitt left. Hewitt himself made for the police station. Few inspectors indeed of the Metropolitan Police force did not know Hewitt by sight, and the one here in charge knew him well. He remembered very well the occasion, six weeks or so before, when Mrs. Clark brought Mrs. Seton's child to the station. He was on duty himself at the time, and he turned up the book containing an entry on the subject. From this it appeared that the lady gave the address' No. 89 Sedgby Road, Belsize Park.

"I suppose you didn't happen to know the lady," Hewitt asked—"by sight or otherwise?"

"No, I didn't, and I'm not sure I could swear to her again," the inspector answered. "She wore a heavy veil, and I didn't see much of her face. One rum thing I noticed though: she seemed rather fond of the baby, and as she stooped down to kiss him before she went away I could see an old scar on her throat. It was just the sort of scar I've seen on a man that's had his throat cut and got over it. She wore a high collar to hide it, but stooping shifted the collar, and so I saw it."

"Did she seem an educated woman?"

"Oh yes; perfect lady; spoke very nice. I told her a baby had been inquired after by Mrs. Seton, and from the description I'd no doubt this was the one. And so it was."

"At what time was this?"

"7.10 p.m. exactly. Here it is, all entered properly."

"Now as to Sedgby Road, Belsize Park. Do you happen to know it?"

"Oh, yes, very well. Very quiet, respectable road indeed. I only know it through walking through."

"I see a suburban directory on the shelf behind you. Do you mind pulling it down? Thanks. Let us find Sedgby Road. Here it is. See, there *is* no No. 89; the highest number is 67."

"No more there is," the inspector answered, running his finger down the column; "and there's no Clark in the road, that's more. False address, that's plain. And so they've lost him again, have they? We had notice yesterday, of course, and I've just got some bills. This last seems a queer sort of affair, don't it? Child sitting inside the house disappeared like a ghost, and all the doors and windows fastened inside."

Hewitt agreed that the affair had very uncommon features, and presently left the station and sought a cab. All the way back to his office he considered the matter deeply. As a matter of fact, he was at a loss. Certain evidence he had seen in the house, but it went a very little way, and beyond that there was merely no clue whatever. There were features of the child's first estrayal also that attracted him, though it might very easily be the case that nothing connected the two events. There was an unknown woman—apparently a lady—who had once had her throat cut, bringing the child back after several hours and giving a false name and address, for since the address was false the same was probably the case with the name. Why was this? This time the child was still absent, and nothing whatever was there to suggest in what direction he might be followed, neither was there anything to indicate why he should be detained anywhere, if detained he was. Hewitt determined, while awaiting any result that the bills might bring, to cause certain inquiries to be made into the antecedents of the Setons. Moreover, other work was waiting, and the Seton business must be put aside for a few hours at least.

Hewitt sat late in his office that evening, and at about nine o'clock Mrs. Seton returned. The poor woman seemed on the verge of serious illness. She had received two anonymous letters, which she brought with her, and with scarcely a word placed before Hewitt's eyes.

The first he opened and read as follows:—

The writer observes that you are offering a reward for the re-covery of your child. There is no necessity for this; Charley is quite safe, happy, and in good hands. Pray do not instruct detectives or take any such steps just yet. The child is well and shall be returned to you. This I swear solemnly. His errand is one of mercy; pray have patience.

Hewitt turned the letter and envelope in his hand. "Good paper, of the same sort as the envelope," he remarked, "but only a half sheet, freshly torn off, probably because the other side bore an address heading; therefore, most likely from a respectable sort of house. The writing is a woman's, and good, though the writer was agitated when she did it. Posted this afternoon, at Willesden."

"You see," Mrs. Seton said anxiously, "she knows his name. She calls him Charley."

"Yes," Hewitt answered; "there may be something in that, or there may not. The name Charles Seton is on the bills, isn't it? And they have been visible publicly all day today. So that the name may be more easily explained than some other parts of the letter. For instance, the writer says that the child's errand' is one of mercy. The little fellow may be very intelligent—no doubt is—but children of two years old as a rule do not practise errands of mercy—nor indeed errands of any sort. Can you think of anything whatever, Mrs. Seton, in connection with your family history, or indeed anything else, that may throw light on that phrase?"

He looked keenly at her as he asked, but her expression was one of blank doubt merely, as she shook her head slowly and answered in the negative. Hewitt turned to the other letter and read this:—

Madam,—If you want your child you had better make an arrangement with me. You fancy he has strayed, but as a matter of fact he has been stolen, and you little know by whom. You will never get him back except through me, you may rest assured of that. Are you prepared to pay me one hundred pounds (£100) if I hand him to you, and no questions asked? Your present reward, £20, is paltry; and you may finally bid goodbye to your child if you will not accept my terms. If you do, say as much in an advertisement to the *Standard*, addressed to Veritas.

"A man's handwriting," Hewitt commented; "fairly well formed, but shaky. The writer is not in first-rate health—each line totters away in a downward slope at the end. I shouldn't be surprised to hear that the gentleman drank. Postmark, 'Hampstead'; posted this afternoon also. But the striking thing is the paper and envelope. They are each of exactly the same kind and size as those of the other letter. The paper also is a half sheet, and torn off on the same side as the other; confirmation of my suspicion that the object is to get rid of the printed address. I shall be surprised if both these were not written in the same house. That looks like a traitor in the enemy's camp; the question is which is the traitor?" Hewitt regarded the letters intently for a few seconds and then proceeded.

"Plainly," he said, "if these letters are written by people who know anything about the matter, one writer is lying. The woman promises that the child shall be returned, without reward or search, and talks generally as if the taking away of the child, or the estrayal, or whatever it was, were a very virtuous sort of proceeding. The man says plainly that the child has been stolen, with no attempt to gloss the matter, and asserts that nothing will get the child back but heavy blackmail—a very different story. On the other hand, can there be any concerted design in these two letters? Are they intended, each from its own side, to play up to a certain result?" Hewitt paused and thought. Then he asked suddenly: "Do you recognise anything familiar either in the handwriting or the stationery of these letters?"

"No, nothing."

"Very well," Hewitt said, "we will come to closer quarters with the blackmailer, I think. You needn't commit yourself to paying anything, of course."

"But, Mr. Hewitt, I will gladly pay or do anything. The hundred pounds is nothing. I will pay it gladly if I can only get my child."

"Well, well, we shall see. The man may not be able to do what he offers after all, but that we will test. It is too late now for an advertisement in tomorrow morning's *Standard,* but there is the *Evening Standard*—he may even mean that—and the next morning's. I will have an advertisement inserted in both, inviting this man to make an appointment, and prove the genuineness of his offer; that will fetch him if he wants the money, and can do anything for it. Have you nothing else to tell me?"

"Nothing. But have you ascertained nothing yourself? Don't say I've to pass another night in such dreadful suspense."

"I'm afraid, Mrs. Seton, I must ask you to be patient a little longer. I have ascertained something, but it has not carried me far as yet. Remember that if there is anything at all in these anonymous letters (and I think there is) the child is at any rate safe, and to be found one way or another. Both agree in that." This he said mainly to comfort his client, for in fact he had learned very little. His news from the City as to Mr. Seton's early history had been but meagre. He was known as a successful speculator, and that was almost all. There was an indefinite notion that he had been married once before, but nothing more.

★★★★★★

All the next day Hewitt did nothing in the case. Another affair, a previous engagement, kept him hard at work in his office all day, and indeed had this not been the case he could have done little. His City inquiries were still in progress, and he awaited, moreover, a reply to the advertisement. But at about half-past seven in the evening this telegram arrived—

Child returned. Come at once.—Seton.

In five minutes Hewitt was making northwest in a hansom, and in half an hour he was ringing the bell at the Setons' house. Within, Mrs. Seton was still semi-hysterical, clasping the child—an intelligent-looking little fellow—in her arms, and refusing to release her hold of him for a moment. Mr. Seton stood before the fire in the same room. He was a smart-looking, scrupulously dressed man of thirty-five or thereabouts, and he began explaining his telegram as soon as he had wished Hewitt good evening.

"The child's back," he said, "and of course that's the great thing. But I'm not satisfied, Mr. Hewitt. I want to know why it was taken away, and I want to punish somebody. It's really very extraordinary. My poor wife has been driving about all day—she called on you, by the bye, but you were out," (Hewitt credited this to Kerrett, who had been told he must not be disturbed) "and she has been all over the place uselessly, unable to rest, of course. Well, I have been at home since half-past four, and at about six I was smoking in the small morning-room—I often use it as a smoking-room—and looking out at the French window. I came away from there, and half an hour or more later, as it was getting dusk, I remembered I had left the French window open, and sent a servant to shut it. She went straight to the room, and there on the floor, where he was seen last, she found the child playing with his toys as though nothing had happened!"

"And how was he dressed—as he is now?"

"Yes, just as he was when we missed him."

Hewitt stepped up to the child as he sat on his mother's lap, and rubbed his cheek, speaking pleasantly to him. The little fellow looked up and smiled, and Hewitt observed: "One thing is noticeable: this linen overall is almost clean. Little boys like this don't keep one white overall clean for three days, do they? And see—those shoes—aren't they new? Those he had were old, I think you said, and tan coloured."

The shoes now on the child's feet were of white leather, with a noticeable sewn ornamentation in silk. His mother had not noticed them before, and as she looked he lifted his little foot higher and said. "Look, mummy, more new shoes!"

"Ask him," suggested Hewitt hurriedly, "who gave them to him."

His father asked him and the little fellow looked puzzled. After a pause he said "Mummy."

"No," his mother answered, "*I* didn't."

He thought a moment and then said, "No, no, not *his* mummy— course not." And for some little while after that the only answer procurable from him was "Course not," which seemed to be a favourite phrase of his.

"Have you asked him where he has been?"

"Yes," his mother answered, "but he only says 'Ta-ta.'"

"Ask him again."

She did. This time, after a little reflection, he pointed his chubby arm toward the door and said. "Been dere."

"Who took you?" asked Mrs. Seton.

Again Charley seemed puzzled. Then, looking doubtfully at his mother, he said "Mummy."

"No, not mummy," she answered, and his reply was "Course not," after which he attempted to climb on her shoulder.

Then, at Hewitt's suggestion, he was asked whom he went to see. This time the reply was prompt.

"Poor daddy," he said.

"What, *this* daddy?"

"No, not *vis* daddy—course not." And that was all that could be got from him.

"He will probably say things in the next day or two which may be useful," Hewitt said, "if you listen pretty sharply. Now I should like to go to the small morning-room."

In time room in question the door was still open. Outside the moon had risen and made the evening almost as clear as day. Hewitt examined the steps and the path at their foot, but all was dry and hard and showed no footmark. Then, as his eye rested on the small gate, "See here," he exclaimed suddenly; "somebody has been in, lifting the gate as I showed Mrs. Seton when I was last here. The gate has been replaced in a hurry and only the top hinge has dropped in its place; the bottom one is disjointed." He lifted time gate once more and set it back. The ground just along its foot was softer than in the parts surrounding, and here Hewitt perceived the print of a heel. It was the heel-mark of a woman's boot, small and sharp and of the usual curved D-shape. Nowhere else within or without was there the slightest mark. Hewitt went some distance either way in the outer lane, but without discovering anything more.

"I think I will borrow those new shoes," Hewitt said on his return. "I think I should be disposed to investigate further in any case, for my own satisfaction. The thing interests me. By the way, Mrs. Seton, tell me, would these shoes be more likely to have been bought at a regular shoemaker's or at a baby-linen shop?"

"Certainly, I should say at a baby-linen shop," Mrs. Seton answered; "they are of excellent quality, and for babies' shoes of this fancy description one would never go to an ordinary shoemaker's."

"So much the better, because the baby-linen shops are fewer than the shoemakers'. I may take these, then? Perhaps before I go you had better make quite certain that there is nothing else not your own about the child."

There was nothing, and with the shoes in his pocket Hewitt re-gained his cab and travelled back to his office. The case, from its very bareness and simplicity, puzzled him. Why was the child taken? Plainly not to keep, for it had been returned almost as it went. Plainly also not for the sake of reward or blackmail, for here was the child safely back, before the anonymous blackmailer had had a chance of earning his money. More, the advertised reward had not been claimed. Also it could not be a matter of malice or revenge, for the child was quite un-harmed, and indeed seems to have been quite happy. No conceivable family complication previous to the marriage of Mr. and Mrs. Seton could induce anybody to take away and return the child, which was undoubtedly Mrs. Seton's. Then who could be the "poor daddy" and "mummy"—not "*vis* daddy" and not "*vis* mummy"—that the child had been with. The Setons knew nothing of them. It was difficult to see what it could all mean.

Arrived at his office Hewitt took a map, and, setting the leg of a pair of compasses on the site of the Setons' house, described a circle, including in its radius all Willesden and Hampstead. Then, with the Suburban Directory to help him, he began searching out and noting all the baby-linen shops in the area. After all, there were not many—about a dozen. This done, Hewitt went home.

In the morning he began his hunt. His design was to call at each of the shops until he laid found in which a pair of shoes of that particular pattern had been sold on the day of little Charley Seton's disappear-ance. The first two shops he tried did not keep shoes of the pattern, and had never had them, and the young ladies behind the counter seemed vastly amused at Hewitt's inquiries. Nothing perturbed, he tried the next shop on his list in the Hampstead district. There they kept such shoes as a rule, but were "out of them at present." Hewitt immediately sent his card to the proprietress requesting a few minutes' interview. The lady—a very dignified lady indeed—in black silk, grey corkscrew curls and spectacles, came out with Hewitt's card between her fingers. He apologised for troubling her, and, stepping out of hear-ing from the counter, explained that his business was urgent.

"A child has been taken away by some unauthorised person, whom I am endeavouring to trace. This person bought this pair of shoes on Monday. You keep such shoes, I find, though they are not in stock at present, and, as they appear to be of an uncommon sort, possibly they were bought here."

The lady looked at them. "Yes," she said, "this pattern of shoe is made especially for me. I do not think you can buy them at other places."

"Then may I ask you to inquire from your assistants if any were sold on Monday, and to whom?"

"Certainly." Then there were consultations behind counters and desks, and examinations of carbon-papered books. In the end the proprietress came to Hewitt, followed by a young lady of rather pert and self-confident aspect. "We find," she said, "that two pairs of these shoes were sold on Monday. But one pair was afterwards brought back and exchanged for others less expensive. This young lady sold both."

"Ah, then possibly she may remember something of the person who bought the pair which was *not* exchanged."

"Yes," the assistant answered at once, addressing herself to the lady, "it was Mrs. Butcher's servant."

The proprietress frowned slightly. "Oh, indeed," she said, "Mrs. Butcher's servant, was it. There have been inquiries about Mrs. Butcher before, I believe, though not *here*. Mrs. Butcher is a woman who takes babies to mind, and is said to make a trade of adopting them, or finding people anxious to adopt them. I know nothing of her, nor do I want to. She lives somewhere not far off, and you can get her address, I believe, from the greengrocer's round the corner."

"This pattern of shoe is made especially for me."

"Does she keep more than one servant?"

"Oh, I think not; but no doubt the greengrocer can say." The lady seemed to feel it an affront that she should be supposed to know anything of Mrs. Butcher, and Hewitt consequently started for the greengrocer's. Now this was just one of those cases in which dependence on information given by other people put Hewitt on the wrong scent. He spent that day in a fatiguing pursuit of Mrs. Butcher's servant, with adventures rather amusing in themselves, but quite irrelevant to the Seton case. In the end, when he had captured her, and proceeded to open a cunning battery of inquiries, under plea of a bet with a friend that the shoes could not be matched, he soon found that *she* had been the purchaser who, after buying just such a pair of shoes, had returned and exchanged them for something cheaper. And the only outcome of his visit to the baby-linen shop was the waste of a day. It was indeed just one of those checks which, while they may hamper the progress of a narrative for popular reading, are nevertheless inseparable from the matter-of-fact experience of Hewitt's profession.

With a very natural rage in his heart, but with as polite an exterior as possible, Hewitt returned to the baby-linen shop in the evening. The whole case seemed barren of useful evidence, and at each turn as yet he had found himself helpless. At the shop the self-confident young lady calmly admitted that soon after he had left something had caused her to remember that it was the other customer who had kept the white shoes and not Mrs. Butcher's servant.

"And do you know the other customer?" he asked.

"No, she was quite a stranger. She brought in a little boy from a cab and bought a lot of things for him—a suit of outdoor clothes, as well as the shoes."

"Ah! now probably this is what I want. Can you remember anything of the child?"

"Yes, he was a pretty little fellow, about two years old or so, with curls. She called him Charley."

"Did she put the things on him in the shop?"

"Not the frock; but she put on the outer coat, the hat and the shoes. I can remember it all now quite well, now I have had time to think."

"Then what shoes did the child wear when he came in?"

"Rather old tan-coloured ones."

"Then I think this is the person I am after. You say you never saw her at any other time before or since. Try to describe her."

"Well, she was a lady well dressed, in black. She had a very high collar to hide a scar on her neck, like the scars people have sometimes after abscesses, I think. I could see it from the side when she stooped down."

"And are you sure she had nothing sent home? Did she take everything with her?"

"Yes; nothing was sent, else we should know her address, you know."

"She didn't happen to pay with a banknote, did she?"

"No, in cash."

Hewitt left with little more ceremony and made the best of his way to his friend the inspector at the police station. Here was the woman with the scarred neck again—Charley's deliverer once, now his kidnapper. If only something else could be ascertained of her— some small clue that might bring her identity into view—the thing would be done.

At the station, however, there was something new. A man had just come in, very drunk, and had given himself into custody for kidnapping the child Charles Seton, whose description was set forth on the bill which still appeared on the notice-board outside the station. When Hewitt arrived the man was lolling, wretched and maudlin, against the rail, and, oblivious of most of the questions addressed to him, was ranting and snivelling by turns. His dress was good, though splashed with mud, and his bloated face, bleared eyes and loose, tremulous mouth proclaimed the habitual drunkard.

"I shay I'll gimmeself up," he proclaimed, with a desperate attempt at dignity; "I'll gimmeself up takin' away lil boy; I'll shacrifishe m'self. Solemn duty shacrifishe m'self f'elpless woman, ain't it? Ver' well then; gimmeself up takin' 'way lil boy, buyin' 'm pair shoes. No harm in that, issher? Hope not. Ver' well then." And be subsided into tears.

"What's your name?" asked the inspector.

"Whash name? Thash my bishnesh. Warrer wan' know name for? Grapert—hence ask gellum'sh name. I'm gellum, thash whit' I am. Besht of shisters too, besht shis'ers"—snivelling again—"an' I'm ungra'ful beasht. But I shacrifishe 'self; she shun' get 'n trouble. D'year? Gimmeself up shtealin' lil boy. Who says I ain' gellum?"

Nothing more intelligible than this could be got out of him, and presently he was taken off to the cells. Then Hewitt asked the inspector, "What will happen to him now?"

The inspector laughed.

"Oh he'll get very sober and sick and sorry by the morning," he said; "and then he'll have to send home for some money, that's all."

"What's your name?" asked the inspector.

"And as to the child?"

"Oh, he'll forget all about that; that's only a drunken freak. The child has been recovered. You know that, I suppose?"

"Yes, but I am still after the person who took it away. It was a woman. Indeed, I've more than a suspicion that it was the woman who brought the child here when he was lost before—the one with the scar on the neck, you know."

"Is that so?" said the inspector. "Well, that's a rum go, ain't it? What did she bring him back here for if she wanted him again?"

"That I want to find out," Hewitt answered. "And now I want you to do me a favour. You say you expect that man below will want to send home in the morning for money. Well, I want to be the messenger."

The inspector opened his eyes.

"Want to be the messenger? Well, that's easily done; if you're here at the time I'll leave word. But why?"

"Well, I've a sort of notion I know something about his family, and I want to make sure. Shall I be here at eight in the morning, or shall we say nine?"

"Which you like; I expect he'll be shouting for bail before eight."

"Very well, we will say eight. Goodnight."

And so Hewitt had to let yet another night go without an explanation of the mystery; but he felt that his hand was on the key at last, though it had only fallen there by chance. Prompt to his time at eight in the morning he was at the police-station, where another inspector was now on duty, who, however, had been told of Hewitt's wish.

"Ah," he said, "you're well to time, Mr. Hewitt. That prisoner's as limp as rags now; he's begging of us to send to his sister."

"Does he say anything about that child?"

"Says he don't know anything about it; all a drunken freak. His name's Oliver Neale, and he lives at 10 Morton Terrace, Hampstead, with his sister. Her name's Mrs. Isitt, and you're to take this note and bring her back with you, or at any rate some money; and you're to say he's truly repentant," the inspector concluded with a grin.

The distance was short, and Hewitt walked it. Morton Terrace was a short row of pleasant old-fashioned villas, ivy-grown and neat, and No. 10 was as neat as any. To the servant who answered his ring Hewitt announced himself as a gentleman with a message from Mrs. Isitt's brother. This did not seem to prepossess the girl in Hewitt's favour, and she backed to the end of the hall and communicated with some-body on the stairs before finally showing Hewitt into a room, where he was quickly followed by Mrs. Isitt.

She was a rather tall woman of perhaps thirty-eight, and had probably been attractive, though now her face bore lines of sad grief. Hewitt noticed that she wore a very high black collar.

"Good-morning, Mrs. Isitt," he said. "I'm afraid my errand is not altogether pleasant. The fact is your brother, Mr. Neale, was not alto-gether sober last night, and he is now at the police station, where he wrote this note."

Mrs. Isitt did not appear surprised, and took the note with no more than a sigh.

"Yes," she said, "it can't be concealed. This is not the first time by many, as you probably know, if you are a friend of his."

She read the note, and as she looked up Hewitt said—

"No, I have not known him long. I happened to be at the station last night, and he rather attracted my attention by insisting, in his intoxi-cated state, on giving himself up for kidnapping a child, Charles Seton."

Mrs. Isitt started as though shot. Pale of cheek, she glanced fear-fully in Hewitt's face and there met a keen gaze that seemed to read her brain. She saw that her secret was known, but for a moment she struggled, and her lips worked convulsively—

"Charles Seton—Charles Seton?" she said.

"Yes, Mrs. Isitt, that is the name. The child, as a matter of fact, was stolen by the person who bought these shoes for it. Do you recognise them?"

He produced the shoes and held them before her. The woman sank on the sofa behind her, terrified, but unable to take her eyes from Hewitt's.

"Come, Mrs. Isitt," he said, "you have been recognised. Here is my card. I am commissioned by the parents of the child to find who removed him, and I think I have succeeded."

She took the card and glanced at it dazedly; then she sank with a groaning sob with her face on the head of the sofa, and as she did so Hewitt could see a scar on the side of her neck peeping above her high collar.

"Oh, my God!" the woman moaned. "Then it has come to this. He will die! he will die!"

The woman's anguish was piteous to see. Hewitt had gained his point, and was willing to spare her. He placed his hand on her heaving shoulder and begged her not to distress herself.

"The matter is rather difficult to understand, Mrs. Isitt," he said. "If you will compose yourself perhaps you can explain. I can assure you that there is no desire to be vindictive. I'm afraid my manner upset you. Pray reassure yourself. May I sit down?"

She sank with a groaning sob with her face on the head of the sofa.

Nobody could by his manner more easily restore confidence and trust than Hewitt, when it pleased him. Mrs. Isitt lifted her head and gazed at him once more with a troubled though quieter expression.

"I think you wrote Mrs. Seton an anonymous letter," Hewitt said, producing the first of those which Mrs. Seton had brought him. "It was kind of you to reassure the poor woman."

"Oh, tell me," Mrs. Isitt asked, "was she much upset at missing the little boy? Did it make her ill?"

"She was upset, of course; but perhaps the joy of recovering him compensated for all."

"Yes; I took him back as soon as I possibly could, really I did, Mr. Hewitt. And, oh! I was so tempted! My life has been so unhappy! If you only knew!" She buried her face in her hands.

"Will you tell me?" Hewitt suggested gently. "You see, whatever happens, an explanation of some sort is the first thing."

"Yes, yes—of course. Oh, I am a wretched woman." She paused for some little while, and then went on: "Mr. Hewitt, my husband is a lunatic." She paused again.

"There was never a man, Mr. Hewitt, so devoted to his wife and children as my husband. He bore even with the continual annoyance of my brother, whom you saw, *because* he was my brother. But a little more than a year ago, as the result of an accident, a tumour formed on his brain. The thing is incurable except, as a remote possibility, by a most dangerous operation, which the doctors fear to attempt except under most favourable conditions. Without that he must die sooner or later. Meantime he is insane, though with many and sometimes long intervals of perfect lucidity. When the disease attacked him there was little warning, except from pains in the head, till one dreadful night. Then he rose from bed a maniac and killed our child, a little girl of six, whom he was devotedly attached to. He also cut my own throat with his razor, but I recovered. I would rather say nothing more of that—it is too dreadful; though indeed I think about little else. There was another child, a baby boy, about a year old when his sister died, and he—he died of scarlet fever scarcely four months ago.

"My husband was taken to a private asylum at Willesden, where he now is. I visited him frequently, and took the baby, and it was almost terrible to see—a part of his insanity, no doubt—how his fondness for that child grew. When it died I never dared to tell him. Indeed, the doctors forbade it. In his state he would have died raving.

"But he asked for it, sometimes earnestly, sometimes angrily, till I almost feared to visit him. Then he began to demand it of the doctors and attendants, and his excitement increased day by day. I was told to prepare for the worst. When I visited him he sometimes failed to recognise me, and at others demanded the child fiercely. I should tell you that it was only just about this time that it was found that the tumour existed, and the idea of the operation was suggested; but of course it was impossible in his disturbed condition. I scarcely dared to go to see him, and yet I did so long to! Dr. Bailey did indeed suggest that possibly we might find he would be quieted by being shown another child; but I myself felt that to be very unlikely.

"It was while things were in this state, and about six or seven weeks ago, that, walking toward Cricklewood one morning, I saw a little fellow trotting along all alone, who actually startled me—startled me very much—by his resemblance to our poor little one. The likeness was one of those extraordinary ones that one only finds among young children. This child was a little bigger and stronger than ours was when he died, but then it was older—probably very nearly the age and size our own would have been had it lived.

"Nobody else was in sight, and I fancied the child looked about to cry, so I went to it and spoke. Plainly it had strayed, and could not tell me where it lived, only that its name was Charley. I took it in my arms and it grew quite friendly. As I talked to it suddenly Dr. Bailey's suggestion came in my mind. If any child could deceive my poor husband surely this was the one. Of course I should have to find its parents—probably through the police; but why not at any rate take it to Willesden in the meantime for an hour or so? I could not resist the temptation—I took the first available cab.

"The result of the experiment almost frightened me. My poor husband received the child with transports of delight, kissed it, and laughed and wept over it like a mother rather than a father, and refused to give it up for hours. The child of course would not answer to its strange name at first, but he seemed an adaptable little thing, and presently began calling my poor husband 'daddy.' I had not been so happy myself for months as I was as I watched them. I. had told Dr. Bailey—what I fear was not strictly true—that I had borrowed the child from a friend. At length I felt I must go and take the boy to the police, and with great difficulty I managed to get it away, my poor husband crying like a child. Well, I took the little fellow to the station I judged nearest to where I found him, and gave him up to the care of the inspector. But I was a little frightened at having kept him so long,

"Daddy!"

and gave a false name and address. Still I learned from the inspector that the child had been inquired after, and by whom.

"My husband was quiet for some days after this, but then he began to ask for his boy with more vehemence than ever. He grew worse and worse, and soon his ravings were terrible. Dr. Bailey urged me to bring the child again, but what could I do? I formed a desperate idea of going to Mrs. Seton, telling her the whole thing, and imploring her to let me take the child again. But then would that be likely? Would she allow her child to be placed in the arms of a lunatic—one indeed who had already killed a child of his own? I felt that the thing was impossible. Still I went to the house and walked about it again and again, I scarcely knew why. And my poor husband in his confinement screamed for his child till I dared not go near him. So it was when one morning—last Monday morning—I had passed the front of the Setons' house and turned up the lane at the side. I could see over the low fence and hedge, and as I came to the French window with the steps I saw that the window was open at one side and little Charley was standing on the top step.

"He recognised me, smiled and called just as my own child would have done; indeed, as I stood there I almost fell into the delusion of my poor mad husband. I took the gate in my hands, shaking it impatiently, and in attempting to open it from the wrong end, found the hinges lift out. I could see that nobody else was in the room behind the French window. There was the temptation—the overwhelming temptation—and I was distracted. I took the little fellow hurriedly in my anus and pulled the window to, so that the bottom bolt fell into the floor socket; then I replaced the gate as I found it and ran to where I knew there was a cabstand. Oh! Mr. Hewitt, was it so very sinful? And I meant to bring him back that same afternoon, I really did.

"The child was in indoor clothes, and had no hat. I called at a baby-linen shop and bought hat, cloak, frock and a new pair of shoes. Then I hurried to Willesden. Again the effect was magical. My husband was happy once more; but when at last I attempted to take the child away he would not let it go. It was terrible. Oh, I can't describe the scene. Dr. Bailey told me that, come what might, I must stay that night in a room his wife would provide for me and keep the child, or perhaps I must sit up with my husband and let the child sleep on my knee. In the end it was the latter that I did.

"By the morning my senses were blunted and I scarcely cared what happened. I determined that as I had gone so far I would keep the child that day at least; indeed, as I say, whether by the influence of my husband I know not, but I almost felt myself falling into his delusion that the child was ours. I went home for an hour at midday, taking the child, and then my wretched brother saw it and got the whole story from me. He told me that reward bills were out about the child, and then I dimly realised that its mother must be suffering pain, and I wrote the note you spoke of. Perhaps I had some little idea of delaying pursuit—I don't know. At any rate I wrote it, and posted it at Willesden as I went back. My husband had been asleep when I left, but now he was awake again and asking for the child once more. There is little more to say. I stayed that night and the next day, and by that time my husband had become tranquil and rational as he had not been for months. If only the improvement can be sustained they think of operating tomorrow or the next day.

"I carried Charley back in the dusk, intending to put him inside one of the gates, ring, and watch him safely in from a little way off, but as I passed down the side lane I saw the French window open again and nobody near. I had been that way before and felt bolder there. I took his hat and cloak (I had already changed his frock) and, after kissing him, put him hastily through the window and came away. But I had forgotten the new shoes. I remembered them, however, when I got home, and immediately conceived a fear that the child's parents might trace me by their means. I mentioned this fear to my brother, and it appeared to frighten him.

"He borrowed some money of me yesterday, and it seems got intoxicated. In that state he is always anxious to do some noble action, though he is capable, I am grieved to say, of almost any meanness when sober. He lives here at my expense, indeed, and borrows money from his friends for drink. These may seem hard things for a sister to say, but everybody knows it. He has wearied me, and I have lost all shame of him. I suppose in his muddled state he got the notion that he would accuse himself of what I had done and so shield me. I expect he repented of his self-sacrifice this morning though."

Hewitt knew that he had, but said nothing. Also he said nothing of the anonymous letter he had in his pocket, wherein Mr. Oliver Neale had covertly demanded a hundred pounds for the restoration of Charley Seton. Ho guessed however that that gentleman had feared making the appointment that the advertisement answering his letter had suggested.

To Mr. and Mrs. Seton Hewitt told the whole story, omitting at first names and addresses. "I saw plainly," he said in course of his talk, "that the child might easily have been taken from the French window. I did not say so, for Mrs. Seton was already sufficiently distressed, and the notion that the child was kidnapped and not simply lost might have made her worse just then. The toys—the cart with the string on it in particular—had been dragged in the direction of the window, and then nothing would be easier than for the child to open the window itself. There was nothing but a drop bolt, working very easily, which the child must often have seen lifted, and you will remember that the catch did not act. Once the child had opened the window and got outside, the whole thing was simple. The gate could be lifted, the child taken, and the window pulled to, so that the bolt would fall into its place and leave all as before.

"As to the previous occasion, I thought it curious at first that the child should stray before lunch and yet not be heard of again till the evening, and then apparently not be over-fatigued. But beyond these little things, and what I inferred from the letter, I had very little to help me indeed. Nothing, in fact, till I got the shoes, and they didn't carry me very far. The drunken rant of the man in the police station attracted me because he spoke not only of taking away the child, but of buying it shoes.

"Now nobody could know of the buying of the shoes who did not know something more. But I knew it was a woman who had taken Charley, as you know, from the heel-mark and the evidence of the shop people, so that when the bemused fool talked of his sister, and sacrificing himself for her, and keeping her out of trouble, and so on, I arranged the case up in my mind, and, so far as I ventured, I guessed it aright. The police inspector knew nothing of the matter of the shoes, nor of the fact of the person I was after being a woman, so thought the thing no more-than a drunken freak.

"And now," Hewitt said, "before I tell you this woman's name, don't you think the poor creature has suffered enough?"

Both Mrs. Seton and her husband agreed that she had, and that so far as they were concerned no further steps should be taken. And when she was told where to go, Mrs. Seton went off at once to offer Mrs. Isitt her forgiveness and sympathy. But Mrs. Isitt's punishment came in twenty-four hours, when her husband died in the surgeon's hands.

THE CASE OF MR. GELDARD'S ELOPEMENT

1.

Any people have been surprised at the information that, in all Martin Hewitt's wide and busy practice, the matrimonial cases whereon he has been engaged have been comparatively few. That he has had many important cases of the sort is true, but among the innumerable cases of different descriptions they make a small percentage. The reason is that so many of the persons wishing to consult him on such concerns were actuated by mere unreasoning or fanciful jealousy that Hewitt would do no more in their cases than urge reconciliation and mutual trust.

The common "private inquiry" offices chiefly flourish on this class of case, and their proprietors present no particular reluctance to taking it up. In any event it means fees for consultation and "watching;" and recent newspaper reports have made it plain that among some of the less scrupulous agents a case may be manufactured from beginning to end according to order. Again, Hewitt had a distaste for the sort of work commonly involved in matrimonial troubles; and with the immense amount of business brought to him, rendering necessary his rejection of so many commissions, it was easy for him to avoid what went against his inclinations. Still, as I have said, matrimonial cases there were, and often of an interesting nature, taking rise in no fanciful nor unreasoning jealousy.

When, on its change of proprietorship, I accepted my appointment on the paper that now claims me, I had a week or two's holiday pending the final turning over of the property. I could not leave town, for I might have been wanted at any moment, but I made an absorbing and instructive use of my leisure as an amateur assistant to Hewitt. I sat in his office much of the time and saw more of the daily routine of his work than I had ever done before; and I was present at one or two interviews that initiated cases that afterwards developed striking features. One of these—which indeed I saw entirely through before I resumed my more legitimate work—was the case of Mr. and Mrs. Geldard.

Hewitt had stepped out for a few minutes, and I was sitting alone in his private room when I became conscious of some disturbance in the outer office. An excited female voice was audible making impatient inquiries. Presently Kerrett, Hewitt's clerk, came in with the message that a lady—Mrs. Geldard, was the name on the visitor's slip that she had filled up—was anxious to see Mr. Hewitt, at once, and failing himself had decided to see me, whom Kerrett had calmly taken it upon himself to describe as Hewitt's confidential assistant. He apologised for this, and explained that he thought, as the lady-seemed excited, it would be as well to let her see me to begin with, if there was no objection, and perhaps she would begin to be coherent and intelligible by Hewitt's arrival, which might occur at any moment.

So the lady was shown in. She was tall, bony, and severe of face, and she began as soon as she saw me: "I've come to get you to get a watch set on my husband. I've endured this sort of thing in silence long enough. I won't have it. I'll see if there's no protection to be had for a woman treated as I am—with his goings out all day 'on business' when his office is shut up tight all the time. I wanted to see Mr. Hewitt himself, but I suppose you'll do, for the present at any rate, though I'll have it sifted to the bottom, and get the best advice to be had, no matter what it costs, though I *am* only a woman with nobody to confide in or to speak a word for me, and I'm not going to be crushed like a fly, as I'll soon let him know."

Here I seized a short opportunity to offer Mrs. Geldard a chair, and to say that I expected Mr. Hewitt in a few minutes.

"Very well, I'll wait and see him. But you have to do with the watching business no doubt, and you'll understand what it is I want done; and I'm sure I'm justified, and mean to sift it to the bottom, whatever happens. Am I to be kept in total ignorance of what my husband does all day when he is supposed to be at business? Is it likely I should submit to that?"

I said I didn't think it likely at all, which was a fact. Mrs. Geldard appeared to be about the least submissive woman I ever saw.

"No, and I won't, that's more. Nice goings on somewhere, no doubt, with his office shut up all day and the business going to ruin. I want you to watch him. I want you to follow him tomorrow morning and find out all he does and let me know. I've followed him myself this morning and yesterday morning, but he gets away somehow from the back of his office, and I can't watch on two staircases at once, so I want you to come and do it, and I'll—"

Here fortunately Hewitt's arrival checked Mrs. Geldard's flow of speech, and I rose and introduced him. I told him shortly that the lady desired a watch to be set on her husband at his office, and a report to be given her of his daily proceedings. Hewitt did not appear to accept the commission with any particular delight, but he sat down to hear his visitor's story. "Stay here, Brett," he said, as he saw my hands stretched towards the door. "We've an engagement presently, you know."

The engagement, I remembered, was merely to lunch, and Hewitt kept me with some notion of restricting the time which this alarming woman might be disposed to occupy. She repeated to Hewitt, in the same manner, what she had already said to me, and then Hewitt, seizing his first opportunity, said, "Will you please tell me, Mrs. Geldard, definitely and concisely, what evidence, or even indication, you have of unbecoming conduct on your husband's part, and substantially what case you wish me to take up?"

"Case? why, I've been telling you." And again Mrs. Geldard repeated her vague catalogue of sufferings, assuring Hewitt that she was determined to have the best advice and assistance, and that therefore she had come to him.

In the end Hewitt answered: "Put concisely, Mrs. Geldard, I take it that your case is simply this. Mr. Geldard is in business as, I think you told me, a general agent and broker, and keeps an office in the city. You have had various disagreements with him—not an uncommon thing, unfortunately, between married people—and you have entertained certain indefinite suspicions of his behaviour. Yesterday you went so far as to go to his office soon after he should have been there, and found him absent and the office shut up. You waited some time, and called again, but the door was still locked, and the caretaker of the building assured you that Mr. Geldard usually kept his office thus shut. You knocked repeatedly, and called through the keyhole, but got no answer. This morning you even followed your husband and saw him enter his office, but when, a little later, you yourself attempted to enter it you once more found it locked and apparently tenantless. From this you conclude that he must have left his rooms by some back way, and you say you are determined to find out where he goes and what he does during the day. For this purpose, you, I gather, wish me to watch him and report his whole day's proceedings to you?"

"Yes, of course; as I said."

"I'm afraid the state of my other engagements just at present will scarcely admit of that. Indeed, to speak quite frankly, this mere watching, especially of husband or wife, is not a sort of business that I care to undertake, except as a necessary part of some definite, tangible case. But apart from that, will you allow me to advise you? Not professionally, I mean, but merely as a man of the world. Why come to third parties with these vague suspicions? Family divisions of this sort, with all sorts of covert mistrust and suspicion, are bad things at best, and once carried as far as you talk of carrying this, go beyond peaceable remedy. Why not deal frankly and openly with your husband? Why not ask him plainly what he has been doing during the days you were unable to get into his office? You will probably find it all capable of a very simple and innocent explanation."

"Am I to understand, then," Mrs. Geldard said, bridling, "that you refuse to help me?"

"I have not refused to help you," Hewitt replied. "On the contrary, I am trying to help you now. Did your husband ever follow any other profession than the one he is now engaged in?"

"Once he was a mechanical engineer, but he got very few clients, and it didn't pay."

"There, now, is a suggestion. Would it be very unlikely that your husband, trained mechanician as he is, may have reverted so far to his old profession as to be conceiving some new invention? And in that case, what more probable than that he would lock himself securely in his office to work out his idea, and take no notice of visitors knocking, in order to admit nobody who might learn something of what he was doing? Does he keep a clerk or office boy?"

"No, he never has since he left the mechanical engineering."

"Well, Mrs. Geldard, I'm sorry I have no more time now, but I must earnestly repeat my advice. Come to an understanding with your husband in a straightforward way as soon as you possibly can. There are plenty of private inquiry offices about where they will watch anybody, and do almost anything, without any inquiry into their clients' motives, and with a single eye to fees. I charge you no fee, and advise you to treat your husband with frankness."

Mrs. Geldard did not seem particularly satisfied, though Hewitt's rejection of a consultation fee somewhat softened her. She left protesting that Hewitt didn't know the sort of man she had to deal with, and that, one way or another, she must have an explanation.

"Come, we'll get to lunch," said Hewitt. "I'm afraid my suggestion as to Mr. Geldard's probable occupation in his office wasn't very brilliant, but it was the pleasantest I could think of for the moment, and the main thing was to pacify the lady. One does no good by aggravating a misunderstanding of that sort."

"Can you make any conjecture," I said, "at what the trouble really is?"

Hewitt raised his eyebrows and shook his head. "There's no telling," he said: "An angry, jealous, pragmatical woman, apparently, this Mrs. Geldard, and it's impossible to judge at first sight how much she really knows and how much she imagines. I don't suppose she'll take my advice. She seems to have worked herself into a state of rancour that must burst out violently somewhere. But lunch is the present business. Come."

The next day I spent at a friend's house a little way out of town, so that it was not till the following morning, about the same Hewitt that I learned from Hewitt that Mrs. Geldard had called again.

"Yes," he said; "she seems to have taken my advice in her own way, which wasn't a judicious one. When I suggested that she should speak frankly to her husband I meant her to do it in a reasonably amicable mood. Instead of that, she appears to have flown at his throat, so to speak, with all the bitterness at her tongue's disposal. The natural result was a row. The man slanged back, the woman threatened divorce, and the man threatened to leave the country altogether. And so yesterday Mrs. Geldard was here again to get me to follow and watch him. I had to decline once more, and got something rather like a slanging myself for my pains. She seemed to think I was in league with her husband in some way. In the end I promised—more to get rid of her than anything else—to take the case in hand if ever there were anything really tangible to go upon; if her husband really did desert her, you know, or anything like that. If, in fact, there were anything more for me to consider than these spiteful suspicions."

"I suppose," I said, "she had nothing more to tell you than she had before?"

"Very little. She seems to have startled Geldard, however, by a chance shot. It seems that she once employed a maid, whom she subsequently dismissed, because, as she tells me, the young woman was a great deal too good-looking, and because she observed, or fancied she observed, signs of some secret understanding between her maid and her husband.

"Moreover, it was her husband who discovered this maid and introduced her into the house, and furthermore, he did all he could to induce Mrs. Geldard not to dismiss her. He even hinted that her dismissal might cause serious trouble, and Mrs. Geldard says it is chiefly since this maid has left the house that his movements have become so mysterious. Well it seems that in the heat of yesterday's quarrel Mrs. Geldard, quite at random, asked tauntingly how many letters Geldard had received from Emma Trennatt lately. Emma Trennatt was the girl's name. This chance shot seemed to hit the target. Geldard (so his wife tells me at any rate) winced visibly, paled a little, and dodged the question. But for the rest of the quarrel he appeared much less at ease, and made more than one attempt to find out how much his wife really knew of the correspondence she had spoken of.

"But as her reference to it was of course the wildest possible fluke, he got little guidance, while his better-half waxed savage in her triumph, and they parted on wild cat terms. She came straight here and

Signs of some secret understanding.

303

evidently thought that after Geldard's reception of her allusion to cor-respondence with Emma Trennatt—which she seemed to regard as final and conclusive confirmation of all her jealousies—I should take the case in hand at once. When she found me still disinclined she gave me a trifling sample of her rhetoric, as no doubt commonly supplied to Mr. Geldard. She said in effect that she had only come to me be-cause she meant having the best assistance possible, but that she didn't think much of me after all, and one man was as bad as another, and so on. I think she was a trifle angrier because I remained calm and civil. And she went away this time without the least reference to a consulta-tion fee one way or another."

I laughed. "Probably," I said, "she went off to some agent who'll watch as long as she likes to pay."

"Quite possibly." But we were quite wrong. Hewitt took his hat and we made for the staircase. As we opened the landing-door there were hurried feet on the stairs below, and as it shut behind Mrs. Geld-ard's bonnet-load of pink flowers hove up before us. She was in a state of fierce alarm and excitement that had oddly enough something of triumph in it, as of the woman who says, "I told you so." Hewitt gave a tragic groan under his breath.

"Here's a nice state of things I'm in for now, Mr. Hewitt," she began abruptly, "through your refusing to do anything for me while there was time, though I was ready to pay you well as I told your young man but no you wouldn't listen to anything and seemed to think you knew my business better than I could tell you and now you've caused this state of affairs by delay perhaps you'll take the case in hand now?"

"But you haven't told me what has happened—" Hewitt began, whereat the lady instantly rejoined, with a shrill pretence of a laugh, "Happened? Why what do you suppose has happened after what I have told you over and over again? My precious husband's gone clean away, that's all. He's deserted me and gone nobody knows where. That's what's happened. You said that if he did anything of that sort you'd take the case up; so now I've come to see if you'll keep your promise. Not that it's likely to be of much use *now.*"

We turned back into Hewitt's private office and Mrs. Geldard told her story. Disentangled from irrelevances, repetitions, opinions and incidental observations, it was this. After the quarrel Geldard had gone to business as usual and had not been seen nor heard of since. After her yesterday's interview with Hewitt Mrs. Geldard had called at her husband's office and found it shut as before. She went home again and waited, but he never returned home that evening, nor all night. In the morning she had gone to the office once more, and finding it still shut had told the caretaker that her husband was missing and insisted on his bringing his own key and opening it for her inspection. Nobody was there, and Mrs. Geldard was astonished to find folded and laid on a cupboard shelf the entire suit of clothes that her husband had worn when he left home on the morning of the previous day. She also found in the waste paper basket the fragments of two or three envelopes addressed to her husband, which she brought for Hewitt's inspection. They were in the handwriting of the girl Trennatt, and with them Mrs. Geldard had discovered a small fragment of one of the letters, a mere scrap, but sufficient to show part of the signature "Emma," and two or three of a row of crosses running beneath, such as are employed to represent kisses. These things she had brought with her.

Hewitt examined them slightly and then asked, "Can I have a photograph of your husband, Mrs. Geldard?"

She immediately produced, not only a photograph of her husband, but also one of the girl Trennatt, which she said belonged to the cook. Hewitt complimented her on her foresight. "And now," he said, "I think we'll go and take a look at Mr. Geldard's office, if we may. Of course I shall follow him up now." Hewitt made a sign to me, which I interpreted as asking whether I would care to accompany him. I assented with a nod, for the case seemed likely to be interesting.

I omit most of Mrs. Geldard's talk by the way, which was almost ceaseless, mostly compounded of useless repetition, and very tiresome.

The office was on a third floor in a large building in Finsbury Pavement. The caretaker made no difficulty in admitting us. There were two rooms, neither very large, and one of them at the back very small indeed. In this was a small locked door.

"That leads on to the small staircase, sir," the caretaker said in response to Hewitt's inquiry. "The staircase leads down to the basement, and it ain't used much 'cept by the cleaners."

"If I went down this back staircase," Hewitt pursued, "I suppose I should have no difficulty in gaining the street?"

"Not a bit, sir. You'd have to go a little way round to get into Finsbury Pavement, but there's a passage leads straight from the bottom of the stairs out to Moorfields behind."

"Yes," remarked Mrs. Geldard bitterly, when the caretaker had left the room, "that's the way he's been leaving the office every day, and in disguise, too." She pointed to the cupboard where her husband's clothes lay. "Pretty plain proof that he was ashamed of his doings, whatever they were."

"Come, come," Hewitt answered deprecatingly, "we'll hope there's nothing to be ashamed of—at any rate till there's proof of it. There's no proof as yet that your husband has been disguising. A great many men who rent offices, I believe, keep dress clothes at them—I do it myself—for convenience in case of an unexpected invitation, or such other eventuality. We may find that he returned here last night, put on his evening dress and went somewhere dining. Illness, or fifty accidents, may have kept him from home."

But Mrs. Geldard was not to be softened by any such suggestion, which I could see Hewitt had chiefly thrown out by way of pacifying the lady, and allaying her bitterness as far as he could, in view of a possible reconciliation when things were cleared up.

"*That* isn't very likely," she said. "If he kept a dress suit here openly I should know of it, and if he kept it here unknown to me, what did he want it for? If he went out in dress clothes last night, who did he go with? Who do you suppose, after seeing those envelopes and that piece of the letter?"

"Well, well, we shall see," Hewitt replied. "May I turn out the pockets of these clothes?"

"Certainly; there's nothing in them of importance," Mrs. Geldard said. "I looked before I came to you."

Nevertheless, Hewitt turned them out. "Here is a cheque-book with a number of cheques remaining. No counterfoils filled in, which is awkward. Bankers, the London Amalgamated. We will call there presently. An ivory pocket paper-knife. A sovereign purse—empty." Hewitt placed the articles on the table as he named them. "Gold pencil case, ivory folding rule, Russia-leather card-case." He turned to Mrs. Geldard. "There is no pocket-book," he said, "no pocket-knife and no watch, and there are no keys. Did Mr. Geldard usually carry any of these things?"

"Yes," Mrs. Geldard replied, "he carried all four." Hewitt's simple methodical calmness, and his plain disregard of her former volubility, appeared by this to have disciplined Mrs. Geldard into a businesslike brevity and directness of utterance.

"As to the watch now. Can you describe it?"

"Oh, it was only a cheap one. He had a gold one stolen—or at any rate he told me so—and since then he has only carried a very common sort of silver one, without a chain."

"The keys?"

"I only know there *was* a bunch of keys. Some of them fitted drawers and bureaux at home, and others, I suppose, fitted locks in this office."

"What of the pocket-knife?"

"That was a very uncommon one. It was a present, as a matter of fact, from an engineering friend, who had had it made specially. It was large, with a tortoise-shell handle and a silver plate with his initials. There was only one ordinary knife-blade in it, all the other implements were small tools or things of that kind. There was a small pair of silver callipers, for instance."

"Like these?" Hewitt suggested, producing those he used for measuring drawers and cabinets in search of secret receptacles.

"Yes, like those. And there were folding steel compasses, a tiny flat spanner, a little spirit level, and a number of other small instruments of that sort. It was very well made indeed; he used to say that it could not have been made for five pounds."

"Indeed?" Hewitt cast his eyes about the two rooms. "I see no signs of books here, Mrs. Geldard—account books I mean, of course. Your husband must have kept account books, I take it?"

"Yes, naturally; he must have done. I never saw them, of course, but every business man keeps books." Then after a pause Mrs. Geldard continued: "And they're gone too. I never thought of *that*. But there, I might have known as much. Who can trust a man safely if his own wife can't? But I won't shield him. Whatever he's been doing with his clients' money he'll have to answer for himself. Thank heaven I've enough to live on of my own without being dependent on a creature like him. But think of the disgrace! My husband nothing better than a common thief—swindling his clients and making away with his books when he can't go on any longer! But he shall be punished, oh yes; *I'll* see he's punished, if once I find him!"

Hewitt thought for a moment, and then asked: "Do you know any of your husband's clients, Mrs. Geldard?"

"No," she answered, rather snappishly, "I don't. I've told you he never let me know anything of his business—never anything at all; and very good reason he had too, that's certain."

"Then probably you do not happen to know the contents of these drawers?" Hewitt pursued, tapping the writing-table as he spoke.

"Oh, there's nothing of importance in them—at any rate in the unlocked ones. I looked at all of them this morning when I first came."

The table was of the ordinary pedestal pattern with four drawers at each side and a ninth in the middle at the top, and of very ordinary quality. The only locked drawer was the third from the top on the left-hand side. Hewitt pulled out one drawer after another. In one was a tin half full of tobacco; in another a few cigars at the bottom of a box; in a third a pile of notepaper headed with the address of the office, and rather dusty; another was empty; still another contained a handful of string. The top middle drawer rather reminded me of a similar drawer of my own at my last newspaper office, for it contained several pipes; but my own were mostly briars, whereas these were all clays.

"There's nothing really so satisfactory," Hewitt said, as he lifted and examined each pipe by turn, "to a seasoned smoker as a well-used clay. Most such men keep one or more such pipes for strictly private use." There was nothing noticeable about these pipes except that they were uncommonly dirty, but Hewitt scrutinised each before returning it to the drawer. Then he turned to Mrs. Geldard and said: "As to the bank now—the London Amalgamated, Mrs. Geldard. Are you known there personally?"

"Oh, yes; my husband gave them authority to pay cheques signed by me up to a certain amount, and I often do it for household expenses, or when he happens to be away."

"Then perhaps it will be best for you to go alone," Hewitt responded. "Of course they will never, as a general thing, give any person information as to the account of a customer, but perhaps, as you are known to them, and hold your husband's authority to draw cheques, they may tell you something. What I want to find out is, of course, whether your husband drew from the bank all his remaining balance yesterday, or any large sum. You must go alone, ask for the manager, and tell him that you have seen nothing of Mr. Geldard since he left for business yesterday morning.

"Mind, you are not to appear angry, or suspicious, or anything of that sort, and you mustn't say you are employing me to bring him back from an elopement. That will shut up the channel of information at once. Hostile inquiries they'll never answer, even by the smallest hint, except after legal injunction. You can be as distressed and as alarmed as you please. Your husband has disappeared since yesterday morning, and you've no notion what has become of him; that is your tale, and a perfectly true one. You would like to know whether or not he has withdrawn his balance, or a considerable sum, since that would indicate whether or not his absence was intentional and premeditated."

Mrs. Geldard understood and undertook to make the inquiry with all discretion. The bank was not far, and it was arranged that she should return to the office with the result.

As soon as she had left Hewitt turned to the pedestal table and probed the keyhole of the locked drawer with the small stiletto attached to his penknife. "This seems to be a common sort of lock," he said. "I could probably open it with a bent nail. But the whole table is a cheap sort of thing. Perhaps there is an easier way."

He drew the unlocked drawer above completely out, passed his hand into the opening and felt about. "Yes," he said, "it's just as I hoped—as it usually is in pedestal tables not of the best quality; the partition between the drawers doesn't go more than two-thirds of the way back, and I can drop my hand into the drawer below. But I can't feel anything there—it seems empty."

He withdrew his hand and we tilted the whole table backward, so as to cause whatever lay in the drawers to slide to the back. This dodge was successful. Hewitt reinserted his hand and withdrew it with two orderly heaps of papers, each held together by a metal clip.

The papers in each clip, on examination, proved to be all of an identical character, with the exception of dates. They were, in fact, rent receipts. Those for the office, which had been given quarterly, were put back in their place with scarcely a glance, and the others Hewitt placed on the table before him. Each ran, apart from dates, in this fashion:

> Received from Mr. J. Cookson 15s., one month's rent of stable at 8 Dragon Yard, Benton Street, to—(here followed the date.) Also rent, feed and care of horse in own stable as agreed, £2.—W. Gask.

The receipts were ill-written, and here and there ill-spelt. Hewitt put the last of the receipts in his pocket and returned the others to the drawer. "Either," he said, "Mr. Cookson is a client who gets Mr. Geldard to hire stables for him, which may not be likely, or Mr. Geldard calls himself Mr. Cookson when he goes driving—possibly with Miss Trennatt. We shall see."

The pedestal table put in order again, Hewitt took the poker and raked in the fireplace. It was summer, and behind the bars was a sort of screen of cartridge paper with a frilled edge, and behind this, various odds and ends had been thrown—spent matches, trade-circulars crumpled up, and torn paper. There were also the remains of several cigars, some only half smoked, and one almost whole. The torn paper Hewitt examined piece by piece, and finally sorted out a number of pieces which he set to work to arrange on the blotting pad. They formed a complete note, written in the same hand as were the envelopes already found by Mrs. Geldard—that of the girl Emma Trennatt. It corresponded also with the solitary fragment of another letter which had accompanied them, by way of having a number of crosses below the signature, and it ran thus:—

Tuesday Night.
Dear Sam,—Tomorrow, to carry. Not late because people are coming for flowers. What you did was no good. The smoke leaks worse than ever, and F. thinks you must light a new pipe or else stop smoking altogether for a bit. Uncle is anxious.—Emma.

Then followed the crosses, filling one line and nearly half the next; seventeen in all.

Hewitt gazed at the fragments thoughtfully. "This is a find," he said—"most decidedly a find. It looks so much like nonsense that it must mean something of importance. The date, you see, is Tuesday night. It would be received here on Wednesday—yesterday—morning. So that it was immediately after the receipt of this note that Geldard left. It's pretty plain the crosses don't mean kisses. The note isn't quite of the sort that usually carries such symbols, and moreover, when a lady fills the end of a sheet of notepaper with kisses she doesn't stop less than half way across the last line—she fills it to the end. These crosses mean something very different. I should like, too, to know what 'smoke' means. Anyway this letter would probably astonish Mrs. Geldard if she saw it. We'll say nothing about it for the present."

He swept the fragments into an envelope, and put away the envelope in his breast pocket. There was nothing more to be found of the least value in the fireplace, and a careful examination of the office in other parts revealed nothing that I had not noticed before, so far as I could see, except Geldard's boots standing on the floor of the cupboard wherein his clothes lay. The whole place was singularly bare of what one commonly finds in an office in the way of papers, handbooks, and general business material.

Mrs. Geldard was not long away. At the bank she found that the manager was absent and his deputy had been very reluctant to say anything definite without his sanction. He gave Mrs. Geldard to understand, however, that there was a balance still remaining to her husband's credit; also that Mr. Geldard had drawn a cheque the previous morning, Wednesday, for an amount "rather larger than usual." And that was all.

"By the way, Mrs. Geldard," Hewitt observed, with an air of recollecting something, "there *was* a Mr. Cookson I believe, if I remember, who knew a Mr. Geldard. You don't happen to know, do you, whether or not Mr. Geldard had a client or an acquaintance of that name?"

"No, I know nobody of the name."

"Ah, it doesn't matter. I suppose it isn't necessary for your husband to keep horses or vehicles of any description in his business?"

"No, certainly not." Mrs. Geldard looked surprised at the question.

"Of course—I should have known that. He does not drive to business, I suppose?"

"No, he goes by omnibus."

"But as to Emma Trennatt now. This photograph is most welcome, and will be of great assistance, I make no doubt. But is there anything individual by which I might identify her if I saw her—anything beyond what I see in the photograph? A peculiarity of step, for instance, or a scar, or what not."

"Yes, there is a large mole—more than a quarter of an inch across I should think—on her left cheek, an inch below the outer corner of her eye. The photograph only shows the other side of the face."

"That will be useful to know. Now has she a relative living at Crouch End, or thereabout?"

"Yes, her uncle; she's living with him now—or she was at any rate till lately. But how did you know that?"

"The Crouch End postmark was on those envelopes you found. Do you know anything of her uncle?"

"Nothing, except that he's a nurseryman, I believe."

"Not his full address?"

"No."

"And Trennatt is his name?"

"Thank you. I think, Mrs. Geldard," Hewitt said, taking his hat, "that I will set out after your husband at once. You, I think, can do no better than stay at home till I have news for you. I have your address. If anything comes to your knowledge, please telegraph it to my office at once."

The office door was locked, the keys were left with the caretaker, and we saw Mrs. Geldard into a cab at the door. "Come," said Hewitt, "we'll go somewhere and look at a directory, and after that to Dragon Yard. I think I know a man in Moorgate Street who'll let me see his directory."

We started to walk down Finsbury Pavement. Suddenly Hewitt caught my arm and directed my eyes toward a woman who had passed hurriedly in the opposite direction. I had not seen her face, but Hewitt had. "If that isn't Miss Emma Trennatt," he said, "it's uncommonly like the notion I've formed of her. We'll see if she goes to Geldard's office."

We hurried after the woman, who, sure enough, turned into the large door of the building we had just left. As it was impossible that she should know us we followed her boldly up the stairs and saw her stop before the door of Geldard's office and knock. We passed her as she stood there—a handsome young woman enough—and well back on her left cheek, in the place Mrs. Geldard had indicated, there was plain to see a very large mole. We pursued our way to the landing above and there we stopped in a position that commanded a view of Geldard's door. The young woman knocked again and waited.

"This doesn't look like an elopement yesterday morning, does it?" Hewitt whispered. "Unless Geldard's left both this one and his wife in the lurch."

The young woman below knocked once or twice more, walked irresolutely across the corridor and back, and in the end, after a parting knock, started slowly back downstairs.

"Brett," Hewitt exclaimed with suddenness, "will you do me a favour? That woman understands Geldard's secret comings and goings, as is plain from the letter. But she would appear to know nothing of where he is now, since she seems to have come here to find him. Perhaps this last absence of his has nothing to do with the others. In any case will you follow this woman? She must be watched; but I want to see to the matter in other places. Will you do it?"

Of course I assented at once. We had been descending the stairs as Hewitt spoke, keeping distance behind the girl we were following. "Thank you," Hewitt now said. "Do it. If you find anything urgent to communicate wire to me in care of the inspector at Crouch End Police Station. He knows me, and I will call there in case you may have sent. But if it's after five this afternoon, wire also to my office. If you keep with her to Crouch End, where she lives, we shall probably meet."

We parted at the door of the office we were at first bound for, and I followed the girl southward.

This new turn of affairs increased the puzzlement I already laboured under. Here was the girl Trennatt—who by all evidence appeared to be well acquainted with Geldard's mysterious proceedings, and in consequence of whose letter, whatever it might mean, he would seem to have absented himself—herself apparently ignorant of his whereabouts and even unconscious that he had left his office. I had at first begun to speculate on Geldard's probable secret employment; I had heard of men keeping good establishments who, unknown to even their own wives, procured the wherewithal by begging or crossing-sweeping in London streets; I had heard also—knew in fact from Hewitt's experience—of well-to-do suburban residents whose actual profession was burglary or coining.

I had speculated on the possibility of Geldard's secret being one of that kind. My mind had even reverted to the case, which I have related elsewhere, in which Hewitt frustrated a dynamite explosion by his timely discovery of a baker's cart and a number of loaves, and I wondered whether or not Geldard was a member of some secret brotherhood of Anarchists or Fenians. But here, it would seem, were two distinct mysteries, one of Geldard's generally unaccountable movements, and another of his disappearance, each mystery complicating the other. Again, what did that extraordinary note mean, with its crosses and its odd references to smoking? Had the dirty clay pipes anything to do with it? Or the half-smoked cigars? Perhaps the whole thing was merely ridiculously trivial after all. I could make nothing of it, however, and applied myself to my pursuit of Emma Trennatt, who mounted an omnibus at the Bank, on the roof of which I myself secured a seat.

2

Here I must leave my own proceedings to put in their proper place those of Martin Hewitt as I subsequently learnt them.

Benton Street, he found by the directory, turned out of the City Road south of Old Street, so was quite near. He was there in less than ten minutes, and had discovered Dragon Yard. Dragon Yard was as small a stable-yard as one could easily find. Only the right-hand side was occupied by stables, and there were only three of these. On the left was a high dead wall bounding a great warehouse or some such building. Across the first and second of the stables stretched a long board with the legend, "W. Gask, Corn, Hay and Straw Dealer," and underneath a shop address in Old Street. The third stable stood blank and uninscribed, and all three were shut fast. Nobody was in the yard, and Hewitt at once proceeded to examine the end stable. The doors were unusually well finished and close-fitting, and the lock was a good one, of the lever variety, and very difficult to pick. Hewitt examined the front of the building very carefully, and then, after a visit to the entrance of the yard, to guard against early interruption, returned and scrambled by projections and fastenings to the roof. This was a roof in contrast to those of the other stables. They were of tiles, seemed old, and carried nothing in the way of a skylight; evidently it was the habit of Mr. Gask and his helpers to do their horse and van business with gates wide open to admit light.

But the roof of this third stable was newer and better made, and carried a good-sized skylight of thick fluted glass. Hewitt took a good look at such few windows as happened to be in sight, and straight away began, with the strongest blade of his pocket-knife, to cut away the putty from round one pane. It was a rather long job, for the putty had hardened thoroughly in the sun, but it was accomplished at length, and Hewitt, with a final glance at the windows in view, prized up the pane from the end and lifted it out.

The interior of the stable was apparently empty. Neither stall nor rack was to be seen; and the place was plainly used as a coach or van house simply. Hewitt took one more look about him and dropped quietly through the hole in the skylight. The floor was thickly laid with straw. There were a few odd pieces of harness, a rope or two, a lantern, and a few sacks lying here and there, and at the darkest end there was, an obscure heap covered with straw and sacking. This heap Hewitt proceeded to unmask, and having cleared away a few sacks left revealed about half-a-dozen rolls of linoleum. One of these he dragged to the light, where it became evident that it had remained thus rolled and tied with cord in two places for a long period. There were cracks in the surface, and when the cords were loosened the linoleum showed no disposition to open out or to become unrolled.

Others of the rolls on inspection exhibited the same peculiarities. Moreover, each roll appeared to consist of no more than a couple of yards of material at most, though all were of the same pattern. Every roll in fact was of the same length, thickness and shape as the others, containing somewhere near two yards of linoleum in a roll of some half dozen thicknesses, leaving an open diameter of some four inches in the centre. Hewitt looked at each in turn and then replaced the heap as he had found it. After this to regain the skylight was not

Half-a-dozen rolls of linoleum.

difficult by the aid of a trestle. The pane was replaced as well as the absence of fresh putty permitted, and five minutes later Hewitt was in a hansom bound for Crouch End.

He dismissed his cab at the police station. Within he had no difficulty in procuring a direction to Trennatt, the nurseryman, and a short walk brought him to the place. A fairly high wall topped with broken glass bounded the nursery garden next the road and in the wall were two gates, one a wide double one for the admission of vehicles, and the other a smaller one of open pales, for ordinary visitors. The garden stood sheltered by higher ground behind, whereon stood a good-sized house, just visible among the trees that surrounded it. Hewitt walked along by the side of the wall. Soon he came to where the ground of the nursery garden appeared to be divided from that of the house by a most extraordinarily high hedge extending a couple of feet above the top of the wall itself. Stepping back, the better to note this hedge, Hewitt became conscious of two large boards, directly facing each other, with scarcely four feet space between them, one erected on a post in the ground of the house and the other similarly elevated from that of the nursery, each being inscribed in large letters, "Trespassers will be prosecuted."

Hewitt smiled and passed on; here plainly was a neighbour's quar-

315

rel of long standing, for neither board was by any means new. The wall continued, and keeping by it Hewitt made the entire circuit of the large house and its grounds, and arrived once more at that part of the wall that enclosed the nursery garden. Just here, and near the wider gate, the upper part of a cottage was visible, standing within the wall, and evidently the residence of the nurseryman. It carried a conspicuous board with the legend, "H. M. Trennatt, Nurseryman." The large house and the nursery stood entirely apart from other houses or enclosures, and it would seem that the nursery ground had at some time been cut off from the grounds attached to the house.

Hewitt stood for a moment thoughtfully, and then walked back to the outer gate of the house on the rise. It was a high iron gate, and as Hewitt perceived, it was bolted at the bottom. Within the garden showed a neglected and weed-choked appearance, such as one associates with the garden of a house that has stood long empty.

A little way off a policeman walked. Hewitt accosted him and spoke of the house. "I was wondering if it might happen to be to let," he said. "Do you know?"

"No, sir," the policeman replied, "it ain't; though anyone might almost think it, to look at the garden. That's a Mr. Fuller as lives there—and a rum 'un too."

"Oh, he's a rum 'un, is he? Keeps himself shut up, perhaps?"

"Yes, sir. On'y 'as one old woman, deaf as a post, for servant, and never lets nobody into the place. It's a rare game sometimes with the milkman. The milkman, he comes and rings that there bell, but the old gal's so deaf she never 'ears it. Then the milkman, he just slips 'is 'and through the gate-rails, lifts the bolt and goes and bangs at the door. Old Fuller runs out and swears a good 'un. The old gal comes out and old Fuller swears at 'er, and she turns round and swears back like anything. She don't care for 'im—not a bit. Then when he ain't 'avin' a row with the milkman and the old gal he goes down the garden and rows with the old nurseryman there down the 'ill. He jores the nurseryman from 'is side o' the hedge and the nurseryman he jores back at the top of 'is voice. I've stood out there ten minutes together and nearly bust myself a-laughin' at them gray-'eaded old fellers a-callin' each other everythink they can think of; you can 'ear 'em 'alf over the parish. Why, each of 'em's 'ad a board painted, 'Trespassers will be Prosecuted,' and stuck 'em up facin' each other, so as to keep up the row."

"Very funny, no doubt."

"Funny? I believe you, sir. Why it's quite a treat sometimes on a dull beat like this. Why, what's that? slowed if I don't think they're beginning again now. Yes, they are. Well, my beat's the other way."

There was a sound of angry voices in the direction of the nursery ground, and Hewitt made toward it. Just where the hedge peeped over the wall the altercation was plain to hear.

"You're an old vagabond, and I'll indict you for a nuisance!"

"You're an old thief, and you'd like to turn me out of house and home, wouldn't you? Indict away, you greedy old scoundrel!"

These and similar endearments, punctuated by growls and snorts, came distinctly from over the wall, accompanied by a certain scraping, brushing sound, as though each neighbour were madly attempting to scale the hedge and personally bang the other.

Hewitt hastened round to the front of the nursery garden and quietly tried first the wide gate and next the small one. Both were fastened securely. But in the manner of the milkman at the gate of the house above, Hewitt slipped his hand between the open slats of the small gate and slid the night-latch that held it. Within the quarrel ran high as Hewitt stepped quietly into the garden. He trod on the narrow grass borders of the beds for quietness' sake, till presently only a line of shrubs divided him from the clamorous nurseryman.

Stooping and looking through an opening which gave him a back view, Hewitt observed that the brushing and scraping noise proceeded, not from angry scramblings, but from the forcing through an inadequate opening in the hedge of some piece of machinery which the nurseryman was most amicably passing to his neighbour at the same time as he assailed him with savage abuse, and received a full return in kind.

It appeared to consist of a number of coils of metal pipe, not unlike those sometimes used in heating apparatus, and was as yet only a very little way through. Something else, of bright copper, lay on the garden-bed at the foot of the hedge, but intervening plants concealed its shape.

Hewitt turned quickly away and made towards the greenhouses, keeping tall shrubs as much as possible between himself and the cottage, and looking sharply about him. Here and there about the garden were stand-pipes, each carrying a tap at its upper end and placed conveniently for irrigation. These in particular Hewitt scrutinised, and presently, as he neared a large wooden outhouse close by the large gate, turned his attention to one backed by a thick shrub. When the thick undergrowth of the shrub was pushed aside a small stone slab, black and dirty, was disclosed, and this Hewitt lifted, uncovering a square hole six or eight inches across, from the fore-side of which the

Some piece of machinery which the nurseryman
was most amicably passing to his neighbour.

stand-pipe rose.

The row went cheerily on over by the hedge, and neither Trennatt nor his neighbour saw Hewitt, feeling with his hand, discover two stop-cocks and a branch pipe in the hole, nor saw him try them both. Hewitt, however, was satisfied, and saw his case plain. He rose and made his way back toward the small gate. He was scarce halfway there when the straining of the hedge ceased, and before he reached it the last insult had been hurled, the quarrel ceased, and Trennatt approached. Hewitt immediately turned his back to the gate, and looking about him inquiringly hemmed aloud as though to attract attention. The nurseryman promptly burst round a corner crying, "Who's that? who's that, eh? What d'ye want, eh?"

"Why," answered Hewitt in a tone of mild surprise, "is it so uncommon to have a customer drop in?"

"I'd ha' sworn that gate was fastened," the old man said, looking about him suspiciously.

"That would have been rash; I had no difficulty in opening it. Come, can't you sell me a button-hole?"

The old man led the way to a greenhouse, but as he went he growled again, "I'd ha' sworn I shut that gate."

"Perhaps you forgot," Hewitt suggested. "You have had a little ex-

The stand-pipe in the nursery garden.

citement with your neighbour, haven't you?"

Trennatt stopped and turned round, darting a keen glance into Hewitt's face.

"Yes," he answered angrily, "I have. He's an old villain. He'd like to turn me out of here, after being here all my life-and a lot o' good the ground 'ud be to him if he kep' it like he keeps his own! And look there!" He dragged Hewitt toward the "Trespassers" boards. "Goes and sticks up a board like that looking over my hedge! As though I wanted to go over among his weeds! So I stuck up another in front of it, and now they can stare each other out o' countenance. Buttonhole, you said, sir, eh?"

The old man saw Hewitt off the premises with great care, and the latter, flower in coat, made straight for the nearest post-office and despatched a telegram. Then he stood for some little while outside the post-office deep in thought, and in the end returned to the gate of the house above the nursery.

With much circumspection he opened the gate and entered the grounds. But instead of approaching the house he turned immediately to the left, behind trees and shrubs, making for the side nearest the nursery.

Soon he reached a long, low wooden shed.

The door was only secured by a button, and turning this he gazed into the dark interior.

Now he had not noticed that close after him a woman had entered the gate, and that that woman was Mrs. Geldard. She would have made for the house, but catching sight of Hewitt, followed him swiftly and quietly over the long grass. Thus it came to pass that his first apprisal of the lady's presence was a sharp drive in the back which pitched him down the step to the low floor of what he had just perceived to be merely a tool-house, after which the door was shut and buttoned behind him.

"Perhaps you'll be more careful in future," game Mrs. Geldard's angry voice from without, "how you go making mischief between husband and wife and poking your nose into people's affairs. Such fellows as you ought to be well punished."

Hewitt laughed softly. Mrs. Geldard had evidently changed her mind. The door presented no difficulty; a fairly vigorous push dislodged the button entirely, and he walked back to the outer gate chuckling quietly. In the distance he heard Mrs. Geldard in shrill altercation with the deaf old woman. "It's no good you a-talking," the old woman was saying. "I can't hear. Nobody ain't allowed in this here place, so you must get out.

His first apprisal of the lady's presence was a sharp drive in the back.

Out you go now!" Outside the gate Hewitt met me.

3.

My own adventure had been simple. I had secured a back seat on the roof of the omnibus whereon Emma Trennatt travelled south from the Bank, from which I could easily observe where she alighted. When she did so I followed, and found to my astonishment that her destination was no other than the Geldards' private house at Camberwell—as I remembered from the address on the visitor's slip which Mrs. Geldard had handed in at Hewitt's office a couple of days before. She handed a letter to the maid who opened the door, and soon after, in response to a message by the same maid, entered the house. Presently the maid reappeared, bonneted, and hurried off, to return in a few minutes in a cab with another following behind.

Almost immediately Mrs. Geldard emerged in company with Emma Trennatt. She hurried the girl into one of the cabs, and I heard her repeat loudly twice the address of Hewitt's office, once to the girl and once to the cabman. Now it seemed plain to me that to follow Emma Trennatt farther would be waste of time, for she was off to Hewitt's office, where Kerrett would learn her message. And knowing where a message would find Hewitt sooner than at his office, I judged it well to tell Mrs. Geldard of the fact. I approached, therefore, as she was entering the other cab and began to explain when she cut me short.

"You go and tell your master to attend to his own business as soon as he pleases, for not a shilling does he get from me. He ought to be ashamed of himself, sowing dissension between man and wife for the sake of what he can make out of it, and so ought you."

I bowed with what grace I might, and retired. The other cab had gone, so I set forth to find one for myself at the nearest rank. I could think of nothing better to do than to make for Crouch End Police Station and endeavour to find Hewitt. Soon after my cab emerged north of the city I became conscious of another cab whose driver I fancied I recognised, and which kept ahead all along the route. In fact, it was Mrs. Geldard's cab, and presently it dawned upon him that we must both be bound for the same place. When it became quite clear that Crouch End was the destination of the lady I instructed my driver to disregard the police station and follow the cab in front. Thus I arrived at Mr. Fuller's house just behind Mrs. Geldard, and thus, waiting at the gate, I met Hewitt as he emerged.

"Hullo, Brett!" he said. "Condole with me. Mrs. Geldard has changed her mind, and considers me a pernicious creature anxious to make mischief between her and her husband; I'm very much afraid I shan't get my fee."

"No," I answered, "she told me you wouldn't."

We compared notes, and Hewitt laughed heartily. "The appearance of Emma Trennatt at Geldard's office this morning is explained," he said. "She went first with a message from Geldard to Mrs. Geldard at Camberwell, explaining his absence and imploring her not to talk of it or make a disturbance. Mrs. Geldard had gone off to town, and Emma Trennatt was told that she had gone to Geldard's office. There she went, and then we first saw her. She found nobody at the office, and after a minute or two of irresolution returned to Camberwell, and then succeeded in delivering her message, as you saw. Mrs. Geldard is apparently satisfied with her husband's explanation. But I'm afraid the revenue officers won't approve of it."

"The revenue officers?"

"Yes. It's a case of illicit distilling—and a big case, I fancy. I've wired to Somerset House, and no doubt men are on their way here now. But Mrs. Geldard's up at the house, so we'd better hurry up to the police station and have a few sent from there. Come along. The whole thing's very clever, and a most uncommonly big thing. If I know all about it—and I think I do—Geldard and his partners have been turning out untaxed spirit by the hundred gallons for a long time past. Geldard is the practical man, the engineer, and probably erected the whole apparatus himself in that house on the hill. The spirit is brought down by a pipe laid a very little way under the garden surface, and carried into one of the irrigation stand-pipes in the nursery ground. There's a quiet little hole behind the pipe with a couple of stop-cocks—one to shut off the water when necessary, the other to do the same with the spirit.

"When the stopcocks are right you just turn the tap at the top of the pipe and you get water or whisky, as the case may be. Fuller, the man up at the house, attends to the still, with such assistance as the deaf old woman can give him. Trennatt, down below, draws off the liquor ready to be carried away. These two keep up an ostentatious appearance of being at unending feud to blind suspicion. Our as yet ungreeted friend Geldard, guiding spirit of the whole thing, comes disguised as a carter with an apparent cart-load of linoleum, and carries away the manufactured stuff. In the pleasing language of

Geldard and Co., 'smoke,' as alluded to in the note you saw, means whisky. Something has been wrong with the apparatus lately, and it has been leaking badly. Geldard has been at work on it, patching, but ineffectually. 'What you did was no good' said the charming Emma in the note, as you will remember. 'Uncle was anxious.' And justifiably so, because not only does a leak of spirit mean a waste, but it means a smell, which some sharp revenue man might sniff. Moreover, if there is a leak, the liquid runs somewhere at random, and with any sudden increase in volume attention might easily be attracted. It was so bad that 'F.' (Fuller) thought Geldard must light another pipe (start another still) or give up smoking (distilling) for a bit.

"There is the explanation of the note. 'Tomorrow, to carry' probably means that he is to call with his cart—the cart in whose society Geldard becomes Cookson—to remove a quantity of spirit. He is not to come late because people are expected on floral business. The crosses I *think* will be found to indicate the amount of liquid to be moved. But that we shall see. Anyhow Geldard got there yesterday and had a busy day loading up, and then set to repairing. The damage was worse than supposed, and an urgent thing. Result, Geldard works into early morning, has a sleep in the place, where he may be called at any moment, and starts again early this morning. New parts have to be ordered, and these are delivered at Trennatt's today and passed through the hedge. Meantime Geldard sends a message to his wife explaining things, and the result you've seen."

At the police station a telegram had already been received from Somerset House. That was enough for Hewitt, who had discharged his duty as a citizen and now dropped the case. We left the police and the revenue officers to deal with the matter and travelled back to town.

"Yes," said Hewitt on the way, after each had fully described his day's experiences, "it seemed pretty plain that Geldard left his office by the back way in disguise, and there were things that hinted what that disguise was. The pipes were noticeable. They were quite unnecessarily dirty, and partly from dirty fingers. Pipes smoked by a man in his office would never look like that. They had been smoked out of doors by a man with dirty hands, and hands and pipes would be in keeping with the rest of the man's appearance. It was noticeable that he had left not only his clothes and hat but his boots behind him. They were quite plain though good boots, and would be quite in keeping with any dress but that of a labourer or some such man in his working clothes. Moreover, the partly-smoked cigars were probably thrown aside because they would appear inconsistent with Geldard's changed dress. The contents of the pockets in the clothes left behind, too, told the same tale. The cheap watch and the necessary keys, pocketbook and pocket-knife were taken, but the articles of luxury, the russia-leather card-case, the sovereign purse and so on were left. Then we came on the receipts for stable-rent. Suggestion—perhaps the disguise was that of a carter.

"Then there was the coach-house. Plainly, if Geldard took the trouble thus to disguise himself, and thus to hide his occupation even from his wife, he had sonic very good reason for secrecy. Now the goods which a man would be likely to carry secretly in a cart or van, as a regular piece of business, would probably be either stolen or smuggled. When I examined those pieces of linoleum I became convinced that they were intended merely as receptacles for some other sort of article altogether. They were old, and had evidently been thus rolled for a very long period. They appeared to have been exposed to weather, but on the outside only. Moreover, they were all of one size and shape, each forming a long hollow cylinder, with plenty of interior room. Now from this it was plainly unlikely that they were intended to hold *stolen* goods.

"Stolen goods are not apt to be always of one size and shape, adaptable to a cylindrical recess. Perhaps they were smuggled. Now the only goods profitable to be smuggled nowadays are tobacco and spirits, and plainly these rolls of linoleum would be excellent receptacles for either. Tobacco could be packed inside the rolls and the ends stopped artistically with narrow rolls of linoleum. Spirits could be contained in metal cylinders exactly fitting the cavity and the ends filled in the same way as for tobacco. But for tobacco a smart man would probably make his linoleum rolls of different sizes, for the sake of a more innocent appearance, while for spirits it would be a convenience to have vessels of uniform measure, to save trouble in quicker delivery and calculation of quantity. Bearing these things in mind I went in search of the gentle nurseryman at Crouch End.

"My general survey of the nursery ground and the house behind it inspired me with the notion that the situation and arrangement were most admirably adapted for the working of a large illicit still—a form of misdemeanour, let me tell you, that is much more common nowadays than is generally supposed. I remembered Geldard's engineering experience, and I heard something of the odd manners of Mr.

Puller; my theory of a traffic in untaxed spirits became strengthened. But why a nursery? Was this a mere accident of the design? There were commonly irrigation pipes about nurseries, and an extra one might easily be made to carry whisky. With this in mind I visited the nursery with the result you know of. The stand-pipe I tested (which was where I expected—handy to the vehicle-entrance) could produce simple New River water or raw whisky at command of one of two stopcocks. My duty was plain. As you know, I am a citizen first and an investigator after, and I find the advantage of it in my frequent intercourse with the police and other authorities.

"As soon as I could get away I telegraphed to Somerset House. But then I grew perplexed on a point of conduct. I was commissioned by Mrs. Geldard. It scarcely seemed the loyal thing to put my client's husband in gaol because of what I had learnt in course of work on her behalf. I decided to give him, and nobody else, a sporting chance. If I could possibly get at him in the time at my disposal, by himself, so that no accomplice should get the benefit of my warning, I would give him a plain hint to run; then he could take his chance. I returned to the place and began to work round the grounds, examining the place as I went; but at the very first outhouse I put my head into I was surprised in the rear by Mrs. Geldard coming in hot haste to stop me and rescue her husband. She most unmistakably gave me the sack, and so now the police may catch Geldard or not, as their luck may be."

They did catch him. In the next day's papers, a report of a great capture of illicit distillers occupied a prominent place. The prisoners were James Fuller, Henry Matthew Trennatt, Sarah Blatten, a deaf woman, Samuel Geldard and his wife Rebecca Geldard. The two women were found on the premises in violent altercation when the officers arrived, a few minutes after Hewitt and I had left the police station on our way home. It was considered by far the greatest haul for the revenue authorities since the seizure of the famous ship's boiler on a waggon in the East-End stuffed full of tobacco, after that same ship's boiler had made about a dozen voyages to the continent and back "for repair." Geldard was found dressed as a workman, carrying out extensive alterations and repairs to the still. And a light van was found in a shed belonging to the nursery loaded with seventeen rolls of linoleum, each enclosing a cylinder containing two gallons of spirits, and packed at each end with narrow linoleum rolls. It will be remembered that seventeen was the number of crosses at the foot of Emma Trennatt's note.

The prisoners were James Fuller, Henry Matthew Trennatt, Sarah Blatten, a deaf woman, Samuel Geldard and his wife Rebecca Geldard.

The subsequent raids on a number of obscure public-houses in different parts of London, in consequence of information gathered on the occasion of the Geldard capture, resulted in the seizure of a large quantity of secreted spirit for which no permit could be shown. It demonstrated also the extent of Geldard's connection, and indicated plainly what was done with the spirit when he had carted it away from Crouch End. Some of the public-houses in question must have acquired a notoriety among the neighbours for frequent purchases of linoleum.

THE CASE OF THE DEAD SKIPPER

1.

It is a good few years ago now that a suicide was investigated by a coroner's jury, before whom Martin Hewitt gave certain simple and direct evidence touching the manner of the death, and testifying to the fact of its being a matter of self-destruction. The public got certain suggestive information from the bare newspaper report, but they never learnt the full story of the tragedy that led up to the suicide that was so summarily disposed of.

The time I speak of was in Hewitt's early professional days, not long after he had left Messrs. Crellan's office, and a long time before I myself met him. At that time fewer of the police knew him and were aware of his abilities, and fewer still appreciated them at their true value. Inquiries in connection with a case had taken him early one morning to the district which is now called "London over the border," and which comprises West Ham and the parts there adjoining. At this time, however, the district was much unlike its present self, for none of the grimy streets that now characterise it had been built, and even in its nearest parts open laud claimed more space than buildings.

Hewitt's business lay with the divisional surgeon of police, who had, he found, been called away from his breakfast to a patient. Hewitt followed him in the direction of the patient's house, and met him returning. They walked together, and presently, as they came in sight of a row of houses, a girl, having the appearance of a maid-of-all-work, came running from the side door of the end house—a house rather larger and more pretentious than the others in the row. Almost immediately a policeman appeared from the front door, and, seeing the girl running, shouted to Hewitt and his companion to stop her. This Hewitt did by a firm though gentle grasp of the arms, and, turning her about, marched her back again. "Come, come," he said, "you'll gain nothing by running away, whatever it is." But the girl shuddered and sobbed, and cried incoherently, "No, no—don't; I'm afraid. I don't like it, sir. It's awful. I can't stop there."

She was a strongly-built, sullen-looking girl, with prominent eyebrows and a rather brutal expression of face, consequently her extreme nervous agitation, her distorted face and her tears were the more noticeable.

"What is all this?" the surgeon asked as they reached the front door of the house. "Girl in trouble?"

The policeman touched his helmet. "It's murder, sir, this time," he said, "that's what it is. I've sent for the inspector, and I've sent for you too, sir; and of course I couldn't allow anyone to leave the house till I'd handed it over to the inspector. Come," he added to the girl, as he saw her indoors, "don't let's have any more o' that. It looks bad, I can tell you."

"Where's the body?" asked the surgeon.

"First-floor front, sir—bed-sittin'-room. Ship's captain, I'm told. Throat cut awful."

"Come," said the surgeon, as he prepared to mount the stairs. "You'd better come up too, Mr. Hewitt. You may spot something that will help if it's a difficult case."

Together they entered the room, and indeed the sight was of a sort that any maidservant might be excused for running away from. Between the central table and the fireplace, the body lay fully clothed, and the whole room was in a great state of confusion, drawers lying about with the contents spilt, boxes open, and papers scattered about. On a table was a bottle and a glass.

"Robbery, evidently," the surgeon said as he bent to his task. "See, the pockets are all emptied and partly protruding at the top. The watch and chain has been torn off, leaving the swivel in the button-hole."

"Yes," Hewitt answered, "that is so." He had taken a rapid glance about the room, and was now examining the stove, a register, with close attention. He shut the trap above it and pushed to the room door. Then very carefully, by the aid of the feather end of a quill pen which lay on the table, he shifted the charred remains of a piece or two of paper from the top of the cold cinders into the fire shovel. He carried them to the sideboard, nearer the light from the window, and examined them minutely, making a few notes in his pocket-book, and then, removing the glass shade from an ornament on the mantelpiece, placed it over them.

"There's something that *may* be of some use to the police," he remarked, "or may not, as the case may be. At any rate there it is, safe from draughts, if they want it. There's nothing distinguishable on one piece, but I think the other has been a cheque."

The surgeon had concluded his first rapid examination and rose to his feet. "A very deep cut," he said, "and done from behind, I think, as he was sitting in his chair. Death at once, without a doubt, and has been dead seven or eight hours I should say. Bed not slept in, you see. Couldn't have done it himself, that's certain."

"The knife," Hewitt added, "is either gone or hidden. But here is the inspector."

The inspector was a stranger to Hewitt, and looked at him inquiringly, till the surgeon introduced him and mentioned his profession. Then he said, with the air of one unwillingly relaxing a rule of conduct, "All right, doctor, if he's a friend of yours. A little practice for you, eh, Mr. Hewitt?"

"Yes," Hewitt answered modestly. "I haven't had the advantage of any experience in the police force, and perhaps I may learn. Perhaps also I may help you."

This did not seem to strike the inspector as a very luminous probability, and he stepped to the landing and ordered up the constable to make his full report. He had brought another man with him, who took charge of the door. By this time, thinly populated as was the neighbourhood, boys had begun to collect outside.

The policeman's story was simple. As he passed on his beat he had been called by three women who had a light ladder planted against the window-sill of the room. They feared something was wrong with the occupant of the room, they said, as they could not make him hear, and his door was locked, therefore they had brought the ladder to look in at the window, but now each feared to go and look. Would he, the policeman, do so? He mounted the ladder, looked in at the window, and saw—what was still visible.

He had then, at the women's urgent request, entered the house, broken in the door, and found the body to be dead and cold. He had told the women at once, and warned them, in the customary manner, that any statement they might be disposed to volunteer would be noted and used as evidence. The landlady, who was a widow, and gave her name as Mrs. Beckle, said that the dead man's name was Abel Pullin, and that he was a captain in the merchant service, who had occupied the room as a lodger since the end of last week only, when he had returned from a voyage. So far as she knew no stranger had been in the house since she last saw Pullin alive on the previous evening, and the only person living in the house, who had since gone out, was Mr. Foster, also a seafaring man, who had been a mate, but for some time had had no ship. He had gone out an hour or so before the discovery was made—earlier than usual, and without breakfast. That was all that Mrs. Beckle knew, and the only other persons in the house were the servant and a Miss Walker, a school teacher. They knew nothing; but Miss Walker was very anxious to be allowed to go to her school, which of course he had not allowed till the inspector should arrive.

"That's all right," the inspector said. "And you're sure the door was locked?"

"Yes, sir, fast."

"Key in the lock?"

"No, sir. I haven't seen any key."

"Window shut, just as it is now?"

"Yes, sir; nothing's been touched."

The inspector walked to the window and opened it. It was a wooden-framed casement window, fastened by the usual turning catch at the side, with a heavy bow handle. He just glanced out and then swung the window carelessly to on its hinges. The catch, however, worked so freely that the handle dropped and the catch banged against the window frame as he turned away. Hewitt saw this and closed the casement properly, after a glance at the sill.

The inspector made a rapid examination of the clothing on the body, and then said, "It's a singular thing about the key. The door was locked fast, but there's no key to be seen inside the room. Seems it must have been locked from the outside."

He mounted the ladder
and looked in at the window.

"Perhaps," Hewitt suggested, "other keys on this landing fit the lock. It's commonly the case in this sort of house."

"That's so," the inspector admitted, with the air of encouraging a pupil. "We'll see."

They walked across the landing to the nearest door. It had a small round brass escutcheon, apparently recently placed there. "Yale lock;" said the inspector. "That's no good." They went to the third door, which stood ajar.

"Seems to be Mr. Foster's room," the inspector remarked; "here's the key inside."

They took it across the landing and tried it. It fitted Captain Pullin's lock exactly and easily. "Hullo!" said the inspector, "look at that!"

Hewitt nodded thoughtfully. Just then he became aware of somebody behind him, who had arrived noiselessly. He turned and saw a mincing little woman, with a pursed mouth and lofty expression, who took no notice of him but addressed the inspector. "I shall be glad to know, if you please," she said, "when I may leave the house and attend to my duties. My school has already been open for three-quarters of an hour, and I cannot conceive why I am detained in this manner."

"Very sorry, ma'am," the inspector replied. "Matter of duty, of course. Perhaps we shall be able to let you go presently. Meanwhile perhaps you can help us. You're not obliged to say anything, of course, but if you do we shall make a note of it. You didn't hear any uncommon noise in the night, did you?"

"Nothing at all. I retired at ten and I was asleep soon after. I know nothing whatever of the whole horrible affair, and I shall leave the house entirely as soon as I can arrange."

"Did you have any opportunity of observing Mr. Pullin's manners or habits?" Hewitt asked.

"Indeed, no. I saw nothing of him. But I could hear him very often, and his language was not of the sort I could tolerate. He seemed to dominate the whole house with his boorish behaviour, and he was frequently intoxicated. I had already told Mrs. Beckle that if his stay were to continue mine should cease. I avoided him, indeed, altogether, and I know nothing of him."

"Do you know how he came here? Did he know Mrs. Beckle or anybody else in the house before?"

"That also I can't say. But Mrs. Beckle, I believe, knew all about him. In fact, I have sometimes thought there was some mysterious connection between them, though what I cannot say. Certainly I cannot understand a landlady keeping so troublesome a lodger."

"You have seen a little more of Mr. Foster, of course?"

"Well, yes. He has been here so much longer. He was more endurable than was Captain Pullin, certainly, though *he* was not always sober. The two did not love one another, I believe."

There the inspector pricked his ears. "They didn't love one another, you say, ma'am. Why was that?"

"Oh, I don't really know. I fancy Mr. Foster wanted to borrow money or something. He used to say Captain Pullin had plenty of money, and had once sunk a ship purposely. I don't know whether or not this was serious, of course."

Hewitt looked at her keenly. "Have you ever heard him called Captain Pullin of the *Egret*?" he asked.

"No, I never heard the name of any vessel."

"There's just one thing, Miss Walker," the inspector said, "that I'm afraid I must insist on before you go. It's only a matter of form, of course. But I must ask you to let me look round your room—I shan't disturb it."

Miss Walker tossed her head. "Very well then," she said, turning toward the door with the Yale lock, and producing the key; "there it is." And she flung the door open.

The inspector stepped within and took a perfunctory glance round. "That will do; thank you," he said; "I am sorry to have kept you. I think you may go now, Miss Walker. You won't be leaving here today altogether; I suppose?"

"No, I'm afraid I can't. Good-morning."

As she disappeared by the foot of the stairs the inspector remarked in a jocular undertone, "Needn't bother about *her*. She isn't strong enough to cut a hen's throat."

Just then Miss Walker appeared again and attempted to take her umbrella from the stand—a heavy, tall oaken one. The ribs, however, had become jammed between the stand and the wall; so Miss Walker, with one hand, calmly lifted the stand and disengaged the umbrella with the other. "My eyes!" observed the inspector, "she's a bit stronger than she looks."

The surgeon came upon the landing. "I shall send to the mortuary now," he said.

"I've seen all I want to see here. Have you seen the landlady?"

"No. I think she's downstairs."

They went downstairs and found Mrs. Beckle in the back room, much agitated, though she was not the sort of woman one would expect to find greatly upset by anything. She was thin, hard and rigid, with the rigidity and sharpness that women acquire who have a long and lonely struggle with poverty. She had at first very little to say. Captain Pullin had lodged with her before. Last night he had been in all the evening and had gone to bed about half-past eleven, and by a quarter past everybody else had done so, and the house was fastened up for the night. The front door was fully bolted and barred, and it was found so in the morning. No stranger had been in the house for some days. The only person who had left before the discovery was Mr. Foster, and he went away when only the servant was up.

This was unusual, as he usually took breakfast in the house. What had frightened the girl so much, she thought, was the fact that after the door had been burst open she peeped into the room, out of curiosity, and was so horrified at the sight that she ran out of the house. She had always been a hardworking girl, though of sullen habits.

The inspector made more particular inquiries as to Mr. Foster, and after some little reluctance Mrs. Beckle gave her opinion that he was very short of money indeed. He had lost his ship sometime back through a neglect of duty, and he was not of altogether sober habits; he had consequently been unable to get another berth as yet. It was a fact, she admitted, that he owed her a considerable sum for rent, but he had enough clothes and nautical implements in his boxes to cover that and more.

Hewitt had been watching Mrs. Beckle's face very closely, and now suddenly asked, with pointed emphasis, "How long have you known Mr. Pullin?"

Mrs. Beckle faltered and returned Hewitt's steadfast gaze with a quick glance of suspicion. "Oh," she said, "I have known him, on and off, for a long time."

"A connection by marriage, of course?" Hewitt's hard gaze was still upon her.

Mrs. Beckle looked from him to the inspector and back again, and the corners of her mouth twitched. Then she sat down and rested her head on her hand. "Well, I suppose I must say it, though I've kept it to myself till now," she said resignedly. "He's my brother-in-law."

"Of course, as you have been told, you are not obliged to say anything now; but the more information you can give the better chance there may be of detecting your brother-in-law's murderer."

"Well, I don't mind, I'm sure. It was a bad day when he married my sister. He killed her—not at once, so that he might have been hung for it, but by a course of regular brutality and starvation. I hated the man!" she said, with a quick access of passion, which however she suppressed at once.

"And yet you let him stay in your house?"

"Oh, I don't know. I was afraid of him; and he used to come just when he pleased, and practically take possession of the house. I couldn't keep him away; and he drove away my other lodgers." She suddenly fired up again. "Wasn't that enough to make anybody desperate? Can you wonder at anything?"

She quieted again by a quick effort, and Hewitt and the inspector exchanged glances.

"Let me see, he was captain of the sailing ship *Egret,* wasn't he?" Hewitt asked. "Lost in the Pacific a year or more ago?"

"Yes."

"If I remember the story of the loss aright, he and one native hand—a Kanaka boy—were the only survivors?"

"Yes, they were the only two. He was the only one that came back to England."

"Just so. And there *were* rumours, I believe, that after all he wasn't altogether a loser by that wreck? Mind, I only say there were rumours;

there may have been nothing in them."

"Yes," Mrs. Beckle replied, "I know all about that. They said the ship had been east away purposely, for the sake of the insurance. But there was no truth in that, else why did the underwriters pay? And besides, from what I know privately, it couldn't have been. Abel Pullin was a reckless scoundrel enough, I know, but he would have taken good care to be paid well for any villainy of that sort."

"Yes, of course. But it was suggested that he was."

"No, nothing of the sort. He came here, as usual, as soon as he got home, and until he got another ship he hadn't a penny. I had to keep him, so I know. And he was sober almost all the time from want of money. Do you mean to say, if the common talk were true, that he would have remained like that without getting money of the owners, his accomplices, and at least making them give him another ship? Not he. I know him too well."

"Yes, no doubt. He was now just back from his next voyage after that, I take it?"

"Yes, in the *Iolanthe* brig. A smaller ship than he has been used to, and belonging to different owners."

"Had he much money this time?"

"No. He had bought himself a gold watch and chain abroad, and he had a ring and a few pounds in money, and sonic instruments, that was all, I think, in addition to his clothes."

"Well, they've all been stolen now," the inspector said. "Have you missed anything yourself?"

"No."

"Nor the other lodgers, so far as you know?"

"No, neither of them."

"Very well, Mrs. Beckle. We'll have a word or two with the servant now, and then I'll get you to come over the house with us."

Sarah Taffs was the servant's name. She seemed to have got over her agitation, and was now sullen and uncommunicative. She would say nothing. "You said I needn't say nothin' if I didn't want to, and I won't." That was all she would say, and she repeated it again and again. Once, however, in reply to a question as to Foster, she flashed out angrily, "If it's Mr. Foster you're after you won't find 'im. 'E's a gentleman, 'e is, and I ain't goin' to tell you nothin'." But that was all.

Then Mrs. Beckle showed the inspector, the surgeon and Hewitt over the house. Everything was in perfect order on the ground floor and on the stairs. The stairs, it appeared, had been swept before the discovery was made. Nevertheless, Hewitt and the inspector scrutinised them narrowly. The top floor consisted of two small rooms only, used as bedrooms by Mrs. Beckle and Sarah Taffs respectively. Nothing was missing, and everything was in order there.

The one floor between contained the dead man's room, Miss Walker's and Foster's. Miss Walker's room they had already seen, and now they turned into Foster's.

The place seemed to betray careless habits on the part of its tenant, and was everywhere in slovenly confusion. The bed-clothes were flung anyhow on the floor, and a chair was overturned. Hewitt looked round the room and remarked that there seemed to be no clothes hanging about, as might have been expected.

2.

"No," Mrs. Beckle replied; "he has taken to keeping them all in his boxes lately."

"How many boxes has he?" asked the inspector.

"Only these two?"

"That is all."

The inspector stooped and tried the lids.

"Both locked," he said. "I think we'll take the liberty of a peep into these boxes."

He produced a bunch of keys and tried them all, but none fitted. Then Hewitt felt about inside the locks very carefully with a match, and then taking a button-hook from his pocket, after a little careful "humouring" work, turned both the locks, one after another, and lifted the lids.

Mrs. Beckle uttered an exclamation of dismay, and the inspector looked at her rather quizzically. The boxes contained nothing but bricks.

"Ah," said the inspector, "I've seen that sort of suits o' clothes before. People have 'em who don't pay hotel bills and such-like. You're a very good pick-lock, by the way, Mr. Hewitt. I never saw anything quicker and neater."

"But I *know* he had a lot of clothes," Mrs. Beckle protested. "I've seen them."

"Very likely—very likely indeed," the inspector answered. "But they're gone now, and Mr. Foster's gone with 'em."

"But—but the girl didn't say he had any bundles with him when he went out?"

The boxes contained nothing but bricks.

"No, she didn't; and she didn't say he hadn't, did she? She won't say anything about him, and she says she won't, plump. Even supposing he *hadn't* got them with him this morning that signifies nothing. The clothes are gone, and anybody intending a job of *that* sort"—the inspector jerked his thumb significantly towards the skipper's room—"would get his things away quietly first so as to have no difficulty about getting away himself afterwards. No; the thing's pretty plain now, I think; and I'm afraid Mr. Foster's a pretty bad lot. Anyway I shouldn't like to be in his shoes."

"Nor I," Hewitt assented. "Evidence of that sort isn't easy to get over."

"Come, Mrs. Beckle," the inspector said, "do you mind coming into the front room with us? The body's covered over with a rug."

The landlady disliked going, it was plain to see, but presently she pulled herself together and followed the men. She peeped once distrustfully round the door to where the body lay and then resolutely turned her back on it.

"His watch and chain are gone and whatever else he had in his pockets," the inspector said. "I think you said he had a ring?"

"Yes, one—a thick gold one."

"Then that's gone too. Everything's turned upside down, and

336

probably other things are stolen too. Do you miss any?"

"Yes," Mrs. Beckle replied, looking round, but avoiding with her eyes the rug-covered heap near the fireplace. "There was a sextant on the mantelpiece; it was *his;* and he kept one or two other instruments in that drawer"—pointing to one which had been turned out—"but they seem to be gone now. And there was a small ship, carved in ivory, and worth money, I believe—that's gone. I don't know about his clothes; some of them may be stolen or they may not." She stepped to the bed and turned back the coverlet. "Oh," she added, "the sheets are gone from the bed too!"

"Usual thing," the inspector remarked; "wrap up the swag in a sheet, you know—makes a convenient bundle. Nothing else missing?"

The landlady took one more look round and said doubtfully, "No, no, I don't think so. Oh, but yes," she suddenly added, "uncle's hook."

"Oh," remarked the inspector with dismal jocularity, "he's took uncle's hook as well as his own, has he? What was uncle's hook like?"

"It wasn't of much value," Mrs. Beckle explained; "but I kept it as a memorial. My great uncle, who died many years ago, was a sea-captain too, and had lost his left hand by accident. He wore a hook in its place—a hook made for him on board his vessel. It was an iron hook screwed into a wooden stock. He had it taken off in his last ill-ness and gave it to me to mind against his recovery. But he never got well, so I've kept it over since. It used to hang on a nail at the side of the chimney-breast."

"No wounds about the body that might have been made with a hook like that, doctor, were there?" the inspector asked.

"No, no wounds at all but the one."

"Well, well," the inspector said, moving toward the door, "we've got to find Foster now, that's plain. I'll see about it. You've sent to the mortuary you say, doctor? All right. You've no particular reason for sending the girl out of doors today, I suppose, Mrs. Beckle?"

"I *can* keep her in, of course," the landlady answered. "It will be inconvenient, though."

"Ah, then keep her in, will you? We mustn't lose sight of her. I'll leave a couple of men here, of course, and I'll tell them she mustn't be allowed out."

Hewitt and the surgeon went downstairs and parted at the door. "I shall be over again tomorrow morning," Hewitt said, "about that other matter I was speaking of. Shall I find you in?"

"Well," the doctor answered, "at any rate they will tell you where

I am. Good morning."

"Good morning," Hewitt answered, and then stopped. "I'm obliged for being allowed to look about upstairs here," he said. "I'm not sure what the inspector has in his mind, by the way; but I should think whatever I noticed would be pretty plain to him, though naturally he would be cautious about talking of it before others, as I was myself. That being the case it might seem rather presumptuous in me to make suggestions, especially as he seems fairly confident. But if you have a chance presently of giving him a quiet hint you might draw his special attention to two things—the charred paper that I took from the fireplace and the missing hook. There is a good deal in that, I fancy. I shall have an hour or two to myself, I expect, this afternoon, and I'll make a small inquiry or two on my own account in town. If anything comes of them, I'll let you know tomorrow when I see you."

"Very well, I shall expect you. Goodbye."

Hewitt did not go straight away from the house to the railway station. He took a turn or two about the row of houses, and looked up each of the paths leading from them across the surrounding marshy fields. Then he took the path for the station. About a hundred yards along, the path reached a deep muddy ditch with a high hedge behind it, and then lay by the side of the ditch for some little distance before crossing it. Hewitt stopped and looked thoughtfully at the ditch for a few moments before proceeding, and then went briskly on his way.

That evening's papers were all agog with the mysterious murder of a ship's captain at West Ham, and in next morning's papers it was announced that Henry Foster, a seafaring man, and lately mate of a trading ship, had been arrested in connection with the crime.

3.

That morning Hewitt was at the surgeon's house early. The surgeon was in, and saw him at once. His own immediate business being transacted, Hewitt learned particulars of the arrest of Foster. "The man actually came back of his own accord in the afternoon," the surgeon said. "Certainly he was drunk, but that seems a very reckless sort of thing, even for a drunken man. One rather curious thing was that he asked for Pullin as soon as he arrived, and insisted on going to him to borrow half-a-sovereign. Of course he was taken into custody at once, and charged, and that seemed to sober him very quickly. He seemed dazed for a bit, and then, when he realised the position he was in, refused to say a word. I saw him at the station. He had certainly been drinking a good deal; but a curious thing was that he hadn't a cent of money on him. He'd soon got rid of it all, anyhow."

"Did you say anything to the inspector as to the things I mentioned to you?"

"Yes, but he didn't seem to think a great deal of them. He took a look at the charred paper and saw that one piece had evidently been a cheque on the Eastern Consolidated Bank, but the other he couldn't see any sort of sign upon. As to the hook, he seemed to take it that that was used to fasten in the knot of the bundle, to carry it the more easily."

"Well," Hewitt said, "I think I told you yesterday that I should make an inquiry or two myself? Yes, I did. I've made those inquiries, and now I think I can give the inspector some help. What is his name, by the way?"

"Truscott. He's a very good sort of fellow, really."

"Very well. Shall I find him at the station?"

"Probably, unless he's off duty; that I don't know about. But I should call at the house first, I think, if I were you. That is much nearer than the station, and he might possibly be there. Even if he isn't, there will be a constable, and he can tell you where to find Truscott."

Hewitt accordingly made for the house, and had the good fortune to overtake Truscott on his way there. "Good morning, inspector," he called cheerily. "I've got some information for you, I think."

"Oh, good morning. What is it?"

"It's in regard to *that* business," Hewitt replied, indicating by a nod the row of houses a hundred yards ahead. "But it will be clearer if we go over the whole thing together and take what I have found out in its proper place. You're not altogether satisfied with your capture of Foster, are you?"

"Well, I mustn't say, of course. Perhaps not. We've traced his doings yesterday after he left the house, and *perhaps* it doesn't help us much. But what do you know?"

"I'll tell you. But first can you get hold of such a thing as a boat-hook? Any long pole with a hook on the end will do."

"I don't know that there's one handy. Perhaps they'll have a garden rake at the house, if that'll do?"

"Excellently, I should thick, if it's fairly long. We will ask."

The garden rake was forthcoming at once, and with it Hewitt and the inspector made their way along the path that led towards the railway station and stopped where it came by the ditch.

"I've brought you here purely on a matter of conjecture," Hewitt said, "and there may be nothing in it; but if there is it will help us. This is a very muddy ditch, with a soft bottom many feet deep probably, judging from the wet nature of the soil hereabout."

He took the rake and plunged it deep into the ditch, dragging it slowly back up the side. It brought up a tangle of duckweed and rushes and slimy mud, with a stick or two among it.

"Do you think the knife's been thrown here?" asked the inspector.

"Possibly, and possibly something else. We'll see." And Hewitt made another dive. They went along thus very thoroughly and laboriously, dragging every part of the ditch as they went, it being frequently necessary for both to pull together to get the rake through the tangle of weed and rubbish. They had worked through seven or eight yards from the angle of the path where it approached the ditch, when Hewitt stopped, with the rake at the bottom.

"Here is something that feels a little different," he said. "I'll get as good a hold as I can and then we'll drag it up slowly and steadily together."

He gave the rake a slight twist and then the two pulled steadily. Presently the sunken object came away suddenly, as though mud-suction had kept it under, and rose easily to the surface. It was a muddy mass, and they had to swill it to and fro a few times in the clearer upper water before it was seen to be a linen bundle. They drew it ashore

It was a muddy mass, and they had to swill it to and fro a few
times in the clearer upper water before it was seen as a linen bundle.

and untied the thick knot at the top. Inside was an Indian shawl, also knotted, and this they opened also. There within, wet and dirty, lay a sextant, a chronometer in a case, a gold watch and chain, a handful of coins, a thick gold ring, a ship carved in ivory, with much of the delicate work broken, a sealskin waistcoat, a door key, a seamen's knife, and an iron hook screwed into a wooden stock.

"Lord!" exclaimed Inspector Truscott, "what's this? It's a queer place to hide swag of this sort. Why, that watch and those instruments must be ruined."

"Yes, I'm afraid so," Hewitt answered. "You see the things are wrapped in the sheets, just as you expected. But those sheets mean something more. There are *two,* you notice."

"Yes, of course; but I don't see what it points to. The whole thing's most odd. Foster certainly would have been a fool to hide the things here; he's a sailor himself, and knows better than to put away chronometers and sextants in a wet ditch—unless he got frightened, and put the things there out of sight because the murder was discovered."

"But you say you have traced his movements after he left. If he had come near here while the police were about he would have been seen from the house. No, you've got the wrong prisoner. The person who put those things there didn't want them again."

"Then do you think robbery wasn't the motive after all?"

"Yes, it was; but not *this* robbery. Conic, we'll talk it over in the house. Let us take these things with us."

Arrived at the house Hewitt immediately locked, bolted and barred the front door.

Then he very carefully and gently unfastened each lock, bolt and bar in order, pressing the door with his hand and taking every precaution to avoid noise. Nevertheless, the noise was considerable. There was a sad lack of oil everywhere, and all the bolts creaked; the lock in particular made a deal of noise, and when the key was half turned its bolt shot back with a loud thump.

"Anybody who had once heard that door fastened or unfastened," said Hewitt, "would hesitate about opening it in the dead of night after committing murder. He would remember the noise. Do you mind taking the things up to the room—the room—upstairs? I will go and ask Mrs Beckle a question."

Truscott went upstairs, and presently

Hewitt followed. "I have just asked Mrs. Beckle," he said, "whether or not the captain went to the front door for any purpose on the evening before his death. She says he stood there for some half an hour or so smoking his pipe before he went to bed. We shall see what that means presently, I. think. Now we will go into the thing in the light of what I have found out."

"Yes, tell me that."

"Very well. I think it will make the thing plainer if I summarise separately all my conclusions from the evidence as a whole from the beginning. Perhaps the same ideas struck you, but I'm sure you'll excuse my going over them. Now here was a man undoubtedly murdered, and the murderer was gone from the room. There were two ways by which he could have gone the door and the window. If he went by the window, then he was somebody who did not live in the place, since nobody seemed to have been missing when the girl came down, though, mind you, it was necessary to avoid relying on all she said, in view of her manner, and her almost acknowledged determination not to incriminate Foster. It seemed at first sight probable that the murderer had gone out by the door, because the key was gone entirely, and if he had left by the window he would probably have left the key in the lock to hinder anybody who attempted to get in with another key, or to peep. But then the blind was *up,* and was found so in the morning. It would probably be pulled down at dark, and the murderer

He stood there smoking his pipe before he went to bed.

342

would be unlikely to raise it except to go out that way.

"But then the casement was shut and fastened. Just so; but can't it be as easily shut and fastened from the outside as from the in? The catch is very loose, and swings by itself. True, this *prevents* the casement shutting when it is just carelessly banged to, but see here." He rose and went to the window. "Anybody from outside who cared to hold the catch back with his finger till the casement was shut as far as the frame could then shut the window completely, and the catch would simply swing into its appointed groove.

"And now see something more. You and I both looked at the sill outside. It is a smooth new sill—the house itself is almost new; but probably you saw in one place a sharply marked pit or depression. Look, it seems to have been drilled with a sharp steel point. It was absolutely new, for there was the powder of the stone about the mark. The wind has since blown the powder away. Now if a man had descended from that sill by means of a rope with a hook at the end that was just the sort of mark I should expect him to leave behind. So that at any rate the balance of probability was that the murderer had left by the window. But there is another thing which confirms this. You will remember that when Mrs. Beckle mentioned that the sheets were gone from the bed you concluded that they had been taken to carry

"The catch would simply
swing into its appointed groove."

343

the swag."

"Yes, and so they were, as we have seen here in the bundle."

"Just so; but why *both* sheets? One would be ample. And since you allude to the bundle, why both sheets as well as the Indian shawl? This last, by the way, is a thing Mrs. Beckle seems not to have missed in the confusion, or perhaps she didn't know that Pullin possessed it. Why all these wrappings, and moreover, *why the hook?* The presumption is clear. The bundle was already made up in the Indian shawl and required no more wrapping. The two sheets were wanted to tie together to enable the criminal to descend from the window, and the hook was the very thing to hold this rope with at the top. It was not necessary to tie it to anything, and it would not prevent the shutting of the window behind. Moreover, when the descent had been made, a mere shake of the rope of sheets would dislodge the hook and bring it down, thus leaving no evidence of the escape—except the mark on the sill, which was very small.

"Then again, there was no noise or struggle heard. Pullin, as you could see, was a powerful, hard-set man, not likely to allow his throat to be cut without a lot of trouble, therefore the murderer must either have entered the room unknown to him—an unlikely thing, for he had not gone to bed—or else must have been there with his permission, and must have taken him by sudden surprise. And now we come to the heart of the thing. Of the two papers burnt in the grate—you have kept them under the shade I see—one bore no trace of the writing that had been on it (many inks and papers do not after having been burnt), but the other bore plain signs of having been a cheque. Now just let us look at it.

"The main body of the paper has burnt to a deep grey ash, nearly black, but the printed parts of the cheque—those printed in coloured inks, that is—are of a much paler grey, quite a light ash colour. That is the colour to which most of the *pink* ink used in printing cheques burns, as you may easily test for yourself with an old cheque of the sort that is printed from a fine plate with water-solution pink ink. The *black* ink, on the other hand, such as the number of the cheque is printed in, has charred black, and by sharp eyes is quite distinguishable against the general dark grey of the paper. The cinder is unfortunately broken rather badly, and the part containing the signature is missing altogether. But one can plainly see in large script letters part of the boldest line of print, the name of the bank. The letters are *e r n C o n s o*, and this must mean the Eastern Consolidated Bank. Of course you saw that for yourself."

"Yes, of course I did."

"Fortunately the whole of the cheque number is unbroken. It is Of course I took a note of that, as well as of the other particulars distinguishable. It is payable to Pullin, clearly, for here is the latter half of his Christian name, Abel, and the first few letters of Pullin. Then on the line where the amount is written at length there are the letters *u s a n d* and *p*. Plainly it was a large cheque, for thousands. At the bottom, where the amount is placed in figures, there is a bad break, but the first figure is a 2. The cheque, then, was one for £2000 at least. And there is one more thing. The cinder is perfect and unbroken nearly all along the top edge, and there is no sign of crossing, so that here is an open cheque which any thief might cash with a little care. That is all we can see, but it is enough, I think. Now would a thief, committing murder for the sake of plunder, *burn* this cheque? Would Pullin, to whom the money was to be paid, burn it? I think not. Then who in the whole world *would* have any interest in burning it? Not a soul, with one single exception—*the man who drew it.*"

"Yes, yes. What! do you mean that the man who drew that cheque must have murdered Pullin in order to get it back and destroy it?"

"That is my opinion. Now who would draw Pullin a cheque for £2000? Anybody in this house? Is it at all likely? Of course not. Again, we are pointed to a stranger. And now remember Pullin's antecedents. On his last voyage but one his ship the *Egret,* from Valparaiso for Wellington, New Zealand, was cast away on the Paumotu Islands, far out of her proper course. There was but a small crew, and, as it happened, all were lost except Pullin and one Kanaka boy. The *Egret* was heavily insured, and there were nasty rumours at Lloyd's that Captain Pullin had made sure of his whereabouts, taken care of himself, and destroyed the ship in collusion with the owners, and that the Kanaka boy had only escaped because he happened to be well acquainted with the islands. But there was nothing positive in the way of proof, and the underwriters paid, with no more than covert grumblings. And, as you remember, Mrs. Heckle told us yesterday Pullin on his return had no money. Now suppose the story of the intentional wreck were true, and for some reason Pullin's payment was put off till after his next voyage. Would the people who sent their men to death in the Pacific hesitate at a single murder to save £2000? I think not.

"After I left you yesterday I made some particular inquiries at Lloyd's through a friend of mine, an underwriter himself. I find that the sole owner of the *Egret* was one Herbert Roofe, trading as Herbert Roofe & Co. The firm is a very small one, as shipping concerns go, and has had the reputation for a long time of being very 'rocky' financially; indeed it was the common talk at Lloyd's that nothing but the wreck of the *Egret* saved Roofe from the Bankruptcy Court, and he is supposed now to be 'hanging on by his eyelashes,' as my friend expresses it, with very little margin to keep him going, and in a continual state of touch-and-go between his debit and credit sides. As to the rumours of the wilful casting away of the *Egret,* my friend assured me that the thing was as certain as anything could be, short of legal proof. There was something tricky about the cargo, and altogether it was a black sort of business. And to complete things he told me that the bankers of Herbert Roofe & Co. were the Eastern Consolidated."

"Phew! This is getting pretty warm, I must say, Mr. Hewitt."

"Wait a minute; my friend aided me a little further still. I told him the whole story—in confidence, of course—and he agreed to help. At my suggestion he went to the manager of the Eastern Consolidated Bank, whom he knew personally, and represented that among a heap of cheques one had got torn, and the missing piece destroyed. This was true entirely, except in regard to the heap—a little fiction which I trust my friend may be forgiven. The cheque, he said, was on the Eastern Consolidated, and its number was B/K63777. Would the manager mind telling him which of his customers had the cheque book from which that had been taken? Trace of where the cheque had come from had been quite lost, and it would save a lot of trouble if the Bank could let him know. 'Certainly,' said the manager; 'I'll inquire.' He did, and presently a clerk entered the room with the information that cheque No. B/K63777 was from a book in the possession of Messrs. Herbert Roofe & Co."

The inspector rose excitedly from his chair. "Come," he said, "this must be followed up. We mustn't waste time; there's no knowing where Roofe may have got to by this."

"Just a little more patience," Hewitt said. "I don't think there will be much difficulty in finding him. He believes himself safe. As soon as my friend told me what the Bank manager had said I went round to Roofe's office to ascertain his whereabouts, prepared with an excuse for the interview in case I should find him in. It was a small office, rather, over a shop in Leadenhall Street. When I asked for Mr. Roofe the clerk informed me that he was at home confined to his room by a bad cold, and had not been at the office since Tuesday—the next day but one before the body was discovered.

"I appeared to be disappointed, and asked if I could send him a message. Yes, I could, the clerk told me. All letters were being sent to him, and he was sending business instructions daily to the office from Chadwell Heath. I saw that the address had slipped inadvertently from the clerk's mouth, for it is a general rule, I know, in city offices, to keep the principals' addresses from casual callers. So I said no more, but contented myself with the information I had got. I took the first opportunity of looking at a suburban directory, and then I found the name of Mr. Roofe's house at Chadwell Heath. It is Scarby Lodge."

"I must be off, then, at once," Truscott said, "and make careful inquiries as to his movements. And those cinders—bless my soul, they're as precious as diamonds now! How shall we keep them from damage?"

"Oh, the glass shade will do, I fancy. But wait a moment; let us review things thoroughly. I will run rapidly over what I suggest has happened between Roofe and Pullin, and you shall stop me if you see any flaw in the argument. It's best to make our impressions clear and definite. Now we will suppose that the *Egret* has been lost, and Pullin has come home to claim the reward of his infamy. We will suppose it is £2000. He goes to Roofe and demands it. Roofe says he can't possibly pay just then; he is very hard up, and the insurance money of the *Egret* has only just saved him from bankruptcy. Pullin insists on having his money. But, says Roofe, that is impossible, because he hasn't got it.

"A cheque for the amount would be dishonoured. The plunder of the underwriters has all been used to keep things going. Roofe says plainly that Pullin must wait for the money. Pullin can't reveal the conspiracy without implicating himself, and Roofe knows it. He promises to pay in a certain time, and gives Pullin an acknowledgment of the debt, an IOU, perhaps, or something of that kind, and with that Pullin has to be contented, and, having no money, he has to go away on another voyage, this time in a ship belonging to somebody else, became it would look worse than ever if Roofe gave him another berth at once. He makes his voyage and he returns, and asks for his money again. But Roofe is as bard up as ever. He cannot pay, and he cannot refuse to pay.

"It is ruin either way. He knows that Pullin will stand no more delay, and may do something desperate, so Roofe does something desperate himself. He tells Pullin that he must not call at his office, nor must anybody see them together anywhere for fear of suspicion. He suggests that he, Roofe, should call at Pullin's lodgings late one night, and bring the money. Pullin is to let him in himself, so that nobody may see him. Pullin consents, and thus assists in the concealment of his own murder. He waits at the front door smoking his pipe (you remember that Mrs. Beckle told me so), waiting for Roofe. When Roofe comes Pullin takes him very quietly up to his room without attracting attention. Roofe, on his part, has prepared things by feigning a bad cold and going to bed early, going out—perhaps through the window—when all his household is quiet. There are plenty of late trains from Chadwell Heath that would bring him to Stratford.

"Well, when they are safely in Pullin's room Roofe hears the front door shut and bolted, with all its squeaks and thumps, and decides that it won't be safe to go out that way after he has committed his crime. The men sit and talk, and Pullin drinks. Roofe doesn't. You will remember the bottle on the table, with only one glass. Roofe produces and writes a cheque for the £2000, and Pullin hands back the IOU, which Roofe burns. *That* would be the lower of the two charred pieces of paper, which we have there with the other, but can't read.

"Then the crime takes place. Perhaps Pullin drinks a little too much. At any rate Roofe gets behind him, uses the sharp seaman's knife he has brought for the purpose, and straightway the skipper is dead at his feet. Then Roofe gets back the cheque and burns *that*. After that he ransacks the whole room. He fears there may be some documentary evidence, which, being examined, may throw some light on the *Egret* affair. Then he sets about his escape. To make the thing look like a murder for ordinary plunder, and at the same time account for the upset room, he takes away all the dead man's valuables tied in that shawl.

"He sees the hook—just the thing he wants—and of course the sheets are an obvious substitute for a rope. He takes away the door-key, to make it seem likely that somebody inside the house had been the criminal, and then he simply goes away through the window, as I have already explained. At 5.45 there would be a train to Chadwell Heath, and that would land him home early enough to enable him to regain his bedroom unobserved. After that he wisely maintains the pretence of illness for a day or two.

"I guessed that the things carried off would be in that ditch, for very simple reasons. I looked about the house, and the ditch seemed the only available hiding-place near. More, it was on the way to the station, the direction Roofe would naturally take. He would seize the very first opportunity of getting rid of his burden, for every possible reason. It was a nuisance to carry; he could not account for it if he were asked; and the further he carried it before getting rid of it the more distinct the clue to the direction he had taken, supposing it ever were found. The behaviour of some of the people in the house might have been suspicious, if I hadn't had so strong a clue in my hand, leading in another direction. Foster probably pawned all his clothes, and put those bricks in his boxes to conceal the fact, so that Mrs. Beckle might not turn him away. He owed her so much that at last he hadn't the face to go and eat her breakfast when he had no money to pay for it. He went out early, met friends, got 'stood' drinks and came back drunk. Probably he had been kind to the girl Taffs at some time or another, so that when she found he was suspected she refused to give any information."

"Yes," the inspector said, "it certainly seems to fit together. There's a future before you, Mr. Hewitt. But now I must go to Chadwell Heath. Are you coming?"

At Chadwell Heath it was found that a first-class return ticket to Stratford had been taken just before the 10.54 train left on the last night Abel Pullin was seen alive, and that the return half had been given up by a passenger who arrived by the first train soon after six in the morning The porter who took the ticket remembered the circumstance, because first-class tickets were rare at that time in the morning,

"Stop, sir! Let me see that!"

but he did not recognise the passenger, who was muffled up.

"But I think there's enough for an arrest without a warrant, at any rate," Truscott said. "I am off to Scarby Lodge. Can't afford to waste any more time."

Scarby Lodge was a rather pretentious house. It was arranged that Truscott should wait aside till Hewitt had sent in a message asking to see Mr. Roofe on a matter of urgent business, and that then both should follow the servant to his room. This was done, and as the parlour maid was knocking at the bedroom door she was astonished to find Hewitt and the police inspector behind her. Truscott at once pushed open the door and the two walked in.

It was a large room, and at the end a man sat in his dressing-gown near a table on which stood several medicine bottles. He frowned as Truscott and Hewitt entered, but betrayed no sign of emotion, carelessly taking one of the small bottles from the table. "What do you want here?" he said.

"Sorry to be so unceremonious," Truscott said, "but I am a police officer, and it is my duty to arrest you on a serious charge of murder on the person of —— Stop, sir! Let me see that!"

But it was too late. Before Truscott could reach him Roofe had swallowed the contents of the small bottle and, swaying once, dropped to the floor as though shot.

Hewitt stooped over the man. "Dead," he said, "dead as Abel Pullin. It is prussic acid. He had arranged for instant action if by any chance the game went against him."

But Inspector Truscott was troubled. "This is a nice thing," he said, "to have a prisoner commit suicide in front of my eyes. But you can testify that I hadn't time to get near him, can't you? Indeed, he *wasn't* a prisoner at the time, for I hadn't arrested him, in fact."

The Case of the "Flitterbat Lancers"

It was late on a summer evening, two or three years back, that I drowsed in my armchair over a particularly solid and ponderous volume of essays on social economy. I was doing a good deal of reviewing at the time, and I remember that this particular volume had a property of such exceeding toughness that I had already made three successive attacks on it, on as many successive evenings, each attack having been defeated in the end by sleep. The weather was hot, my chair was very comfortable, and the book had somewhere about its strings of polysyllables an essence as of laudanum. Still something had been done on each evening, and now on the fourth I strenuously endeavoured to finish the book. I was just beginning to feel that the words before me were sliding about and losing their meanings, when a sudden crash and a jingle of broken glass behind me woke me with a start, and I threw the book down. A pane of glass in my window was smashed, and I hurried across and threw up the sash to see, if I could, whence the damage had come.

The building in which my chambers (and Martin Hewitt's office) were situated was accessible—or rather visible, for there was no entrance—from the rear. There was, in fact, a small courtyard, reached by a passage from the street behind, and into this courtyard, my sitting-room window looked.

"Hullo, there!" I shouted. But there came no reply. Nor could I distinguish anybody in the courtyard. Some men had been at work during the day on a drainpipe, and I reflected that probably their litter had provided the stone with which my window had been smashed. As I looked, however, two men came hurrying from the passage into the court, and going straight into the deep shadow of one corner, presently appeared again in a less obscure part, hauling forth a third man, who must have already been there in hiding. The third man struggled fiercely, but without avail, and was dragged across toward the passage

"A pane of glass in my window was smashed."

The man struggled fiercely.

leading to the street beyond. But the most remarkable feature of the whole thing was the silence of all three men. No cry, no exclamation, escaped any of them. In perfect silence the two hauled the third across the courtyard, and in perfect silence he swung and struggled to resist and escape.

The matter astonished me not a little, and the men were entering the passage before I found voice to shout at them. But they took no notice, and disappeared. Soon after I heard cab wheels in the street beyond, and had no doubt that the two men had carried off their prisoner.

I turned back into my room a little perplexed. It seemed probable that the man who had been borne off had broken my window. But why? I looked about on the floor, and presently found the missile. It was, as I had expected, a piece of broken concrete, but it was wrapped up in a worn piece of paper, which had partly opened out as it lay on my carpet, thus indicating that it had just been crumpled round the stone.

I disengaged the paper and spread it out. Then I saw it to be a rather hastily written piece of manuscript music, whereof I append a reduced facsimile:

This gave me no help. I turned the paper this way and that, but could make nothing of it. There was not a mark on it that I could discover, except the music and the scrawled title, "Flitterbat Lancers," at the top.

The paper was old, dirty, and cracked. What did it all mean? One might conceive of a person in certain circumstances sending a message—possibly an appeal for help—through a friend's window, wrapped round a stone, but this seemed to be nothing of that sort.

Once more I picked up the paper, and with an idea to hear what the Flitterbat Lancers sounded like, I turned to my little pianette and strummed over the notes, making my own time and changing it as seemed likely. But I could by no means extract from the notes anything resembling an air. I half thought of trying Martin Hewitt's office door, in case he might still be there and offer a guess at the meaning of my smashed window and the scrap of paper, when Hewitt himself came in. He had stayed late to examine a bundle of papers in connection with a case just placed in his hands, and now, having finished, came to find if I were disposed for an evening stroll before turning in. I handed him the paper and the piece of concrete, observing, "There's a little job for you, Hewitt, instead of the stroll." And I told him the complete history of my smashed window.

Hewitt listened attentively, and examined both the paper and the fragment of paving. "You say these people made absolutely no sound whatever?" he asked.

"None but that of scuffling, and even that they seemed to do quietly."

"Could you see whether or not the two men gagged the other, or placed their hands over his mouth?"

"No, they certainly didn't do that. It was dark, of course, but not so dark as to prevent my seeing generally what they were doing."

Hewitt stood for half a minute in thought, and then said, "There's something in this, Brett—what, I can't guess at the moment, but something deep, I fancy. Are you sure you won't come out now?"

I told Hewitt that I was sure, and that I should stick to my work.

"Very well," he said; "then perhaps you will lend me these articles?" holding up the paper and the stone.

353

"Delighted," I said. "If you get no more melody out of the clinker than I did out of the paper, you won't have a musical evening. Goodnight!"

Hewitt went away with the puzzle in his hand, and I turned once more to my social economy, and, thanks to the gentleman who smashed my window, conquered.

At this time my only regular daily work was on an evening paper so that I left home at a quarter to eight on the morning following the adventure of my broken window, in order, as usual, to be at the office at eight; consequently, it was not until lunchtime that I had an opportunity of seeing Hewitt. I went to my own rooms first, however, and on the landing by my door I found the housekeeper in conversation with a shortish, sun-browned man, whose accent at once convinced me that he hailed from across the Atlantic. He had called, it appeared, three or four times during the morning to see me, getting more impatient each time. As he did not seem even to know my name, the housekeeper had not considered it expedient to give him any information about me, and he was growing irascible under the treatment. When I at last appeared, however, he left her and approached me eagerly.

"See here, sir," he said, "I've been stumpin' these here durn stairs o' yours half through the mornin'. I'm anxious to apologise, and fix up some damage."

He had followed me into my sitting-room, and was now standing with his back to the fireplace, a dripping umbrella in one hand, and the forefinger of the other held up boulder-high and pointing, in the manner of a pistol, to my window, which, by the way, had been mended during the morning, in accordance with my instructions to the housekeeper.

"Sir," he continued, "last night I took the extreme liberty of smashin' your winder."

"Oh," I said, "that was you, was it?"

"It was, sir—me. For that I hev come humbly to apologize. I trust the draft has not discommoded you, sir. I regret the accident, and I wish to pay for the fixin' up and the general inconvenience." He placed a sovereign on the table. "I 'low you'll call that square now, sir, and fix things friendly and comfortable as between gentlemen, an' no ill will. Shake."

And he formally extended his hand.

I took it at once. "Certainly," I said. "As a matter of fact, you haven't

354

inconvenienced me at all; indeed, there were some circumstances about the affair that rather interested me." And I pushed the sovereign toward him.

"Say now," he said, looking a trifle disappointed at my unwillingness to accept his money, "didn't I startle your nerves?"

"Not a bit," I answered, laughing. "In fact, you did me a service by preventing me going to sleep just when I shouldn't; so we'll say no more of that."

"Well—there was one other little thing," he pursued, looking at me rather sharply as he pocketed the sovereign. "There was a bit o' paper round that pebble that came in here. Didn't happen to notice that, did you?"

"Yes, I did. It was an old piece of manuscript music."

"That was it—exactly. Might you happen to have it handy now?"

"Well," I said, "as a matter of fact a friend of mine has it now. I tried playing it over once or twice, as a matter of curiosity, but I couldn't make anything of it, and so I handed it to him."

"Ah!" said my visitor, watching me narrowly, "that's a puzzler, that Flitterbat Lancers—a real puzzler. It whips 'em all. Ha, ha'." He laughed suddenly—a laugh that seemed a little artificial. "There's music fellers as 'lows to set right down and play off anything right away that can't make anything of the Flitterbat Lancers. That was two of 'em that was monkeyin' with me last night. They never could make anythin' of it at all, and I was tantalising them with it all along till they got real mad, and reckoned to get it out o' my pocket and learn it at home. Ha, ha! So I got away for a bit, and just rolled it round a stone and heaved it through your winder before they could come up, your winder being the nearest one with a light in it. Ha, ha! I'll be considerable obliged you'll get it from your friend right now. Is he stayin' hereabout?"

The story was so ridiculously lame that I determined to confront my visitor with Hewitt, and observe the result. If he had succeeded in making any sense of the Flitterbat Lancers, the scene might be amusing. So I answered at once, "Yes; his office is on the floor below; he will probably be in at about this time. Come down with me."

We went down, and found Hewitt in his outer office. "This gentleman," I told him with a solemn intonation, "has come to ask for his piece of manuscript music, the Flitterbat Lancers. He is particularly proud of it, because nobody who tries to play it can make any sort of tune out of it, and it was entirely because two dear friends of his were anxious to drag it out of his pocket and practice it over on the quiet that he flung it through my windowpane last night, wrapped round a piece of concrete."

The stranger glanced sharply at me, and I could see that my manner and tone rather disconcerted him. Burt Hewitt came forward at once. "Oh, yes," he said "just so—quite a natural sort of thing. As a matter of fact, I quite expected you. Your umbrella's wet—do you mind putting it in the stand? Thank you. Come into my private office."

We entered the inner room, and Hewitt, turning to the stranger, went on: "Yes, that is a very extraordinary piece of music, that Flitterbat Lancers. I have been having a little bit of practice with it myself, though I'm really nothing of a musician. I don't wonder you are anxious to keep it to yourself. Sit down."

The stranger, with a distrustful look at Hewitt, complied. At this moment, Hewitt's clerk, Kerrett, entered from the outer office with a slip of paper. Hewitt glanced at it, and crumpled it in his hand. "I am engaged just now," was his remark, and Kerrett vanished.

"And now," Hewitt said, as he sat down and suddenly turned to the stranger with an intent gaze, "and now, Mr Hoker, we'll talk of this music."

The stranger started and frowned. "You've the advantage of me, sir," he said; "you seem to know my name, but I don't know yours."

Hewitt smiled pleasantly. "My name," he said, "is Hewitt, Martin Hewitt, and it is my business to know a great many things. For instance, I know that you are Mr Reuben B. Hoker, of Robertsville, Ohio."

Mr. Hoker.

The visitor pushed his chair back, and stared. "Well—that gits me," he said. "You're a pretty smart chap, Mr Hewitt. I've heard your name before, of course. And—and so you've been a-studyin' the Flitterbat Lancers, have you?" This with a keen glance at Hewitt's face. "Well, s'pose you have. What's your idea?"

"Why," answered Hewitt, still keeping his steadfast gaze on Hoker's eyes, "I think it's pretty late in the century to be fishing about for the Wedlake jewels."

These words astonished me almost as much as they did Mr Hoker. The great Wedlake jewel robbery is, as many will remember, a traditional story of the 'sixties. I remembered no more of it at the time than probably most men do who have at some time or another read the *causes célèbres* of the century. Sir Francis Wedlake's country house had been robbed, and the whole of Lady Wedlake's magnificent collection of jewels stolen. A man named Shiels, a strolling musician, had been arrested and had been sentenced to a long term of penal servitude. Another man named Legg—one of the comparatively wealthy scoundrels who finance promising thefts or swindles and pocket the greater part of the proceeds—had also been punished, but only a very few of the trinkets, and those quite unimportant items, had been recovered. The great bulk of the booty was never brought to light. So much I remembered, and Hewitt's sudden mention of the Wedlake jewels in connection with my broken window, Mr Reuben B. Hoker, and the Flitterbat Lancers, astonished me not a little.

As for Hoker, he did his best to hide his perturbation, but with little success. "Wedlake jewels, eh?" he said; "and—and what's that to do with it, anyway?"

"To do with it?" responded Hewitt, with an air of carelessness. "Well, well, I had my idea, nothing more. If the Wedlake jewels have nothing to do with it, we'll say no more about it, that's all. Here's your paper, Mr Hoker—only a little crumpled." He rose and placed the article in Mr Hoker's hand, with the manner of terminating the interview.

Hoker rose, with a bewildered look on his face, and turned toward the door. Then he stopped, looked at the floor, scratched his cheek, and finally sat down and put his hat on the ground. "Come," he said, "we'll play a square game. That paper has something to do with the Wedlake jewels, and, win or lose, I'll tell you all I know about it. You're a smart man and whatever I tell you, I guess it won't do me no harm; it ain't done me no good yet, anyway."

"Say what you please, of course," Hewitt answered, "but think first. You might tell me something you'd be sorry for afterward."

"Say, will you listen to what I say, and tell me if you think I've been swindled or not? My two hundred and fifty dollars is gone now, and I guess I won't go skirmishing after it anymore if you think it's no good. Will you do that much?"

"As I said before," Hewitt replied, "tell me what you please, and if I can help you I will. But remember, I don't ask for your secrets."

"That's all right, I guess, Mr Hewitt. Well, now, it was all like this." And Mr Reuben B. Hoker plunged into a detailed account of his adventures since his arrival in London.

Relieved of repetitions, and put as directly as possible, it was as follows: Mr Hoker was a wagon-builder, had made a good business from very humble beginnings, and intended to go on and make it still a better. Meantime, he had come over to Europe for a short holiday—a thing he had promised himself for years. He was wandering about the London streets on the second night after his arrival in the city, when he managed to get into conversation with two men at a bar. They were not very prepossessing men, though flashily dressed. Very soon they suggested a game of cards. But Reuben B. Hoker was not to be had in that way, and after a while, they parted. The two were amusing enough fellows in their way, and when Hoker saw them again the next night in the same bar, he made no difficulty in talking with them freely. After a succession of drinks, they told him that they had a speculation on hand—a speculation that meant thousands if it succeeded—and to carry out which they were only waiting for a paltry sum of £50. There was a house, they said, in which was hidden a great number of jewels of immense value, which had been deposited there by a man who was now dead.

Exactly in what part of the house the jewels were to be found they did not know. There was a paper, they said, which was supposed to contain some information, but as yet they hadn't been quite able to make it out. But that would really matter very little if once they could get possession of the house. Then they would simply set to work and search from the topmost chimney to the lowermost brick, if necessary. The only present difficulty was that the house was occupied, and that the landlord wanted a large deposit of rent down before he would consent to turn out his present tenants and give them possession at a higher rental. This deposit would come to £50, and they hadn't the money. However, if any friend of theirs who meant business would put the necessary sum it their disposal, and keep his mouth shut, they would make him an equal partner in the proceeds with themselves; and as the value of the whole haul would probably be something not very far off £20,000, the speculation would bring a tremendous return to the man who was smart enough to put down his £50.

Hoker, very distrustful, sceptically demanded more detailed particulars of the scheme. But these the two men (Luker and Birks were their names, he found, in course of talking) inflexibly refused to communicate.

"Is it likely," said Luker, "that we should give the 'ole thing away to anybody who might easily go with his fifty pounds and clear out the bloomin' show? Not much. We've told you what the game is, and if you'd like to take a flutter with your fifty, all right; you'll do as well as anybody, and we'll treat you square. If you don't—well, don't, that's all. We'll get the oof from somewhere—there's blokes as 'ud jump at the chance. Anyway, we ain't going to give the show away before you've done somethin' to prove you're on the job, straight. Put your money in, and you shall know as much as we do."

Then there were more drinks, and more discussion. Hoker was still reluctant, though tempted by the prospect, and growing more venturesome with each drink.

"Don't you see," said Birks, "that if we was a-tryin' to 'ave you we should out with a tale as long as yer arm, all complete, with the address of the 'ouse and all. Then I s'pose you'd lug out the pieces on the nail, without askin' a bloomin' question. As it is, the thing's so perfectly genuine that we'd rather lose the chance and wait for some other bloke to find the money than run a chance of givin' the thing away. It's a matter o' business, simple and plain, that's all. It's a question of either us trustin' you with a chance of collarin' twenty thousand pounds or you trustin' us with a paltry fifty. We don't lay out no 'igh moral sentiments, we only say the weight o' money is all on one side. Take it or leave it, that's all. 'Ave another Scotch?"

The talk went on and the drinks went on, and it all ended, at "chucking-out time," in Reuben B. Hoker handing over five £10 notes, with smiling, though slightly incoherent, assurances of his eternal friendship for Luker and Birks.

In the morning he awoke to the realisation of a bad head, a bad tongue, and a bad opinion of his proceedings of the previous night. In his sober senses it seemed plain that he had been swindled. All day he cursed his fuddled foolishness, and at night he made for the bar that had been the scene if the transaction, with little hope of seeing either Luker or Birks, who had agreed to be there to meet him. There they were, however, and, rather to his surprise, they made no demand for more money. They asked him if he understood music, and showed him the worn old piece of paper containing the Flitterbat Lancers. The exact spot, they said, where the jewels were hidden was supposed to be indicated somehow on that piece of paper. Hoker did not understand music, and could find nothing on the paper that looked in the least like a direction to a hiding-place for jewels or anything else.

Luker and Birks then went into full particulars of their project. First, as to its history. The jewels were the famous Wedlake jewels, which had been taken from Sir Francis Wedlake's house in 1866 and never heard of again. A certain Jerry Shiels had been arrested in connection with the robbery, had been given a long sentence of penal servitude, and had died in jail. This Jerry Shiels was an extraordinarily clever criminal, and travelled about the country as a street musician. Although an expert burglar, he very rarely perpetrated robberies himself, but acted as a sort of traveling fence, receiving stolen property and transmitting it to London or out of the country. He also acted as the agent of a man named Legg, who had money, and who financed any likely looking project of a criminal nature that Shiels might arrange.

Jerry Shiels travelled with a "pardner"—a man who played the harp and acted as his assistant and messenger in affairs wherein Jerry was reluctant to appear personally. When Shiels was arrested, he had in his possession a quantity of printed and manuscript music, and after his first remand his "pardner," Jimmy Snape, applied for the music to be given up to him, in order, as he explained, that he might earn his living. No objection was raised to this, and Shiels was quite willing that Snape should have it, and so it was handed over. Now among the music was a small slip, headed Flitterbat Lancers, which Shiels had shown to Snape before the arrest. In case of Shiels being taken, Snape was to take this slip to Legg as fast as he could.

But as chance would have it, on that very day Legg himself was arrested, and soon after was sentenced also to a term of years. Snape hung about in London for a little while, and then emigrated. Before leaving, however, he gave the slip of music to Luker's father, a rag-shop keeper, to whom he owed money. He explained its history, and Luker senior made all sorts of fruitless efforts to get at the information concealed in the paper. He had held it to the fire to bring out concealed writing, had washed it, had held it to the light till his eyes ached, had gone over it with a magnifying glass—all in vain. He had got musicians to strum out the notes on all sorts of instruments—backwards, forwards, alternately, and in every other way he could think of. If at any time he fancied a resemblance in the resulting sound to some familiar song-tune, he got that song and studied all its words with loving care, upside-down, right-side up—every way.

He took the words Flitterbat Lancers and transposed the letters in all directions, and did everything else he could think of. In the end he gave it up, and died. Now, lately, Luker junior had been impelled with a desire to see into the matter. He had repeated all the parental experiments, and more, with the same lack of success. He had taken his "pal" Birks into his confidence, and together they had tried other experiments till at last they began to believe that the message had probably been written in some sort of invisible ink which the subsequent washings had erased altogether. But he had done one other thing: he had found the house which Shiels had rented at the time of his arrest, and in which a good quantity of stolen property—not connected with the Wedlake case—was discovered.

Here, he argued, if anywhere, Jerry Shiels had hidden the jewels. There was no other place where he could be found to have lived, or over which he had sufficient control to warrant his hiding valuables therein. Perhaps, once the house could be properly examined, something about it might give a clue as to what the message of the Flitterbat Lancers meant.

Hoker, of course, was anxious to know where the house in question stood, but this Luker and Birks would on no account inform him. "You've done your part," they said, "and now you leave us to do ours. There's a bit of a job about gettin' the tenants out. They won't go, and it'll take a bit of time before the landlord can make them. So you just hold your jaw and wait. When we're safe in the 'ouse, and there's no chance of anybody else pokin' in, then you can come and help find the stuff."

Hoker went home that night sober, but in much perplexity. The thing might be genuine, after all; indeed, there were many little things that made him think it was. But then, if it were, what guarantee had he that he would get his share, supposing the search turned out successful? None at all. But then it struck him for the first time that these jewels, though they may have lain untouched so long, were stolen property after all. The moral aspect of the affair began to trouble him a little, but the legal aspect troubled him more. That consideration however, he decided to leave over for the present. He had no more than the word of Luker and Birks that the jewels (if they existed) were those of Lady Wedlake, and Luker and Birks themselves only professed to know from hearsay. At any rate, he made up his mind to have some guarantee for his money. In accordance with this resolve, he suggested, when he met the two men the next day, that he should take charge of the slip of music and make an independent study of it. This proposal, however, met with an instant veto.

Hoker resolved to make up a piece of paper, folded as like the slip of music as possible, and substitute one for the other at their next meeting. Then he would put the Flitterbat Lancers in some safe place, and face his fellow conspirators with a hand of cards equal to their own. He carried out his plan the next evening with perfect success, thanks to the contemptuous indifference with which Luker and Birks had begun to regard him. He got the slip in his pocket, and left the bar. He had not gone far, however, before Luker discovered the loss, and soon he became conscious of being followed. He looked for a cab, but he was in a dark street, and no cab was near. Luker and Birks turned the corner and began to run. He saw they must catch him. Everything now depended on his putting the Flitterbat Lancers out of their reach, but where he could himself recover it. He ran till he saw a narrow passageway on his right, and into this he darted. It led into a yard where stones were lying about, and in a large building before him he saw the window of a lighted room a couple of floors up. It was a desperate expedient, but there was no time for consideration. He wrapped a stone in the paper and flung it with all his force through the lighted window. Even as he did it he heard the feet of Luker and Birks as they hurried down the street. The rest of the adventure in the court I myself saw.

Luker and Birks kept Hoker in their lodgings all that night. They searched him unsuccessfully for the paper; they bullied, they swore, they cajoled, they entreated, they begged him to play the game square with his pals. Hoker merely replied that he had put the Flitterbat Lancers where they couldn't easily find it, and that he intended playing the game square as long as they did the same. In the end they released him, apparently with more respect than they had before entertained, advising him to get the paper into his possession as soon as he could.

"And now," said Mr Hoker, in conclusion of his narrative, "perhaps you'll give me a bit of advice. Am I playin' a fool-game running after these toughs, or ain't I?"

Hewitt shrugged his shoulders. "It all depends," he said, "on your friends Luker and Birks. They may want to swindle you, or they may not. I'm afraid they'd like to, at any rate. But perhaps you've got some little security in this piece of paper. One thing is plain: they certainly believe in the deposit of the jewels themselves, else they wouldn't have taken so much trouble to get the paper back."

"Then I guess I'll go on with the thing, if that's it."

"That depends, of course, on whether you care to take trouble to get possession of what, after all, is somebody else's lawful property."

Hoker looked a little uneasy. "Well," he said, "there's that, of course. I didn't know nothin' of that at first, and when I did I'd parted with my money and felt entitled to get something back for it. Anyway, the stuff ain't found yet. When it is, why then, you know, I might make a deal with the owner. But, say, how did you find out my name, and about this here affair being jined up with the Wedlake jewels?"

Hewitt smiled. "As to the name and address, you just think it over a little when you've gone away, and if you don't see how I did it. You're not so cute as I think you are. In regard to the jewels—well, I just read the message of the Flitterbat Lancers, that's all."

"You read it? Whew! And what does it say? How did you do it?" Hoker turned the paper over eagerly in his hands as he spoke.

"See, now," said Hewitt, "I won't tell you all that, but I'll tell you something, and it may help you to test the real knowledge of Luker and Birks. Part of the message is in these words, which you had better write down: 'Over the coals the fifth dancer slides, says Jerry Shield the homey.'"

"What?" Hoker exclaimed, "fifth dancer slides over the coals? That's mighty odd. What's it all about?"

"About the Wedlake jewels, as I said. Now you can go and make a bargain with Luker and Birks. The only other part of the message is an address, and that they already know, if they have been telling the truth about the house they intend taking. You can offer to tell them what I have told you of the message, after they have told you where the house is, and proved to you that they are taking the steps they talked of. If they won't agree to that, I think you had best treat them as common rogues and charge them with obtaining your money under false pretences."

Nothing more would Hewitt say than that, despite Hoker's many questions; and when at last Hoker had gone, almost as troubled and perplexed as ever, my friend turned to me and said, "Now, Brett, if you haven't lunched and would like to see the end of this business, hurry!"

"The end of it?" I said. "Is it to end so soon? How?"

"Simply by a police raid on Jerry Shiels's old house with a search warrant. I communicated with the police this morning before I came here."

"Poor Hoker!" I said.

"Oh, I had told the police before I saw Hoker, or heard of him, of course. I just conveyed the message on the music slip—that was enough. But I'll tell you all about it when there's more time; I must be off now. With the information I have given him, Hoker and his friends may make an extra push and get into the house soon, but I couldn't resist the temptation to give the unfortunate Hoker some sort of sporting chance—though it's a poor one, I fear. Get your lunch as quickly as you can, and go at once to Colt Row, Bankside—South-wark way, you know. Probably we shall be there before you. If not, wait."

Colt Row was not difficult to find. It was one of those places that decay with an excess of respectability, like Drury Lane and Clare Market. Once, when Jacob's Island was still an island, a little farther down the river, Colt Row had evidently been an unsafe place for a person with valuables about him, and then it probably prospered, in its own way. Now it was quite respectable, but very dilapidated and dirty. Perhaps it was sixty yards long—perhaps a little more. It was certainly a very few yards wide, and the houses at each side had a patient and forlorn look of waiting for a metropolitan improvement to come along and carry them away to their rest.

I could see no sign of Hewitt, nor of the police, so I walked up and down the narrow pavement for a little while. As I did so, I became conscious of a face at the window of the least ruinous house in the row, a face that I fancied expressed particular interest in my movements. The house was an old gabled structure, faced with plaster. What had apparently once been a shop-window on the ground floor was now shuttered up, and the face that watched me—an old woman's—looked out from the window above. I had noted these particulars with some curiosity, when, arriving again at the street corner, I observed Hewitt approaching, in company with a police inspector, and followed by two unmistakable plainclothesmen.

"Well," Hewitt said, "you're first here after all. Have you seen any more of our friend Hoker?"

"No, nothing."

"Very well—probably he'll be here before long, though."

The party turned into Colt Row, and the inspector, walking up to the door of the house with the shuttered bottom window, knocked sharply. There was no response, so he knocked again, equally in vain.

"All out," said the inspector.

"No," I said; "I saw a woman watching me from the window above not three minutes ago."

"Ho, ho!" the inspector replied. "That's so, eh? One of you—you, Johnson—step round to the back, will you?"

One of the plainclothesmen started off, and after waiting another minute or two the inspector began a thundering cannonade of knocks that brought every available head out of the window of every inhabited room in the Row. At this the woman opened the window, and began abusing the inspector with a shrillness and fluency that added a street-corner audience to that already congregated at the windows.

"Go away, you blaggards!" the lady said, "you ought to be 'orse-w'ipped, every one of ye! A-comin' 'ere a-tryin' to turn decent people out o' 'ouse and 'ome! Wait till my 'usband comes 'ome—'e'll show yer, ye mutton-cadgin' scoundrels! Payin' our rent reg'lar, and good tenants as is always been—and I'm a respectable married woman, that's what I am, ye dirty great cowards!"—this last word with a low, tragic emphasis.

Hewitt remembered what Hoker had said about the present tenants refusing to quit the house on the landlord's notice. "She thinks we've come from the landlord to turn her out," he said to the inspector. "We're not here from the landlord, you old fool!" the inspector said. "We don't want to turn you out. We're the police, with a search warrant, and you'd better let us in or you'll get into trouble."

"'Ark at 'im!" the woman screamed, pointing at the inspector. "'Ark at 'im! Thinks I was born yesterday, that feller! Go 'ome, ye dirty pie-stealer, go 'ome!"

The audience showed signs of becoming a small crowd, and the inspector's patience gave out. "Here, Bradley," he said, addressing the remaining plainclothesman, "give a hand with these shutters," and the two—both powerful men—seized the iron bar which held the shutters and began to pull. But the garrison was undaunted, and, seizing a broom, the woman began to belabour the invaders about the shoulders and head from above.

But just at this moment, the woman, emitting a terrific shriek, was suddenly lifted from behind and vanished. Then the head of the

The woman began to belabour the invaders
about the shoulders and head from above.

plainclothesman who had gone round to the back appeared, with the calm announcement, "There's a winder open behind, sir. But I'll open the front door if you like."

In a minute the bolts were shot, and the front door swung back. The placid Johnson stood in the passage, and as we passed in he said, "I've locked 'er in the back room upstairs."

"It's the bottom staircase, of course," the inspector said; and we tramped down into the basement. A little way from the stair-foot Hewitt opened a cupboard door, which enclosed a receptacle for coals. "They still keep the coals here, you see," he said, striking a match and passing it to and fro near the sloping roof of the cupboard. It was of plaster, and covered the underside of the stairs.

"And now for the fifth dancer," he said, throwing the match away and making for the staircase again. "One, two, three, four, five," and he tapped the fifth stair from the bottom.

The stairs were uncarpeted, and Hewitt and the inspector began a careful examination of the one he had indicated. They tapped it in different places, and Hewitt passed his hands over the surfaces of both tread and riser. Presently, with his hand at the outer edge of the riser, Hewitt spoke. "Here it is, I think," he said; "it is the riser that slides."

He took out his pocketknife and scraped away the grease and paint

366

from the edge of the old stair. Then a joint was plainly visible. For a long time, the plank, grimed and set with age, refused to shift; but at last, by dint of patience and firm fingers, it moved, and was drawn clean out from the end.

Within, nothing was visible but grime, fluff, and small rubbish. The inspector passed his hand along the bottom angle. "Here's something," he said. It was the gold hook of an old-fashioned earring, broken off short.

Hewitt slapped his thigh. "Somebody's been here before us," he said "and a good time back too, judging from the dust. That hook's a plain indication that jewellery was here once. There's plainly nothing more, except—except this piece of paper." Hewitt's eyes had detected—black with loose grime as it was—a small piece of paper lying at the bottom of the recess. He drew it out and shook off the dust. "Why, what's this?" he exclaimed. "More music!"

We went to the window, and there saw in Hewitt's hand a piece of written musical notation, thus:—

Hewitt pulled out from his pocket a few pieces of paper. "Here is a copy I made this morning of the Flitterbat Lancers, and a note or two of my own as well," he said. He took a pencil, and, constantly referring to his own papers, marked a letter under each note on the last-found slip of music. When he had done this, the letters read:

"You are a clever cove whoever you are but there was a cleverer says Jim Snape the horney's mate."

"You see." Hewitt said handing the inspector the paper. "Snape, the unconsidered messenger, finding Legg in prison, set to work and got the jewels for himself. The thing was a cryptogram, of course, of a very simple sort, though uncommon in design. Snape was a humorous soul, too, to leave this message here in the same cipher, on the chance of somebody else reading the Flitterbat Lancers."

"But," I asked, "why did he give that slip of music to Laker's father?"

"Well, he owed him money, and got out or it that way. Also, he avoided the appearance of 'flushness' that paying the debt might have given him, and got quietly out of the country with his spoils."

The shrieks upstairs had grown hoarser, but the broom continued vigorously. "Let that woman out," said the inspector, "and we'll go and report. Not much good looking for Snape now, I fancy. But there's some satisfaction in clearing up that old quarter-century mystery."

We left the place pursued by the execrations of the broom wielder, who bolted the door behind us, and from the window defied us to come back, and vowed she would have us all searched before a magistrate for what we had probably stolen. In the very next street we hove in sight of Reuben B. Hoker in the company of two swell-mob-looking fellows, who sheered off down a side turning in sight of our group. Hoker, too, looked rather shy at the sight of the inspector.

"The meaning of the thing was so very plain," Hewitt said to me afterwards, "that the duffers who had the Flitterbat Lancers in hand for so long never saw it at all. If Shiels had made an ordinary clumsy cryptogram, all letters and figures, they would have seen what it was at once, and at least would have tried to read it; but because it was put in the form of music, they tried everything else but the right way. It was a clever dodge of Shiels's, without a doubt. Very few people, police officers or not, turning over a heap of old music, would notice or feel suspicious of that little slip among the rest. But once one sees it is a cryptogram (and the absence of bar lines and of notes beyond the stave would suggest that) the reading is as easy as possible. For my part I tried it as a cryptogram at once. You know the plan—it has been described a hundred times.

"See here—look at this copy of the Flitterbat Lancers. Its only difficulty—and that is a small one—is that the words are not divided. Since there are positions for less than a dozen notes on the stave, and there are twenty-six letters to be indicated, it follows that crotchets, quavers, and semiquavers on the same line or space must mean different letters. The first step is obvious. We count the notes to ascertain which sign occurs most frequently, and we find that the crotchet in the top space is the sign required—it occurs no less than eleven times. Now the letter most frequently occurring in an ordinary sentence of English is e. Let us then suppose that this represents e. At once a coincidence strikes us. In ordinary musical notation in the treble clef the note occupying the top space would be E. Let us remember that presently.

"Now the most common word in the English language is '*the*.' We know the sign for *e*, the last letter of this word, so let us see if in more than one place that sign is preceded by two others identical in each case. If so, the probability is that the other two signs will represent *t* and *h*, and the whole word will be '*the*.' Now it happens in no less than four places the sign e is preceded by the same two other signs—once in the first line, twice in the second, and once in the fourth. No word of three letters ending in e would be in the least likely to occur four times in a short sentence except '*the*.' Then we will call it '*the*', and note the signs preceding the *e*. They are a quaver under the bottom line for the *t*, and a crotchet on the first space for the *h*. We travel along the stave, and wherever these signs occur we mark them with *t* or *h*, as the case may be.

"But now we remember that *e*, the crotchet in the top space, is in its right place as a musical note, while the crotchet in the bottom space means *h*, which is no musical note at all. Considering this for a minute, we remember that among the notes which are expressed in ordinary music on the treble stave, without the use of ledger lines, *d*, *e* and *f* are repeated at the lower and at the upper part of the stave. Therefore, anybody making a cryptogram of musical notes would probably use one set of these duplicate positions to indicate other letters, and as *a* is in the lower part of the stave, that is where the variation comes in. Let us experiment by assuming that all the crotchets above *f* in ordinary musical notation have their usual values, and let us set the letters over their respective notes. Now things begin to shape. Look toward the end of the second line: there is the word *the* and the letters *f f t h*, with another note between the two *f*'s. Now that word can only possibly be *fifth*, so that now we have the sign for *i*. It is the crotchet on the bottom line. Let us go through and mark the *i*'s.

"And now observe. The first sign of the lot is *i*, and there is one other sign before the word '*the*.' The only words possible here beginning with *i*, and of two letters, are *it*, *if*, *is* and *in*. Now we have the signs for *t* and *f*, so we know that it isn't *it* or *if*. Is would be unlikely here, because there is a tendency, as you see, to regularity in these signs, and *t*, the next letter alphabetically to *s*, is at the bottom of the stave. Let us try *n*. At once we get the word *dance* at the beginning of line three. And now we have got enough to see the system of the thing. Make a stave and put *G A B C* and the higher *D E F* in their proper musical places.

"Then fill in the blank places with the next letters of the alphabet downward, *h i j*, and we find that *h* and *I* fall in the places we have already discovered for them as crotchets. Now take quavers, and go on with *k l m n o*, and so on as before, beginning on the A space. When you have filled the quavers, do the same with semiquavers—there are only six alphabetical letters left for this—*u v w x y z*. Now you will find that this exactly agrees with all we have ascertained already, and if you will use the other letters to fill up over the signs still unmarked you will get the whole message:

In the Colt Row ken over the coals the fifth dancer slides says Jerry Shiels the horney.

"'Dancer,' as perhaps you didn't know, is thieves' slang for a stair, and 'horney' is the strolling musician's name for cornet player. Of course the thing took a little time to work out, chiefly because the sentence was short, and gave one few opportunities. But anybody with the key, using the cipher as a means of communication, would read it easily.

"As soon as I had read it, of course I guessed the purport of the Flitterbat Lancers. Jerry Shiels's name is well-known to anybody with half my knowledge of the criminal records of the century, and his connection with the missing Wedlake jewels, and his death in prison, came to my mind at once. Certainly here was something hidden, and as the

"The fifth dancer slides."

370

Wedlake jewels seemed most likely, I made the shot in talking to Hoker."

"But you terribly astonished him by telling him his name and address. How was that?" I asked curiously.

Hewitt laughed aloud. "That," he said; "why, that was the thinnest trick of all. Why, the man had it engraved on the silver band of his umbrella handle. When he left his umbrella outside, Kerrett (I had indicated the umbrella to him by a sign) just copied the lettering on one of the ordinary visitors' forms, and brought it in. You will remember I treated it as an ordinary visitor's announcement." And Hewitt laughed again.

★★★★★★

On the afternoon of the next day Reuben B. Hoker called on Hewitt and had half-an-hour's talk with him in his private room. After that he came up to me with half-a-crown in his hand. "Sir," he said, "everything has turned out a durned sell. I don't want to talk about it anymore. I'm goin' out of this durn country. Night before last I broke your winder. You put the damage at half-a-crown. Here is the money. Good-day to you, sir."

And Reuben B. Hoker went out into the tumultuous world.

THE CASE OF THE LATE MR. REWSE

1.

Of this case I personally saw nothing beyond the first advent in Hewitt's office of Mr. Horace Bowyer, who put the case in his hands, and then I merely saw Mr. Bowyer's back as I passed down stairs from my rooms. But I noted the case in full detail after Hewitt's return from Ireland, as it seemed to me one not entirely without interest, if only as an exemplar of the fatal ease with which a man may unwittingly dig a pit for his own feet—a pit from which there is no climbing out.

A few moments after I had seen the stranger disappear into Hewitt's office, Kerrett brought to Hewitt in his inner room a visitor's slip announcing the arrival on argent business of Mr. Horace Bowyer. That the visitor was in a hurry was plain from a hasty rattling of the closed wicket in the outer room where Mr. Bowyer was evidently making impatient attempts to follow his announcement in person. Hewitt showed himself at the door and invited Mr. Bowyer to as soon as Kerrett had with much impetuosity florid gentleman with a loud voice and a large stare.

"Mr. Hewitt," he said, "I must claim your immediate attention to a business of the utmost gravity. Will you please consider yourself commissioned, wholly regardless of expense, to set aside whatever you may have in hand and devote yourself to the case I shall put in your hands?"

"Certainly not," Hewitt replied with a slight smile. "What I have in hand are matters which I have engaged to attend to, and no mere compensation for loss of fees could persuade me to leave my clients in the lurch, else what would prevent some other gentleman coming here tomorrow with a bigger fee than yours and bribing me away from you?"

"But this—this is a most serious thing, Mr. Hewitt. A matter of life or death—it is indeed!"

"Quite so," Hewitt replied; "but there are a thousand such matters at this moment pending of which you and I know nothing, and there are also two or three more of which you know nothing but on which I am at work. So that it becomes a question of practicability. If you will tell me your business I can judge whether or not I may be able to accept your commission concurrently with those I have in hand. Some operations take months of constant attention; some can be conducted intermittently; others still are a mere matter of a few days many of hours simply."

"I will tell you then," Mr. Bowyer replied. "In the first place, will you have the kindness to read that? It is a cutting from the *Standard's* column of news from the provinces of two days ago."

Hewitt took the cutting and read as follows:—

"The epidemic of smallpox in County Mayo, Ireland, shows few signs of abating. The spread of the disease has been very remarkable considering the widely-scattered nature of the population, though there can be no doubt that the market towns are the centres of infection, and that it is from these that the germs of contagion are carried into the country by people from all parts who resort thither on market days. In many cases the disease has assumed a particularly malignant form, and deaths have been very rapid and numerous. The comparatively few medical men available are sadly overworked, owing largely to the distances separating their different patients. Among those who have succumbed within the last few days is Mr. Algernon Rewse, a young English gentleman who has been staying with a friend at a cottage a few miles from Cullanin, on a fishing excursion."

Hewitt placed the cutting on the table at his side. "Yes?" he said inquiringly.

"It is to Mr. Algernon Rewse's death you wish to draw my attention?"

"It is," Mr. Bowyer answered; "and the reason I come to you is that

I very much suspect—more than suspect, indeed—that Mr. Algernon Rewse has *not* died by smallpox, but has been murdered—murdered cold-bloodedly, and for the most sordid motives, by the friend who has been sharing his holiday."

"In what way do you suppose him to have been murdered?"

"That I cannot say—that, indeed, I want you to find out, among other things—chiefly perhaps, the murderer himself, who has made off."

"And your own status in the matter," queried Hewitt, "is that of—?"

"I am trustee under a will by which Mr. Rewse would have benefited considerably had he lived but a month or two longer. That circumstance indeed lies rather near the root of the matter. The thing stood thus. Under the will I speak of that of young Rewse's uncle, a very old friend of mine in his lifetime—the money lay in trust till the young fellow should attain twenty-five years of age. His younger sister, Miss Mary Rewse, was also benefited, but to a much smaller extent. She was to come into her property also on attaining the age of twenty-five, or on her marriage, whichever event happened first. It was further provided that in case either of these young people died before coming into the inheritance, his or her share should go to the survivor: I want you particularly to remember this.

"You will observe that now, in consequence of young Algernon

Algernon Rewse.

373

Rewse's death, barely two months before his twenty-fifth birthday, the whole of the very large property—all personalty, and free from any tie or restriction—which would otherwise have been his, will, in the regular course, pass, on her twenty-fifth birthday, *or on her marriage,* to Miss Mary Rewse, whose own legacy was comparatively trifling. You will understand the importance of this when I tell you that the man whom I suspect of causing Algernon Rewse's death, and who has been his companion on his otherwise lonely holiday, is engaged to be married to Miss Rewse."

Mr. Bowyer paused at this, but Hewitt only raised his eyebrows and nodded.

"I have never particularly liked the man," Mr. Bowyer went on. "He never seemed to have much to say for himself. I like a man who holds up his head and opens 'his mouth. I don't believe in the sort of modesty that he showed so much of-it isn't genuine. A man can't afford to be genuinely meek and retiring who has his way to make in the world—and he was clever enough to know *that.*"

"He is poor, then?" Hewitt asked.

"Oh yes, poor enough. His name, by-the-bye, is Main Stanley Main—and he is a medical man. He hasn't been practising, except as assistant, since he became qualified, the reason being, I understand, that he couldn't afford to buy a good practice. He is the person who will profit by young Rewse's death—or at any rate who intended to; but we will see about that. As for Mary, poor girl, she wouldn't have lost her brother for fifty fortunes."

"As to the circumstances of the death, now?"

"Yes, yes, I am coming to that. Young Algernon Rewse, you must know, had rather run down in health, and Main persuaded him that he wanted a change. I don't know what it was altogether, but Rewse seemed to have been having his own little love troubles and that sort of thing, you know. He'd been engaged, I think, or very nearly so, and the young lady died, and so on. Well, as I said, he had run down and got into low health and spirits, and no doubt a change of some sort would have done him good. This Stanley Main always seemed to have a great influence over the poor boy—he was about four or five years older than Rewse—and somehow he persuaded him to go away, the two together, to some outlandish wilderness of a place in the West of Ireland for salmon-fishing.

"It seemed to me at the time rather a ridiculous sort of place to go to, but Main had his way, and they went. There was a cottage—rather a good sort of cottage, I believe, for the district—which some friend of Main's, once a landowner in the district, had put up as a convenient box for salmon-fishing, and they rented it. Not long after they got there this epidemic of small-pox got about in the district—though that, I believe, has had little to do with poor young Rewse's death. All appeared to go well until a day over a week ago, when Mrs. Rewse received this letter from Main." Mr. Bowyer handed Martin Hewitt a letter, written in an irregular and broken hand, as though of a person writing under stress of extreme agitation. It ran thus:—

My dear Mrs. Rewse,—You will probably have heard through the newspapers—indeed I think Algernon has told you in his letters—that a very bad epidemic of small-pox is abroad in this district. I am deeply grieved to have to tell you that Algernon himself has taken the disease in a rather bad form. He showed the first symptoms today (Tuesday), and he is now in bed in the cottage. It is fortunate that I, as a medical man, happen to be on the spot, as the nearest local doctor is five miles off at Cullanin, and he is working and travelling night and day as it is. I have my little medicine chest with me, and can get whatever else is necessary from Cullanin, so that everything is being done for Algernon that is possible, and I hope to bring him up to scratch in good health soon, though of course the disease is a dangerous one. Pray don't unnecessarily alarm yourself, and don't think about coming over here, or anything of that sort. You can do no good, and will only run risk yourself. I will take care to let you know how things go on, so please don't attempt to come. The journey is long and would be very trying to you, and you would have no place to stay at nearer than Cullanin, which is quite a centre of infection. I will write again tomorrow.—Yours most sincerely,
Stanley Main.

Not only did the handwriting of this letter show signs of agitation, but here and there words had been repeated, and sometimes a letter had been omitted. Hewitt placed the letter on the table by the newspaper cutting, and Mr. Bowyer proceeded.

"Another letter followed on the next day," he said, handing it to Hewitt as he spoke; "a short one, as you see; not written with quite such signs of agitation. It merely says that Rewse is very bad, and repeats the former entreaties that his mother will not think of going to him."

Hewitt glanced at the letter and placed it with the other, while Mr. Bowyer continued:

"Notwithstanding Main's persistent anxiety that she should stay at home, Mrs. Rewse, who was of course terribly worried about her only son, had almost made up her mind, in spite of her very delicate health, to start for Ireland, when she received a third letter announcing Algernon's death. Here it is. It is certainly the sort of letter that one might expect to be written in such circumstances, and yet there seems to me at least a certain air of disingenuousness about the wording. There are, as you see, the usual condolences, and so forth. The disease was of the malignant type, it says, which is terribly rapid in its action, often carrying off the patient even before the eruption has time to form. Then—and this is a thing I wish you especially to note—there is once more a repetition of his desire that neither the young man's mother nor his sister shall come to Ireland. The funeral must take place immediately, he says, under arrangements made by the local authorities, and before they could reach the spot. Now doesn't this obtrusive anxiety of his that no connection of young Rewse's should be near him during his illness, nor even at the funeral, strike you as rather singular?"

"Well, possibly it is; though it may easily be nothing but zeal for the health of Mrs. Rewse and her daughter. As a matter of fact, what Main says is very plausible. They could do no sort of good in the circumstances, and might easily run into danger themselves, to say nothing of the fatigue of the journey and general nervous upset. Mrs. Rewse is in weak health, I think you said?"

"Yes, she's almost an invalid in fact; she is subject to heart disease. But tell me now, as an entirely impartial observer, doesn't it seem to you that there is a very forced, unreal sort of tone in all these letters?"

"Perhaps one may notice something of the sort, but fifty things may cause that. The case from the beginning may have been worse than he made it out. What ensued on the receipt of this letter?"

"Mrs. Rewse was prostrated, of course. Her daughter communicated with me as a friend of the family, and that is how I heard of the whole thing for the first time. I saw the letters, and it seemed to me, looking at all the circumstances of the case, that somebody at least ought to go over and make certain that everything was as it should be. Here was this poor young man, staying in a lonely cottage with the only man in the world who had any reason to desire his death, or any profit to gain by it, and he had a very great inducement indeed. Moreover, he was a medical man, *carrying his medicine chest with him,* remember, as he says himself in his letter. In this situation Rewse suddenly dies, with nobody about him, so far as there is anything to show, but Main himself. As his medical attendant it would be Main who would certify and register the death, and no matter what foul play might have taken place he would be safe as long as nobody was on the spot to make searching inquiries might easily escape even then, in fact. When one man is likely to profit much by the death of another a doctor's medicine chest is likely to supply but too easy a means to his end."

"Did you say anything of your suspicions to the ladies?"

"Well—well I hinted perhaps—no more than hinted, you know. But they wouldn't hear of it—got indignant, and 'took on' as people call it, worse than ever, so that I had to smooth them over. But since it seemed somebody's duty to see into the matter a little more closely, and there seemed to be nobody to do it but myself, I started off that very evening by the night mail. I was in Dublin early the next morning and spent that day getting across Ireland. The nearest station was ten miles from Cullanin, and that, as you remember, was five miles from the cottage, so that I drove over on the morning of the following day. I must say Main appeared very much taken aback at seeing me. His manner was nervous and apprehensive, and made me more suspicious than ever. The body had been buried, of course, a couple of days or more. I asked a few rather searching questions about the illness, and so forth, and his answers became positively confused. He had burned the clothes that Rewse was wearing at the time the disease first showed itself, he said, as well as all the bedclothes, since there was no really efficient means of disinfection at hand.

"His story in the main was that he had gone off to Cullanin one morning on foot to see about a top joint of a fishing-rod that was to be repaired. When he returned early in the afternoon he found Algernon Rewse sickening of smallpox, at once put him to bed, and there nursed him till he died. I wanted to know, of course, why no other medical man had been called in. He said that there was only one available, and it was doubtful if he could have been got at even a day's notice, so overworked was he; moreover, he said this man, with his hurry and over-strain, could never have given the patient such efficient attention as he himself, who had nothing else to do.

"After a while I put it to him plainly that it would at any rate have

377

been more prudent to have had the body at least inspected by some independent doctor, considering the fact that he was likely to profit so largely by young Rewse's death, and I suggested that with an exhumation order it might not be too late now, as a matter of justice to himself. The effect of that convinced me. The man gasped and turned blue with terror. It was a full minute, I should think, before he could collect himself sufficiently to attempt to dissuade me from doing what I had hinted at. He did so as soon as he could by every argument he could think of—entreated me in fact almost desperately.

"That decided me. I said that after what he had said, and particularly in view of his whole manner and bearing, I should insist, by every means in my power, on having the body properly examined, and I went off at once to Cullanin to set the telegraph going, and see whatever local authority might be proper. When I returned in the afternoon Stanley Main had packed his bag and vanished, and I have not heard nor seen anything of him since. I stayed in the neighbourhood that day and the next, and left for London in the evening. By the help of my solicitors proper representations were made at the Home Office, and, especially in view of Main's flight, a prompt order was made for exhumation and medical examination preliminary to an inquest.

"I am expecting to hear that the disinterment has been effected to-day. What I want you to do of course is chiefly to find Main. The Irish constabulary in that district are fine big men, and no doubt most excellent in quelling a faction fight or shutting up a shebeen, but I doubt their efficiency in anything requiring much more finesse. Perhaps also you may be able to find out something of the means by which the murder—it is plain it is one—was committed. It is quite possible that Main may have adopted some means to give the body the appearance, even to a medical man, of death from smallpox."

"That," Hewitt said, "is scarcely likely, else, indeed, why did he not take care that another doctor should see the body before the burial? That would have secured him. But that is not a thing one can deceive a doctor over. Of course in the circumstances exhumation is desirable, but if the case *is* one of smallpox, I don't envy the medical man who is to examine. At any rate the business is, I should imagine, not likely to be a very long one, and I can take it in hand at once. I will leave tonight for Ireland by the 6.30 train from Euston."

"Very good. I shall go over myself, of course. If anything comes to my knowledge in the meanwhile, of course I'll let you know."

An hour or two after this a cab stopped at the door, and a young lady dressed in black sent in her name and a minute later was shown into Hewitt's room. It was Miss Mary Rewse. She wore a heavy veil, and all she said she uttered in evidently deep distress of mind. Hewitt did what he could to calm her, and waited patiently.

At length she said: "I felt that I must come to you, Mr. Hewitt, and yet now that I am here I don't know what to say. Is it the fact that Mr. Bowyer has commissioned you to investigate the circumstances of my poor brother's death, and to discover the whereabouts of Mr. Main?"

"Yes, Miss Rewse, that is the fact. Can you tell me anything that will help me?"

"No, no, Mr. Hewitt, I fear not. But it is such a dreadful thing, and Mr. Bowyer is—I'm afraid he is so much prejudiced against Mr. Main that I felt I ought to do something—to say something at least to prevent you entering on the case with your mind made up that he has been guilty of such an awful thing. He is really quite incapable of it, I assure you."

"Pray, Miss Rewse," Hewitt replied, "don't allow that apprehension to disturb you. If Mr. Main is, as you say, incapable of such an act as perhaps he is suspected of, you may rest assured no harm will come to him. So far as I am concerned at any rate I enter the case with a perfectly open mind. A man in my profession who accepted prejudices at the beginning of a case would have very poor results to show indeed. As yet I have no opinion, no theory, no prejudice—nothing indeed but a bare outline of fads. I shall derive no opinion and no theory from anything but a consideration of the actual circumstances and evidences on the spot. I quite understand the relation in which Mr. Main stands in regard to yourself and your family Have you heard from him lately?"

"Not since the letter informing us of my brother's death."

"Before then?"

Miss Rewse hesitated.

"Yes," she said, "we corresponded. But—but there was really nothing—the letters were of a personal and private sort—they were—"

"Yes, yes, of course," Hewitt answered, with his eyes fixed keenly on the veil which Miss Rewse still kept down. "Of course I understand that. Then there is nothing else you can tell me?"

"No, I fear not. I can only implore you to remember that no matter what you may see and hear, no matter what the evidence may be, I am sure, sure, *sure* that poor Stanley could never do such a thing." And Miss Rewse buried her face in her hands.

Hewitt kept his eyes on the lady, though he smiled slightly, and asked, "How long have you known Mr. Main?"

"For some five or six years now. My poor brother knew him at school, though of course they were in different forms, Mr. Main being the elder."

"Were they always on good terms?"

"They were always like brothers."

Little more was said. Hewitt condoled with Miss Rewse as well as he might, and she presently took her departure. Even as she descended the stairs a messenger came with a short note from Mr. Bowyer enclosing a telegram just received from Cullanin. The telegram ran thus:—

Body exhumed. death from shot-wound. No trace of small-pox. Nothing yet heard of Main. have communicated with coroner.—O'Reilly.

2

Hewitt and Mr. Bowyer travelled towards Mayo together, Mr. Bowyer restless and loquacious on the subject of the business in hand, and Hewitt rather bored thereby. He resolutely declined to offer an opinion on any single detail of the case till he had examined the available evidence, and his occasional remarks on matters of general

"How long have you known Mr. Main?"

380

interest, the scenery and so forth, struck his companion, unused to business of the sort which had occasioned the journey, as strangely cold-blooded and indifferent. Telegrams had been sent ordering that no disarrangement of the contents of the cottage was to be allowed pending their arrival, and Hewitt well knew that nothing more was practicable till the site was reached. At Ballymaine, where the train was left at last, they stayed for the night, and left early the next morning for Cullanin, where a meeting with Dr. O'Reilly at the mortuary had been appointed. There the body lay stripped of its shroud, calm and grey, and beginning to grow ugly, with a scarcely noticeable breach in the flesh of the left breast.

"The wound has been thoroughly cleansed, closed and stopped with a carbolic plug before interment," Dr. O'Reilly said. He was a middle-aged, grizzled man, with a face whereon many recent sleepless nights had left their traces. "I have not thought it necessary to do anything in the way of dissection. The bullet is not present, it has passed clean through the body, between the ribs both back and front, piercing the heart on its way. The death must have been instantaneous."

Hewitt quickly examined the two wounds, back and front, as the doctor turned the body over, and then asked: "Perhaps, Dr. O'Reilly, you have had some experience of a gunshot wound before this?"

The doctor smiled grimly. "I think so," he answered, with just enough of brogue in his words to hint his nationality and no more. "I was an army surgeon for a good many years before I came to Cullanin, and saw service in Ashanti and in India."

"Come then," Hewitt said, "you're an expert. Would it have been possible for the shot to have been fired from behind?"

"Oh, no. See! the bullet entering makes a wound of quite a different character from that of the bullet leaving."

"Have you any idea of the weapon used?"

"A large revolver, I should think; perhaps of the regulation size; that is, I should judge the bullet to have been a conical one of about the size fitted to such a weapon—smaller than that from a rifle."

"Can you form an idea of from what distance the shot was fired?"

Dr. O'Reilly shook his head. "The clothes have all been burned," he said, "and the wound has been washed, otherwise one might have looked for powder blackening."

"Did you know either the dead man or Dr. Main personally?"

"Only very slightly. I may say I saw just such a pistol as might cause that sort of wound in his hands the day before he gave out that Rewse had been attacked by smallpox. I drove past the cottage as he stood in the doorway with it in his hand. He had the breach opened, and seemed to be either loading or unloading it—which it was I couldn't say."

"Very good, doctor, that may be important. Now is there any single circumstance, incident or conjecture that you can tell me of in regard to this case that you have not already mentioned?"

Doctor O'Reilly thought for a moment, and replied in the negative.

"I heard of course," he said, "of the reported new case of smallpox, and that Main had taken the case in hand himself. I was indeed relieved to hear it, for I had already more on my hands than one man can safely be expected to attend to. The cottage was fairly isolated, and there could have been nothing gained by removal to an asylum—indeed there was practically no accommodation. So far as I can make out nobody seems to have seen young Rewse, alive or dead, after Main had announced that he had the smallpox. He seems to have done everything himself, laying out the body and all, and you may be pretty sure that none of the strangers about was particularly anxious to have anything to do with it. The undertaker (there is only one here, and he is down with the smallpox himself now) was as much overworked as I was myself, and was glad enough to send off a coffin by a market cart and leave the laying out and screwing down to Main, since he had got those orders. Main made out the death certificate himself, and, since he was trebly qualified, everything seemed in order."

"The certificate merely attributed the death to smallpox, I take it, with no qualifying remarks?"

"Smallpox simply."

Hewitt and Mr. Bowyer bade Dr. O'Reilly good morning, and their car was turned in the direction of the cottage where Algernon Rewse had met his death. At the Town Hall in the market place, however, Hewitt stopped the car and set his watch by the public clock. "This is more than half an hour before London time," he said, "and we mustn't be at odds with the natives about the time."

As he spoke Dr. O'Reilly came running up breathlessly. "I've just heard something," he said. "Three men heard a shot in the cottage as they were passing, last Tuesday week."

"Where are the men?"

"I don't know at the moment; but they can be found. Shall I set about it?"

"If you possibly can," Hewitt said, "you will help us enormously. Can you send them messages to be at the cottage as soon as they can get there today? Tell them they shall have half-a-sovereign apiece."

"Right, I will. Good-day."

"Tuesday week," said Mr. Bowyer as they drove off; "that was the date of Main's first letter, and the day on which, by his account, Rewse was taken ill. Then if that was the shot that killed Rewse he must have been lying dead in the place while Main was writing those letters reporting his sickness to his mother. The cold-blooded scoundrel!"

"Yes," Hewitt replied, "I think it probable in any case that Tuesday was the day that Rewse was shot. It wouldn't have been safe for Main to write the mother lying letters about the smallpox before. Rewse might have written home in the meantime, or something might have occurred to postpone Main's plans, and then there would be impossible explanations required."

Over a very bad road they jolted on and in the end arrived where the road, now become a mere path, passed a tumble-down old farmhouse.

"This is where the woman lives who cooked and cleaned house for Rewse and Main," Mr. Bowyer said. "There is the cottage, scarce a hundred yards off, a little to the right of the track."

"Well," replied Hewitt, "suppose we stop here and ask her a few questions? I like to get the evidence of all the witnesses as soon as possible. It simplifies subsequent work wonderfully."

They alighted, and Mr. Bowyer roared through the open door and tapped with his stick. In reply to his summons a decent-looking woman of perhaps fifty, but wrinkled beyond her age, and better dressed than any woman Hewitt had seen since leaving Cullanin, appeared from the hinder buildings and curtsied pleasantly.

"Good morning, Mrs. Hurley, good morning," Mr. Bowyer said, "this is Mr. Martin Hewitt, a gentleman from London, who is going to look into this shocking murder of our young friend Mr. Rewse and sift it to the bottom. He would like you to tell him something, Mrs. Hurley."

The woman curtsied again. "An' it's the jintleman is welcome, sor, sad doin's as ut is." She had a low, pleasing voice, much in contrast with her unattractive appearance, and characterised by the softest and broadest brogue imaginable. "Will ye not come in? Mother av Hiven! An' thim two livin' together, an' fishin' an' readin' an' all, like brothers! An' trut' ut is he was a foine young jintleman indade, indade!"

"I suppose, Mrs. Hurley," Hewitt said, "you've seen as much of the life of those two gentlemen here as anybody?"

"True ut is, sor; none more—nor as much."

"Did you ever hear of anybody being on bad terms with Mr. Rewse—anybody at all, Mr. Main or another?"

"Niver a soul in all Mayo. How could ye? Such a foine young jintleman, an' fair-spoken an' all."

"Tell me all that happened on the day that you heard that Mr. Rewse was ill—Tuesday week."

"In the mornin', sor, 'twas much as ord'nary. I was over there at half afther sivin, an' 'twas half an hour afther that I cud hear the jintleman dhressin'. They tuk their breakfast—though Mr. Rewse's was a small wan. It was half afther nine that Mr. Main wint off walkin' to Cullanin, Mr. Rewse stayin' in, havin' letthers to write. Half an hour later I came away mesilf. Later than that (it was nigh elivin) I wint across for a pail from the yard, an' then, through the windy as I passed I saw the dear young jintleman sittin' writin' at the table calm an' peaceful—an' saw him no more in this warrl'."

"And after that?"

"Afther that, sor, I came back wid the pail, an' saw nor heard no more till two o'clock, whin Mr. Main came back from Cullanin."

"Did you see him as he came back?"

"That I did, sor, as I stud there nailin' the fence where the pig bruk ut. I'd been there an' had me of down the road lookin' for him an hour past, expectin' he might be bringin' somethin' for me to cook for their dinner. An' more by token he gave me the toime from his watch, set by the Town Hall clock."

"And was it two o'clock?"

"It was that to the sthroke, an' me own ould clock was right too whin I wint to set ut. An'—"

"One moment; may I see your clock?"

Mrs. Hurley turned and shut an open door which had concealed an old hanging clock. Hewitt produced his watch and compared the time. "Still right I see, Mrs. Hurley," he said; "your clock, keeps excellent time."

"It does that, sor, an' nivir more than claned twice by Rafferty since me own father (rest his soul!) lift ut here. 'Tis no bad clock, as Mr. Rewse himsilf said oft an' again; an' I always kape ut by the Town Hall toime. But as I was sayin', Mr. Main came back an' gave me the toime; thin he wint sthraight to his house, an' no more av him I saw

"Mrs. Hurley." he said. "your clock keeps excellent time."

till may be half afther three."

"And then?"

"An' thin, sor, he came across in a sad Lakin', wid a letther. 'Take ut,' sez he, 'an' have ut posted at Cullanin by the first that can get there. Mr. Rewse has the sickness on him awful bad,' he sez, 'an' ye must not be near the place or ye'll take ut. I have him to bed, an' his clothes I shall burn behin' the cottage,' sez he, 'so if ye see smoke ye'll know what ut is. There'll be no docthor wanted. I'm wan mesilf, an' I'll do all for 'um. An' sure I knew him for a docthor ivir since he come. 'The cottage ye shall not come near,' he sez, 'till ut's over one way or another, an' yez can lave whativir av food an' dhrink we want mid-betwixt the houses an' go back, an' I'll come and fetch ut. But have the letther posted,' he sez, 'at wanst. 'Tis not contagious,' he sez, 'bein' as I've dishinfected it mesilf. But kape yez away from the cottage.' An' I kept."

"And then did he go back to the cottage at once?"

"He did that, sor, an' a sore stew was he in to all seemin'—white as paper, and much need, too, the murtherin' Scutt! An' him always so much the jintleman an' all. Well I saw no more av him that day. Next day he laves another letther wid the dirtily' plates there mid-betwixt the houses, an' shouts for ut to be posted. 'Twas for the poor young jintleman's mother, sure, as was the other wan. An' the day afther there was another letther, an' wan for the undhertaker, too, for he tells me it's all over, an' he's dead. An' they buried him next day followin'."

"So that from the time you went for the pail and saw Mr. Rewse writing, till after the funeral, you were never at the cottage at all?"

"Nivir, sor; an' can ye blame me? Wid children an' Terence himself sick wid bronchitis in this house?"

"Of course, of course, you did quite right—indeed you only obeyed orders. But now think; do you remember on any one of those three days hearing a shot, or any other unusual noise in the cottage?"

"Nivir at all, sor. 'Tis that I've been thryin' to bring to mind these four days. Such may have been, but not that I heard."

"After you went for the pail, and before Mr. Main returned to the house, did Mr. Rewse leave the cottage at all, or might he have done so?"

"He did not lave at all, to my knowledge. Sure he *might* have gone an' he might have come back widout my knowin'. But see him I did not."

"Thank you, Mrs. Hurley. I think we'll go across to the cottage now. If any people come will you send them after us? I suppose a policeman is there?"

"He is, sor. An' the serjint is not far away. They've been in chyarge since Mr. Bowyer wint away last—but shlapin' here."

Hewitt and Mr. Bowyer walked towards the cottage. "Did you notice," said Mr. Bowyer, "that the woman saw Rewse *writing letters?* Now what were those letters, and where are they? He has no correspondents that I know of but his mother and sister, and they heard nothing from him. Is this something else?—some other plot? There is something very deep here."

"Yes," Hewitt replied thoughtfully, "I think our inquiries may take us deeper than we have expected; and in the matter of those letters— yes, I think they may he near the kernel of the mystery."

Here they arrived at the cottage—an uncommonly substantial structure for the district. It was square, of plain, solid brick, with a slated roof. On the patch of ground behind it there were still signs of the fires wherein Main had burnt Rewse's clothes and other belongings. And sitting on the window-sill in front was a big member of the R.I.C., soldierly and broad, who rose as they came and saluted Mr. Bowyer.

"Good-day, constable," Mr. Bowyer said. "I hope nothing has been disturbed?"

"Not a shtick, sor. Nobody's as much as gone in."

"Have any of the windows been opened or shut?" Hewitt asked.

"This wan was, sor," the policeman said, indicating the one behind him, "when they took away the corrpse, an' so was the next round the corrner. 'Tis the bedroom windier they are, an' they opened thim to give ut a bit av air. The other windy behin'—sittin'-room windy—has not been opened."

"Very well," Hewitt answered, "we'll take a look at that unopened window from the inside."

The door was opened and they passed inside. There was a small lobby, and on the left of this was the bedroom with two single beds. The only other room of consequence was the sitting-room, the cottage consisting merely of these, a small scullery and a narrow closet used as a bathroom, wedged between the bedroom and the sitting-room. They made for the single window of the sitting-room at the back. It was an ordinary sash window, and was shut, but the catch was not fastened. Hewitt examined the catch, drawing Mr. Bowyer's attention to a bright scratch on the grimy brass. "See," he said, "that nick in the catch exactly corresponds with the narrow space between the two frames of the window. And look"—he lifted the bottom sash a little as he spoke—"there is the mark of a knife on the frame of the top sash. Somebody has come in by that window, forcing the catch with a knife."

"Yes, yes!" cried Mr. Bowyer, greatly excited, "and he has gone out that way too, else why is the window shut and the catch not fastened? Why should he do that? What in the world does *this* thing mean?"

Before Hewitt could reply the constable put his head into the room and announced that one Larry Shanahan was at the door, and had been promised half-a-sovereign.

"One of the men who heard a shot," Hewitt said to Mr. Bowyer. "Bring him in, constable."

The constable brought in Larry Shanahan, and Larry Shanahan brought in a strong smell of whisky. He was an extremely ragged person, with only one eye, which caused him to hold his head aside as he regarded Hewitt, much as a parrot does. On his face sun-scorched brown and fiery red struggled for mastery, and his voice was none of the clearest. He held his hat against his stomach with one hand and with the other pulled his forelock.

"An' which is the honourable jintleman," he said, "as do be burrnin' to prisint me wid a bit o' goold?"

"Here I am," said Hewitt, jingling money in his pocket, "and here is the half-sovereign. It's only waiting where it is till you have answered a few questions. They say you heard a shot fired hereabout?

"Faith, an' that I did, sor. 'Twas a shot in this house, indade, no other."

"And when was it?"

"Sure, 'twas in the afthernoon."

"But on what day?"

"Last Tuesday sivin-noight, sor, as I know by rayson av Ballyshiel fair that I wint to."

"Tell me all about it."

"I will, sor. 'Twas pigs I was dhrivin' that day, sor, to Ballyshiel fair from just beyond Cullanin, sor, I dhropped in wid Danny Mulcahy, that intentioned thravellin' the same way, an' while we tuk a thrifle av a dhrink in comes Dennis Grady, that was to go to Ballyshiel similarously. An' so we had another thrifle av a dhrink, or maybe a thrifle more, an' we wint togedther, passin' this way, sor, as ye may not know, bein' likely a shtranger. Well, sor, ut was as we were just forninst this place that there came a divil av a bang that makes us shtop simultaneous. 'What's that?' sez Dan. ''Tis a gunshot,' sez I, an' 'tis in the brick house too.' 'That is so,' sez Dennis; 'nowhere else.' And we lukt at wan

"An' which is the honourable gentleman as
do be burnin' to prisint me wid a bit o' goold?"

388

another. 'An' what'll we do?' sez I. 'What would yez?' sez Dan; "Tis none av our business.' 'That is so,' sez Dennis again, and we wint on. Ut was quare, maybe, but it might aisily be wan av the jiritlemen emptyin' a barr'l out o' windy or what not. An'—an' so—an' so Mr. Shanahan scratched his ear, an' so—we wint."

"And do you know at what time this was?"

Larry Shanahan ceased scratching, and seized his ear between thumb and forefinger, gazing severely at the floor with his one eye as he did so, plunged in computation. "Sure," he said, "'twould be— 'twould be—let's see—'twould be—" he looked up, "'twould be half-past two maybe, or maybe a thrifle nearer three."

"And Main was in the place all the time after two," Mr. Bowyer said, bringing down his fist on his open hand. "That finishes it. We've nailed him to the minute."

"Had you a watch with you?" asked Hewitt.

"Divil of a watch in the company, sor. I made an internal calcula-tion. 'Tis foive mile from Cullanin, and we never lift till near half an hour after the Town Hall clock had struck twelve. 'Twould take us two hours and a thrifle more, considherin' the pigs, an' the rough road, an' the distance, an' an' the thrifle of dhrink." His eye rolled slyly as he said it. "That was my calculation, sor."

Here the constable appeared with two more men. Each had the usual number of eyes, but in other respects they were very good copies of Mr. Shanahan. They were both ragged, and neither bore any violent likeness to a teetotaller. "Dan Mulcahy and Dennis Grady," announced the constable.

Mr. Dan Mulcahy's tale was of a piece with Mr. Larry Shanahan's, and Mr. Dennis Grady's was the same. They had all heard the shot it was plain. What Dan had said to Dennis and what Dennis had said to Larry mattered little. Also they were all agreed that the day was Tuesday by token of the fair. But as to the time of day there arose a disagreement.

"'Twas nigh soon afther wan o'clock," said Dan Mulcahy.

"Soon afther wan!" exclaimed Larry Shanahan with scorn. "Soon afther your grandmother's pig! 'Twas half afther two at laste. Ut sthruck twelve nigh half an hour before we lift Cullanin. Why, yez heard ut!"

"That I did not. Ut sthruck eleven, an' we wint in foive minutes."

"What fool-talk ye shpake Dan Mulcahy. 'Twas twelve sthruck; I counted ut."

"Thin ye counted wrong. I counted ut, an' 'twas elivin."

"Yez nayther av yez right," interposed Dennis Grady. "'Twas not elivin when we lift; 'twas not, be the mother av Moses!"

"I wondher at ye, Dennis Grady; ye must have been dhrunk as a Kerry cow," and both Mulcahy and Shanahan turned upon the obstinate Grady, and the dispute waxed clamorous till Hewitt stopped it.

"Come, come," he said, "never mind the time then. Settle that between you after you've gone. Does either of you remember—not calculate, you know, but *remember*—the time you got to Ballyshiel?— the actual time by a clock—not a guess."

Not one of the three had looked at a clock at Ballyshiel.

"Do you remember anything about coming home again?"

They did not. They looked furtively at one another and presently broke into a grin.

"Ah! I see how *that* was," Hewitt said good-humouredly. "That's all now, I think. Come, it's ten shillings each, I think." And he handed over the money. The men touched their forelocks again, stowed away the money and prepared to depart. As they went Larry Shanahan stepped mysteriously back again and said in a whisper, "Maybe the jintlemen wud like me to kiss the book on ut? An' as to the toime—"

"Oh, no thank you," Hewitt laughed. "We take your word for it Mr. Shanahan." And Mr. Shanahan pulled his forelock again and vanished.

"There's nothing but confusion to be got from them," Mr. Bowyer remarked testily. "It's a mere waste of time."

"No, no, not a waste of time," Hewitt replied, "nor a waste of money. One thing is made pretty plain. That is that the shot was fired on Tuesday. Mrs. Hurley never noticed the report, but these three men were close by, and there is no doubt that they heard it. It's the only single thing they agree about at all. They contradict one another over everything else, but they agree completely in that. Of course I wish we could have got the exact time; but that can't be helped. As it is it is rather fortunate that they disagreed so entirely. Two of them are certainly wrong, and perhaps all three. In any case it wouldn't have been safe to trust to mere computation of time by three men just beginning to get drunk, who had no particular reason for remembering. But if by any chance they had agreed on the time we might have been led into a wrong track altogether by taking the thing as fact.

"But a gunshot is not such a doubtful thing. When three independent witnesses hear a gunshot together there can be little doubt that a shot has been fired. Now I think you'd better sit down. Perhaps you can find something to read. I'm about to make a very minute examination of this place, and it will probably bore you if you've nothing else to do."

But Mr. Bowyer would think of nothing but the business in hand. "I don't understand that window," he said, shaking his finger towards it as he spoke. "Not at all. Why should Main want to get in and out by a window? He wasn't a stranger."

Hewitt began a most careful inspection of the whole surface of floor, ceiling, walls and furniture of the sitting-room. At the fireplace he stooped and lifted with great care a few sheets of charred paper from the grate. These he put on the window-ledge. "Will you just bring over that little screen," he asked, "to keep the draught from this burnt paper? Thank you. It looks like letter paper, and thick letter paper, since the ashes are very little broken. The weather has been fine, and there has been no fire in that grate for a long time. These papers have been carefully burned with a match or a candle."

"Ah! perhaps the letters poor young Rewse was writing in the morning. But what can they tell us?"

"Perhaps nothing—perhaps a great deal." Hewitt was examining the cinders keenly, holding the surface sideways to the light. "Come," he said, "see if I can guess Rewse's address in London. 17 Mountjoy Gardens, Hampstead. Is that it?"

"Yes. Is it there? Can you read it? Show me." Mr. Bowyer hurried across the room, eager and excited.

"You can sometimes read words on charred paper," Hewitt replied, "as you may have noticed. This has curled and crinkled rather too much in the burning, but it is plainly notepaper with an embossed heading, which stands out rather clearly. He has evidently brought some notepaper with him from home in his trunk. See, you can just see the ink lines crossing out the address; but there's little else. At the beginning of the letter there is 'My d——' then a gap, and then the last stroke of 'M' and the rest of the word 'mother.' 'My dear Mother,' or 'My dearest Mother' evidently. Something follows too in the same line, but that is unreadable. 'My dear Mother and Sister' perhaps. After that there is nothing recognisable. The first letter looks rather like 'W,' but even that is indistinct. It seems to be a longish letter—several sheets, but they are stuck together in the charring. Perhaps more than one letter."

"The thing is plain," Mr. Bowyer said. "The poor lad was writing home, and perhaps to other places, and Main, after his crime, burned the letters, because they would have stultified his own with the lying tale about smallpox."

Hewitt said nothing, but resumed his general search. He passed his hand rapidly over every inch of the surface of everything in the room. Then he entered the bedroom and began an inspection of the same sort there. There were two beds, one at each end of the room, and each inch of each piece of bed linen passed rapidly under his sharp eye. After the bedroom he betook himself to the little bath-room, and then to the scullery. Finally, he went outside and examined every board of a close fence that stood a few feet from the sitting-room window, and the brick-paved path lying between.

When it was all over he returned to Mr. Bowyer. "Here is a strange thing," he said. "The shot passed clean through Rewse's body, striking no bones, and meeting no solid resistance. It was a good-sized bullet, as Dr. O'Reilly testifies, and therefore must have had a large charge of powder behind it in the cartridge. After emerging from Rewse's back it *must* have struck something else in this confined place. Yet on nowhere—ceiling, floor, wall nor furniture—can I find the mark of a bullet nor the bullet itself."

"The bullet itself Main might easily have got rid of."

"Yes, but not the mark. Indeed, the bullet would scarcely be easy to get at if it had struck anything I have seen about here; it would have buried itself. Just look round now. Where could a bullet strike in this place without leaving its mark?"

Mr. Bowyer looked round. "Well, no," he said, "nowhere. Unless the window was open and it went out that way."

"Then it must have hit the fence or the brick paving between, and there is no sign of a bullet there," Hewitt replied. "Push the sash as high as you please, the shot couldn't have passed *over* the fence without hitting the window first. As to the bedroom windows, that's impossible. Mr. Shanahan and his friends would not only have heard the shot, they would have seen it—which they didn't."

"Then what's the meaning of it?"

"The meaning of it is simply this: either Rewse was shot somewhere else and his body brought here afterwards, or the article, whatever it was, that the bullet struck must have been taken away."

"Yes, of course. It's just another piece of evidence destroyed by Main, that's all. Every step we go we see the diabolical completeness of his plans. But now every piece of evidence missing only tells the more against him. The body alone condemns him past all redemption."

Hewitt was gazing about the room thoughtfully. "I think we'll have Mrs. Hurley over here," he said; "she should tell us if anything is missing. Constable, will you ask Mrs. Hurley to step over here?"

Mrs. Hurley came at once and was brought into the sitting-room. "Just look about you, Mrs. Hurley," Hewitt said, "in this room and everywhere else, and tell me if anything is missing that you can remember was here on the morning of the day you last saw Mr. Rewse."

She looked thoughtfully up and down the room. "Sure, sor," she said, "'tis all there as ord'nary." Her eyes rested on the mantelpiece and she added at once, "Except the clock, indade."

"Except the clock?"

"The clock ut is, sure. Ut stud on that same mantelpiece on that mornin' as ut always did."

"What sort of clock was it?"

"Just a plain round wan wid a metal case—an American clock they said ut was. But ut kept nigh as good time as me own."

"It *did* keep good time, you say?"

"Faith an' ut did, sor. Mine an' this ran together for weeks wid nivir a minute betune thim."

"Thank you, Mrs. Hurley, thank you; that will do," Hewitt exclaimed, with something of excitement in his voice. He turned to Mr. Bowyer. "We must find that clock," he said. "And there's the pistol; nothing has been seen of that. Come, help me search. Look for a loose board."

"But he'll have taken them away with him, probably."

"The pistol perhaps—althought that isn't likely. The clock, no. It's evidence, man, evidence!" Hewitt darted outside and walked hurriedly round the cottage, looking this way and that about the country adjacent.

Presently he returned. "No," he said, "I think it's more likely in the house." He stood for a moment and thought. Then he made for the fireplace and flung the fender across the floor. All round the hearthstone an open crack extended. "See there!" he exclaimed as he pointed to it. He took the tongs, and with one leg levered the stone up till he could seize it in his fingers. Then he dragged it out and pushed it across the linoleum that covered the floor. In the space beneath lay a large revolver and a common American round nickel-plated clock. "See here!" he cried, "see here!" and he rose and placed the articles on the mantel-piece. The glass before the clock-face was smashed to atoms, and there was a gaping rent in the face itself. For a few seconds

393

Hewitt regarded it as it stood, and then he turned to Mr. Bowyer. "Mr. Bowyer," he said, "we have done Mr. Stanley Main a sad injustice. Poor young Rewse committed suicide. There is proof undeniable," and he pointed to the clock.

"Proof? How? Where? Nonsense, man. Pooh! Ridiculous! If Rewse committed suicide, why should Main go to all that trouble and tell all those lies to prove that he died of smallpox? More even than that, what has he run away for?"

"I'll tell you, Mr. Bowyer, in a moment. But first as to this clock. Remember, Main set his watch by the Cullanin Town Hall clock, and Mrs. Hurley's clock agreed exactly. That we have proved ourselves today by my own watch. Mrs. Hurley's clock still agrees. *This* clock was always kept in time with Mrs. Hurley's. Main returned at two exactly. Look at the time by that clock—the time when the bullet crashed into and stopped it."

The time was three minutes to one.

Hewitt took the clock, unscrewed the winder and quickly stripped off the back, exposing the works. "See," he said, "the bullet is lodged firmly among the wheels, and has been torn into snags and strips by the impact. The wheels themselves are ruined altogether. The central axle which carries the hands is bent. See there! Neither hand will move in the slightest. That bullet struck the axle and fixed those hands immovably at the moment of time when Algernon Rewse died. Look at the mainspring. It is less than half rim out. Proof that the clock was going when the shot struck it. Main left Rewse alive and well at half-past nine. He did not return till two—when Rewse had been dead more than an hour."

"But then, hang it all! How about the lies, and the false certificate, and the bolting?"

"Let me tell you the whole tale, Mr. Bowyer, as I conjecture it to have been. Poor young Rewse was, as you told me, in a bad state of health—thoroughly run down, I think you said. You said something of his engagement and the death of the lady. This pointed clearly to a nervous—a mental upset. Very well. He broods, and so forth. He must go away and find change of scene and occupation. His intimate friend Main brings him here. The holiday has its good effect perhaps, at first, but after a while it gets monotonous, and brooding sets in again. I do not know whether or not you happen to know it, but it is a fact that four-fifths of all persons suffering from melancholia have suicidal tendencies. This may never have been suspected by Main, who otherwise might not have left him so long alone.

"At any rate he *is* left alone, and he takes the opportunity. He writes a note to Main and a long letter to his mother—an awful, heart-breaking letter, with a terrible picture of the mental agony wherein he was to die—perhaps with a tincture of religious mania in it, and prophesying merited hell for himself in the hereafter. This done, he simply stands up from this table, at which he has been writing, and with his back to the fire-place shoots himself. There he lies till Main returns an hour later. Main finds the door shut and nobody answers his knock. He goes round to the sitting-room window, looks through, and perhaps he sees the body.

"Anyway he pushes back the catch with his knife, opens the window and gets in, and *then* he sees. He is completely knocked out of time. The thing is terrible. What shall he—what can he do? Poor Rewse's mother and sister dote on him, and his mother is an invalid—heart disease. To let her see that awful letter would be to kill her. He burns the letter, also the note to himself. Then an idea strikes him. Even without the letter the news of her boy's suicide will probably kill the poor old lady. Can she be prevented hearing of it? Of his death she must know—that's inevitable. But as to the manner? Would it not be possible to concoct some kind lie? And then the opportunities of the situation occur to him. Nobody but himself knows of it. He is a medical man, fully qualified, and empowered to give certificates of death.

"More, there is an epidemic of smallpox in the neighbourhood. What easier, with a little management, than to call the death one by smallpox? Nobody would be anxious to examine too closely the corpse of a smallpox patient. He decides that he will do it. He writes the letter to Mrs. Rewse announcing that her son has the disease, and he forbids Mrs. Hurley to come near the place for fear of infection. He cleans the floor—it is linoleum here, you see, and the stains were fresh—burns the clothes, cleans and stops the wound. At every turn his medical knowledge is of use. He puts the smashed clock and the pistol out of sight under the hearth. In a word he carries out the whole thing rather cleverly, and a terrible few days he must have passed. It never strikes him that he has dug a frightful pit for his own feet. You are suspicious, and you come across.

"In a perhaps rather peremptory manner You tell him how suspicious his conduct has been. And then a sense of his terrible position comes upon him like a thunderclap. He sees it all. He has deliberately of his own motion destroyed every evidence of the suicide. There

He took the tongs, and with one leg levered the stone up.

is no evidence in the world that Rewse did not die a natural death, except the body, and that you are going to dig up. He sees now (you remind him of it in fact) that *he* is the one man alive who can profit by Rewse's death. And there is the shot body, and there is the false death certificate, and there are the lying letters, and the tales to the neighbours and everything. He has himself destroyed everything that proves suicide. All that remains points to a foul murder and to him as the murderer. Can you wonder at his complete breakdown and his flight? What else in the world could the poor fellow do?"

"Well well—yes, yes," Mr. Bowyer replied thoughtfully, "it seems very plausible of course. But still, look at probabilities, my dear sir, look at probabilities."

"No, but look at *possibilities*. There is that clock. Get over it if you can. Was there ever a more insurmountable alibi? Could Main possibly be here shooting Rewse and half way between here and Cullanin at the same time? Remember, Mrs. Hurley saw him come back at two, and she had been watching for an hour, and could see more than half a mile up the road."

"Well, yes, I suppose you're right. And what must we do now?"

"Bring Main back. I think we should advertise to begin with. Say, 'Rewse is proved to have died over an hour before you came. All safe.

Your evidence is wanted,' or something of that sort. And we must set the telegraph going. The police already are looking for him, no doubt. Meanwhile I will look here for a clue myself."

The advertisement was successful in two days. Indeed, Main afterwards said that he was at the time, once the first terror was over, in doubt whether or not it would be best to go back and face the thing out, trusting to his innocence. He could not venture home for money, nor to his bank, for fear of the police. He chanced, upon the advertisement as he searched the paper for news of the case, and that decided him. His explanation of the matter was precisely as Hewitt had expected. His only thought till Mr. Bowyer first arrived at the cottage had been to smother the real facts and to spare the feelings of Mrs. Rewse and her daughter, and it was not till that gentleman put them so plainly before him that he in the least realised the dangers of his position. That his fears for Mrs. Rewse were only too well grounded was proved by events, for the poor old lady only survived her son by a month.

These events took place some little while ago, as may be gathered from the fact that Miss Rewse has now been Mrs. Stanley Main for nearly three years.

THE CASE OF THE WARD LANE TABERNACLE

1.

Among the few personal friendships that Martin Hewitt has allowed himself to make there is one for an eccentric but very excellent old lady named Mrs. Mallett. She must be more than seventy now, but she is of robust and active, not to say masculine, habits, and her relations with Hewitt are irregular and curious. He may not see her for many weeks, perhaps for months, until one day she will appear in the office, push Kerrett (who knows better than to attempt to stop her) into the inner room, and salute Hewitt with a shake of the hand and a savage glare of the eye which would appal a stranger, but which is quite amiably meant. As for myself, it was long ere I could find any resource but instant retreat before her gaze, though we are on terms of moderate toleration now.

After her first glare she sits in the chair by the window and directs her glance at Hewitt's small gas grill and kettle in the fireplace—a glance which Hewitt, with all expedition, translates into tea. Slightly mollified by the tea, Mrs. Mallett condescends to remark in tones of tragic truculence, on passing matters of conventional interest—the weather, the influenza, her own health, Hewitt's health, and so forth, any reply of Hewitt's being commonly received with either disregard or contempt.

In half an hour's time or so she leaves the office with a stern command to Hewitt to attend at her house and drink tea on a day and at a time named—a command which Hewitt obediently fulfils, when he passes through a similarly exhilarating experience in Mrs. Mallett's back drawing-room at her little freehold house in Fulham. Altogether Mrs. Mallett, to a stranger, is a singularly uninviting personality, and indeed, except Hewitt, who has learnt to appreciate her hidden good qualities, I doubt if she has a friend in the world. Her studiously concealed charities are a matter of as much amusement as gratification to Hewitt, who naturally, in the course of his peculiar profession, comes across many sad examples of poverty and suffering, commonly among the decent sort, who hide their troubles from strangers' eyes and suffer in secret. When such a case is in his mind it is Hewitt's practice to inform Mrs. Mallett of it at one of the tea ceremonies. Mrs. Mallett

Slightly mollified by the tea...

receives the story with snorts of incredulity and scorn but takes care, while expressing the most callous disregard and contempt of the troubles of the sufferers, to ascertain casually their names and addresses; twenty-four hours after which Hewitt need only make a visit to find their difficulties in some mysterious way alleviated.

Mrs. Mallett never had any children, and was early left a widow. Her appearance, for some reason or another, commonly leads strangers to believe her an old maid. She lives in her little detached house with its square piece of ground, attended by a house-keeper older than herself and one maid-servant. She lost her only sister by death soon after the events I am about to set down, and now has, I believe, no relations in the world. It was also soon after these events that her present housekeeper first came to her in place of an older and very deaf woman, quite useless, who had been with her before. I believe she is moderately rich, and that one or two charities will benefit considerably at her death; also I should be far from astonished to find Hewitt's own name in her will, though this is no more than idle conjecture.

The one possession to which she clings with all her soul—her one pride and treasure—is her great-uncle Joseph's snuff-box, the lid of which she steadfastly believes to be made of a piece of Noah's original ark discovered on the top of Mount Ararat by some intrepid explorer of vague identity about a hundred years ago. This is her one weakness, and woe to the unhappy creature who dares hint a suggestion that possibly the wood of the ark rotted away to nothing a few thousand years before her great-uncle Joseph ever took snuff. I believe he would be bodily assaulted. The box is brought for Hewitt's admiration at every tea ceremony at Fulham, when Hewitt handles it reverently and expresses as much astonishment and interest as if he had never seen or heard of it before.

It is on these occasions only that Mrs. Mallett's customary stiffness relaxes. The sides of the box are of cedar of Lebanon, she explains (which very possibly they are), and the gold mountings were worked up from spade guineas (which one can believe without undue strain on the reason). And it is usually these times, when the old lady softens under the combined influence of tea and uncle Joseph's snuff-box, that Hewitt seizes to lead up to his hint of some starving governess or distressed clerk, with the full confidence that the more savagely the story is received the better will the poor people be treated as soon as he turns his back.

It was her jealous care of uncle Joseph's snuff-box that first brought Mrs. Mallett into contact with Martin Hewitt, and the occasion, though not perhaps testing his acuteness to the extent that some did, was nevertheless one of the most curious and fantastic on which he has ever been engaged She was then some ten or twelve years younger than she is now, but Hewitt assures me she looked exactly the same; that is to say, she was harsh, angular, and seemed little more than fifty years of age. It was before the time of Kerrett, and another youth occupied the outer office. Hewitt sat late one afternoon with his door ajar when he heard a stranger enter the outer office, and a voice, which he afterwards knew well as Mrs. Mallett's, ask "Is Mr. Martin Hewitt in?"

"Yes, ma'am, I think so. If you will write your name and——"

"Is he in there?" And with three strides Mrs. Mallett was at the inner door and stood before Hewitt himself, while the routed office-lad stared helplessly in the rear.

"Mr. Hewitt," Mrs. Mallet said, "I have come to put an affair into your hands, which I shall require to be attended to at once."

Hewitt was surprised, but he bowed politely, and said, with some suspicion of a hint in his tone, "Yes—I rather supposed you were in a hurry."

She glanced quickly in Hewitt's face and went on: "I am not accustomed to needless ceremony, Mr. Hewitt. My name is Mallett—Mrs. Mallett—and here is my card. I have come to consult you on a matter of great annoyance and some danger to myself. The fact is I am being watched and followed by a number of persons."

Hewitt's gaze was steadfast, but he reflected that possibly this curious woman was a lunatic, the delusion of being watched and followed by unknown people being perhaps the most common of all; also it was no unusual thing to have a lunatic visit the office with just such a complaint. So he only said soothingly, "Indeed? That must be very annoying."

"Yes, yes, the annoyance is bad enough perhaps," she answered shortly, "but I am chiefly concerned about my great-uncle Joseph's snuff-box."

This utterance sounded a trifle more insane than the other, so Hewitt answered, a little more soothingly still: "Ah, of course. A very important thing, the snuff-box, no doubt."

"It is, Mr. Hewitt—it is important, as I think you will admit when you have seen it. Here it is," and she produced from a small handbag the article that Hewitt was destined so often again to see and affect an interest in. "You may be incredulous, Mr. Hewitt, but it is nevertheless a fact that the lid of this snuff-box is made of the wood of the original ark that rested on Mount Ararat."

She handed the box to Hewitt, who murmured, "Indeed! Very interesting—very wonderful, really," and returned it to the lady immediately.

"That, Mr. Hewitt, was the property of my great-uncle, Joseph Simpson, who once had the honour of shaking hands with his late Majesty King George the Fourth. The box was presented to my uncle by——," and then Mrs. Mallett plunged into the whole history and adventures of the box, in the formula wherewith Hewitt subsequently became so well acquainted, and which need not be here set out in detail. When the box had been properly honoured Mrs. Mallett proceeded with her business.

"I am convinced, Mr. Hewitt," she said, "that systematic attempts are being made to rob me of this snuff-box. I am not a nervous or weak-minded woman, or perhaps I might have sought your assistance before. The watching and following of myself I might have disregarded, but when it comes to burglary I think it is time to do something."

"Certainly," Hewitt agreed.

"Well, I have been pestered with demands for the box for some time past. I have here some of the letters which I have received, and I am sure I know at whose instigation they were sent." She placed on the table a handful of papers of various sizes, which Hewitt examined one after another. They were mostly in the same handwriting, and all were unsigned. Everyone was couched in a fanatically toned imitation of scriptural diction, and all sorts of threats were expressed with many emphatic underlinings. The spelling was not of the best, the writing was mostly uncouth, and the grammar was in ill shape in many places, the "thous" and "thees" and their accompanying verbs falling over each other disastrously. The purport of the messages was rather vaguely expressed, but all seemed to make a demand for the restoration of some article held in extreme veneration. This was alluded to in many figurative ways as the "token of life," the "seal of the woman," and so forth, and sometimes Mrs. Mallett was requested to restore it to the "ark of the covenant." One of the least vague of these singular documents ran thus:—

Thou of no faith put the bond of the woman clothed with the sun on the stoan sete in thy back garden this night or thy blood beest on your own hed. Give it back to us the five righteous only in this citty, give us that what saves the faithful when the erth is swalloed up.

Hewitt read over these fantastic missives one by one till he began to suspect that his client, mad or not, certainly corresponded with mad Quakers. Then he said, "Yes, Mrs. Mallett, these are most extraordinary letters. Are there any more of them?"

"Bless the man, yes, there were a lot that I burnt. All the same crack-brained sort of thing."

"They are mostly in one handwriting," Hewitt said, "though some are in another. But I confess I don't see any very direct reference to the snuff-box."

"Oh, but it's the only thing they can mean," Mrs. Mallett replied with great positiveness. "Why, he wanted me to sell it him; and last night my house was broken into in my absence and everything ransacked and turned over, but not a thing was taken. Why? Because I had the box with me at my sister's; and this is the only sacred relic in my possession. And what saved the faithful when the world was swallowed up? Why, the ark of course." The old lady's manner was odd, but notwithstanding the bizarre and disjointed character of her complaint Hewitt had now had time to observe that she had none of the unmistakable signs of the lunatic. Her eye was steady and clear, and she had none of the restless habits of the mentally deranged. Even at that time Hewitt had met with curious adventures enough to teach him not to be astonished at a new one, and now he set himself seriously to get at his client's case in full order and completeness.

"Come, Mrs. Mallett," he said, "I am a stranger, and I can never understand your case till I have it, not as it presents itself to your mind, in the order of importance of events, but in the exact order in which they happened. You had a great-uncle, I understand, living in the early part of the century, who left you at his death the snuff-box which you value so highly. Now you suspect that somebody is attempting to extort or steal it from you. Tell me as clearly and simply as you can whom you suspect and the whole story of the attempts."

"That's just what I'm coming to," the old lady answered, rather pettishly. "My uncle Joseph had an old housekeeper, who of course knew all about the snuff-box, and it is her son Reuben Penner who is trying to get it from me. The old woman was half crazy with one extraordinary religious superstition and another, and her son seems to be just the same. My great-uncle was a man of strong common-sense and a churchman (though he did think he could write plays), and if it hadn't been for his restraint I believe—that is I have been told—Mrs. Penner would have gone clean demented with religious mania. Well, she died in course of time, and my great-uncle died sometime after, leaving me the most important thing in his possession (I allude to the snuff-box of course), a good bit of property, and a tin box full of his worthless manuscript. I became a widow at twenty-six, and since then I have lived very quietly in my present house in Fulham.

"A couple of years ago I received a visit from Reuben Penner. I didn't recognise him, which wasn't wonderful, since I hadn't seen him for thirty years or more. He is well over fifty now, a large heavy-faced man with uncommonly wild eyes for a greengrocer—which is what he is, though he dresses very well, considering. He was quite respectful at first, and very awkward in his manner. He took a little time to get his courage, and then he began questioning me about my religious feelings. Well, Mr. Hewitt, I am not the sort of person to stand a lecture from a junior and an inferior, whatever my religious opinions may be, and I pretty soon made him realise it. But somehow he persevered. He wanted to know if I would go to some place of worship that he called his 'Tabernacle.' I asked him who was the pastor. He said himself. I asked him how many members of the congregation there were, and (the man was as solemn as an owl.)

"I assure you, Mr. Hewitt) he actually said five! I kept my countenance and asked why such a small number couldn't attend church, or at any rate attach itself to some decent Dissenting chapel. And then the man burst out; mad—mad as a hatter. He was as incoherent as such people usually are, but as far as I could make out he talked, among a lot of other things, of some imaginary woman—a woman standing on the moon and driven into a wilderness on the wings of an eagle. The man was so madly possessed of his fancies that I assure you for a while he almost ceased to look ridiculous. He was so earnest in his rant. But I soon cut him short.

"It's best to be severe with these people—it's the only chance of bringing them to their senses. 'Reuben Penner,' I said, 'shut up! Your mother was a very decent person in her way, I believe, but she was half a lunatic with her superstitious notions, and you're a bigger fool than she was. Imagine a grown man, and of your age, coming and asking me, of all people in the world, to leave my church and make another fool in a congregation of five, with you to rave at me about women in the moon! Go away and look after your greengrocery, and go to church or chapel like a sensible man. Go away and don't play the fool any longer; I won't hear another word!'

"When I talk like this I am usually attended to, and in this case

"Reuben Penner," I said, "shut up!"

Penner went away with scarcely another word. I saw nothing of him for about a month or six weeks and then he came and spoke to me as I was cutting roses in my front garden. This time he talked—to begin with, at least—more sensibly. 'Mrs. Mallett,' he said, 'you have in your keeping a very sacred relic.'

"'I have,' I said, 'left me by my great-uncle Joseph. And what then?'

"'Well'—he hummed and hawed a little—'I wanted to ask if you might be disposed to part with it.'

"'What?' I said, dropping my scissors—'sell it?'

"'Well, yes,' he answered, putting on as bold a face as he could.

"The notion of selling my uncle Joseph's snuff-box in any possible circumstances almost made me speechless. 'What!' I repeated. 'Sell it?—sell it? It would be a sinful sacrilege!'

"His face quite brightened when I said this, and he replied, 'Yes, of course it would; I think so myself, ma'am; but I fancied you thought otherwise. In that case, ma'am, not being a believer yourself, I'm sure you would consider it a graceful and a pious act to present it to my little Tabernacle, where it would be properly valued. And it having been my mother's property——'

"He got no further. I am not a woman to be trifled with, Mr. Hewitt, and I believe I beat him out of the garden with my basket. I was so infuriated I can scarcely remember what I did. The suggestion

404

"I am not a woman to be trifled with."

that I should sell my uncle Joseph's snuff-box to a greengrocer was bad enough; the request that I should actually give it to his 'Tabernacle' was infinitely worse. But to claim that it had belonged to his mother—well I don't know how it strikes you, Mr. Hewitt, but to me it seemed the last insult possible."

"Shocking, shocking, of course," Hewitt said, since she seemed to expect a reply. "And he called you an unbeliever, too. But what happened after that?"

"After that he took care not to bother me personally again; but these wretched anonymous demands came in, with all sorts of darkly hinted threats as to the sin I was committing in keeping my own property. They didn't trouble me much. I put 'em in the fire as fast as they came, until I began to find I was being watched and followed, and then I kept them."

"Very sensible," Hewitt observed, "very sensible indeed to do that. But tell me as to these papers. Those you have here are nearly all in one handwriting, but some, as I have already said, are in another. Now before all this business, did you ever see Reuben Penner's handwriting?"

"No, never."

"Then you are not by any means sure that he has written any of these things?"

"But then who else could?"

"That of course is a thing to be found out. At present, at any rate, we know this: that if Penner has anything to do with these letters he is not alone, because of the second handwriting. Also we must not bind ourselves past other conviction that he wrote any one of them. By the way, I am assuming that they all arrived by post?"

"Yes, they did."

"But the envelopes are not here. Have you kept any of them?"

"I hardly know; there may be some at home. Is it important?"

"It may be; but those I can see at another time. Please go on."

"These things continued to arrive, as I have said, and I continued to burn them till I began to find myself watched and followed, and then I kept them. That was two or three months ago. It is a most unpleasant sensation, that of feeling that some unknown person is dogging your footsteps from corner to corner and observing all your movements for a purpose you are doubtful of. Once or twice I turned suddenly back, but I never could catch the creatures, of whom I am sure Penner was one."

"You saw these people, of course?"

"Well, yes, in a way—with the corner of my eye, you know. But it was mostly in the evening. It was a woman once, but several times I feel certain it was Penner. And once I saw a man come into my garden at the back in the night, and I feel quite sure that was Penner."

"Was that after you had this request to put the article demanded on the stone seat in the garden?"

"The same night. I sat up and watched from the bathroom window, expecting someone would come. It was a dark night, and the trees made it darker, but I could plainly see someone come quietly over the wall and go up to the seat."

"Could you distinguish his face?"

"No, it was too dark. But I feel sure it was Penner."

"Has Penner any decided peculiarity of form or gait?"

"No, he's just a big common sort of man. But I tell you I feel certain it was Penner."

"For any particular reason?"

"No, perhaps not. But who else could it have been? No, I'm very sure it must have been Penner."

Hewitt repressed a smile and went on. "Just so," he said. "And what happened then?"

"He went up to the seat, as I said, and looked at it, passing his hand over the top. Then I called out to him. I said if I found him on my premises again by day or night I'd give him in charge of the police. I assure you he got over the wall the second time a good deal quicker than the first. And then I went to bed, though I got a shocking cold in the head sitting at that open bathroom window. Nobody came about the place after that till last night. A few days ago my only sister was taken ill. I saw her each day, and she got worse. Yesterday she was so bad that I wouldn't leave her. I sent home for some things and stopped in her house for the night. Today I got an urgent message to come home, and when I went I found that an entrance had been made by a kitchen window and the whole house had been ransacked, but not a thing was missing."

"Were drawers and boxes opened?"

"Everywhere. Most seemed to have been opened with keys, but some were broken. The place was turned upside down, but, as I said before, not a thing was missing. A very old woman, very deaf, who used to be my housekeeper, but who does nothing now, was in the house, and so was my general servant. They slept in rooms at the top and were not disturbed. Of course the old woman is too deaf to have heard anything, and the maid is a very heavy sleeper. The girl was very frightened, but I pacified her before I came away. As it happened, I took the snuff-box with me. I had got very suspicious of late, of course, and something seemed to suggest that I had better so I took it. It's pretty strong evidence that they have been watching me closely, isn't it, that they should break in the very first night I left the place?"

"And are you quite sure that nothing has been taken?"

"Quite certain. I have spent a long time in a very careful search."

"And you want me, I presume, to find out definitely who these people are, and get such evidence as may ensure their being punished?"

"That is the case. Of course I know Reuben Penner is the moving spirit—I'm quite certain of that. But still I can see plainly enough that as yet there's no legal evidence of it. Mind, I'm not afraid of him—not a bit. That is not my character. I'm not afraid of all the madmen in England; but I'm not going to have them steal my property—this snuff-box especially."

"Precisely. I hope you have left the disturbance in your house exactly as you found it?"

"Oh, of course, and I have given strict orders that nothing is to be touched. Tomorrow morning I should like you to come and look at it."

"I must look at it, certainly," Hewitt said, "but I would rather go at once."

"Pooh—nonsense!" Mrs. Mallett answered, with the airy obstinacy that Hewitt afterwards knew so well. "I'm not going home again now to spend an hour or two more. My sister will want to know what has become of me, and she mustn't suspect that anything is wrong, or it may do all sorts of harm. The place will keep till the morning, and I have the snuff-box safe with me. You have my card, Mr. Hewitt, haven't you? Very well. Can you be at my house tomorrow morning at half-past ten? I will be there, and you can see all you want by daylight. We'll consider that settled. Good-day." Hewitt saw her to his office door and waited till she had half descended the stairs. Then he made for a staircase window which gave a view of the street. The evening was coming on murky and foggy, and the street lights were blotchy and vague. Outside a four-wheeled cab stood, and the driver eagerly watched the front door. When Mrs. Mallett emerged he instantly began to descend from the box with the quick invitation, "Cab, mum, cab?"

He seemed very eager for his fare, and though Mrs. Mallett hesitated a second she eventually entered the cab. He drove off, and Hewitt tried in vain to catch a glimpse of the number of the cab behind. It was always a habit of his to note all such identifying marks throughout

"Cab, mum?"

408

a case, whether they seemed important at the time or not, and he has often had occasion to be pleased with the outcome. Now, however, the light was too bad. No sooner had the cab started than a man emerged from a narrow passage opposite, and followed. He was a large, rather awkward, heavy-faced man of middle age, and had the appearance of a respectable artisan or small tradesman in his best clothes. Hewitt hurried downstairs and followed the direction the cab and the man had taken, toward the Strand.

But the cab by this time was swallowed up in the Strand traffic, and the heavy-faced man had also disappeared. Hewitt returned to his office a little disappointed, for the man seemed rather closely to answer Mrs. Mallett's description of Reuben Penner.

2.

Punctually at half-past ten the next morning Hewitt was at Mrs. Mallett's house at Fulham. It was a pretty little house, standing back from the road in a generous patch of garden, and had evidently stood there when Fulham was an outlying village. Hewitt entered the gate, and made his way to the front door, where two young females, evidently servants, stood. They were in a very disturbed state, and when he asked for Mrs. Mallett, assured him that nobody knew where she was, and that she had not been seen since the previous afternoon.

"But," said Hewitt, "she was to stay at her sister's last night, I believe."

"Yes, sir," answered the more distressed of the two girls—she in a cap—"but she hasn't been seen there. This is her sister's servant, and she's been sent over to know where she is, and why she hasn't been there." This the other girl—in bonnet and shawl—corroborated. Nothing had been seen of Mrs. Mallett at her sister's since she had received the message the day before to the effect that the house had been broken into.

"And I'm so frightened," the other girl said, whimperingly. "They've been in the place again last night."

"Who have?"

"The robbers. When I came in this morning——"

"But didn't you sleep here?"

"I—I ought to ha' done sir, but—but after Mrs. Mallett went yesterday I got so frightened I went home at ten." And the girl showed signs of tears, which she had apparently been already indulging in.

"And what about the old woman—the deaf woman; where was

she?"

"She was in the house, sir. There was nowhere else for her to go, and she was deaf and didn't know anything about what happened the night before, and confined to her room, and—and so I didn't tell her."

"I see," Hewitt said with a slight smile. "You left her here. She didn't see or hear anything, did she?"

"No sir; she can't hear, and she didn't see nothing."

"And how do you know thieves have been in the house?"

"Everythink's tumbled about worse than ever, sir, and all different from what it was yesterday; and there's a box o' papers in the attic broke open, and all sorts o' things."

"Have you spoken to the police?"

"No, sir; I'm that frightened I don't know what to do. And missis was going to see a gentleman about it yesterday, and——"

"Very well, I am that gentleman—Mr. Martin Hewitt. I have come down now to meet her by appointment. Did she say she was going anywhere else as well as to my office and to her sister's?"

"No, sir. And she—she's got the snuff-box with her and all." This latter circumstance seemed largely to augment the girl's terrors for her mistress's safety.

"Very well," Hewitt said, "I think I'd better just look over the house now, and then consider what has become of Mrs. Mallett—if she isn't heard of in the meantime." The girl found a great relief in Hewitt's presence in the house, the deaf old house-keeper, who seldom spoke and never heard, being, as she said, "worse than nobody."

"Have you been in all the rooms?" Hewitt asked.

"No, sir; I was afraid. When I came in I went straight upstairs to my room, and as I was coming away I see the things upset in the other attic. I went into Mrs. Perks' room, next to mine (she's the deaf old woman), and she was there all right, but couldn't hear anything. Then I came down and only just peeped into two of the rooms and saw the state they were in, and then I came out into the garden, and presently this young woman came with the message from Mrs. Rudd."

"Very well, we'll look at the rooms now," Hewitt said, and they proceeded to do so. All were in a state of intense confusion. Drawers, taken from chests and bureaux, littered about the floor, with their contents scattered about them. Carpets and rugs had been turned up and flung into corners, even pictures on the walls had been disturbed, and while some hung awry others rested on the floor and on chairs. The things, however, appeared to have been fairly carefully handled, for nothing was damaged except one or two framed engravings, the brown paper on the backs of which had been cut round with a knife and the wooden slats shifted so as to leave the backs of the engravings bare. This, the girl told Hewitt, had not been done on the night of the first burglary; the other articles also had not on that occasion been so much disturbed as they now were.

Mrs. Mallett's bedroom was the first floor front. Here the confusion was, if possible, greater than in the other rooms. The bed had been completely unmade and the clothes thrown separately on the floor, and everything else was displaced. It was here indeed that the most noticeable features of the disturbance were observed, for on the side of the looking-glass hung a very long old-fashioned gold chain untouched, and on the dressing-table lay a purse with the money still in it. And on the looking-glass, stuck into the crack of the frame, was a half sheet of notepaper with this inscription scrawled in pencil:—

"To Mr. Martin Hewitt.

Mrs. Mallett is alright and in frends hands. She will return soon alright, if you keep quiet. But if you folloe her or take any steps the conseqinses will be very serious."

This paper was not only curious in itself, and curious as being addressed to Hewitt, but it was plainly in the same handwriting as were the most of the anonymous letters which Mrs. Mallett had produced the day before in Hewitt's office. Hewitt studied it attentively for a few moments and then thrust it in his pocket and proceeded to inspect the rest of the rooms. All were the same—simply well-furnished rooms turned upside down. The top floor consisted of three comfortable attics, one used as a lumber-room and the others used respectively as bedrooms for the servant and the deaf old woman. None of these rooms appeared to have been entered, the girl said, on the first night, but now the lumber-room was almost as confused as the rooms downstairs. Two or three boxes were opened and their contents turned out. One of these was what is called a steel trunk—a small one—which had held old papers, the others were filled chiefly with old clothes.

The servant's room next this was quite undisturbed and untouched; and then Hewitt was admitted to the room of Mrs. Mallett's deaf old pensioner. The old woman sat propped up in her bed and looked with half-blind eyes at the peak in the bedclothes made by her bent knees. The servant screamed in her ear, but she neither moved nor spoke.

Hewitt laid his hand on her shoulder and said, in the slow and distinct tones he had found best for reaching the senses of deaf people,

"I hope you are well. Did anything disturb you in the night?" But she only turned her head half toward him and mumbled peevishly, "I wish you'd bring my tea. You're late enough this morning." Nothing seemed likely to be got from her, and Hewitt asked the servant, "Is she altogether bedridden?"

"No," the girl answered; "leastways she needn't be. She stops in bed most of the time, but she can get up when she likes—I've seen her. But missis humours her and lets her do as she likes—and she gives plenty of trouble. I don't believe she's as deaf as she makes out."

"Indeed!" Hewitt answered. "Deafness is convenient sometimes, I know. Now I want you to stay here while I make some inquiries. Perhaps you'd better keep Mrs. Rudd's servant with you if you want company. I don't expect to be very long gone, and in any case it wouldn't do for her to go to her mistress and say that Mrs. Mallett is missing, or it might upset her seriously." Hewitt left the house and walked till he found a public-house where a post-office directory was kept. He took a glass of whisky and water, most of which he left on the counter, and borrowed the directory. He found "Greengrocers" in the "Trade" section and ran his finger down the column till he came on this address:— "Penner, Reuben, 8, Little Marsh Row, Hammersmith, W." Then he returned the directory and found the best cab he could to take him to Hammersmith.

Little Marsh Row was not a vastly prosperous sort of place, and the only shops were three—all small. Two were chandlers', and the third was a sort of semi-shed of the greengrocery and coal persuasion, with the name "Penner" on a board over the door.

The shutters were all up, though the door was open, and the only person visible was a very smudgy boy who was in the act of wheeling out a sack of coals. To the smudgy boy Hewitt applied himself. "I don't see Mr. Penner about," he said; "will he be back soon?"

The boy stared hard at Hewitt. "No," he said, "he won't. 'E's guv' up the shop. 'E paid 'is next week's rent this mornin' and retired."

"Oh!" Hewitt answered sharply. "Retired, has he? And what's become of the stock, eh! Where are the cabbages and potatoes?"

"'E told me to give 'em to the pore, an' I did. There's lots o' pore lives round 'ere. My mother's one, an' these 'ere coals is for 'er, an' I'm goin' to 'ave the trolley for myself."

"Dear me!" Hewitt answered, regarding the boy with amused interest. "You're a very business-like almoner. And what will the Tabernacle do without Mr. Penner?"

The boy stared hard at Hewitt.

"I dunno," the boy answered, closing the door behind him. "I dunno nothin' about the Tabernacle—only where it is."

"Ah, and where is it? I might find him there, perhaps."

"Ward Lane—fust on left, second on right. It's a shop wot's bin shut up; next door to a stable-yard." And the smudgy boy started off with his trolley.

The Tabernacle was soon found. At some very remote period it had been an unlucky small shop, but now it was permanently shuttered, and the interior was lighted by holes cut in the upper panels of the shutters. Hewitt took a good look at the shuttered window and the door beside it and then entered the stable-yard at the side. To the left of the passage giving entrance to the yard there was a door, which plainly was another entrance to the house, and a still damp mud-mark on the step proved it to have been lately used. Hewitt rapped sharply at the door with his knuckles.

Presently a female voice from within could be heard speaking through the keyhole in a very loud whisper. "Who is it?" asked the voice.

Hewitt stooped to the keyhole and whispered back, "Is Mr. Penner here now?"

"No."

"Then I must come in and wait for him. Open the door." A bolt was pulled back and the door cautiously opened a few inches. Hewitt's foot was instantly in the jamb, and he forced the door back and entered. "Come," he said in a loud voice, "I've come to find out where Mr. Penner is, and to see whoever is in here." Immediately there was an assault of fists on the inside of a door at the end of the passage, and a loud voice said, "Do you hear? Whoever you are I'll give you five pounds if you'll bring Mr. Martin Hewitt here. His office is 25 Portsmouth Street, Strand. Or the same if you'll bring the police." And the voice was that of Mrs. Mallett.

Hewitt turned to the woman who had opened the door, and who now stood, much frightened, in the corner beside him. "Come," he said, "your keys, quick, and don't offer to stir, or I'll have you brought back and taken to the station." The woman gave him a bunch of keys without a word. Hewitt opened the door at the end of the passage, and once more Mrs. Mallett stood before him, prim and rigid as ever, except that her bonnet was sadly out of shape and her mantle was torn.

"Thank you, Mr. Hewitt," she said. "I thought you'd come, though where I am I know no more than Adam. Somebody shall smart severely for this. Why, and that woman—that woman," she pointed contemptuously at the woman in the corner, who was about two-thirds her height, "was going to search me—me! Why——" Mrs. Mallett, blazing with suddenly revived indignation, took a step forward and the woman vanished through the outer door.

"Come," Hewitt said, "no doubt you've been shamefully treated; but we must be quiet for a little. First I will make quite sure that nobody else is here, and then we'll get to your house." Nobody was there. The rooms were dreary and mostly empty. The front room, which was lighted by the holes in the shutters, had a rough reading-desk and a table, with half a dozen wooden chairs. "This," said Hewitt, "is no doubt the Tabernacle proper, and there is very little to see in it. Come back now, Mrs. Mallett, to your house, and we'll see if some explanation of these things is not possible. I hope your snuff-box is quite safe?"

Mrs. Mallett drew it from her pocket and exhibited it triumphantly. "I told them they should never get it," she said, "and they saw I meant it, and left off trying." As they emerged in the street she said: "The first thing, of course, is to bring the police into this place."

"No, I think we won't do that yet," Hewitt said. "In the first place the case is one of assault and detention, and your remedy is by summons or action; and then there are other things to speak of. We shall get a cab in the High Street, and you shall tell me what has happened to you."

Mrs. Mallett's story was simple. The cab in which she left Hewitt's office had travelled west, and was apparently making for the locality of her sister's house; but the evening was dark, the fog increased greatly, and she shut the windows and took no particular notice of the streets through which she was passing. Indeed, with such a fog that would have been impossible. She had a sort of undefined notion that some of the streets were rather narrow and dirty, but she thought nothing of it, since all cabmen are given to selecting unexpected routes. After a time, however, the cab slowed, made a sharp turn, and pulled up. The door was opened, and "Here you are mum," said the cabby. She did not understand the sharp turn, and had a general feeling that the place could not be her sister's, but as she alighted she found she had stepped directly upon the threshold of a narrow door into which she was immediately pulled by two persons inside. This, she was sure, must have been the side-door in the stable-yard, through which Hewitt himself had lately obtained entrance to the Tabernacle.

Before she had recovered from her surprise the door was shut behind her. She struggled stoutly and screamed, but the place she was in was absolutely dark; she was taken by surprise, and she found resistance useless. They were men who held her, and the voice of the only one who spoke she did not know. He demanded in firm and distinct tones that the "sacred thing" should be given up, and that Mrs. Mallett should sign a paper agreeing to prosecute nobody before she was allowed to go. She however, as she asserted with her customary emphasis, was not the sort of woman to give in to that. She resolutely declined to do anything of the sort, and promised her captors, whoever they were, a full and legal return for their behaviour.

Then she became conscious that a woman was somewhere present, and the man threatened that this woman should search her. This threat Mrs. Mallett met as boldly as the others. She should like to meet the woman who would dare attempt to search her, she said. She defied anybody to attempt it. As for her uncle Joseph's snuff-box, no matter where it was, it was where they would not be able to get it. That they should never have, but sooner or later they should have something very unpleasant for their attempts to steal it. This declaration had an immediate effect. They importuned her no more, and she was left in an inner room and the key was turned on her. There she sat, dozing occasionally, the whole night, her indomitable spirit remaining proof through all those doubtful hours of darkness. Once or twice she heard people enter and move about, and each time she called aloud to offer, as Hewitt had heard, a reward to anybody who should bring the police or communicate her situation to Hewitt. Day broke and still she waited, sleepless and unfed, till Hewitt at last arrived and released her.

On Mrs. Mallett's arrival at her house Mrs. Rudd's servant was at once despatched with reassuring news and Hewitt once more addressed himself to the question of the burglars. "First, Mrs. Mallett," he said, "did you ever conceal anything—anything at all mind—in the frame of an engraving?"

"No, never."

"Were any of your engravings framed before you had them?"

"Not one that I can remember. They were mostly uncle Joseph's, and he kept them with a lot of others in drawers. He was rather a collector, you know."

"Very well. Now come up to the attic. Something has been opened there that was not touched at the first attempt."

"See now," said Hewitt, when the attic was reached, "here is a box full of papers. Do you know everything that was in it?"

"No, I don't," Mrs. Mallett replied. "There were a lot of my uncle's manuscript plays. Here you see 'The Dead Bridegroom, or the Drum of Fortune,' and so on; and there were a lot of autographs. I took no interest in them, although some were rather valuable, I believe."

"Now bring your recollection to bear as strongly as you can," Hewitt said. "Do you ever remember seeing in this box a paper bearing nothing whatever upon it but a wax seal?"

"Oh yes, I remember that well enough. I've noticed it each time I've turned the box over—which is very seldom. It was a plain slip of vellum paper with a red seal, cracked and rather worn—some celebrated person's seal, I suppose. What about it?" Hewitt was turning the papers over one at a time. "It doesn't seem to be here now," he said. "Do you see it?"

"No," Mrs. Mallett returned, examining the papers herself, "it isn't. It appears to be the only thing missing. But why should they take it?"

"I think we are at the bottom of all this mystery now," Hewitt answered quietly. "It is the Seal of the Woman."

"The what? I don't understand. The fact is, Mrs. Mallett, that these people have never wanted your uncle Joseph's snuff-box at all, but that seal."

"Not wanted the snuff-box? Nonsense! Why, didn't I tell you Penner asked for it—wanted to buy it?"

"Yes, you did, but so far as I can remember you never spoke of a single instance of Penner mentioning the snuff-box by name. He spoke of a sacred relic, and you, of course, very naturally assumed he spoke of the box. None of the anonymous letters mentioned the box, you know, and once or twice they actually did mention a seal, though usually the thing was spoken of in a roundabout and figurative way. All along, these people—Reuben Penner and the others—have been after the seal, and you have been defending the snuff-box."

"But why the seal?"

"Did you never hear of Joanna Southcott?"

"Oh yes, of course; she was an ignorant visionary who set up as prophetess eighty or ninety years ago or more."

"Joanna Southcott gave herself out as a prophetess in 1790. She was to be the mother of the Messiah, she said, and she was the woman driven into the wilderness, as foretold in the twelfth chapter of the Book of Revelation. She died at the end of 1814, when her followers numbered more than 100,000, all fanatic believers. She had made rather a good thing in her lifetime by the sale of seals, each of which was to secure the eternal salvation of the holder. At her death, of course, many of the believers fell away, but others held on as faithfully as ever, asserting that 'the holy Joanna' would rise again and fulfil all the prophecies.

"These poor people dwindled in numbers gradually, and although they attempted to bring up their children in their own faith, the whole belief has been practically extinct for years now. You will remember that you told me of Penner's mother being a superstitious fanatic of some sort, and that your uncle Joseph possessed her extravagances. The thing seems pretty plain now. Your uncle Joseph possessed himself of Joanna Southcott's seal by way of removing from poor old Mrs. Penner an object of a sort of idolatry, and kept it as a curiosity. Reuben Penner grew up strong in his mother's delusions, and to him and the few believers he had gathered round him at his Tabernacle, the seal was an object worth risking anything to get.

"First he tried to convert you to his belief. Then he tried to buy it; after that, he and his friends tried anonymous letters, and at last, grown desperate, they resorted to watching you, burglary and kidnapping. Their first night's raid was unsuccessful, so last night they tried kidnapping you by the aid of a cabman. When they had got you, and you had at last given them to understand that it was your uncle Joseph's snuff-box you were defending, they tried the house again, and this time were successful. I guessed they had succeeded then, from a simple circumstance. They had begun to cut out the backs of framed engravings for purposes of search, but only some of the engravings were so treated.

"That meant either that the article wanted was found behind one of them, or that the intruders broke off in their picture-examination to search somewhere else, and were then successful, and so under no necessity of opening the other engravings. You assured me that nothing could have been concealed in any of the engravings, so I at once assumed that they had found what they were after in the only place wherein they had not searched the night before—the attic—and probably among the papers in the trunk."

"But then if they found it there why didn't they return and let me go?"

"Because you would have found where they had brought you. They probably intended to keep you there till the dark of the next evening, and then take you away in a cab again and leave you some distance off. To prevent my following and possibly finding you they left here on your looking-glass this note" (Hewitt produced it) "threatening all sorts of vague consequences if you were not left to them. They knew you had come to me, of course, having followed you to my office. And now Penner feels himself anything but safe. He has relinquished his greengrocery and dispensed his stock in charity, and probably, having got the seal he has taken himself off. Not so much perhaps from fear of punishment as for fear the seal may be taken from him, and with it the salvation his odd belief teaches him it will confer."

Mrs. Mallett sat silently for a little while and then said in a rather softened voice, "Mr. Hewitt, I am not what is called a woman of sentiment, as you may have observed, and I have been most shamefully treated over this wretched seal. But if all you tell me has been actually what has happened I have a sort of perverse inclination to forgive the man in spite of myself. The thing probably had been his mother's—or at any rate he believed so—and his giving up his little all to attain the object of his ridiculous faith, and distributing his goods among the poor people and all that—really it's worthy of an old martyr, if only it were done in the cause of a faith a little less stupid—though of course he thinks his is the only religion, as others do of theirs. But then"—Mrs. Mallett stiffened again—"there's not much to prove your theories, is there?"

Hewitt smiled. "Perhaps not," he said, "except that, to my mind at any rate, everything points to my explanation being the only possible one. The thing presented itself to you, from the beginning, as an attempt on the snuff-box you value so highly, and the possibility of the seal being the object aimed at never entered your mind. I saw it whole from the outside, and on thinking the thing over after our first interview I remembered Joanna Southcott. I think I am right."

"Well, if you are, as I said, I half believe I shall forgive the man. We will advertise if you like, telling him he has nothing to fear if he can give an explanation of his conduct consistent with what he calls his religious belief, absurd as it may be."

★★★★★★

That night fell darker and foggier than the last. The advertisement went into the daily papers, but Reuben Penner never saw it. Late the next day a bargeman passing Old Swan Pier struck some large object with his boat-hook and brought it to the surface. It was the body of a drowned man, and it was afterwards identified as that of Reuben Penner, late greengrocer, of Hammersmith. How he came into the water there was nothing to show. There was no money nor any valuables found on the body, and there was a story of a large, heavy-faced man who had given a poor woman—a perfect stranger—a watch and chain and a handful of money down near Tower Hill on that foggy evening. But this again was only a story, not definitely authenticated. What was certain was that, tied securely round the dead man's neck with a cord, and gripped and crumpled tightly in his right hand, was a soddened piece of vellum paper, blank, but carrying an old red seal, of which the device was almost entirely rubbed and cracked away. Nobody at the inquest quite understood this.

THE AFFAIR OF SAMUEL'S DIAMONDS

1.

I have already recorded many of the adventures of my friend Martin Hewitt, but among them there have been more of a certain few which were discovered to be related together in a very extraordinary manner; and it is to these that I am now at liberty to address myself. There may have been others—cases which gave no indication of their connection with these; some of them indeed I may have told without a suspicion of their connection with the Red Triangle; but the first in which that singular accompaniment became apparent was the matter of Samuel's diamonds. The case exhibited many interesting features, and I was very anxious to report it, with perhaps even less delay than I had thought judicious in other cases; but Hewitt restrained me.

"No, Brett," he said, "there is more to come of this. This particular case is over, it is true, but there is much behind. I've an idea that I shall see that Red Triangle again. I may, or, of course, I may not; but there is deep work going on—very deep work, and whether we see more of it or not, I must keep prepared. I can't afford to throw a single card upon the table. So, as many notes as you please, Brett, for future reference; but no publication yet—none of your journalism!"

Hewitt was right. It was not so long before we heard more of the Red Triangle, and after that more, though the true connection of some of the cases with the mysterious symbol and the meaning of the symbol itself remained for a time undiscovered. But at last Hewitt was able to unmask the hideous secret, and for ever put an end to the evil influence that gathered about the sign; and now there remains no reason why the full story should not be told.

I have told elsewhere of my first acquaintance with Martin Hewitt, of his pleasant and companionable nature, his ordinary height, his stoutness, his round, smiling face—those characteristics that aided him so well in his business of investigator, so unlike was his appearance and manner to that of the private detective of the ordinary person's imagination. Therefore, I need only remind my readers that my bachelor chambers were, during most of my acquaintance with Hewitt, in the old building near the Strand, in which Hewitt's office stood at the top of the first flight of stairs; where the plain ground-glass of the door bore as inscription the single word "Hewitt," and the sharp lad, Kerrett, first received visitors in the outer office.

Next door to this old house, at the time I am to speak of, a much newer building stood, especially built for letting out in offices. It happened that one day as Hewitt left his office for a late lunch, he became aware of a pallid and agitated Jew who was pervading the front door of this adjoining building. The man exhibited every sign of nervous expectancy, staring this way and that up and down the busy street, and once or twice rushing aimlessly half-way up the inner stairs, and as often returning to the door. Apprehension was plain on his pale face, and he was clearly in a state that blinded his attention to the ordinary matters about him, just as happens when a man is in momentary and nervous expectation of some serious event.

Noting these things as he passed, with no more than the observation that was his professional habit, Hewitt proceeded to his lunch. This done with, he returned to his office, perceiving, as he passed the next-door building, that the distracted Jew was no longer visible. It seemed plain that the person or the event he had awaited with such obvious nervousness had arrived and passed; one more of the problems, anxieties or crises that join and unravel moment by moment in the human ant-hill of London, had perhaps closed for good or ill within the past half-hour; perhaps it had only begun.

A message awaited Hewitt at his office—an urgent message. The housekeeper had come in from next door, Kerrett reported, with an urgent request that Mr. Martin Hewitt would go immediately to the offices of Mr. Denson, on the third floor. The housekeeper seemed to know little or nothing of the business, except that a Mr. Samuel was alone in Mr. Denson's office, and had sent the message.

With no delay Hewitt transferred himself to the next-door offices. There the housekeeper, who inhabited a uniform and a glass box opposite the foot of the first flight of stairs, directed Hewitt, with the remark that the gentleman was very impatient and very much upset. "Third floor, sir, second door on the right; name Denson on the door. There's no lift."

"W. F. Denson" was the complete name, followed by the line "Foreign and Commission Agent." This Hewitt read with some little difficulty, for the door was open, and on the threshold stood that same agitated Jew whom Hewitt had seen at the front door.

A little less actively perturbed now, he was nevertheless still nervously pale. "Mr. Martin Hewitt?" he cried, while Hewitt was still only at the head of the stairs. "Is it Mr. Martin Hewitt?"

Hewitt came quietly along the corridor, using eyes and ears as he came. The Jew was a man of middle height, very obviously Jewish, and with a slight accent that hinted a Continental origin.

"I have just received your message," Hewitt said, "and, as you see, I am here with no delay. Is Mr. Denson in?"

"No—good heafens no—I would gif anything if he was, Mr. Hewitt. Come in, do! I haf been robbed—robbed by Denson himself, wit'out a wort of doubt. It is terrible—terrible! Fifteen t'ousant pounds! It ruins me, Mr. Hewitt, ruins me! Unless you can recover it! If you recover it, I will pay—pay—oh, I will pay fery well indeed!"

There was a characteristically sudden moderation of the client's emphasis when he came to the engagement to pay. Hewitt had observed it in other clients, but it did not disturb him.

"First," he said, "you must tell me your difficulty. You say you have been robbed of fifteen thousand pounds——"

"Tiamonts, Mr. Hewitt—tiamonts! All from the case—here is the case, empty——"

"Let us be methodical. We will shut the door and sit down." Hewitt pressed his client into a chair and produced his note-book. "It will be better to begin at the beginning. First, I should like to know your name, and a few such particulars as that."

"Lewis Samuel, Hatton Garden—150, Hatton Garden—tiamont merchant."

"Yes. And what is your connection with Mr. Denson?"

"Business—just business," Samuel responded. He pronounced it "pishness," and it seemed his favourite word. "Like this; I will tell you. I haf known him some time, and did at first small pishness. He bought a little tiamont and haf it set in pracelet, and he pay—straightforward pishness. Then he bought some very good paste stones, all set in gold, and he pay—quite straightforward pishness. At the same time, he says, 'I am pishness man myself, Mr. Samuel,' he says, 'and I like to make a little moneys as well as pay out sometimes. Don't you want any little agencies done? I do all foreign commissions, and I can forwart and receive and clear at dock and custom house. If you send any tiamonts I can consign and insure—very cheapest rates to you, special. If you want brokerage or buy and sell for you, confidential, I can do it with lowest commission. Especially I haf good connection with America. I haf many rich Americans, principals and customers,' he says, 'and often I could do pishness for you when they come over.'"

"By which he meant he might sell them diamonds?" Hewitt queried.

"Just so, Mr. Hewitt—reg'lar pishness. And after that two or three little parcels of tiamonts he bought—for American customers, he says. But he says he can do bigger pishness soon. Ay, so he has—goot heavens, he has! But I tell you. I do also one or two small pishnesses with him, and that is all right—he treat me very well and I pay when it suits. Then he says, 'Samuel,' he says, very friendly now inteet, 'Samuel, could you get a nice large lot of tiamonts for an American customer I expect here soon?' And I say, 'Of course I can.' 'Enough,' he says, 'to fit out a rich man's wife—that is, to pegin. He is not long rich, and he will want more soon—ah, she will make him pay! But to pegin—a good fit-out of tiamonts, eh?'

"I tell him yes, and I offer usual commission. But no, says Denson, he wants no commission; he will make his own profit. That I don't mind so long as I get mine; so I agree to put the tiamonts in at a price. The American, he says, is to come over about a big company deal, and when it is through he will pay well. So last week I pring a peautiful collection all cut but unset, and I wait out in that room while Denson shows them to his customer."

"You mean you let them out of your sight?"

"Yes—that is not so uncommon; reg'lar pishness. You see I was out here—this is the only way out. Denson was in the inner office with the stones and the American. Neither could get out without passing here. And I had done pishness with him alretty."

"Well?"

"You see I wait downstairs with my case—this case—till Denson sends down. He doesn't want me to show—fery natural, you see, in pishness. When I sell to make a profit, perhaps for somebody else, I don't want that somebody to know my customer, else he sells direct and I lose my profit—fery natural. See?"

"Of course, I understand. It's a point of business among you gentlemen to keep your own customers to yourselves. And often, no doubt, diamonds pass through several hands before reaching the eventual customer, leaving a profit in each."

"Always, Mr. Hewitt—always, you might say. Well, you see, Denson sends down that his customer is in, and I come up. Denson comes out from the inner office, takes my case, and I wait in there."

The case which Samuel showed Hewitt was of black leather, perhaps eighteen inches long by a foot wide. The arrangement of the office was simple. In this, the outer room, a small space was partitioned off by means of a ground glass screen, and it was in there that Samuel meant that he had waited.

"Well, he took the case in, and I could hear some sound of talking—but not much, you see, the door being shut. After a time, the door opens and I hear Denson say: 'Very well, think over it; but don't be long or you'll lose the chance. Excuse me while I put them back in the safe.' Then he shuts the door and brings the case to me and goes back. But of course I stay till I haf looked very carefully through all the tiamonts, in the different compartments of the case, in case one might haf dropped on the floor, or got changed, you know. That is pishness."

"Just so. And they were all right?"

"All right and same as the list—I know well a tiamont that I haf seen once. So I go away, and afterwards Denson tells me that the

American liked much the stones but wouldn't quite come up to price. That, of course, is fery usual pishness. 'But he will rise, Samuel,' Denson says. 'I know him quite well, and them tiamonts is as good as sold with a good profit for me; and a good one for you, too, I bet,' he says. I was putting the lot to him for fifteen t'ousant pounds, and it would have been a nice profit in that for me. And then Denson he chaffs me and he says, 'Ah! Samuel,' he says, 'wasn't you afraid my customer and me would hook it out o' the window with all your stones?' I don't like that sort o' joke in pishness, you see, but I say, 'All right—I wasn't afraid o' that. The window was a mile too high, and besides I could see it from where I was a-sitting.' And so I could, you see, plain enough to see if it was opened."

The ground-glass partition, in fact, cut off a part of the window of the outer office, which, being at an angle with the inner room, gave a side view of the window that lighted that apartment.

"Denson laughed at that," Samuel went on. "'Ha-ha!' says he, 'I never thought of that. Then you could see the American's hat hanging up just by the window—rum hat, ain't it?' And that was quite true, for I had noticed it—a big, grey wideawake, almost white."

Hewitt nodded approvingly. "You are quite right," he said, "to tell me everything you recollect, even of the most trivial sort; the smallest thing may be very valuable. So you took your diamonds away the first time, last week. What next?"

"Well, I came again, just the same, today, by appointment. Just the same I sat in that place, and just the same Denson took the case into the inner room. 'He's come to buy this time, I can see,' Denson whispers, and winks. 'But he'll fight hard over the price. We'll see!' and off he goes into the other room. Well, I waited. I waited and I waited a long time. I looked out sideways at the window, and there I see the American's big wideawake hat hanging up just inside the other window, same as last time. So I think they are a long time settling the price, and I wait some more. But it is such a very long time, and I begin to feel uneasy. Of course, I know you cannot sell fifteen t'ousant wort' of tiamonts in five minutes—that is not reasonable pishness. But I could hear nothing at all now—not a sound. And the boy—the boy that came down to call me up—he wasn't come back.

"But there I could see the big wideawake hat still hanging inside the window, and of course I knew there was only one door out of the inner room, right before me, so it seemed foolish to be uneasy. So I waited longer still, but now it was so late, I thought they should have come out to lunch before this, and then I was fery uneasy—fery uneasy inteet. So I thought I would pretend to be a new caller, and I opened the outer office door and banged it, and walked in very loud and knocked on the boy's table. I thought Denson would come when he heard that, but no—there was not a sound. So I got more uneasy, and I opened the window and leaned out as far as I could, to look in at the other window. There I could see nothing but the big hat and the back of a chair and a bit of the room—empty. So I went and banged the outer door again, and called out, 'Hi! Mr. Denson, you're wanted! Hi! d'y'ear?' and knocked with my umbrella on the inner door; and, Mr. Hewitt—you might have knocked me down with half a feather when I got no answer at all—not a sound! I opened the door, Mr. Hewitt, and there was nobody there—nobody! There was my leather case on the table, open—and empty! Fifteen t'ousant pounds in tiamonts, Mr. Hewitt—it ruins me!"

Hewitt rose, and flung wide the inner office door. "This is certainly the only door," he said, "and that is the only window—quite well in view from where you sat. There is the wideawake hat still hanging there—see, it is quite new; obviously brought for you to look at, it would seem. The door and the window were not used, and the chimney is impossible—register grate. But there was one other way—there."

The inner wall of each of the rooms was the wall of the corridor into which all the offices opened, and this corridor was lighted—and the offices partly ventilated—by a sort of hinged casement or fanlight close up by the ceiling, oblong, and extending the most of the length of each room. Plainly an active man, not too stout, might mount a chair-back, and climb very quietly through the opening. "That's the only way," said Hewitt, pointing.

"Yes," answered Samuel, nodding and rubbing his knuckles together nervously. "I saw it—saw it when it was too late. But who'd have thought o' such a thing beforehand? And the American—either there wasn't an American at all, or he got out the same way. But, anyway, here I am, and the tiamonts are gone, and there is nothing here but the furniture—not worth twenty pound!"

"Well," Hewitt said, "so far, I think I understand, though I may have questions to ask presently. But go on."

"Go on? But there is no more, Mr. Hewitt! Quite enough, don't you think? There is no more—I am robbed!"

"But when you found the empty room, and the case, what did you do? Send for the police?"

The Jew's face clouded slightly. "No, Mr. Hewitt," he said, "not for the police, but for you. Reason plain enough. The police make a great fuss, and they want to arrest the criminal. Quite right—I want to arrest him, and punish him too, plenty. But most I want the tiamonts back, because if not it ruins me. If it was to make choice between two things for me, whether to punish Denson or get my tiamonts, then of course I take the tiamonts, and let Denson go—I cannot be ruined. But with the police, if it is their choice, they catch the thief first, and hold him tight, whether it loses the property or not; the property is only second with them—with me it is first and second, and all. So I take no more risks than I can help, Mr. Hewitt. I have sent for you to get first the stones—afterwards the thief if you can. But first my property; you can perhaps find Denson and make him give it up rather than go to prison. That would be better than having him taken and imprisoned, and perhaps the stones put away safe all the time ready for him when he came out."

"Still, the police can do things that I can't," Hewitt interposed; "stop people leaving or landing at ports, and the like. I think we should see them."

Samuel was anxiously emphatic. "No, Mr. Hewitt," he said, "certainly not the police. There are reasons—no, *not* the police, Mr. Hewitt, at any rate, not till you have tried. I cannot haf the police—just yet."

Martin Hewitt shrugged his shoulders. "Very well," he said, "if those are your instructions, I'll do my best. And so you sent for me at once, as soon as you discovered the loss?"

"Yes, at once."

"Without telling anybody else?"

"I haf tolt nobody."

"Did you look about anywhere for Denson—in the street, or what not?"

"No—what was the good? He was gone; there was time for him to go miles."

"Very good. And speaking of time, let me judge how far he may have gone. How long were you kept waiting?"

"Two hours and a quarter, very near—within five minutes."

"By your watch?"

"Yes—I looked often, to see if it was so long waiting as it seemed."

"Very good. Do you happen to have a piece of Denson's writing about you?"

Samuel looked round him. "There's nothing about here," he said, "but perhaps we can find—oh here—here's a post-card." He took the card from his pocket, and gave it to Hewitt.

"There is nothing else to tell me, then?" queried Hewitt. "Are you sure that you have forgotten nothing that has happened since you first arrived—*nothing at all?*" There was meaning in the emphasis, and a sharp look in Hewitt's eyes.

"No, Mr. Hewitt," Samuel answered, hastily; "there is nothing else I can tell you."

"Then I will think it over at once. You had better go back quietly to your office, and think it over yourself, *in case* you have forgotten something; and I need hardly warn you to keep quiet as to what has passed between us—unless you tell the police. I think I shall take the liberty of a glance over Mr. Denson's office, and since his office boy still stays away, I will lend him my clerk for a little. He will keep his eyes open if any callers come, and his ears too. Wait while I fetch him."

2.

It was at this point that my humble part in the case began, for Hewitt hurried first to my rooms.

"Brett," he exclaimed, "are you engaged this afternoon?"

"No—nothing important."

"Will you do me a small favour? I have a rather interesting case. I want a man watched for an hour or so, and I haven't a soul to do it. Kerrett *may* be known, and I *am* known. Besides, there is another job for Kerrett."

Of course, I expressed myself willing to do what I could.

"Capital," replied Hewitt. "Come along—you like these adventures, I know, or I wouldn't have asked you; and you know the dodges in this sort of observation. The man is one Samuel, a Jew, of 150 Hatton Garden, diamond dealer. I'll tell you more afterwards. Kerrett and I are going into the offices next door, and I want you to wait thereabout. Presently I will come downstairs with him and he will go away. An hour or so will be enough, probably."

I followed Hewitt downstairs. He took Kerrett with him and locked his office door. I saw them both disappear within the large new building, and I waited near a convenient postal pillar-box, prepared to seem very busy with a few old letters from my pocket until my man's back was turned.

In a very few minutes Hewitt reappeared, this time with a man—a

427

Jew, obviously—whom I remembered having seen already at the door of that office more than an hour before, as I had passed on the way from the bookseller's at the corner. The man walked briskly up the street, and I, on the opposite side, did the same, a little in the rear.

He turned the corner, and at once slackened his pace and looked about him. He took a peep back along the street he had left, and then hailed a cab.

For a hundred yards or more I was obliged to trot, till I saw another cab drop its fare just ahead, and managed to secure it and give the cabman instructions to follow the cab in front, before it turned a corner. The chase was difficult, for the horse that drew me was a poor one, and half a dozen times I thought I had lost sight of the other cab altogether; but my cabman was better than his animal, and from his high perch he kept the chase in view, turning corners and picking out the cab ahead among a dozen others with surprising certainty. We went across Charing Cross Road by way of Cranborne Street, past Leicester Square, through Coventry Street and up the Quadrant and Regent Street. At Oxford Circus the Jew's cab led us to the left, and along Oxford Street we chased it past Bond Street end. Suddenly my cab pulled up with a jerk, and the driver spoke through the trapdoor. "That fare's getting down, sir," he said, "at the corner o' Duke Street."

I thrust a half-crown up through the hole and sprang out. "'E's crossing the road, sir," the cabman finally reported, and I hurried across the street accordingly.

The man I was watching was strikingly Jewish enough, and easy to distinguish in a crowd. I had almost overtaken him before he had gone a dozen yards up the northern end of Duke Street. He walked on into Manchester Square. There a small, neat brougham, with blinds drawn, was being driven slowly round the central garden. I saw Samuel walk hurriedly up to this brougham, which stopped as he approached. He stepped quickly into the carriage and shut the door behind him. The brougham resumed its slow progress, and I loitered, keeping it in view, though the blinds were drawn so close that it was impossible to guess who might be Samuel's companion, if he had one. I think I have said that when the Jew came to the office door with Hewitt I perceived that he was a man I had seen before that day. I was now convinced that I had also seen that same brougham, at the same time; but of this presently.

The carriage made one slow circuit, and then Samuel got out and shut the door quickly again. I took the precaution of turning my back

428

and letting him overtake and pass me on his way back through Duke Street. At the end of the street he mounted an omnibus going east, and I took another seat in the same vehicle. The rest was uninteresting. He went direct to No. 150 Hatton Garden, and there remained. I read his name on the door-post among a score of others, and after a twenty-minutes' wait I returned to my rooms. I had no doubt that it was the meeting in the brougham that Hewitt wished reported, and I remembered his rule was never to watch a man a moment after the main object was secured.

Hewitt was out, and he did not return till after dusk. Then he came straightway to my rooms.

"Well, Brett," he said, "what's the report? As a matter of fact, Samuel is my client, as I shall explain presently. I don't like spying on a client, as a rule, but I was convinced that he was keeping something back from me, and there was something odd about his whole story. But what did you see?"

I told Hewitt the tale of my pursuit as I have told it here. "I came away," I concluded, "after it seemed that he was settled in his office for a bit. But there is another thing you should know. When he first came out with you I recognised him at once as a man I had seen at that same door a little after two o'clock—say a quarter past."

"Yes?" answered Hewitt. "I saw him there myself a little sooner—something like two, I should say. What was he doing?"

"Well," I replied, "he was doing pretty well what he did in Manchester Square. For as a matter of fact the brougham also was here then—just outside the next-door office. I think I might swear to that same brougham—though of course I didn't notice it so particularly that first time."

Hewitt whistled. "Oh!" he said. "Tell me about this. Did he get into the brougham this time?"

"Yes. He came out of the office door with a black leather case in his hand and a very scared look on his face. And he popped into the brougham, leather case, scared look and all."

"Ho—ho!" said Hewitt, thoughtfully, and whistled again. "A black leather case, eh! Come, come, the plot thickens. And what happened? Did the carriage go off?"

"No; I saw nothing more—shouldn't have noticed so much, in fact, if the whole thing hadn't looked a trifle curious. Nervous, pallid Jew with a black case—as though he thought it was dynamite and might go off at any moment—closed brougham, blinds drawn, Jew

429

skipped in and banged the door, but brougham didn't move; and I fancied—perhaps only fancied—that I saw a woman's black veil inside. But then I turned in here and saw no more."

Hewitt sat thoughtfully silent for a few moments. Then he rose and said, "Come next door, and I'll tell you how we stand. The housekeeper will let us in, and we'll see if you can identify that black case anywhere."

It seemed that Hewitt had by this established a good understanding with the housekeeper next door. "Nobody's been, sir," the man said, as he admitted us and closed the heavy doors. "Office boy not come back, nor nothing."

We went up to Denson's office on the third floor, the door of which the housekeeper opened; and having turned on the electric light, he left us.

"Now, is that anything like the case?" Hewitt asked, when the housekeeper was gone; and he lifted from under the table the very black case I had seen Samuel take into the brougham.

I said that I felt as sure of the case as of the brougham. And then Hewitt told me the whole tale of Samuel and his loss of fifteen thousand pounds' worth of diamonds, just as it appears earlier in this narrative.

"Now, see here," said Hewitt, when he had made me acquainted with his client's tale, "there is something odd about all this. See this post-card which Samuel gave me. It is from Denson, and it makes this morning's appointment. See! 'Be down below at eleven sharp' is the message. He came and he waited just two hours and a quarter, as he tells me, being certain to the time within five minutes. That brings, us to a quarter-past one—the time when he finds he is robbed; and he came downstairs in a very agitated state at a quarter-past one, as I have since ascertained. At two I pass and see him still dancing distractedly on the front steps—certainly very much like a man who has had a serious misfortune, or expects one. At a quarter-past two—that was about it, I think?" (I nodded) "At a quarter-past two you see him, still agitated, diving into the brougham with this black case in his hand; and a little afterward—after all this, mind—he tells me this story of a robbery of diamonds from that very case, and assures me that he sent for me the moment he discovered the loss—that is to say, at a quarter-past one, a positive lie—and has told nobody else. He further assures me that he has told me everything that has happened up to the moment he meets me. Then he goes away—to his office, as he tells me. But you find him posting to Manchester Square in a cab, and there once more plunging into that same mysterious closed brougham. Now why should he do that? He has seen the person in that brougham, presumably, an hour before, and there can be nothing more to communicate, except the result of his interview with me—a thing I warned him to keep to himself. It's odd, isn't it?"

"It is. What can be his motive?"

"I want to know his motive. I object to working for a client who deceives me—indeed, it's unsafe. I may be making myself an accomplice in some criminal scheme. You observe that he never called for the police—a natural impulse in a robbed man. Indeed, he expressly vetoes all communication with the police."

"Of course he gave reasons."

"But the reasons are not good enough. I can't stop a man leaving this country anywhere round the coast except by going to the police."

"Can it be," I suggested, "that Samuel and Denson are working in collusion, and have perhaps insured the stones, and now want your help to make out a case of loss?"

"Scarcely that, I think, for more than one reason. First, it isn't a risk any insurer would take, in the circumstances. Next, the insurer would certainly want to know why the police were not informed at once. But there is more. I have not been idle this while, as you would know. I will tell you some of the things I have ascertained. To begin with, Samuel is known in Hatton Garden only as a dealer on a very small and peddling scale. A dabbler in commissions, in fact, rather than a buyer and seller of diamonds in quantities on his own account. His office is nothing but a desk in a small room he shares with two others—small dealers like himself. When I spoke to the people most likely to know, of his offering fifteen thousand pounds' worth of diamonds on his own account, they laughed. An investment of two or three hundred pounds in stones was about his limit, they said. Now that fact offers fresh suggestions, doesn't it?" Hewitt looked at me significantly.

"You mean," I said after a little consideration, "that Samuel may have been entrusted with the diamonds to sell by the real owner, and has made all these arrangements with Denson to get the gems for themselves and represent them as stolen?"

Hewitt nodded thoughtfully. "There's that possibility," he said. "Though even in that case the owner would certainly want to know why the police had not been told, and I don't know what satisfactory answer Samuel could make. And more, I find that no such robbery has been reported to any of the principal dealers in Hatton Garden to-day; and, so far as I can ascertain, none of them has entrusted Samuel with anything like so large a quantity of diamonds as he talks of—lately, at any rate."

"Isn't it possible that the diamonds are purely imaginary?" I suggested. "Mightn't there be some trick played on that basis? Perhaps a trick on the American customer—if there was one."

Hewitt was thoughtful. "There are many possibilities," he said, "which I must consider. The diamonds may even be stolen property to begin with; that would account for a great deal, though perhaps not all. But the whole thing is so oddly suspicious, that unless my client is willing to let me a great deal further into his confidence tomorrow morning I shall throw up the case."

"Did you direct any inquiries after Denson?"

"Of course; which brings me to the other things I have ascertained. He has not been here long—a few months. I cannot find that he has been doing any particular business all the time with anybody except Samuel. With him, however, he seems to have been very friendly. The housekeeper speaks of them as being 'very thick together.' The rooms are cheaply furnished, as you see. And here is another thing to consider. The housekeeper vows that he never left his glass box at the foot of the stairs from the time Samuel went upstairs first to the time when he came down again, vastly agitated, at a quarter-past one, and sent a message; and during all that time *Denson never passed the box*! And the main door is the only way out."

"But wasn't he there at all?"

"Yes, he was there, certainly, when Samuel came. But note, now. Observe the sequence of things as we know them now. First, there is Denson in his office; I can find nothing of any American visitor, and I am convinced that he is a total fiction, either of Denson's or Samuel and Denson together. Denson is in his office. To him comes Samuel. Neither leaves the place till Samuel comes down at a quarter-past one o'clock. I told you he sent some sort of message. The housekeeper tells me that he called a passing commissionaire and gave him something, though whether it was a telegram or a note he did not see; nor does he know the commissionaire, nor his number—though he could easily be found if it became necessary, no doubt.

"Samuel sends the message, and waits on the steps, watching, in an agitated manner (as would be natural, perhaps, in a man engaged in an anxious and ticklish piece of illegality) for an hour, when this mysterious brougham appears. He takes this black case into the brougham, and he obviously brings it out again, for here it is. Whatever has happened, he brings it out empty. Then he sends the housekeeper for me. When at length I arrive, Denson has certainly gone, but there was an opportunity for that while the housekeeper was absent on the message to my office—*after* all Samuel's agitation, and after he had carried his case to and from the brougham."

"The whole thing is odd enough, certainly, and suspicious enough. Have you found anything else?"

"Yes. Denson lives, or lived, in a boarding house in Bloomsbury. He has only been there two months, however, and they know practically nothing of him. Today he came home at an unusual time, letting himself in with his latchkey, and went away at once with a bag, but the accounts of the exact time are contradictory. One servant thought it was before twelve, and another insisted that it was after one. He has not been back."

"And the office boy—can't you get some information out of him?"

"He hasn't been seen since the morning. I expect Denson told him to take a whole holiday. I can't find where he lives, at the moment, but no doubt he will turn up tomorrow. Not that I expect to get much from him. But I shan't bother. Unless Mr. Samuel will answer satisfactorily some very plain questions I shall ask—and I don't expect he will—I shall throw up the commission. He called, by the way, not long ago, but I was out. We shall see him in the morning, I expect."

A look round Denson's office taught me no more than it had taught Hewitt already. There were two small rooms, one inside the other, with ordinary and cheap office furniture. It was quite plain that any man of ordinary activity and size could have got out of the inner room into the corridor by the means which Samuel suggested—through the hinged wall-light, near the ceiling. Hewitt had meddled with nothing—he would do no more till he was satisfied of the *bonâ fides* of his client; certainly he would not commit himself to breaking open desks or cupboards. And so, the time for my attendance at the office approaching—I was working on the *Morning Ph[oe]nix* then, and ten at night saw my work begin—we shut Denson's office, and went away.

3.

In the morning I was awakened by an impatient knocking at my bedroom door. Going to bed at two or three I was naturally a late riser, and this was about nine. I scrambled sleepily out of bed, and turned the key. Hewitt was standing in my sitting-room, with a newspaper in his hand.

"Sorry to break your morning sleep, Brett," he said, "but something interesting has happened in regard to that business you helped me with yesterday, and you may like to know. Crawl back into bed if you like."

But I was already in my dressing-gown, and groping for my clothes. "No, no, come in and tell me," I said. "What is it?"

Hewitt sat on the bed. "I'll tell you in due order," he said. "First, I saw Samuel again last night—after you had gone away. You remember I went back to my office; I had a letter or two to write which I had set aside in the afternoon. Well, I wrote the letters, shut up, and went downstairs. I opened the outer door, and there was Samuel, in the act of ringing the housekeeper's bell. He said he was very anxious, and couldn't sleep without coming to hear if I had made any progress; he had called before, but I was out. I half thought of taking him back to my office, but decided that it wasn't worthwhile. So I walked along to the corner of the Strand, till I got him well under the lights. Then I stopped and talked to him. 'You ask about the progress in your case, Mr. Samuel,' I said. 'Now, I have sometimes met people who seem to consider me a sort of prophet, seer, or diviner. As a matter of fact, I am nothing but a professional investigator, and even if I were possessed of such an amazing genius as I lay no claim to, I could never succeed in a case, nor even make progress in it, if my client started me with false information, or only told me half the truth. More, when I find that such is the state of affairs, and that if I am to succeed I must begin by investigating my client before I proceed with his case, I throw that case up on the instant—invariably. Do you understand that? Now I must tell you that I have made no progress with your case, none; for that very reason.'"

"He protested, of course—vowed he had told me the simple truth, and so forth. I replied by asking him certain definite questions. First, I asked him whose the diamonds were. He repeated that they were his own. To that I simply replied, 'Good evening, Mr. Samuel,' and turned away. He came after me beseechingly, and prevaricated. He said something about another party having an interest, but the matter being confidential. To that I responded by asking him with whom he had communicated before sending for me, and who was the person in the brougham which he had twice entered. That flabbergasted him.

He said that he couldn't answer those questions without bringing other parties into the matter, to which I answered that it was just those other parties that I meant to know about, if I were to move a step in the matter.

"At this he got into a sad state—imploring, actually imploring, me not to desert him. He said he should do something desperate—something terrible—that night if I didn't relieve his mind, and undertake the case. What he meant he'd do I didn't know, of course, but it didn't move me. I said finally that I would deal only with principals, and that until I had the personal instructions of the actual owner of the diamonds, in addition to a complete explanation of the brougham incident, I should do nothing, and I recommended him to go to the police; and with that I left him."

"And you got nothing more from him than that?"

"Nothing more; but it was something, you see. He admitted, to all intents, that the diamonds were not his own. And now see here. I suppose I left him about ten o'clock. Here is a paragraph in one of this morning's newspapers. It is only in the one paper; the matter seems to have occurred rather late for press."

Hewitt gave me the paper in his hand, pointing to the following paragraph:

"Horrible Discovery.—A shocking discovery was made just before midnight last night, near the York column, where a police-constable found the dead body of a man lying on the stone steps. The body, which was fully clothed in the ordinary dress of a labouring man, bore plain marks of strangulation, and it was evident that a brutal murder had been committed. A singular circumstance was the presence of a curious reddish mark upon the forehead, at first taken for a wound, but soon discovered to be a mark apparently drawn or impressed on the skin. At the time of going to press, no arrest had been made, and so far the affair appears a mystery."

"Well," I said, "this certainly seems curious, especially in the matter of the mark on the forehead. But what has it all to do——"

"To do with Samuel and his diamonds, you mean? I'll tell you. *That dead man is Denson!*"

"Denson?" I exclaimed. "Denson? How?"

"I get it from the housekeeper next door. It seems that when the police came to examine the body they found, among other things—money and a watch, and the like—a piece of an addressed envelope, used to hold a few pins—the pins stuck in and the paper rolled up, you know. There was just enough of it to guess the address by—that of the office next door; and it was the only clue they had. So they came along here at once and knocked up the housekeeper. He went with them and instantly recognised Denson, disguised in labourer's clothes, but Denson, he says, unmistakably."

"And the mark on the forehead?"

"That is very odd. It is an outlined triangle, rather less than an inch along each side. It is quite red, he says, and seems to be done in a greasy, sticky sort of ink or colour."

"Was anything found—the diamonds?"

"No. He says there was money—two or three five-pound notes, I believe, some small change, a watch, keys and so forth; but there's not a word of diamonds."

I paused in my dressing. "Does that mean that the murderer has got them?" I asked. Hewitt pursed his lips and shook his head. "It *may* mean that," he said, "but does it look altogether like it when five-pound notes are left? On the other hand, there is the disguise; the only reason that we know of for that would be that he was bolting with the diamonds. But the really puzzling thing is the mark on the forehead. Why that? Of course, the picturesque and romantic thing to suppose is that it is the mark of some criminal club or society. But criminal associations, such as exist, don't do silly things like that. When criminals rob and murder, they don't go leaving their tracks behind them purposely—they leave nothing that could possibly draw attention to them if they can help it; also, they don't leave five-pound notes. But I'm off to have a look at that mark. Inspector Plummer is in charge of the case—you remember Plummer, don't you, in the Stanway Cameo case, and two or three others? Well, Plummer is an old friend of mine, and not only am I interested in this matter myself, but now that it becomes a case of murder, I must tell the police all I know, merely as a loyal citizen. I've an idea they will want to ask our friend Mr. Samuel some very serious questions."

"Will you go now?"

"Yes, I must waste no more time. You get your breakfast and look out for me, or for a message."

Hewitt was off to Vine Street, and I devoted myself to my toilet and my breakfast, vastly mystified by this tragic turn in a matter already puzzling enough.

★★★★★★

It was not a messenger, but Hewitt himself, who came back in less than an hour. "Come," he said, "Plummer is below, and we are going next door, to Denson's office. I've an idea that we may get at something at last. The police are after Samuel hot-foot. They think he should be made sure of in any case without delay; and I must say they have some reason, on the face of it."

We joined Plummer at once—I have already spoken of Plummer in my accounts of several of Hewitt's cases in which I met him—and we all turned into the office next door. There we found a very frightened and bewildered office boy, whom Denson had given a holiday yesterday, after sending him down to Samuel. He had come to his work as usual, only to meet the housekeeper's tale of the murder of his master and the end of his business prospects. He had little or no information to impart. He had only been employed for a month or six weeks, and during that time his work had been practically nothing.

Plummer nodded at this information, and sniffed comprehensively at the office furniture. "I know this sort o' stuff," he said. "This is the way they fit up long firm offices and such. This place was taken for the job, that's plain, by one or both of 'em."

The boy's address was taken, and he was given a final holiday, and asked to send up the housekeeper as he went out. Plummer passed Hewitt a bunch of keys.

The housekeeper entered. "Now, Hutt," said Martin Hewitt, "you were saying yesterday, I think, that the main front door was the only entrance and exit for this building?"

"That's so, sir—the only one as anybody can use, except me."

"Oh! then there *is* another, then?"

"Well, not exactly to say an entrance, sir. There's a small private door at the back into the court behind, but that's only opened to take in coals and such, and I always have the key. This house isn't like yours, sir; you have no back way into the court as we have. It's a convenience, sometimes."

"Ah, I've no doubt. Do you happen to have the key with you?"

"It's on the bunch hanging up in my box, sir. Shall I fetch it?"

"I should like to see it, if you will."

The housekeeper disappeared, and presently returned with a large bunch of keys.

"This is the one, Mr. Hewitt," he explained, lifting it from among the rest.

Hewitt examined it closely, and then placed beside it one from the bunch Plummer had given him. "It seems you're not the only person who ever had a key exactly like that, Hutt," he said. "See here—this was found in Mr. Denson's pocket."

Plummer nodded sagaciously. "All in the plant," he said. "See—it's brand new; clean as a new pin, and file marks still on it."

"Take us to this back door, Hutt," Hewitt pursued. "We'll try this key. Is there a back staircase?"

There *was* a small back staircase, leading to the coal-cellars, and only used by servants. Down this we all went, and on a lower landing we stopped before a small door. Hewitt slipped the key in the lock and turned it. The door opened easily, and there before us was the little courtyard which I think I have mentioned in one of my other narratives—the courtyard with a narrow passage leading into the next street.

Martin Hewitt seemed singularly excited. "See there," he said, "that is how Denson left the building without passing the housekeeper's box! And now I'm going to make another shot. See here. This key on Denson's bunch attracted my attention because of its noticeable newness compared with most of the others. *Most* of the others, I say, because there is one other just as bright—see! This small one. Now, Hutt, do you happen to have a key like that also?"

Hutt turned the key over in his hand and glanced from it to his own bunch. "Why, yes, sir!" he said presently. "Yes, sir! It's the same as the key of the fire-hose cupboards!"

"Does that key fit them all? How many fire-hose cupboards are there?"

"Two on each floor, sir, one at each end, just against the mains. And one key fits the lot."

"Show us the nearest to this door."

A short, narrow passage led to the main ground-floor corridor, where a cupboard lettered "Fire Hose" stood next the main and its fittings. "We have to keep the hose-cupboards locked," the housekeeper explained apologetically, "'cause o' mischievous boys in the offices."

This key fitted as well as the other. A long coil of brown leather hose hung within, and in a corner lay a piece of chamois leather evidently used for polishing the brass fittings. This Hewitt pulled aside, and there beneath it lay another and cleaner piece of chamois leather, neatly folded and tied round with cord. Hewitt snatched it up. He unfastened the cord; he unrolled the leather, which was sewn into a sort of bag or satchel; and when at last he spread wide the mouth of this satchel, light seemed to spring from out of it, for there lay a glittering heap of brilliants!

"What!" cried Plummer, who first got his speech. "Diamonds! Samuel's diamonds!"

"Diamonds, at any rate," replied Hewitt, "whether Samuel's or somebody else's. But they can't have been there long. How often is this cupboard opened?"

"Every Saturday reg'lar, sir," replied the housekeeper; "just to dust it out and see things is right."

"Now, see here!" said Martin Hewitt, "I've had luck in my conjectures as yet, and I'll try again. Here is what I believe has happened. Every word that Samuel told me about the theft of those diamonds was true, except as to their ownership. Denson has planned all along to rob him of as big a collection of diamonds as he could prompt him to get together, and he has played up to this for months. His smaller dealings one way and another were ground-bait. Very artfully he let Samuel take the diamonds safely away once, in order that he should be less watchful and less suspicious the second time. This second time he does the trick exactly as we see. He hangs up the imaginary American's hat, he escapes by the fanlight, and he goes out by the back way to avoid the housekeeper's observation. He has arranged beforehand for this, too. He has seized an opportunity when the housekeeper has been out of his box to get wax impressions of these two keys, and he has made copies of them.

"And here we come on a curious thing. It is easy enough to understand why he should foresee and get himself a key for the back door, in order to make his escape. But why the key of the hose-cupboard? Why, indeed, should he leave the diamonds behind him at all? It is plain that he meant to come back for them—probably at night. He would have been wholly free from observation in that quiet courtyard, and he could let himself in, get the diamonds, and leave again without exciting the smallest alarm or suspicion. But why take all the trouble? Why not stick to the plunder from the beginning? The plain inference is that he feared somebody or something. He feared being stopped and searched, or he feared being waylaid *sometime during yesterday*. By whom? There's the puzzle, and I can't see the bottom of it, I confess. If I could, perhaps I might know something of last night's murder.

"As to Samuel's prevarications, there is only one explanation that will fit, now that the rest is made clear. He must have been entrusted with these diamonds by a private owner, for sale—secretly. Some lady of conspicuous position in difficulties, probably—perhaps unknown to her husband. Such things occur every day. A common expedient is to sell the stones and have good paste substituted, in the same settings. Samuel would be just the man to carry through a transaction of that sort. That would account for everything. The jewels are *en suite*, cut, but unset—taken from a set of jewellery, and paste substituted. Samuel arranges it all for the lady, finds a customer—Denson—who treats him exactly as he has told us. When he realises the loss Samuel doesn't know what to do. He mustn't call the police, being bound to secrecy on the lady's behalf. He sends her a hasty message, and remains keeping watch by Denson's office.

"She hurries to him with all possible secrecy, keeping her carriage blinds down; he dashes into the brougham to describe the disaster, taking his case with him in his frantic desire to explain things fully. The lady fears publicity, and won't hear of the police—she instructs him to consult me: and consequently, of course, when I recommend communicating with the police he won't listen to the suggestion. Samuel has arranged with the lady to hurry off and report progress as soon as he has consulted me, and this he does, the lady having appointed Manchester Square for the interview. Perhaps she hints some suspicion of Samuel's honesty—rather natural, perhaps, in the circumstances. That terrifies him more than ever, and leads to his frantic appeals to me when I throw the case up. Come, there's my guess at the facts of the case, and I'll back it with twopence and a bit more. Eh, Plummer?"

"I don't take your bet," answered Plummer. "The thing's plain enough; except the murder. There's something deeper there."

Hewitt became grave. "That's true," he said, "and something I can see no way into, as yet. But come—you take this parcel of diamonds, as representing the law. And here comes one of your men, I think."

We had been approaching the front door during this talk, and now a police constable appeared, and saluted Plummer. "Samuel's just been brought in, sir," he reported. "He's half dead with fright, and he's sent a message to Lady H—— in P—— Square; and he says he wants Mr. Martin Hewitt to come and speak for him."

"Poor Samuel!" Hewitt commented. "Come, we'll go and make him happy. Here are the diamonds, and, those safely accounted for, there's no evidence to connect him with the murder. We'll get him out of the mess as soon as possible."

And so they did. Hewitt's reading of the case was correct to a tittle, as it turned out, and with very little delay Samuel was released. But with the message from the police station, the fat was in the fire as regarded Lady H——. Her husband necessarily became acquainted with everything, and there was serious domestic trouble.

Samuel was glad enough to get quit of the business with no worse than a bad fright, as may well be supposed. He showed himself most grateful to Hewitt in after times, giving him excellent confidential advice and information more than once in matters connected with the diamond trade. He is still in business, I believe, in a much larger way, and I have no doubt he is the wiser for his experience, and for the lesson which Hewitt did not forget to rub well in: that it is useless and worse to place a confidential matter in the hands of a man of Hewitt's profession, and at the same time withhold particulars of the case, however unessential they may appear to be.

★★★★★★

But meantime, on the way to Vine Street I asked Hewitt what led him to suppose that the new key on Denson's bunch fitted a lock in that particular office building.

"Call it a lucky guess, if you like," Hewitt answered; "but as a matter of fact it was prompted by pure common sense. Plummer showed me the things found on the body, and I saw at once that the keys offered the only chance of immediate information. I went through them one by one. There was his latchkey—the key with which he had gone into his lodgings to fetch away the disguise. There was another largish key, equally old—probably the key of his office door. There were other smaller keys, also old—plainly belonging to bags and trunks and drawers and so forth. And then there was the large, perfectly new key. What was that? It was not the key of any bag or drawer, clearly—it was the key of a door—a door with a lever lock. What door? Had Denson some other office? Perhaps he had, but first it was best to begin by trying it on places we were already acquainted with. At once I thought of Denson's disappearance unobserved by the housekeeper. Could this be the key of some private exit from the office building? I resolved to test that conjecture first, and it turned out to be the right one. Being successful so far, of course I turned to the other new key and tried that, as you saw."

"But what of that triangular mark on the man's forehead?"

Martin Hewitt became deeply thoughtful. "That," he said, "is a matter wholly beyond me at present, as indeed is the whole business of the murder. Whether we shall ever know more I can't guess, but the matter is deep—deep and difficult and dark. As to the mark itself, that seems to have been impressed from an engraved stamp of some sort. It is a plain equilateral triangle in red outline, measuring about an inch on each side. It is in a greasy, sticky sort of red ink, which may be smeared, but is very difficult, if not impossible, to rub away. What it means I can't at present conjecture. I have told you my reasons for not thinking it the sign of any gang of criminals. But whose sign is it? Surely not that of some self-constituted punisher of crime?

"For such a person, with no risk to himself, could have handed Denson over to the police, if he knew of his offence. Can he have been murdered by an accomplice? But he used no accomplice; if one thing is plain in all that story of the stolen diamonds it is that Denson did the thing wholly by himself. Besides, an accomplice would have taken the keys and have gone and secured the diamonds for himself; else why the murder at all? But no keys were taken—nothing was taken, as far as we can tell. And why was the body placed in that conspicuous position? It is pretty certain that the crime cannot have happened where the body was found—somebody must have heard or seen a struggle in such a place as that. As it is, I should say, the body was probably brought quietly to the spot in a cab, or some such conveyance.

"But mystery envelops this crime everywhere. So far as I can see, there is no clue whatever beyond the Red Triangle, which, as yet, I cannot understand. The strangling points to the murder being committed by a powerful man, certainly, and it is a form of crime that may have been perpetrated silently. But beyond that I can see nothing. The apparent motivelessness of the thing makes the mystery all the darker, and the circumstances we are acquainted with, instead of helping us, seem to complicate the puzzle.

"What was it that Denson feared when he left those diamonds behind him, when he might have carried them away? And why should he fear it in daytime and not at night, since it would seem plain that he meant to have returned for the stones at night? Where did he go to disguise himself yesterday—we know it was not in his lodgings—and where has he left the clothes he discarded?"

All these doubts and mysteries were destined to be cleared up, in more or less degree; but it was not till Hewitt and I had witnessed other singular adventures that the answer came to the problem, the real meaning of the Red Triangle was made apparent, and its connection with the theft of Samuel's diamonds grew clear. For indeed the connection proved in the end to be very intimate indeed. Once, a little later, we were allowed to see a shade farther into the mystery, as

I shall tell in the proper place; but even then the real secret remained hidden from us till the appointed end.

So ended the case of Samuel's diamonds, so far as concerned Samuel himself and the owner; but the case of the Red Triangle had only begun.

THE CASE OF MR. JACOB MASON

1.

The mystery of Denson's death remained a mystery, despite all the police could do. The coroner's jury returned a verdict of "Murder by some person or persons unknown"—which, indeed, was all that could be expected of them; for they had no more before them than the bare fact that the body, disguised in the clothes of a labourer, had been found on the steps near the Duke of York's column, just before midnight, by a police constable. But for the housekeeper's identification, even the name of the victim would have been unknown. The jury certainly wasted some time in idle speculation as to the strange triangular mark found on the forehead, without a speck of evidence to help them; but in the end they returned their verdict, and went home.

But the police knew a little more than the jury, though that little rather confused than helped them. They exercised their judgment at the inquest in withholding all evidence of the theft of diamonds on which the victim had been engaged, the curious particulars of which I have already related. In this they followed their usual course in cases where the evidence withheld could give the jury no help in arriving at their verdict, and at the same time might easily hamper further investigations if revealed. For the theft had been frustrated by Martin Hewitt's exertions, as we have seen, and in any case the thief was now dead and beyond the reach of human punishment. The one matter now remaining for the police was inquiry into the murder of this same thief, and the one object of their exertions the apprehension of the murderer or murderers.

The case, as I have already said, was in the hands of Inspector Plummer, an intelligent officer and an old friend of Hewitt's. A few days' work after the inquest yielded Plummer so little result that he called at Hewitt's office to talk matters over.

"I suppose," Plummer began, "it's no use asking if you've heard anything more of that matter of Denson's murder?"

Hewitt shook his head. "I haven't heard a word," he said. "If I had, it would have come on to you at once. But I hope you've had some luck yourself?"

"Not a scrap; time wasted; and the few off-chance clues I tried have led nowhere, so that I'm where I was at the start. The thing is quite the oddest in all my experience. See how we stand. Here's a man, Denson, who has just pulled off one of the cleverest jewel robberies ever attempted. He so arranges it that he walks safely off with fifteen thousand pounds' worth of diamonds, leaving the victim, Samuel, stuck patiently in an office for an hour or two before he even begins to suspect anything is wrong, and *then* unable to set the police after him, for the reasons you discovered. But this Denson doesn't carry the plunder off straightway, as he so easily might have done—he conceals it in the very house where the robbery was committed, taking with him a key by aid of which he may return and get it. Why?

"As you explained, it was probably because he feared somebody— feared being stopped and searched *on the day of the robbery*—not after, since it was plain he meant to return for his booty at night. Who could this have been, and why did Denson fear him? Mystery number one. Then this Denson is found dead that same night disguised in the clothes of a labourer, in a most conspicuous spot in London—the last place in the world one would expect a murderer to select for depositing his victim's body, for it is evidently *not* the place where the murder was committed. More, on the forehead there is this extraordinary impressed mark of a Red Triangle. Now, what can all that mean? Robbery, perhaps one thinks. But the body isn't robbed! There are three five-pound notes on it, besides a sovereign or two and some small change, a watch and chain, keys and all the rest of it.

"Then one guesses at the diamonds. Perhaps it was an accomplice in the robbery, who finds that Denson is about to bolt with the whole lot. But if there's one thing plain in this amazing business it is that Denson *had* no accomplice; he did the whole thing alone, as you discovered, and he needed no help. More than that, if this were the work of an accomplice why didn't he get the jewels? There were the keys to his hand and he left them! And would such a person actually go out of his way to put the body where it must be discovered at once, instead of concealing it till he could himself get away with the diamonds? Of course not. But there was no accomplice, and it's useless to labour that farther. All these arguments apply equally against the theory that it was the work of some criminal gang. They would have taken all they could get, notes, keys, diamonds and all, and they wouldn't have been so foolish as to exhibit the body with that extraordinary mark;

criminal gangs are not such fools as to take unnecessary chances and gratuitously leave tracks behind them, as you know well enough. Well then, there we stand. So far, do you see any more in it than I do?"

Hewitt shook his head. "No," he said, "I can't say I do. All the considerations you have mentioned have already occurred to me. I talked them over, in fact, with my friend Brett. My connection with the case ceased, of course, with the discovery of the jewels, and about the murder I know no more than has been told me. I never saw the body, and so had no opportunity of picking up any overlooked clue; though doubtless you have seen to that. I know not a tittle more than you have just summarised, and on that alone the thing seems mystery pure and unadulterated."

"All there is beyond that was ascertained by the divisional surgeon on examination of the body. The man died from strangulation, as you know, and the natural presumption from that was that the murderer must have been a powerful man. But the surgeon is of the positive opinion—he is certain, in fact—that Denson was strangled with an instrument—a tourniquet."

"A tourniquet?"

"Yes, a surgeon's tourniquet, such as is used to compress a leg or arm and so stop a flow of blood. He considers the marks unmistakable. Now that might point to the murderer being a medical man."

"Conjecturally, yes; though, of course, it justifies nothing more than conjecture."

"Precisely. Well, that was something, but precious little. A tourniquet is a common thing enough—no more than a band with screw fittings, and there was nothing to show that the tourniquet used was any different from a thousand others; and I can see no particular reason why a doctor should commit a murder like this any more than any other man; in which the divisional surgeon agreed with me. And doctor or none, that Red Triangle was altogether unaccounted for. About that, too, by the way, the divisional surgeon told me a little, but a very useless little. The mark was not properly dried, owing to its slightly greasy nature, and although it was almost impossible to remove it wholly, it *was* possible to scrape off a little of the ink, or colour. Here is a little of it on a paper—quite dried now, of course."

Plummer carefully took from his pocket a small folded paper, unfolded it, and revealed a smaller paper within. On this were two little smears of a bright red colour. "There—that's the stuff," he said. "The surgeon examined it, and he reports it to be rather oddly constituted—so as to bear some affinity of meaning, possibly, to the triangle. For the stuff is a compound of three substances—animal, vegetable and mineral; there is a fine vegetable oil, he says, some waxy preparation, certainly of animal origin, and a mineral—cinnabar: vermilion, in fact. But though there *may* be some connection between the triangle and the substances representing the three natural kingdoms, it gives nothing practical—nothing to go on."

Martin Hewitt had been closely examining the marks on the paper, and now he answered, "I'm not so sure of that, though, Plummer. I think at least that it gives us another conjecture. I should guess that the man you want, as well as being acquainted with the use of the tourniquet, has at some time travelled in, or to, China."

"Why?"

"Unless I am wider of the mark than usual, this is the pigment used on Chinese seals. A Chinaman's seal acts for his signature on all sorts of documents; it is impressed or printed by hand pressure from a little engraved stone die, precisely as this triangle seems to have been, and the ink or colour is almost always red, compounded of vermilion, wax, and oil of sesamum."

Plummer sat up with a whistle. "Phew! Then it may have been done by a Chinaman!"

Hewitt shrugged his shoulders. "It's possible," he said; "of course, though, the sign, the triangle, is not a Chinese character. As a character, of course it is the Greek *Delta*. But it may be no character at all. In the signs of the ancient Cabala, the triangle, apex upward as it was in this case, was the symbol of fire; apex downward, it signified water."

Plummer patted the side of his head distractedly. "Heavens!" he said, "don't tell me I'm to search all China, and Greece, and—wherever the cabalistic pundits come from!"

"Well, no," Hewitt answered with a smile. "I think I should, at any rate, begin in this country. I rather think you might make a beginning at Denson. That is what I should do if the case were mine. See if anything can be ascertained of his previous life—probably under another name or names. *He* may have been in China. Yes, certainly, as we stand at present, I should begin at Denson."

"I think I will," the inspector replied, "though there's precious little to begin on there. I'd like to have you with me on this job, but, of course, that's impossible, since it's purely a police matter. But something, some information, may come your way, and in that case you'll let me know at once, of course."

"Of course I shall—it's a serious matter, as well as a strange one. I wish you all luck!"

Plummer departed to grapple with his difficulties, but in fact it was Hewitt who first heard fresh news of the Red Triangle, and that from a wholly unexpected quarter.

It was, indeed, only two days after Plummer's visit that Kerrett brought into Hewitt's private room the card of the Rev. James Potswood, with a request for a consultation. Mr. Potswood's name was known to Hewitt, as, indeed, it was to many people, as that of a most devoted clergyman, rector of a large parish in north-west London, who devoted not only all his time and personal strength to his work, but also spent every penny of his private income on his parish. It was not a small income that Mr. Potswood spent in this unselfish way, for he came of a wealthy family, and though a good part of his parish was inhabited by well-to-do people, there was quite enough poverty and distress in the poorer quarters to cause this excellent man often to regret that his resources were not even larger. He was a spare active grey-whiskered man of nearly sixty, with prominent and not very handsome features, though his face was full of frank and simple kindliness.

"My errand, Mr. Hewitt," he said, "is of a rather vague, not to say visionary, character, and I doubt if you can help me. But at any rate I will explain the trouble as well as I can. In the first place, am I right in supposing that you were in some way professionally engaged in connection with that extraordinary case of murder a week or so ago—the case in which a man named Denson was found dead on the steps by the Duke of York's column?"

"Yes—and no," Hewitt answered. "I was professionally engaged on a certain matter about which you will not wish me to particularise—since it is the business of a client—and in course of it I came upon the other affair."

"Then before I ask what you know of that mysterious event, Mr. Hewitt, I will tell you my story, so that you may judge whether you are able to reveal anything, or to do anything. Of course, what I say is in the strictest confidence."

"Of course."

"I have a parishioner, a Mr. Jacob Mason, of whom I have seen very little of late years—scarcely anything at all, in fact, till a few days ago. He is fairly well to do, I believe, living a somewhat retired life in a house not far from my rectory. For many years he has laboured at natural science—chemistry in particular—and he has a very excellently fitted laboratory attached to his house. He is a widower, with no children of his own, but his orphan niece, a Miss Creswick, lives under his guardianship. Mr. Mason was never a very regular church-goer, but years ago I saw much more of him than I have of late. I must be perfectly frank with you, Mr. Hewitt, if you are to help me, and therefore I must tell you that we disagreed on points of religion, in such a way that I found it difficult to maintain my former regard for Mr. Mason. He had a curiously fantastic mind, and he was constantly being led to tamper with things that I think are best left alone—what is called spiritualism, for instance, and that horrible form of modern superstition which we hear whispers of at times from the Continent—the alleged devil-propitiation or worship.

"It was not that he did anything I thought morally wrong, you understand—except that he dabbled. And he was always running after some new thing—animal magnetism, or telepathy, or crystal-gazing, or theosophy, or some one of the score of such things that have an attraction for a mind of that sort. And it was a characteristic of each new enthusiasm with him that it prompted him to try to convert *me*; and that in such terms—terms often applied to the doctrines of that religion of which I am a humble minister—as I could in nowise permit in my presence. So that our friendly intercourse, though not interrupted by any definite breaking off, fell away to almost nothing. For which reason I was a little surprised to receive a visit from Mr. Mason on the afternoon of the day on which the newspapers printed the report of the finding of the body of Denson. You may remember that only one morning paper mentioned the matter, and that very briefly; but there were full reports in all the evening papers."

"Yes, the discovery was made very late the previous night."

"So I gathered. Well, I was told that Mr. Mason had been shown into my study, and there I found him. He was in an extremely nervous and agitated state, and he had an evening paper in his hand. With scarcely a preliminary word he burst out, 'Have you seen this in the paper? This—this murder? There—there's the report.' And he thrust the paper into my hands.

"I had not seen or heard anything of the matter, in fact, till that moment, and now he gave me little leisure to read the report. He walked up and down the room, nervously clasping his hands, sometimes together, sometimes at his sides, sometimes before him, shaking his head in a shuddering sort of way, and bursting out once or twice as though the words were uncontrollable, 'What ought I to do? What *can* I do?'

"I looked up from the paper, and he went on, 'Have you read it? It's a murder—a horrid murder. The poor wretched fellow was trying to escape, but he couldn't. It's a murder!'

"'It certainly seems so,' I said. 'But what—did you know this man, Denson?'

"'No, of course not,' Mason replied, 'but there it is, plain enough, and here's another paper with just the same report, but a little shorter.' He pulled the second paper from his pocket. 'I got what different papers I could, but these are the two fullest. It's plain enough it's a brutal murder, isn't it? And the man was a merchant, or an agent, or something, in Portsmouth Street, but he was found in labourer's clothes— proof that he feared it and was trying to escape it; but he couldn't—he couldn't—no! nor anybody. It's awful, awful!'

"'But I don't understand,' I said. 'Won't you sit down?' For Mason continued to pace distractedly about the room. 'What is it you think this unfortunate man was trying to escape? And what am I to do in the matter?'

"He stopped, pressed both hands to his head, and seemed to control himself by a great effort. 'You must excuse me,' he said. 'I'm a bit run down lately, and my nerves are all wrong. I'm talking rather wildly, I'm afraid. I really hardly know why I came to you, except that I haven't a soul I can talk to about—well, about anything, scarcely.'

"He took a chair, and sat for a little while with his head forward on his hand and his eyes directed towards the floor. Then he said, in a musing way, rather as though he was thinking aloud than talking to me, 'You were right, after all, Potswood, and I was a fool to disregard your warnings. I oughtn't to have dabbled—I should have left those things alone.'

"I said nothing, thinking it best not to disturb him, but to leave him free to say what he wanted to say in his own way. He remained quiet for a minute or two more, and then sat up with an appearance of much greater composure. 'You mustn't mind me, Potswood,' he said. 'As I've told you, I'm in a bad state of nerves, and at best I'm an impulsive sort of person, as you know. I needn't have bothered you like this—I came rushing round here without thinking, and if the house had been a bit farther off I should have come to my senses before I reached you. After all, there's nothing so much to disturb one's-self about, and this man—this Denson—may very well have deserved his fate. Don't you think that likely?'

"He added this last question with an involuntary eagerness that scarcely accorded with the indifferent tone with which he had begun. I answered guardedly. I said of course nobody could say what the unhappy man's sins might have been, but that whatever they were they could never justify the fearful sin of murder. 'And,' I added, 'if you know anything of the matter, Mason, or have the smallest suspicion as to who is the guilty person, I'm sure you won't hesitate in your duty.'

"'My duty?' he said. 'Oh yes, of course; my duty. You mean, of course, that any law-abiding citizen who knows of evidence should bring it out. Just so. Of course I haven't any evidence—that paper gave me the first news of the thing.'

"'I think,' I rejoined, 'that anybody who was possessed of even less than evidence—of any suspicion which might lead to evidence—should go at once and place the authorities in possession of all he knows or suspects.'

"'Yes,' he said—very calmly now, though it seemed at cost of a great effort—'so he should; so he should, no doubt, in any ordinary case. But sometimes there are difficulties, you know—great difficulties.' He stopped and looked at me furtively and uneasily. 'A man might fear for his own safety—he might even know that to say what he knew would be to condemn himself to sudden death; and more, perhaps, more. Suppose—it might be, you know—suppose, for instance, a man was placed between the alternatives of neglecting this duty and of breaking a—well an oath, a binding oath of a very serious—terrible—character? An oath, we will say, made previously, without any foreknowledge of the crime?'

"I said that any such oath taken without foreknowledge of the crime could not have contemplated such an event, and that however wrong the taking of such an oath might have been in itself, to assist in concealing such a crime as this murder was infinitely worse—infinitely worse than taking the oath, and infinitely worse than breaking it. Though as to the latter, I repeated that any such engagement made without contemplation or foreknowledge of such a crime would seem to be void in that respect. I went further—much further. I conjured him to make no secret of anything he might know, and not to burden his conscience with complicity—for that was what concealment would amount to—in such a terrible crime. I added some further exhortations which I need not repeat now, and presently his assumed calmness departed utterly, and he became even more agitated than when first he came. He would say nothing further, however, and in the end he went away, saying he would 'think over the matter very seriously.'

"It was quite plain to me that my poor friend was suffering acutely from the burden of some terrible secret, and that in his impulsive way he had rushed to confide in me at the first shock of the news of this murder, and that afterwards his courage had failed him. But I conceived it my duty not to allow such a matter to stand thus. Therefore, giving Mason a few hours for calm consideration, I called on him in the evening. I was told that he was not very well and had gone to bed; he had, however, left a message, in case I should call, to the effect that he would come and see me in the morning. I waited the whole of that next morning and the whole of the afternoon, and saw nothing of him. In the evening urgent parish work took me away, but next morning I called again at Mason's house and saw him. This time he avoided the subject—tried to dodge it, in fact.

"But I was not to be denied, and the result was another scene of alternate agitation and forced calmness. I will not weary you, Mr. Hewitt, with useless repetition, but I may say that I have seen Mason twice since then without bringing him to any definite resolve. As a matter of fact, I believe that he is restrained from saying anything further by fear—sheer terror. He has even gone so far as to deny absolutely that he knows anything of the matter—and then has contradicted himself a minute afterwards. At last, this morning, I have brought him a degree further.

"In the last few days I made it my business to acquaint myself, as far as possible, with the exact circumstances of the tragedy, so far as they are known, and in course of my inquiries I saw the housekeeper of the offices next door—the man who identified the body as Denson's. He either could not, or would not, tell me very much, but he *did* say that you had been working in some way in connection with the case, and that you knew as much of it as anybody. That gave me an idea. This morning I told Mason that not only he, but I also had a duty in respect to this matter, and my duty was to see that nothing in connection with such a crime as this should be hushed up on any consideration or for anybody's fancies. I said that if he liked he need tell me no more, but might take *you* into consultation professionally, as your client, allowing me first to see you and to assure you that, consistently with his own safety, he was anxious to further the ends of justice.

"I said that, as your client, your first duty would be to protect him, that your professional practice would keep your mouth absolutely sealed, and that you already knew a good deal about the crime—perhaps more than he suspected. I protested that this seemed to me the very least he could do, and I warned him that if he refused to do even this, I should have to consider whether it was consistent with my character, as a clergyman and a loyal citizen, any longer to conceal the fact that he was keeping back information that might lead to the apprehension of the murderer. This frightened him, and between the fear of the threat and the fear that you might already know more than he suspected, he authorised me—he was even eager about it—to come and see you; always, of course, under a pledge of strict professional secrecy."

"So far your account is quite clear, Mr. Potswood," Hewitt said. "You have done your best, now I must do mine. You wish me to see Mason at once, no doubt?"

"I arranged to bring you to his house, if you were willing and your engagements permitted, at three this afternoon. Will that do? I have been keeping you, I see—it is past one already. Will you lunch with me at my club?"

"With great pleasure—more especially as I have a few questions to ask as we go along. Is it far?"

"Just at this end of Pall Mall—we will walk, if you like."

"Tell me now," said Hewitt as they went, "anything you know about Mr. Mason's habits, family connections, and so forth, as fully and as minutely as you please. Has he any friends connected with China, for instance?"

"China? Why, no, I think not; except—but I'll tell you all I know. Mr. Mason has no family connections, so far as I am aware—at any rate, in London—except his niece, Miss Creswick. She is within a few months of twenty-one, a charming girl, but horribly shut in, for Mason has almost no visitors. Miss Creswick was his sister's daughter; she lost her mother first and then her father, and was left to the guardianship of her uncle. He was also trustee under the will, and he has, I believe, discretion to keep charge of her property, if he thinks fit, till she reaches the age of twenty-five; though in case of his death she is to inherit in the ordinary way, on coming of age. She is a very dutiful and, indeed, an affectionate niece; though I must say he is scarcely fair to her, keeping her, as he does, so completely secluded from the society of young people of her own age.

"Mere thoughtlessness, I think; he has had no children of his own, his mind is wholly occupied with his science and his fads, and he makes himself a recluse without a thought of the girl. And that brings me to what I was about to say at first, when you asked me if Mr. Mason had any friends connected with China. There is a young doctor— Lawson is his name—some very distant connection of the family, I think, who had a professional appointment of some sort in Shanghai for a year or two, but who is now in London trying to work up a small practice of his own. If you hadn't mentioned China I shouldn't have thought of him, since he never goes to the house now—or, at any rate, is supposed not to go."

"Doesn't go to the house? And why is that?"

"Well, there was a disagreement. What it was I don't quite know, but in the first place it had some connection with some of Mason's experiments—something which Lawson declined to help him with for professional reasons, or else something he declined to do for Lawson, I don't know which. But the thing went further, for, as a matter of fact, there was something between the young people—Lawson is only twenty-eight—and Mason put an end to that. It had been something like a formal engagement, I think, but in the quarrel—Mason was always quarrelling with somebody when he *had* friends, and that's why he has so few now—in the quarrel things were said that ended in a rupture. Whether young Lawson was fortune-hunting or not I cannot say, but Mason certainly accused him of it, and promised to keep back the girl's money as long as he could. In the meantime, Mason declared an end to the engagement, and poor Helen was broken-hearted; for as I have said, she is an affectionate girl, and she hadn't a friend to confide in. But I'm boring you—you don't want to know all these things, surely?"

"On the contrary, I can't possibly know too much, and the particulars can't possibly be too minute. Nine cases out of ten I bring to an issue by means of a triviality. You were saying a little while back that there were almost *no* visitors at Mr. Mason's house; but you said 'almost,' and that means there are some. Who are they?"

"Very occasionally—rarely, in fact—there are one or two members of learned societies with whom he had been in correspondence, or who are old friends. There is a Professor Hutton and a Dr. Burge, I believe; but they don't appear once in six months; and there is Mr. Everard Myatt, who is more frequent. He does not profess to be a great man of science, but he is interested in chemistry as an amateur, and is, I fancy, a sort of disciple of Mason's. He has noticed a sad difference in Mason just lately, and he even called on me yesterday, though I hardly knew him by sight, in the hope that I would back up his urgent suggestion that Mason should go off for a change and a rest. Beyond these I don't think I know of a single visitor. But here we are at the Megatherium."

2.

Mr. Jacob Mason's house stood in its own grounds in a quiet suburban road. It was not a very large house, but it straggled about comfortably in the manner of detached houses built in the suburbs at a time when space was less valuable than now, and it consisted of two floors only. The front door was not far from the road, and was clearly visible to passengers who might chance to look through either of the two iron gates that opened one on each end of the semi-circular drive.

All these things Martin Hewitt noticed as the Rev. Mr. Potswood pushed open one of these gates, and the two walked up the drive. The front door stood in a portico, and a French window gave access to the roof of this portico from a bedroom or dressing-room. As Hewitt and his companion approached the house the French window was pushed open, and a man appeared—a middle-aged, slightly stoutish man with a short, grey beard; commonplace enough in himself, but now convulsed with noisy anger, shaking his fists and stamping on the portico-roof.

"Get out!" he shouted. "Don't come near my house again, or I'll have you flung out! Go away and take your friends with you! D'you hear? Go away, sir, and don't come here annoying me! Go! Go at once!"

Mr. Potswood absolutely staggered with amazement. "Why," he gasped, "it's Mason! He's mad—clean mad! Why, Mason, my poor friend, don't you know me?"

"Get out, I say!" cried Mason. "Give me no more of your talk! I won't have you here!" And now Hewitt caught a glimpse of a girl's face at the window behind the man—a pale and handsome face, drawn with anxiety and fear.

Hewitt seized the clergyman quickly by the arm. "Come," he whispered hurriedly, "come away at once. There is a reason for this. Get away at once. If you can answer back angrily, do so, but at any rate, come away."

He hurried back to the gate, half dragging the astounded rector, who was all too honest a soul to be able to counterfeit an anger he did not feel, even if his amazement had not made him speechless. Hewitt closed the gate behind him and said as he walked, "Where is the rectory? We will go there. He may have sent a message while you were out."

Mechanically the rector took the first turning. "But he's mad!" he protested. "Mad, poor fellow! Merciful heavens, Mr. Hewitt, his whole tale must have been a delusion! A mere madman's fancy! Poor fellow! We must go back, Mr. Hewitt—we really must! We can't leave that poor girl there alone with a raving maniac!"

"No," Hewitt insisted, "come to the rectory. That is no madness, Mr. Potswood. Couldn't you see the colour of the man under the eyes, and the shaking of his beard? That was not anger and it was not madness. It was terror, Mr. Potswood—sheer, sick terror! Terror, or some emotion very much like it."

"But, if terror, why that outburst? What does it mean? If it were terror, why not rather welcome our company and help?"

"Don't you see, Mr. Potswood?" answered Hewitt. "Don't you guess? *Mason is watched, and he knows it!* He was acting his anger before unseen eyes—and he knew they were on him!"

"God be merciful to us all," ejaculated the clergyman. "Poor man—poor sinner! What is this unspeakable thing which has him in its clutches? What had he done to give himself over to such a power?"

"We can tell nothing, and guess nothing, as yet," Hewitt answered. "Let us see if he has sent you a message. It seems likely. If he has it may help us. If not—then I think we must do something decisive at once. But don't hurry so! It is hard to restrain one's self, I know, but there may be eyes on us, Mr. Potswood, and we must not seem to be persisting in our errand."

So they went through the quiet streets for the two or three furlongs that seemed so many miles to the good parson. Arrived at the rectory, Mr. Potswood pushed impatiently through the gate, and was hurrying toward the house, when he perceived a bent little old man standing among some shrubs with his own gardener, who was digging.

"There's Mason's gardener!" the rector exclaimed, and went to meet him.

The old man touched his hat, looked sharply towards Hewitt, who was waiting near the rectory door, and then disappeared round a corner of the house, the rector following. In a few seconds Mr. Potswood reappeared, with a slip of paper in his hand. "Here," he said, "see this! The old man was told to give it to nobody but me, and in nobody else's presence. He's been waiting since one o'clock."

Scrawled on the paper, in trembling and straggling letters, were these words:—

> You must not bring Mr. Martin Hewitt to my house this afternoon. I am watched. It is hopeless. Do not desert me. Bring him tonight after dark at eight. I shall want his best skill, and you shall know all. After dark. Come to the back gate in the lane, which will be ajar, and through the conservatory at the side, where my niece will be waiting at eight, after dark. Burn this and do not let it out of your sight first. Send a line by this man to say you will do as I ask, but do not say what it is, for fear of accidents. Send at once. Do come at eight, with Mr. Hewitt.

"We must do as he says," remarked Hewitt. "We know nothing of this matter, and we must be guided till we do. Just write an unsigned note—'All shall be as you request,' or words to that effect, and be sure the man gives it to him. Let him out behind through the churchyard, if possible, and tell him not to go straight from one house to the other. Is he an intelligent man?"

"Yes—uncommonly shrewd, I believe. He says he can't have been followed. He knows several gardeners hereabout, and he seems to have called on each of them on his way—in at the front of the garden and out at the back each time, after a few minutes' conversation. Gipps is rather a cunning old fellow."

"Ah," said Hewitt admiringly, "that's the sort of messenger I often want. I'll give him half a crown for himself and the money to pay for a telegram on his way. He knows nothing essential, of course?"

"No—only that his master is in some sort of trouble, and warned him that he might be followed."

"That is good. I shall telegraph to Detective-Inspector Plummer, of Scotland Yard. All right—I quite understand that all I have heard is confidential. I shall tell Plummer nothing till I may—indeed, as yet I have very little to tell that would help him. But I think it will be well to have the police within call—we may want them at a moment's notice; I have no police powers, you see, and Plummer has the Denson case in hand. I will ask him to be here, at this house, before a quarter to eight, if you will allow me."

And so the telegram went to Plummer, and Hewitt, accepting the rector's invitation to an early dinner before starting on their visit, resigned himself to wait. He did not like the waste of time, as he frankly told Mr. Potswood. He would have preferred to see Mason at once, at any risk, and to take what means he thought necessary without delay. But as it seemed that the risk was to be chiefly Mason's, and as Mason knew all of which both he and the rector were ignorant, Mason must be allowed to choose his own time.

The excellent Mr. Potswood endured agonies of suspense, though he also insisted that Mason's wishes must be observed exactly. "What is it all—what can it be?" he ejaculated again and again. "What dreadful influence can thus compass a man about, here in London, in these times?"

★★★★★★

It was autumn, and night fell early. Dinner was over at last, and they had scarcely left the table when Plummer arrived, anxious and eager.

"You'll have to trust me a little, Plummer," Hewitt said, when he had made him known to the rector. "I can tell you nothing now—know nothing, in fact, or very little more than nothing. The fact is, I'm going to see a man who promises information to me alone, in confidence, as his client, and I don't know how long I may have to keep you in the dark. But this is where the trail lies hot, and I know that's where you want to be. More, if you're wanted suddenly you'll be at hand. You have a man or two with you, I suppose, as I suggested?"

"Three of the best of them. They will follow us up. Is it far?"

"No, close enough. It is a house in a walled garden—not a high wall. We go in at a gate from the lane behind, and I think you should wait at that gate, and put your men at hand. We mustn't go in as a crowd. The rector had better go first, and you and I will follow on the opposite side of the road."

So the procession was formed, and it was still some three minutes short of eight o'clock when Hewitt and Plummer joined the clergyman at the door in the garden wall behind Mason's house. The door was ajar as had been promised in Mason's note. Leaving Plummer on guard without, Martin Hewitt and the rector stepped as silently as possible through the little kitchen garden and across a strip of lawn toward where a dull light illuminated the conservatory, at the right-hand end of the house. The door of the conservatory was ajar also, and this the rector pushed open.

"Miss Creswick!" the rector called, in a loud whisper. "Miss Creswick!" And with that a girl appeared within.

"Oh, Mr. Potswood," she said, "I'm so glad you've come! I can't think what's wrong with poor uncle! I'm afraid he must be going

457

mad! He is terrified at something, and he has been getting worse, till he could hardly speak or walk. Dr. Lawson has been—about an hour ago, and since then uncle has been much quieter, in his study."

They were entering the dimly-lighted drawing-room now. "Dr. Lawson?" queried the rector. "Rather an unusual visitor, isn't he? How long has he been gone?"

Miss Creswick flushed slightly through all her paleness and grief. "I don't know," she said. "He let himself out, I fancy. He said he could not stay long when he came, but I didn't hear him go; I have been upstairs, and the servants are in the kitchen—they say uncle's mad, and I'm really afraid he is!"

They left the drawing-room, and walked along the corridor and the hall to the opposite side of the house, where the study lay. Miss Creswick tapped gently at the door, but there was no answer. She tapped again, louder, and then came the faint sound of a quick step on the carpet, and then a slight scraping noise, as when a door is closed over a carpet it will scarcely pass. "That's the window into the garden," said Miss Creswick. "Why is he going out? Uncle! Uncle Jacob!"

But now the silence was wholly unbroken. Hewitt snatched quickly at the door-handle. "Locked!" he said. "Come—the quickest way into the garden!"

They ran out at the front door, and round toward the study window. It was a French window, exactly at the opposite end of the house to the conservatory, and now the gas-light streamed out through one half of it, which stood curtainless and ajar, while the curtain was drawn across the other half. Hewitt was the least familiar with the place, but he was quickest on his legs, and more seriously alarmed than the others. He reached the window first—and instantly turned and thrust the rector back against Miss Creswick. "Quick! take her away," he said; "we are too late!" and in the same moment, even as Hewitt dashed over the threshold, he snatched a whistle from his pocket, and blew his hardest.

There on the floor lay Mason, his face dreadful and staring and black; tight in his neck was the band of a tourniquet, and fresh and wet on his forehead was the Red Triangle.

Hewitt snatched at the screw of the tourniquet behind the neck, and loosened it as quickly as hands could turn. But it was too late. Too late, the examining surgeon afterwards said, by a quarter of an hour.

Plummer was at the window with his men at his heels even before the tourniquet was half unscrewed.

"Round the wall of the garden," shouted Hewitt, "and whistle up the police! He's only this moment out!"

The house was alive with shouts and screams. The rector came running back, and Hewitt, busy with his useless attempt at restoration, called now for a doctor. People were scampering in the street, and Hewitt left the victim to the care of the rector, and himself joined Plummer, all in fewer seconds than it may be told in.

But Plummer and his men were beaten, for nothing—not so much as a moving shadow—was seen in the garden or about the walls. Worse, the general trampling would obliterate possible tracks. Plummer set a guard of police about the wall, and came in for consultation with Hewitt.

The body was carried into another room, and Hewitt and Plummer began an examination of the study.

"No signs of a struggle," commented Plummer, "and there was no noise, they say. That's very odd."

"From what I have seen and heard today," said Hewitt, "it is as I should have expected. I believe the man was almost killed by terror before he was strangled—dazed, stricken dumb, paralysed, deafened by it—everything but blinded, poor wretch. And to have been blinded would have been a mercy."

And then, as they made their examination systematically, calmly and without flurry, Hewitt told the whole tale of his day's adventures, together with all he had heard from the rector. "The man's dead," he said, "and his confidence is at an end. Indeed, I never had it—the case, so far as I am concerned, is over before I have even touched it. I haven't had a chance, Plummer; and the thing is deep and dark, deep and dark. Oh, if only the man had let me come to him in the daylight, spite of all! This might all have been averted . . . . There has been a close search here, too. See how everything is turned over. But, stay!"

A low fire smouldered in the grate, and on it lay ashes of many burnt papers. Hewitt passed the shovel carefully under these ashes, lifted them out and placed them gently on the table under the light of the gas-pendant.

"I must leave you," said Plummer. "There'll be an inspector here from the station in a moment—he won't interfere with you, and if anybody can get information out of this room it's you. The next thing for me is plain. I must make sure of Dr. Lawson, if he can be found."

"That is quite right, without a doubt," Hewitt responded. "I may find anything or nothing in this room, and, meanwhile, he was the last person known to have been here, and the only visitor, and he was not heard to go out, unless we heard him go when we were outside the study door. More, it was plainly some one familiar with the place who was able to get away so quickly by the window and the garden."

"And his interest in getting rid of Mason, too—the girl of age in a few months, and all obstacles to getting hold of her, and her money, removed. And—and the surgical tourniquet, the Chinese colour and everything!"

"Quite right, you must make sure of him, as you say. You will get his address from the rector. Meanwhile I'll try to begin my little contribution to the case—to begin it as best I can, after all the chances have made it useless."

3.

It was after nine when Plummer returned. The rector had just rejoined Hewitt in the study, having left poor Miss Creswick, utterly broken down, in her room, in charge of a scarcely less terrified servant. Plummer tapped, and pushed the study door open.

"That's done clean and sure enough," he said, with professional calmness. "And he's a cool hand, is that Dr. Lawson. But have you found anything more? We shall want all we can get."

"We shall," Hewitt assented, "and we shall find more than we've got now, or I'm grievously mistaken. But tell me first what you've done."

He removed the blotting pad, on which the paper ashes still lay, and very carefully shut it away in a wide drawer where no draught could disturb it; he also shut another drawer which stood open.

"We had no difficulty in finding Dr. Lawson," Plummer began. "We met him, in fact, leaving his surgery. I went back with him into the gas-light, and there put it to him plump. Well, he was staggered, badly. Any man would be, of course. But he pulled himself together wonderfully soon, and the first thing he said was that he was just on his way to Mason's house. I thought at first, of course, that he meant to deny that he had been there already, and I gave him the usual warning about what he said being used in evidence. But he went on, and I've got it all safely noted. He admitted that he had been here, at about seven o'clock or just before, and he said he came because Mr. Mason sent for him. That doesn't seem likely, does it, on the facts as we know them?"

"Why, no," said the rector. "The last time he was here he was ordered out, and I know of no reason why he should have been asked to come today. We must ask if anybody was sent."

"I have asked," replied Plummer, "just now, and none of the servants was sent. But Lawson's story is that he *was* sent for and came, though he said he shouldn't say what Mason wanted to see him about till he knew more of the case. Looks as though he hadn't quite got his story ready yet, doesn't it? He had thought over the point about not being seen to go away, though; he said he had let himself out at about half-past seven, being familiar with the ways of the house. And he said that Mason was rather unwell—nervously upset—when he left him, but that was all."

"It's terrible," said the rector, "terrible. It seems impossible to believe it of young Lawson; and yet—and yet!" And then after a pause—"Good heavens!" he burst out again. "Why, I only realise it now! There is the other crime, too! Denson! Two murders! Two—and most certainly by the same hand! Mr. Plummer, I *can't* believe it! Oh, there's more behind, more behind, Mr. Hewitt."

"There *is* more," said Hewitt, "as you will see when I tell you the little I have been able to ascertain. There *is* more behind, though I see little of it yet. First——"

There was a sharp knock at the front door, followed by a ring, muffled in the distant kitchen. Hewitt started up. "Who is this late visitor at this unvisited house?" he said. "If it is the police, well enough. But if anybody else—*anybody*—you may call me Doctor, or anything you please, except Martin Hewitt. Don't forget that!"

There were hurried steps in the hall, a question or two, and the study door was pushed open. Two servants—they would not venture from the kitchen singly this dreadful night—made a confused announcement of "Mr. Myatt," and were instantly pushed aside by Mr. Myatt himself, anxious and agitated.

The late Mr. Mason's closest scientific friend was a palish, black-bearded man, of above middle height, with stooping shoulders and a very quick pair of eyes. There was something about his face that somehow reminded Hewitt of portraits he had seen of John Knox, and yet it was not such a face as his; it seemed oddly unlike in its very likeness.

"What is this dreadful news, Mr. Potswood?" he cried. "I heard people talking in the next street on my way home. Is it true? But the servants have told me so. They say our poor friend—but there has been an arrest, hasn't there?"

The rector nodded gravely.

"And who? Tell me about it, Mr. Potswood—tell me!"

"I think I must see how Miss Creswick is doing," said Hewitt, speaking across to Plummer and making for the door.

"Certainly, doctor, certainly!" answered Plummer with a nod.

Hewitt closed the door behind him, leaving the rector in the full tide of his account of the day's events; but Hewitt's way took him to the kitchen, where the servants were cowering and whispering together, frightened and bewildered.

"Is there any paint or varnish of any sort in the place?" he asked sharply. "Give me anything there is—black, if possible—and a brush, quickly."

"There's—there's Brunswick black, sir, for the stove," said the cook.

"That will do; be quick. Oh, there's Gipps, the gardener! You're just the man I want, Gipps. Come and find me a board or a plank, quick as you please!" And Hewitt pushed the old gardener before him into the garden by the kitchen door.

★★★★★★

A quarter of an hour later, Mr. Everard Myatt, having heard all that was to be told of his friend's terrible death and the arrest of Mr. Lawson, turned to go, meeting Hewitt at the study door on his way.

"And how is poor Miss Creswick by now, doctor?" he asked anxiously.

Hewitt shook his head. "No better than you could expect," he said, "but, on the whole, no worse. She mustn't be seen tonight, of course, but, perhaps, if you could call round in the morning with the rector——"

"Of course—of course! Poor girl—and Dr. Lawson suspected, too—what a terrible blow for her! Anything I can do, doctor, of course, as I said to Mr. Potswood—anything I can do I will do as gladly as such sad circumstances permit."

The rector had been coming to the door with Mr. Myatt, but Plummer, catching a sign from Hewitt, restrained him unseen, and Hewitt and the visitor walked into the hall together.

"They have put out the light, it seems," Hewitt said. "I wonder why—unless people from the crowd have been coming into the garden and staring in through the glass panels. I wonder if we can find the door-handle. Yes, here it is. Dark outside, too! Good-night—mind how you go on the steps!"

Mr. Myatt checked and stumbled in the dark porch, and reached quickly downward.

"There's a board standing across the porch," he said.

"A board?" replied Hewitt. "So there is. Let me move it, or it'll upset somebody. Goodnight!"

Mr. Myatt strode off into the dark night, and Hewitt, noiselessly lifting the board he had himself placed in position, hastened back to the study.

He swung up the board, all sticky and shiny with Brunswick black, and laid it across a spread newspaper, on the table. There on the top, in the midst of the black varnish, were the prints of all five finger-tips of a hand, where Mr. Myatt had felt for the obstruction in the porch.

Hewitt opened the drawer he had shut a little while back, and took therefrom a sheet of writing-paper. And when, with the lens from his pocket, he began to examine that paper in comparison with the finger-marks on the board, Plummer and the rector could see that there were also two distinct finger-marks on the paper and one faint one—all red. Plummer came to look.

"What's this?" he said. "Was this what you were going to tell us about?"

Hewitt did not reply for a few moments, but continued his examination. Then he rose and turned to Plummer.

"You've still got that piece of paper in your pocket, I suppose," he said, "with the little red smudges of colour put there by the police surgeon?"

"Yes—here it is," and the detective took it from his waistcoat pocket.

"Thanks," said Hewitt. "Now, see here. That is a little of the red stuff taken from the mark on Denson's forehead a week ago, and found to consist of vermilion, oil and wax. You have seen the second impression of that awful mark on the forehead of your poor friend Mason, Mr. Potswood, tonight. This room has been searched for papers before we began, and papers have been burnt. In the search this drawer was opened—containing, as you see, nothing but a supply of new headed note-paper. The note-paper was hastily lifted to see if anything else lay beneath, and here, on the bottom sheet, these finger-marks were left in that same adhesive, freely marking red—a sort of stuff that sticks to and marks whatever it touches. The hand that lifted that paper was the hand that impressed that ghastly mark; and the hand that left its print on this black varnish was Mr. Everard Myatt's! Now compare the two!"

Plummer had snatched the lens, and was narrowly comparing the marks ere Hewitt had well finished speaking.

"They are!" he cried, as the rector bent excitedly over him. "They are the same! See—forefinger and middle finger—the same, every line!"

"I needn't tell you," pursued Hewitt, "certainly I needn't tell Plummer, that that is the most certain and scientific method of identification known. The police know that—and use it. But now there is some more. You saw me take that charred paper from the fire. Sometimes words may be read on charred paper—it depends on the paper and the ink. Most of the cinders were too much broken to yield any information, though we may try again by daylight. But one was suggestive. See it!" Hewitt very carefully pulled out the flat drawer that held the cinders.

"You see," he went on, "that one—this—is different from the rest. It has retained its original form better, and has been less broken, because of being of thicker paper. It is a crumpled envelope. Look at the flap—it has never been closed down. Moreover, on that same flap you may read in embossed letters, still visible, part of the name of this house. Plain inference—this was an envelope intended for a letter never sent, and so crumpled up and dropped into the waste-paper basket. But why should such an apparently unimportant thing as that be carefully brought from the waste-paper basket and burnt? Somebody was anxious that the smallest scrap of paper evidencing a certain correspondence should be destroyed.

"But look closely at the front of the envelope—the ink shows a rather lighter grey than the paper. The address is incomplete—at any rate, no more than some of the first line and a little of the second is at all visible now; but it is plain that the first line begins with an E. The letters immediately following are not distinct, but next there is a capital M beginning a name which is clearly Myatt or Myall. Now, *that* is why, when Myatt came here, I took the first steps to hand to get an impression of his finger-tips, in order to compare them with the marks on that paper."

"But why," asked the astonished rector, "why did he come back?"

"Nothing but a bold measure to see how things were going—he came as his own spy, that's all. He's a keen and dangerous man. Don't you remember telling me how he called on you yesterday, though you hardly knew him by sight, merely to ask you to persuade Mason to take a holiday? It struck me as a little odd at the time. He was pumping you, Mr. Potswood—he wanted to find what Mason had been saying! And he is not alone—plainly he is not alone, for poor Mason knew they were watching everywhere. But come—this is no time for speculation. Plummer—you must hold him safely—we'll pick up evidence enough when you've got him. I wouldn't leave it, Plummer—I'd take him tonight!"

"You're right—right, as usual, Mr. Hewitt," Plummer agreed. "More especially as the rector was—well, a little incautious in talking to him just now."

"I? What did I say?" Mr. Potswood asked, astonished. "I had no suspicions—how could I have——"

"No, Mr. Potswood," the detective replied, "you had no suspicions, and for that very reason, in the excitement of the narrative, you called Mr. Martin Hewitt by his right name at least twice! And after I had called him 'doctor,' too!" he added regretfully.

"Is that so?" asked Hewitt.

The poor rector was sadly abashed. "But I really wasn't aware of it, Mr. Hewitt!" he protested. "I hardly think I could—but, there, perhaps I did! Of course, if Inspector Plummer remembers it——"

"He'll be off!" exclaimed Hewitt. "With that hint, and finding the black stuff on his hands, he'll smell a rat instantly! Come, Mr. Potswood—you can show us the nearest way to his house, at any rate! Come—we may get him yet!"

★★★★★★

But the good rector's slip of the tongue was fatal, and Myatt was not yet to meet the fate that fitted him. The house was not far—less than a mile away. It was a detached house, but quite a small one—smaller than Mason's. Plummer blocked every exit with a man, but his caution was wasted. Myatt was gone.

There was the house and the furniture and two servants, just as it might have been any day in the year when Myatt was out for an hour. But now he was out for good. The police watched and waited all night, and all the next day; they waited and watched for a week, and the house was under observation after that, but Myatt never returned. He had made his plans, it was plain, for just such a flight, whenever the necessity might arise; and when he was assured that danger threatened, he simply vanished in the dark of a London night. Search brought no information—not a scrap of telltale paper lay in Calton Lodge—not a letter, not a line. Though, indeed, the police were to see more of Myatt's work yet—and so was Hewitt.

Dr. Lawson's detention did not last the night out. The unhappy Mason had indeed sent to him, by a chance messenger, having grown desperate in long waiting for the return of Gipps from the rectory. Mason was ready to call in any aid, to recall any of the friendships he had sacrificed in the past. But Lawson was long in coming, having received the note after a long professional round, and when at last he arrived, Mason was a little reassured by the promise of Hewitt's visit. Therefore, he did not tell the doctor so much as he might have done. Nevertheless, he talked wildly and vaguely, so that Dr. Lawson feared some disturbance of his reason. The doctor quieted and soothed him, however, and when he left he promised to return after his consultation hour at the surgery was over. He must have been watched away from the house, and then the blow fell that sealed for ever the lips of Jacob Mason.

Poor Miss Creswick was taken from the old house in which she could no longer remain, and for a few months she stayed at the rectory, tended lovingly by the rector's excellent wife—stayed there, in fact, till her wedding-day, which took place early the next year; so that for her and Dr. Lawson the tragedy ended in happiness, after all.

★★★★★★

"God forgive me," cried the rector in the grey of the morning, when it became clear that Myatt had escaped—"God forgive me! Through my stupidity a horrible creature has been set loose in the world to work his diabolical will afresh!"

"Never mind," said Hewitt. "It was not stupidity, Mr. Potswood—nothing but your openness of character. You were not trained to the cunning that we must use in my profession. And there will be more than Myatt to take—he was not alone! It is plain that Mason was found to be wavering in whatever horrible allegiance he had bound himself, and he was watched. No, Myatt was not alone!"

"No, I fear not," replied the clergyman. "I fear not: there is horrible mystery still. The watching and besetting that terrified him so much; the fact that he seems to have yielded up his life without a struggle—and that with help so near; and the connection—what could it have been?—between Mason and the other victim—Denson. That is a deep mystery indeed! And that horrible sign! Mr. Hewitt, you have done much—but not all!"

"No," replied Martin Hewitt, "not nearly all. It is even doubtful whether or not it will be my lot to come across the thing again; but it will be in the hands of the police. And, after all, we have achieved something. For we know that if Myatt can be captured we shall be at the heart of the mystery."

THE CASE OF THE LEVER KEY

1.

In some of the cases which we now know to have been connected with the Red Triangle, there was nothing, in the first place, to show any such association. In some of these cases the connection has become apparent only since the final clearing up of the whole mystery, and with these cases we have no present concern; but in others it revealed itself during the investigation of the case. It was to this second category that the next case belonged—the next at all connectible, that is, after that of the mysterious death of Mr. Jacob Mason and the flight of Everard Myatt.

The case was remarkable in other respects also; first, because in one of its features it had a resemblance to the case of Samuel's diamonds, which first brought the Red Triangle to Hewitt's notice; next, because in its course Hewitt encountered what he declared to be the most ingenious and baffling cryptogram that he had ever seen in the length of his strange experience; and thirdly, because I was the means of placing that cryptogram in his hands, owing to one of those odd chances that arise again and again in real life—are, indeed, so common as to pass almost unregarded—and yet might be thought improbable if offered in the guise of a mere story. Hewitt has often alluded to the curious persistence of such chances in his experience.

I think I have elsewhere mentioned a certain police officer's prolonged search after a criminal for whose arrest he held a warrant, ending in the discovery—because of a misdirected call—that the man had been living all the time next door to himself; and I have also told of the other detective inspector, who, being sent in search of a criminal of whom he had but the meagrest and most unsatisfactory particulars, and whom he scarcely hoped ever to run down, actually *fell over* the man as he was leaving the office where he had received his information, in the doorway of which the fellow had stooped to tie his shoe-lace! But, as Hewitt would say, nothing but the exceptional nature of the surrounding circumstances makes these things seem extraordinary. What more ordinary experience, for example, than to meet a friend in some London street—perhaps one friend of the only dozen or so you have among the four millions of people about you? The odds against you two, of all the millions, choosing the one street of the thousands in London to walk down at the same minute of time, would seem incalculable; and yet the chance comes off so often as to be a matter of the most ordinary experience.

On this occasion I was expecting orders from my editor to produce certain articles on the subject of the London hospitals. It will be remembered that the matter was very much in the air a few years ago, and as nothing is professionally more uncomfortable than to be called on suddenly for an accurate and reasonable leading article on a subject one knows nothing about, I wrote to my friend, Barton McCarthy, who is house-surgeon at St. Augustine's, and he replied by an offer to tell me anything I cared to ask if I would call at the hospital.

I set out accordingly some little time after a breakfast even later than ordinary, and called in at Hewitt's office on my way downstairs, to say that I should not be lunching at our usual place that day.

"No," Hewitt answered, "nor shall I, I expect. I'm off to the City, at once. I have an urgent message to go immediately to Kingsley, Bell and Dalton's, in Broad Street, where a big bond robbery has just been discovered. Perhaps I can give you a lift in my cab?"

We hurried off together accordingly. Hewitt knew nothing of the case he had to examine, and so could tell me nothing, beyond the short urgent request that he would come at once, and that the matter involved the loss of bonds to a very large amount; and he dropped me at a convenient spot, whence my walk to the hospital was but a short one.

I saw my friend McCarthy, and bothered him very successfully for nearly an hour, getting all the information I had expected, and more, during a very interesting walk through the great hospital.

"You get some idea in a place like this," said McCarthy, as we came at last into the receiving room for accident cases, "you get some idea, Brett, of the size of this great London machine working about us. You might walk about the streets for a week and never see a serious accident, or even an accident at all, and yet, you see, here they come all day long—a stream of people damaged or killed in the machine."

A decent workman was having a gashed hand dressed and strapped, and a navvy with bandages about his head was being led away by a friend. Nurses and dressers were waiting ready to take their orderly turns at the incoming casualties, and as we looked a more serious case was brought in on an ambulance by two policemen. The patient was a ragged, disreputable-looking fellow of middle age, in grimy and tattered clothes, whose head had been roughly bandaged by the policemen who brought him. He had been knocked down and kicked on the head by a butcher's cart-horse, it seemed, in Moorgate Street, and he was quite insensible. A very short examination showed that the case was nothing trivial, and McCarthy sent me to sit in his private room to wait lunch, while he gave the matter his personal attention.

When he returned he brought a small crumpled envelope in his hand. "That case is put to bed," he said, "still insensible."

"Is it very bad?" I asked.

"Slight fracture of the occipital, and, of course, concussion of the brain—probably contusion, too, I expect we shall find presently. Not so over serious for a healthy man, but I'm afraid he's an old soaker— the sort that crumple up at a touch. Nobody knows him, and there's nothing to identify him in the pockets—a few coppers, an old knife, and so on. So we can't send to tell his friends—unless we bring in your friend Martin Hewitt to trace 'em out, which would come too expensive. Besides," McCarthy added, dropping into a seat before his desk, "if he's got any friends they'll come, sooner or later, when they miss him. This is the only thing he'd got beside what's in the pockets—he'd been sent on a message, probably."

My friend held up the crumpled envelope and took from it a small key. "He'd got this envelope gripped tightly in his hand," he said, "but there was no address on it, so we tore it open in the hope of finding one inside. But there was nothing there but the key. If you were a very promising pupil of your friend Hewitt, I should expect you to take a glance at it and tell us the man's address at once, together with his age, birthplace, when vaccinated, and the residence of his maternal grandmother. But you're not, so I'll let you off."

McCarthy turned the key idly about in his hand and tried it on a lock in his desk. "Stopped up," he remarked, withdrawing it, and peeping into the barrel; "not dirt, either—stopped up with paper! What's that for?"

He took a pin to clear the barrel, and the paper came away quite readily. It was a tight little roll, which the surgeon pulled out into a small strip rather less than three inches long and about half-an-inch broad.

"Hullo!" he exclaimed. "Look here! Here's a job for Martin Hewitt, after all! Figures! What does that mean? And what an amazing place to put them in! A key barrel! By Jove, Brett, this looks like one of your favourite adventures. Somebody sends a key in an envelope, and a row of incomprehensible figures rolled up inside the key. Look at it!"

I took the key and the paper. The key was of a good sort; small, inscribed "Tripp's Patent" on the bow, and it evidently belonged to a superior lever lock. The paper which had come from the barrel was very thin and tough—a kind I have seen used in typewriters. It had been very carefully and closely rolled, and then pushed into the key so that its natural tendency to open out held it tightly within. Written upon it with a fine pen appeared a series of very minute figures, thus:—

```
9, 8, 14, 4, 20, 18, 5, 9 ; 15, 19, 20,
0, 3, 9, 8, 5 ; 3, 23, 0, 0, 5, 13, 14,
19 ; 19, 20, 0, 0, 0, 0, 6, 1 ; 5, 20, 0,
0, 0, 0, 3, 22 ; 1, 15, 0, 0, 0  0, 18,
5 ; 1, 8, 20, 11, 18, 9, 5, 20 ; 12, 5,
23, 14, 14, 1, 1, 20.
```

"Well," inquired McCarthy, "what do you make of it?"

"Not much as yet," I admitted. "But it's pretty certain it must be a cryptogram or code-writing of some sort; and if that's the case, I *think* I might back myself to read it—with a little time." For I well remembered the case of the "Flitterbat Lancers," and the lesson in cypher-reading which Hewitt then gave me.

"Come," my friend replied, much interested, "let's see how you do it. Meantime we'll get on with our lunch."

I took a pencil and a spare sheet of paper, and I studied those figures all through lunch and for some little time after. It soon became plain that the problem was much more difficult than it looked, and I said so. "At the first glance," I said, "it looked a fairly easy cypher; but as a matter of fact, I don't think it's easy at all. One assumes, of course, that the figures stand for letters, and on that assumption two or three peculiarities are noticeable. First, the highest number written here is 23, so that all the letters indicated, in whatever order they may come, are within the compass of the twenty-six letters of the alphabet. Next, the numbers most frequently repeated, if we except the noughts, are 5 and 20, which occur seven times each.

"Now, the vowel most frequently occurring in average English writing is e, and you will at once perceive that e is number five in the alphabet, counting from the beginning. More, if we go on counting so, we shall find that 20 is *t*, which is one of the most frequently occurring consonants. This would seem to hint that the cypher is of the very simplest description, consisting of the mere substitution of figures for letters in the exact order of the alphabet. But what, then, of the noughts? What can they mean? More especially when we consider that in three places there are actually four noughts in succession; for, of course, no letter is repeated four times successively in any English word, nor in any foreign word that I can imagine. But let us put down the letters in substitution for the figures, on the supposition that the figures stand for letters in their alphabetical order, leaving the noughts as they are. Then we get this."

I rapidly pencilled the letters on the spare paper, thus:—*i, h, n, d, t, r, e, i; o, s, t, o, c, i, h, e; c, w, o, o, e, m, n, s; s, t, o, o, o, o, f, a; e, t, o, o, o, o, c, v; a, o, o, o, o, o, r, e; a, h, t, k, r, i, e, t; l, e, w, n, n, a, a, t.*

"See there," I said. "Now, I can make nothing of that. When I come to examine the comparative frequency of the different letters, I find them much as they might be expected to be in a sentence of normal English, and any change would destroy the proportion. *E* and *t* are the most frequent, and then come *a, n, i, r, s,* and *c*. But as they stand they all mean nothing. It is possible that this may be one of the difficult variable letter cyphers, which Hewitt might read, but I can't. But even then, if the values of the letters change as they would do, they would get out of their normal proportions of frequency; so that a variable letter cypher seems unlikely. And there is another oddity. Look, and you will see that, counting the noughts in, the letters go in groups of eight, with a semi-colon at the end of each group.

"Now, it is impossible that the message can be a sentence in which every word has exactly eight letters—or, at least, I should think so. It can scarcely be that the semi-colon itself means a letter—it would be singular for one letter to occur with such curious regularity as that. There is no other visible division between the words, nor any single one of the usual aids by which the reader of secret cypher is able to take a hold of his work. No, I'm afraid I must give it up; for the present, at any rate. But I really think it is a thing that would vastly interest Hewitt, if I might show it to him. I suppose I mustn't?"

"Well," McCarthy answered, "perhaps it isn't strictly according to rule, but I think I might venture to lend it to you till tomorrow, if that will do. Indeed, I think, on second thoughts, that I may consider my-self quite justified, since it may lead to the man's identification, and it will be a sufficient answer to any inquiry to say that I have shown it to Mr. Martin Hewitt for that purpose. But you'll be careful of it, won't you? Do you want the key, too?"

"I think, if I may, I will take the key and the envelope all together. You can never tell what may or what may not help him, and the three things may hang together, and perhaps explain each other in some mysterious way."

"Very good—here's the whole bag of tricks. It's a queer business altogether, and I must say I feel inquisitive; certainly, if Hewitt can get anything out of those figures I shall be mighty curious to know how he does it. You'll come in again tomorrow, then?"

I promised I would, and walked off with the crumpled envelope, the little key, and the puzzling strip of figures. Since the lesson from Hewitt which I have alluded to, I had often amused myself with cryptogram reading, and I had never found a cypher message in a newspaper "agony-column" the meaning of which I could not get at with a little trouble. But this was something altogether beyond me; and if I have any reader who prides himself on his ability to read secret cypher, I recommend him to try his skill on this one before he reads further.

The circumstances, too, seemed as puzzling as the writing itself. Why, if any person wished to send a note and a key in a closed envelope, should he take the trouble to pack the note inside the key? Why, especially when the note was already written in so baffling a cypher? Whither had this ragged messenger been going with the mysterious package, and who had sent him, and why?

Guessing and musing, I reached home, and found that Hewitt had returned before me. I made my way into his office, and came on him sitting at his desk with a large lens, attentively examining a broken brass padlock.

"Am I bothering you?" I asked. "Are you on the bond robbery, now?"

Martin Hewitt nodded, with a jerk of the hand toward the padlock. "It's a tough job," he said, "and I shall shut myself up presently and think hard over it; just now I can't see my way into it at all. But what have you got there?"

"Never mind," I said, "you're too busy now. I came across something very odd at the hospital, which I thought would interest you—that's all."

"Very well, let me see it. I haven't begun my bout of cogitation yet. Show me."

I put the envelope, the key and the paper on the table before him. Hewitt, with a glance of surprise, picked up the key and examined it. "That's curious," he said, and straightway began fitting the key to the broken padlock on the desk.

"Why, man alive!" he cried, with a sudden burst of excitement, "where did you get this? This—this is the article—the key—the very thing I want!" He sprang to his feet and stared in my face in sheer amazement. "Heavens, Brett, the thing's almost supernatural! I've a broken lever padlock here, and of all things in the world I wanted to find the one key that fitted it; and you calmly walk in and clap down the very thing under my nose! Where did you get it?"

I told him the tale of the man who had been knocked down in Moorgate Street, and I explained exactly how the paper, the key and the envelope were found in relation to each other, and why I had brought them.

"And when was the man knocked over?" Hewitt asked.

"Sometime between one and two o'clock, I should say," I replied. "They brought him in well before two, at any rate."

Hewitt stared into vacancy for a moment, thinking hard. Then he said, "Brett, I believe you've saved my reputation—not that it could have suffered much, perhaps, in such a desperate case. But as a fact I had already advised the calling in of the police, and should, perhaps, even have given up the part of the case still left me. But this ought to put me on the proper track. You see, every one of these patent lever locks differs in some slight degree from all the rest, and only its own key will fit it; and here, by this amazing piece of good luck, is the one key for this very lock, and the man who had it is detained in hospital. Come, I'm off to see him. Insensible, you say, when you left?"

"Yes," I answered, "and likely to be so for some time, McCarthy thinks; so you probably won't get much information out of him just yet. But the cypher——"

"I'll examine the cypher as I go along, I think. But I should like to take a look at the man, at any rate, even if he can't tell me anything. Will you give me a note to your friend McCarthy?"

"Of course," I answered, readily, and sat down to scribble the few lines necessary to introduce Hewitt.

When I had finished, Hewitt, who had been examining the cryptogram meanwhile, remarked: "This cypher is something out of the common, Brett. I certainly don't expect to be able to read it in the cab-journey—perhaps not in a week of study. The man who devised this is a man of abilities altogether beyond the average."

"I have had my best try at it," I said, "but it beats me wholly. I brought it purely as a matter of curiosity, to show you; it was the merest chance that I brought the key as well."

"And if you hadn't I should probably have put the cypher aside until the case was over, and so have missed the whole thing. Another lesson never to despise what seem like trifles. If you have studied the cypher you have no doubt observed—but there, we'll talk that over afterwards, and the whole case if you like. I'll go now, and I'll tell you all about the business when time permits."

2.

Here is the case of the bond robbery as it had been presented to Martin Hewitt that morning, while I was at St. Augustine's Hospital, and as I learned it from him later. I had been a little puzzled to hear Hewitt say that the case had seemed so desperately hopeless that he advised the calling in of the police, because my experience had rather been that it was Hewitt who was commonly called in—often too late—when the police were beaten, and I had never before heard of a case in which this order of things was reversed. It turned out, however, as will be seen, that in the state of the matter as it first presented itself the only measures that seemed possible were such as it was in the power of the police alone to adopt.

Messrs. Kingsley, Bell, and Dalton were an old-established firm of brokers whose operations were not enormous nor much in the eye of the public, but who carried on a steady and reputable business in a set of offices high up in a great building in Broad Street—a building so large that the notice "Offices to let" was a permanent fixture in the front porch. The firm's clients were chiefly steady-going investors of the old-fashioned sort, who wished to avoid all speculative fireworks, and to deal through a firm whose habits were conformable to their own. The last Kingsley had left the firm and soon afterward died, some few years back, and now the head of the firm was Mr. Robert Stanstead Bell, a gentleman of some sixty years of age. There were a couple of sleeping partners—relations—but the one other active partner was Mr. Clarence Dalton, a young man but recently advanced to partnership, and, it was said, likely to become Mr. Bell's son-in-law whenever the old gentleman's daughter Lilian should be married.

The steady, even round of business to which Kingsley, Bell, and Dalton, and their clerks were accustomed was suddenly interrupted by an appalling loss. It was discovered that bonds were missing from the safe, bonds to the amount of some £25,000; and whence, how, or when they were taken was an utter mystery. It was this loss which had occasioned the urgent message to Hewitt.

When Hewitt reached the spot he was shown at once into an inner office, where Mr. Bell sat waiting. The old gentleman was in a sad state of agitation, and it was with some difficulty that Hewitt got from him a reasonably connected account of the trouble.

"The loss comes at such a time, Mr. Hewitt," the senior partner explained, "that I don't know but it may ruin us utterly, unless my clients' property can be recovered. We have had to pay out heavy sums of late to the representatives of dead or retiring partners, and other circumstances combine with these to make the matter in this way even more terribly serious than the very large amount of the loss would seem to suggest. So I beg you will do what you can."

"That of course," responded Hewitt. "But please tell me, as clearly as you can, the precise circumstances of the case. Where were the bonds taken from?"

"This safe," Mr. Bell answered, turning toward a very large and heavy one, which might almost have been called a small strong room. "They were kept, together with others, in this box, one of several, as you see. The box was fastened, like the rest, with a Tripp's patent lever padlock, the only key of which I kept, together with the key of the safe."

The box indicated was one of ordinary thin sheet iron, japanned black—something like what is called a deed box.

"The padlock has been broken open, I see," Hewitt observed.

"Yes, but I did that myself this morning. It had been blocked up in some way, so that the key wouldn't turn—doubtless in order to cause delay when next the box should come to be opened. As it was I might have desisted and put off opening it till later, but I had a reason for wishing to refer at once to a list which was in the box, and so I decided to break the padlock. It was more difficult than one might expect, with such a small padlock."

"And then you discovered your loss?"

"Then I discovered the loss, Mr. Hewitt, though it was a mere chance even then. For see! All the bonds have not been taken, and those left are placed on the top, while the space below is filled with dummies. I hardly know why I turned them over—for the list was at the top—but I did, and then——" Mr. Bell finished with a despairing gesture.

"And this was some time this morning?"

"At about half-past eleven."

"And when did you last open the box before that?"

"Ten days ago at least, I should think—and even then the bonds may have been gone, for I only opened it to refer to the same list, and

I examined nothing else."

"You say that some bonds are left and others are gone. I presume those taken are such as would be easy to negotiate, and those left are such as would be difficult. Is that the fact?"

"Precisely."

"Then the thief evidently knows the ropes, and altogether the matter would seem awkward. For anything short of ten days, you see, and quite possibly for even a longer time than that, these bonds have been in the undisturbed possession of some person who could easily dispose of them, and would certainly do so without a moment's delay."

Mr. Bell nodded sadly. "Quite true," he said.

"But now tell me a little more. You say you yourself keep the only key of the padlock, as well as the key of the safe. So that you open the safe every morning yourself and close it at night?"

"Just so."

"And do you never entrust the keys to anybody else?"

"The key of the safe is on a separate bunch from the key of the box. This second bunch, with the key of the box, is *always* in my pocket, and not a soul else ever touches it. The other bunch, with the outer key of the safe, I sometimes hand to my partner, or to the head clerk, Mr. Foster, if something is wanted from the safe when I am busy. Though, as a rule, the safe door is open so long as I am about the place. Nothing but the books can be taken out without the use of other keys for the drawers and boxes, which I keep on the private bunch."

"And would it be possible for anybody—anybody at all, mind—to get at that private bunch of keys in such a way, for instance, as to be able to take a wax impression of the key of that bond-box?"

"No, certainly not," Mr. Bell answered with decision. "Certainly not. At any rate, not in this office," he added.

"Ah, not in this office. Anywhere else?"

"No, nor anywhere else, I should think," the other replied, though this time a little more thoughtfully. "There's only my own family at home and the servants and——"

"Anybody who has access to this room of the office?" Hewitt asked keenly.

Mr. Bell seemed a little startled.

"Why, no," he said, "nobody at home comes to the office—not even a visitor, except, of course, my junior partner, who visits the room pretty frequently."

"Very well. You don't remember ever mislaying the keys temporarily, I suppose, either here or at home?"

"No-o," Mr. Bell replied slowly. "I can't say that I do remember anything of the sort. No—and I believe I should be sure to remember if I had."

"Ah! And when you realised your loss what did you do? Told your partner first, I suppose?"

"No—he doesn't know of the discovery. He went out just before I made it, and I don't expect him in again today." But as Mr. Bell spoke there grew plain in his face the pallor of a new fear.

Martin Hewitt observed it, but kept his thoughts to himself. "Well," he said, "you didn't tell your partner. Nor the police?"

"No, Mr. Hewitt. You see, of course, the first thing the police attempt is to catch and punish the thief, and they make the recovery of the property a subsidiary object. But for me, Mr. Hewitt, the recovery of the property, as I have explained, is the one great consideration. Punish the thief by all means, but first save me from ruin, Mr. Hewitt! That is why I sent for you; for that, and because I thought it might be advisable to keep the matter quiet, till you had taken some steps."

"There is something in that consideration, certainly. So you have told nobody of the loss, except me?"

"Nobody but Foster, my head clerk—an old and faithful servant. It was he, in fact, who suggested sending for you. As he put it very forcibly, you can act for *me* and my interests, while the police act for themselves, and—very properly, of course, as police—in the interest of the community."

"Very well. I see you have several clerks in the outer office. Do they ever come into this room?"

"Never, unless they are sent for."

"If you and your partner were out, and one of the clerks came in *without* being sent for, the rest would know it, of course?"

"Certainly."

"I observe three private rooms opening out of this. What are they?"

"This is a sort of extra inner room where I have private interviews with clients—I was in there with a client for half an hour this morning before I discovered the loss. The next is a mere little box of a room where the correspondence clerk sits and works. The other is a larger place—it is shared between my partner, Mr. Clarence Dalton, and the head clerk, Mr. Foster."

"Now let me have your broken padlock—and the key. I see you have forced up the front plate with a screw-driver. I will borrow that

477

screwdriver, if you please, and force it off completely."

Hewitt's client produced a screwdriver from a drawer, and in a very few moments the interior of the little padlock lay uncovered. Hewitt examined the lock attentively for some few minutes, trying the key several times against the levers. Then he stood up and said—

"Mr. Bell, you have made a mistake. This is not your lock at all!"

"Not my lock!" exclaimed the broker. "What do you mean? I tell you it is the lock of that box, and I broke it open myself!"

"Yes," answered Hewitt calmly, "it was on that box, and you broke it open yourself; but all the same it is not your lock. Let me explain. These are very good little padlocks, with an excellent lever action, 'dogged against detent,' as the technical phrase goes; so that only the key properly made for each lock will open it. They are so good, indeed, as locks, that it would be a waste of time to try picking them, when, because of their small size, it is so very easy to break them apart, just as you have done yourself, and just as I could probably have done in half the time, having had rather more experience. Now that is what has been done with *your* lock by the person who has your bonds. But of course a broken lock has one disadvantage as compared with a skilfully picked lock—it shows at the first glance what has happened. In this case, Mr. Bell, *your* lock has been broken and taken away, and the thief, having first provided himself with another padlock of precisely the same make and size, has substituted *that*, locked it with its proper key and so left it!"

"What! Then that was why——"

"That, of course, was why you supposed it to be out of order when you attempted to open it with *your* key. As a matter of fact, it is even now in perfectly good order, except for the damage we have jointly committed with the screw-driver. And now, observe! That lock was shut by another key; if the man that did that is as sharp as I suppose he is, he will have got rid of that key at once. But perhaps he hasn't; and if not, then the man who has that key is the thief. At any rate, the key is the clue we must hunt for. Let us have your clerks in one by one, and look at their keys. Some are out at lunch by this time, probably?"

"No—I said they might be wanted, so kept them. I thought you might prefer to see them before they went out."

"Very well thought of, but perhaps scarcely judicious, on the whole. Because if there *is* a guilty person among them it may give him a hint; and the odds are rather against its being very useful, considering the possibility—even probability—that the bonds and the collateral evidence left here days ago. But we'll look at their keys, by all means, and then they may go to lunch as soon as you please. Let me do the talking, or perhaps you'll start a scare. Send for the nearest clerks first, then the others. As each comes in, mention his name, so that I can hear it. Say, 'Oh, Mr. Brown'—or Jones, or what not—'have you some keys about you?' Don't mention my name, and I will do the rest. Push to the door of the safe, and lock this drawer in the table."

Mr. Bell did as Hewitt directed, and then called the head clerk, Mr. Foster, from his room, with the prescribed inquiry about keys.

"Yes, Mr. Foster," Hewitt added pleasantly, "I'm not sure that the lock is quite in order, but I promised to open it for Mr. Bell, so we'll try."

Mr. Foster, a slim, active old gentleman, grown grey in the firm's service, pulled a bunch of keys from his pocket, and Hewitt scrutinised each narrowly. "No," he said, "I'm afraid none of these will do. Stay," he added suddenly, and turning his back, carried the bunch to the window. "No," he concluded, as he came back to the table and tried one of the keys fruitlessly. "No, I'm afraid none of those will do. Thank you, Mr. Foster. You don't happen to have any more, do you?"

No, Mr. Foster hadn't any more, and he retired to his room. Then Mr. Bell called the correspondence clerk, Mr. Henning. Mr. Henning was a much younger man than the head clerk—twenty-six or so—pale and blue-eyed, with weak whiskers and a straggling moustache. His keys were just as readily produced as Mr. Foster's, but again Hewitt's examination was unsuccessful. The only other key he had belonged to the typewriter, and *that* did not fit.

Then came Mr. Potter, the book-keeper, round, and tubby, and puffy, and his keys went under inspection in the same way, taking a little longer this time, with two separate dashes to the light of the window. Then there was Mr. Robson, young and spruce, Mr. Clancy, older and less tidy, and four or five more. All the keys were examined, all with the same lack of success, and all the clerks were sent away to take their turns at lunch.

"No," Hewitt reported, as soon as he and Mr. Bell were alone again, "it was certainly none of those keys. Though indeed, my little attempt was desperate at best. A man would be a fool to keep *that* key longer than he needed it, and especially to string it with his others. Still, of course, it is by just such blunders as that that nine criminals out of ten are discovered. And now let me take a good look at that box and its contents."

He lifted the box from the safe to the table, and narrowly scrutinised its exterior, especially about the hasp, where the padlock had been. "Either the thief was an experienced hand," he said, "or he took some steady practice with a few such padlocks as this before setting to work. There are no signs of banging about or slipping of tools anywhere."

"But, of course, banging or anything violent would have been noticed in a place like this," Mr. Bell remarked.

"In office hours, yes," responded Hewitt. "But we mustn't forget that office hours are only seven or eight out of the twenty-four."

"But you don't suspect burglary, do you?"

"I'm afraid, as yet, I've precious little ground for suspecting anything definite," Hewitt answered; "but we must keep awake to every possibility. Now let us see the dummies." He turned them over, and loosened them wherever they were tied. "Yes," he remarked, "quite neatly done. Filled in with ordinary blank foolscap, such as, no doubt, you have in your office—but, then, it is in every other office, too; every stationer has it by the ream. No marks anywhere—no old newspapers, nothing that could give the shadow of a clue." He dropped the last of the papers, and turned to his client. "Mr. Bell," he said, "this thing has been thought out to the last inch. There is something like genius in this robbery—if genius is the capacity for taking pains. My advice to you is to call in the Scotland Yard people at once."

"Do you mean you can do nothing?" asked Mr. Bell despairingly. "Don't tell me that, Mr. Hewitt!"

"No, I don't mean that," Hewitt answered. "I mean that until I have had time to think the thing over very thoroughly I can't tell what I can or ought to do. Meantime, I think the police should know; not because I think they can see farther into the thing than I can—for, indeed, I don't think they can; but simply because the thief is getting a longer start every moment, and the police are armed with powers that are not at my disposal. They can get search warrants, stop people at ports and railway stations, arrest suspects—do a score of things that will be necessary. Send to Scotland Yard and get Detective Inspector Plummer, if he's available—he's as good a man as they have.

"Tell him that you've engaged me, or, better still, write a note to the Scotland Yard authorities, and let me have it, to send or not as I think best, after I have turned the thing over in my mind. I shall take one good look round this office, and then run back to my rooms for an hour or two's hard consideration of whatever I may see. One or two small things I *have* seen already—though I'd rather not mention them till I've made up my mind how they bear. Matters seem likely to have gone so far that perhaps the regular police course of catching the thief first will be the best plan, if it can be done. Meantime, it will be my business to keep my eye first on the recovery of the bonds. But I think we must have the police, Mr. Bell. Now, I'll take my general look round."

3.

After Martin Hewitt had rushed off to St. Augustine's Hospital with the key, the envelope, and the cypher I had brought him, I heard nothing of him till dusk fell—about six. Then I received this telegram:—

Cypher read. Most interesting case. If you can spare an hour be outside 120 Broad Street at six thirty.—Hewitt.

I had to be at my office between eight and nine, and to keep Hewitt's appointment I should probably have to sacrifice my dinner. But I was particularly curious to know the meaning of that cypher, and just as curious to know how it could be read; and, moreover, I knew that any case that Hewitt called interesting would probably be interesting above the common. So I took my hat and sought a cab.

I was first at the meeting-place—indeed, a little before my time. No. 120 Broad Street was a great new building of offices, most, if not all, closed at this time—a fact indicated by the shutting of one of the halves of the big front door, where a char-woman was sweeping the steps under the board which announced that offices were to be let. I waited nearly a quarter of an hour, and then at last a hansom stopped and deposited Hewitt and another older gentleman before me.

"Hope we haven't kept you waiting, Brett," Hewitt said. "This is Mr. Bell, of Kingsley, Bell and Dalton; it took me a little longer than I expected to reach him. His offices are shut, and the clerks all gone, but we are going to turn up the lights for a bit. The lift man is gone too, I expect, so we shall have a good long stair-climb."

As to the lift man Hewitt was right, and during our long climb I received, briefly, an account of the loss Mr. Bell's firm had suffered. "I have told Mr. Bell," Hewitt said, "that it was you who happened across the key in such an odd fashion, and when I wired I was sure he would be glad to let you see the upshot of your strange bit of luck. I was also pretty sure that you would like to see it, too. For I really believe that this case—which I confess seemed pretty near hopeless a few hours ago—is coming to an issue now, and here."

"Did you get any information out of the man in the hospital?" I asked.

"Not a scrap," Hewitt replied. "He was still insensible, and though I saw his clothes, and they told me a good deal about the gentleman's personal habits—which are not dazzlingly noble, to put it mildly—they told me nothing else whatever, except that he had recently been knocked down in the mud, which I knew already. But the cypher has told me something, as I will explain presently."

By this time, we had reached the high floor in which the offices stood, and Mr. Bell, all wonder and pale agitation, unlocked the outer door, and turned on the electric light.

"Now," cried Hewitt, "show me your ventilators!"

There were some, it seemed, in the top panes of the windows, but these were not what Hewitt wanted. There were others in the form of upright chambers or flues, made of metal, and painted the same colour as the walls about them. They rose from the floor in corners and wall angles, and could be shut or opened by means of lids over their upper ends. These were more to Hewitt's mind, and he went about from one to another, groping under the lids, and poking down into the flues with a walking-stick. There was a wire-grating, or diaphragm, it seemed, in each of them, two or three feet down, and we could hear the end of the stick raking on this at each investigation. One after another of these ventilators Hewitt examined, till he had examined them all, in outer and inner rooms, without result; and I could see that he was disappointed.

"There must be another somewhere," he said, and hunted afresh.

But plainly he had tried them all, and now he could do no more than try them all again, with as little result.

"It *is* a ventilator," he said, positively. "Unless——" he broke off thoughtfully and stood silent for a few moments. "Ah! of course!" he resumed presently. "We'll send for the housekeeper and a candle. Which is the nearest empty office—the nearest office to let? Is there one on this floor?"

"I think not," Mr. Bell answered. "But there's one on the floor below, just opposite the lift—I see the bill on the door every day as I come up."

"We'll try that, then. I'll rake out every ventilator in this palatial edifice before I'll call myself beaten. Come, call the housekeeper. Is there a speaking tube? Tell him to bring a light."

The housekeeper came, wonderingly, with a watch-man's oil-lantern, and we all went to the floor below. Opposite the lift was a glass door from which a bill had recently been torn.

"Why, it's let!" said Mr. Bell.

"Yes, sir," assented the housekeeper. "Let a day or two ago to a Mr. Catherton Hunt. Or, at least, a deposit was paid."

"But see—the door's not locked," Hewitt observed, pushing it open. "I think we'll trespass on Mr. Catherton Hunt's new offices, since they seem quite empty, and he hasn't taken possession. Come—ventilators!"

It was a small office—an outer room of moderate size, and one smaller inner room. Hewitt at once attacked the ventilators in the larger apartment—there were two of them—but retired disappointed from each. There was one ventilator only in the small room. Hewitt tilted the lid, which was at about the level of his eyes, thrust in his hand, and drew forth a bundle of folded papers; thrust in his hand again and drew forth another bundle; did it again, and drew forth more!

Mr. Bell fell upon the first bundle almost as a dog falls upon a bone; and now he snatched eagerly at each successive paper or bundle, till Hewitt raked the grating with his stick, and declared that there were no more. "Is that all?" he asked.

Mr. Bell went tremblingly from paper to paper, and, at last, said that he believed it really was. "I can verify it by the list upstairs," he added, "if you are sure there are no more."

"No more," repeated Hewitt, rattling his stick in the ventilator again. "Let us go and verify, by all means."

We sent the puzzled housekeeper away, and returned to the office above, and presently Mr. Bell, now beginning so far to recover from his amazement as to express incoherent gratitude, reported that the bonds were correct and complete to the last and least.

"Very well," said Hewitt, "then my part of the business is done, though I must say I've had luck, or rather, Brett has had it for me. But the police must come on now. I think, Mr. Bell, we'll go along to Scotland Yard when we leave here. They'll be wanting to see Mr. Catherton Hunt, I expect, whoever he is—and somebody in your office, too, if I'm not sadly mistaken."

"Who?" gasped Mr. Bell.

"That, perhaps, you can help to point out. See here—do you know whose figures they are?" and Hewitt produced the small slip of paper containing the cypher.

"They're very small," remarked Mr. Bell, putting on his glasses; "very small indeed; but I think—why they're Henning's, I do believe!"

"Ah! one or two other little things seemed to point that way. Henning is your correspondence clerk, I believe, and I expect this thin little slip is a specimen of your typewriter paper. Have you any of his written figures for comparison?"

"Well no—I hardly think—you see he typewrites his letters, and although I know his writing very well I can't at the moment put my hand on any figures of his."

"Never mind—it's mere matter of curiosity; the police will ask him questions in the morning. What *I* believe has happened is this. Our friend Henning—if he's the man—has a friend outside a great deal cleverer than himself—though he would seem to have his share of cunning, too. Between them they resolved to rob you in the way they have done—temporarily. Henning was to take advantage of his position in that little inner room to get at the safe some day when it was open and when you were engaged in your own private inner room with a client, so leaving the safe unwatched. He was provided with a spare patent padlock and key, of the sort you used on that black box, and his confederate had drilled him in the trick of breaking that particular sort of padlock open, with other spare specimens. He got his opportunity this morning."

"Only this morning?"

"This morning, I think, else we should never have got these bonds back, nor even have heard of them again. I think you said you were engaged with a client for half an hour?"

"Yes, from about half-past ten to eleven."

"That was his chance, and he took it. He broke the padlock, took out the bonds, substituted the dummies he had already prepared in his own desk, and locked the box again with the new padlock. Meantime Hunt had paid a deposit, pending references, on the office below— the nearest empty room. Of course, he wouldn't get the key until the tenancy was finally accepted—which he never intended it should be. But he easily arranged to have the door left unlocked for a day or two, on some convenient excuse—arranging decorations, or what not. And the bill was taken down, so that prospective and prospecting tenants were kept away. The bonds being stolen, Henning took the first opportunity of carrying them to the empty office—probably piecemeal—a thing he could easily manage almost under your nose, before you were aware of your loss. There he was to conceal them, either in the chimney, under the boards, or in the ventilator, as he might find convenient—and he found the ventilator most convenient.

"Then he was to apprise his confederate of the fact that the robbery had been effected in order that Hunt might come and quietly fetch the plunder away. The message was to take an ingenious form. Hunt was to have a fellow waiting about in the street, and as soon as Henning could get out—say to lunch—he was just to *send the key* by this messenger—the key with which he had locked the new padlock on the black box. You see the advantages of that simple arrangement. First, the key, which is evidence, is got rid of in a safe and effectual way—a thing that couldn't be done as well by merely flinging it away on or near the premises, where it might be found. Next, the message is perfectly secret—the messenger could never guess what the key meant, nor could any other person not in the confederate's confidence. And, at the same time, the key tells all that is necessary; the robbery has been effected—come and remove the plunder.

"But something unforeseen happens. No sooner are the bonds stolen and safely hidden than you go to the box, find something wrong with the lock, break it open and discover the loss. This was a thing that they trusted would not happen till after the bonds were safely got away. More, I am sent for, the clerks are kept in from lunch, and so on. Henning gets into a funk, and resolves to send a message of special urgency to his confederate. For that purpose he uses a cypher which the two have agreed upon—the most ingenious cypher I have ever seen used for the purpose. He doesn't wish to make his message any more conspicuous than he need, so he writes his cypher on this scrap of paper and rolls it inside the key—probably another expedient agreed upon in case of necessity. Then the key goes into an envelope, for greater security of the cypher message, and the messenger gets it when Henning is at last released for lunch. What happened to the message we know; and here it is.

"Now I will not weary you with a detailed account of the different ways in which I attacked this cypher, but I will take the shortest possible cut to the true interpretation. A very short examination of the cryptogram shows that while no number is included above 23, the numbers, in their relative frequency, roughly agree with the relative frequency of the corresponding letters of the alphabet, *a* for 1, *b* for 2, and so on."

Here I handed Hewitt the pencilled note I had made at the hospital, with letters substituted for the figures, thus:—*i, h, n, d, t, r, e, i; o, s, t, o, c, i, h, e; c, w, o, o, e, m, n, s; s, t, o, o, o, o, f, a; e, t, o, o, o, o, c, v; a, o, o, o, o, o, r, e; a, h, t, k, r, i, e, t; l, e, w, n, n, a, a, t.*

Hewitt took the paper and went on. "If that were all the thing would be childishly simple. But you will see that we seem as far from the solution as ever; for the letters as they stand mean nothing, though in fact they are in normal relative frequency; so that if they mean other letters, all the rules are upset, and we are at a standstill. I admit that for a long time the thing bothered me. But a peculiarity struck me. Not only were the figures, or letters, disposed in groups of *eight*, but there were also *eight* such groups—sixty-four altogether. What did that suggest? What but a chessboard?"

"A chessboard?" I queried.

"Just so—a chessboard. Eight squares each way—sixty-four altogether. So I drew a rough representation of a chessboard, and set out the letters on it, in their order, like this:—

i	*h*	*n*	*d*	*t*	*r*	*e*	*i*
o	*s*	*t*	*o*	*c*	*i*	*h*	*e*
c	*w*	*o*	*o*	*e*	*m*	*n*	*s*
s	*t*	*o*	*o*	*o*	*o*	*f*	*a*
e	*t*	*o*	*o*	*o*	*o*	*c*	*v*
a	*o*	*o*	*o*	*o*	*o*	*r*	*e*
a	*h*	*t*	*k*	*r*	*i*	*e*	*t*
i	*e*	*w*	*n*	*n*	*a*	*a*	*t*

"Now, there was my chessboard with my letters on it. I tried reading them downward, across, upward and diagonally, in the direction of the moves of different chess pieces—king, queen, rook and bishop. Nothing came of that, whatever I did; the thing was as unreadable as ever. But there remained one chess-move to try—the eccentric move of the knight; the move of one square forward, backward or sideways, and then one square diagonally, or, as it has sometimes been more concisely expressed, the move to the next square but one of a different colour from that on which it rests. I tried the knight's move, and I read the cypher.

"I began at the top left-hand corner, just as one does in reading a book. I read the moves downward—*I* to *w*, *e* and *h*, and found that led to nothing. So I took the one alternative move, and, with a little consideration, skipped along from *I* to *t* in the second line of squares, *t* in the top line, *h* in the second line, *e* in the third, *r* in the top and *e* in the second. That gave me an idea. There were the letters *i, t, t,* followed by the word *here.* I tried back from the *I* again, and taking in the reverse order the *w, e* and *h* which I had first given up, I read my own name, as you can see it, from the *h* on the bottom line but one, moving upward. So I had the words *Hewitt here.* I need not carry you through all the steps, which will now be plain enough to you. But I found that the message actually began in the *right*-hand corner, and read thus, the noughts counting for nothing—

Invent loss disc take at once Martin Hewitt here fear watch.

"The noughts were plainly merely inserted to fill in unneeded squares, and keep the rest of the figures in their proper relative places when the cypher was written in line. At first I was a little puzzled to understand what seemed to be the first word *invent.* But it was quite clear that *loss disc* meant 'loss discovered,' so I concluded that here in the beginning was a contraction also, and that *in* was a separate word. In that case *vent* could be a contraction for no other word but 'ventilator,' in accordance with the sense of the words. So I concluded that the meaning of the whole sentence was simply this: 'The plunder is in the ventilator, the loss is discovered, take away the booty at once; Martin Hewitt is here, and I fear I may be watched.' There is the reading, and our little adventure this evening is what it has led to.

"Of course, the confederate wouldn't go groping about the squares so painfully as I have had to do. To him the reading would be simple enough, for the order of the moves would be preconcerted. Each of the conspirators would have, as a guide, both to reading and writing the cypher, a drawn set of squares, numbered in the order of the moves—1 where we have the *i*, 2 where we have the *n*, 3 where we have the *v*, and so on. With that before him, either reading or writing in this extraordinary cryptogram would be easy and quick enough. And now for Scotland Yard!"

4.

We learned late on the following day that Henning had not appeared at the office. From that we assumed that he must have met his confederate in the evening, and, finding that he had not received the message sent, conceived that something was wrong, and made himself safe. The confederate, Hunt, however, made his appearance early next morning, but escaped.

What happened is best told in Plummer's words when he called on Hewitt in the afternoon.

"I went round this morning," he said, "as I said I would last night. I took a good man with me, and we got the dummy bonds that had been put in Bell's box and popped 'em in the ventilator, where the real ones had been hidden. You see, we'd got nothing *legal* against Catherton Hunt as yet, but if we could only grab him with those dummy bonds on him it might help, with the other evidence we could scrape up (and especially if we could take Henning), to sustain a charge of conspiracy to steal. Well, he came so quick he was on us before we were quite ready. We'd got the dummies in their place, and I was in front of the door telling my man the likeliest corner to wait in, when suddenly up pops the lift right in front of me, with a gentleman in it—clean-shaven.

"I looked at him and he looked at me. I had a sort of distant notion that I might have seen him before, and it's pretty certain he had something more than a distant notion about me. 'Down again,' he says to the lift man, before the gate was swung, 'I've forgotten something!' And down the lift went. You'll understand I had no idea he was the man we wanted; but as the lift went down and my eyes were on the man's face, I saw who he was! When he stood straight before me I had no more than a vague notion that I'd seen him somewhere before. But down the lift went, and in the flash of time when he'd nearly disappeared, and the bottom part of his face was hidden by the sill of the lift opening—the part of his face where his beard had been when we met him last—I saw it was Myatt!"

"Myatt? Good heavens!"

"Everard Myatt, Mr. Hewitt, the man that murdered Mr. Jacob Mason! Everard Myatt, for a thousand, with his beard shaved! And we've lost him again! What could we do? We shouted and ran downstairs, and that was all. He'd gone, of course. And when we asked the hall porter he told us that Mr. Catherton Hunt had just come down the lift and hurried out!"

The Case of the Burnt Barn

1.

Everard Myatt—or Catherton Hunt—was lost again. Martin Hewitt had been wholly successful, for he had recovered Mr. Bell's missing bonds; but the police caught neither of the conspirators. Investigation at Henning's lodgings showed that careful preparations must have been made for an immediate flight if it should become necessary, and the flight had taken place. The man in the hospital, who had been knocked down in carrying from one to the other the extraordinary message that Hewitt deciphered, remained insensible for a few days, and could not be questioned till sometime later still. Then he professed to have forgotten all about the message on which he was going when he met his accident, and the medical men in attendance informed the police that it was quite possible that the fellow's statement was true.

He said that he *did* carry messages sometimes, when he could get a job, but he could remember nothing of the message of the key, nor of who had sent him, nor where he was to go. Nevertheless, the police, although they professed to accept his statement, kept a wary eye on him after his discharge from the hospital, for they had a very great suspicion that he knew more than he chose to tell. But nothing more was heard of the accomplices till another case of Martin Hewitt's brought the news, and that in a manner strange enough.

The matter began, as so many matters of Hewitt's did, with the receipt of a telegram, followed immediately by another. For the first having been handed in at a country office not very long before eight the previous evening, it was not delivered at Hewitt's office till the morning, in accordance with the ancient manners and customs observed in the telegraphic system of this country. It had been despatched from Throckham, in Middlesex, and it was simply a very urgently worded request to Hewitt to come at once, signed "Claire Peytral." The second telegram, which came even as Hewitt was reading the first, on his arrival at his office, ran thus:—

Did you receive telegram? See newspapers. Matter life or death. Would come personally but cannot leave mother. Pray answer.—Peytral.

The answer went instantly that Hewitt would come by the next train, for he had seen the morning paper and from that knew the urgency of the case. But a consultation of the railway guide showed that trains to Throckham were fewer than one might suppose, considering the proximity of the village to London, and that the next would leave in about an hour and a quarter; so that I saw Hewitt before he started. He came up to my rooms, in fact, as I was beginning to breakfast.

"See here," he said, "I am sent for in the Throckham case. Have you seen the report?"

As a leader writer, I had little business with the news side of my paper, and indeed I had no more than a vague recollection of some such heading as: "Tragedy in a barn," in one evening paper of the day before, and "Murder at Throckham" in another. So I could claim no very exact knowledge of the affair.

"Here you have a paper, I see," Hewitt said, reaching for it. "Perhaps their report is fuller than that in mine." He gave me his own newspaper and began searching in the other. "No," he said presently, "much the same. News agency report to both papers, no doubt."

The report which I read ran as follows:—

Singular Tragedy.—An extraordinary occurrence is reported from Throckham, a small village within fifteen miles of London, involving a tragic fatality that has led to a charge of murder. On Thursday evening an old barn, for some time disused, was discovered to be on fire, and it was only by extraordinary exertions on the part of the villagers that the fire was extinguished. Upon an examination of the place yesterday morning the body of Mr. Victor Peytral, a gentleman who had lived in the neighbourhood for some time, and who had been missing since shortly before the discovery of the fire, was found in the ruins. The body was burnt almost beyond recognition, but not so much as to conceal the fact that the unfortunate gentleman had not perished in the fire, but had been the victim of foul play. The throat was very deeply cut, and there can be no doubt that the murderer must have fired the barn with the object of destroying all traces of the crime. The police have arrested Mr. Percy Bowmore, a frequent visitor at the house of the deceased.

"My telegram," said Hewitt, "is plainly from a relative of this Mr. Peytral who is dead—perhaps a daughter, since she speaks of being unable to leave her mother. In that case, probably an only child, since there is no other to leave."

"Unless the others are too young," I suggested.

"Just so," Hewitt replied. "Well, Brett," he added, "today is Saturday."

Saturday was, of course, my "off" day, and I understood Hewitt to hint that if I pleased I might accompany him to Throckham. "Saturday it is," I said, "and I have no engagements. Would you care for me to come?"

"As you please, of course. I can guess very little of the case as yet, naturally, beyond what I have read in the paper; but the subtle sense of my experience tells me that there is all the chance of an interesting case in this. That's *your* temptation. As for myself, I don't mind admitting that—especially in these country cases, where the resources of civilisation are not always close at hand—I'm never loth to have a friend with me who isn't too proud to be made use of. That's *my* temptation!"

No persuasion was needed, and in due time we set out together.

2.

It is my experience that places are to be found within twenty miles of London far more rural, far sleepier, far less influenced by the great city that lies so near, than places thrice and four times as far away. They are just too far out to be disturbed by suburban traffic, and too near to feel the influence of the great railway lines. These main lines go by, carrying their goods and their passengers to places far beyond, and it is only by awkward little branch lines, with slow and rare trains, that any part of this mid-lying belt is reached, and even then it is odds but that one must drive a good way to his destination.

Throckham was just such a place as I speak of, and that was the reason why we had such ample time to catch the first of the half-dozen leisurely trains by which one might reach the neighbourhood during the day. The station was Redfield, and Throckham was three miles beyond it.

At Redfield a coachman with a dogcart awaited Hewitt—only one gentleman having been expected, as the man explained, in offering to give either of us the reins. But Hewitt wished to talk to the coachman, and I willingly took the back seat, understanding very well that my friend would get better to work if he first had as many of the facts as possible from a calm informant before discussing them with the dead man's relations, probably confused and distracted with their natural emotions.

The coachman was a civil and intelligent fellow, and he gave Hewitt all he knew of the case with perfect clearness, as I could very well hear.

"It isn't much I can tell you, sir," he said, "beyond what I expect you know. I suppose you didn't know Mr. Peytral, my master, that's dead?"

"No. But he was a foreigner, I suppose—French, from the name."

"Well, no, sir," the coachman replied, thoughtfully; "not French exactly, I think, though sometimes he talked French to the mistress. They came from somewhere in the West Indies, I believe, and there's a trifle of—well, of dark blood in 'em, sir, I should think; though, of course, it ain't for me to say."

"Yes—there are many such families in the French West Indies. Did you ever hear of Alexandre Dumas?"

"No, sir, can't say I did."

"Well, he was a very great Frenchman indeed, but he had as much 'dark blood' as your master had—probably more; and it came from the West Indies, too. But go on."

"Mr. Peytral, you must understand, sir, has lived here a year or two—I've only been with him nine months. He talked English always—as good as you or me; and he was always called *Mr.* Peytral—not *Monsieur*, or *Signor*, or any o' them foreign titles. I think he was naturalised. Mrs. Peytral, she's an invalid—came here an invalid, I'm told. She never comes out of her bedroom 'cept on an invalid couch, which is carried. Miss Claire, she's the daughter, an' the only one, and she was hoping you'd ha' been down last night, sir, by the last train. She's in an awful state, as you may expect, sir."

"Naturally, to lose her father in such a terrible way."

"Yes, sir, but it's wuss than that even, for her. You see, this Mr. Bowmore, that they've took up, he's been sort of keepin' company with Miss Claire for some time, an' there's no doubt she was very fond of him. That makes it pretty bad for her, takin' it both ways, you see."

"Of course—terrible. But tell me how the thing happened, and why they took this Mr. Bowmore."

"Well, sir, it ain't exactly for me to say, and, of course, I don't know the rights of it, bein' only a servant, but they say there was a sudden quarrel last night between Mr. Peytral and Mr. Bowmore. I think myself that Mr. Peytral was getting a bit excitable lately, whatever it was. On Thursday night, just after dinner, he went strolling off in the dusk, alone, and presently Mr. Bowmore—he came down in the afternoon—went strolling off after him. It seems they went down toward the Penn's Meadow barn, Mr. Peytral first, and Mr. Bowmore catching him up from behind. A man saw them—a gamekeeper. He was lyin' quiet in a little wood just the other side of Penn's Meadow, an' they didn't see him as they came along together. They were quarrelling, it seems, though Grant—that's the gamekeeper—couldn't hear exactly what about; but he heard Mr. Peytral tell Mr. Bowmore to go away. He 'preferred to be alone' and he'd 'had enough' of Mr. Bowmore, from what Grant could make out. 'Get out o' my sight, sir, I tell you!' the old gentleman said at last, stamping his foot, and shaking his fist in the young gentleman's face. And then Bowmore turned and walked away."

"One moment," Hewitt interposed. "You are telling me what Grant saw and heard. How did it come to your knowledge?"

"Told me hisself, sir—told me every word yesterday. Told me twice, in fact. First thing in the morning when they found the body, and then again after he'd been to Redfield and had it took down by the police. It was because of that they arrested Mr. Bowmore, of course."

"Just so. And is this gamekeeper Grant in the same employ as yourself?"

"Oh, no, sir! Mr. Peytral's is only just an acre or two of garden and a paddock. Grant's master is Colonel White, up at the Hall."

"Very good. You were saying that Mr. Peytral told Mr. Bowmore to get out of his sight, and that Mr. Bowmore walked away. What then?"

"Well, Grant saw Mr. Bowmore walk away, but it was only a feint—a dodge, you see, sir. He walked away to the corner of the little wood where Grant was, and then he took a turn into the wood and began following Mr. Peytral up, watching him from among the trees. Came close by where Grant was sitting, following up Mr. Peytral and watching him; and so Grant lost sight of 'em."

"Did Grant say what he was doing in the wood?"

"He said he'd found marks of rabbit-snares there, and he was watching to see if anybody came to set any more."

"Yes—quite an ordinary part of his duty, of course. What next?"

"Well, Grant didn't see any more. He waited a bit, and then moved off to another part of the wood, and he didn't notice anything else particular till the barn was on fire. It was dark, then, of course."

"Yes—you must tell me about the fire. Who discovered it?"

"Oh, a man going home along the lane. He ran and called some people, and they fetched the fire-engine from the village and pumped out of the horse-pond just close by. It was pretty much of a wreck by the time they got the fire out, but it wasn't all gone, as you might have expected. You see, it had been out of use for some time, sir, and there was mostly nothing but old broken ploughs and lumber there; and what's more, there was a deal of rain early in the week, as you may remember, sir, so the thatch was pretty sodden, being out o' repair and all—and so was the timber, for the matter o' that, for there's no telling when it was last painted. So the fire didn't go quite so fierce as it might, you see; else I should expect it had been all over before they got to work on it."

"Not at all a likely sort of place to catch fire, it would seem, either," Hewitt commented. "Old ploughs and such lumber are not very combustible."

"Quite so, sir; that's what makes 'em think it so odd, I suppose. But there *was* a bundle or two of old pea-straw there, shied in last summer, they say, being over bundles from the last load, and there left."

"And when was Mr. Bowmore seen next?"

"He came strolling back, sir, and told the young lady he'd left her father outside, or something of that sort, I think; said nothing of the quarrel, I believe. But he said the barn was on fire—which he must have known pretty early, sir, for 'tis a mile from the house off that way;" and the coachman pointed with his whip.

"Nothing was suspected of the murder, it seems, till yesterday morning?"

"No, sir. Miss Claire got frightful worried when her father didn't come home, as you would expect, and specially at him not coming home all night. But when the fire was quite put out, o' course the people went away home to bed, and it wasn't till the morning that anybody went in to turn the place over. Then they found the body."

"Badly burnt, I believe?"

"Horrid burnt, sir. If it wasn't for Mr. Peytral's being missing, I doubt if they'd have known it was him at all. It took a doctor's examination to see clear that the throat had been cut. But cut it had been, and deep, so the doctor said. And now the body's gone over to Redfield mortuary."

Hewitt asked a few questions more, and got equally direct answers, except where the coachman had to confess ignorance. But presently we were at the house to which Hewitt had been summoned.

It was a pleasant house enough, standing alone, apart from the village, a little way back from a loop of road that skirted a patch of open green. As we came in at the front gate, I caught an instant's glimpse of a pale face at an upper window, and before we could reach the drawing-room door Miss Claire Peytral had met us.

She was a young lady of singular beauty, which the plain signs of violent grief and anxiety very little obscured. Her complexion, of a very delicate ivory tinge, was scarcely marred by the traces of sleeplessness and tears that were nevertheless clear to see. Her eyes were large and black, and her jetty hair had a slight waviness that was the only distinct sign about her of the remote blend of blood from an inferior race.

"Oh, Mr. Hewitt," she cried, "I am so glad you have come at last! I have been waiting—waiting so long! And my poor mother is beginning to suspect!"

"You have not told her, then?"

"No, it will kill her when she knows, I'm sure—kill her on the spot. I have only said that father is ill at—at Redfield. Oh, what shall I do?"

The poor girl seemed on the point of breakdown, and Hewitt spoke sharply and distinctly.

"What you must do is this," he said. "You must attend to me, and tell me all I want to know as accurately and as tersely as you can. In that case I will do whatever I can, but if you give way you will cripple me. It all depends on you, remember. This is my intimate friend, Mr. Brett, who is good enough to offer to help us. Now, first, I think I know the heads of the case, from the newspapers, and, more especially, from your coachman. But when you sent for me, no doubt you had some definite idea or intention in your mind. What was it?"

"Oh, he is innocent, Mr. Hewitt—he is, really! The only friend I have in the world—the only friend we all have!"

"Steady—steady," Hewitt said, pressing her kindly and firmly into a seat. "You *must* keep steady, you know, if I am to do anything. I expected that would be your belief. Now tell me why you are so sure."

"Mr. Hewitt, if you knew him you wouldn't ask. He would never injure my poor father—he went out after him purely out of kindness, because I was uneasy. He would never hurt him, Mr. Hewitt, never, never! I can't say it strongly enough—he never would! Oh! my poor father, and now———"

"Steady again!" cried Hewitt, more sharply still. I could see that he feared the hysterical breakdown that might come at any moment after the lengthened suspense Miss Peytral had suffered. "Listen, now—you mustn't frighten yourself too much. If Mr. Bowmore is innocent—and you say you are so certain of it—then I've no doubt of finding a way to prove it if only you'll make your best effort to help me, and keep your wits about you. As far as I can see at present there's nothing against him that we need be afraid of if we tackle it properly, and, of course, the police make arrests of this sort by way of precaution in a case like this, on the merest hint. Come now, you say you were uneasy when your father went out after dinner on Thursday night. Why?"

"I don't know, quite, Mr. Hewitt. It was my mother that was uneasy, really, about something she never explained to me. My father had taken to going out in the evening after dinner, just in the way he did on Thursday night. I don't know why, but I think it had something to do with my mother's anxiety."

"Did he dress for dinner?"

"No, not lately. He used to dress always, but he has dropped it of late."

Hewitt paused for a moment, thoughtfully. Then he said, "Mrs. Peytral is an invalid, I know, and no doubt none the better for her anxiety. But if it could be managed I should like to ask her a few questions. What do you think?"

But this Miss Peytral was altogether against. Her mother was suffering from spinal complaint, it appeared, with very serious nervous complications, and there was no answering for the result of the smallest excitement. She never saw strangers, and, if it could possibly be avoided, it must be avoided now.

"Very well, Miss Peytral, I will first go and look at some things I must see, and I will do without your mother's help as long as I possibly can. But now you must answer a few more questions yourself, please."

Hewitt's questions produced little more substantial information, it seemed to me, than he had already received. Mr. Peytral had taken the house in which we were sitting—it was called "The Lodge" simply—two years ago. Before that the family had lived in Surrey, but they had not moved direct from there; there was a journey to America between, on some business of Mr. Peytral's, and it was on the return voyage that they had met Mr. Percy Bowmore. Mr. Bowmore had no friends nearer than Canada, and he was reading for the Bar—in a very desultory way, as I gathered. Miss Peytral's childhood had been passed in the West Indies, at the town of San Domingo, in fact, where her father had been a merchant.

Her mother had been a helpless invalid ever since Miss Peytral could remember. As to the engagement with Bowmore, it would seem to have had the full approval of both parents all along. But a rather curious change had come over her father, she thought, a few months ago. What it was that had caused it she could not say, but he grew nervous and moody, often absent-minded, and sometimes even short-tempered and snappish, a thing she had never known before. Also he read the daily papers with much care and eagerness. It was plain that Miss Peytral had no idea of any cause which might have led to a quarrel between Bowmore and her father, and Hewitt's most cunning questions failed to elicit the smallest suggestion of reason for such an occurrence.

Ten days or so ago, Mr. Peytral had returned from a short walk after dinner, very much agitated; and from that day he had made a practice of going out immediately after dinner every evening regularly, walking off across the paddock, and so away in the direction of Penn's Meadow. The first visit of Percy Bowmore after this practice had begun was on Thursday, but the presence of the visitor made no difference, as Miss Peytral had expected it would. Her father rose abruptly after dinner and went off as before; and this time Mrs. Peytral, who had been brought down to dinner, displayed a singular uneasiness about him. She had experienced the same feeling, curiously enough, on other occasions, Miss Peytral remarked, when her husband had been unwell or in difficulties, even at some considerable distance. This time the feeling was so strong that she begged Bowmore to hurry after Mr. Peytral and accompany him in his walk. This the young man had done; but he returned alone after a while, saying simply that he had lost sight of Mr. Peytral, whom he had supposed might have come home by some other way; and mentioning also that he had been told that Penn's Meadow barn was on fire.

When it grew late, and Mr. Peytral failed to return, Bowmore went out again and made inquiry in all directions. It grew necessary to concoct a story to appease Mrs. Peytral, who had been taken back to her bedroom. Bowmore spent the whole night in fruitless search and inquiry, and then, with the morning, came the terrible news of the discovery in the burnt barn; and late in the afternoon Bowmore was arrested.

The poor girl had a great struggle to restrain her feelings during the conversation, and, at its close, Hewitt had to use all his tact to keep her going. Physical exhaustion, as well as mental trouble, were against her, and stimulus was needed. So Hewitt said, "Now you must try your best, and if you will keep up as well as you have done a little longer, perhaps I may have good news for you soon. I must go at once and examine things. First, I should like to have brought to me every single pair of boots or shoes belonging to your father. Send them, and then go and look after your mother. Remember, you are helping all the time."

3.

Hewitt examined the boots and shoes with great rapidity, but with a singularly quick eye for peculiarities.

"He liked a light shoe," he said, "and he preferred to wear shoes rather than boots. There are few boots, and those not much worn, although he was living in the country. Trod square on the right foot, inward on the left, and wore the left heel more than the right. It's plain he hated nails, for these are all hand-sewn, with scarcely as much as a peg visible in the lot; and they are all laced, boots and shoes alike. Come, this is the best-worn pair; it is also a pair of the same sort the maid tells me he must have been wearing, since they are missing; low shoes, laced; we'll take them with us."

We left the house and sought our friend the coachman. He pointed out quite clearly the path by which his master had gone on his last walk; showed us the gate, still fastened, over which he had climbed to gain the adjoining meadow, and put us in the way of finding the small wood and the barn.

Both within and without the gate there was a small patch bare of grass, worn by feet; and here Martin Hewitt picked up his trail at once.

"The ground has hardened since Thursday night," he said; "and so much the better—it keeps the marks for us. Do you see what is here?"

There were footmarks, certainly, but so beaten and confused that

I could make nothing of them. Hewitt's practised eye, however, read them as I might have read a rather illegibly written letter.

"Here is the right foot, plain enough," he said, carefully fitting the shoe he had brought in the mark. "He alighted on that as he came over the gate. Half over it is another footmark—Bowmore's, I expect, for I can see signs of others, in both directions—going and coming. But we shall know better presently."

He rose, and we followed the irregular track across the meadow. Like most such field-tracks, its direction was plainly indicated by the thin and beaten grass, with a bare spot here and there. Hewitt troubled to take no more than a glance at each of these spots as we passed, but that was all he needed. The meadow was bounded by a hedge, with a stile; and at the farther side of this stile my friend knelt again, with every sign of attention.

"A little piece of luck," he reported. "The left shoe has picked up a tiny piece of broken thorn-twig just here. See the mark? The shoe was a little soddened in the sole by this time, and the thorn stuck. I hope it stuck altogether. If it did it may help us wonderfully when we get to the barn, for the trouble there will be the trampling all round of the people at the fire."

So we went on till we reached the edge of the little wood. The field-path skirted this, and here Hewitt dropped on his knees and set to work with great minuteness.

"Keep away from the track, Brett," he warned me, "or you may make it worse. The police have been here, I see, and quite recently, coming from the direction of Redfield. Here are two pairs of un-mistakable police boots and another heavy pair with them; no doubt they brought the gamekeeper along with them, to have things fully explained."

From the corner of the wood to a point forty yards along the path; back to the corner again, and then into the wood Hewitt went, care-fully examining every inch of the ground as he did so. Then at last he rejoined me.

"I think the gamekeeper has told the truth," he said. "It's pretty plain, thanks to the soft ground hereabout, notwithstanding the po-licemen's boots. Here they came together—the thorn-twig sticks to the shoe still, you see—and here they stopped. The marks face about, and Bowmore's steps are retraced to the corner of the wood. Peytral's turn again and go on, and Bowmore's turn into the edge of the wood and come along among the trees. You don't see them in the grassy parts quite as well as I do, I expect, but there they are. We'll keep after Peytral's prints. Bowmore's come back in the same track, I see."

The next stile led to Penn's Meadow. This meadow—a large one—stretched over a rather steep hump of land, at the other side of which the barn stood. From the stile two paths could be discerned—one rising straight over the meadow in the direction of the barn, and the other skirting it to the left, parallel with the hedge.

"Here the footprints part," Hewitt observed, musingly; "and what does that mean? Manoeuvring—or what?"

He thought a moment, and then went on: "We'll leave the tracks for the present and see the barn. That is straight ahead, I take it."

When we reached the top of the rise the barn came in view, a blackened and sinister wreck. The greater part of the main structure was still standing, and even part of the thatched roof still held its place, scorched and broken. Off to the right from where we stood the village roofs were visible, giving indication of the position of the road to Redfield. A single human figure was in sight—that of a policeman on guard before the barn.

"Now we must get rid of that excellent fellow," said Hewitt, "or he'll be offering objections to the examination I want to make. I wonder if he knows my name?"

We walked down to the barn, and Hewitt, assuming the largest possible air, addressed the policeman.

"Constable," he said, "I am here officially—here is my card. Of course you will know the name if you have had any wide experience—London experience especially. I am looking into this case on behalf of Miss Peytral—co-operating with the police, of course. Where is your inspector?"

He was a rather stupid countryman, this policeman, but he was visibly impressed—even flurried—by Hewitt's elaborate bumptiousness. He saluted, tried to look unnaturally sagacious, and confessed that he couldn't exactly say where the inspector was, things being put about so just now. He might be in Throckham village, but more likely he was at Redfield.

"Ah!" Hewitt replied, with condescension. "Now, if he is in the village, you will oblige me, constable, by telling him that I am here. If he is not there, you will return at once. I will be responsible here till you come back. Don't be very long, now."

The man was taken by surprise, and possibly a trifle doubtful. But Hewitt was so extremely lofty and so very peremptory and official, that the inferior intelligence capitulated feebly, and presently, after another uneasy salute, the village policeman had vanished in the direction of the road. The moment he had disappeared Hewitt turned to the ruined barn. The door was gone, and the scorched and charred lumber that littered the place had a look of absolute ghostliness—perhaps chiefly the effect of my imagination in the knowledge of the ghastly tragedy that the place had witnessed. Well in from the doorway was a great scatter of light ashes—plainly the pea-straw that the coachman had spoken of. And by these ashes and partly among them, marked in some odd manner on the floor, was a horrible black shape that I shuddered to see, as Hewitt pointed it out with a moving forefinger, which he made to trace the figure of a prostrate human form.

"Did you never see that before in a burnt house?" Hewitt asked in a hushed voice. "I have, more than once. That sort of thing always leaves a strange stain under it, like a shadow."

But business claimed Martin Hewitt, and he stepped carefully within. Scarcely had he done so, when he stood suddenly still, with a low whistle, pointing toward something lying among the dirt and ashes by the foot of that terrible shape.

"See?" he said. "Don't disturb anything, but look!"

I crept in with all the care I could command, and stooped. The place was filled with such a vast confusion of lumber and cinder and ash that at first I failed to see at all what had so startled Hewitt's attention. And even when I understood his direction, all I saw was about a dozen little wire loops, each a quarter of an inch long or less, lying among a little grey ash that clung about the ends of some of the loops in clots. Even as I looked another thing caught Hewitt's eye. Among the straw-ashes there lay some cinders of paper and card, and near them another cinder, smaller, and plainly of some other substance. Hewitt took my walking-stick, and turned this cinder over. It broke apart as he did so, and from within it two or three little charred sticks escaped. Hewitt snatched one up and scrutinised it closely.

"Do you see the tin ferrule?" he said. "It has been a brush; and that was a box of colours!" He pointed to the cinder at his feet. "That being so," he went on, "that paper and card was probably a sketch-book. Brett! come outside a bit. There's something amazing here!"

We went outside, and Hewitt faced me with a curious expression that for the life of me I could not understand.

"Suppose," he said, "*that Mr. Victor Peytral is not dead after all?*"

"Not dead?" I gasped; "but—but he is! We know——"

"It seems to me," Hewitt pursued, with his eyes still fixed on mine, "that we know very little indeed of this affair, as yet. The body was unrecognisable, or very near it. You remember what the coachman said? 'If it wasn't for Mr. Peytral's being missing,' he said, 'I doubt if they'd have known it was him at all.' I think those were his exact words. More, you must remember that the body has not been seen by either of Peytral's relatives."

"But then," I protested, "if it isn't his body whose is it?"

"Ah, indeed," Hewitt responded, "whose is it? Don't you see the possibilities of the thing? There's a colour-box and a sketch-book burned. Who carried a colour-box and a sketch-book? Not Peytral, or we should have heard of it from his daughter; she made a particular point of her father's evening strolls being quite aimless, so far as her knowledge or conjecture went; she knew nothing of any sketching. And another thing—don't you see what *those* things mean?" He pointed toward the place of the little wire loops.

"Not at all."

"Man, don't you see they've been boot-buttons? When the boots shrivelled, the threads were burnt and the buttons dropped off. Boot-buttons are made of a sort of composition that burns to a grey ash, once the fire really gets hold of them—as you may try yourself, any time you please. You can see the ash still clinging to some of the shanks; and there the shanks are, lying in two groups, six and six, as they fell! Now Peytral came out in laced shoes."

"But if Peytral isn't dead, where is he?"

"Precisely," rejoined Hewitt, with the curious expression still in his eyes. "As you say, where is he? And as you said before, who is the dead man? Who is the dead man, and where is Peytral, and why has he gone? Don't you see the possibilities of the case *now?*"

Light broke upon me suddenly. I saw what Hewitt meant. Here was a possible explanation of the whole thing—Peytral's recent change of temper, his evening prowlings, his driving away of Bowmore, and lastly, of his disappearance—his flight, as it now seemed probable it was. The case had taken a strange turn, and we looked at one another with meaning eyes. It might be that Hewitt, begged by the unhappy girl we had but just left to prove the innocence of her lover, would by that very act bring her father to the gallows.

"Poor girl!" Hewitt murmured, as we stood staring at one another. "Better she continued to believe him dead, as she does! Brett, there's many a good man would be disposed to fling these proofs away for the girl's sake and her mother's, seeing how little there can be to hurt Bowmore. But justice must be done, though the blow fall—as it commonly does—on innocent and guilty together. See, now, I've another idea. Stay on guard while I try."

He hurried out toward the farther side of the broad band of trampled ground which surrounded the burnt barn, and began questing to and fro, this way and that, receding farther from me as he went, and nearing the horse-pond and the road. At last he vanished altogether, and left me alone with the burnt barn, my thoughts, and—that dim shape on the barn floor. It was broad day, but I felt none too happy; and I should not have been at all anxious to keep the police watch at night.

Perhaps Hewitt had been gone a quarter of an hour, perhaps a little more, when I saw him again, hurrying back and beckoning to me. I went to meet him.

"It's right enough," he cried. "I've come on his trail again! There it is, thorn-mark and all, by the roadside, and at a stile—going to Redfield—probably to the station. Come, we'll follow it up! Where's that fool of a policeman? Oh, the muddle they *can* make when they really try!"

"Need we wait for him?" I asked.

"Yes, better now, with those proofs lying there; and we must tell him not to be bounced off again as I bounced him off. There he comes!"

The heavy figure of the local policeman was visible in the distance, and we shouted and beckoned to hurry him. Agility was no part of that policeman's nature, however, and beyond a sudden agitation of his head and his shoulders, which we guessed to be caused by a dignified spasm of leisurely haste, we saw no apparent acceleration of his pace.

As we stood and waited we were aware of a sound of wheels from the direction of Redfield, and as the policeman neared us from the right, so the sound of wheels approached us from the left. Presently a fly hove in sight—the sort of dusty vehicle that plies at every rural railway station in this country; and as he caught sight of us in the road the driver began waving his whip in a very singular and excited manner. As he drew nearer still he shouted, though at first we could not distinguish his words. By this time the policeman, trotting ponderously, was within a few yards. The passenger in the fly, a thin, dark, elderly man, leaned over the side to look ahead at us, and with that the policeman pulled up with a great gasp and staggered into the ditch.

"'Ere 'e is!" cried the fly-driver, regardless of the angry remonstrances of his fare. "'Ere 'e is! 'E's all right! It ain't 'im! 'Ere he is!"

"Shut your mouth, you fool!" cried the angry fare. "*Will* you stop making a show of me?"

"Not me!" cried the eccentric cabman. "I don't want no fare, sir! I'm drivin' you 'ome for honour an' glory, an' honour an' glory I'll make it! 'Ere 'e is!"

Hewitt took in the case in a flash—the flabbergasted policeman, the excited cabman and the angry passenger. He sprang into the road and cried to the cabman, who pulled up suddenly before us.

"Mr. Victor Peytral, I believe?" said Martin Hewitt.

"Yes, sir," answered the dark gentleman snappishly, "but I don't know you!"

"There has been a deal of trouble here, Mr. Peytral, over your absence from home, as no doubt you have become aware; and I was telegraphed for by your daughter. My name is Hewitt—Martin Hewitt."

Peytral's face changed instantly. "I know your name well, Mr. Hewitt," he said. "There's a matter—but who is this?"

"My friend, Mr. Brett, who is good enough to help me today. If I may detain you a moment, I should like a word with you aside."

"Certainly."

Mr. Peytral alighted, and the two walked a little apart.

I saw Hewitt talking and pointing toward the burnt barn, and I well guessed what he was saying. He was giving Peytral warning of what he had discovered in the barn, explaining that he must give the information to the police, and asking if, in those circumstances, Peytral wished to go home, or to make other arrangements. Often Hewitt's duty to his clients and his duty as a law-upholding citizen between them put him in some such delicate position.

But there was no hesitation in Mr. Victor Peytral. Plainly he feared nothing, and he was going home.

"Very well, then," I heard Hewitt say as they turned towards us, "perhaps we had better go on slowly and let my friend cut across the fields first to break the news. Brett—I knew you would be useful, sooner or later."

And so I hurried off, with the happy though delicate mission to restore both father and lover to Miss Claire Peytral.

4.

Miss Peytral had to be put to bed under care of a nurse, for the revulsion was very great, and so was her physical prostration. Bowmore, now set free, and in himself a very pleasant young fellow, came with hurried inquiries and congratulations, and then rushed off to London to cable to his friends in Canada, for fear of the effect of newspaper telegrams.

When at last Hewitt and I sat with Mr. Peytral in his study, "Mr. Hewitt," said Peytral, "I am not sure how far explanations may go between us. There is more in that death in the barn than the police will ever guess."

Peytral was haggard and drawn, for, as he had let slip already, he had scarce slept an hour since leaving home on Thursday.

"I am tired," he said, "and worn out, but that is not a novelty with me; and I'm not sure but we may be of use to each other. Did my daughter tell you why she sent Mr. Bowmore after me on Thursday night?"

Hewitt explained the thing as briefly as possible, just as he had heard it from Miss Peytral.

"Ah," said Peytral, thoughtfully. "So she thought my manner became moody a few months back. It did, no doubt, for I had memories; and more, I had apprehensions. Mr. Hewitt, I think I read in the papers that you were in some way engaged in the extraordinary case of the murder of Mr. Jacob Mason?"

"That is quite correct. I was."

"There was another case, a little while before, which possibly you may not have heard of. A man was found strangled near the York column, by Pall Mall, with just such a mark on his forehead as was found on Mr. Mason's."

"I know that case, too, as well as the other."

"Do you know the name of the murderer?"

"I think I do. We speak in confidence, of course, as client and professional man?"

"Of course. What was his name?"

"I have heard two—Everard Myatt and Catherton Hunt."

"Neither is his real name, and I doubt if anybody but himself knows it. Twenty years ago and more I knew him as Mayes. He was a Jamaican. Mr. Hewitt, that man's foul life has been justly forfeit a thousand times, but if it belongs to anybody it belongs to me!"

It was terrible to see the sudden fiery change in the old man. His lassitude was gone in a flash, his eyes blazed and his nostrils dilated.

For a little while he sat so, his mouth awork with passion; then he sank back in his chair with a sigh.

"I am getting old," he said, more quietly, "and perhaps I am not strong enough to lose my temper. . . . Well, as I said, Mayes was a Jamaican, a renegade white. Do you remember that in the black rebellion of 1865, there was a traitorous white man among the negroes? Eyre hanged a few rebels, and rightly, but the worst creature on all that island escaped—probably escaped by the aid of that very white skin that should have ensured him a greater punishment than the rest. He escaped to Hayti. Now you have probably heard something of Hayti, and of the common state of affairs there?"

We both had heard, and, indeed, the matter had been particularly brought to Hewitt's notice by the case which I have told elsewhere as "The Affair of the Tortoise." As for me, I had read Sir Spenser St. John's book on the black republic, and I had been greatly impressed by the graphic picture it gives of the horrible, blood-stained travesty of regular government there prevailing. Nothing in the worst of the South American Republics is to be remotely compared to it. In the worst periods there was not a crime imaginable that could not be, and was not, committed openly and with impunity by anybody on the right side of the so-called "government"; and the "government" was nothing but an organised crime in itself.

"Well," Peytral pursued, "then I need not expatiate on it, and you will understand the sort of place that Mayes fled to, and how it suited him. He was a man of far greater ability than any of the coarse scoundrels in power, and he was worse than all of them. He was not such a fool as to aim at ostensible political power—that way generally led to assassination. He was the jackal, the contriver, the power behind the throne, the instigator of half the devilry set going in that unhappy place, and he profited by it with little risk; he was the confidential adviser of that horrible creature Domingue. If you know anything of Hayti you will know what that means.

"At this time I was comparatively a young man, and a merchant at Port-au-Prince. It was a bad place, of course, and business was risky enough, but, for that very reason, profits were large, and that was an attraction to a sanguine young man like myself. I did very well, and I had thoughts of getting out of it with what I had made. But it was a fatal thing to be supposed wealthy in Port-au-Prince, unless you were a villain in power, or partner with one. I was neither, and I was judged a suitable victim by Mayes. Not I alone, either—no, nor even only I and my fortune. Gentlemen, gentlemen, my poor wife, who now lies——"

Peytral's utterance failed him. He rose as if choking, and Hewitt rose to quiet him. "Never mind," he said, "sit quiet now. We understand. Rest a moment."

The old man sank back in his chair, and for a little while buried his face in his hands. Then he went on.

"I needn't go into details," he said, huskily. "It is enough to say that every devilish engine of force and cunning was put in operation against me. So it came that at last, on a hint from a hanger-on of the police-office, who had enough humanity in him to remember a kindness he had experienced at my hands, that we took flight in the middle of the night—my poor wife, myself, and our three children, with nothing in the world but our bare lives and the clothes we wore. I might have tried to get aboard a foreign ship in the harbour, but I knew that would be useless. I should have been given up on whatever criminal charge Mayes chose to present, and my wife and children with me. I had hope of somehow getting to San Cristobel, where I had a friend—over the border in the other government of the island, the Dominican Republic. That was eighty miles away and more, across swamps, and forests and mountains. Well, we did it—we did it. We did it, Mr. Hewitt, and I dream of it still. They hunted us, sir—hunted us with dogs. We hid from them a whole day among the rank weeds—up to our shoulders in the water of a pestilential fever-swamp; Claire, the baby, on her mother's back, and both the boys on mine. They died— they died next day. My two beautiful boys, gentlemen, died in my arms, and I was too weak even to bury them!"

There was another long pause, and the man's head was bowed in his hands once more. Presently he went on again, but at first without lifting his head.

"We did it, gentlemen," he said—"we did it. We crawled into San Cristobel at the end of five days; and from that moment my dear wife has never once stood upright on her feet. So we came out of it, and the baby, Claire, was the one that suffered least. She was too young to understand, and her mother—her mother saved her, when I could not save the boys!"

He paused again, and presently sat up, pale, but in full command of himself. "You will excuse me, gentlemen, I am sure, and make allowances for my feelings," he said. "There is not a great deal more to tell. Mayes did not last long in Hayti. Domingue was overthrown, and Mayes left the island, I was told, and made for another part of the world. Years afterward I heard of his being in China, though what truth there may have been in the rumour I cannot say.

"My friend in San Cristobel—he was a cousin, in fact—put me on my legs again, and after a while he helped me to begin business at San Domingo, under my present name, Peytral, which, in fact, was my mother's maiden name. There came a sudden push in trade with the United States about this time, and I went into my affairs with the more energy to distract my thoughts. In fifteen years—to cut a long story short—I had made the small competency which I have brought to England with me, with the idea of a peaceful end to my life and my wife's; though I doubt if I am to have that now. I doubt it, and I will tell you why. Mr. Hewitt, when I went away without warning on Thursday night I was dogging Mayes!"

Hewitt nodded, with no sign of surprise. "And the man killed in the barn?"

"That is one more of his thousand crimes, without a doubt. Though it differs. Do you know what drew my attention to the murders of the men Denson and Mason, and so set me thinking? In each case the murder was by strangulation, and the medical evidence at the inquests showed that it was effected by means of a tourniquet. In fact, in the second case, the tourniquet itself was left behind."

"Yes," Hewitt replied, "I loosened it myself—but, unfortunately, I was too late."

"Well, now," Peytral went on, "in Hayti, in my time, Mayes's enemies had a habit of dying suddenly in the night, by strangulation, and a tourniquet was always the instrument. And just as murder was quite a popular procedure in that accursed place, so strangulation by tourniquet became for a while the most common form of the crime. It was rapid, effective, and silent, you see. So that a murder by tourniquet, quite an unknown thing in this country, took my attention at once, and when another followed it so soon, I felt something like certainty. And the triangle was suggestive, too."

"Were Mayes's victims marked in that way in Hayti?"

"No, there was no mark. But"—here Mr. Peytral's features assumed a curious expression—"there are things which are not believed in this country—which are laughed at, in fact, and called superstition. You know something of Hayti, and therefore you must have heard of Voodoo—the witchcraft and devil-worship of the West Indies. Well, Mayes was as deep in that as he was in every other species of wickedness. It sounds foolish, perhaps, here in civilised England, and you may laugh, but I tell you that Mayes could make men do as he wished, with their consent or against it! And he used a thing—it was generally known that he used a thing marked with a triangle—a Red Triangle—by the use of which he could bend men to his will!"

Hewitt was listening intently, with no sign of laughter at all, notwithstanding his client's apprehension. And I remembered the case of Mr. Jacob Mason, and how that victim had so fervently expressed his wish to the excellent clergyman, Mr. Potswood, that he had never dabbled in the strange devilries of Myatt—or Mayes, as we were now learning to call him.

"At any rate," Peytral resumed, "you will understand that the conjunction of the tourniquet with the Red Triangle in the two cases you know of caused me some excitement. My daughter, as you have said, noticed a change in my habits from that time; my wife did more—she knew the reason. Mr. Hewitt, I am an older man, but there is hotter blood in my veins than in yours. My father was English—though you might scarcely suppose it—but my mother, to whose name I have reverted, was a French Creole. So perhaps my natural instincts come nearer to those of our savage ancestry than do yours. Whether or not you will understand me I do not know, but I can tell you that even now, in cold blood—for my paroxysm has exhausted itself and me—it seems to me that it would be my duty, not to say my sacred duty, to tear that man to pieces with my hands whenever and wherever I could put them on him! My old passions may have slept, I find, but they are alive still, and I found them waking when I realised that Mayes was alive and in England. The words 'sane' and 'insane' are elastic in their application, but I doubt if you would have called me strictly sane of late. I evolved mad schemes for the destruction of this wretch, and I was ready to devote myself and everything I possessed to the purpose.

"More than once I contemplated coming to you—seeing that you had met the man in one of his villainies—with the idea of enlisting your aid. But I reflected that you would probably make yourself no party to a plan of private revenge, and I hesitated. And then—then, a little more than a week ago, I saw the man himself! Changed, without doubt, but not half as much changed as I am myself. Nevertheless, sure as I am of him now, I hesitated then. For it was here in the meadow that you know, near the barn, and the thing seemed so likely to be illusion that I almost suspected my senses. It was dusk, and he was walking and talking with another man, a good deal younger. And presently, while I was still confounded with surprise, and as they passed behind a clump of trees, Mayes was gone, and I saw his companion alone. He was a young man—an artist, it would seem, with sketch-book and colours."

I started, and Hewitt and I glanced at each other. Peytral saw it and paused. "Never mind," said Hewitt. "Please go on."

"After that I came out every night, in the hope of seeing my enemy again. On several evenings I saw the young artist waiting by the barn expectantly, but nobody joined him. I found that this young man was lodging at a cottage in the village, and I resolved not to lose sight of him.

"At last, on Thursday night, I saw Mayes again. Mr. Bowmore was here, and when I left the house he troubled me much by coming after me. I was obliged to tell him that I wished to be alone, and I was in a nervously explosive state when I did it. He seemed reluctant to go; my anger blazed out, and I violently ordered him off. From what he has told me it seems that he followed me still, but lost sight of me near Penn's Meadow. Well, be that as it may, I saw Mayes and the young artist again. I watched from a rather awkward spot, and dusk was falling, so that I could not see all that passed; but presently I was aware that Mayes was making off by the road alone, and I followed him.

"From that moment I think I really was mad, though my madness did not drive me to attack him at once. I had a feeling of curiosity to see where he would go, and a curious cruel idea of letting him run for a little first—as a cat feels, I suppose, with a mouse. You may judge that I was not in my normal state of mind from the fact that all through yesterday and part of today I never as much as thought of telegraphing home to say that I had gone to London. For it was to London I followed him. I took no ticket at the station—I got on the platform by stealth, and entered the train unobserved, for he and one boy were the only passengers, and I feared attracting attention. It was easy enough, in such a station as Redfield, and I paid my fare at London. And after all I lost him! Lost him in London!"

"How?"

"Like a fool. I saw him enter a house, and waited. Followed him again, and waited at another. I might have flung him into the river from the Embankment, and I refrained. And then—whether it began at a dark corner or in a group of people I cannot tell, but I suddenly discovered that I was following a stranger—a stranger of about Mayes's form and stature. It was what I should have expected, and provided for, in London streets at night!

"If I have been mad, it was then I was worst. I suppose by that time it must have been too late to get back home, but I never thought of that. I ran the streets the whole night, like a fool, hunting for Mayes. I kept on all day yesterday. I waited and watched hours at the two houses he had visited; and it was not till early this morning that I flung myself on a bed in a private hotel in Euston Road. I slept a little, and my paroxysm was over. Perhaps I am more fortunate than I am disposed to think, since I am as yet in no danger of trial for murder."

This passionate, wayward, stricken man was plainly the object of fascinated interest to Hewitt. My friend waited a moment, and then said—"The houses he called at—I should like to know them. And where you lost sight of him."

Peytral sat back, and gazed thoughtfully for fully half a minute in Hewitt's face. "Do you know," he said at length, "I don't think I'll answer that question now. I'd like to leave it for a day or two. Yesterday I wouldn't have told you, even on the rack—no, not a word! I should have said, 'Take your own chances, and get him if you can. As for me, I consider him *my* prey, and what scent I have picked up I shall use myself!' A mad fancy, you will think, perhaps. For me the question is, was I sanest then or now? I will take a day or two to think."

5.

In less than a day or two the identity of the victim of the burnt barn was established. For Hewitt had his idea, and he communicated with Plummer, of Scotland Yard. The man with the buttoned boots and the sketch-book was the artist who had been staying at the cottage in the village, but who, singularly enough, had never been seen to draw, and had left no drawings behind him. He had warned the people of the cottage that he might be away for a night or two, and he had stayed away for two nights before; so that his disappearance did not disturb them, and when they heard that Mr. Peytral's body had been found in the barn they accepted the news as fact. They recognised at once a photograph produced by Plummer as that of their late lodger. And the photograph had been procured from Messrs. Kingsley, Bell and Dalton, the intended victims in the bond case, and it was one of Henning, their vanished correspondence clerk!

That his death would be convenient to Mayes, the greater scoundrel, was plain enough. The bond robbery had been brought to naught, thanks to Martin Hewitt, and Henning was now useless. Worse, he might be caught, or give himself up, and was thus a perpetual danger. And probably he wanted money. This being so, it was a singular fact that at the inquest the surgeon who had examined the wound gave it as his most positive opinion that it had been self-inflicted. And it was inflicted with a razor, Henning's own, as was very clearly proved after inquiry. For the razor was found in the barn by the police, entangled with the blackened frame of an old lantern. Here was still another puzzle; one to which the final revelation of the mystery of the Red Triangle gave an answer, as will be seen in due place.

THE CASE OF THE ADMIRALTY CODE

1.

Quick on the heels of the case of the Burnt Barn followed the next of the Red Triangle affairs. Indeed, the interval was barely two days. Mr. Victor Peytral, it will be remembered, had declined to reveal to Hewitt the addresses of the two houses in London which he had seen Mayes visit, desiring to think the matter over for a few days first; but before any more could be heard from him, news of another sort was brought by Inspector Plummer.

It may give some clue to the period whereabout the whole mystery of the Red Triangle began to be cleared up if I say that at the time of Plummer's visit this country was on the very verge of war with a great European State. It is a State with which the present relations of England are of the friendliest description, and, since the dreaded collision was happily averted, there is no need to particularise in the matter now, especially as the name of the country with which we were at variance matters nothing as regards the course of events I am to relate. Though most readers will recognise it at once when I say that the war, had it come to that, would have been a naval war of great magnitude; and that during the time of tension swift but quiet preparations were going forward at all naval depots, and movements and dispositions of our fleet were arranged that extended to the remotest parts of the ocean.

It was at the height of the excitement, and, as I have said, two days after the return of Hewitt and myself from Throckham, when the case of the Burnt Barn had been disposed of, that Detective-Inspector Plummer called. I was in Hewitt's office at the time, having, in fact, called in on my way to learn if he had heard more from Mr. Victor Peytral, for, as may be imagined, I was as eager to penetrate the mystery of the Triangle as Hewitt himself—perhaps more so, since Hewitt was a man inured to mysteries. I had hardly had time to learn that Peytral had not yet made up his mind so far as to write, when Plummer pushed hurriedly into the room.

"Excuse my rushing in like this," he said, "but your lad told me that it was Mr. Brett who was with you, and the matter needs hurry. You've heard no more of that fellow—Myatt, Hunt, Mayes, whatever his name is last—since the barn murder, of course? Has Peytral given you the tip he half promised?"

Hewitt shook his head again. "Brett has this moment come to ask the same question," he said. "I have heard nothing."

"I must have it," said Plummer, emphatically. "Do you think he will tell me?"

Hewitt shook his head again. "Scarcely likely," he said. "He's an odd fellow, this Mr. Peytral—a foreigner, with revenge in his blood. I have done him and his daughter some little service, and he told me all his private history; but he seemed even then disposed to keep Mayes to himself and let nobody interfere with his own vengeance. But I will wire if you like. What is it?"

"I'll tell you," said Plummer, pushing the door close behind him. "I'll tell you—in confidence, of course—because you've seen more of this mysterious rascal than I have, and—equally in confidence, of course—Mr. Brett may hear, too, since he's been in several of the cases already. Well, of course, we all know well enough that we want this creature—Mayes, we may as well call him, I suppose, now—for three murders, at least, to say nothing of other things. That's all very well, and we might have got him with time. But now we want him for something else; and it's such a thing that *we must have him at once*, or else"—and Plummer pursed his lips and snapped his fingers significantly. "We can't wait over this, Mr. Hewitt; *we've got to have that man today*, if it can be done. And there's more than ordinary depending on it. It's the country this time. The Admiralty telegraphic code has been stolen!"

"By Mayes?"

Plummer shrugged his shoulders. "That's to be proved," he said; "but he was seen leaving the office at about the time the loss occurred, and that's enough to set me after him; and there's not another clue of any sort. Mr. Hewitt, I wish you were in the official service!"

Hewitt smiled. "You flatter me," he said, "as you have done before. But why in this case particularly?"

"It's a case altogether out of the ordinary, and one of a string of such, all of which you have at your fingers' ends. And I don't mind confessing that this man Mayes is a little too big a handful for one—

513

for me, at any rate. I wish you could work with me over this; in fact, in the special circumstances I've a good mind to ask to have you retained, as an exceptional measure. But the thing's urgent, and there's red-tape!"

Hewitt had taken a glance at his desk tablet, which he now flung down.

"I'll do it for love," he said, "if necessary. My appointment list is uncommonly slack just now, and even if it weren't, I'd make a considerable sacrifice rather than be out of this. This fellow Mayes is a dangerous man; and I feel it a point of honour that he shall not continue to escape. Moreover, I have begun to form a certain theory as to the Red Triangle, and all there is at the back of it—a theory I would rather keep to myself till I see a little more, since as it stands it may only strike you as fantastic, and if it is wrong it may lead some of us off the track; but it is a theory I wish to test to the end. So I'm with you, Plummer, if you'll allow it; and you can make your official application for a special retainer or not, just as you please."

Plummer was plainly delighted.

"Most certainly I will," he said. "Shall I give you the heads of the case, or will you come to the Admiralty and see for yourself?"

"Both, I think," said Hewitt. "But first I will send a telegram to Peytral. Then you can give me the heads of the case as we go along, and I will look at the place for myself. I am in this case heart and soul, pay or no pay—and I expect my friend Brett would like to be in it, too. Is there any objection?"

"Well," Plummer answered, a little doubtfully, "we're glad of outside help, of course, but I'm not sure, officially——"

"Of course you are always glad of outside help," Hewitt interrupted, "and in this case we may possibly find Brett more useful than you think. Consider now. He has seen a good deal of these cases—quite as much as you, in fact—but he is the only one of the three of us whom Mayes does not know by sight. Remember, Mayes saw us both in the affair of Mr. Jacob Mason, and he saw you again in the case of the Lever Key—escaped, in fact, because he instantly recognised you. I'll answer for Brett's discretion, and I'm sure he'll be glad to help, even if, for official reasons, you may not find it possible to admit him wholly into your counsels."

Of course I willingly assented, and the conditions understood, Plummer offered no further objection. Hewitt despatched his telegram, and in a very few minutes we were in a cab on the way to the

Admiralty.

"This is the way of it," Plummer said. "You will remember that when we lost Mayes at the end of the Lever Key case, I was waiting for him in that city office, with an assistant, and that we only saw him for an instant in the lift. Well, that assistant was a very intelligent man of mine, named Corder—a fellow with a wonderful memory for a face. Now Corder is on another case just now, and we'd put him on, dressed like a loafer, to hang about Whitehall and the neighbourhood, watching for someone we want. Well, this morning there came an urgent message to the Yard from the Admiralty, to ask for a responsible official at once, and I was sent. As I came along I saw Corder lounging about, and of course I took no notice—it would not do for us people from the Yard to recognise each other too readily in the street. But Corder came up, and made pretence to ask me for a match to light his pipe; and under cover of that he told me that he had seen Mayes not an hour before, coming out of the Admiralty.

"At this, of course, I pricked up my ears. I didn't know what they wanted me for, but if there was mischief, and that fellow had been there, it was likely at least that he might have been in it. Corder was quite positive that it was the man, although he had only seen him for a moment in the lift. He hadn't seen him go into the Admiralty office, but he was passing as he came out, and noted the time exactly, so that he might report to me at the first opportunity. The time was 11.32, and Mayes jumped into a hansom and drove off. He walked right out into the middle of the road to stop the hansom—you know how wide the road is there—so that Corder couldn't hear his direction to the cabman, but he took the number as the cab went off. Corder ought to have collared him then and there, I think, but he was in a difficult position. It would have endangered the case he was on, which is very important; and besides, he didn't realise how much we wanted him for, having only been brought in as an assistant at the tail of our bond case. Still less did he guess—any more than myself—what I was going to hear at the Admiralty office."

"At any rate," interrupted Hewitt, "you've got the number of the cab?"

"Here it is," Plummer answered, "and I've already set a man to get hold of the cabman. You'd better note the number—92,873."

Hewitt duly noted the number, and advised me to do the same, in case I should chance to meet the cab during the afternoon; and as we neared our destination Plummer gave us the rest of the case in outline.

515

"In the office," he said, "I found them in a great state. A copy of the code, or cypher, in which confidential orders and other messages are sent to the fleet all over the world, and in which reports and messages are sent back, had disappeared during the morning. It was in charge of a Mr. Robert Telfer, a clerk of responsibility and undoubted integrity. He kept it in a small iron safe, which is let into the wall of his private room. It was safe when he arrived in the morning, and he immediately used it in order to code a telegram, and locked it in the safe again at 10.20. Two hours later, at 12.20, he went to the safe for it again, in order to de-code a message just received, and it was gone!

"And the lock of the safe is one that would take hours to pick, I should judge. There isn't a shade of a clue, so far as I can see, except this circumstance of Mayes being seen leaving by Corder—just between Telfer's two visits to the safe, you perceive. And of course there may be nothing in that, except for the character of the man. And that's all there is to go on, as far as I can see. I needn't tell you how important the thing is at a time like this, and how much would be paid for that secret code by a certain foreign government. We have made hurried arrangements to have certain places watched, and as soon as I have taken you to the office I must rush off and make a few more arrangements still. But here we are."

Mr. Robert Telfer's room was at the side of a long and gloomy corridor on the upper floor, and the door was distinguished merely by a number and the word "Private" painted thereon. We found Mr. Telfer sitting alone, and plainly in a state of great nervous tension. He was a man of forty or thereabout, thin, alert, and using a single eye-glass. Plummer introduced us by name, and rapidly explained our business.

"I told you the name of the party I am after, Mr. Telfer," Plummer said, "and I went straight to Mr. Martin Hewitt, as being most likely to have information of him. Mr. Hewitt, whose name you know already, of course, is kind enough, seeing we're in a bad pinch, and pushed for time, to come in and give us all the help he can. Both he and his friend, Mr. Brett, know a good deal of the doings of the person we're after, and their assistance is likely to be of the very greatest value. Do you mind giving Mr. Hewitt any information he may ask? I must rush over to the Yard to put some other inquiries on foot, and to set an observation or two, but I'll be back presently."

"Certainly," Mr. Telfer answered, "I'm only too anxious to give any information whatever—so long as it is nothing departmentally forbidden—which will help to put this horrible matter right. Please ask me anything, and be patient if my answers are not very clear. I have been much overworked lately, as you may imagine, and have had very little sleep; and now this terrible misfortune has upset me completely; for, of course, I am held responsible for that copy of the code, and if it isn't recovered, and quickly, I am ruined—to say nothing, of course, of the far more serious consequences in other directions."

"That is the safe in which it was kept, I presume?" Hewitt said, indicating a small one let into the wall. "May I examine it?"

"Certainly." Mr. Telfer turned and produced the keys from his pocket. "The code was here, lying on this shelf when I needed it this morning at ten. I took it out, used it, returned it to the same place exactly, and locked the safe door. Then I took the draft of the telegram, together with the copy in cypher, into the controller's room, gave it into safe hands, and returned here."

Hewitt narrowly examined the lock of the safe with his pocket lens. "There are no signs of the lock having been picked," he said, "even if that were possible. As a matter of fact, this is a lock that would take half a day to pick, even with a heavy bag of tools. No, I don't think that was the way of it. You have no doubt about locking the safe door at 10.20, I suppose, before you went to the controller's room?"

"No possible doubt whatever. You see, I left the whole bunch of keys hanging in the lock while I coded the telegram. It was a short one, and was soon done. Then I returned the code to its place, locked the safe, and then used another key on the bunch to lock a drawer in this desk. I had no occasion to go to the safe again till about 12.20, when the controller's secretary came here with a telegram to be decoded. The safe was still locked then, but when it was opened the code was gone."

"You had had no occasion to go to the safe in the meantime?"

"None at all. I locked it at 10.20, and I unlocked it two hours later, and that was all."

"You were not in the room the whole of the time, of course?"

"Oh, no. I have told you that at 10.20 I went to the controller's room, and after that I went out two or three times on one occasion or another. But each time I locked the door of the room."

"Oh, you did? That is important. And you took all your keys with you, I presume?"

"Yes, all. The keys on the bunch I took in my pocket, of course, and the room door key I also took. There are one or two rather important papers on my desk, you see, and anybody from the corridor might come in if the door were left unlocked."

"The lock of the door would be a good deal easier to pick than that of the safe," Hewitt observed, after examining it. "But that would be of no great use with the safe locked. Shortly, then, the facts are these. You locked the code safely away at 10.20, you left the room two or three times, but each time the door, as well as the safe, was locked, and the keys in your pocket; and then, at 12.20, or two hours exactly after the code had been put safely away, you opened the safe again in presence of the controller's secretary, and the code had vanished. That is the whole matter in brief, I take it?"

"Precisely." Mr. Telfer was pallid and bewildered. "It seems a total impossibility," he said; "a total, absolute, physical impossibility; but there it is."

"But as no such thing as a physical impossibility ever happens," Hewitt replied calmly, "we must look further. Now, are there any other ways into this room than by that door into the corridor? I see another door here. What is that?"

"That door has been locked for ages. The room on the other side is one like this, with a door in the corridor; it is used chiefly to store old documents of no great importance, and I believe that whole stacks of them, in bundles, are piled against the other side of that same door. We will send for the key and see, if you like."

The key was sent for, and the door from the corridor opened. As Telfer had led us to expect, the place was full of old papers in bundles and parcels, thick with ancient dust, and these things were piled high against the door next his room, and plainly had not been disturbed for months, or even years.

"There remains the skylight," said Hewitt, "for I perceive, Mr. Telfer, that your room is lighted from above, and has no window; while the grate is a register. There seems to be no opening in that skylight but the revolving ventilator. Am I right?"

"Quite so. There is no getting in by the skylight without breaking it, and, as you see, it has not been broken. Certainly there are men on the roof repairing the leads, but it is plain enough that nobody has come that way. The thing is wholly inexplicable."

"At present, yes," Hewitt said, musingly. He stood for a few moments in deep thought.

"Plummer is longer away than I expected," he said presently. "By the way, what was the external appearance of the missing code?"

"It was nothing but a sort of thin manuscript book, made of a few sheets of foolscap size, sewn in a cover of thickish grey paper. I left it in the safe doubled lengthwise, and tied with tape in the middle."

"Its loss is a very serious thing, of course?"

"Oh, terribly, terribly serious, Mr. Hewitt," Telfer replied, despairingly. "I am responsible, and it will put an end to my career, of course. But the consequences to the country are more important, and they may be disastrous—enormously so. A great sum would be paid for that code on the Continent, I need hardly say."

"But now that you know it is taken, surely the code can be changed?"

"It's not so easy as it seems, Mr. Hewitt," Telfer answered, shaking his head. "It means time, and I needn't tell you that with affairs in their present state we can't afford one moment of time. Some expedients are being attempted, of course, but you will understand that any new code would have to be arranged with scattered items of the fleet in all parts of the world, and that probably with the present code in the hands of the enemy. Moreover, all our messages already sent will be accessible with very little trouble, and they contain all our strategical coaling and storing dispositions for a great war, Mr. Hewitt; and they can't, they *can't* be altered at a moment's notice! Oh, it is terrible!... But here is Inspector Plummer. No news, I suppose, Mr. Plummer?"

"Well, no," Plummer answered deliberately. "I can't say I've any news for *you*, Mr. Telfer, just yet. But I want to talk about a few things to Mr. Hewitt. Hadn't we better go and see if your telegram is answered, Mr. Hewitt? Unless you've heard."

"No, I haven't," Hewitt replied. "We'll go on at once. Good-day for the present, Mr. Telfer. I hope to bring good news when next I see you."

"I hope so, too, Mr. Hewitt, most fervently," Telfer answered; and his looks confirmed his words.

We walked in silence through the corridor, down the stairs, and out by the gates into the street. Then Plummer turned on his heel and faced Hewitt.

"That man's a wrong 'un," he said, abruptly, jerking his thumb in the direction of the office we had just left. "I'll tell you about it in the cab."

As soon as our cab was started on its way back to Hewitt's office Plummer explained himself.

"He's been watched," he said, "has Mr. Telfer, when he didn't know it; and he'll be watched again for the rest of today, as I've arranged.

What's more, he won't be allowed to leave the office this evening till I have seen him again, or sent a message. No need to frighten him too soon—it mightn't suit us. But he's in it, alone or in company!"

"How do you know?"

"I'll tell you. It seems the lead roofs are being repaired at the Admiralty, and the plumbers are walking about where they like. Now I needn't tell you I've had a man or two fishing about among the door-keepers and so on at the Admiralty, and one of them found a plumber he knew slightly, working on the roof. That plumber happens to be no fool—a bit smarter than the detective-constable, it seems to me, in fact. Anyhow, he seems to have got more out of my man than my man got out of him; and soon after I reached the Yard he turned up, asking to see me. He said he'd heard that a valuable paper was missing (he didn't know what) from the room with the skylight in the top floor, where the gentleman with the single eye-glass was, and where the safe was let in the wall; and he wanted to know what would be the reward for anybody giving information about it.

"Of course I couldn't make any promise, and I gave him to understand that he would have to leave the amount of the reward to the authorities, if his information was worth anything; also, that we were getting to work fast, and that if he wished to be first to give information he'd better be quick about it; but I promised to make a special report of his name and what he had to say if it were useful. And it will be, or I'm vastly mistaken! For just you see here. Our friend, Mr. Telfer, says he put that code safely away at 10.20 in the safe, and that he never went to the safe again till 12.20, when the controller's secretary was with him; never went to it for anything whatever, observe.

"Well, the plumber happened to be near the skylight at half-past eleven, and he is prepared to swear that he saw Mr. Telfer—'the gent with the eye-glass,' as he calls him—go to the safe, unlock it, take out a grey paper, folded lengthwise, with red tape round it, re-lock the safe, and carry that paper out into the corridor! The plumber was kneeling by a brazier, it seems, which was close by the skylight, and he is so certain of the time because he was regulating his watch by Westminster Hall clock, and compared it when the half-hour struck, which was just while Telfer was absent in the corridor with the paper. He was only gone a second or two, and you will remember that Corder saw Mayes leaving the premises within two minutes of that time!"

"Yes!"

"Well, Telfer was back in a second or two, *without the paper*, and went on with his affairs as before. That's pretty striking, eh?"

"Yes," Hewitt answered thoughtfully, "it is."

"It was a sort of shot in the dark on the part of the plumber, for he knew nothing else—nothing about Telfer legitimately having the keys of the safe, nor any of the particulars we have been told. He merely knew that a paper was missing, and having seen a paper taken out of the safe he got it into his head that he had possibly witnessed the theft; and he kept his knowledge to himself till he could see somebody in authority. Mighty keen, too, about a reward!"

"And now you are having Telfer supervised?"

"I am. Not that we're likely to get the code from him; that's passed out, sure enough, in Mayes's hands—or else his pockets."

To this confident expression of opinion Hewitt offered no reply, and presently we alighted at his office, eager to learn if Peytral had given the information Hewitt so much desired. Sure enough a telegram was there, and it ran thus:

"On the night you know of, Mayes went first to 37 Raven Street, Blackfriars, then to 8 Norbury Row, Barbican. Message follows."

"Now we're at work," Hewitt said, briskly, "and for a while we part. I shall make a few changes of dress, and go to take a look at 37 Raven Street, Blackfriars. Will you two go on to Norbury Row? You'll have to be careful, Plummer, and not show yourself. That is where Brett will be useful, since he isn't known; if anybody is to be seen let it be him. I shall be very careful myself—though I shall have some little disguise; and I fancy I shall not be so likely to be seen as you."

"What are we to do?" I asked.

"Well, of course, if you see Mayes in the open, grab him instantly. I needn't tell Plummer *that*. I think Plummer would naturally seize him on the spot, rush him off to the nearest station and go back with enough men to clear out No. 8 Norbury Row. If you don't see him you'll keep an observation, according to Plummer's discretion. But, unless some exceptional chance occurs, I hope you won't go rushing in till we communicate with each other—we must work together, and I may have news. My instinct seems to tell me that yours is the right end of the stick, at Barbican. But we must neglect nothing, and that is why I want you to hold on there while I make the necessary examination at the other end. Do you know this Norbury Row, Plummer?"

"I think I know every street and alley in the City," Plummer answered. "There is a very good publican at the corner of Norbury Row, who's been useful to the police a score of times. He keeps his eyes open, and I shall be surprised if he can't give us *some* information about No. 8, anyhow. Moon's his name, and the house is 'The Compasses.' I shall go there first. And if you've any message to send, send it through him. I'll tell him."

On the stairs Plummer and I encountered another of his assistants. "I've got the cab, sir," he reported. "Waiting outside now. Took up a fare in Whitehall, opposite the Admiralty, and drove him to Charterhouse Street; got down just by the Meat Market. That's all the man seems to know."

Plummer questioned the cabman, and found that as a matter of fact that was all he did know. So, telling him to wait to take us our little journey, we returned and reported his information to Hewitt.

"Just as I expected," he said, quietly. "He stopped the cab a bit short of his destination, of course,—just as you will, no doubt. There's not a great deal in the evidence, but it confirms my idea."

2.

We followed Mayes's example by stopping the cab in Charterhouse Street, and walking the short remaining distance to Barbican. Norbury Row was an obscure street behind it, at the corner of which stood "The Compasses," the public-house which Plummer had mentioned. We did not venture to show ourselves in Norbury Row, but hastened into the nearest door of "The Compasses," which chanced to be that of the private bar.

A stout, red-faced, slow-moving man with one eye and a black patch, stood behind the bar. Plummer lifted his finger and pointed quickly toward the bar-parlour; and at the signal the one-eyed man turned with great deliberation and pulled a catch which released the door of that apartment, close at our elbows. We stepped quickly within, and presently the one-eyed man came rolling in by the other door.

"Well, good art'noon, Mr. Plummer, sir," he said, with a long intonation and a wheeze. "Good art'noon, sir. You've bin a stranger lately."

"Good afternoon, Mr. Moon," Plummer answered, briskly. "We've come for a little information, my friend and I, which I'm sure you'll give us if you can."

"All the years I've been knowed to the police," answered Mr. Moon, slower and wheezier as he went on, "I've allus give 'em all the information I could, an' that's a fact. Ain't it, Mr. Plummer?"

"Yes, of course, and we don't forget it. What we want now———"

"Allus tell 'em what—ever I knows," rumbled Mr. Moon, turning to me, "allus; an' glad to do it, too. 'Cause why? Ain't they the police? Very well then, I tells 'em. Allus tells 'em!"

Plummer waited patiently while Mr. Moon stared solemnly at me after this speech. Then, when the patch slowly turned in my direction and the eye in his, he resumed, "We want to know if you know anything about No. 8 Norbury Row?"

"Number eight," Mr. Moon mused, gazing abstractedly out of the window; "num—ber eight. Ground-floor, Stevens, packing-case maker; first-floor, Hutt, agent in fancy-goods; second-floor, dunno. Name o' Richardson, bookbinder, on the door, but that's bin there five or six year now, and it ain't the same tenant. Richardson's dead, an' this one don't bind no books as I can see. I don't even remember seein' him *very* often. Tallish, darkish sort o' gent he is, and don't seem to have many visitors. Well, then there's the top-floor—but I s'pose it's the same tenant. Richardson used to have it for his workshop. That's all."

"Have you got a window we can watch it from?"

Mr. Moon turned ponderously round and without a word led the way to the first floor, puffing enormously on the stairs.

"You *can* see it from the club-room," he said at length, "but this 'ere little place is better."

He pushed open a door, and we entered a small sitting-room. "That's the place," he said, pointing. "There's a new packing-case a-standing outside now."

Norbury Row presented an appearance common enough in parts of the city a little way removed from the centre. A street of houses that once had sheltered well-to-do residents had gradually sunk in the world to the condition of tenement-houses, and now was on the upward grade again, being let in floors to the smaller sort of manufacturers, and to such agents and small commercial men as required cheap offices. No. 8 was much like the rest. A packing-case maker had the ground-floor, as Moon had said, and a token of his trade, in the shape of a new packing-case, stood on the pavement. The rest of the building showed nothing distinctive.

"There y'are, gents," said Mr. Moon, "if you want to watch, you're welcome, bein' the p'lice, which I allus does my best for, allus. But you'll have to excuse me now, 'cos o' the bar."

Mr. Moon stumped off downstairs, leaving Plummer and myself watching at the window.

"Your friend the publican seems very proud of helping the police," I remarked.

Plummer laughed. "Yes," he said, "or at any rate, he is anxious we shan't forget it. You see, it's in some way a matter of mutual accommodation. We make things as easy as possible for him on licensing days, and as he has a pretty extensive acquaintance among the sort of people we often want to get hold of, he has been able to show his gratitude very handsomely once or twice."

The house on which our eyes were fixed was a little too far up the street for us to see perfectly through the window of the second-floor, though we could see enough to indicate that it was furnished as an office. We agreed that the unknown second-floor tenant was more likely to be our customer, or connected with him, than either of the others. Still, we much desired a nearer view, and presently, since the coast seemed clear, Plummer announced his intention of taking one.

He left me at the post of observation, and presently I saw him lounging along on the other side of the way, keeping close to the houses, so as to escape observation from the upper windows. He took a good look at the names on the door-post of No. 8, and presently stepped within.

I waited five or six minutes, and then saw him returning as he had come.

"It's the top floors we want," he said, when he rejoined me in Mr. Moon's sitting-room. "The packing-case maker is genuine enough, and very busy. So is the fancy-goods agent. I went in, seeing the door wide open, and found the agent, a little, shop-walkery sort of chap, hard at work with his clerk among piles of cardboard boxes. I wouldn't go further, in case I were spotted. Do you think you'd be cool enough to do it without arousing suspicion? Mayes doesn't know you, you see. What do you think? We don't want to precipitate matters till we hear from Hewitt, but on the other hand I don't want to sit still as long as anything can be ascertained. You might ask a question about book-binding."

"Of course," I said. "If you will let me I'll go at once—glad of the chance to get a peep. I'll bespeak a quotation for binding and lettering a thousand octavos in paste grain, on behalf of some convenient firm of publishers. That would be technical enough, I think?"

I took my hat and walked out as Plummer had done, though, of course, I approached the door of No. 8 with less caution. The packing-case maker's men were hammering away merrily, and as I mounted the stairs I saw the little fancy-goods agent among his cardboard boxes, just as Plummer had said. The upper part of the house was a silent contrast to the busy lower floors, and as I arrived at the next landing I was surprised to see the door ajar.

I pushed boldly in, and found myself alone in a good-sized room plainly fitted as an office. There were two windows looking on the street, and one at the back, more than half concealed behind a ground glass partition or screen. I stepped across and looked out of this window. It looked on a narrow space, or well, of plain brick wall, containing nothing but a ladder, standing in one corner. And the only other window giving on this narrow square space was in the opposite wall, but much lower, on the ground level.

I saw these things in a single glance, and then I turned—to find myself face to face with a tallish, thin, active man, with a pale, shaven, ascetic face, dark hair, and astonishingly quick glittering black eyes. He stood just within the office door, to which he must have come without a sound, looking at me with a mechanical smile of inquiry, while his eyes searched me with a portentous keenness.

"Oh," I said, with the best assumption of carelessness I could command, "I was looking for you, Mr. Richardson. Do you care to give a quotation for binding at per thousand crown octavo volumes in paste grain, plain, with lettering on back?"

"No," answered the man with the eyes, "I don't; I'm afraid my carelessness has led you into a mistake. I am not Richardson the bookbinder. He was my predecessor in this office, and I have neglected to paint out his name on the door-post."

I hastened to apologise. "I am sorry to have intruded," I said. "I found the door ajar and so came in. You see the publishing season is beginning, and our regular binders are full of work, so that we have to look elsewhere. Good-day!"

"Good-day," the keen man responded, turning to allow me to pass through the door. "I'm sorry I cannot be of service to you—on this occasion."

From first to last his eyes had never ceased to search me, and now as I descended the stairs I could *feel* that they were fixed on me still.

I took a turn about the houses, in order not to be observed going direct to "The Compasses," and entered that house by way of the private bar, as before.

"That is Mayes, and no other," said Plummer, when I had made my report and described the man with the eyes. "I've seen him twice, once with his beard and once without. The question now is, whether we hadn't best sail in straight away and collar him. But there's the window at the back, and a ladder, I think you said. Can he reach it?"

"I think he might—easily."

"And perhaps there's the roof, since he's got the top floor too. Not good enough without some men to surround the house. We must go gingerly over this. One thing to find out is, what is the building behind? Ah, how I wish Mr. Hewitt were here now! If we don't hear from him soon we must send a message. But we mustn't lose sight of No. 8 for a moment."

There was a thump at the sitting-room door, and Mr. Moon came puffing in and shouldered himself confidentially against Plummer. "Bloke downstairs wants to see you," he said, in a hoarse grunt that was meant for a low whisper. "Twigged you outside, I think, an' says he's got somethink partickler to tell yer. I believe 'e's a 'nark'; I see him with one o' your chaps the other day."

"I'll go," Plummer said to me hurriedly. "Plainly somebody's spotted me in the street, and I may as well hear him."

I knew very well, of course, what Moon meant by a 'nark.' A 'nark' is an informer, a spy among criminals who sells the police whatever information he can scrape up. Could it be possible that this man had anything to tell about Mayes? It was scarcely likely, and I made up my mind that Plummer was merely being detained by some tale of a petty local crime.

But in a few minutes he returned with news of import. "This fellow is most valuable," he said. "He knows a lot about Mayes, whom, of course, he calls by another name; but the identity's certain. He saw me looking in at No. 8, he says, and guessed I must be after him. He seems to have wondered at Mayes's mysterious movements for a long time, and so kept his eye on him and made inquiries. It seems that Mayes sometimes uses a back way, through the window you saw on the opposite side of the little area, by way of that ladder you mentioned. It's quite plain this fellow knows something, from the particulars about that ladder. He wants half a sovereign to show me the way through a stable passage behind and point out where our man can be trapped to a certainty. It'll be a cheap ten shillingsworth, and we mustn't waste time. If Hewitt comes, tell him not to move till I come back or send a message, which I can easily do by this chap I'm going with. And be sure to keep your eye on the front door of No. 8 while I'm gone."

The thing had begun to grow exciting, and the fascination of the pursuit took full possession of my imagination. I saw Plummer pass across the end of the street in company with a shuffling, out-at-elbows-looking man with dirty brown whiskers, and I set myself to watch the door of the staircase by the packing-case maker's with redoubled attention, hoping fervently that Mayes might emerge, and so give me the opportunity of capping the extraordinary series of occurrences connected with the Red Triangle by myself seizing and handing him over to the police.

So I waited and watched for something near another quarter of an hour. Then there came another thump at the door, and once more I beheld Mr. Moon.

"Man askin' for you in the bar, sir," he said.

"Asking for me?" I asked, a little astonished. "By name?"

"Mr. Brett, 'e said, sir. He's the same chap, you know. He's got a message from Inspector Plummer, 'e says."

"May he come up here?" I asked, mindful of maintaining my watch.

"Certainly, sir, if you like. I'll bring him."

Presently the shuffling man with the dirty whiskers presented himself. He was a shifty, villainous-looking fellow of middle height, looking a "nark" all over. He pulled off his cap and delivered his message in a rum-scented whisper. "Inspector Plummer says the front way don't matter now," he said. "'E can cop 'im fair the other way if you'll go round to him at once. If Mr. Martin Hewitt's here 'e'd rather 'ave 'im, but on'y one's to come now."

Naturally, I thought, Plummer would prefer Hewitt; but in this case I should for once be ahead of my friend, and have the pleasure of relating the circumstances of the capture to him, instead of listening, as usual, to his own quiet explanations of the manner in which the case had been brought to a successful issue. So I took my hat and went.

"Best let me go in front," whispered the "nark." "You bein' a toff might be noticed." It was a reasonable precaution, and I followed him accordingly.

We went a little way down Barbican, and presently, taking a very narrow turning, plunged into a cluster of alleys, through which, however, I could plainly perceive that our way lay in the direction of the back of the house in Norbury Row. At length my guide stopped at what seemed a stable yard, pushed open a wicket gate, and went in, keeping the gate open for me to follow.

It was, indeed, a stable yard, littered with much straw, which the "nark" carefully picked to walk on as noiselessly as possible, motioning me to do the same. It was a small enough yard, and dark, and when my guide very carefully opened the door of a stable I saw that that was darker still.

He pushed the door wide so as to let a little light fall on another door which I now perceived in the brick wall which formed the side of the stable. After listening intently for a moment at this door, the guide stepped back and favoured me with another puff of rum and a whisper. "There's no light in that there passage," he said, "an' we'd better not strike one. I'll catch hold of your hand."

He pulled the stable door to, and took me by the hand. I heard the inner door open quietly, and we stepped cautiously forward. We had gone some five or six yards in the darkness when I felt something cold touch the wrist of the hand by which I was being led. There was a loud click, my hand was dropped, and I felt my wrist held fast, while I could hear my late guide shuffling away in the darkness.

I could not guess whether to cry out or remain quiet. I called after the man in a loud whisper, but got no answer. I used my other hand to feel at my right wrist, and found that it was clipped in one of a pair of handcuffs, the other being locked in a staple in the wall. I tugged my hardest to loosen this staple, but it held firm. The thing had been so sudden and stealthy that I scarce had time to realise that I was in serious danger, and that, doubtless, Plummer had preceded me, when a light appeared at an angle ahead. It turned the corner, and I perceived, coming toward me, carrying a lamp, the pale man of the eyes, whom I had encountered not an hour before—in a word, Mayes.

His eyes searched me still, but he approached me with a curiously polite smile.

"No, Mr. Brett," he said, "my name is not Richardson, and I am not a bookbinder. Not that I am particular about such a thing as a name, for you have heard of me under more than one already, and you are quite at liberty to call me Richardson if you like. I am sorry to have to talk to you in this uncomfortable place, but the circumstances are exceptional. But, at least, I should give you a chair."

He stepped back a little way and pressed a bell-button. Presently the fellow who had decoyed me there appeared, and Mayes ordered him to bring me a chair at once, which he did, with stolid obedience. I sat in it, so that my wrist rested at somewhere near the level of my shoulder.

"Mr. Brett," Mayes pursued, when his man was gone, "I am not so implacable a person as you perhaps believe me; in fact, I can assure you that my disposition is most friendly."

"Then unfasten this handcuff," I said.

"I am sorry that that is a little precaution I find it necessary to take till we understand each other better. I am glad to see you, Mr. Brett, though I am sure you will not think me rude if I say that I should have preferred Mr. Martin Hewitt in your place. But perhaps his turn will come later. I have a proposition to make, Mr. Brett. I should like you to join me."

"To join you?"

"Exactly." He nodded pleasantly. "You needn't shrink; I shan't ask you to do anything vulgar, or even anything that, with your present prejudices, you might consider actively criminal. You can help me, you see, in your own profession as a journalist; and in other ways. And my enterprise is greater than you may imagine. Join me, and you shall be a great man in an entirely new sphere. A small matter of initiation is necessary, and that is all. You have only to consent to that."

I said nothing.

"You seem reluctant. Well, perhaps it is natural, in your present ignorance. This is no vulgar criminal organisation that I have, understand. I have taken certain measures to provide myself with the necessary tools in the shape of money, and so forth, but my aims are larger than you suspect—perhaps larger than you can understand. And I work with a means more wonderful than you have experience of. For instance, here is today's work. You know about the lost Naval Code, of course—it is what you came about. That document is now lying in the desk you stood by in the room where we spoke of paste grain book covers and the like. It was there then at your elbow. It will be sold for many thousands of pounds by tomorrow, and all the puny watchings and dodgings that have been devised cannot prevent it. The money will go to aid me in the attainment of the power of which you may have a part, if you wish. The means of attaining this I scruple no more about than you did today about the story of the book-bindings." He bowed with a slight smile and went on.

"Come now, Mr. Brett, put aside your bourgeois prejudices and join me. Your friend Plummer is coming gladly, I feel sure, and he will be useful, too. And from what I have seen from Mr. Martin Hewitt, I have no doubt I can make it right with him. If I can't it will be very bad for him, I can assure you; you have heard and seen something of my powers, and I need say no more. But Hewitt is a man of sense, and will come in, of course, and you had better come with your friends. I want one or two superior men. Mason—you know about Jacob Mason, of course—Mason was a fool, and he was lost—inevitably.

The others"—he made a gesture of contempt—"they are mere vulgar tools. They will have their rewards if they are faithful, of course; if not—well, you remember Denson in the Samuel diamond business? He was *not* faithful, and there was an end of him. I may tell you that Denson was made an example, for one was needed. I assigned him a certain operation, and, having brought it to success, he endeavoured to embezzle—did embezzle—the proceeds. He was made a conspicuous example, in a most conspicuous public place, to impress the others. They didn't know *him*, but they knew well enough what the Red Triangle meant! Ah, my excellent recruit—for so I count you already—there is more in that little sign than you can imagine! It is more than a sign—it is an implement of very potent power; and you shall learn its whole secret in that little form of initiation I spoke of. See now, a present example. Telfer, the Admiralty clerk, gave up that document at my mere spoken word. He will deny it to his dying day, and he will be ruined for the act; but he gave me the paper himself, at my mere order. If he were one of my own—if he had passed through the initiation I offer you, I would have protected him; as it is, he must take his punishment, and though it is only I who will benefit, he will still deny the fact! Ha! Mr. Brett, do you begin to perceive that I do not boast when I tell of powers beyond your understanding?"

Truly I was amazed, though I could not half understand. The circumstances of the loss of the Admiralty code had been so inexplicable, and now these incredible suggestions of the prime actor in the matter were more mysterious still.

"Ha! you are amazed," he went on, "but if you will come further into my counsels I will amaze you more. What are you now? A drudge of a journalist, and if ever you make a thousand a year to feed yourself with you will be lucky. Come to me and you shall be a man of power. There is a place beyond the sea where I may be king, and you a viceroy. Don't think I am raving! It is true enough that I am an enthusiast, but I have power, power to do anything I please, I tell you! What are the greatest powers among men on this earth? Some will say the pen, or the sword, or love, or what not. Men of the world will say, money and lies; and they will be very nearly right. Money and lies will move continents, but I have one greater power still—the very apex of the triangle! That power I revealed to Jacob Mason. He thought to betray it, and it killed him. That power I will reveal to you, if you will accept the alternative I offer."

"The alternative?"

"Yes, the alternative, for an alternative it is, of course. If you will go through the form of initiation, I shall keep you here a little till I can trust you—which will be very soon. But if not—well, Mr. Brett, I wish to be as friendly as you please, but having been at the trouble of catching you, and having got you here safely, you who know so much now, you who could be so dangerous if you ever got away—eh? Well, you know my methods, and you have seen them exemplified, and you will understand."

There was no anger in his voice as he uttered this threat, nor even, I thought, in his eyes. But what there was was worse.

"But I'm sure you will not make things unpleasant," he concluded. "You will go through the little form I have arranged, if only for curiosity. Just think over it for a moment, while I go to close my little office."

He took the lamp and turned away, but as he reached the angle of the passage, there came a sound that checked his steps. I could hear a noise of feet and hurried voices, and then suddenly arose a shout in a voice which seemed to be Plummer's. "Here!" it cried. "Help! This way, Hewitt! Brett!"

I shouted back at the top of my voice, wondering where Plummer was, and what it might all mean. And with that Mayes turned, and I saw that he was about to make for the door I had entered by. I resolved he should not pass me if I could prevent it, and I sprang up and seized my chair in my left hand, shouting aloud for help as I did so.

Mayes came with a bound, and flung his lighted lamp full at my head. It struck the chair and smashed to a thousand pieces, and in that instant of time Mayes was on me. Plainly he had no weapon, or he would have used it; but I was at disadvantage enough, with my right wrist chained to the wall. I clung with all my might, and endeavoured to swing my enemy round against the wall in order that I might clasp my hands about him, and I shouted my loudest as I did it. But the chair and the broken glass hampered me, and Mayes was desperate. The agony in my right wrist was unbearable, and just as I was conscious of a rush of approaching feet a heavy blow took me full in the face, and I felt Mayes rush over me while I fell and hung from the wrist.

I had a stunned sense of lights and voices and general confusion, and then I remembered nothing.

3.

I came to myself on the floor of a lighted room, with Hewitt's face over mine. My wrist seemed broken, though it was free, there was oil and blood on my clothes, and in my left hand I still gripped a piece of Mayes's coat.

"Stop him!" I cried. "He's gone by the stable! Have they got him?"

"No good, Brett," Hewitt answered soberly. "You did your best, but he's gone, and Peytral after him!"

"Peytral?"

"Yes. He brought his own message to town. But see if you can stand up."

I was well enough able to do that, and, indeed, I had only fainted from the pain of the strain on my wrist. Several policemen were in the room, beside Hewitt and Plummer. Mayes's stronghold was in the hands of his enemies.

Then I suddenly remembered.

"The Admiralty code!" I cried. "It was in the office desk. Have you got it?"

"No," Hewitt answered. "Come, Plummer, up the ladder!"

Little time was lost in forcing Mayes's desk, and there the document was found, grey cover, red tape and all intact. The police were left to make a vigorous search for any possible copy, and the original was handed to Plummer, as chief representative of the law present. He had been trapped precisely as I had been, except that he had been led further, and shut in a cellar as well as fastened by the wrist. Mayes, it seemed, had wasted very little time in attempting to pervert him, and I have no doubt that, whatever fate might have been reserved for me, Plummer would never have left the place alive had it not been for the timely irruption of Hewitt, with Peytral and the police.

In half an hour Peytral returned. He had dashed out in chase of the fugitive, but failed even to see him—lost him wholly in the courts, in fact. For some little while he persevered, but found it useless.

The dirty-whiskered man made no attempt to escape, though there was talk of another man having got away in the confusion by way of the stable roof. The police were left in charge of the place, and we deferred a complete exploration till the next day.

Hewitt's tale was simple enough. He had endued himself in some-what seedy clothes, and had visited 37 Raven Street, Blackfriars, which he found to be merely a tenement house. It took some time to make inquiries there, with the necessary caution, because of the number of lodgers; and then the inquiries led to nothing. It was an experi-ence common enough in his practice, but none the less an annoying delay, and when he returned to his office he found Mr. Peytral already awaiting him. Peytral described his following of Mayes at much greater length and detail than before, and he and Hewitt had come on to Norbury Row at once and asked news of Mr. Moon.

Mr. Moon's description of the successive disappearances of Plummer and myself, and of our continued absence, so aroused Hewitt's suspicions that he instantly procured help from the nearest station, and approached the door of Mayes's office. A knock being unanswered, the door was instantly broken in. The room was found to be unoccupied, but the ladder was still standing at the open window, by which Mayes had descended to the back premises. Down this ladder Hewitt went, with the police after him. The rest I had seen myself.

"But what," I said, "what is this mystery? Why did Telfer give up the code, and what is the power that Mayes talks of?"

"It is a power," replied Hewitt, "that I have suspected for some time, and now I am quite sure of it. A secret, dangerous and terrible power which I have encountered before, though never before have I known its possibilities carried so far. It is hypnotism!"

"Hypnotism!" I exclaimed. "But can a person be hypnotised against his will?"

"In a sense, in most cases, he cannot. That is the explanation of Mayes's proposals to you to go through a 'form of initiation.' If you had consented, the 'form' would have been a process of hypnotism. Once or twice repeated, and you would have been wholly under his control, so that if he willed it and forbade you, you could tell nothing of what he wished kept secret, and you would have committed any crime he might suggest. Consider poor Jacob Mason! Remember how he struggled to tell what he knew, oppressed by the horror of it, and how it all ended! And remember Henning the clerk, Mayes's tool in that case of bond robbery! What has happened to him? He committed suicide, as you know, immediately after Mayes had left him at the barn. Brett, this power of hypnotism, a power for healing in the hands of a good man, may become a terrible power for evil in the hands of a villain!"

"But Telfer, today? He seems to have known nothing of Mayes, and he was not one of his regular creatures—Mayes himself told me so."

"About that I don't know. But I expect we shall find that he has been willingly hypnotised at some time or another, perhaps more than once, by this same scoundrel Mayes. Possibly in one of Mayes's appearances in respectable society, at an evening party, or the like. In a case of that sort the hypnotist may impress a certain formula—a word, a name, or a number—on the subject's mind, by the repetition of which, at any future time, that same subject may be instantly hypnotised. So that, once having become hypnotised, on any innocent occasion, the subject is in the power of the hypnotist, more or less, ever after. The hypnotist says: 'When I repeat such and such a sentence or number to you in future, you will be hypnotised,' and hypnotised the subject duly is, instantly. Supposing such a case in this matter of Mr. Telfer, it would only be necessary for Mayes to meet him in the corridor, repeat his formula and command the victim to bring out the paper he specified. This done he could similarly order him to *forget the whole transaction*, and this the victim would do, infallibly."

It is only necessary to say here, parenthetically, that later inquiry proved the truth of Hewitt's supposition. Twice or three times Mr. Telfer had been hypnotised in a friend's chambers, by a plausible tall man whose acquaintance his host had made at some public scientific gathering. And in the end it became possible to identify this man with Mayes.

Mr. Moon, of "The Compasses," was of great comfort to me that evening. My cuts and bruises were washed in his house, and my inner man revived with his food and drink.

"Allus glad to oblige the p'lice," said Mr. Moon; "allus. 'Cos why? Ain't they the p'lice? Very well then!"

The Adventure of Channel Marsh

1.

Mayes's stronghold was taken, but Mayes had escaped us once again; the cage was in our hands, but the bird had flown.

Martin Hewitt, however, had his plans, as he was soon to show. The recovery of the Admiralty code was a good stroke, and was a satisfactory ending to an important case; but that, and even the capture of the curious premises behind the Barbican, made but a halting-place in his pursuit of Mayes, and as soon as I was in some degree recovered from my struggle, and the captured place had been hastily searched, the chase was resumed without a moment's delay; and that adventure was entered upon which saw the end of the Red Triangle and its unholy doings—which came terribly near to seeing the end of Hewitt himself, in fact.

I have not described the den near the Barbican with any great particularity, but I have said that the office, accessible from the open street, was only connected with the hidden premises behind—premises, as was afterwards discovered, held under a separate tenancy—by an easily-shifted ladder. It was in these hidden premises, approached by the maze of courts and the stable-yard, that the main evidences of Mayes's way of life were observable. The passage where my wrist had been locked to the wall, and the room or cellar in which Plummer had been confined, were the only parts of the lower premises fitted for the detention of prisoners, with the exception of one very low and wholly unlighted cellar, entered by a trapdoor and a very steep flight of brick steps. This place smelt horribly faint and stagnant; but it produced on my mind, both then and when I examined it later, an effect of horror and repulsion more than could be accounted for by the smell alone. Of its history nothing was discovered, and perhaps the feeling (though others experienced it as well as myself) was the effect of mere fancy; but I have never got rid of a conviction that that black cellar, or rather pit—for it was very narrow—had been the instrument of crimes never to be told.

There were one or two rooms sparely furnished—one as a bed-room, a larger room, with a long table, a sofa, and several chairs; and in one of the smaller rooms was found a stove, ladles and crucibles for the melting down of metals—gold or silver. It was in this same room also that the table stood, in the drawers of which were found papers, let-ters and formulæ—things giving more than a hint of the use to which Mayes had put his friendship with Mr. Jacob Mason, for of every pos-sible manner and detail in which science—more particularly the sci-ence of chemistry—could aid in the commission of crime, there were notes in these same drawers. But most of these things were observed in detail later. The thing that set us once more on the trail of Mayes, that very night and that very hour, was found in the isolated office facing the street. It was a cheque-book, quite full of unused cheques.

"This cheque-book," said Hewitt to Inspector Plummer and my-self, "was in the drawer below that in which we discovered the Admi-ralty code. The Eastern Consolidated is the bank, as you see—Upper Holloway branch. Now we must follow this at once, before waiting to search any further. There may be something more important as a clue, or there may not, but at any rate, while we are looking for it we are losing time. This may bring us to him at once."

"You mean that he may have some address in Holloway," suggested Plummer, "and we may get it from the bank?"

"There's that possibility, and another," Hewitt answered. "He has had to bolt without warning or preparation, with nothing but the clothes he ran in—probably very little money. Money he will want at once, and he would rather not wait till the morning to get it; if he can get it at once it will mean thirteen or fourteen hours' start at least. More, he will know very well that this place will be searched, that this cheque-book will be discovered soon enough, and that consequently the bank will be watched. This is what he will do—what he is doing now, very likely. He will knock up the resident manager of that bank and try to get a cheque cashed tonight. I don't think that can be done; in which case he will probably try to make some arrangement to have money sent him. Either way, we must be at the Upper Holloway branch of the Eastern Consolidated Bank as soon as a hansom can get us there."

Thus it was settled, and Hewitt and Plummer went off at once, leaving Plummer's men, with the City police, in charge of the raided premises; leaving some of them also to make inquiries in the neighbourhood. Mr. Victor Peytral had shown himself anxious to accompany Hewitt and Plummer, but had been dissuaded by Hewitt. I guessed that Hewitt feared that some hasty indiscretion on the part of this terribly wronged man might endanger his plans. Peytral, however, seemed tractable enough, and left immediately after them; he had business, he said, which he expected would occupy him for a day or two, and when it was completed he would see us again.

As for myself I only remained long enough to ascertain that the police could find no trace of the direction of Mayes's flight in the immediate neighbourhood. They had little to aid them. He had gone without a hat, and his dress was in some degree disordered by his struggle with me; but the latter defect he might easily have remedied in the courts as he ran, and they could gather no tidings of a hatless man. So I took my way to my office, my wrist growing stiffer and more painful as I went, so that I was not sorry to arrange for another member of the staff to take my duty for the night, and to get to bed a few hours earlier than usual, after the day's fatigue and excitement.

2.

Going to bed uncommonly soon I woke correspondingly early in the morning; but I was no earlier than Hewitt, who was at my door, in fact, ere my breakfast was well begun.

"Well," I asked eagerly, almost before my friend had entered, "have you got him at last?"

"Not yet," Hewitt answered. "But he did exactly as I had expected.

Plummer and I knocked up the bank manager, who lives over the premises at the Upper Holloway branch. He was a very decent fellow—rather young for the post—but he was naturally a bit surprised, possibly irritated, at being bothered by one and another after office hours. I showed him the cheque-book, and asked him if it belonged to any customer of his.

"'Why, yes,' he said, examining the numbers, 'I remember this because it is the first of a new series, and we issued it the day before yesterday to a new customer. Where did you get it?'

"'We are very anxious to see that customer,' I said. 'Has he been here this evening?'

"The manager seemed a trifle surprised, but answered readily enough. 'Yes,' he said, 'he was here not an hour ago.'

"'Wanting to draw money?' I asked. But that the manager wouldn't tell me, of course. So that it was necessary for Plummer to step in and reveal the facts that this was a police matter, and that he was a detective-inspector. That made some difference. The manager told us that our man had opened an account at the bank only two days before; and I'd like you to guess what name he had opened it under."

"Not Myatt?" I said. "After the chase——"

"No, not Myatt."

"Catherton Hunt?"

"No, nor Catherton Hunt. He had opened it in the name of Mayes!"

"What! his actual name?"

"His actual original name, according to Peytral. The account was transferred, it would seem, from another bank; and I have an idea we may find that he has been shifting his money about from one bank to another as safety suggested, using his real name with it. You remember we could find no trace of a banking account when the police raided and ransacked Calton Lodge after Mason was killed? Quite probably he has had small current accounts in other names at various times to aid in his schemes, but his main account has always stood in his real name; and by that, you see, we get some confirmation of Peytral's story. Well, as I say, the account was opened in the name of Mayes, and the cheque-book was issued which we discovered last night. The Upper Holloway branch saw no more of its customer till yesterday evening, long after hours, when he drove up in a hansom."

"Oh," I said, "in a hansom, was it? The men left behind could get no news of him."

"Yes, we ascertained that last night; we called back, of course, the last thing. I expect he got the first cab visible and drove off to a hatter's a fair distance away, and then on to the bank. At any rate, he knocked up the manager and told him that he had a sudden need for money that very night; could he have some?

"The manager told him it would be impossible. Even if he had been willing to do it, against all regulations, it would still be impossible. For the strong-room and every cash receptacle in it was locked with two separate locks with different keys, and though he had one of these keys himself, it was useless without the other, which was in the possession of his second in command, who lived some distance out of London. This course is the usual precaution adopted in branch banks of this sort; opening and closing, morning and evening, have to be done by chief and assistant together. And I tell you, Brett, I believe that it was only the being informed of this fact that prevented Mayes from trying some of his hypnotic tricks on the bank manager; in which case there would have been a big bank robbery—perhaps something worse in addition."

"Murder?"

"Murder with a tourniquet, perhaps—perhaps with some other weapon; but, at any rate, probably with the Red Triangle. You know, of course—indeed I told you, I think—that in most cases—not all—it is necessary to get the subject's consent to the *first* exercise of hypnotism on him. I told you also it is possible for the practised hypnotist, while the subject is under the influence of the *first* experiment, to suggest to him a certain word or formula, or even a silent sign, which shall bring him under the influence at any other time, whenever the hypnotist chooses to repeat it—just as must have been done with Mr. Telfer, in the case of the Admiralty code. The first suggestion would not be the difficult thing it might seem—it would only require a little time and persuasion. Nothing would be said about hypnotism, of course; perhaps something about a little physical experiment, or the like, and then in a moment or two the subject would be in this creature's power for ever. Remember the little 'ceremony of initiation' that the scoundrel attempted to persuade you to submit to! That meant hypnotism—perhaps death.

"But this is mere speculation. Mayes found that the keys on the premises were not enough to release his money, even if the strict rules of the bank had permitted the cashing of a cheque out of hours. But the manager suggested that perhaps some neighbouring tradesman would exchange cash for a cheque, and, with the view of obliging the new customer, went with him as far as the shop of Mr. Isaac Trenaman, a grocer and cheesemonger with a rather large shop at the corner of the road. Mr. Trenaman, introduced and assured by the manager, was willing to give as much cash as he could find in the till against Mr. Mayes's cheque, and did so to the extent of twenty-seven pounds, a cheque for which sum was duly drawn on one of the tradesman's own cheque forms, and left with him. This done, the bank's new customer took himself off, with thanks and apologies; carrying with him, however, two blank cheque forms from Mr. Trenaman's book, the pennies for which he punctiliously paid over the counter. Having no cheque forms with him, he explained, he might find them useful if he could come across some friend who could provide the cash he wished to use that night. And having completed this business so far, this charming new customer of the bank made off into the night."

"And is that all you know of his movements?"

"Yes, as yet. He seems to have made no very definite excuse to the manager for wanting the money in such a hurry—just said something had occurred which made cash necessary, and was very polite and apologetic, generally. The manager formed a notion that it must be for some gambling purpose—he fancied that Mayes said something distantly alluding to that, but wasn't sure."

"Did you ask about the address given to the bank?"

"Of course; but there we gained nothing. The manager couldn't remember it exactly, and the books, of course, were locked up. But we know it already—for what the manager *could* remember was that it was an office address, and somewhere near Barbican! So that we are back at the Barbican den again, where I am going now, with Plummer, to give a day to a minute investigation of the whole place. Meanwhile a watch is being set at the bank in Holloway."

"Do you expect him back there, then?"

"Hardly. You see he knows that by this time we must have found his cheque-book, and will be on the watch. But there is just a chance—a very remote one—that he may send a message; perhaps send some-body to cash a cheque. Though I don't expect it, for he is no fool—he is, indeed, a sort of genius—and that would be a mistake, I think. Still, he is bold, and that is where his money is, and he may make a dash at it. So a couple of Plummer's men are to be waiting there, this morn-ing, in the manager's office, and if anybody comes from Mayes he will be detained. Perhaps you would like to be with them? You can't be of much use with me, and the job will be dull. But there you *may* have a chance of excitement, and you will be useful to come and report if anything does happen. Why, you may even bag Mayes himself!"

"Of course—I'll go anywhere you please. They told you last night, I suppose, that Peytral had business, and had gone off?"

"Yes, and I'm not sorry. He is too dangerous a man to have about us, with his hot blood and the terrible injuries he keeps in memory. As likely as not, if we get Mayes, we should next have to collar Peytral for shooting him, or something. So I'm not sorry he is out of it for a bit. But can you start now? Plummer is in my office and the two men are in a cab outside. The bank opens at nine, and that is in Upper Holloway."

I seized my hat and made ready.

"You should keep your eyes open," Hewitt hinted, "before you get to the bank and when you leave, as well as while you're there. Do you remember how poor Mason was watched? Well, there is probably some watching going on now. Last night, on our way to the bank and back, I believe Plummer and I were watched pretty closely."

3.

Plummer's two plain-clothes men and I reached the neighbourhood of the bank with a quarter of an hour to spare, or rather more. We dismissed the cab at some little distance from the spot, and approached singly, so that it was not difficult for us to slip in separately among the dozen or fifteen clerks as they arrived. We passed directly into the manager's room, the door of which opened into the space left for the public before the counter. From this room the whole of the outer office was visible through the glass of the partition. The manager, Mr. Blockley, a quick, intelligent man of thirty-six or so, gave us chairs and pointed out how best we could watch the counter without ourselves being observed.

"If a letter is sent," he said, "it will be brought here to me, of course, and I will bring the messenger in. If a cheque is presented from Mayes, I have told the cashier to slide that big ledger off his desk accidentally with his elbow. That will be your signal, and then you can do whatever you think proper. I don't think I can do any more than that."

We took our positions and waited. I felt pretty sure that if Mayes sent at all it would be early, for obvious reasons. And I was right, for the very first customer was our man.

He stepped in briskly scarcely a minute after the manager had ceased speaking, and I remembered having seen him waiting at the street corner as I came along. He was a well-dressed, smart enough looking man, in frock coat and tall hat. He took a letter-case from his pocket, picked out a cheque from the rest of the papers in it, and passed it under the wire grille of the counter. The cashier took it, turned it over, and shifted mechanically to post the amount in the book on his desk. As he did so his elbow touched the heavy ledger which the manager had pointed out to us, and it fell with a crash. The cashier calmly put his pen behind his ear, and stooped to pick up the book, but even as he did it the two Scotland Yard men were out before the counter, and had sidled up to the stranger, one on each side.

"May we see that cheque, if you please?" asked one, and the cashier turned its face toward him. "Ah, just so; a hundred pounds—Mayes. We must just trouble you to come with us, if you please. There is some explanation wanted about that cheque."

I had followed the two men from the manager's room, and now I saw that while one had laid his hand on the stranger's shoulder the other had taken him by the opposite arm. "Why," said the former, looking into his face, "it's Broady Sims!"

"All right," the man growled resignedly. "It's a cop. I'll go quiet."

But as he spoke I saw the free hand steal out behind him and pitch away a crumpled fragment of paper. One of the policemen saw it too, followed it with his eyes, and saw me snatch it up.

"That's right, sir," he said, "take care of that; and we'll have a cab, in case anything else drops accidentally. It's just a turning over, Broady, that's what it is."

I spread out the piece of paper, and was astonished to find inscribed on it just such another series of figures, in groups of eight, as was found in the cypher message in the Case of the Lever Key.

Here was a great find—a secret message as clear to me as to Mayes himself, and as likely as not the scrap of paper that would hang him! I took one of the plain-clothes men aside while the other kept his hold of Broady Sims.

"This is very important," I said. "It is a cypher message which Mr. Hewitt can read—or I, myself, in fact, with a little time. Must you take it with you? If so, I'll make a copy now."

"Well, sir, we're responsible, you see," the man said, "so I think we must take it; so perhaps you'd better make a copy, as you suggest."

"Very well," I said, "that is done in a few seconds. You can take your man off, and I will go direct to Mr. Hewitt and Inspector Plummer with the copy." And with that I made the copy, which read thus:—

> 23, 19, 15, 1, 9, 14, 9, 2; 20, 8, 1,
> 20, 14, 14, 20, 8; 14, 5, 12, 4, 9, 7,
> 5, 14; 3, 8, 18, 23, 0, 14, 1, 8; 22,
> 9, 6, 1, 18, 3, 5, 1; 19, 14, 15, 21,
> 9, 0, 20, 12; 18, 12, 21, 1, 6, 23, 20,
> 12; 9, 18, 15, 5, 18, 13, 12, 20.

It struck me to ask the manager if the cheque just presented were one of those procured from Mr. Trenaman the night before, and I found that it was. Then I left the policemen with their prisoner and made for the nearest cab-rank. This cypher message, no doubt conveying Mayes's instructions to the man just captured, was probably of the utmost importance, and Hewitt must see it at once; and as the cab ambled along towards Barbican I busied myself in deciphering the figures according to the plan of the knight's move in chess, as Hewitt had explained to me.

I could only see two noughts among the numbers, so plainly it was a longer message than the one then deciphered—one of sixty-two letters, in fact. I turned the figures into the letters corresponding in the alphabet, *a* for 1, *b* for 2, and so on, as Hewitt had done, and I arranged these letters in the squares of a roughly drawn chessboard, so that they stood thus:—

w	*s*	*o*	*a*	*i*	*n*	*i*	*b*
t	*h*	*a*	*t*	*n*	*n*	*t*	*h*
n	*e*	*l*	*d*	*i*	*g*	*e*	*n*
c	*h*	*r*	*w*	*o*	*n*	*a*	*h*
v	*i*	*f*	*a*	*t*	*c*	*e*	*a*
s	*n*	*o*	*u*	*t*	*o*	*t*	*l*
r	*l*	*u*	*a*	*f*	*w*	*t*	*l*
i	*r*	*o*	*e*	*r*	*m*	*l*	*t*

The letters thus set out, to read off the message was a simple task enough, in view of the key Hewitt had given me. I began, as in the case of the Lever Key message, at the right-hand top corner, and taking the knight's move from *b* to *e* in the last square but one of the third line, thence to *a* at the end of the fifth line, and so to *t* in the seventh line, and from that to *r* (fifth square in bottom line), *u* in seventh line and so on, in the order shown by the Lever Key message, a copy of which I kept as a curiosity in my pocket-book. So I read the message through, and I set it down thus:—

Be at ruin Channel Marsh tonight twelve; wait in hall for instruc. Word final.

The general meaning of this seemed clear enough. The man whom the policeman had recognised as Broady Sims was to be at some spot—a ruined building, it would seem—in a place called Channel Marsh, at midnight, there to wait in the hall for instructions; no doubt for instructions where to take the hundred pounds he was to have got from the bank. "Word final" was not so clear, though I judged—and I think rightly—that it meant that the word "final" was to be used as a password by which the two messengers should know each other.

I was almost at my destination, and was cogitating the message and its meaning, when the cab checked at some traffic in Barbican, just by the "Compasses" public-house, and Mr. Victor Peytral hailed me and climbed on the step of the cab.

"I was just going to see if Mr. Hewitt was at the place," he said, "and if so to ask him for news. But I am rather in a hurry, and perhaps you can tell me?"

"We are on the track, I think," I answered, "and I have just come across this, which I am taking to Hewitt," and with that I showed him my translation of the cypher, and gave him its history in half a dozen sentences.

"That's good," Peytral answered. "I don't know Channel Marsh, do you? But probably Mr. Hewitt does. I won't keep you any longer—I see you're hurrying. But I hope to see you again before long."

He dropped off the step and disappeared, and the cab went on round the corner by the "Compasses."

I found Hewitt and Plummer in the office where, on pretence of bookbindery, I had first seen Mayes face to face the day before. They were near the completion of their examination of this office and all its contents, and soon would begin as systematically on the premises behind. I gave Hewitt my copy of the cypher message, and my translation, with an exact account of how it had come into my possession.

Martin Hewitt studied the message for a minute or two, and then relapsed into grave thought. So he sat for some little time, while Plummer left the room by the window and descended the ladder to speak with his men on guard below.

Presently Hewitt looked up and said: "Brett, this message is most important—probably as important as you suppose it to be. But at the

543

same time I believe you have made a great mistake about it."

"But I haven't misread it, have I? Is there any other way——"

"No, you haven't misread it; you've read every word as it was intended to be read. But it is a very different thing from what you suppose it to be."

"What is it, then?"

Martin Hewitt put the paper on the table and looked keenly in my face. "It is a trap," he said. "It is a trap to catch *me*—unless I flatter myself unduly."

I could not understand. "A trap?" I repeated. "But how?"

"Why should Mayes need to send his confederate instructions by written note? We know the nature of his hold over his subordinates, and we know that it means personal communication. Also, the cheque was in Mayes's own hands last night. More, Mayes knows very well that I have read that cypher—has known it for some time; otherwise how could we have discovered the bonds in the case of the Lever Key? Also, Mayes knows that we have his cheque-book and know his bank. Didn't I assure you we were watched last night? I believe he knows all we have done. In such circumstances he might risk his jackal's liberty by sending him on the desperate chance of cashing a cheque, but, knowing the risk, he would never have let him come with information on him.

"And least of all would he have let him come carrying a vital secret written in that very cypher which he knows I read many weeks ago. And then see how that message, instead of being concealed, was positively brought to your notice! That man Broady Sims is a cunning rascal, and the police know him of old as a skilful swindler and bill-forger. A man like that doesn't get rid of a compromising scrap of paper by trundling it out under your nose just at the moment he is arrested, when the attention of everybody is directed to him; no, he would wait his opportunity, and then he would probably slip it into his mouth and swallow it. As it is, he would seem to have succeeded in dropping this paper full in your sight, with an elaborate pretence of secrecy. Now this is what has been done, Brett. That man has been sent to cash a cheque, with very little hope of success, or none, because the first move that Mayes would anticipate on our part would be the watching for him and his cheques at the bank in Upper Holloway. If by any chance the cheques had been cashed, well and good, no harm would have been done, and then Mayes could have gone on to arrange for drawing the rest of his balance—could probably have quite safely come himself to draw it. But if on the other hand, as he fully anticipated, Sims was arrested, what then?

"Nothing was lost but a penny cheque-form, and even Sims—though Mayes would care nothing about that—could only be searched and then released, for the cheque was perfectly genuine, and there was no charge against him. But since he would certainly be searched, that cypher note was given him, with instructions to make a conspicuous show of attempting to get rid of it. Now that note was written in a cypher which Mayes knew was as plain as print—to whom? To *me*. I am on his trail, and this note is deliberately flung in my way, open as the day, but with every appearance of secrecy. I am his dangerous enemy, and he knows it—as he told you, in fact, yesterday. If he can clear me away, he can take breath and make himself safe. The purpose of this note is to induce me to go, alone, to this place on Channel Marsh tonight at twelve, in the hope of learning where to find Mayes. There I am to be got rid of—murdered in some way, for which preparation will be made. Mayes judges my character pretty well. He knows that, in such circumstances as he represents, Sims being kept away from his appointment, I should certainly go and take his place, and use his password, to learn what I could. And, Brett, *that is precisely what I shall do!*"

"What? You will go?" I exclaimed. "But you mustn't—the danger! We'd better both go together."

Hewitt smiled. "Why not forty of us?" he said. "No. Here is a chance of bagging our man, for, however I am to be arranged for—whether by shot, steel, or the tourniquet, I make no doubt it is Mayes himself who is to do it. You shall come, however, you and Plummer at least. But we will not go in a bunch—you shall follow me and watch, ready to help when needful. This Channel Marsh is an empty, dark space between two channels of the Lea. It is among the Hackney Marshes, lying between Stratford and Homerton, and I fancy there is a deserted house there, though I can't remember ever having seen it. Do you know it?"

"No; not in the least."

"Well, I must reconnoitre today, and that with a lot of care. I think I told you I was convinced of being watched, and that is a thing you can't prevent in a place like London, if it is skilfully done. Now, Brett, you have done very well this morning. If you want to be on the scene of action tonight at twelve, you must get leave from your editor, mustn't you? How's your wrist?"

It was still extremely stiff, and I told Hewitt that I doubted my ability to hold a pen for two or three days.

"Very well, then; get off and convey your excuses as soon as you please. I shall have a talk with Plummer, and then I shall take a few hours to myself, by myself, in somebody else's clothes. Be in your rooms all the evening, for you may expect a message."

4.

It was at a little past nine in the evening that I next saw Hewitt. He came into my rooms in an incongruous get-up. He wore corduroy trousers, a very dirty striped jersey, a particularly greasy old jacket, and a twisted neckcloth; but overall was an excellent overcoat, and on his head a tall hat of high polish.

"Brought to me by Kerrett," he said, in explanation of the hat and overcoat. "He's been waiting with them for a long time in a court by Milford Lane. A good hat and overcoat will cover anything, and I preferred to enter this building in my own character. I've been wearing that this afternoon," and he pulled out of his pocket an old peaked cap with ear-pieces tied over the top.

"You mustn't bring your best clothes," he went on, "or you'll spoil them scrambling about boats and groping in ditches. I have done my ditch-groping for the day, and I'm going to change. You had best be putting on older things while I get into newer."

"What sort of place is this Channel Marsh?" I asked.

"Well, I should think there must be a great many better places to spend a night in. It must be the dreariest, wettest flat within many miles of London, and I should like to see the portrait of the man who had the idea of building a house there. For a house there is, or rather the ruins of it—deserted for years, and half carried away by rats and people who wanted slates and firewood and water pipes."

"Is that the place where you intend waiting tonight?"

"It is. I haven't examined it nearly so closely as I should like, for fear of raising a scare. Channel Marsh is almost an island, with a narrow neck of an entrance at each end. A foot-track runs the whole length, and a person in the ruined house can easily see anybody entering the Marsh from either end. For that reason, I reconnoitred from a boat—the boat you will go in tonight. I think it is the very dirtiest old tub I ever saw, so that it suited my rig out. I discovered it at a wharf some little way down the river, and I paid a shilling for the hire of it. Channel Marsh is banked a bit on one side, and I crept up under cover of the bank. I learned very little, beyond the general lie of the land, because I was so mighty cautious. I judged it better to be content with half an examination, rather than drive away the game. And even as it is I've an idea I have been seen. I lay up among some reeds till dark, but after that I am *sure* there was somebody on the Marsh—and skulking, too, like me. So after waiting and scouting for a little I gave it up and paddled quietly back."

"But look here, Hewitt," I said, "this seems a bit mad. Why go and risk yourself as you talk of doing? You believe Mayes will be there, at the ruin, or will come there at twelve. Very well, then, why can't the police send enough men to surround the place and capture him for certain?"

Hewitt smiled and shook his head. "My dear Brett," he said, "you haven't seen the place, and I have. It will be hard enough job for you and Plummer to get near the spot unobserved, guided by a man who knows every inch. A trampling crowd of policemen would have as much chance as a herd of elephants, and on such light nights as we are having now they would be seen a mile off. And who knows what scouts he may have out? No, as I say, it will be a great piece of luck if you get through unobserved as it is, and even now I'm not perfectly certain that I couldn't do best alone. However, arrangements are made now, and you are coming, three of you."

"Then what are the arrangements?" I asked.

"Just these. You are to leave here first. Make the best of your way to Mile End Gate, where an old inn stands in the middle of the road. Go to the corner of the turning opposite this, at the south side of the road. At eleven o'clock a four-wheeler will drive up, with Plummer and one of his men in it. The man is one who knows all the geography of Channel Marsh, and he also knows exactly where to find the boat I used today. You will drive to a little way beyond Bow Bridge, and then Plummer's man will lead you to the boat. You had better scull and leave the others to look out. They will know what to do. You will pull along to a place where you can watch till you see me coming on to the Marsh by the path. As soon as you see me you will slip quietly along to a place the policeman will show you, close to the ruin, and watch again. That's all. I don't know whether or not you think it worthwhile to take a pistol. I certainly shall; but then I'm most likely to want it. Plummer will have one."

I thought it well worthwhile, and I took my regulation "Webley"—a relic of my old Volunteer captaincy. Then, by way of the underground railway, I gained the neighbourhood of Mile End, and interested myself about its back streets till the time approached to look for Plummer's cab.

Plummer was more than punctual—indeed, he was two or three minutes before his time. The cab drew near the kerb and scarcely stopped, so quickly did I scramble in.

"Good," said Plummer; "we're well ahead of time. Mr. Hewitt quite right?"

"Yes," I said. "I left him so an hour and a half ago at his office." And we sat silent while the cab rattled and rumbled over the stony road to Bow Bridge, and the shopkeepers on the way put up their shutters and extinguished their lights.

Bow Bridge was reached and passed, and presently we stopped the cab and alighted. Here Styles, Plummer's man, took the lead, and a little way farther along the road we turned into a dark and muddy lane on the left. We floundered through this for some hundred and fifty yards or so, and then suddenly drew in at an opening on the right. Here we stood for a few moments while our guide groped his way down toward the muddy water we could smell, rather than see, a little way before us. There were a few broken steps and a broad black thing which was the boat. We got into it as silently as we could manage, and cast off. It was a clumsy, broad-beamed, leaky old conveyance, and that it was as dirty as Hewitt had described it I could feel as I groped for the sculls and got them out. The night was light and dark by turns—changing with the clouds. We shipped the rudder, and Styles steered, or I should probably have run ashore more than once, for the banks were not always distinct, and the channel was narrow and dark. We passed the black forms of several factories with tall chimneys, and then drew out among the Marshes, flat and grey, with wisps of mist lying here and there. So we went in silence for a while, till at last we drew in against the bank on the left and laid hold by a post at a landing-place.

"This is the Channel Marsh," whispered Styles, as we climbed cautiously ashore. "We can't see the house very well from here, but there's where Mr. Hewitt will come through."

Looking over the top of the low bank, we could discern a path which traversed the length of the marsh, entering it by a broken gate at a neck of land which we must have passed on our way. Here we crouched and waited. We had heard the half-hour struck on some distant clock soon after entering the boat, and now we waited anxiously for the three-quarters. So long did the time seem to my excited perceptions that I had quite decided that the clock must have stopped, or, at any rate, did not chime quarters, when at last the strokes came, distant and plaintive, over the misty flats.

"A quarter of an hour," Plummer remarked. "He won't be a minute late, nor a minute too early, from what I know of him. How long will it take him from that gate to the ruin?"

"Eight or nine minutes, good," Styles answered.

"Then we shall see him in seven minutes or six minutes, as the case may be," Plummer rejoined in the same low tones.

Slowly the minutes dragged, with not a sound about us save the sucking and lapping of the muddy river and the occasional flop of a water-rat. The dark clouds were now fewer, and the moon was high and only partially obscured by the thinner clouds that traversed its face. More than once I fancied a sound from the direction of the ruin, and then I doubted my fancy; when at last there was a sound indeed, but from the opposite direction, and in a moment we saw Hewitt, muffled close about the neck, walking briskly up the path.

We regained the boat with all possible speed and silence, and I pulled my best, regardless of my stiff wrist. During our watch I had had time to perceive the wisdom of the arrangements which had been made. We had been watching from a place fairly out of sight from the ruin, yet sufficiently near it to be able to reach its neighbourhood before Hewitt; and certainly it was better to approach the actual spot at the same time as Hewitt himself, for then, if he were being watched for, the attention of the watcher would be diverted from us.

Presently we reached the reed-bed that Hewitt had spoken of, and I could see a sort of little creek or inlet. Here I ceased to pull, and Styles cautiously punted us into the creek with one of the sculls. The boat grounded noiselessly in the mud, and we crept ashore one at a time through mud and sedge.

The creek was edged with a bank of rough, broken ground, grown with coarse grass and bramble, and as we peeped over this bank the ruined house stood before us—so near as to startle me by its proximity. It must have been a large house originally—if, indeed, it was ever completed. Now it stood roofless, dismantled, and windowless, and in many places whole rods of brickwork had fallen and now littered the ground about. The black gap of the front door stood plain to see, with a short flight of broken steps before it, and by the side of these a thick timber shore supported the front wall. It struck me then that the ruin was perhaps largely due to a failure of the marshy foundation.

The place seemed silent and empty. Hewitt's footsteps were now plain to hear, and presently he appeared, walking briskly as before. He could not see us, and did not look for us, but made directly for the broken steps. He mounted these, paused on the topmost, and struck a match. It seemed a rather large hall, and I caught a momentary glimpse of bare rafters and plasterless wall. Then the match went out and Hewitt stepped within. Almost on the instant there came a loud jar, and a noise of falling bricks; and then, in the same instant of time I heard a terrific crash, and saw Hewitt leap out at the front door—leap out, as it seemed, from a cloud of dust and splinters.

I sprang to my feet, but Plummer pulled me down again. "Steady!" he said, "lie low! He isn't hurt. Wait and see before we show ourselves."

It seemed that the floor above had fallen on the spot where Hewitt had been standing. He had alighted from his leap on hands and knees, but now stood facing the house, revolver in hand, watching.

There was a moment's pause, a sound of movement from the upper part of the ruin, another quiet moment, and then a bang and a flash from high on the wall to the right. Hewitt sprang to shelter behind the heavy shore, and another shot followed him, scoring a white line across the thick timber.

Plummer was up, and Styles and I were after him.

"There he is!" cried Plummer, "up on the coping!" I pulled out my own pistol.

"Don't shoot!" cried Hewitt. "We'll take him alive!"

Far to the right, on the topmost coping of the front wall, I could see a crouching figure. I saw it rise to its knees, and once more raise an arm to take aim at Hewitt; and then, with a sudden cry, another human figure appeared from behind the coping and sprang upon the first. There was a moment of struggle, and then the rotten coping crumbled, and down, down, came bricks and men together.

I sickened. I can only explain my feeling by saying that never before had I seen anything that seemed so long in falling as those two men. And then with a horrid crash they struck the broken ground, and the pistol fired again with the shock.

We reached them in a dozen strides, and turned them over, limp, oozing, and lifeless. And then we saw that one was Mayes, and the other—Victor Peytral!

We kept no silence now, but Plummer blew his whistle loud and long, and I fired my revolver into the air, chamber after chamber. Styles started off at a run along the path towards the town lights, to fetch what aid he might.

But even then we had doubt if any aid would avail Mayes. He was the under man in the fall, and he had dropped across a little heap of bricks. He now lay unconscious, breathing heavily, with a terrible wound at the back of the head, and Hewitt foretold—and rightly—that when the doctor did come he would find a broken spine. Peytral, on the other hand, though unconscious, showed no sign of injury, and just before the doctor came sighed heavily and turned on his side.

First there came policemen, and then in a little time a hastily dressed surgeon, and after him an ambulance. Mayes was carried off to hospital, but with a good deal of rubbing and a little brandy, Peytral came round well enough to be helped over the Marshes to a cab.

The trap which had been laid for Hewitt was simple, but terribly effective. The floor above the hall—loose and broken everywhere—was supported on rafters, and the rafters were crossed underneath and supported at the centre by a stout beam. The rafters had been sawn through at both ends, and the rotten floor had been piled high with broken brick and stone to a weight of a ton or more. The end of a loose beam had been wedged obliquely under the end of the one timber now supporting the whole weight, so that a pull on the opposite end of this long lever would force away the bricks on which the beam rested and let the whole weight fall. It was the jar of the beam and the fall of the first few loose bricks that had so far warned Hewitt as to enable him to leap from under the floor almost as it fell.

Peytral's sudden appearance, when we had time to reflect on it, gave us a suspicion as to some at least of the espionage to which Hewitt had been subjected—a suspicion confirmed, later, by Peytral himself after his recovery from the shock of the fall. For fresh news of his enemy had re-awakened all his passion, and since he alone could not find him, he was willing enough to let Hewitt do the tracking down, if only he himself might clutch Mayes's throat in the end. This explained the "business" that had called him away after the Barbican stronghold had been captured; finding both Hewitt and Plummer somewhat uncommunicative, and himself somewhat "out of it," he had drawn off, and had followed Hewitt's every movement, confident that he would be led to his old enemy at last.

What I had told him of the cypher message had led him to hunt out Channel Marsh in the afternoon, and to return at midnight. He, of course, regarded the message, as I did myself at the time, as a perfectly genuine instruction from Mayes to Sims, and he came to the rendezvous wholly in ignorance as to what Hewitt was doing, and with no better hope than that he might hear something that would lead him in the direction of Mayes. He had entered the marsh after dark from the upper end, and had lain concealed by the other channel till near midnight; then he had crept to the rear of the ruin and climbed to where an opening seemed to offer a good chance of hearing what might pass in the hall. He had heard Hewitt approach from the front, and the crash that followed. The rest we had seen.

5.

Mayes never recovered consciousness, and was dead when we visited the hospital the day after; both skull and spine were badly fractured. And the very last we saw of the Red Triangle was the implement with which it had been impressed, which was found in his pocket.

It was a small triangular prism of what I believe is called soapstone. It was perhaps four inches long, and the face at the end corresponded with the mark that Hewitt had seen on the forehead of Mr. Jacob Mason. It fitted closely in a leather case, in the end of which was a small, square metal box full of the red, greasy pigment with which the mark had been impressed. It was from Broady Sims that we learnt the exact use and meaning of this implement: though he would not say a word till he had seen with his own eyes Mayes lying dead in the mortuary. Then he gasped his relief and said, "That's the end of something worse than slavery for me! I'll turn straight after this."

Sims's story was long, and it went over ground that concerns none of Hewitt's adventures. But what we learned from it was briefly this. It had been Mayes's way to meet clever criminals as they left gaol after a term of imprisonment. In this manner he had met Sims. He had made great promises, had spoken of great ideas which they could put into execution together, had lent him money, and then at last had "initiated" him, as he called it. He had put him to lie back in a chair and had directed his gaze on the Red Triangle held in the air before him: and then the Triangle had descended gently, and he felt sleepy, till at the cold touch of the thing on his forehead his senses had gone.

This was done more than once, and in the end the victim found that Mayes had only to raise the Triangle before him to send him to sleep instantly. Then he found that he must do certain things, whether he wanted or not. And it ended in complete subservience; so that Mayes could set him to perpetrate a robbery and then appropriate the proceeds for himself, for by post-hypnotic suggestion he could force him to bring and hand over every penny. More, the poor wretch was held in constant terror, for he knew that his very life depended on the lift of his master's hand. He could be sent into lethargy by a gesture and killed in that state.

That very thing was done, in fact, as we have seen, in two cases.

Sims was but one of a gang of such criminals, brought to heel and made victims. Their minds and souls, such as they were, had passed into the miscreant's keeping, and terror reinforced the power of hypnotism. They committed crimes, and when they failed they took the punishment; when they succeeded Mayes took the gains, or at any rate the greater part of them. He went, also, among people who were not yet criminals, and by degrees made them so, to his own profit. The case of Henning, the correspondence clerk, was one that had come under Hewitt's eyes. He used his faculty also with great cunning in other ways—as we had seen in the matter of the Admiralty code. And it was even said among the gang that a man he had once hypnotised he could force by suggestion to commit suicide when he became useless or inconvenient.

Sims and the ragged fellow who had decoyed me into Mayes's den were the only members of the gang whom we could identify after his death, but many others must have shared their relief; and I sincerely hope—though I hardly expect—that they all availed themselves of their liberty to abandon their evil courses. As in fact the two I speak of did, and took to honest work.

All that had remained mysterious in the earlier cases now became clear. In the first, the case of Samuel's diamonds, Denson had been put into the office where Samuel had found him, by Mayes, with the express design of effecting a diamond robbery. The robbery was effected, and the unhappy Denson formed a plan of making a bolt of it himself with the diamonds. He was, perhaps, what is called a difficult subject in hypnotism—amenable enough to direct influence, but not sufficiently retentive of post-hypnotic suggestion. He hid the jewels and adopted a disguise, but Mayes was watching him better than he supposed. The diamonds were lost, but Denson was found and done to death—probably not in that retreat near Barbican, but at night in some empty street. The diamonds were not found on him, and the body, with the mark of the Triangle still on it, was taken by night to a central spot in London and there left.

Mayes probably thought that a notable example like this, so boldly displayed and so conspicuously reported in the Press, would impress his auxiliaries throughout London with the terror that was one of his weapons; for they would well understand the meaning of the Red Triangle, and they would receive a striking illustration of the consequences of rebellion or bad faith. The money and the watch were left in the pockets because they were trifles after the loss of fifteen thousand pounds' worth of diamonds, and their presence in the pockets made the murder the less easy to understand—which was a point gained. And as to the keys—Mayes knew nothing of where the diamonds were hidden, and so had no use for them. For where could he use them? Denson had left his lodgings, and as to the office, that, he would guess, would be in the hands of the police, on Samuel's complaint. The immediate result of this affair on the only honest member of Mayes's circle I have told in the case of Mr. Jacob Mason. He was not yet thoroughly in Mayes's hands, but he had "dabbled," as he remorsefully confessed, and Mayes had already found him useful. He was dangerous, and his end came quickly. Another victim who had probably begun innocently enough was Henning, the clerk to Kingsley, Bell and Dalton, and his death in the Penn's Meadow barn leaves a mystery that never can be positively cleared up. Was it murder or was it suicide by post-hypnotic suggestion? It will be remembered that the fire burst out in the barn after Mayes had left it.

The case of Mr. Telfer was explained clearly enough by Hewitt at the time; but it is an example of the snares that lie open for the most innocent person who allows himself to be made the subject of hypnotic experiments at the hands of persons with whom, and with whose objects, he is not thoroughly acquainted. And it must be remembered that at this time there are persons advertising to teach the practice of hypnotism to anybody who will pay; to anybody who may use the terrible power as he pleases. More, the danger is so great that it has led two eminent men of science to issue a public protest and warning, with an urgent plea that the practice of hypnotism be restricted by law at least as closely as that of vivisection.

As to what would have happened if Plummer and I had yielded to Mayes's threats so far as to undergo the "initiation" he proposed, at the time we were helpless in his hands—of that I have little doubt. I cannot suppose that he would have wasted much time over me, once I had fallen lethargic. When Hewitt burst in he would have found me lying dead, with the Red Triangle on my forehead. It would have saved Mayes a lot of noise and struggle, at least. But I often wonder whether or not there was anything in his reference to the place beyond the sea, where he would make me a great man if I did as he wished. Was it his design, having accumulated sufficient wealth, to return and take his natural place among the enlightened rulers of Hayti? He would not have been so much worse than some of the others.

The Horace Dorrington Cases

I shall here set down in language as simple and straightforward as I can command, the events which followed my recent return to England; and I shall leave it to others to judge whether or not my conduct has been characterised by foolish fear and ill-considered credulity. At the same time, I have my own opinion as to what would have been the behaviour of any other man of average intelligence and courage in the same circumstances; more especially a man of my exceptional upbringing and retired habits.

I was born in Australia, and I have lived there all my life till quite recently, save for a single trip to Europe as a boy, in company with my father and mother. It was then that I lost my father. I was less than nine years old at the time, but my memory of the events of that European trip is singularly vivid.

My father had emigrated to Australia at the time of his marriage, and had become a rich man by singularly fortunate speculations in land in and about Sydney. As a family we were most uncommonly self-centred and isolated. From my parents I never heard a word as to their relatives in England; indeed, to this day I do not as much as know what was the Christian name of my grandfather. I have often supposed that some serious family quarrel or great misfortune must have preceded or accompanied my father's marriage. Be that as it may, I was never able to learn anything of my relatives, either on my mother's or my father's side. Both parents, however, were educated people, and indeed I fancy that their habit of seclusion must first have arisen from this circumstance, since the colonists about them in the early days, excellent people as they were, were not as a class distinguished for extreme intellectual culture. My father had his library stocked from England, and added to by fresh arrivals from time to time; and among his books he would pass most of his days, taking, however, now and again an excursion with a gun in search of some new specimen to add to his museum of natural history, which occupied three long rooms in our house by the Lane Cove River.

I was, as I have said, eight years of age when I started with my parents on a European tour, and it was in the year 1873. We stayed but a short while in England at first arrival, intending to make a longer stay on our return from the Continent. We made our tour, taking Italy last, and it was here that my father encountered a dangerous adventure.

We were at Naples, and my father had taken an odd fancy for a picturesque-looking ruffian who had attracted his attention by a complexion unusually fair for an Italian, and in whom he professed to recognise a likeness to Tasso the poet. This man became his guide in excursions about the neighbourhood of Naples, though he was not one of the regular corps of guides, and indeed seemed to have no regular occupation of a definite sort. "Tasso," as my father always called him, seemed a civil fellow enough, and was fairly intelligent; but my mother disliked him extremely from the first, without being able to offer any very distinct reason for her aversion. In the event her instinct was proved true.

"Tasso"—his correct name, by the way, was Tommaso Marino— persuaded my father that something interesting was to be seen at the Astroni crater, four miles west of the city, or thereabout; persuaded him, moreover, to make the journey on foot; and the two accordingly set out. All went well enough till the crater was reached, and then, in a lonely and broken part of the hill, the guide suddenly turned and attacked my father with a knife, his intention, without a doubt, being murder and the acquisition of the Englishman's valuables. Fortunately, my father had a hip-pocket with a revolver in it, for he had been warned of the danger a stranger might at that time run wandering in the country about Naples. He received a wound in the flesh of his left arm in an attempt to ward off a stab, and fired, at wrestling distance, with the result that his assailant fell dead on the spot. He left the place with all speed, tying up his arm as he went, sought the British consul at Naples, and informed him of the whole circumstances. From the authorities there was no great difficulty. An examination or two, a few signatures, some particular exertions on the part of the consul, and my father was free, so far as the officers of the law were concerned.

But while these formalities were in progress no less than three attempts were made on his life—two by the knife and one by shoot-

HIS ASSAILANT FELL DEAD.

ing—and in each his escape was little short of miraculous. For the dead ruffian, Marino, had been a member of the dreaded Camorra, and the Camorristi were eager to avenge his death. To anybody acquainted with the internal history of Italy—more particularly the history of the old kingdom of Naples—the name of the Camorra will be familiar enough. It was one of the worst and most powerful of the many powerful and evil secret societies of Italy, and had none of the excuses for existence which have been from time to time put forward on behalf of the others. It was a gigantic club for the commission of crime and the extortion of money. So powerful was it that it actually imposed a regular tax on all food material entering Naples—a tax collected and paid with far more regularity than were any of the taxes due to the lawful Government of the country. The carrying of smuggled goods was a monopoly of the Camorra, a perfect organisation existing for the purpose throughout the kingdom.

The whole population was terrorised by this detestable society, which had no less than twelve centres in the city of Naples alone. It contracted for the commission of crime just as systematically and calmly as a railway company contracts for the carriage of merchandise. A murder was so much, according to circumstances, with extras for disposing of the body; arson was dealt in profitably; maimings and kidnappings were carried out with promptitude and despatch; and any diabolical outrage imaginable was a mere matter of price. One of the staple vocations of the concern was of course brigandage. After the coming of Victor Emanuel and the fusion of Italy into one kingdom the Camorra lost some of its power, but for a long time gave considerable trouble. I have heard that in the year after the matters I am describing two hundred Camorristi were banished from Italy.

As soon as the legal forms were complied with, my father received the broadest possible official hint that the sooner and the more secretly he left the country the better it would be for himself and his family. The British consul, too, impressed it upon him that the law would be entirely unable to protect him against the machinations of the Camorra; and indeed it needed but little persuasion to induce us to leave, for my poor mother was in a state of constant terror lest we were murdered together in our hotel; so that we lost no time in returning to England and bringing our European trip to a close.

In London we stayed at a well-known private hotel near Bond Street. We had been but three days here when my father came in one evening with a firm conviction that he had been followed for something like two hours, and followed very skilfully too. More than once he had doubled suddenly with a view to confront the pursuers, who he felt were at his heels, but he had met nobody of a suspicious appearance. The next afternoon I heard my mother telling my governess (who was travelling with us) of an unpleasant-looking man, who had been hanging about opposite the hotel door, and who, she felt sure, had afterwards been following her and my father as they were walking. My mother grew nervous, and communicated her fears to my father. He, however, pooh-poohed the thing, and took little thought of its meaning.

Nevertheless, the dogging continued, and my father, who was never able to fix upon the persons who caused the annoyance—indeed he rather felt their presence by instinct, as one does in such cases, than otherwise—grew extremely angry, and had some idea of consulting the police. Then one morning my mother discovered a little paper label stuck on the outside of the door of the bedroom occupied by herself and my father. It was a small thing, circular, and about the size of a sixpenny-piece, or even smaller, but my mother was quite certain that it had not been there when she last entered the door the night before, and she was much terrified. For the label carried a tiny device, drawn awkwardly in ink—a pair of knives of curious shape, crossed: the sign of the Camorra. Nobody knew anything of this label, or how it came where it had been found. My mother urged my father to place himself under the protection of the police at once, but he delayed.

Indeed, I fancy he had a suspicion that the label might be the production of some practical joker staying at the hotel who had heard of his Neapolitan adventure (it was reported in many newspapers) and designed to give him a fright. But that very evening my poor father was found dead, stabbed in a dozen places, in a short, quiet street not forty yards from the hotel. He had merely gone out to buy a few cigars of a particular brand which he fancied, at a shop two streets away, and in less than half an hour of his departure the police were at the hotel door with the news of his death, having got his address from letters in his pockets.

It is no part of my present design to enlarge on my mother's grief, or to describe in detail the incidents that followed my father's death, for I am going back to this early period of my life merely to make more clear the bearings of what has recently happened to myself. It will be sufficient therefore to say that at the inquest the jury returned a verdict of wilful murder against some person or persons unknown; that it was several times reported that the police had obtained a most important clue, and that being so, very naturally there was never any arrest. We returned to Sydney, and there I grew up.

I should perhaps have mentioned ere this that my profession—or I should rather say my hobby—is that of an artist. Fortunately, or unfortunately, as you may please to consider it, I have no need to follow any profession as a means of livelihood, but since I was sixteen years of age my whole time has been engrossed in drawing and painting. Were it not for my mother's invincible objection to parting with me, even for the shortest space of time, I should long ago have come to Europe to work and to study in the regular schools. As it was I made shift to do my best in Australia, and wandered about pretty freely, struggling with the difficulties of moulding into artistic form the curious Australian landscape. There is an odd, desolate, uncanny note m characteristic Australian scenery, which most people are apt to regard as of little value for the purposes of the landscape painter, but with which I have always been convinced that an able painter could do great things. So I did my feeble best.

Two years ago my mother died. My age was then twenty-eight, and I was left without a friend in the world, and, so far as I know, without a relative. I soon found it impossible any longer to inhabit the large house by the Lane Cove river. It was beyond my simple needs, and the whole thing was an embarrassment, to say nothing of the associations of the house with my dead mother, which exercised a painful and depressing effect on me. So I sold the house, and cut myself adrift. For a year or more I pursued the life of a lonely vagabond in New South Wales, painting as well as I could its scattered forests of magnificent trees, with their curious upturned foliage. Then, miserably dissatisfied with my performance, and altogether filled with a restless spirit, I determined to quit the colony and live in England, or at any rate somewhere in Europe. I would paint at the Paris schools, I promised myself, and acquire that technical mastery of my material that I now felt the lack of.

The thing was no sooner resolved on than begun. I instructed my solicitors in Sydney to wind up my affairs and to communicate with their London correspondents in order that, on my arrival in England, I might deal with business matters through them. I had more than half resolved to transfer all my property to England, and to make the old country my permanent headquarters; and in three weeks from the date of my resolve I had started. I carried with me the necessary letters of introduction to the London solicitors, and the deeds appertaining to certain land in South Australia, which my father had bought just before his departure on the fatal European trip. There was workable copper in this land, it had since been ascertained, and I believed I might profitably dispose of the property to a company in London.

I found myself to some extent out of my element on board a great passenger steamer. It seemed no longer possible for me in the constant association of shipboard to maintain that reserve which had become with me a second nature. But so much had it become my nature that I shrank ridiculously from breaking it, for, grown man as I was, it must be confessed that I was absurdly shy, and indeed I fear little better than an overgrown schoolboy in my manner. But somehow I was scarce a day at sea before falling into a most pleasant acquaintanceship with another passenger, a man of thirty-eight or forty, whose name was Dorrington. He was a tall, well-built fellow, rather handsome, perhaps, except for a certain extreme roundness of face and fullness of feature; he had a dark military moustache, and carried himself erect, with a swing as of a cavalryman, and his eyes had, I think, the most penetrating quality I ever saw. His manners were extremely engaging, and he was the only good talker I had ever met. He knew everybody, and had been everywhere. His fund of illustration and anecdote was inexhaustible, and during all my acquaintance with him I never heard him tell the same story twice.

Nothing could happen—not a bird could fly by the ship, not a dish could be put on the table, but Dorrington was ready with a pungent remark and the appropriate anecdote. And he never bored nor wearied one. With all his ready talk he never appeared unduly obtrusive nor in the least egotistic. Mr. Horace Dorrington was altogether the most charming person I had ever met. Moreover, we discovered a community of taste in cigars.

"By the way," said Dorrington to me one magnificent evening as we leaned on the rail and smoked, "Rigby isn't a very common name in Australia, is it? I seem to remember a case, twenty years ago or more, of an Australian gentleman of that name being very badly treated in London—indeed, now I think of it, I'm not sure that he wasn't murdered. Ever hear anything of it?"

"Yes," I said, "I heard a great deal, unfortunately. He was my father, and he was murdered."

"Your father? There—I'm awfully sorry. Perhaps I shouldn't have mentioned it; but of course I didn't know."

"Oh," I replied, "that's all right. It's so far back now that I don't mind speaking about it. It was a very extraordinary thing altogether." And then, feeling that I owed Dorrington a story of some sort, after listening to the many he had been telling me, I described to him the whole circumstances of my father's death.

"Ah," said Dorrington when I had finished, "I have heard of the Camorra before this—I know a thing or two about it, indeed. As a matter of fact, it still exists; not quite the widespread and open thing it once was, of course, and much smaller; but pretty active in a quiet way, and pretty mischievous. They were a mighty bad lot, those Camorristi. Personally I'm rather surprised that you heard no more of them. They were the sort of people who would rather any day murder three people than one, and their usual idea of revenge went a good way beyond the mere murder of the offending party; they had a way of including his wife and family, and as many relatives as possible. But at any rate you seem to have got off all right, though I'm inclined to call it rather a piece of luck than otherwise."

Then, as was his invariable habit, he launched into anecdote. He told me of the crimes of the Mafia, that Italian secret society, larger even and more powerful than the Camorra, and almost as criminal;

tales of implacable revenge visited on father, son, and grandson in succession, till the race was extirpated. Then he talked of the methods; of the large funds at the disposal of the Camorra and the Mafia, and of the cunning patience with which their schemes were carried into execution; of the victims who had discovered too late that their most trusted servants were sworn to their destruction, and of those who had fled to remote parts of the earth and hoped to be lost and forgotten, but who had been shadowed and slain with barbarous ferocity in their most trusted hiding-places. Wherever Italians were, there was apt to be a branch of one of the societies, and one could never tell where they might or might not turn up. The two Italian forecastle hands on board at that moment might be members, and might or might not have some business in hand not included in their signed articles.

I asked if he had ever come into personal contact with either of these societies or their doings.

"With the Camorra, no, though I know things about them that would probably surprise some of them not a little. But I have had professional dealings with the Mafia—and that without coming off second best, too. But it was not so serious a case as your father's; one of a robbery of documents and blackmail."

"Professional dealings?" I queried.

Dorrington laughed. "Yes," he answered. "I find I've come very near to letting the cat out of the bag. I don't generally tell people who I am when I travel about, and indeed I don't always use my own name, as I am doing now. Surely you've heard the name at some time or another?"

I had to confess that I did not remember it. But I excused myself by citing my secluded life, and the fact that I had never left Australia since I was a child.

"Ah," he said, "of course we should be less heard of in Australia. But in England we're really pretty well known, my partner and I. But, come now, look me all over and consider, and I'll give you a dozen guesses and bet you a sovereign you can't tell me my trade. And it's not such an uncommon or unheard-of trade, neither."

Guessing would have been hopeless, and I said so. He did not seem the sort of man who would trouble himself about a trade at all. I gave it up.

"Well," he said, "I've no particular desire to have it known all over the ship, but I don't mind telling you—you'd find it out probably before long if you settle in the old country—that we are what is called private inquiry agents—detectives—secret service men—whatever you like to call it."

"Indeed!"

"Yes, indeed. And I think I may claim that we stand as high as any—if not a trifle higher. Of course I can't tell you, but you'd be rather astonished if you heard the names of some of our clients. We have had dealings with certain royalties, European and Asiatic, that would startle you a bit if I could tell them. Dorrington & Hicks is the name of the firm, and we are both pretty busy men, though we keep going a regiment of assistants and correspondents. I have been in Australia three months over a rather awkward and complicated matter, but I fancy I've pulled it through pretty well, and I mean to reward myself with a little holiday when I get back. There—now you know the worst of me. And D. & H. present their respectful compliments, and trust that by unfailing punctuality and a strict attention to business they may hope to receive your esteemed commands whenever you may be so unfortunate as to require their services. Family secrets extracted, cleaned, scaled, or stopped with gold. Special attention given to wholesale orders." He laughed and pulled out his cigar-case. "You haven't another cigar in your pocket," he said, "or you wouldn't smoke that stump so low. Try one of these."

I took the cigar and lit it at my remainder. "Ah, then," I said, "I take it that it is the practice of your profession that has given you such a command of curious and out-of-the-way information and anecdote. Plainly you must have been in the midst of many curious affairs."

"Yes, I believe you," Dorrington replied. "But, as it happens, the most curious of my experiences I am unable to relate, since they are matters of professional confidence. Such as I can tell I usually tell with altered names, dates, and places. One learns discretion in such a trade as mine."

"As to your adventure with the Mafia, now. Is there any secrecy about that?"

Dorrington shrugged his shoulders. "No," he said, "none in particular. But the case was not particularly interesting. It was in Florence. The documents were the property of a wealthy American, and some of the Mafia rascals managed to steal them. It doesn't matter what the documents were—that's a private matter—but their owner would have parted with a great deal to get them back, and the Mafia held them for ransom. But they had such a fearful notion of the American's wealth, and of what he ought to pay, that, badly as he wanted the papers back, he couldn't stand their demands, and employed us to negotiate and to do our best for him. I think I might have managed to get the things stolen back again—indeed I spent some time thinking a plan over—but I decided in the end that it wouldn't pay. If the Mafia were tricked in that way they might consider it appropriate to stick somebody with a knife, and that was not an easy thing to provide against. So I took a little time and went another way to work. The details don't matter—they're quite uninteresting, and to tell you them would be to talk mere professional 'shop'; there's a deal of dull and patient work to be done in my business. Anyhow, I contrived to find out exactly in whose hands the documents lay. He wasn't altogether a blameless creature, and there were two or three little things that, properly handled, might have brought him into awkward complications with the law. So I delayed the negotiations while I got my nets effectually round this gentleman, who was the president of that particular branch of the Mafia, and when all was ready I had a friendly interview with him, and just showed him my hand of cards. They served as no other argument would have done, and in the end we concluded quite an amicable arrangement on easy terms for both parties, and my client got his property back, including all expenses, at about a fifth of the price he expected to have to pay. That's all. I learnt a deal about the Mafia while the business lasted, and at that and other times I learnt a good deal about the Camorra too."

Dorrington and I grew more intimate every day of the voyage, till he knew every detail of my uneventful little history, and I knew many of his own most curious experiences. In truth he was a man with an irresistible fascination for a dull home-bird like myself. With all his gaiety he never forgot business, and at most of our stopping places he sent off messages by cable to his partner. As the voyage drew near its end he grew anxious and impatient lest he should not arrive in time to enable him to get to Scotland for grouse-shooting on the twelfth of August. His one amusement, it seemed, was shooting, and the holiday he had promised himself was to be spent on a grouse-moor which he rented in Perthshire. It would be a great nuisance to miss the twelfth, he said, but it would apparently be a near shave. He thought, however, that in any case it might be done by leaving the ship at Plymouth, and rushing up to London by the first train.

"Yes," he said, "I think I shall be able to do it that way, even if the boat is a couple of days late. By the way," he added suddenly, "why not come along to Scotland with me? You haven't any particular business in hand, and I can promise you a week or two of good fun."

The invitation pleased me. "It's very good of you," I said, "and as a matter of fact I haven't any very urgent business in London. I must see those solicitors I told you of, but that's not a matter of hurry; indeed, an hour or two on my way through London would be enough. But as I don't know any of your party and "

"Pooh, pooh, my dear fellow," answered Dorrington, with a snap of his fingers, "that's all right. I shan't have a party. There won't be time to get it together. One or two might come down a little later, but if they do they'll be capital fellows, delighted to make your acquaintance, I'm sure. Indeed, you'll do me a great favour if you'll come, else I shall be all alone, without a soul to say a word to. Anyway, I won't miss the twelfth, if it's to be done by any possibility. You'll really have to come you know—you've no excuse. I can lend you guns and anything you want, though I believe you've such things with you. Who is your London solicitor, by the way?"

"Mowbray, of Lincoln's Inn Fields."

"Oh, Mowbray? We know him well; his partner died last year. When I say we know him well, I mean as a firm. I have never met him personally, though my partner (who does the office work) has regular dealings with him. He's an excellent man, but his managing clerk's frightful; I wonder Mowbray keeps him. Don't you let him do anything for you on his own hook; he makes the most disastrous messes, and I rather fancy he drinks. Deal with Mowbray himself; there's nobody better in London. And by the way, now I think of it, it's lucky you've nothing urgent for him, for he's sure to be off out of town for the twelfth; he's a rare old gunner, and never misses a season. So that now you haven't a shade of an excuse for leaving me in the lurch, and we'll consider the thing settled."

Settled accordingly it was, and the voyage ended uneventfully. But the steamer was late, and we left it at Plymouth and rushed up to town on the tenth. We had three or four hours to prepare before leaving Euston by the night train. Dorrington's moor was a long drive from Crieff station, and he calculated that at best we could not arrive there before the early evening of the following day, which would, however, give us comfortable time for a good long night's rest before the morning's sport opened. Fortunately, I had plenty of loose cash with me, so that there was nothing to delay us in that regard. We made ready in Dorrington's rooms (he was a bachelor) in Conduit Street, and got off comfortably by the ten o'clock train from Euston.

Then followed a most delightful eight days. The weather was fine, the birds were plentiful, and my first taste of grouse-shooting was a complete success. I resolved for the future to come out of my shell and mix in the world that contained such charming fellows as Dorrington, and such delightful sports as that I was then enjoying. But on the eighth day Dorrington received a telegram calling him instantly to London.

"It's a shocking nuisance," he said; "here's my holiday either knocked on the head altogether or cut in two, and I fear it's the first rather than the second. It's just the way in such an uncertain profession as mine. There's no possible help for it, however; I must go, as you'd understand at once if you knew the case. But what chiefly annoys me is leaving you all alone."

I reassured him on this point, and pointed out that I had for a long time been used to a good deal of my own company. Though indeed, with Dorrington away, life at the shooting-lodge threatened to be less pleasant than it had been.

"But you'll be bored to death here," Dorrington said, his thoughts jumping with my own. "But on the other hand it won't be much good going up to town yet. Everybody's out of town, and Mowbray among them. There's a little business of ours that's waiting for him at this moment—my partner mentioned it in his letter yesterday. Why not put in the time with a little tour round? Or you might work up to London by irregular stages, and look about you. As an artist you'd like to see a few of the old towns—probably, Edinburgh, Chester, Warwick, and so on. It isn't a great programme, perhaps, but I hardly know what else to suggest. As for myself I must be off as I am by the first train I can get."

I begged him not to trouble about me, but to attend to his business. As a matter of fact, I was disposed to get to London and take chambers, at any rate for a little while. But Chester was a place I much wanted to see—a real old town, with walls round it—and I was not indisposed to take a day at Warwick. So in the end I resolved to pack up and make for Chester the following day, and from there to take train for Warwick. And in half an hour Dorrington was gone.

Chester was all delight to me. My recollections of the trip to Europe in my childhood were vivid enough as to the misfortunes that followed my father, but of the ancient buildings we visited I remembered little. Now in Chester I found the mediaeval town I had so often read of. I wandered for hours together in the quaint old "Rows," and walked on the city wall. The evening after my arrival was fine and moonlight, and I was tempted from my hotel. I took a stroll about the town and finished by a walk along the wall from the Watergate toward the cathedral. The moon, flecked over now and again by scraps of cloud, and at times obscured for half a minute together, lighted up all the Roodee in the intervals, and touched with silver the river beyond. But as I walked I presently grew aware of a quiet shuffling footstep some little way behind me. I took little heed of it at first, though I could see nobody near me from whom the sound might come. But soon I perceived that when I stopped, as I did from time to time to gaze over the parapet, the mysterious footsteps stopped also, and when I resumed my walk the quiet shuffling tread began again. At first I thought it might be an echo; but a moment's reflection dispelled that idea. Mine was an even, distinct walk, and this which followed was a soft, quick, shuffling step—a mere scuffle. Moreover, when, by way of test, I took a few silent steps on tip-toe, the shuffle still persisted. I was being followed.

Now I do not know whether or not it may sound like a childish fancy, but I confess I thought of my father. When last I had been in England, as a child, my father's violent death had been preceded by just such followings. And now after all these years, on my return, on the very first night I walked abroad alone, there were strange footsteps in my track. The walk was narrow, and nobody could possibly pass me unseen. I turned suddenly, therefore, and hastened back. At once I saw a dark figure rise from the shadow of the parapet and run. I ran too, but I could not gain on the figure, which receded farther and more indistinctly before me. One reason was that I felt doubtful of my footing on the unfamiliar track. I ceased my chase, and continued my stroll. It might easily have been some vagrant thief, I thought, who had a notion to rush, at a convenient opportunity, and snatch my watch. But ere I was far past the spot where I had turned there was the shuffling footstep behind me again. For a little while I feigned not to notice it; then, swinging round as swiftly as I could, I made a quick rush. Useless again, for there in the distance scuttled that same indistinct figure, more rapidly than I could run. What did it mean? I liked the affair so little that I left the walls and walked toward my hotel.

The streets were quiet. I had traversed two, and was about emerging into one of the two main streets, where the Rows are, when, from the farther part of the dark street behind me, there came once more the sound of the now unmistakable footstep. I stopped; the footsteps

stopped also. I turned and walked back a few steps, and as I did it the sounds went scuffling away at the far end of the street.

It could not be fancy. It could not be chance. For a single incident perhaps such an explanation might serve, but not for this persistent recurrence. I hurried away to my hotel, resolved, since I could not come at my pursuer, to turn back no more. But before I reached the hotel there were the shuffling footsteps again, and not far behind.

It would not be true to say that I was alarmed at this stage of the adventure, but I was troubled to know what it all might mean, and altogether puzzled to account for it. I thought a great deal, but I went to bed and rose in the morning no wiser than ever.

Whether or not it was a mere fancy induced by the last night's experience I cannot say, but I went about that day with a haunting feeling that I was watched, and to me the impression was very real indeed. I listened often, but in the bustle of the day, even in quiet old Chester, the individual characters of different footsteps were not easily recognisable. Once, however, as I descended a flight of steps from the Rows, I fancied I heard the quick shuffle in the curious old gallery I had just quitted. I turned up the steps again and looked. There was a shabby sort of man looking in one of the windows, and leaning so far as to hide his head behind the heavy oaken pilaster that supported the building above. It might have been his footstep, or it might have been my fancy. At any rate I would have a look at him. I mounted the top stair, but as I turned in his direction the man ran off, with his face averted and his head ducked, and vanished down another stair. I made all speed after him, but when I reached the street he was nowhere to be seen.

What *could* it all mean? The man was rather above the middle height, and he wore one of those soft felt hats familiar on the head of the London organ-grinder. Also his hair was black and bushy, and protruded over the back of his coat-collar. Surely this was no delusion; surely I was not imagining an Italian aspect for this man simply because of the recollection of my father's fate?

Perhaps I was foolish, but I took no more pleasure in Chester. The embarrassment was a novel one for me, and I could not forget it. I went back to my hotel, paid my bill, sent my bag to the railway station, and took train for Warwick by way of Crewe.

It was dark when I arrived, but the night was near as fine as last night had been at Chester. I took a very little late dinner at my hotel, and fell into a doubt what to do with myself. One rather fat and very sleepy commercial traveller was the only other customer visible, and the billiard room was empty. There seemed to be nothing to do but to light a cigar and take a walk.

I could just see enough of the old town to give me good hopes of tomorrow's sight-seeing. There was nothing visible of quite such an interesting character as one might meet in Chester, but there were a good few fine old sixteenth century houses, and there were the two gates with the chapels above them. But of course the castle was the great show-place, and that I should visit on the morrow, if there were no difficulties as to permission. There were some very fine pictures there, if I remembered aright what I had read. I was walking down the incline from one of the gates, trying to remember who the painters of these pictures were, besides Van Dyck and Holbein, when—that shuffling step was behind me again!

I admit that it cost me an effort, this time, to turn on my pursuer. There was something uncanny in that persistent, elusive footstep, and indeed there was something alarming in my circumstances, dogged thus from place to place, and unable to shake off my enemy, or to understand his movements or his motive. Turn I did, however, and straightway the shuffling step went off at a hastened pace in the shadow of the gate. This time I made no more than half-a-dozen steps back. I turned again, and pushed my way to the hotel. And as I went the shuffling step came after. The thing was serious. There must be some object in this unceasing watching, and the object could bode no good to me. Plainly some unseen eye had been on me the whole of that day, had noted my goings and comings and my journey from Chester. Again, and irresistibly, the watchings that preceded my father's death came to mind, and I could not forget them.

I could have no doubt now that I had been closely watched from the moment I had set foot at Plymouth. But who could have been waiting to watch me at Plymouth, when indeed I had only decided to land at the last moment? Then I thought of the two Italian forecastle hands on the steamer—the very men whom Dorrington had used to illustrate in what unexpected quarters members of the terrible Italian secret societies might be found. And the Camorra was not satisfied with single revenge; it destroyed the son after the father, and it waited for many years, with infinite patience and cunning.

Dogged by the steps, I reached the hotel and went to bed. I slept but fitfully at first, though better rest came as the night wore on. In the early morning I woke with a sudden shock, and with an indefinite sense of being disturbed by somebody about me. The window was directly opposite the foot of the bed, and there, as I looked, was the face of a man, dark, evil, and grinning, with a bush of black hair about his uncovered head, and small rings m his ears.

It was but a flash, and the face vanished. I was struck by the terror that one so often feels on a sudden and violent awakening from sleep, and it was some seconds ere I could leave my bed and get to the window. My room was on the first floor, and the window looked down on a stableyard. I had a momentary glimpse of a human figure leaving the gate of the yard, and it was the figure that had fled before me in the Bows, at Chester. A ladder belonging to the yard stood under the window, and that was all.

I rose and dressed; I could stand this sort of thing no longer. If it were only something tangible, if there were only somebody I could take hold of, and fight with if necessary, it would not have been so bad. But I was surrounded by some mysterious machination, persistent, unexplainable, that it was altogether impossible to tackle or to face. To complain to the police would have been absurd—they would take me for a lunatic. They are indeed just such complaints that lunatics so often make to the police—complaints of being followed by indefinite enemies, and of being besieged by faces that look in at windows. Even if they did not set me down a lunatic, what could the police of a provincial town do for me in a case like this? No, I must go and consult Dorrington.

I had my breakfast, and then decided that I would at any rate try the castle before leaving. Try it I did accordingly, and was allowed to go over it. But through the whole morning I was oppressed by the horrible sense of being watched by malignant eyes. Clearly there was no comfort for me while this lasted; so after lunch I caught a train which brought me to Euston soon after half-past six.

I took a cab straight to Dorrington's rooms, but he was out, and was not expected home till late. So I drove to a large hotel near Charing Cross—I avoid mentioning its name for reasons which will presently be understood—sent in my bag, and dined.

I had not the smallest doubt but that I was still under the observation of the man or the men who had so far pursued me; I had, indeed, no hope of eluding them, except by the contrivance of Dorrington's expert brain. So as I had no desire to hear that shuffling footstep again—indeed it had seemed, at Warwick, to have a physically painful effect on my nerves—I stayed within and got to bed early.

I had no fear of waking face to face with a grinning Italian here. My window was four floors up, out of reach of anything but a fire-escape. And, in fact, I woke comfortably and naturally, and saw nothing from my window but the bright sky, the buildings opposite, and the traffic below. But as I turned to close my door behind me as I emerged into the corridor, there, on the muntin of the frame, just below the bedroom number, was a little round paper label, perhaps a trifle smaller than a sixpence, and on the label, drawn awkwardly in ink, was a device of two crossed knives of curious, crooked shape. The sign of the Camorra!

I will not attempt to describe the effect of this sign upon me. It may best be imagined, in view of what I have said of the incidents preceding the murder of my father. It was the sign of an inexorable fate, creeping nearer step by step, implacable, inevitable, and mysterious. In little more than twelve hours after seeing that sign my father had been a mangled corpse. One of the hotel servants passed as I stood by the door, and I made shift to ask him if he knew anything of the label. He looked at the paper, and then, more curiously, at me, but he could offer no explanation. I spent little time over breakfast, and then went by cab to Conduit Street. I paid my bill and took my bag with me.

Dorrington had gone to his office, but he had left a message that if I called I was to follow him; and the office was in Bedford Street, Covent Garden. I turned the cab in that direction forthwith.

"Why," said Dorrington as we shook hands, "I believe you look a bit out of sorts! Doesn't England agree with you?"

"Well," I answered, "it has proved rather trying so far." And then I described, in exact detail, my adventures as I have set them down here.

Dorrington looked grave. "It's really extraordinary," he said, "most extraordinary: and it isn't often that I call a thing extraordinary neither, with my experience. But it's plain something must be done something to gain time at any rate. We're in the dark at present, of course, and I expect I shall have to fish about a little before I get at anything to go on. In the meantime, I think you must disappear as artfully as we can manage it." He sat silent for a little while, thoughtfully tapping his forehead with his finger-tips. "I wonder," he said presently, "whether or not those Italian fellows on the steamer are in it or not. I suppose you haven't made yourself known anywhere, have you?"

"Nowhere. As you know, you've been with me all the time till you left the moor, and since then I have been with nobody and called on nobody."

"Now there's no doubt it's the Camorra," Dorrington said—"that's pretty plain. I think I told you on the steamer that it was rather wonderful that you had heard nothing of them after your father's death. What has caused them all this delay there's no telling—they know best themselves; it's been lucky for you, anyway, so far. What I'd like to find out now is how they have identified you, and got on your track so promptly. There's no guessing where these fellows get their information—it's just wonderful; but if we can find out, then perhaps we can stop the supply, or turn on something that will lead them into a pit. If you had called anywhere on business and declared yourself—as you might have done, for instance, at Mowbray's—I might be inclined to suspect that they got the tip in some crooked way from there. But you haven't. Of course, if those Italian chaps on the steamer *are* in it, you're probably identified pretty certainly; but if they're not, they may only have made a guess. We two landed together, and kept together, till a day or two ago; as far as any outsider would know, I might be Rigby and you might be Dorrington. Come, we'll work on those lines. I think I smell a plan. Are you staying anywhere?"

"No. I paid my bill at the hotel and came along here with my bag."

"Very well. Now there's a house at Highgate kept by a very trustworthy man, whom I know very well, where a man might be pretty comfortable for a few days, or even for a week, if he doesn't mind staying indoors, and keeping himself out of sight. I expect your friends of the Camorra are watching in the street outside at this moment; but I think it will be fairly easy to get you away to Highgate without letting them into the secret, if you don't mind secluding yourself for a bit. In the circumstances, I take it you won't object at all?"

"Object? I should think not."

"Very well, that's settled. You can call yourself Dorrington or not, as you please, though perhaps it will be safest not to shout 'Rigby' too loud. But as for myself, for a day or two at least I'm going to be Mr. James Rigby. Have you your card-case handy?"

"Yes, here it is. But then, as to taking my name, won't you run serious risk?"

Dorrington winked merrily. "I've run a risk or two before now," he said, "in course of my business. And if I don't mind the risk, you needn't grumble, for I warn you I shall charge for risk when I send you my bill. And I think I can take care of myself fairly well, even with the Camorra about. I shall take you to this place at Highgate, and then you won't see me for a few days. It won't do for me, in the character of Mr. James Rigby, to go dragging a trail up and down between this place and your retreat. You've got some other identifying papers, haven't you?"

"Yes, I have." I produced the letter from my Sydney lawyers to Mowbray, and the deeds of the South Australian property from my bag.

"Ah," said Dorrington, "I'll just give you a formal receipt for these, since they're valuable; it's a matter of business, and we'll do it in a business-like way. I may want something solid like this to support any bluff I may have to make. A mere case of cards won't always act, you know. It's a pity old Mowbray's out of town, for there's a way in which he might give a little help, I fancy. But never mind—leave it all to me. There's your receipt. Keep it snug away somewhere, where inquisitive people can't read it."

He handed me the receipt, and then took me to his partner's room and introduced me. Mr. Hicks was a small, wrinkled man, older than Dorrington, I should think, by fifteen or twenty years, and with all the aspect and manner of a quiet old professional man.

Dorrington left the room, and presently returned with his hat in his hand. "Yes," he said, "there's a charming dark gentleman with a head like a mop, and rings in his ears, skulking about at the next corner. If it was he who looked in at your window, I don't wonder you were startled. His dress suggests the organ-grinding interest, but he looks as though cutting a throat would be more in his line than grinding a tune; and no doubt he has friends as engaging as himself close at call. If you'll come with me now I think we shall give him the slip. I have a growler ready for you—a hansom's a bit too glassy and public. Pull down the blinds and sit back when you get inside."

He led me to a yard at the back of the building wherein the office stood, from which a short flight of steps led to a basement. We followed a passage in this basement till we reached another flight, and ascending these, we emerged into the corridor of another building. Out at the door at the end of this, and we passed a large block of model dwellings, and were in Bedfordbury. Here a four-wheeler was waiting, and I shut myself in it without delay.

I was to proceed as far as King's Cross in this cab, Dorrington had arranged, and there he would overtake me in a swift hansom. It fell out as he had settled, and, dismissing the hansom, he came the rest of the journey with me in the four-wheeler.

We stopped at length before one of a row of houses, apparently recently built—houses of the over-ornamented, gabled and tiled sort that abound in the suburbs.

"Crofting is the man's name," Dorrington said, as we alighted. "He's rather an odd sort of customer, but quite decent in the main, and his wife makes coffee such as money won't buy in most places."

A woman answered Dorrington's ring—a woman of most extreme thinness. Dorrington greeted her as Mrs. Crofting, and we entered.

"We've just lost our servant again, Mr, Dorrington," the woman said in a shrill voice, "and Mr. Crofting ain't at home. But I'm expecting him before long."

"I don't think I need wait to see him, Mrs. Crofting," Dorrington answered. "I'm sure I can't leave my friend in better hands than yours. I hope you've a vacant room?"

"Well, for a friend of yours, Mr. Dorrington, no doubt we can find room."

"That's right. My friend Mr."—Dorrington gave me a meaning look—"Mr. Phelps, would like to stay here for a few days. He wants to be quite quiet for a little—do you understand? "

"Oh, yes, Mr. Dorrington, I understand."

"Very well, then, make him as comfortable as you can, and give him some of your very best coffee. I believe you've got quite a little library of books, and Mr. Phelps will be glad of them. Have you got any cigars?" Dorrington added, turning to me.

"Yes; there are some in my bag."

"Then I think you'll be pretty comfortable now. Goodbye. I expect you'll see me in a few days—or at any rate you'll get a message. Meantime be as happy as you can."

Dorrington left, and the woman showed me to a room upstairs, where I placed my bag. In front, on the same floor, was a sitting-room, with, I suppose, some two or three hundred books, mostly novels, on shelves. The furniture of the place was of the sort one expects to find in an ordinary lodging-house—horsehair sofas, loo tables, lustres, and so forth. Mrs. Crofting explained to me that the customary dinner hour was two, but that I might dine when I liked. I elected, however, to follow the custom of the house, and sat down to a cigar and a book.

At two o'clock the dinner came, and I was agreeably surprised to find it a very good one, much above what the appointments of the house had led me to expect. Plainly Mrs. Crofting was a capital cook. There was no soup, but there was a very excellent sole, and some well-done cutlets with peas, and an omelet; also a bottle of Bass. Come, I felt that I should not do so badly in this place after all. I trusted that Dorrington would be as comfortable in his half of the transaction, bearing my responsibilities and troubles. I had heard a heavy, blundering tread on the floor below, and judged from this that Mr. Crofting had returned.

After dinner I lit a cigar, and Mrs. Crofting brought her coffee. Truly it was excellent coffee, and brewed as I like it—strong and black, and plenty of it. It had a flavour of its own too, novel, but not unpleasing. I took one cupful, and brought another to my side as I lay on the sofa with my book. I had not read six lines before I was asleep.

I woke with a sensation of numbing cold in my right side, a terrible stiffess in my limbs, and a sound of loud splashing in my ears. All was pitch dark, and—what was this? Water! Water all about me. I was lying in six inches of cold water, and more was pouring down upon me from above. My head was afflicted with a splitting ache. But where was I? Why was it dark? And whence all the water? I staggered to my feet, and instantly struck my head against a hard roof above me. I raised my hand; there was the roof or whatever place it was, hard, smooth and cold, and little more than five feet from the floor, so that I bent as I stood. I spread my hand to the side; that was hard, smooth and cold

575

too. And then the conviction struck me like a blow—I was in a covered iron tank, and the water was pouring in to drown me!

I dashed my hands frantically against the lid, and strove to raise it. It would not move. I shouted at the top of my voice, and turned about to feel the extent of my prison. One way I could touch the opposite sides at once easily with my hands, the other way it was wider—perhaps a little more than six feet altogether. What was this? Was this to be my fearful end, cooped in this tank while the water rose by inches to choke me? Already the water was a foot deep. I flung myself at the sides, I beat the pitiless iron with fists, face and head, I screamed and implored. Then it struck me that I might at least stop the inlet of water. I put out my hand and felt the falling stream, then found the inlet and stopped it with my fingers. But water still poured in with a resounding splash; there was another opening at the opposite end, which I could not reach without releasing the one I now held! I was but prolonging my agony. Oh, the devilish cunning that had devised those two inlets, so far apart! Again I beat the sides, broke my nails with tearing at the corners, screamed and entreated in my agony. I was mad, but with no dulling of the senses, for the horrors of my awful, helpless state, overwhelmed my brain, keen and perceptive to every ripple of the unceasing water.

In the height of my frenzy I held my breath, for I heard a sound from outside. I shouted again—implored some quicker death. Then there was a scraping on the lid above me, and it was raised at one edge, and let in the light of a candle. I sprang from my knees and forced the lid back, and the candle flame danced before me. The candle was held by a dusty man, a workman apparently, who stared at me with scared eyes, and said nothing but, "Goo' lor'!"

Overhead were the rafters of a gabled roof, and tilted against them was the thick beam which, jammed across from one sloping rafter to another, had held the tank-lid fast. "Help me!" I gasped. "Help me out!"

The man took me by the armpits and hauled me, dripping and half dead, over the edge of the tank, into which the water still poured, making a noise in the hollow iron that half drowned our voices. The man had been at work on the cistern of a neighbouring house, and hearing an uncommon noise, he had climbed through the spaces left in the party walls to give passage along under the roofs to the builders' men. Among the joists at our feet was the trap-door through which, drugged and insensible, I had been carried, to be flung into that horrible cistern.

With the help of my friend the workman I made shift to climb through by the way he had come. We got back to the house where he had been at work, and there the people gave me brandy and lent me dry clothes. I made haste to send for the police, but when they arrived Mrs. Crofting and her respectable spouse had gone. Some unusual noise in the roof must have warned them. And when the police, following my directions further, got to the offices of Dorrington and Hicks, those acute professional men had gone too, but in such haste that the contents of the office, papers and everything else, had been left just as they stood.

The plot was clear now. The followings, the footsteps, the face at the window, the label on the door—all were a mere humbug arranged by Dorrington for his own purpose, which was to drive me into his power and get my papers from me. Armed with these, and with his consummate address and knowledge of affairs, he could go to Mr. Mowbray in the character of Mr. James Rigby, sell my land in South Australia, and have the whole of my property transferred to himself from Sydney. The rest of my baggage was at his rooms; if any further proof were required it might be found there. He had taken good care that I should not meet Mr. Mowbray—who, by the way, I afterwards found had not left his office, and had never fired a gun in his life. At first I wondered that Dorrington had not made some operations had been of a more than questionable sort. And among their papers were found complete sets, neatly arranged in dockets, each containing in skeleton a complete history of a case.

Many of these cases were of a most interesting character, and I have been enabled to piece together, out of the material thus supplied, the narratives which will follow this. As to my own case, it only remains to say that as yet neither Dorrington, Hicks, nor the Croftings have been caught. They played in the end for a high stake (they might have made six figures of me if they had killed me, and the first figure would not have been a one) and they lost by a mere accident. But I have often wondered how many of the bodies which the coroners' juries of London have returned to be "Found Drowned" were drowned, not where they were picked up, but in that horrible tank at Highgate. What the drug was that gave Mrs. Crofting's coffee its value in Dorrington's eyes I do not know, but plainly it had not been sufficient in my case to keep me unconscious against the shock of cold water till I could be drowned altogether. Months have passed since my adventure, but even now I sweat at the sight of an iron tank.

THE CASE OF JANISSARY

1

In this case (and indeed in most of the others) the notes and other documents found in the dockets would, by themselves, give but a faint outline of the facts, and, indeed, might easily be unintelligible to many people, especially as for much of my information I have been indebted to outside inquiries. Therefore, I offer no excuse for presenting the whole thing digested into plain narrative form, with little reference to my authorities. Though I knew none of the actors in it, with the exception of the astute Dorrington, the case was especially interesting to me, as will be gathered from the narrative itself.

The only paper in the bundle which I shall particularly allude to was a newspaper cutting, of a date anterior by nine or ten months to the events I am to write of. It had evidently been cut at the time it appeared, and saved, in case it might be useful, in a box in the form of a book, containing many hundreds of others. From this receptacle it had been taken, and attached to the bundle during the progress of the case. I may say at once that the facts recorded had no direct concern with the case of the horse Janissary, but had been useful in affording a suggestion to Dorrington in connection therewith. The matter is the short report of an ordinary sort of inquest, and I here transcribe it.

> Dr. McCulloch held an inquest yesterday on the body of Mr. Henry Lawrence, whose body was found on Tuesday morning last in the river near Vauxhall Bridge. The deceased was well known in certain sporting circles. Sophia Lawrence, the widow, said that deceased had left home on Monday afternoon at about five, in his usual health, saying that he was to dine at a friend's and she saw nothing more of him till called upon to identify the body. He had no reason for suicide, and so far as witness knew, was free from pecuniary embarrassments. He had, indeed, been very successful in betting recently. He habitually carried a large pocket-book, with papers in it.
>
> Mr. Robert Naylor, commission agent, said that deceased dined with him that evening at his house in Gold Street, Chelsea, and left for home at about half-past eleven. He had at the time a sum of nearly four hundred pounds upon him, chiefly in notes, which had been paid him by witness in settlement of a bet. It was a fine night, and deceased walked in the direction of Chelsea Embankment.

That was the last witness saw of him. He might not have been perfectly sober, but he was not drunk, and was capable of taking care of himself. The evidence of the Thames police went to show that no money was on the body when found, except a few coppers, and no pocket-book. Dr. William Hodgetts said that death was due to drowning. There were some bruises on the arms and head which might have been caused before death. The body was a very healthy one. The coroner said that there seemed to be a strong suspicion of foul play, unless the pocket-book of the deceased had got out of his pocket in the water; but the evidence was very meagre, although the police appeared to have made every possible inquiry. The jury returned a verdict of 'Found Drowned, though how the deceased came into the water there was no evidence to show'.

I know no more of the unfortunate man Lawrence than this, and I have only printed the cutting here because it probably induced Dorrington to take certain steps in the case I am dealing with. With that case the fate of the man Lawrence has nothing whatever to do. He passes out of the story entirely.

2.

Mr. Warren Telfer was a gentleman of means, and the owner of a few—very few—racehorses. But he had a great knack of buying hidden prizes in yearlings, and what his stable lacked in quantity it often more than made up for in quality. Thus he had once bought a St. Leger winner for as little as a hundred and fifty pounds. Many will remember his bitter disappointment of ten or a dozen years back, when his horse, Matfelon, starting an odds-on favourite for the Two Thousand, never even got among the crowd, and ambled in streets behind everything. It was freely rumoured (and no doubt with cause) that Matfelon had been "got at" and in some way "nobbled". There were hints of a certain bucket of water administered just before the race—a bucket of water observed in the hands, some said of one, some said of another person connected with Ritter's training establishment. There was no suspicion of pulling for plainly the jockey was doing his best with the animal all the way along, and never had a tight rein. So a nobbling it must have been, said the knowing ones, and Mr. Warren Telfer said so too, with much bitterness. More, he immediately removed his horses from Ritter's stables, and started a small training place of his own for his own horses merely; putting an old steeplechase jockey in charge, who had come out of a bad accident permanently lame, and had fallen on evil days.

The owner was an impulsive and violent-tempered man, who, once a notion was in his head, held to it through everything, and in spite of everything. His misfortune with Matfelon made him the most insanely distrustful man alive. In everything he fancied he saw a trick, and to him every man seemed a scoundrel. He could scarce bear to let the very stable-boys touch his horses, and although for years all went as well as could be expected in his stables, his suspicious distrust lost nothing of its virulence. He was perpetually fussing about the stables, making surprise visits, and laying futile traps that convicted nobody. The sole tangible result of this behaviour was a violent quarrel between Mr. Warren Telfer and his nephew Richard, who had been making a lengthened stay with his uncle.

Young Telfer, to tell the truth, was neither so discreet nor so exemplary in behaviour as he might have been, but his temper was that characteristic of the family, and when he conceived that his uncle had an idea that he was communicating stable secrets to friends outside, there was an animated row, and the nephew betook himself and his luggage somewhere else. Young Telfer always insisted, however, that his uncle was not a bad fellow on the whole, though he had habits of thought and conduct that made him altogether intolerable at times. But the uncle had no good word for his graceless nephew; and indeed Richard Telfer betted more than he could afford, and was not so particular in his choice of sporting acquaintances as a gentleman should have been.

Mr. Warren Telfer's house, Blackhall, and his stables were little more than two miles from Redbury, in Hampshire; and after the quarrel Mr. Richard Telfer was not seen near the place for many months—not, indeed, till excitement was high over the forthcoming race for the Redbury Stakes, for which there was an entry from the stable—Janissary, for long ranked second favourite; and then the owner's nephew did not enter the premises, and, in fact, made his visit as secret as possible.

I have said that Janissary was long ranked second favourite for the Redbury Stakes, but a little more than a week before the race he became first favourite, owing to a training mishap to the horse fancied first, which made its chances so poor that it might have been scratched at any moment. And so far was Janissary above the class of the field (though it was a two-year-old race, and there might be a surprise) that it at once went to far shorter odds than the previous favourite, which, indeed, had it run fit and well, would have found Janissary no easy colt to beat.

Mr. Telfer's nephew was seen near the stables but two or three days before the race, and that day the owner despatched a telegram to the firm of Dorrington Hicks. In response to the telegram, Dorrington caught the first available train for Redbury, and was with Mr. Warren Telfer in his library by five in the afternoon.

"It is about my horse Janissary that I want to consult you, Mr. Dorrington," said Mr. Telfer. "It's right enough now—or at least was right at exercise this morning—but I feel certain that there's some diabolical plot on hand somewhere to interfere with the horse before the Redbury Stakes day, and I'm sorry to have to say that I suspect my own nephew to be mixed up in it in some way. In the first place I may tell you that there is no doubt whatever that the colt, if let alone, and bar accident, can win in a canter. He could have won even if Herald, the late favourite, had kept well, for I can tell you that Janissary is a far greater horse than anybody is aware of outside my establishment—or at any rate, than anybody ought to be aware of, if the stable secrets are properly kept.

"His pedigree is nothing very great, and he never showed his quality till quite lately, in private trials. Of course it has leaked out somehow that the colt is exceptionally good—I don't believe I can trust a soul in the place. How should the price have gone up to five to four unless somebody had been telling what he's paid not to tell? But that isn't all, as I have said. I've a conviction that something's on foot—somebody wants to interfere with the horse. Of course we get a tout about now and again, but the downs are pretty big, and we generally manage to dodge them if we want to. On the last three or four mornings, however, whenever Janissary might be taking his gallop, there was a big, hulking fellow, with a red beard and spectacles—not so much watching the horse as trying to get hold of the lad. I am always up at five, for I've found to my cost—you remember about Matfelon—that if a man doesn't want to be ramped he must never take his eye off things.

"Well, I have scarcely seen the lad ease the colt once on the last three or four mornings without that red-bearded fellow bobbing up from a knoll, or a clump of bushes, or something, close by—especially if Janissary was a bit away from the other horses, and not under my nose, or the head lad's, for a moment. I rode at the fellow, of course, when I saw what he was after, but he was artful as a cartload of monkeys, and vanished somehow before I could get near him. The head lad believes he has seen him about just after dark, too; but I am keeping the stable lads in when they're not riding, and I suppose he finds he has no chance of getting at them except when they're out with the horses. This morning, not only did I see this fellow about, as usual, but, I am ashamed to say, I observed my own nephew acting the part of a common tout. He certainly had the decency to avoid me and clear out, but that was not all, as you shall see.

"This morning, happening to approach the stables from the back, I suddenly came upon the red-bearded man—giving money to a groom of mine! He ran off at once, as you may guess, and I discharged the groom where he stood, and would not allow him into the stables again. He offered no explanation or excuse, but took himself off, and half an hour afterwards I almost sent away my head boy too. For when I told him of the dismissal, he admitted that he had seen that same groom taking money off my nephew at the back of the of stables, an hour before, and had not informed me! He said that he thought that as it was 'only Mr. Richard' it didn't matter. Fool! Anyway, the groom has gone, and, so far as I can tell as yet, the colt is all right. I examined him at once, of course; and I also turned over a box that Weeks, the groom, used to keep brushes and odd things in. There I found this paper full of powder. I don't yet know what it is, but it's certainly nothing he had any business with in the stable. Will you take it?

"And now," Mr. Telfer went on, "I'm in such an uneasy state that I want your advice and assistance. Quite apart from the suspicious— more than suspicious—circumstances I have informed you of, I am certain—I know it without being able to give precise reasons—I am certain that some attempt is being made at disabling Janissary before Thursday's race. I feel it in my bones, so to speak. I had the same suspicion just before that Two Thousand, when Matfelon was got at. The thing was in the air, as it is now. Perhaps it's a sort of instinct; but I rather think it is the result of an unconscious absorption of a number of little indications about me. Be it as it may, I am resolved to leave no opening to the enemy if I can help it, and I want to see if you can suggest any further precautions beyond those I am taking. Come and look at the stables."

Dorrington could see no opening for any piece of rascality by which he might make more of the case than by serving his client loyally, so he resolved to do the latter. He followed Mr. Telfer through the training stables, where eight or nine thoroughbreds stood, and could suggest no improvement upon the exceptional precautions that already existed.

"No," said Dorrington, "I don't think you can do any better than this—at least on this, the inner line of defence. But it is best to make the outer lines secure first. By the way, this isn't Janissary, is it? We saw him farther up the row, didn't we?"

"Oh no, that's a very different sort of colt, though he does look like, doesn't he? People who've been up and down the stables once or twice often confuse them. They're both bays, much of a build, and about the same height, and both have a bit of stocking on the same leg, though Janissary's is bigger, and this animal has a white star. But you never saw two creatures look so like and run so differently. This is a dead loss—not worth his feed. If I can manage to wind him up to something like a gallop I shall try to work him off in a selling plate somewhere; but as far as I can see he isn't good enough even for that. He's a disappointment. And his stock's far better than Janissary's too, and he cost half as much again! Yearlings are a lottery. Still, I've drawn a prize or two among them, at one time or another."

"Ah yes, so I've heard. But now as to the outer defences I was speaking of. Let us find out who is trying to interfere with your horse. Do you mind letting me into the secrets of the stable commissions?"

"Oh no. We're talking in confidence, of course. I've backed the colt pretty heavily all round, but not too much anywhere. There's a good slice with Barker—you know Barker, of course; Mullins has a thousand down for him, and that was at five to one, before Herald went amiss. Then there's Ford and Lascelles—both good men, and Naylor—he's the smallest man of them all, and there's only a hundred or two with him, though he's been laying the horse pretty freely everywhere, at least until Herald went wrong. And there's Pedder. But there must have been a deal of money laid to outside backers, and there's no telling who may contemplate a ramp."

"Just so. Now as to your nephew. What of your suspicions in that direction?"

"Perhaps I'm a little hasty as to that," Mr. Telfer answered, a little ashamed of what he had previously said. "But I'm worried and mystified, as you see, and hardly know what to think. My nephew Richard is a little erratic, and he has a foolish habit of betting more than he can afford. He and I quarrelled some time back, while he was staying here, because I had an idea that he had been talking too freely outside. He had, in fact; and I regarded it as a breach of confidence. So there was a quarrel and he went away."

"Very well. I wonder if I can get a bed at the 'Crown' at Redbury: I'm afraid it'll be crowded, but I'll try."

"But why trouble? Why not stay with me, and be near the stables?"

"Because then I should be of no more use to you than one of your lads. People who come out here every morning are probably staying at Redbury, and I must go there after them."

3.

The "Crown" at Redbury was full in anticipation of the races, but Dorrington managed to get a room ordinarily occupied by one of the landlord's family, who undertook to sleep at a friend's for a night or two. This settled, he strolled into the yard, and soon fell into animated talk with the hostler on the subject of the forthcoming races. All the town was backing Janissary for the Stakes, the hostler said, and he advised Dorrington to do the same.

During this conversation two men stopped in the street, just outside the yard gate, talking. One was a big, heavy, vulgar-looking fellow in a box-cloth coat, and with a shaven face and hoarse voice; the other was a slighter, slimmer, younger and more gentlemanlike man, though there was a certain patchy colour about his face that seemed to hint of anything but teetotalism.

"There," said the hostler, indicating the younger of these two men, "that's young Mr. Telfer, him as whose uncle's owner o' Janissary. He's a young plunger, he is, and he's on Janissary too. He give me the tip, straight, this mornin'. 'You put your little bit on my uncle's colt,' he said. 'It's all right. I ain't such pals with the old man as I was, but I've got the tip that his money's down on it. So don't neglect your opportunities, Thomas,' he says; and I haven't. He's stoppin' in our house, is young Mr. Richard."

"And who is that he is talking to? A bookmaker?"

"Yes, sir, that's Naylor—Bob Naylor. He's got Mr. Richard's bets. P'raps he's puttin' on a bit more now."

The men at the gate separated, and the bookmaker walked off down the street in the fast gathering dusk. Richard Telfer, however, entered the house, and Dorrington followed him. Telfer mounted the stairs and went into his room. Dorrington lingered a moment on the stairs and then went and knocked at Telfer's door.

"Hullo!" cried Telfer, coming to the door and peering out into the gloomy corridor.

"I beg pardon," Dorrington replied courteously. "I thought this was Naylor's room."

"No—it's No. 23, by the end. But I believe he's just gone down the street."

Dorrington expressed his thanks and went to his own room. He took one or two small instruments from his bag and hurried stealthily to the door of No. 23.

All was quiet, and the door opened at once to Dorrington's pick-lock, for there was nothing but the common tumbler rim-lock to secure it. Dorrington, being altogether an unscrupulous scoundrel, would have thought nothing of entering a man's room thus for purposes of mere robbery. Much less scruple had he in doing so in the present circumstances. He lit the candle in a little pocket lantern, and, having secured the door, looked quickly about the room. There was nothing unusual to attract his attention, and he turned to two bags lying near the dressing-table. One was the usual bookmaker's satchel, and the other was a leather travelling-bag; both were locked.

Dorrington unbuckled the straps of the large bag and produced a slender picklock of steel wire, with a sliding joint, which, with a little skilful "humouring", turned the lock in the course of a minute or two. One glance inside was enough. There on the top lay a large false beard of strong red, and upon the shirts below was a pair of spectacles. But Dorrington went farther, and felt carefully below the linen till his hand met a small, flat, mahogany box. This he withdrew and opened. Within, on a velvet lining, lay a small silver instrument resembling a syringe. He shut and replaced the box, and, having rearranged the contents of the bag, shut, locked and strapped it, and blew out his light. He had found what he came to look for. In another minute Mr. Bob Naylor's door was locked behind him, and Dorrington took his picklocks to his own room.

It was a noisy evening in the Commercial Room at the "Crown". Chaff and laughter flew thick, and Richard Telfer threatened Naylor with a terrible settling day. More was drunk than thirst strictly justified, and everybody grew friendly with everybody else. Dorrington, sober and keenly alert, affected the reverse, and exhibited especial and extreme affection for Mr. Bob Naylor. His advances were unsuccessful at first, but Dorrington's manner and the "Crown" whisky overcame the bookmaker's reserve, and at about eleven o'clock the two left the house arm in arm for a cooling stroll in the High Street. Dorrington blabbed and chattered with great success, and soon began about Janissary.

"So you've pretty well done all you want with Janissary, eh? Book full? Ah! nothing like keeping a book even all round—it's the safest way—'specially with such a colt as Janissary about. Eh, my boy?" He nudged Naylor genially. "Ah! no doubt it's a good colt, but old Telfer has rum notions about preparation, hasn't he?"

"I dunno," replied Naylor. "How do you mean?"

"Why, what does he have the horse led up and down behind the stable for, half an hour every afternoon?"

"Didn't know he did."

"Ah! but he does. I came across it only this afternoon. I was coming over the downs, and just as I got round behind Telfer's stables there I saw a fine bay colt, with a white stocking on the off hind leg, well covered up in a suit of clothes, being led up and down by a lad, like a sentry—up and down, up and down—about twenty yards each way, and nobody else about. 'Hullo!' says I to the lad, 'hullo! what horse is this?' 'Janissary,' says the boy—pretty free for a stable-lad. 'Ah!' says I. 'And what are you walking him like that for?' 'Dunno,' says the boy, 'but it's gov'nor's orders. Every afternoon, at two to the minute, I have to bring him out here and walk him like this for half an hour exactly, neither more or less, and then he goes in and has a handful of malt. But I dunno why.' 'Well,' says I, 'I never heard of that being done before. But he's a fine colt,' and I put my hand under the cloth and felt him—hard as nails and smooth as silk."

"And the boy let you touch him?"

"Yes; he struck me as a bit easy for a stable-boy. But it's an odd trick, isn't it, that of the half-hour's walk and the handful of malt? Never hear of anybody else doing it, did you?"

"No, I never did."

They talked and strolled for another quarter of an hour and then finished up with one more drink.

4.

The next was the day before the race, and in the morning Dorrington, making a circuit, came to Mr. Warren Telfer's from the farther side. As soon as they were assured of privacy: "Have you seen the man with the red beard this morning?" asked Dorrington.

"No; I looked out pretty sharply, too."

"That's right. If you like to fall in with my suggestions, however, you shall see him at about two o'clock, and take a handsome rise out of him."

"Very well," Mr. Telfer replied. "What's your suggestion?"

"I'll tell you. In the first place, what's the value of that other horse that looks so like Janissary?"

"Hamid is his name. He's worth—well, what he will fetch. I'll sell him for fifty and be glad of the chance."

"Very good. Then you'll no doubt be glad to risk his health temporarily to make sure of the Redbury Stakes, and to get longer prices for anything you may like to put on between now and tomorrow afternoon. Come to the stables and I'll tell you. But first, is there a place where we may command a view of the ground behind the stables without being seen?"

"Yes, there's a ventilation grating at the back of each stall."

"Good! Then we'll watch from Hamid's stall, which will be empty. Select your most wooden-faced and most careful boy, and send him out behind the stable with Hamid at two o'clock to the moment. Put the horse in a full suit of clothes—it is necessary to cover up that white star—and tell the lad he must lead it up and down slowly for twenty yards or so. I rather expect the red-bearded man will be coming along between two o'clock and half-past two. You will understand that Hamid is to be Janissary for the occasion. You must drill your boy to appear a bit of a fool, and to overcome his stable education sufficiently to chatter freely—so long as it is the proper chatter. The man may ask the horse's name, or he may not. Anyway, the boy mustn't forget it is Janissary he is leading. You have an odd fad, you must know (and the boy must know it too) in the matter of training. This ridiculous fad is to have your colt walked up and down for half an hour exactly at two o'clock every afternoon, and then given a handful of malt as he comes in. The boy can talk as freely about this as he pleases, and also about the colt's chances, and anything else he likes; and he is to let the stranger come up, talk to the horse, pat him in short, to do as he pleases. Is that plain?"

"Perfectly. You have found out something about this red-bearded chap then?"

"Oh, yes—it's Naylor the bookmaker, as a matter of fact, with a false beard."

"What! Naylor?"

"Yes. You see the idea, of course. Once Naylor thinks he has nobbled the favourite he will lay it to any extent, and the odds will get longer. Then you can make him pay for his little games."

"Well, yes, of course. Though I wouldn't put too much with Naylor in any case. He's not a big man, and he might break and lose me the lot. But I can get it out of the others."

"Just so. You'd better see about schooling your boy now, I think. I'll tell you more presently."

A minute or two before two o'clock Dorrington and Telfer, mounted on a pair of steps, were gazing through the ventilation grating of Hamid's stall, while the colt, clothed completely, was led around. Then Dorrington described his operations of the previous evening.

"No matter what he may think of my tale," he said. "Naylor will be pretty sure to come. He has tried to bribe your stablemen, and has been baffled. Every attempt to get hold of the boy in charge of Janissary has failed, and he will be glad to clutch at any shadow of a chance to save his money now. Once he is here, and the favourite apparently at his mercy, the thing is done. By the way, I expect your nephew's little present to the man you sacked was a fairly innocent one. No doubt he merely asked the man whether Janissary was keeping well, and was thought good enough to win, for I find he is backing it pretty heavily. Naylor came afterwards, with much less innocent intentions, but fortunately you were down on him in time. Several considerations induced me to go to Naylor's room.

"In the first place, I have heard rather shady tales of his doings on one or two occasions, and he did not seem a sufficiently big man to stand to lose a great deal over your horse. Then, when I saw him, I observed that his figure bore a considerable resemblance to that of the man you had described, except as regards the red beard and the spectacles—articles easily enough assumed, and, indeed, often enough used by the scum of the ring whose trade is welshing. And, apart from these considerations, here, at any rate, was one man who had an interest in keeping your colt from winning, and here was his room waiting for me to explore. So I explored it, and the card turned up trumps."

As he was speaking, the stable-boy, a stolid-looking youngster, was leading Hamid back and forth on the turf before their eyes.

"There's somebody," said Dorrington suddenly, "over in that clump of trees. Yes—our man, sure enough. I felt pretty sure of him after you had told me that he hadn't thought it worthwhile to turn up this morning. Here he comes."

Naylor, with his red beard sticking out over the collar of his big coat, came slouching along with an awkwardly assumed air of carelessness and absence of mind.

"Hullo!" he said suddenly, as he came abreast of the horse, turning as though but now aware of its presence, "that's a valuable sort of horse, ain't it, my lad?"

"Yes," said the boy, "it is. He's goin' to win the Redbury Stakes tomorrow. It's Janissary."

"Oh! Janey Sairey, is it?" Naylor answered, with a quaint affectation of gaping ignorance. "Janey Sairey, eh? Well, she do look a fine 'orse, what I can see of 'er. What a suit o' clo'es! An' so she's one o' the 'orses that runs in races, is she? Well, I never! Pretty much like other 'orses, too, to look at, ain't she? Only a bit thin in the legs."

The boy stood carelessly by the colt's side, and the man approached. His hand came quickly from an inner pocket, and then he passed it under Hamid's cloths, near the shoulder. "Ah, it do feel a lovely skin, to be sure!" he said. "An' so there's goin' to be races at Redbury to-morrow, is there? I dunno anythin' about races myself, an'—Oo my!"

Naylor sprang back as the horse, flinging back its ears, started suddenly, swung round, and reared. "Lor," he said, "what a vicious brute! Jist because I stroked her! I'll be careful about touching racehorses again." His hand passed stealthily to the pocket again, and he hurried on his way, while the stable-boy steadied and soothed Hamid.

Telfer and Dorrington sniggered quietly in their concealment. "He's taken a deal of trouble, hasn't he?" Dorrington remarked. "It's a sad case of the biter bit for Mr. Naylor, I'm afraid. That was a prick the colt felt—hypodermic injection with the syringe I saw in the bag, no doubt. The boy won't be such a fool as to come in again at once,

"THE HORSE STARTED SUDDENLY, SWUNG ROUND, AND REARED."

will he? If Naylor's taking a look back from anywhere, that may make him suspicious."

"No fear. I've told him to keep out for the half-hour, and he'll do it. Dear, dear, what an innocent person Mr. Bob Naylor is! 'Well, I never! Pretty much like other horses!' He didn't know there were to be races at Redbury! 'Janey Sairey,' too—it's really very funny!"

Ere the half-hour was quite over, Hamid came stumbling and dragging into the stable yard, plainly all amiss, and collapsed on his litter as soon as he gained his stall. There he lay, shivering and drowsy.

"I expect he'll get over it in a day or two," Dorrington remarked. "I don't suppose a vet could do much for him just now, except, perhaps, give him a drench and let him take a rest. Certainly, the effect will last over tomorrow. That's what it is calculated for."

5

The Redbury Stakes were run at three in the afternoon, after two or three minor events had been disposed of. The betting had undergone considerable fluctuations during the morning, but in general it ruled heavily against Janissary. The story had got about, too, that Mr. Warren Telfer's colt would not start. So that when the numbers went up, and it was seen that Janissary was starting after all, there was much astonishment, and a good deal of uneasiness in the ring.

"It's a pity we can't see our friend Naylor's face just now, isn't it?" Dorrington remarked to his client, as they looked on from Mr. Telfer's drag.

"Yes; it would be interesting," Telfer replied. "He was quite confident last night, you say."

"Quite. I tested him by an offer of a small bet on your colt, asking some points over the odds, and he took it at once. Indeed, I believe he has been going about gathering up all the wagers he could about Janissary, and the market has felt it. Your nephew has risked some more with him, I believe, and altogether it looks as though the town would spoil the 'bookies' badly."

As the horses came from the weighing enclosure, Janissary was seen conspicuous among them, bright, clean, and firm, and a good many faces lengthened at the sight. The start was not so good as it might have been, but the favourite (the starting-price had gone to evens) was not left, and got away well in the crowd of ten starters. There he lay till rounding the bend, when the Telfer blue and chocolate was seen among the foremost, and near the rails. Mr. Telfer almost trembled as he watched through his glasses.

"Hang that Willett!" he said, almost to himself. "He's too clever against those rails before getting clear. All right, though, all right! He's coming!"

Janissary, indeed, was showing in front, and as the horses came along the straight it was plain that Mr. Telfer's colt was holding the field comfortably. There were changes in the crowd; some dropped away, some came out and attempted to challenge for the lead, but the favourite, striding easily, was never seriously threatened, and in the end, being a little let out, came in a three-lengths winner, never once having been made to show his best.

"I congratulate you, Mr. Telfer," said Dorrington, "and you may congratulate me."

"Certainly, certainly," said Mr. Telfer hastily, hurrying off to lead in the winner.

It was a bad race for the ring, and in the open parts of the course many a humble fielder grabbed his satchel ere the shouting was over, and made his best pace for the horizon; and more than one pair of false whiskers, as red as Naylor's, came off suddenly while the owner betook himself to a fresh stand. Unless a good many outsiders sailed home before the end of the week there would be a bad Monday for layers. But all sporting Redbury was jubilant. They had all been "on" the local favourite for the local race, and it had won.

6

Mr. Bob Naylor "got a bit back", in his own phrase, on other races

"CAME IN THREE LENGTHS THE WINNER."

by the end of the week, but all the same he saw a black settling day ahead. He had been done—done for a certainty. He had realized this as soon as he saw the numbers go up for the Redbury Stakes. Janissary had not been drugged after all. That meant that another horse had been substituted for him, and that the whole thing was an elaborate plant. He thought he knew Janissary pretty well by sight, too, and rather prided himself on having an eye for a horse. But clearly it was a plant—a complete do. Telfer was in it, and so of course was that gentlemanly stranger who had strolled along Redbury High Street with him that night, telling that cock-and-bull story about the afternoon walks and the handful of malt. There was a nice schoolboy tale to take in a man who thought himself broad as Cheapside! He cursed himself high and low. To be done, and to know it, was a galling thing, but this would be worse.

The tale would get about. They would boast of a clever stroke like that, and that would injure him with everybody; with honest men, because his reputation, as it was, would bear no worsening, and with knaves like himself, because they would laugh at him, and leave him out when any little co-operative swindle was in contemplation. But though the chagrin of the defeat was bitter bad enough, his losses were worse. He had taken everything offered on Janissary after he had nobbled the wrong horse, and had given almost any odds demanded. Do as he might, he could see nothing but a balance against him on Monday, which, though he might pay out his last cent, he could not cover by several hundred pounds.

But on the day he met his customers at his club, as usual, and paid out freely. Young Richard Telfer, however, with whom he was heavily "in", he put off till the evening. "I've been a bit disappointed this morning over some ready that was to be paid over," he said, "and I've used the last cheque-form in my book. You might come and have a bit of dinner with me tonight, Mr. Telfer, and take it then."

Telfer assented without difficulty.

"All right, then, that's settled. You know the place—Gold Street. Seven sharp. The missis'll be pleased to see you, I'm sure, Mr. Telfer. Let's see—it's fifteen hundred and thirty altogether, isn't it?"

"Yes, that's it. I'll come."

Young Telfer left the club, and at the corner of the street ran against Dorrington. Telfer, of course, knew him as his late fellow-guest at the "Crown" at Redbury, and this was their first meeting in London after their return from the races.

"Ah!" said Telfer. "Going to draw a bit of Janissary money, eh?"

"Oh, I haven't much to draw," Dorrington answered. "But I expect your pockets are pretty heavy, if you've just come from Naylor."

"Yes, I've just come from Naylor, but I haven't touched the merry sovs just yet," replied Telfer cheerfully. "There's been a run on Naylor, and I'm going to dine with him and his respectable missis this evening, and draw the plunder then. I feel rather curious to see what sort of establishment a man like Naylor keeps going. His place is in Gold Street, Chelsea."

"Yes, I believe so. Anyhow, I congratulate you on your haul, and wish you a merry evening." And the two men parted.

Dorrington had, indeed, a few pounds to draw as a result of his "fishing" bet with Naylor, but now he resolved to ask for the money at his own time. This invitation to Telfer took his attention, and it reminded him oddly of the circumstances detailed in the report of the inquest on Lawrence, transcribed at the beginning of this paper. He had cut out this report at the time it appeared, because he saw certain singularities about the case, and he had filed it, as he had done hundreds of other such cuttings. And now certain things led him to fancy that he might be much interested to observe the proceedings at Naylor's house on the evening after a bad settling-day. He resolved to gratify himself with a strict professional watch in Gold Street that evening, on chance of something coming of it. For it was an important thing in Dorrington's rascally trade to get hold of as much of other people's private business as possible, and to know exactly in what cupboard to find every man's skeleton. For there was no knowing but it might be turned into money sooner or later. So he found the number of Naylor's house from the handiest directory, and at six o'clock, a little disguised by a humbler style of dress than usual, he began his watch.

Naylor's house was at the corner of a turning, with the flank wall blank of windows, except for one at the top; and a public-house stood at the opposite corner. Dorrington, skilled in watching without attracting attention to himself, now lounged in the public-house bar, now stood at the street corner, and now sauntered along the street, a picture of vacancy of mind, and looking, apparently, at everything in turn, except the house at the corner. The first thing he noted was the issuing forth from the area steps of a healthy-looking girl in much gaily beribboned finery. Plainly a servant taking an evening out. This was an odd thing, that a servant should be allowed out on an evening when a guest was expected to dinner; and the house looked like one where it was more likely that one servant would be kept than two. Dorrington hurried after the girl, and, changing his manner of address, to that of a civil labourer, said—

"Beg pardon, Miss, but is Mary Walker still in service at your 'ouse?"

"Mary Walker?" said the girl. "Why, no. I never 'eard the name. And there ain't nobody in service there but me."

"Beg pardon—it must be the wrong 'ouse. It's my cousin, Miss, that's all."

Dorrington left the girl and returned to the public-house. As he reached it he perceived a second noticeable thing. Although it was broad daylight, there was now a light behind the solitary window at the top of the side-wall of Naylor's house. Dorrington slipped through the swing-doors of the public-house and watched through the glass.

It was a bare room behind the high window—it might have been a bathroom—and its interior was made but dimly visible from outside by the light. A tall, thin woman was setting up an ordinary pair of house-steps in the middle of the room. This done, she turned to the window and pulled down the blind, and as she did so Dorrington noted her very extreme thinness, both of face and body. When the blind was down the light still remained within. Again there seemed some significance in this. It appeared that the thin woman had waited until her servant had gone before doing whatever she had to do in that room. Presently the watcher came again into Gold Street, and from there caught a passing glimpse of the thin woman as she moved busily about the front room over the breakfast parlour.

Clearly, then, the light above had been left for future use. Dorrington thought for a minute, and then suddenly stopped, with a snap of the fingers. He saw it all now. Here was something altogether in his way. He would take a daring course.

He withdrew once more to the public-house, and ordering another drink, took up a position in a compartment from which he could command a view both of Gold Street and the side turning. The time now, he saw by his watch, was ten minutes to seven. He had to wait rather more than a quarter of an hour before seeing Richard Telfer come walking jauntily down Gold Street, mount the steps, and knock at Naylor's door. There was a momentary glimpse of the thin woman's face at the door, and then Telfer entered.

It now began to grow dusk, and in about twenty minutes more

Dorrington took to the street again. The room over the breakfast-parlour was clearly the dining-room. It was lighted brightly, and by intent listening the watcher could distinguish, now and again, a sudden burst of laughter from Telfer, followed by the deeper grunts of Naylor's voice, and once by sharp tones that it seemed natural to suppose were the thin woman's.

Dorrington waited no longer, but slipped a pair of thick sock-feet over his shoes, and, after a quick look along the two streets, to make sure nobody was near, he descended the area steps. There was no light in the breakfast-parlour. With his knife he opened the window-catch, raised the sash quietly and stepped over the sill, and stood in the dark room within.

All was quiet, except for the talking in the room above. He had done but what many thieves—"parlour-jumpers" do every day; but there was more ahead. He made his way silently to the basement passage, and passed into the kitchen. The room was lighted, and cookery utensils were scattered about, but nobody was there. He waited till he heard a request in Naylor's gruff voice for "another slice" of something, and noiselessly mounted the stairs. He noticed that the dining-room door was ajar, but passed quickly on to the second flight, and rested on the landing above. Mrs. Naylor would probably have to go downstairs once or twice again, but he did not expect anybody in the upper part of the house just yet. There was a small flight of stairs above the landing whereon he stood, leading to the servant's bedroom and the bathroom. He took a glance at the bathroom with its feeble lamp, its steps, and its open ceiling-trap, and returned again to the bedroom landing. There he stood waiting watchfully.

Twice the thin woman emerged from the dining-room, went downstairs and came up again, each time with food and plates. Then she went down once more, and was longer gone. Meantime Naylor and Telfer were talking and joking loudly at the table.

When once again Dorrington saw the crown of the thin woman's head rising over the bottom stair, he perceived that she bore a tray set with cups already filled with coffee. These she carried into the dining-room, whence presently came the sound of striking matches. After this the conversation seemed to flag, and Telfer's part in it grew less and less, till it ceased altogether, and the house was silent except for a sound of heavy breathing. Soon this became almost a snore, and then there was a sudden noisy tumble as of a drunken man; but still the snoring went on, and the Naylors were talking in whispers.

There was a shuffling and heaving sound, and a chair was knocked over. Then at the dining-room door appeared Naylor, walking backward, and carrying the inert form of Telfer by the shoulders, while the thin woman followed supporting the feet. Dorrington retreated up the small stair-flight, cocking a pocket revolver as he went.

Up the stairs they came, Naylor puffing and grunting with exertion, and Telfer still snoring soundly on, till at last, having mounted the top flight, they came in at the bathroom door, where Dorrington stood to receive them, smiling and bowing pleasantly, with his hat in one hand and his revolver in the other.

The woman, from her position, saw him first, and dropped Telfer's legs with a scream. Naylor turned his head and then also dropped his end. The drugged man fell in a heap, snoring still.

Naylor, astounded and choking, made as if to rush at the interloper, but Dorrington thrust the revolver into his face, and exclaimed, still smiling courteously, "Mind, mind! It's a dangerous thing, is a revolver, and apt to go off if you run against it!"

He stood thus for a second, and then stepped forward and took the woman—who seemed like to swoon—by the arm, and pulled her into the room. "Come, Mrs. Naylor," he said, "you're not one of the fainting sort, and I think I'd better keep two such clever people as you under my eye, or one of you may get into mischief. Come now, Naylor, we'll talk business."

Naylor, now white as a ghost, sat on the edge of the bath, and stared at Dorrington as though in a fascination of terror. His hands rested on the bath at each side, and an odd sound of gurgling came from his thick throat.

"We will talk business," Dorrington resumed. "Come, you've met me before now you know—at Redbury. You can't have forgotten Janissary, and the walking exercise and the handful of malt. I'm afraid you're a clumsy sort of rascal, Naylor, though you do your best. I'm a rascal myself (though I don't often confess it), and I assure you that your conceptions are crude as yet. Still, that isn't a bad notion in its way, that of drugging a man and drowning him in your cistern up there in the roof, when you prefer not to pay him his winnings. It has the very considerable merit that, after the body has been fished out of any river you may choose to fling it into, the stupid coroner's jury will never suspect that it was drowned in any other water but that. Just as happened in the Lawrence case, for instance. You remember that, eh? So do I, very well, and it was because I remembered that that I paid you this visit tonight. But you do the thing much too clumsily, really.

"When I saw a light up here in broad daylight I knew at once it must be left for some purpose to be executed later in the evening; and when I saw the steps carefully placed at the same time, after the servant had been sent out, why the thing was plain, remembering, as I did, the curious coincidence that Mr. Lawrence was drowned the very evening he had been here to take away his winnings. The steps must be intended to give access to the roof, where there was probably a tank to feed the bath, and what more secret place to drown a man than there? And what easier place, so long as the man was well drugged, and there was a strong lid to the tank? As I say, Naylor, your notion was meritorious, but your execution was wretched—perhaps because you had no notion that I was watching you."

He paused, and then went on. "Come," he said, "collect your scattered faculties, both of you. I shan't hand you over to the police for this little invention of yours; it's too useful an invention to give away to the police. I shan't hand you over, that is to say, as long as you do as I tell you. If you get mutinous, you shall hang, both of you, for the Lawrence business. I may as well tell you that I'm a bit of a scoundrel myself, by way of profession. I don't boast about it, but it's well to be frank in making arrangements of this sort. I'm going to take you into my service. I employ a few agents, and you and your tank may come in very handy from time to time. But we must set it up, with a few improvements, in another house—a house which hasn't quite such an awkward window. And we mustn't execute our little suppressions so regularly on settling-day; it looks suspicious. So as soon as you can get your faculties together we'll talk over this thing."

The man and the woman had exchanged glances during this speech, and now Naylor asked, huskily, jerking his thumb toward the man on the floor, "An'—an' what about 'im?"

"What about him? Why, get rid of him as soon as you like. Not that way, though." (He pointed toward the ceiling trap.) "It doesn't pay me, and I'm master now. Besides, what will people say when you tell the same tale at his inquest that you told at Lawrence's? No, my friend, bookmaking and murder don't assort together, profitable as the combination may seem. Settling-days are too regular. And I'm not going to be your accomplice, mind. You are going to be mine. Do what you please with Telfer. Leave him on somebody's doorstep if you like."

"But I owe him fifteen hundred, and I ain't got more than half of it! I'll be ruined!"

"Very likely," Dorrington returned placidly. "Be ruined as soon as possible, then, and devote all your time to my business. You're not to ornament the ring any longer, remember—you're to assist a private inquiry agent, you and your wife and your charming tank. Repudiate the debt if you like it's a mere gaming transaction, and there is no legal claim or leave him in the street and tell him he's been robbed. Please yourself as to this little roguery—you may as well, for it's the last you will do on your own account. For the future your respectable talents will be devoted to the service of Dorrington Hicks, private inquiry agents; and if you don't give satisfaction, that eminent firm will hang you, with the assistance of the judge at the Old Bailey. So settle your business yourselves, and quickly, for I've a good many things to arrange with you."

And, Dorrington watching them continually, they took Telfer out by the side gate in the garden wall and left him in a dark corner.

Thus I learnt the history of the horrible tank that had so nearly ended my own life, as I have already related. Clearly the Naylors had changed their name to Crofting on taking compulsory service with Dorrington, and Mrs. Naylor was the repulsively thin woman who had drugged me with her coffee in the house at Highgate. The events I have just recorded took place about three years before I came to England. In the meantime, how many people, whose deaths might be turned to profit, had fallen victims to the murderous cunning of Dorrington and his tools?

The Case of "The Mirror of Portugal"

Whether or not this case has an historical interest is a matter of conjecture. If it has none, then the title I have given it is a misnomer. But I think the conjecture that some historical interest attaches to it is by no means an empty one, and all that can be urged against it is the common though not always declared error that romance expired fifty years at least ago, and history with it. This makes it seem improbable that the answer to an unsolved riddle of a century since should be found today in an inquiry agent's dingy office in Bedford Street, Covent Garden. Whether or not it has so been found the reader may judge for himself, though the evidence stops far short of actual proof of the identity of the "Mirror of Portugal" with the stone wherewith this case was concerned.

But first, as to the "Mirror of Portugal." This was a diamond of much and ancient fame. It was of Indian origin, and it had lain in the possession of the royal family of Portugal in the time of Portugal's ancient splendour. But three hundred years ago, after the extinction of the early line of succession, the diamond, with other jewels, fell into the possession of Don Antonio, one of the half-dozen pretenders who were then scrambling for the throne. Don Antonio, badly in want of money, deposited the stone in pledge with Queen Elizabeth of England, and never redeemed it.

Thus it took its place as one of the English Crown jewels, and so remained till the overthrow and death of Charles the First. Queen Henrietta then carried it with her to France, and there, to obtain money to satisfy her creditors, she sold it to the great Cardinal Mazarin. He bequeathed it, at his death, to the French Crown, and among the Crown jewels of France it once more found a temporary abiding place. But once more it brought disaster with it in the shape of a revolution, and again a king lost his head at the executioner's hands. And in the riot and confusion of the great Revolution of 1792 the "Mirror of Portugal," with other jewels, vanished utterly. Where it went to, and who took it, nobody ever knew. The "Mirror of Portugal" disappeared as suddenly and effectually as though fused to vapour by electric combustion.

So much for the famous "Mirror." Whether or not its history is germane to the narrative which follows, probably nobody will ever certainly know. But that Dorrington considered that it was, his notes on the case abundantly testify.

For some days before Dorrington's attention was in any way given to this matter, a poorly-dressed and not altogether prepossessing Frenchman had been haunting the staircase and tapping at the office door, unsuccessfully attempting an interview with Dorrington, who happened to be out, or busy, whenever he called. The man never asked for Hicks, Dorrington's partner; but this was very natural. In the first place, it was always Dorrington who met all strangers and conducted all negotiations, and in the second, Dorrington had just lately, in a case regarding a secret society in Soho, made his name much known and respected, not to say feared, in the foreign colony of that quarter; wherefore it was likely that a man who bore evidence of residence in that neighbourhood should come with the name of Dorrington on his tongue.

The weather was cold, but the man's clothes were thin and threadbare, and he had no overcoat. His face was of a broad, low type, coarse in feature and small in forehead, and he wore the baggy black linen peaked cap familiar on the heads of men of his class in parts of Paris. He had called unsuccessfully, as I have said, sometimes once, sometimes more frequently, on each of three or four days before he succeeded in seeing Dorrington. At last, however, he intercepted him on the stairs, as Dorrington arrived at about eleven in the morning.

"Pardon, *m'sieu*," he said, laying his finger on Dorrington's arm, "it is M. Dorrington—not?"

"Well—suppose it is, what then?" Dorrington never admitted his identity to a stranger without first seeing good cause.

"I 'ave beesness—very great beesness; beesness of a large profit for you if you please to take it. Where shall I tell it?"

"Come in here," Dorrington replied, leading the way to his private room. The man did not look like a wealthy client, but that signified nothing. Dorrington had made profitable strokes after introductions even less promising.

The man followed Dorrington, pulled off his cap, and sat in the chair Dorrington pointed at.

"In the first place," said Dorrington, "what's your name?"

"Ah, yas—but before—all that I tell is for ourselves alone, is it not? It is all in confidence, eh?"

"Yes, yes, of course," Dorrington answered, with virtuous impatience. "Whatever is said in this room is regarded as strictly confidential. What's your name?"

"Jacques Bouvier."

"Living at—?"

"Little Norham Street, Soho."

"And now the business you speak of."

"The beesness is this. My cousin, Leon Bouvier—he is *coquin*—a rrrascal!"

"Very likely."

"He has a great jewel—it is, I have no doubt, a diamond—of a great value. It is not his! There is no right of him to it! It should be mine. If you get it for me one-quarter of it in money shall be yours! And it is of a great value."

"Where does your cousin live? What is he?"

"Beck Street, Soho. He has a shop—a *café*—Café des Bons Camarades. And he give me not a crrrust—if I starve!"

It scarcely seemed likely that the keeper of a little foreign cafe in a back street of Soho would be possessed of a jewel a quarter of whose value would be prize enough to tempt Dorrington to take a new case up. But Dorrington bore with the man a little longer. "What is this jewel you talk of?" he asked. "And if you don't know enough about it to be quite sure whether it is a diamond or not, what *do* you know?"

"Listen! The stone I have never seen; but that it is a diamond makes probable. What else so much value? And it is much value that gives my cousin so great care and trouble—*cochon!* Listen! I relate to you. My father—he was charcoal-burner at Bonneuil, department of Seine. My uncle—the father of my cousin—also was charcoal-burner. The grandfather—charcoal-burner also; and his father and his grandfather before him—all burners of charcoal, at Bonneuil. Now perceive. The father of my grandfather was of the great Revolution—a young man, great among those who stormed the Bastille, the Tuileries, the Hotel de Ville, brave, and a leader. Now, when palaces were burnt and heads were falling there was naturally much confusion. Things were lost—things of large value. What more natural? While so many were losing the head from the shoulders, it was not strange that some should lose jewels from the neck. And when these things were lost, who might have a greater right to keep them than the young men of the Revolution, the brave, and the leaders, they who did the work?"

"If you mean that your respectable great-grandfather stole something, you needn't explain it anymore," Dorrington said. "I quite understand."

"I do not say stole; when there is a great revolution a thing is anybody's. But it would not be convenient to tell of it at the time, for the new government might believe everything to be its own. These things I do not know, you will understand—I suggest an explanation, that is all. After the great Revolution, my great-grandfather lives alone and quiet, and burns the charcoal as before. Why? The jewel is too great to sell so soon. So he gives it to his son and dies. He also, my grandfather, still burns the charcoal. Again, why? Because, as I believe, he is too poor, too common a man to go about openly to sell so great a stone. More, he loves the stone, for with that he is always rich; and so he burns his charcoal and lives contented as his father had done, and he is rich, and nobody knows it. What then? He has two sons. When he dies, which son does he leave the stone to? Each one says it is for himself—that is natural. I say it was for my father. But however that may make itself, my father dies suddenly. He falls in a pit—by accident, says his brother; not by accident, says my mother; and soon after, she dies, too. By accident too, perhaps you ask? Oh yes, by accident too, no doubt." The man laughed disagreeably.

"So I am left alone, a little boy, to burn charcoal. When I am a bigger boy there comes the great war, and the Prussians besiege Paris. My uncle, he, burning charcoal no more, goes at night, and takes things from the dead Prussians. Perhaps they are not always quite dead when he finds them—perhaps he makes them so. Be that as it will, the Prussians take him one dark night; and they stand him against a garden wall, and *pif! paf!* they shoot him. That is all of my uncle; but he dies a rich man, and nobody knows. What does his wife do? She has the jewel, and she has a little money that has been got from the dead Prussians. So when the war is over, she comes to London with my cousin, the bad Leon, and she has the *café*—Café des Bons Camarades.

"And Leon grows up, and his mother dies, and he has the *café*, and with the jewel is a rich man—nobody knowing; nobody but me. But, figure to yourself; shall I burn charcoal and starve at Bonneuil with a rich cousin in London—rich with a diamond that should be mine? Not so. I come over, and Leon, at first he lets me wait at the *café*. But I do not want that—there is the stone, and I can never see it, never find it. So one day Leon finds me looking in a box, and—*chut!* out I go. I tell Leon that I will share the jewel with him or I will tell the police. He laughs at me—there is no jewel, he says—I am mad. I do not tell the police, for that is to lose it altogether. But I come here and I offer you one quarter of the diamond if you shall get it."

"Steal it for you, eh?"

Jacques Bouvier shrugged his shoulders. "The word is as you please," he said. "The jewel is not his. And if there is delay it will be gone. Already he goes each day to Hatton Garden, leaving his wife to keep the Café des Bons Camarades. Perhaps he is selling the jewel today! Who can tell? So that it will be well that you begin at once."

"Very well. My fee in advance will be twenty guineas."

"What? *Dieu!*—I have no money, I tell you! Get the diamond, and there is one quarter—twenty-five *per cent.*—for you!"

"But what guarantee do you give that this story of yours isn't all a hoax? Can you expect me to take everything on trust, and work for nothing?"

The man rose and waved his arms excitedly. "It is true, I say!" he exclaimed. "It is a fortune! There is much for you, and it will pay! I have no money, or you should have some. What can I do? You will lose the chance if you are foolish!"

"It rather seems to me, my friend, that I shall be foolish to give valuable time to gratifying your cock-and-bull fancies. See here now.

I'm a man of business, and my time is fully occupied. You come here and waste half an hour or more of it with a long rigmarole about some valuable article that you say yourself you have never seen, and you don't even know whether it is a diamond or not. You wander at large over family traditions which you may believe yourself or may not. You have no money, and you offer no fee as a guarantee of your *bona fides,* and the sum of the thing is that you ask me to go and commit a theft—to purloin an article you can't even describe, and then to give you three-quarters of the proceeds. No, my man, you have made a mistake. You must go away from here at once, and if I find you hanging about my door again I shall have you taken away very summarily. Do you understand? Now go away."

"Mon Dieu! But—"

"I've no more time to waste," Dorrington answered, opening the door and pointing to the stairs. "If you stay here any longer you'll get into trouble."

Jacques Bouvier walked out, muttering and agitating his hands. At the top stair he turned and, almost too angry for words, burst out, "Sir—you are a ver' big fool—a fool!" But Dorrington slammed the door.

He determined, however, if he could find a little time, to learn a little more of Leon Bouvier—perhaps to put a man to watch at the Café des Bons Camarades. That the keeper of this place in Soho

"SIR—YOU ARE A VER' BIG FOOL—A FOOL!"

should go regularly to Hatton Garden, the diamond market, was curious, and Dorrington had met and analysed too many extraordinary romances to put aside unexamined Jacques Bouvier's seemingly improbable story. But, having heard all the man had to say, it had clearly been his policy to get rid of him in the way he had done. Dorrington was quite ready to steal a diamond, or anything else of value, if it could be done quite safely, but he was no such fool as to give three-quarters of his plunder—or any of it—to somebody else. So that the politic plan was to send Jacques Bouvier away with the impression that his story was altogether pooh-poohed and was to be forgotten.

2

Dorrington left his office late that day, and the evening being clear, though dark, he walked toward Conduit Street by way of Soho; he thought to take a glance at the Café des Bons Camarades on his way, without being observed, should Jacques Bouvier be in the vicinity.

Beck Street, Soho, was a short and narrow street lying east and west, and joining two of the larger streets that stretch north and south across the district. It was even a trifle dirtier than these by-streets in that quarter are wont to be. The Café des Bons Camarades was a little green-painted shop the window whereof was backed by muslin curtains, while upon the window itself appeared in florid painted letters the words "*Cuisine Francaise.*" It was the only shop in the street, with the exception of a small coal and firewood shed at one end, the other buildings consisting of the side wall of a factory, now closed for the night, and a few tenement houses. An alley entrance—apparently the gate of a stable-yard—stood next the *café*.

As Dorrington walked by the steamy window, he was startled to hear his own name and some part of his office address spoken in excited tones somewhere in this dark alley entrance; and suddenly a man rather well dressed, and cramming a damaged tall hat on his head as he went, darted from the entrance and ran in the direction from which Dorrington had come. A stoutly built Frenchwoman, carrying on her face every indication of extreme excitement, watched him from the gateway, and Dorrington made no doubt that it was in her voice that he had heard his name mentioned. He walked briskly to the end of the short street, turned at the end, and hurried round the block of houses, in hope to catch another sight of the man. Presently he saw him, running, in Old Compton Street, and making in the direction of Charing Cross Road. Dorrington mended his pace, and followed. The man emerged where Shaftesbury Avenue meets Charing Cross Road, and, as he crossed, hesitated once or twice, as though he thought of hailing a cab, but decided rather to trust his own legs.

He hastened through the byways to St. Martin's' Lane, and Dorrington now perceived that one side and half the back of his coat was dripping with wet mud. Also it was plain, as Dorrington had suspected, that his destination was Dorrington's own office in Bedford Street. So the follower broke into a trot, and at last came upon the muddy man wrenching at the bell and pounding at the closed door of the house in Bedford Street, just as the housekeeper began to turn the lock.

"M'sieu Dorrington—M'sieu Dorrington!" the man exclaimed, excitedly, as the door was opened.

"'E's gawn 'ome long ago," the caretaker growled; "you might 'a known that. Oh, 'ere 'e is though—good evenin', sir."

"I am Mr. Dorrington," the inquiry agent said politely. "Can I do anything for you?"

"Ah yes—it is important—at once! I am robbed!"

"Just step upstairs, then, and tell me about it."

Dorrington had but begun to light the gas in his office when his visitor broke out, "I am robbed, M'sieu Dorrington, robbed by my cousin—*coquin!* Rrrobbed of everything! Rrrobbed I tell you!" He seemed astonished to find the other so little excited by the intelligence.

"Let me take your coat," Dorrington said, calmly. "You've had a downer in the mud, I see. Why, what's this?" he smelt the collar as he went toward a hat-peg, "Chloroform!"

"Ah yes—it is that rrrascal Jacques! I will tell you. This evening I go into the gateway next my house—Café des Bons Camarades—to enter by the side-door, and—*paf!*—a shawl is fling across my face from behind—it is pull tight—there is a knee in my back—I can catch nothing with my hand—it smell all hot in my throat—I choke and I fall over—there is no more. I wake up and I see my wife, and she take me into the house. I am all muddy and tired, but I feel—and I have lost my property—it is a diamond—and my cousin Jacques, he has done it!"

"Are you sure of that?"

"Sure? Oh yes—it is certain, I tell you—certain!"

"Then why not inform the police?"

The visitor was clearly taken aback by this question. He faltered, and looked searchingly in Dorrington's face. "That is not always the convenient way," he said. "I would rather that you do it. It is the diamond that I want—not to punish my cousin—thief that he is!"

Dorrington mended a quill with ostentatious care, saying encouragingly as he did so, "I can quite understand that you may not wish to prosecute your cousin—only to recover the diamond you speak of. Also I can quite understand that there may be reasons—family reasons perhaps, perhaps others—which may render it inadvisable to make even the existence of the jewel known more than absolutely necessary. For instance, there may be other claimants, Monsieur Leon Bouvier."

The visitor started. "You know my name then?" he asked. "How is that?"

Dorrington smiled the smile of a sphinx. "M. Bouvier," he said, "it is my trade to know everything—everything." He put the pen down and gazed whimsically at the other. "My agents are everywhere. You talk of the secret agent of the Russian police—they are nothing. It is my trade to know all things. For instance"—Dorrington unlocked a drawer and produced a book (it was but an office diary), and, turning its pages, went on. "Let me see—B. It is my trade, for instance, to know about the Café des Bons Camarades, established by the late Madame Bouvier, now unhappily deceased. It is my trade to know of Madame Bouvier at Bonneuil, where the charcoal was burnt, and where Madame Bouvier was unfortunately left a widow at the time of the siege of Paris, because of some lamentable misunderstanding of her husband's with a file of Prussian soldiers by an orchard wall. It is my trade, moreover, to know something of the sad death of that husband's brother—in a pit—and of the later death of his widow. Oh yes. More" (turning a page attentively, as though following detailed notes), "it is my trade to know of a little quarrel between those brothers—it might even have been about a diamond, just such a diamond as you have come about tonight—and of jewels missed from the Tuileries in the great Revolution a hundred years ago."

He shut the book with a bang and returned it to its place. "And there are other things—too many to talk about," he said, crossing his legs and smiling calmly at the Frenchman.

During this long pretence at reading, Bouvier had slid farther and farther forward on his chair, till he sat on the edge, his eyes staring wide, and his chin dropped. He had been pale when he arrived, but now he was of a leaden grey. He said not a word.

Dorrington laughed lightly. "Come," he said, "I see you are astonished. Very likely. Very few of the people and families whose *dossiers* we have here" (he waved his hand generally about the room) "are aware of what we know. But we don't make a song of it, I assure you, unless it is for the benefit of clients. A client's affairs are sacred, of course, and our resources are at his disposal. Do I understand that you become a client?"

Bouvier sat a little farther back on his chair and closed his mouth. "A—a—yes," he answered at length, with an effort, moistening his lips as he spoke. "That is why I come."

"Ah, now we shall understand each other," Dorrington replied genially, opening an ink-pot and clearing his blotting-pad. "We're not connected with the police here, or anything of that sort, and except so far as we can help them we leave our client's affairs alone. You wish to be a client, and you wish me to recover your lost diamond. Very well, that is business. The first thing is the usual fee in advance—twenty guineas. Will you write a cheque?"

Bouvier had recovered some of his self-possession, and he hesitated. "It is a large fee," he said.

"Large? Nonsense! It is the sort of fee that might easily be swallowed up in half a day's expenses. And besides—a rich diamond merchant like yourself!"

Bouvier looked up quickly. "Diamond merchant?" he said. "I do not understand. I have lost my diamond—there was but one."

"And yet you go to Hatton Garden every day."

"What!" cried Bouvier, letting his hand fall from the table, "you know that too?"

"Of course," Dorrington laughed, easily; "it is my trade, I tell you. But write the cheque."

Bouvier produced a crumpled and dirty chequebook and complied, with many pauses, looking up dazedly from time to time into Dorrington's face.

"Now," said Dorrington, "tell me where you kept your diamond, and all about it."

"It was in an old little wooden box—so." Bouvier, not yet quite master of himself, sketched an oblong of something less than three inches long by two broad. "The box was old and black—my grandfather may have made it, or his father. The lid fitted very tight, and the inside was packed with fine charcoal powder with the diamond resting in it. The diamond—oh, it was great; like that—so." He made another sketch, roughly square, an inch and a quarter across. "But it looked even much greater still, so bright, so wonderful! It is easy to understand that my grandfather did not sell it—beside the danger. It is so beautiful a thing, and it is such great riches—all in one little box.

Why should not a poor charcoal-burner be rich in secret, and look at his diamond, and get all the few things he wants by burning his charcoal? And there was the danger. But that is long ago. I am a man of beesness, and I desired to sell it and be rich. And that Jacques—he has stolen it!"

"Let us keep to the point. The diamond was in a box. Well, where was the box?"

"On the outside of the box there were notches—so, and so. Bound the box at each place there was a tight, strong, silk cord—that is two cords. The cords were round my neck, under my shirt, so. And the box was under my arm—just as a boy carries his satchel, but high up—in the armpit, where I could feel it at all times. Tonight, when I come to myself, my collar was broken at the stud—see—the cords were cut—and all was gone!"

"You say your cousin Jacques has done this. How do you know?"

"Ah! But who else? Who else could know? And he has always tried to steal it. At first, I let him wait at the Café des Bons Camarades. What does he do? He prys about my house, and opens drawers; and I catch him at last looking in a box, and I turn him out. And he calls me a thief! *Sacri!* He goes—I have no more of him; and so—he does this!"

"Very well. Write down his name and address on this piece of paper, and your own." Bouvier did so. "And now tell me what you have been doing at Hatton Garden."

"Well, it was a very great diamond—I could not go to the first man and show it to sell. I must make myself known."

"It never struck you to get the stone cut in two, did it?"

"Eh? What?—*Nom de chien!* No!" He struck his knee with his hand. "Fool! Why did I not think of that? But still"—he grew more thoughtful—"I should have to show it to get it cut, and I did not know where to go. And the value would have been less."

"Just so—but it's the regular thing to do, I may tell you, in cases like this. But go on. About Hatton Garden, you know."

"I thought that I must make myself known among the merchants of diamonds, and then, perhaps, I should learn the ways, and one day be able to sell. As it was, I knew nothing—nothing at all. I waited, and I saved money in the *café*. Then, when I could do it, I dressed well and went and bought some diamonds of a dealer—very little diamonds, a little trayful for twenty pounds, and I try to sell them again. But I have paid too much—I can only sell for fifteen pounds. Then I buy more, and sell them for what I give. Then I take an office in Hatton

Garden—that is, I share a room with a dealer, and there is a partition between our desks. My wife attends the cafe, I go to Hatton Garden to buy and sell. It loses me money, but I must lose till I can sell the great diamond. I get to know the dealers more and more, and then tonight, as I go home—" he finished with an expressive shrug and a wave of the hand.

"Yes, yes, I think I see," Dorrington said. "As to the diamond again. It doesn't happen to be a *blue* diamond, does it?"

"No—pure white; perfect."

Dorrington had asked because two especially famous diamonds disappeared from among the French Crown jewels at the time of the great Revolution. One blue, the greatest coloured diamond ever known, and the other the "Mirror of Portugal." Bouvier's reply made it plain that it was certainly not the first which he had just lost.

"Come," Dorrington said, "I will call and inspect the scene of your disaster. I haven't dined yet, and it must be well past nine o'clock now."

They returned to Beck Street. There were gates at the dark entry by the side of the Café des Bons Camarades, but they were never shut, Bouvier explained. Dorrington had them shut now, however, and a lantern was produced. The paving was of rough cobble stones, deep in mud.

"Do many people come down here in the course of an evening?" Dorrington asked.

"Never anybody but myself."

"Very well. Stand away at your side door."

Bouvier and his wife stood huddled and staring on the threshold of the side door, while Dorrington, with the lantern, explored the muddy cobble stones. The pieces of a broken bottle lay in a little heap, and a cork lay a yard away from them. Dorrington smelt the cork, and then collected together the broken glass (there were but four or five pieces) from the little heap. Another piece of glass lay by itself a little way off, and this also Dorrington took up, scrutinising it narrowly. Then he traversed the whole passage carefully, stepping from bare stone to bare stone, and skimming the ground with the lantern. The mud lay confused and trackless in most places, though the place where Bouvier had been lying was indicated by an appearance of sweeping, caused, no doubt, by his wife dragging him to his feet. Only one other thing beside the glass and cork did Dorrington carry away as evidence, and that the Bouviers knew nothing of; for it was the remembrance of the mark of a sharp, small boot-heel in more than one patch of mud between the stones.

"Will you object, Madame Bouvier," he asked, as he handed back the lantern, "to show me the shoes you wore when you found your husband lying out here?"

Madame Bouvier had no objection at all. They were what she was then wearing, and had worn all day. She lifted her foot and exhibited one. There was no need for a second glance. It was a loose easy cashmere boot, with spring sides and heels cut down flat for indoor comfort.

"And this was at what time?"

It was between seven and eight o'clock, both agreed, though they differed a little as to the exact time. Bouvier had recovered when his wife raised him, had entered the house with her, at once discovered his loss, and immediately, on his wife's advice, set out to find Dorrington, whose name the woman had heard spoken of frequently among the visitors to the cafe in connection with the affair of the secret society already alluded to. He had felt certain that Dorrington would not be at his office, but trusted to be directed where to find him.

"Now," Dorrington asked of Bouvier (the woman had been called away), "tell me some more about your cousin. "Where does he live?"

"DORRINGTON, WITH THE LANTERN, EXPLORED THE MUDDY COBBLE STONES."

"In Little Norham Street; the third house from this end on the right and the back room at the top. That is unless he has moved just lately."

"Has he been ill recently?"

"Ill?" Bouvier considered. "Not that I can say—no. I have never heard of Jacques being ill." It seemed to strike him as an incongruous and new idea. "Nothing has made him ill all his life—he is too good in constitution, I think."

"Does he wear spectacles?"

"Spectacles? *Mais non!* Never! Why should he wear spectacles? His eyes are good as mine."

"Very well. Now attend. Tomorrow you must not go to Hatton Garden—I will go for you. If you see your cousin Jacques you must say nothing, take no notice; let everything proceed as though nothing had happened; leave all to me. Give me your address at Hatton Garden."

"But what is it you must do there?"

"That is my business. I do my business in my own way. Still I will give you a hint. Where is it that diamonds are sold? In Hatton Garden, as you so well know—as I expect your cousin knows if he has been watching you. Then where will your cousin go to sell it? Hatton Garden, of course. Never mind what I shall do there to intercept it. I am to be your new partner, you understand, bringing money into the business. You must be ill and stay at home till you hear from me. Go now and write me a letter of introduction to the man who shares the office with you. Or I will write it if you like, and you shall sign it. What sort of a man is he?"

"Very quiet—a tall man, perhaps English, but perhaps not."

"Ever buy or sell diamonds with him?"

"Once only. It was the first time. That is how I learned of the half-office to let."

The letter was written, and Dorrington stuffed it carelessly into his pocket. "Mr. Hamer is the name, is it?" he said. "I fancy I have met him somewhere. He is short-sighted, isn't he?"

"Oh yes, he is short-sighted. With *pince-nez.*"

"Not very well lately?"

"No—I think not. He takes medicine in the office. But you will be careful, eh? He must not know."

"Do you think so? Perhaps I may tell him, though."

"Tell him? *Ciel*—no! You must not tell people! No!"

"Shall I throw the whole case over, and keep your deposit fee?"

"No—no, not that. But it is foolish to tell to people!"

"I am to judge what is foolish and what wise, M. Bouvier. Good evening!"

"Good evening, M. Dorrington; good evening." Bouvier followed him out to the gate. "And will you tell me—do you think there is a way to get the diamond? Have you any plan?"

"Oh yes, M. Bouvier, I have a plan. But, as I have said, that is my business. It may be a successful plan, or it may not; that we shall see."

"And—and the *dossier*. The notes that you so marvellously have, written out in the book you read. "When this business is over you will destroy them, eh? You will not leave a clue?"

"The notes that I have in my books," answered Dorrington, without relaxing a muscle of his face, "are my property, for my own purposes, and were mine before you came to me. Those relating to you are a mere item in thousands. So long as you behave well, M. Bouvier, they will not harm you, and, as I said, the confidences of a client are sacred to Dorrington & Hicks. But as to keeping them—certainly I shall. Once more—good evening!"

Even the stony-faced Dorrington could not repress a smile and something very like a chuckle as he turned the end of the street and struck out across Golden Square towards his rooms in Conduit Street. The simple Frenchman, only half a rogue—even less than half—was now bamboozled and put aside as effectually as his cousin had been. Certainly there was a diamond, and an immense one; if only the Bouvier tradition were true, probably the famous "Mirror of Portugal"; and nothing stood between Dorrington and absolute possession of that diamond but an ordinary sort of case such as he dealt with every day. And he had made Bouvier pay a fee for the privilege of putting him completely on the track of it! Dorrington smiled again.

His dinner was spoilt by waiting, but he troubled little of that. He spread before him, and examined again, the pieces of glass and the cork. The bottle had been a druggist's ordinary flat bottle, graduated with dose-marks, and altogether seven inches high, or thereabout. It had, without a doubt, contained the chloroform wherewith Leon Bouvier had been assaulted, as Dorrington had judged from the smell of the cork. The fact of the bottle being corked showed that the chloroform had not been bought all at once—since in that case it would have been put up in a stoppered bottle. More probably it had been procured in very small quantities (ostensibly for toothache, or something of that kind) at different druggists, and put together in this larger bottle, which had originally been used for something else. The bottle had been distinguished by a label—the usual white label affixed by the druggist, with directions as to taking the medicine—and this label had been scraped off; all except a small piece at the bottom edge by the right hand side, whereon might be just distinguished the greater part of the letters N, E. The piece of glass that had lain a little way apart from the bottle was not a part of it, as a casual observer might have supposed. It was a fragment of a concave lens, with a channel ground in the edge.

3.

At ten precisely next morning, as usual, Mr. Ludwig Hamer mounted the stairs of the house in Hatton Garden, wherein he rented half a room as office. He was a tall, fair man, wearing thick convex *pince-nez*. He spoke English like a native, and, indeed, he called himself an Englishman, though there were those who doubted the Briticism of his name. Scarce had he entered his office when Dorrington followed him.

The room had never been a very large one, and now a partition divided it in two, leaving a passage at one side only, by the window. On each side of this partition stood a small pedestal table, a couple of chairs, a copying-press, and the other articles usual in a meagerly furnished office. Dorrington strode past Bouvier's half of the room and came upon Hamer as he was hanging his coat on a peg. The letter of introduction had been burnt, since Dorrington had only asked for it in order to get Hamer's name and the Hatton Garden address without betraying to Bouvier the fact that he did not already know all about it.

"Good morning, Mr. Hamer," said Dorrington, loudly. "Sorry to see you're not well"—he pointed familiarly with his stick at a range of medicine bottles on the mantelpiece—"but it's very trying weather, of course. You've been suffering from toothache, I believe?"

Hamer seemed at first disposed to resent the loudness and familiarity of this speech, but at the reference to toothache he started suddenly and set his lips.

"Chloroform's a capital thing for toothache, Mr. Hamer, and for— for other things. I'm not in your line of business myself, but I believe it has even been used in the diamond trade."

"What do you mean?" asked Hamer, flushing angrily.

"Mean? Why, bless me—nothing more than I said. By the way,

I'm afraid you dropped one of your medicine bottles last night. I've brought it back, though I'm afraid it's past repair. It's a good job you didn't quite clear the label off before you took it out with you, else I might have had a difficulty." Dorrington placed the fragments on the table. "You see you've just left the first letter of 'E.C.' in the druggist's address, and the last 'N' of Hatton Garden, just before it. There doesn't happen to be any other Garden in E.C. district that I know of, nor does the name of any other thoroughfare end in N—they are mostly streets, or lanes, or courts, you see. And there seems to be only one druggist in Hatton Garden—capital fellow, no doubt—the one whose name and address I observe on those bottles on the mantelpiece."

Dorrington stood with his foot on a chair, and tapped his knee carelessly with his stick. Hamer dropped into the other chair and regarded him with a frown, though his face was pale. Presently he said, in a strained voice, "Well?"

"Yes; there *is* something else, Mr. Hamer, as you appear to suggest. I see you're wearing a new pair of glasses this morning; pity you broke the others last night, but I've brought the piece you left behind." He gathered up the broken bottle, and held up the piece of concave lens. "I think, after all, it's really best to use a cord with *pince-nez*. It's awkward, and it catches in things, I know, but it saves a breakage, and you're liable to get the glasses knocked off, you know—in certain circumstances."

Hamer sprang to his feet with a snarl, slammed the door, locked it, and turned on Dorrington. But now Dorrington had a revolver in his hand, though his manner was as genial as ever.

"Yes, yes," he said; "best to shut the door, of course. People listen, don't they? But sit down again. I'm not anxious to hurt you, and, as you will perceive, you're quite unable to hurt me. "What I chiefly came to say is this: last evening my client, M. Leon Bouvier, of this office and the Café des Bons Camarades, was attacked in the passage adjoining his house by a man who was waiting for him, with a woman—was it really Mrs. Hamer? but there, I won't ask—keeping watch. He was robbed of a small old wooden box, containing charcoal and—a diamond. My name is Dorrington—firm of Dorrington & Hicks, which you may have heard of. That's my card. I've come to take away that diamond."

Hamer was pale and angry, but, in his way, was almost as calm as Dorrington. He put down the card without looking at it. "I don't understand you," he said. "How do you know I've got it?"

"Come, come, Mr. Hamer," Dorrington replied, rubbing the barrel of his revolver on his knee, "that's hardly worthy of you. You're a man of business, with a head on your shoulders—the sort of man I like doing business with, in fact. Men like ourselves needn't trifle. I've shown you most of the cards I hold, though not all, I assure you. I'll tell you, if you like, all about your little tour round among the druggists with the convenient toothache, all about the evenings on which you watched Bouvier home, and so on. But, really, need we, as men of the world, descend to such peddling detail?"

"Well, suppose I have got it, and suppose I refuse to give it you. What then?"

"What then? But why should we talk of unpleasant things? You won't refuse, you know."

"Do you mean you'd get it out of me by help of that pistol?"

"Well," said Dorrington, deliberately, "the pistol is noisy, and it makes a mess, and all that, but it's a useful thing, and I *might* do it with that, you know, in certain circumstances. But I wasn't thinking of it—there's a much less troublesome way."

"Which?"

"You're a slower man than I took you for, Mr. Hamer—or perhaps you haven't quite appreciated *me* yet. If I were to go to that window and call the police, what with the little bits of evidence in my pocket, and the other little bits that the druggists who sold the chloroform would give, and the other bits in reserve, that I prefer not to talk about just now—there would be rather an awkwardly complete case of robbery with violence, wouldn't there? And you'd have to lose the diamond after all, to say nothing of a little rest in gaol and general ruination."

"That sounds very well, but what about your client? Come now, you call me a man of the world, and I am one. How will your client account for the possession of a diamond worth eighty thousand pounds or so? He doesn't seem a millionaire. The police would want to know about him as well as about me, if you were such a fool as to bring them in. Where did *he* steal it, eh?"

Dorrington smiled and bowed at the question. "That's a very good card to play, Mr. Hamer," he said, "a capital card, really. To a superficial observer it might look like winning the trick. But I think I can trump it." He bent farther forward and tapped the table with the pistol-barrel. "Suppose I don't care one solitary dump what becomes of my client? Suppose I don't care whether he goes to gaol or stays out of it—in short, suppose I prefer my own interests to his?"

"Ho! ho!" Hamer cried. "I begin to understand. You want to grab the diamond for yourself then?"

"I haven't said anything of the kind, Mr. Hamer," Dorrington replied, suavely. "I have simply demanded the diamond which you stole last night, and I have mentioned an alternative."

"Oh, yes, yes, but we understand one another. Come, we'll arrange this. How much do you want?"

Dorrington stared at him stonily. "I—I beg your pardon," he said, "but I don't understand. I want the diamond you stole."

"But come now, we'll divide. Bouvier had no right to it, and he's out. You and I, perhaps, haven't much right to it, legally, but it's between us, and we're both in the same position."

"Pardon me," Dorrington replied, silkily, "but there you mistake. We are *not* in the same position, by a long way. You are liable to an instant criminal prosecution. I have simply come, authorised by my client, who bears all the responsibility, to demand a piece of property which you have stolen. That is the difference between our positions, Mr. Hamer. Come now, a policeman is just standing opposite. Shall I open the window and call him, or do you give in?"

"Oh, I give in, I suppose," Hamer groaned. "But you're a deal too hard. A man of your abilities shouldn't be so mean."

"That's right and reasonable," Dorrington answered briskly. "The wise man is the man who knows when he is beaten, and saves further trouble. You may not find me so mean after all, but I must have the stone first. I hold the trumps, and I'm not going to let the other player make conditions. Where's the diamond?"

"It isn't here—it's at home. You'll have to get it out of Mrs. Hamer. Shall I go and wire to her?"

"No, no," said Dorrington, "that's not the way. We'll just go together, and take Mrs. Hamer by surprise, I think. I mustn't let you out of sight, you know. Come, we'll get a hansom. Is it far?"

"Bessborough Street, Pimlico. You'll find Mrs. Hamer has a temper of her own."

"Well, well, we all have our failings. But before we start, now, observe." For a moment Dorrington was stern and menacing. "You wriggled a little at first, but that was quite natural. Now you've given in; and at the first sign of another wriggle I stop it once and for all. Understand? No tricks, now."

They entered a hansom at the door. Hamer was moody and silent at first, but under the influence of Dorrington's gay talk he opened out after a while. "Well," he said, "you're far the cleverest of the three, no doubt, and perhaps in that way you deserve to win. It's mighty smart for you to come in like this, and push Bouvier on one side and me on the other, and both of us helpless. But it's rough on me after having all the trouble."

"Don't be a bad loser, man!" Dorrington answered. "You might have had a deal more trouble and a deal more roughness too, I assure you."

"Oh yes, so I might. I'm not grumbling. But there's one thing has puzzled me all along. Where did Bouvier get that stone from?"

"He inherited it. It's the most important of the family jewels, I assure you."

"Oh, skittles! I might have known you wouldn't tell me, even if you knew yourself. But I should like to know. What sort of a duffer must it have been that let Bouvier do him for that big stone—Bouvier of all men in the world? Why, he was a record flat himself—couldn't tell a diamond from a glass marble, I should think. Why, he used to buy peddling little trays of rotters in the garden at twice their value! And then he'd sell them for what he could get. I knew very well he wasn't going on systematically dropping money like that for no reason at all. He had some axe to grind, that was plain. And after a while he got asking timid questions as to the sale of big diamonds, and how it was done, and who bought them, and all that. That put me on it at once.

All this buying and selling at a loss was a blind. He wanted to get into the trade to sell stolen diamonds, that was clear; and there was some value in them too, else he couldn't afford to waste months of time and lose money every day over it. So I kept my eye on him. I noticed, when he put his overcoat on, and thought I wasn't looking, he would settle a string of some sort round his neck, under his shirt-collar, and feel to pack up something close under his armpit.

"Then I just watched him home, and saw the sort of shanty he lived in. I mentioned these things to Mrs. H., and she was naturally indignant at the idea of a chap like Bouvier having something valuable in a dishonest way, and agreed with me that if possible it ought to be got from him, if only in the interests of virtue." Hamer laughed jerkily. "So at any rate we determined to get a look at whatever it was hanging round his neck, and we made the arrangements you know about. It seemed to me that Bouvier was pretty sure to lose it before long, one way or another, if it had any value at all, to judge by the way he was done in other matters. But I assure you I nearly fell down like Bouvier himself when I saw what it was. No wonder we left the bottle behind where I'd dropped it, after soaking the shawl—I wonder I didn't leave the shawl itself, and my hat, and everything. I assure you we sat up half last night looking at that wonderful stone!"

"No doubt. I shall have a good look at it myself, I assure you. Here is Bessborough Street. Which is the number?"

They alighted, and entered a house rather smaller than those about it. "Ask Mrs. Hamer to come here," said Hamer, gloomily, to the servant.

The men sat in the drawing-room. Presently Mrs. Hamer entered—a shortish, sharp, keen-eyed woman of forty-five. "This is Mr. Dorrington," said Hamer, "of Dorrington & Hicks, private detectives. He wants us to give him that diamond."

The little woman gave a sort of involuntary bounce, and exclaimed. "What? Diamond? What d'ye mean?"

"Oh, it's no good, Maria," Hamer answered dolefully. "I've tried it every way myself. One comfort is we're safe, as long as we give it up. Here," he added, turning to Dorrington, "show her some of your evidence—that'll convince her."

Very politely Dorrington brought forth, with full explanations, the cork and the broken glass; while Mrs. Hamer, biting hard at her thin lips, grew shinier and redder in the face every moment, and her hard grey eyes flashed fury.

"And you let this man," she burst out to her husband, when Dorrington had finished, "you let this man leave your office with these things in his possession after he had shown them to you, and you as big as he is, and bigger! Coward!"

"My dear, you don't appreciate Mr. Dorrington's forethought, hang it! I made preparations for the very line of action you recommend, but he was ready. He brought out a very well kept revolver, and he has it in his pocket now!"

Mrs. Hamer only glared, speechless with anger.

"You might just get Mr. Dorrington a whisky and soda, Maria," Hamer pursued, with a slight lift of the eyebrows which he did not intend Dorrington to see. The woman was on her feet in a moment.

"Thank you, no," interposed Dorrington, rising also, "I won't trouble you. I'd rather not drink anything just now, and, although I fear I may appear rude, I can't allow either of you to leave the room. In short," he added, "I must stay with you both till I get the diamond."

"And this man Bouvier," asked Mrs. Hamer, "what is his right to the stone?"

"Really, I don't feel competent to offer an opinion, do you know," Dorrington answered sweetly. "To tell the truth, M. Bouvier doesn't interest me very much."

"No go, Maria!" growled Hamer. "I've tried it all. The fact is we've got to give Dorrington the diamond. If we don't he'll just call in the police—then we shall lose diamond and everything else too. He doesn't care what becomes of Bouvier. He's got us, that's what it is. He won't even bargain to give us a share."

Mrs. Hamer looked quickly up. "Oh, but that's nonsense!" she said. "We've got the thing. We ought at least to say halves."

Her sharp eyes searched Dorrington's face, but there was no encouragement in it. "I am sorry to disappoint a lady," he said, "but this time it is my business to impose terms, not to submit to them. Come, the diamond!"

"Well, you'll give us something, surely?" the woman cried.

"Nothing is sure, madam, except that you will give me that diamond, or face a policeman in five minutes!"

The woman realised her helplessness. "Well," she said, "much good may it do you. You'll have to come and get it—I'm keeping it somewhere else. I'll go and get my hat."

Again Dorrington interposed. "I think we'll send your servant for the hat," he said, reaching for the bell-rope. "I'll come wherever you like, but I shall not leave you till this affair is settled, I promise you. And, as I reminded your husband a little time ago, you'll find tricks come expensive."

The servant brought Mrs. Hamer's hat and cloak, and that lady put them on, her eyes ablaze with anger. Dorrington made the pair walk before him to the front door, and followed them into the street. "Now," he said, "where is this place? Remember, no tricks!"

Mrs. Hamer turned towards Vauxhall Bridge. "It's just over by Upper Kennington Lane," she said. "Not far."

She paced out before them, Dorrington and Hamer following, the former affable and businesslike, the latter apparently a little puzzled. When they came about the middle of the bridge, the woman turned suddenly. "Come, Mr. Dorrington," she said, in a more subdued voice than she had yet used, "I give in. It's no use trying to shake you off, I can see. I have the diamond with me. Here."

She put a little old black wooden box in his hand. He made to open the lid, which fitted tightly, and at that moment the woman, pulling her other hand free from under her cloak, flung away over the parapet something that shone like fifty points of electric light.

"There it goes!" she screamed aloud, pointing with her finger. "There's your diamond, you dirty thief! You bully! Go after it now, you spy!"

The great diamond made a curve of glitter and disappeared into the river.

"THERE'S YOUR DIAMOND, YOU DIRTY THIEF!"

For the moment Dorrington lost his cool temper. He seized the woman by the arm. "Do you know what you've done, you wild cat?" he exclaimed.

"Yes, I do!" the woman screamed, almost foaming with passion, while boys began to collect, though there had been but few people on the bridge. "Yes, I do! And now you can do what you please, you thief! you bully!"

Dorrington was calm again in a moment. He shrugged his shoulders and turned away. Hamer was frightened. He came at Dorrington's side and faltered, "I—I told you she had a temper. What will you do?"

Dorrington forced a laugh. "Oh, nothing," he said. "What can I do? Locking you up now wouldn't fetch the diamond back. And besides I'm not sure that Mrs. Hamer won't attend to your punishment faithfully enough." And he walked briskly away.

"What did she do, Bill?" asked one boy of another.

"Why, didn't ye see? She chucked that man's watch in the river."

"Garn! that wasn't his watch!" interrupted a third, "it was a little glass tumbler. I see it!"

"Have you got my diamond?" asked the agonised Leon Bouvier of Dorrington a day later.

"No, I have not," Dorrington replied drily. "Nor has your cousin Jacques. But I know where it is, and you can get it as easily as I."

"Mon Dieu! Where?"

"At the bottom of the river Thames, exactly in the centre, rather to the right of Vauxhall Bridge, looking from this side. I expect it will be rediscovered in some future age, when the bed of the Thames is a diamond field."

The rest of Bouvier's savings went in the purchase of a boat, and in this, with a pail on a long rope, he was very busy for some time afterward. But he only got a great deal of mud into his boat.

THE AFFAIR OF THE "AVALANCHE BICYCLE & TYRE CO., LTD."

1

Cycle companies were in the market everywhere. Immense fortunes were being made in a few days and sometimes little fortunes were being lost to build them up. Mining shares were dull for a season, and any company with the word "cycle" or "tyre" in its title was certain to attract capital, no matter what its prospects were like in the eyes of the expert. All the old private cycle companies suddenly were offered to the public, and their proprietors, already rich men, built themselves houses on the Riviera, bought yachts, ran racehorses, and left business for ever. Sometimes the shareholders got their money's worth, sometimes more, sometimes less—sometimes they got nothing but total loss; but still the game went on. One could never open a newspaper without finding, displayed at large, the prospectus of yet another cycle company with capital expressed in six figures at least, often in seven. Solemn old dailies, into whose editorial heads no new thing ever found its way till years after it had been forgotten elsewhere, suddenly exhibited the scandalous phenomenon of "broken columns" in their advertising sections, and the universal prospectuses stretched outrageously across half or even all the page—a thing to cause apoplexy in the bodily system of any self-respecting manager of the old school.

In the midst of this excitement it chanced that the firm of Dorrington & Hicks were engaged upon an investigation for the famous and long-established "Indestructible Bicycle & Tricycle Manufacturing Company," of London and Coventry. The matter was not one of sufficient intricacy or difficulty to engage Dorrington's personal attention, and it was given to an assistant. There was some doubt as to the validity of a certain patent having reference to a particular method of tightening the spokes and truing the wheels of a tricycle, and Dorrington's assistant had to make inquiries (without attracting attention to the matter) as to whether or not there existed any evidence, either documentary or in the memory of veterans, of the use of this method, or anything like it, before the year 1885. The assistant completed his inquiries and made his report to Dorrington. Now I think I have said that, from every evidence I have seen, the chief matter of Dorrington's solicitude was his own interest, and just at this time he had heard, as had others, much of the money being made in cycle companies.

Also, like others, he had conceived a great desire to get the confidential advice of somebody "in the know"—advice which might lead him into the "good thing" desired by all the greedy who flutter about at the outside edge of the stock and share market. For this reason, Dorrington determined to make this small matter of the wheel patent an affair of personal report. He was a man of infinite resource, plausibility and good-companionship, and there was money going in the cycle trade. Why then should he lose an opportunity of making himself pleasant, in the inner groves of that trade, and catch whatever might come his way—information, syndicate shares, directorships, anything? So that Dorrington made himself master of his assistant's information, and proceeded to the head office of the "Indestructible" company on Holborn Viaduct, resolved to become the entertaining acquaintance of the managing director.

On his way his attention was attracted by a very elaborately fitted cycle shop which his recollection told him was new. "The Avalanche Bicycle & Tyre Company" was the legend gilt above the great plate-glass window, and in the window itself stood many brilliantly enamelled and plated bicycles, each labelled on the frame with the flaming red and gold transfer of the firm; and in the midst of all was another bicycle covered with dried mud, of which, however, sufficient had been carefully cleared away to expose a similar glaring transfer to those that decorated the rest—with a placard announcing that on this particular machine somebody had ridden some incredible distance on bad roads in very little more than no time at all. A crowd stood about the window; and gaped respectfully at the placard, the bicycles, the transfers and the mud, though they paid little attention to certain piles of folded white papers, endorsed in bold letters with the name of the company, with the suffix "limited" and the word "prospectus" in bloated black letter below.

These, however, Dorrington observed at once, for he had himself that morning, in common with several thousand other people, received one by post. Also half a page of his morning paper had been filled with a copy of that same prospectus, and the afternoon had brought another copy in the evening paper. In the list of directors there was a titled name or two, together with a few unknown names—doubtless the "practical men." And below this list there were such positive promises of tremendous dividends, backed up and proved beyond dispute by such ingenious piles of business-like figures, every line of figures referring to some other line for testimonials to its perfect genuineness and accuracy, that any reasonable man, it would seem, must instantly sell the hat off his head and the boots off his feet to buy one share at least, and so make his fortune for ever. True, the business was but lately established, but that was just it. It had rushed ahead with such amazing rapidity (as was natural with an avalanche) that it had got altogether out of hand, and orders couldn't be executed at all; wherefore the proprietors were reluctantly compelled to let the public have some of the luck.

This was Thursday. The share list was to be opened on Monday morning and closed inexorably at four o'clock on Tuesday afternoon, with a merciful extension to Wednesday morning for the candidates for wealth who were so unfortunate as to live in the country. So that it behoved everybody to waste no time lest he be numbered among the unlucky whose subscription-money should be returned in full, failing allotment. The prospectus did not absolutely say it in so many words, but no rational person could fail to feel that the directors were fervently hoping that nobody would get injured in the rush.

Dorrington passed on and reached the well-known establishment of the "Indestructible Bicycle Company." This was already a limited company of a private sort, and had been so for ten years or more. And before that the concern had had eight or nine years of prosperous experience. The founder of the firm, Sir Paul Mallows, was now the managing director, and a great pillar of the cycling industry. Dorrington gave a clerk his card, and asked to see Mr. Mallows.

Mr. Mallows was out, it seemed, but Mr. Stedman, the secretary, was in, and him Dorrington saw. Mr. Stedman was a pleasant, young-ish man, who had been a famous amateur bicyclist in his time, and was still an enthusiast. In ten minutes business was settled and dismissed, and Dorrington's tact had brought the secretary into a pleasant discursive chat, with much exchange of anecdote. Dorrington expressed much interest in the subject of bicycling, and, seeing that Stedman had been a racing man, particularly as to bicycling races.

"There'll be a rare good race on Saturday, I expect," Stedman said. "Or rather," he went on, "I expect the fifty miles' record will go. I fancy our man Gillett is pretty safe to win, but he'll have to move, and I quite expect to see a good set of new records on our advertisements next week. The next best man is Lant—the new fellow, you know—who rides for the 'Avalanche' people."

"Let's see, they're going to the public as a limited company, aren't they?" Dorrington asked, casually.

Stedman nodded, with a little grimace.

"You don't think it's a good thing, perhaps," Dorrington said, noticing the grimace. "Is that so?"

"Well," Stedman answered, "of course I can't say. I don't know much about the firm—nobody does, as far as I can tell—but they seem to have got a business together in almost no time; that is, if the business is as genuine as it looks at first sight. But they want a rare lot of capital, and then the prospectus—well I've seen more satisfactory ones, you know. I don't say it isn't all right, of course, but still I shan't go out of my way to recommend any friends of mine to plunge on it."

"You won't?"

"No, I won't. Though no doubt they'll get their capital, or most of it. Almost any cycle or tyre company can get subscribed just now. And this 'Avalanche' affair is both, and it is so well advertised, you know. Lant has been winning on their mounts just lately, and they've been booming it for all they're worth. By Jove, if they could only screw him up to win the fifty miles on Saturday, and beat our man Gillett, that would give them a push! Just at the correct moment too. Gillett's never been beaten yet at the distance, you know. But Lant can't do it—though, as I have said, he'll make some fast riding—it'd be a race, I tell you!"

"I should like to see it."

"Why not come? See about it, will you? And perhaps you'd like to run down to the track after dinner this evening and see our man training—awfully interesting, I can tell you, with all the pacing machinery and that. Will you come?"

Dorrington expressed himself delighted, and suggested that Stedman should dine with him before going to the track. Stedman, for his part, charmed with his new acquaintance—as everybody was at a first meeting with Dorrington—assented gladly.

At that moment the door of Stedman's room was pushed open and a well-dressed, middle-aged man, with a shaven, flabby face, appeared. "I beg pardon," he said, "I thought you were alone. I've just ripped my finger against the handle of my brougham door as I came in—the screw sticks out. Have you a piece of sticking plaster?" He extended a bleeding finger as he spoke. Stedman looked doubtfully at his desk.

"Here is some court plaster," Dorrington exclaimed, producing his pocket-book. "I always carry it—it's handier than ordinary sticking plaster. How much do you want?"

"Thanks—an inch or so."

"This is Mr. Dorrington, of Messrs. Dorrington & Hicks, Mr. Mallows," Stedman said. "Our managing director, Mr. Paul Mallows, Mr. Dorrington."

Dorrington was delighted to make Mr. Mallows' acquaintance, and he busied himself with a careful strapping of the damaged finger. Mr. Mallows had the large frame of a man of strong build who has had much hard bodily work, but there hung about it the heavier, softer flesh that told of a later period of ease and sloth. "Ah, Mr. Mallows," Stedman said, "the bicycle's the safest thing, after all! Dangerous things these broughams!"

"Ah, you younger men," Mr. Mallows replied, with a slow and rounded enunciation, "you younger men can afford to be active! We elders——"

"Can afford a brougham," Dorrington added, before the managing director began the next word. "Just so—and the bicycle does it all; wonderful thing the bicycle!"

Dorrington had not misjudged his man, and the oblique reference to his wealth flattered Mr. Hallows. Dorrington went once more through his report as to the spoke patent and then Mr. Mallows bade him goodbye.

"Good day, Mr. Dorrington, good day," he said. "I am extremely obliged by your careful personal attention to this matter of the patent. We may leave it with Mr. Stedman now, I think. Good day. I hope soon to have the pleasure of meeting you again." And with clumsy stateliness Mr. Mallow's vanished.

2

"So you don't think the 'Avalanche' good business as an investment?" Dorrington said once more as he and Stedman, after an excellent dinner, were cabbing it to the track.

"No, no," Stedman answered, "don't touch it! There's better things than that coming along presently. Perhaps I shall be able to put you in for something you know a bit later; but don't be in a hurry. As to the 'Avalanche,' even if everything else were satisfactory, there's too much 'booming' being done just now to please me. All sorts of rumours, you know, of their having something 'up their sleeve,' and so on; mysterious hints in the papers, and all that; as to something revolutionary being in hand with the 'Avalanche' people. Perhaps there is. But why they don't fetch it out in view of the public subscription for shares is more than I can understand, unless they don't want too much of a rush. And as to that well they don't look like modestly shrinking from anything of that sort up to the present."

They were at the track soon after seven but Gillett was not yet riding. Dorrington remarked that Gillett appeared to begin late.

"Well," Stedman explained, "he's one of those fellows that afternoon training doesn't seem to suit, unless it is a bit of walking exercise. He just does a few miles in the morning and a spurt or two, and then he comes on just before sunset for a fast ten or fifteen miles—that is when he is getting fit for such a race as Saturday's. Tonight will be his last spin of that length before Saturday, because tomorrow will be the day before the race. Tomorrow he'll only go a spurt or two, and rest most of the day."

They strolled about inside the track, the two highly "banked" ends whereof seemed to a near-sighted person in the centre to be solid erect walls, along the face of which the training riders skimmed, fly-fashion. Only three or four persons beside themselves were in the enclosure when they first came, but in ten minutes' time Mr. Paul Mallows came across the track.

"Why," said Stedman to Dorrington, "here's the governor! It isn't often he comes down here. But I expect he's anxious to see how Gillett's going, in view of Saturday."

"Good evening Mr. Mallows," said Dorrington. "I hope the finger's all right? Want any more plaster?"

"Good evening, good evening," responded Mr. Mallows heavily. "Thank you, the finger's not troubling me a bit." He held it up, still decorated by the black plaster. "Your plaster remains, you see—I was a little careful not to fray it too much in washing, that was all." And Mr. Mallows sat down on a light iron garden-chair (of which several stood here and there in the enclosure) and began to watch the riding.

The track was clear, and dusk was approaching when at last the great Gillett made his appearance on the track. He answered a friendly question or two put to him by Mallows and Stedman, and then, giving his coat to his trainer, swung off along the track on his bicycle, led in front by a tandem and closely attended by a triplet. In fifty yards his pace quickened, and he settled down into a swift even pace, regular as clockwork. Sometimes the tandem and sometimes the triplet went to the front, but Gillett neither checked nor heeded as, nursed by his pacers, who were directed by the trainer from the centre, he swept along mile after mile, each mile in but a few seconds over the two minutes.

"Look at the action!" exclaimed Stedman with enthusiasm. "Just watch him. Not an ounce of power wasted there! Did you ever see more regular ankle work? And did anybody ever sit a machine quite so well as that? Show me a movement anywhere above the hips!"

"Ah," said Mr. Hallows, "Gillett has a wonderful style—a wonderful style, really!"

The men in the enclosure wandered about here and there on the grass, watching Gillett's riding as one watches the performance of a great piece of art—which, indeed, was what Gillett's riding was. There were, besides Mallows, Stedman, Dorrington and the trainer, two officials of the Cyclists' Union, an amateur racing man named Sparks, the track superintendent and another man. The sky grew darker, and gloom fell about the track. The machines became invisible, and little could be seen of the riders across the ground but the row of rhythmically working, legs and the white cap that Gillett wore. The trainer had just told Stedman that there would be three fast laps and then his man would come off the track.

"Well, Mr. Stedman," said Mr. Mallows, "I think we shall be all right for Saturday."

"Rather!" answered Stedman confidently. "Gillett's going great guns, and steady as a watch!"

The pace now suddenly increased. The tandem shot once more to the front, the triplet hung on the rider's flank, and the group of swishing wheels flew round the track at a "one-fifty" gait. The spectators turned about, following the riders round the track with their eyes. And then swinging into the straight from the top bend, the tandem checked suddenly and gave a little jump. Gillett crashed into it from behind, and the triplet, failing to clear, wavered and swung, and crashed over and along the track too. All three machines and six men were involved in one complicated smash.

Everybody rushed across the grass, the trainer first. Then the cause of the disaster was seen. Lying on its side on the track, with men and bicycles piled over and against it, was one of the green painted light iron garden-chairs that had been standing in the enclosure. The triplet men were struggling to their feet, and though much cut and shaken, seemed the least hurt of the lot. One of the men of the tandem was insensible, and Gillett, who from his position had got all the worst of it, lay senseless too, badly cut and bruised, and his left arm was broken.

The trainer was cursing and tearing his hair. "If I knew; who'd done this," Stedman cried, "I'd pulp him with that chair!"

"Oh, that betting, that betting!" wailed Mr. Mallows, hopping about distractedly; "see what it leads people into doing! It can't have been an accident, can it?"

"Accident? Skittles! A man doesn't put a chair on a track in the dark and leave it there by accident. Is anybody getting away there from the outside of the track?"

"No, there's nobody. He wouldn't wait till this, he's clear off a minute ago and more. Here, Fielders! Shut the outer gate, and we'll see who's about."

But there seemed to be no suspicious character. Indeed, except for the ground-man, his boy, Gillett's trainer, and a racing man, who had just finished dressing in the pavilion, there seemed to be nobody about beyond those whom everybody had seen standing in the enclosure. But there had been ample time for anybody, standing unnoticed at the outer rails, to get across the track in the dark, just after the riders had passed, place the obstruction, and escape before the completion of the lap.

The damaged men were helped or carried into the pavilion, and the damaged machines were dragged after them. "I will give fifty pounds gladly—more, a hundred," said Mr. Mallows, excitedly, "to anybody who will find out who put that chair on the track. It might have ended in murder. Some wretched bookmaker, I suppose, who has taken too many bets on Gillett. As I've said a thousand times, betting is the curse of all sport nowadays."

"The governor excites himself a great deal about betting and bookmakers," Stedman said to Dorrington, as they walked toward the pavilion, "but, between you and me, I believe some of the 'Avalanche' people are in this. The betting bee is always in Mallows' bonnet, but as a matter of fact there's very little betting at all on cycle races, and what there is is little more than a matter of half-crowns or at most half-sovereigns on the day of the race. No bookmaker ever makes a heavy book first. Still there may be something in it this time, of course. But look at the 'Avalanche' people. With Gillett away their man can certainly win on Saturday, and if only the weather keeps fair he can almost as certainly beat the record; just at present the fifty miles is fairly easy, and it's bound to go soon. Indeed, our intention was that Gillett should pull it down on Saturday. He was a safe winner, bar accidents, and it was good odds on his altering the record, if the weather were any good at all.

"With Gillett out of it Lant is just about as certain a winner as our man would be if all were well. And there would be a boom for the 'Avalanche' company, on the very eve of the share subscription! Lant, you must know, was very second-rate till this season, but he has improved wonderfully in the last month or two, since he has been with the 'Avalanche' people. Let him win, and they can point to the machine as responsible for it all. 'Here,' they will say in effect, 'is a man who could rarely get in front, even in second-class company, till he rode an 'Avalanche.' Now he beats the world's record for fifty miles on it, and makes rings round the topmost professionals!' Why, it will be worth thousands of capital to them. Of course the subscription of capital won't hurt us, but the loss of the record may, and to have Gillett knocked out like this in the middle of the season is serious."

"Yes, I suppose with you it is more than a matter of this one race."

"Of course. And so it will be with the 'Avalanche' company. Don't you see, with Gillett probably useless for the rest of the season, Lant will have it all his own way at anything over ten miles. That'll help to boom up the shares and there'll be big profit made on trading in them. Oh, I tell you this thing seems pretty suspicious to me."

"Look here," said Dorrington, "can you borrow a light for me, and let me run over with it to the spot where the smash took place? The people have cleared into the pavilion, and I could go alone."

"Certainly. Will you have a try for the governor's hundred?"

"Well, perhaps. But any way there's no harm in doing you a good turn if I can, while I'm here. Someday perhaps you'll do me one.'

"Right You are—I'll ask Fielders, the ground-man."

A lantern was brought, and Dorrington betook himself to the spot where the iron chair still lay, while Stedman joined the rest of the crowd in the pavilion.

Dorrington minutely examined the grass within two yards of the place where the chair lay, and then, crossing the track and getting over the rails, did the same with the damp gravel that paved the outer ring. The track itself was of cement, and unimpressionable by footmarks, but nevertheless he scrutinized that with equal care, as well as the rails. Then he turned his attention to the chair. It was, as I have said, a light chair made of flat iron strip, bent to shape and riveted. It had seen good service, and its present coat of green paint was evidently far from being its original one. Also it was rusty in places, and parts had been repaired and strengthened with cross pieces secured by bolts and square nuts, some rusty and loose. It was from one of these square nuts, holding a cross-piece that stayed the back at the top, that Dorrington secured some object—it might have been a hair—which he carefully transferred to his pocket-book. This done, with one more glance round, he betook himself to the pavilion.

A surgeon had arrived, and he reported well of the chief patient. It was a simple fracture, and a healthy patient. When Dorrington entered, preparations were beginning for setting the limb. There was a sofa in the pavilion and the surgeon saw no reason for removing the patient till all was made secure.

"Found anything?" asked Stedman in a low tone of Dorrington.

Dorrington shook his head. "Not much," he answered at a whisper.

"I'll think over it later."

Dorrington asked one of the Cyclists' Union officials for the loan of a pencil, and, having made a note with it, immediately, in another part of the room, asked Sparks, the amateur, to lend him another. Stedman had told Mr. Mallows of Dorrington's late employment with the lantern, and the managing director now said quietly, "You remember what I said about rewarding anybody who discovered the perpetrator of this outrage, Mr. Dorrington? Well, I was excited at the time, but I quite hold to it. It is a shameful thing. You have been looking about the grounds, I hear. I hope you have come across something that will enable you to find something out! Nothing will please me more than to have to pay you, I'm sure."

"Well," Dorrington confessed, "I'm afraid I haven't seen anything very big in the way of a clue, Mr. Mallows; but I'll think a bit. The worst of it is, you never know who these betting men are, do you, once they get away? There are so many, and it may be anybody. Not only that, but they may bribe anybody."

"Yes, of course—there's no end to their wickedness, I'm afraid. Stedman suggests that trade rivalry may have had something to do with it. But that seems an uncharitable view, don't you think? Of course we stand very high, and there are jealousies and all that, but this is a thing I'm sure no firm would think of stooping to, for a moment. No, it's betting that is at the bottom of this, I fear. And I hope, Mr. Dorrington that you will make some attempt to find the guilty parties."

Presently Stedman spoke to Dorrington again. "Here's something that may help you," he said. "To begin with, it must have been done by someone from the outside of the track."

"Why?"

"Well, at least every probability's that way. Everybody inside was directly interested in Gillett's success, excepting the Union Officials and Sparks, who's a gentleman and quite above suspicion, as much so, in deed, as the Union officials. Of course, there was the ground-man, but he's all right, I'm sure."

"And the trainer?"

"Oh, that's altogether improbable—altogether. I was going to say——"

"And there's that other man who was standing about; I haven't heard who he was."

"Right you are. I don't know him, either. Where is he now?"

But the man had gone.

"Look here, I'll make some quiet inquiries about that man," Stedman pursued. "I forgot all about him in the excitement of the moment. I was going to say that although whoever did it could easily have got away by the gate before the smash came, he might not have liked to go that way in case of observation in passing the pavilion. In that case he could have got away (and indeed he could have got into the grounds to begin with) by way of one of those garden walls that bound the ground just by where the smash occurred. If that were so he must either live in one of the houses, or he must know somebody that does. Perhaps you might put a man to smell about along that road—it's only a short one; Chisnall Road's the name."

"Yes, yes," Dorrington responded patiently. "There might be something in that."

By this time Gillett's arm was in a starched bandage and secured by splints, and a cab was ready to take him home. Mr. Mallows took Stedman away with him, expressing a desire to talk business, and Dorrington went home by himself. He did not turn down Chisnall Road. But he walked jauntily along toward the nearest cab-stand, and once or twice he chuckled, for he saw his way to a delightfully lucrative financial operation in cycle companies, without risk of capital.

The cab gained, he called at the lodgings of two of his men assistants and gave them instant instructions. Then he packed a small bag at his rooms in Conduit Street, and at midnight was in the late fast train for Birmingham.

3

The prospectus of the "Avalanche Bicycle & Tyre Company" stated that the works were at Exeter and Birmingham. Exeter is a delightful old town, but it can scarcely be regarded as the centre of the cycle trade; neither is it in especially easy and short communication with Birmingham. It was the sort of thing that any critic anxious to pick holes in the prospectus might wonder at, and so one of Dorrington's assistants had gone by the night mail to inspect the works. It was from this man that Dorrington, in Birmingham, about noon on the day after Gillett's disaster, received this telegram—

> Works here old disused cloth-mills just out of town. Closed and empty but with big new signboard and notice that works now running are at Birmingham. Agent says only deposit paid—tenancy agreement not signed.—Farrish.

The telegram increased Dorrington's satisfaction, for he had just taken a look at the Birmingham works. They were not empty, though nearly so, nor were they large; and a man there had told him that the chief premises, where most of the work was done, were at Exeter. And the hollower the business the better prize he saw in store for himself. He had already, early in the morning, indulged in a telegram on his own account, though he had not signed it. This was how it ran—

Mallows, 58 Upper Sandown Place,
London, W.
Fear all not safe here. Run down by 10.10 train without fail.

Thus it happened that at a little later than half-past eight Dorrington's other assistant, watching the door of No. 58 Upper Sandown Place, saw a telegram delivered, and immediately afterward Mr. Paul Mallows in much haste dashed away in a cab which was called from the end of the street. The assistant followed in another. Mr. Mallows dismissed his cab at a theatrical wig-makers in Bow Street and entered. When he emerged in little more than forty minutes' time, none but a practiced watcher, who had guessed the reason of the visit, would have recognized him. He had not assumed the clumsy disguise of a false beard. He was "made up" deftly. His colour was heightened, and his face seemed thinner. There was no heavy accession of false hair, but a slight crepe-hair whisker at each side made a better and less pronounced disguise. He seemed a younger, healthier man. The watcher saw him safely off to Birmingham by the ten minutes past ten train, and then gave Dorrington note by telegraph of the guise in which Mr. Mallows was travelling.

Now this train was timed to arrive at Birmingham at one, which was the reason that Dorrington had named it in the anonymous telegram. The entrance to the "Avalanche" works was by a large gate, which was closed, but which was provided with a small door to pass a man. Within was a yard, and at a little before one o'clock Dorrington pushed open the small door, peeped and entered. Nobody was about in the yard, and what little noise could be heard came from a particular part of the building on the right. A pile of solid "export" crates stood to the left, and these Dorrington had noted at his previous call that morning as making a suitable hiding-place for temporary use. Now he slipped behind them and awaited the stroke of one. Prompt at the hour a door on the opposite side of the yard swung open, and two more and a boy emerged and climbed one after another through the little door in the big gate. Then presently another man, not a workman, but apparently a sort of overseer, came from the opposite door, which he carelessly let fall-to behind him, and he also disappeared through the little door, which he then locked. Dorrington was now alone in the sole active works of the "Avalanche Bicycle & Tyre Company, Limited."

He tried the door opposite and found it was free to open. Within he saw in a dark corner a candle which had been left burning, and opposite him a large iron enamelling oven, like an immense safe, and round about, on benches, were strewn heaps of the glaring red and gold transfer which Dorrington had observed the day before on the machines exhibited in the Holborn Viaduct window. Some of the frames had the label newly applied, and others were still plain. It would seem that the chief business of the "Avalanche Bicycle & Tyre Company, Limited," was the attaching of labels to previously nondescript machines. But there was little time to examine further, and indeed Dorrington presently heard the noise of a key in the outer gate. So he stood and waited by the enamelling oven to welcome Mr. Mallows. As the door was pushed open Dorrington advanced and bowed politely. Mallows started guiltily, but, remembering his disguise, steadied himself and asked gruffly, "Well sir, and who are you?"

"I," answered Dorrington with perfect composure, 'I am Mr. Paul Mallows—you may have heard of me in connection with the 'Indestructible Bicycle Company.'"

Mallows was altogether taken aback. But then it struck him that perhaps the detective, anxious to win the reward he had offered in the matter of the Gillett outrage, was here making inquiries in the assumed character of the man who stood, impenetrably disguised, before him. So after a pause he asked again, a little less gruffly, "And what may be your business?"

"Well," said Dorrington, "I did think of taking shares in this company. I suppose there would be no objection to the managing director of another company taking shares in this?"

"No," answered Mallows, wondering what all this was to lead to.

"Of course not; I'm sure you don't think so, eh?" Dorrington, as he spoke, looked in the other's face with a sly leer, and Mallows began to feel altogether uncomfortable. "But there's one other thing," Dorrington pursued, taking out his pocket-book, though still maintaining his leer in Mallows' face—"one other thing. And by the way, will you have another piece of court plaster now I've got it out? Don't say no.

It's a pleasure to oblige you, really." And Dorrington, his leer growing positively fiendish, tapped the side of his nose with the case of court plaster.

Mallows paled under the paint, gasped, and felt for support. Dorrington laughed pleasantly. "Come, come," he said, encouragingly, "don't be frightened. I admire your cleverness, Mr. Mallows, and I shall arrange everything pleasantly, as you will see. And as to the court plaster, if you'd rather not have it you needn't. You have another piece on now, I see. Why didn't you get them to paint it over at Clarkson's? They really did the face very well, though! And there again you were quite right. Such a man as yourself was likely to be recognised in such a place as Birmingham, and that would have been unfortunate for both of us—both of us, I assure you. . . . Man alive, don't look as though I was going to cut your throat! I'm not, I assure you. You're a smart man of business, and I happen to have spotted a little operation of yours, that's all. I shall arrange easy terms for you. . . . Pull yourself together end talk business before the men come back. Here, sit on this bench."

Mallows, staring amazedly in Dorrington's face, suffered himself to be led to a bench, and sat on it.

"Now," said Dorrington, "the first thing is a little matter of a hundred pounds. That was the reward you promised if I should discover who broke Gillett's arm last night. Well I have. Do you happen to have any notes with you? If not, make it a cheque."

"But—but—how—I mean who—who——"

"Tut, tut! Don't waste time, Mr. Mallows. Who? Why, yourself, of course. I knew all about it before I left you last night, though it wasn't quite convenient to claim the reward then, for reasons you'll under-

"TAPPED THE SIDE OF HIS NOSE WITH THE CASE."

stand presently. Come, that little hundred."

"But what—what proof have you? I'm not to be bounced like this, you know," Mr. Mallows was gathering his faculties again.

"Proof? Why, man alive, be reasonable! Suppose I have none—none at all? What difference does that make? Am I to walk out and tell your fellow directors where I have met you—here—or am I to have that hundred? More, am I to publish abroad that Mr. Paul Mallows is the moving spirit in the rotten 'Avalanche Bicycle Company'?"

"Well," Mallows answered reluctantly, "if you put it like that——"

"But I only put it like that to make you see things reasonably. As a matter of fact your connection with this new company is enough to bring your little performance with the iron chair pretty near proof. But I got at it from the other side. See here—you're much too clumsy with your fingers, Mr. Mallows. First you go and tear the tip of your middle finger opening your brougham door, and have to get court plaster from me. Then you let that court plaster get frayed at the edge, and you still keep it on. After that you execute your very successful chair operation. When the eyes of the others are following the bicycles you take the chair in the hand with the plaster on it, catching hold of it at the place where a rough, loose, square nut protrudes, and you pitch it on to the track so clumsily and nervously that the nut carries away the frayed thread of the court plaster with it.

"Here it is, you see, still in my pocket-book, where I put it last night by the light of the lantern; just a sticky black silk thread, that's all. I've only brought it to show you I'm playing a fair game with you. Of course, I might easily have got a witness before I took the thread off the nut, if I had thought you were likely to fight the matter. But I knew you were not. You can't fight, you know, with this bogus company business known to me. So that I am only shoving you this thread as an act of grace, to prove that I have stumped you with perfect fairness. And now the hundred. Here's a fountain pen, if you want one."

"Well," said Mallows glumly, "I suppose I must, then." He took the pen and wrote the cheque. Dorrington blotted it on the pad of his pocket-book and folded it away.

"So much for that!" he said. "That's just a little preliminary, you understand. We've done these little things just as a guarantee of good faith—not necessarily for publication, though you must remember that as yet there's nothing to prevent it. I've the done you a turn by finding out who upset those bicycles, as you so ardently wished me to do last night, and you've loyally fulfilled your part of the contract by paying the promised reward—though I must say that you haven't paid with all the delight and pleasure you spoke of at the time. But I'll forgive you that, and now that the little *hors d'oeuvre* is disposed of, we'll proceed to serious business."

Mallows looked uncomfortably glum.

"But you mustn't look so ashamed of yourself, you know," Dorrington said, purposely misinterpreting his glumness. "It's all business. You were disposed for a little side flutter, so to speak—a little speculation outside your regular business. Well, you mustn't be ashamed of that."

"No," Mallows observed, assuming something of his ordinarily ponderous manner; "no, of course not. It's a little speculative deal. Everybody does it, and there's a deal of money going."

"Precisely. And since everybody does it, and there is so much money going, you are only making your share."

"Of course." Mr. Mallows was almost pompous by now.

"Of course." Dorrington coughed slightly. "Well now, do you know, I am exactly the same sort of man as yourself—if you don't mind the comparison. I am disposed for a little side butter, so to speak—a little speculation outside my regular business. I also am not ashamed of it. And since everybody does it, and there is so much money going— why, I am thinking of making my share. So that we are evidently a pair, and naturally intended for each other!"

Mr. Paul Mallows here looked a little doubtful.

"See here, now," Dorrington proceeded. "I have lately taken it into my head to operate a little on the cycle share market. That was why I came round myself about that little spoke affair, instead of sending an assistant. I wanted to know somebody who understood the cycle trade, from whom I might get tips. You see I'm perfectly frank with you. Well, I have succeeded uncommonly well. And I want you to understand that I have gone every step of the way by fair work. I took nothing for granted, and I played the game fairly. When you asked me (as you had anxious reason to ask) if I had found anything, I told you there was nothing very big—and see what a little thing the thread was! Before I came away from the pavilion I made sure that you were really the only man there with black court plaster on his fingers.

"I had noticed the hands of every man but two, and I made all excuse of borrowing something, to see those. I saw your thin presence of suspecting the betting men, and I played up to it. I have had a telegraphic report on your Exeter works this morning—a deserted

637

cloth mills with nothing on it of yours but a sign-board, and only a deposit of rent paid. There they referred to the works here. Here they referred to the works there. It was very clever, really! Also I have had a telegraphic report of your make-up adventure this morning. Clarkson does it marvellously, doesn't he? And, by the way, that telegram bringing you down to Birmingham was not from your confederate here, as perhaps you fancied. It was from me. Thanks for coming so promptly. I managed to get a quiet look round here just before you arrived, and on the whole the conclusion I come to as to the 'Avalanche Bicycle & Tyre Company, Limited,' is this: A clever man, whom it gives me great pleasure to know," with a bow to Mallows, "conceives the notion of offering the public the very rottenest cycle company ever planned, and all without appearing in it himself. He finds what little capital is required, his two or three confederates help to make up a board of directors, with one or two titled guinea-pigs, who know nothing of the company and care nothing, and the rest's easy.

"A professional racing man is employed to win races and make records, on machines which have been specially made by another firm (perhaps it was the 'Indestructible,' who knows?) to a private order and afterwards decorated with the name and style of the bogus company on a transfer. For ordinary sale, bicycles of the 'trade' description are bought—so much a hundred from the factors, and put your own name on 'em. They come cheap, and they sell at a good price—the profit pays all expenses and perhaps a bit over; and by the time they all break down the company will be successfully floated, the money—the capital—will be divided, the moving spirit and his confederates will have disappeared, and the guinea-pigs will be left to stand the racket—if there is a racket. And the moving spirit will remain unsuspected, a man of account in the trade all the time! Admirable! All the work to be done at the 'works' is the sticking on of labels and a bit of enamelling. Excellent, all round! Isn't that about the size of your operations?"

"Well, yes," Mallows answered, a little reluctantly, but with something of modest pride in his manner, "that was the notion since you speak so plainly."

"And it shall be the notion. All—everything—shall be as you have planned it, with one exception, which is this. The moving spirit shall divide his plunder with me."

"You? But—but—why, I gave you a hundred just now!"

"Dear, dear! Why will you harp so much on that vulgar little hundred? That's settled and done with. That's our little personal bargain in the matter of the lamentable accident with the chair. We are now talking of bigger business—not hundreds but thousands, and not one of them, but a lot. Come now, a mind like yours should be wide enough to admit of a broad and large view of things. If I refrain from exposing this charming scheme of yours I shall be promoting a piece of scandalous robbery. Very well then, I want my promotion money, in the regular way. Can I shut my eyes and allow a piece of iniquity like this to go on unchecked, without getting anything by way of damages for myself? Perish the thought! When all expenses are paid, and the confederates are sent off with as little as they will take, you and I will divide fairly, Mr. Mallows, respectable brothers in rascality.

"Mind, I might say we'd divide to begin with; and leave you to pay expenses, but I am always fair to a partner in anything of this sort. I shall just want a little guarantee, you know—it's safest in such matters as these; say a bill at six months for ten thousand pounds—which is very low. When a satisfactory division is made you shall have the bill back. Come—I have a bill-stamp ready being so much convinced of your reasonableness as to buy it this morning, though it cost five pounds."

"But that's nonsense—you're trying to impose. I'll give you any-thing reasonable—half is out of the question. What, after all the trou-ble and worry and risk that I've had——"

"Which would suffice for no more than to put you in gaol if I held up my finger!"

"But, hang it, be reasonable! You're a mighty clever man, and you've got me on the hip, as I admit. Say ten *per cent.*"

"You're wasting time, and presently the men will be back. Your choice is between making half, or making none, and going to gaol into the bargain. Choose!"

"But just consider——"

"Choose!"

Mallows looked despairingly about him. "But really," he said, "I want the money more than you think. I——"

"For the last time—choose!"

Mallows' despairing gaze stopped at the enamelling oven. "Well, well," he said, "if I most, I must, I suppose. But I warn you you may regret it."

"Oh dear no, I'm not so pessimistic. Come, you wrote a cheque—now I'll write the bill. 'Six months after date, pay to me or my order the sum of ten thousand pounds for value received'—excellent value too, I think. There you are!"

When the bill was written and signed Mallows scribbled his acceptance with more readiness than might have been expected. Then he rose, and said with something of brisk cheerfulness in his tone, "Well, that's done, and the least said the soonest mended. You've won it, and I won't grumble any more. I think I've done this thing pretty neatly, eh? Come and see the 'works.'"

Every other part of the place was empty of machinery. There were a good many finished frames and wheels, bought separately, and now in course of being fitted together for sale, and there were many more complete bicycles of cheap but showy make to which nothing needed to be done but to fix the red and gold "transfer" of the "Avalanche" company. Then Mallows opened the tall iron door of the enamelling oven.

"See this," he said, "this is the enamelling oven. Get in and look round. The frames and other different parts hang on the racks after the enamel is laid on, and all those gas jets are lighted to harden it by heat. Do you see that deeper part there by the back?—go closer."

Dorrington felt a push at his back and the door was swung to with a bang, and the latch dropped. He was in the dark, trapped in a great iron chamber. And instantly Dorrington's nostrils were filled with the smell of escaping gas. He realised his peril on the instant. Mallows had given him the bill with the idea of silencing him by murder and recovering it. He had pushed him into the oven and had turned on the gas. It was dark, but to light a match would mean death instantly, and without the match it must be death by suffocation and poison of gas in a very few minutes. To appeal to Hallow was useless—Dorrington knew too much. It would seem that at last a horribly-fitting retribution had overtaken Dorrington in death by a mode parallel to that which he and his creatures had prepared for others.

Dorrington's victims had drowned in water—or at least Crofton's had, for I never ascertained definitely whether anybody had met his death by the tank after the Croftons had taken service with Dorrington—and now Dorrington himself was to drown in gas. The oven was of sheet iron, fastened by a latch in the centre. Dorrington flung himself desperately against the door, and it gave outwardly at the extreme bottom. He snatched a loose angle-iron with which his hand came in contact, dashed against the door once more, and thrust the iron through where it strained open. Then, with another tremendous plunge, he drove the door a little more outward and raised the angle-iron in the crack; then once more, and raised it again. He was near to losing his senses, when, with one more plunge the catch of the latch, not designed for such treatment, suddenly gave way, the door flew open, and Dorrington, blue in the face, staring, stumbling and gasping, came staggering out into the fresher air, followed by a gush of gas.

Mallows had retreated to the rooms behind, and thither Dorrington followed him, gaining vigour and fury at every step. At sight of him the wretched Mallows sank in a corner, sighing and shivering with terror. Dorrington hauled the struggling wretch across the room, tearing off the crepe whiskers as he came, while Mallows supplicated and whined, fearing that it might be the other's design to imprison him in the enamelling oven. But at the door of the room against that containing the oven their progress came to an end, for the escaped gas had reached the lighted candle, and with one loud report the partition wall fell in, half burying Mallows where he lay, and knocking Dorrington over.

Windows fell out of the building, and men broke through the front gate, climbed into the ruined rooms and stopped the still escaping gas. When the two men and the boy returned, with the conspirator who had been in charge of the works, they found a crowd from the hardware and cycle factories thereabout, surveying with great interest the spectacle of the extrication of Mr. Paul Mallows, managing director of the "Indestructible Bicycle Company," from the broken bricks, mor-

"DORRINGTON HAULED THE STRUGGLING WRETCH ACROSS THE ROOM."

tar, bicycles and transfers of the "Avalanche Bicycle & Tyre Company, Limited," and the preparations for carrying him to a surgeon's where his broken leg might be set. And in a couple of hours it was all over Birmingham, and spreading to other places, that the business of the "Avalanche Bicycle & Tyre Company" consisted of sticking brilliant labels on factors' bicycles, bought in batches. So that when, next day, Lant won the fifty miles race in London, he was greeted with ironical shouts of "Gum on yer transfer!" "Hi! mind yer label!" "Where did you steal that bicycle?" "Sold yer shares?" and so forth.

Somehow the "Avalanche Bicycle & Tyre Company, Limited," never went to allotment. It was found politic, also, that Mr. Paul Mallows should retire from the directorate of the "Indestructible Bicycle Company."

As for Dorrington, he had his hundred pounds reward. But the bill for £10,000 he never presented. Why, I do not altogether know, unless he found that Mr. Mallows' financial position, as he had hinted, was not altogether so good as was supposed.

The Case of Mr. Loftus Deacon

1

This was a case that helped to give Dorrington much of that reputation which unfortunately too often enabled him to profit himself far beyond the extent to which his clients intended. It occurred some few years back, and there was such a stir at the time over the mysterious death of Mr. Loftus Deacon that it well paid Dorrington to use his utmost diligence in an honest effort to uncover the mystery. It gave him one of his best advertisements, though indeed it occasioned him less trouble in the unravelling than many a less interesting case. There were scarcely any memoranda of the affair among Dorrington's papers, beyond entries of fees paid, and I have almost entirely relied upon the account given me by Mr. Stone, manager in the employ of the firm owning the premises in which Mr. Deacon died.

These premises consisted of a large building let out in expensive flats, one of the first places built with that design in the West-End of London. The building was one of three, all belonging to the firm I have mentioned, and numbered 1, 2 and 3, Bedford Mansions. They stood in the St. James's district, and Mr. Loftus Deacon's quarters were in No. 2.

Mr. Deacon's magnificent collection of oriental porcelain will be remembered as long as any in the national depositories; much of it was for a long while lent, and, by Mr. Deacon's will, passed permanently into possession of the nation. His collection of oriental arms, however, was broken up and sold, as were also his other innumerable objects of Eastern art—lacquers, carvings, and so forth. He was a wealthy man, this Mr. Deacon, a bachelor of sixty, and his whole life was given to his collections. He was currently reported to spend some £15,000 a year on them, and, in addition, would make inroads into capital for special purchases at the great sales. People wondered where all the things were kept. And indeed they had reason, for Mr. Deacon's personal establishment was but a suite of rooms on the ground floor of Bedford Mansions. But the bulk of the collections were housed at various museums—indeed it was a matter of banter among his acquaintances that Mr. Loftus Deacon made the taxpayers warehouse most of his things; moreover, the flat was a large one—it occupied almost the whole of the ground-floor of the building, and it overflowed with the choicest of its tenant's possessions.

There were eight large and lofty rooms, as well as the lobby, scullery and so forth, and every one was full. The walls were hung with the most precious *kakemono* and *nishikiyi* of Japan; and glass cabinets stood everywhere, packed with porcelain and faience—celadon, peach-bloom, and blue and white, Satsuma, Raku, Ninsei, and Arita—many a small piece worth its weight in gold over and over and over again. At places on the wall, among the *kakemono* and pictures of the *ukioye,* were trophies of arms. Two suits of ancient Japanese armour, each complete and each the production of one of the most eminent of the Miochin family, were exhibited on stands, and swords stood in many corners and lay in many racks. Innumerable drawers contained specimens of the greatest lacquer ware of Korin, Shunsho, Kajikawa, Koyetsu, and Ritsuo, each in its wadded brocade *fukusa* with the light wooden box encasing all.

In more glass cabinets stood *netsuke* and *okimono* of ivory, bronze, wood, and lacquer. There were a few gods and goddesses, and conspicuous among them two life-sized gilt Buddhas beamed mildly over all from the shelves on which they were raised. By the operation of natural selection, it came about that the choicest of all Mr. Deacon's possessions were collected in these rooms. Here were none of the great cumbersome pots, good in their way, but made of old time merely for the European market. Of all that was Japanese every piece was of the best and rarest, consequently, in almost every case, of small dimensions, as is the way of the greatest of the wares of old Japan. And of all the precious contents of these rooms everything was oriental in its origin except the contents of one case, which displayed specimens of the most magnificent goldsmiths' and silversmiths' work of medieval Europe. It stood in the room which Mr. Loftus Deacon used as his sitting-room, and more than one of his visitors had wondered that such valuable property was not kept at a banker's.

This view, however, always surprised and irritated Mr. Deacon. "Keep it at a banker's?" he would say. "Why not melt it down at once? The things are works of art, things of beauty, and that's why I have them, not merely because they're gold and silver. To shut them up in a strong-room would be the next thing to destroying them altogether. Why not lock the whole of my collections in safes, and never look at them? They are all valuable. But if they are not to be seen I would rather have the money they cost." So the gold and silver stood in its case, to the blinking wonderment of messengers and porters whose errands took them into Mr. Loftus Deacon's sitting-room. The contents of this case were the only occasion, however, of Mr. Deacon's straying from oriental paths in building up his collection. There they stood, but he made no attempt to add to them. He went about his daily hunting, bargaining, cataloguing, cleaning, and exhibiting to friends, but all his new treasures were from the East, and most were Japanese.

His chief visitors were travelling buyers of curiosities; little Japanese who had come to England to study medicine and were paying their terms by the sale of heirlooms in pottery and lacquer; porters from Christie's and Poster's; and sometimes men from Copleston's—the odd emporium by the riverside where lions and monkeys, porcelain and savage weapons were bought and sold close by the ships that brought them home. The travellers were suspicious and cunning; the Japanese were bright, polite, and dignified, and the men from Copleston's were wiry, hairy and amphibious; one was an enormously muscular little hunchback nicknamed Slackjaw—a quaint and rather repulsive compound of showman, sailor and half-caste rough; and all were like mermen, more or less. These curious people came and went, and Mr. Deacon went on buying, cataloguing, and joying in his possessions. It was the happiest possible life for a lonely old man with his tastes and his means of gratifying them, and it went placidly on till one Wednesday mid-day. Then Mr. Deacon was found dead in his rooms in most extraordinary and, it seemed, altogether unaccountable circumstances.

There was but one door leading into Mr. Deacon's rooms from

the open corridor of the building, and this was immediately opposite the large street door. When one entered from the street one ascended three or four broad marble steps, pushed open one of a pair of glazed swing doors and found oneself facing the door by which Mr. Deacon entered and left his quarters. There had originally been other doors into the corridor from some of the rooms, but those Mr. Deacon had had blocked up, so making the flat entirely self-contained. Just by the glazed swing doors which I have spoken of, and in full view of the old gentleman's door, the hall-porter's box stood.

It was glazed on all sides, and the porter sat so that Mr. Deacon's door was always before his eyes, and, so long as he was there, it was very unlikely that anybody or anything could leave or enter by that door unobserved by him. It is important to remember this, in view of what happened on the occasion I am writing of. There was one other exterior door to Mr. Deacon's flat, and one only. It gave upon the back spiral staircase, and was usually kept locked. This staircase had no outlet to the corridors, but merely extended from the housekeeper's rooms at the top of the building to the basement. It was little used, and then only by servants, for it gave access only to the rooms on its own side. There was no way from this staircase to the outer street except through the private rooms of the tenants, or through those of the housekeeper.

That Wednesday morning things had happened precisely in the ordinary way. Mr. Deacon had risen and breakfasted as usual. He was alone, with his newspaper and his morning letters, when his breakfast was taken in and when it was removed. He had remained in his rooms till between twelve and one o'clock. Goods had arrived for him (this was an almost daily occurrence), and one or two ordinary visitors had called and gone away again. It was Mr. Deacon's habit to lunch at his club, and at about a quarter to one, or thereabout, he had come out, locked his door, and leaving his usual message that he should be at the club for an hour or two, in case anybody called, he had left the building. At about one, however, he had returned hurriedly, having forgotten some letters. "I didn't give you any letters for the post, did I, Beard, before I went out?" he asked the porter. And the porter replied that he had not. Mr. Deacon thereupon crossed the corridor, entered his door, and shut it behind him.

He had been gone but a few seconds, when there arose an outcry from within the rooms—a shout followed in a breath by a loud cry of pain, and then silence. Beard, the porter, ran to the door and knocked,

645

but there was no reply. "Did you call, sir?" he shouted, and knocked again, but still without response. The door was shut, and it had a latch lock with no exterior handle. Beard, who had had an uncle die of apoplexy, was now thoroughly alarmed, and shouted up the speaking-tube for the housekeeper's keys. In course of a few minutes they were brought, and Beard and the housekeeper entered.

The lobby was as usual, and the sitting-room was in perfect order. But in the room beyond Mr. Loftus Deacon lay in a pool of blood, with two large and fearful gashes in his head. Not a soul was in any of the rooms, though the two men, first shutting the outer door, searched diligently. All windows and doors were shut, and the rooms were ten-antless and undisturbed, except that on the floor lay Mr. Deacon in his blood at the foot of a pedestal whereupon there squatted, with serenely fierce grin, the god Hachiman, gilt and painted, carrying in one of his four hands a snake, in another a mace, in a third a small human figure, and in the fourth a heavy, straight, guardless sword; and all around furniture, cabinets, porcelain, lacquer and everything else lay undisturbed.

At first sight of the tragedy the porter had sent the lift-man for the police, and soon they arrived, and a surgeon with them. For the surgeon there was very little to do. Mr. Deacon was dead. Either of the two frightful gashes in the head would have been fatal, and they had obviously both been delivered with the same instrument—something

"MR. LOFTUS DEACON LAY IN A POOL OF BLOOD"

heavy and exceedingly sharp.

The police now set themselves to close investigation. The porter was certain that nobody had entered the rooms that morning who had not afterwards left. He was sure that nobody had entered unobserved, and he was sure that Mr. Deacon had re-entered his chambers unaccompanied. Working, therefore, on the assumption that the murderer could not have entered by the front door, the police turned their attention to the back door and the windows. The door to the back staircase was locked, and the key was in the lock and inside. Therefore, they considered the windows. There were but three of these that looked upon the street, two in one room and one in another, but these were shut and fastened within. Other rooms were lighted by windows looking upon lighting-wells, some being supplied with reflectors. All these windows were found to be quite undisturbed, and fastened within, except one.

This window was in the bedroom, and, though it was shut, the catch was not fastened. The porter declared that it was Mr. Deacon's practice invariably to fasten every shut window, a thing he was always very careful about. Moreover, the window now found unfastened and shut was always left open a foot or so all day, to air the bedroom. More, a housemaid was brought who had that morning made the bed and dusted the room. The window was opened, she said, when she had entered the room, and she had left it so, as she always did. Therefore, shut as it was, but not fastened, it seemed plain that this window must have given exit to the murderer, since no other way appeared possible. Also, to shut the window behind him would be the fugitive's natural policy. The lower panes were of ground glass, and at least pursuit would be delayed.

The window looked upon a lighting-well, and the concreted floor of the basement was but fifteen or twenty feet below. Careful inquiries disclosed the fact that a man had been at work painting the joinery about this well-bottom. He was a man of very indifferent character—had in fact "done time"—and he was employed for odd jobs by way of charity, being some sort of connection of a member of the firm owning the buildings. He had, indeed, received a good education, fitted to place him in a very different position from that in which he now found himself, but he was a black sheep. He drank, he gambled, and finally he stole. His relatives helped him again and again, but their efforts were useless, and now he was indebted to one of them for his present occupation at a pound a week. The police, of course, knew something of him, and postponed questioning him directly until they had investigated a little further. It might be that Mr. Deacon's death was the work of a conspiracy wherein more than one had participated.

2

The next morning (Thursday) Mr. Henry Colson was an early caller at Dorrington's office. Mr. Colson was a thin, grizzled man of sixty or thereabout, who had been a close friend—the only intimate friend, indeed—of Mr. Loftus Deacon. He was a widower, and he lived in rooms scarce two hundred yards distant from Bedford Mansions, where his friend had died.

"My business, Mr. Dorrington," he said, "is in connection with the terrible death of my old friend Mr. Loftus Deacon, of which you no doubt have heard or read in the morning papers."

"Yes," Dorrington assented, "both in this morning's papers and the evening papers of yesterday."

"Very good. I may tell you that I am sole executor under Mr. Deacon's will. The will indeed is in my possession (I am a retired solicitor), and there happens to be a sum set apart in that will out of which I am to defray any expenses that may arise in connection with his death. It really seems to me that I should be quite justified in using some part of that sum in paying for inquiries to be conducted by such an experienced man as yourself, into the cause of my poor friend's death. At any rate, I wish you to make such inquiries, even if I have to pay the fees myself. I am convinced that there is something very extraordinary—something very deep—in the tragedy. The police are pottering about, of course, and keeping very mysterious as to the matter, but I expect that's simply because they know nothing. They have made no arrest, and perhaps every minute of delay is making the thing more difficult. As executor, of course, I have access to the rooms. Can you come and look at them now?"

"Oh yes," Dorrington answered, reaching for his hat. "I suppose there's no doubt of the case being one of murder? Suicide is not likely, I take it?"

"Oh no—certainly not. He was scarcely the sort of man to commit suicide, I should say. And he was as cheerful as he could be the afternoon before, when I last saw him . . . Besides, the surgeon says it's nothing of the kind. A man committing suicide doesn't gash himself twice over the head, or even once. And in this case the first blow would have made him incapable of another."

"I have heard nothing about the weapon," Dorrington remarked, as they entered a cab. "Has it been found?"

"That's a difficulty," Mr. Colson answered. "It would seem not. Of course there are numbers of weapons about the place—Japanese swords and what not—any one of which *might* have caused such injuries. But there are no bloodstains on any of them."

"Is any article of value missing?"

"I believe not. Everything seemed to be in its place, so far as I noticed yesterday. But then I was not there long, and was too much agitated to notice very particularly. At any rate the old gold and silver plate had not been disturbed. He kept that in a large case in his sitting-room, and it would certainly be the plate that the murderer would have made for first, if robbery had been his object."

Mr. Colson gave Dorrington the other details of the case, already set forth in this account, and presently the cab stopped before No. 2, Bedford Mansions. The body, of course, had been removed, but otherwise the rooms had not been disturbed. The porter let them into the chambers by aid of the housekeeper's key.

"They don't seem to have found his keys," Mr. Colson explained, "and that will be troublesome for me, I expect, presently. He usually carried them with him, but they were not on the body when found."

"That may be important," Dorrington said. "But let us look at the rooms."

They walked through the large apartments one after the other, and Dorrington glanced casually about him as he went. Presently Mr. Colson stopped, struck with an idea. "Ah!" he said, more to himself than to Dorrington. "I will just see."

He turned quickly back into the room they had just quitted, and made for the broad shelf that ran the length of the wall at about the height of an ordinary table. "Yes!" he cried. "It is! It's gone!"

"What is gone?"

"The sword—the Masamune!"

The whole surface of the shelf, covered with a silk cloth, was occupied by Japanese swords and dirks with rich mountings. Most lay on their sides in rows, but two or three were placed in the lacquered racks. Mr. Colson stood and pointed at a rack which was standing alone and swordless. "That is where it was," he said. "I saw it—was talking about it, in fact—the afternoon before. No, it's nowhere about. It's not like any of the others. Let me see." And Mr. Colson, much excited, hurried from room to room wherever swords were kept, searching for the missing specimen.

"No," he said at last, looking strangely startled. "It's gone. And I think we are near the soul of the mystery." He spoke in hushed, uneasy tones, and his eyes gave token of strange apprehension.

"What is it?" Dorrington asked. "What about this sword?"

"Come into the sitting-room." Mr. Colson led Dorrington away from the scene of Mr. Deacon's end, away from the empty sword rack and from under the shadow of the grinning god with its four arms, its snake, and its threatening sword. "I don't think I'm very superstitious," Mr. Colson proceeded, "but I really feel that I can talk more freely about the matter in here."

They sat at the table, over against the case of plate, and Mr. Colson went on. "The sword I speak of," he said, "was much prized by my poor friend, who brought it with him from Japan nearly twenty years back—not many years after the civil war there, in fact. It was a very ancient specimen—of the fourteenth century, I think—and the work of the famous swordsmith Masamune. Masamune's work is very rarely met with, it seems, and Mr. Deacon felt himself especially fortunate in securing this example. It is the only piece of Masamune's work in the collection. I may tell you that a sword by one of the great old masters is one of the rarest of all the rarities that come from Japan. The possessors of the best keep them rather than sell them at any price. Such swords were handed down from father to son for many generations, and a Japanese of the old school would have been disgraced had he parted with his father's blade even under the most pressing necessity. The mounts he might possibly sell, if he were in very bad circumstances, but the blade never.

"Of course, such a thing *has* occurred—and it occurred in this very case, as you shall hear. But as an almost invariable rule the Japanese *samurai* would part with his life by starvation rather than with his father's sword by sale. Such swords would never be stolen, either, for there was a firm belief that a faithful spirit resided in each, which would bring terrible disaster on any wrongful possessor. Each sword had its own name, just as the legendary sword of King Arthur had, and a man's social standing was judged, not by his house nor by his dress, but by the two swords in his girdle. The ancient sword-smiths wore court dress and made votive offerings when they forged their best blades, and the gods were supposed to assist and to watch over the career of the weapon. Thus you will understand that such an article was apt to become an object almost of worship among the *samurai* or warrior-class in Old Japan. And now to come to the sword in question. It was a long sword or *katana* (the swords, as you know, were worn in pairs, and the smaller was called the *wakizashi*), and it was mounted very handsomely with fittings by a great metal worker of the Goto family.

"The signature of the great Masamune himself was engraved in the usual place—on the iron tang within the hilt. Mr. Deacon bought the weapon of its possessor, a man of some distinction before the overthrow of the Shogun in 1868, but who was reduced to deep poverty by the change in affairs. Mr. Deacon came across him in his direst straits, when his children were near to starvation, and the man sold the sword for a sum that was a little fortune to him, though it only represented some four or five pounds of our money. Mr. Deacon was always very proud of his treasure—indeed it was said to be the only blade by Masamune in Europe; and the two Japanese things that he had always most longed for, I have heard him say, were a Masamune sword and a piece of violet lacquer—that precious lacquer the secret of making which died long ago. The Masamune he acquired, as I have been telling you, but the violet lacquer he never once encountered.

"Six months or so back, Deacon received a visit from a Japanese—taller than usual for a Japanese (I have seen him myself) and with the refined type of face characteristic of some of the higher class of his country. His name was Keigo Kanamaro, his card said, and he introduced himself as the son of Keigo Kiyotaki, the man who had sold Deacon his sword. He had come to England and had found my friend after much inquiry, he said, expressly to take back his father's *katana*. His father was dead, and he desired to place the sword in his tomb, that the soul of the old man might rest in peace, undisturbed by the disgrace that had fallen upon him by the sale of the sword that had been his and his ancestors' for hundreds of years back. The father had vowed when he had received the sword in his turn from Kanamaro's grandfather, never to part with it, but had broken his vow under pressure of want. He (the son) had earned money as a merchant (an immeasurable descent for a *samurai* with the feelings of the old school), and he was prepared to buy back the Masamune blade with the Goto mountings for a much higher price than his father had received for it."

"And I suppose Deacon wouldn't sell it?" Dorrington asked.

"No," Mr. Colson replied. "He wouldn't have sold it at any price, I'm sure. Well, Kanamaro pressed him very urgently, and called again and again. He was very gentlemanly and very dignified, but he was very earnest. He apologised for making a commercial offer, assured Deacon that he was quite aware that he was no mere buyer and seller, but pleaded the urgency of his case. 'It is not here as in Japan,' he said, 'among us, the *samurai* of the old days. You have your beliefs, we have ours. It is my religion that I must place the *katana* in my father's grave. My father disgraced himself and sold his sword in order that I might not starve when I was a little child. I would rather that he had let me die, but since I am alive, and I know that you have the sword, I must take it and lay it by his bones. I will make an offer. Instead of giving you money, I will give you another sword—a sword worth as much money as my father's—perhaps more. I have had it sent from Japan since I first saw you. It is a blade made by the great Yukiyasu, and it has a scabbard and mountings by an older and greater master than the Goto who made those for my father's sword.'

"But it happened that Deacon already had two swords by Yukiyasu, while of Masamune he had only the one. So he tried to reason the Japanese out of his fancy. But that was useless. Kanamaro called again and again and got to be quite a nuisance. He left off for a month or two, but about a fortnight ago he appeared again. He grew angry and forgot his oriental politeness. 'The English have the English ways,' he said, 'and we have ours—yes, though many of my foolish countrymen are in haste to be the same as the English are. We have our beliefs, and we have our knowledge, and I tell you that there are things which you would call superstition, but which are very real! Our old gods are not all dead yet, I tell you! In the old times no man would wear or keep another man's sword. Why? Because the great sword has a soul just as a man has, and it knows and the gods know! No man kept another's sword who did not fall into terrible misfortune and death, sooner or later. Give me my father's *katana* and save yourself.

"'My father weeps in my ears at night, and I must bring him his *katana!*' I was talking to poor Deacon, as I told you, only on Tuesday afternoon, and he told me that Kanamaro had been there again the day before, in a frantic state—so bad, indeed, that Deacon thought of applying to the Japanese legation to have him taken care of, for he seemed quite mad. 'Mind, you foolish man!' he said. 'My gods still live, and they are strong! My father wanders on the dark path and cannot go to his gods without the swords in his girdle. His father asks of his vow! Between here and Japan there is a great sea, but my father may walk even here, looking for his *katana,* and he is angry! I go away for a little. But my gods know, and my father knows!' And then he took

himself off. And now"—Mr. Colson nodded towards the next room and dropped his voice—"now poor Deacon is dead and the sword is gone!"

"Kanamaro has not been seen about the place, I suppose, since the visit you speak of, on Monday?" Dorrington asked.

"No. And I particularly asked as to yesterday morning. The hall-porter swears that no Japanese came to the place."

"As to the letters, now. You say that when Mr. Deacon came back, after having left, apparently to get his lunch, he said he came for forgotten letters. Were any such letters afterwards found?"

"Yes—there were three, lying on this very table, stamped ready for postage."

"Where are they now?"

"I have them at my chambers. I opened them in the presence of the police in charge of the case. There was nothing very important about them—appointments and so forth, merely—and so the police left them in my charge, as executor."

"Nevertheless I should like to see them. Not just now, but present-ly. I think I must see this man presently—the man who was painting in the basement below the window that is supposed to have been shut by the murderer in his escape. That is if the police haven't frightened him."

"Very well, we'll see after him as soon as you like. There was just

653

one other thing—rather a curious coincidence, though of course there can't be anything in such a superstitious fancy—but I think I told you that Deacon's body was found lying at the feet of the four-handed god in the other room?"

"Yes."

"Just so." Mr. Colson seemed to think a little more of the superstitious fancy than he confessed. "Just so," he said again. "At the feet of the god, and immediately under the hand carrying the sword; it is not wooden, but an actual steel sword, in fact."

"I noticed that."

"Yes. Now that is a figure of Hachiman, the Japanese god of war—a recent addition to the collection and a very ancient specimen. Deacon bought it at Copleston's only a few days ago—indeed it arrived here on Wednesday morning. Deacon was telling me about it on Tuesday afternoon. He bought it because of its extraordinary design, showing such signs of Indian influence. Hachiman is usually represented with no more than the usual number of a man's arms, and with no weapon but a sword. This is the only image of Hachiman that Deacon ever saw or heard of with four arms. And after he had bought it he ascertained that this was said to be one of the idols that carry with them ill-luck from the moment they leave their temples.

"One of Copleston's men confided to Deacon that the *lascar* seamen and stokers on board the ship that brought it over swore that everything went wrong from the moment that Hachiman came on board—and indeed the vessel was nearly lost off Finisterre. And Copleston himself, the man said, was glad to be quit of it. Things had disappeared in the most extraordinary and unaccountable manner, and other things had been found smashed (notably a large porcelain vase) without any human agency, after standing near the figure. Well," Mr. Colson concluded, "after all that, and remembering what Kanamaro said about the gods of his country who watch over ancient swords, it *does* seem odd, doesn't it, that as soon as poor Deacon gets the thing he should be found stricken dead at its feet?"

Dorrington was thinking. "Yes," he said presently, "it is certainly a strange affair altogether. Let us see the odd-job man now—the man who was in the basement below the window. Or rather, find out where he is and leave me to find him."

Mr. Colson stepped out and spoke with the hall-porter. Presently he returned with news. "He's gone!" he said. "Bolted!"

"What—the man who was in the basement?"

"Yes. It seems the police questioned him pretty closely yesterday, and he seized the first opportunity to cut and run."

"Do you know what they asked him?"

"Examined him generally, I suppose, as to what he had observed at the time. The only thing he seems to have said was that he heard a window shut at about one o'clock. Questioned further, he got into confusion and equivocation, more especially when they mentioned a ladder which is kept in a passage close by where he was painting. It seems they had examined this before speaking to him, and found it had been just recently removed and put back. It was thick with dust, except just where it had been taken hold of to shift, and there the hand-marks were quite clean. Nobody was in the basement but Dowden (that is the man's name), and nobody else could have shifted that ladder without his hearing and knowing of it. Moreover, the ladder was just the length to reach Deacon's window. They asked if he had seen anybody move the ladder, and he most anxiously and vehemently declared that he had not. A little while after he was missing) and he hasn't reappeared."

"And they let him go!" Dorrington exclaimed. "What fools!"

"He *may* know something about it, of course," Colson said dubiously; "but with that sword missing, and knowing what we do of Kanamaro's anxiety to get it at any cost, and—and"—he glanced toward the other room where the idol stood—"and one thing and another, it seems to me we should look in another direction."

"We will look in all directions," Dorrington replied. "Kanamaro may have enlisted Dowden's help. Do you know where to find Kanamaro?"

"Yes. Deacon has had letters from him, which I have seen. He lived in lodgings near the British Museum."

"Very well. Now, do you happen to know whether a night porter is kept at this place?"

"No, there is none. The outer door is shut at twelve. Anybody coming home after that must ring up the housekeeper by the electric bell."

"The tenants do not have keys for the outer door?"

"No; none but keys for their own rooms."

"Good. Now, Mr. Colson, I want to think things over a little. Would you care to go at once and ascertain whether or not Kanamaro is still at the address you speak of?"

"Certainly, I will. Perhaps I should have told you that, though he knows me slightly, he has never spoken of his father's sword to me, and does not know that I know anything about it. He seems, indeed, to have spoken about it to nobody but Deacon himself. He was very proud and reticent in the matter; and now that Deacon is dead, he probably thinks nobody alive knows of the matter of the sword but himself. If he is at home what shall I do?"

"In that case keep him in sight and communicate with me, or with the police. I shall stay here for a little while. Then I shall get the hall-porter (if you will instruct him before you go) to show me the ladder and the vicinity of Dowden's operations. Also, I think I shall look at the back staircase."

"But that was found locked, with the key inside."

"Well, well, there *are* ways of managing that, as you would know if you knew as much about housebreaking as I do. But we'll see."

3

Mr. Colson took a cab for Kanamaro's lodgings. Kanamaro was not in, he found, and he had given notice to leave his rooms. The servant at the door thought that he was going abroad, since his boxes were being packed, apparently for that purpose. The servant did not know at what time he would be back.

Mr. Colson thought for a moment of reporting these facts at once to Dorrington, but on second thoughts he determined to hurry to the City and make inquiry at some of the shipping offices as to the vessels soon to leave for Japan. On the way, however, he bethought him to buy a shipping paper and gather his information from that. He found what he wanted from the paper, but he kept the cab on its way, for he happened to know a man in authority at the Anglo-Malay Company's office, and it might be a good thing to take a look at their passenger list. Their next ship for Yokohama was to sail in a few days.

But he found it unnecessary to see the passenger list. As he entered one of the row of swing doors which gave access to the large general and inquiry office of the steamship company, he perceived Keigo Kanamaro leaving by another. Kanamaro had not seen him. Mr. Colson hesitated for a moment, and then turned and followed him.

And now Mr. Colson became suddenly seized with a burning fancy to play the subtle detective on his own account. Plainly Kanamaro feared nothing, walking about thus openly, and taking his passage for Japan at the chief office of the first line of steamships that anybody would think of who contemplated a voyage to Japan, instead of leaving the country, as he might have done, by some indirect route, and shipping for Japan from a foreign port. Doubtless, he still supposed that nobody knew of his errand in search of his father's sword. Mr. Colson quickened his pace and came up beside the Japanese.

Kanamaro was a well-made man of some five feet eight or nine—remarkably tall for a native of Dai Nippon. His cheek-bones had not the prominence noticeable in the Japanese of the lower classes, and his pale oval face and aquiline nose gave token of high *sikozu* family. His hair only was of the coarse black that is seen on the heads of all Japanese. He perceived Mr. Colson, and stopped at once with a grave bow.

"Good morning," Mr. Colson said. "I saw you leaving the steamship office, and wondered whether or not you were going to leave us."

"Yes—I go home to Japan by the next departing ship," Kanamaro answered. He spoke with an excellent pronunciation, but with the intonation and the suppression of short syllables peculiar to his countrymen who speak English. "My beesness is finished."

Mr. Colson's suspicions were more than strengthened—almost confirmed. He commanded his features, however, and replied, as he walked by Keigo's side, "Ah! your visit has been successful, then?"

"It has been successful," Kanamaro answered, "at a very great cost."

"At a very great cost?"

"Yes—I did not expect to have to do what I have done—I should once not have believed it possible that I *could* do it. But"—Kanamaro checked himself hastily and resumed his grave reserve—"but that is private beesness, and not for me to disturb you with."

Mr. Colson had the tact to leave that line of fishing alone for a little. He walked a few yards in silence, and then asked, with his eyes furtively fixed on the face of the Japanese, "Do you know of the god Hachiman?"

"It is Hachiman the warrior; him of eight flags," Kanamaro replied. "Yes, I know, of course."

He spoke as though he would banish the subject. But Mr. Colson went on—

"Did he preside over the forging of ancient sword-blades in Japan?" he asked.

"I do not know of preside—that is a new word. But the great workers of the steel, those who made the *katana* in the times of Yoshitsune and Taiko-Sama, they hung curtains and made offerings to Hachiman when they forged a blade—yes. The great Muramasa and the great Masamune and Sanenori—they forged their blades at the

657

foot of Hachiman. And it is believed that the god Inari came unseen with his hammer and forged the steel too. Though Hachiman is Buddhist and Inari is Shinto. But these are not things to talk about. There is one religion, which is yours, and there is another religion, which is mine, and it is not good that we talk together of them. There are things that people call superstition when they are of another religion, though they may be very true."

They walked a little farther, and then Mr. Colson, determined to penetrate Kanamaro's mask of indifference, observed—

"It's a very sad thing this about Mr. Deacon."

"What is that?" asked Kanamaro, stolidly.

"Why, it is in all the newspapers!"

"The newspapers I do not read at all."

"Mr. Deacon has been killed—murdered in his rooms! He was found lying dead at the feet of Hachiman the god."

"Indeed!" Kanamaro answered politely, but with something rather like stolid indifference. "That is very sad. I am sorry. I did not know he had a Hachiman."

"And they say," Mr. Colson pursued, "that *something* has been taken!"

"Ah, yes," Kanamaro answered, just as coolly; "there were many things of much value in the rooms." And after a little while he added, "I see it is a little late. You will excuse me, for I must go to lunch at my lodgings. Good-day."

He bowed, shook hands, and hailed a cab. Mr. Colson heard him direct the cabman to his lodgings, and then, in another cab, Mr. Colson made for Dorrington's office.

Kanamaro's stolidity, the lack of anything like surprise at the news of Mr. Deacon's death, his admission that he had finished his business in England successfully—these things placed the matter beyond all doubt in Mr. Colson's mind. Plainly he felt so confident that none knew of his errand in England, that he took things with perfect coolness, and even ventured so far as to speak of the murder in very near terms—to say that he did not expect to have to do what he had done, and would not have believed it possible that he *could* do it—though, to be sure, he checked himself at once before going farther. Certainly Dorrington must be told at once. That would be better than going to the police, perhaps, for possibly the police might not consider the evidence sufficient to justify an arrest, and Dorrington may have ascertained something in the meantime.

Dorrington had not been heard of at his office since leaving there early in the morning. So Mr. Colson saw Hicks, and arranged that a man should be put on to watch Kanamaro, and should be sent instantly, before he could leave his lodgings again. Then Mr. Colson hurried to Bedford Mansions.

There he saw the housekeeper. From him he learned that Dorrington had left some time since, promising either to be back or to telegraph during the afternoon. Also, he learned that Beard, the hall-porter, was in a great state of indignation and anxiety as a consequence of the discovery that he was being watched by the police. He had got a couple of days leave of absence to go and see his mother, who was ill, and he found his intentions and destination a matter of pressing inquiry. Mr. Colson assured the housekeeper that he might promise Beard a speedy respite from the attentions of the police, and went to his lunch.

4

After his lunch Mr. Colson called and called again at Bedford Mansions, but neither Dorrington nor his telegram had been heard of. At something near five o'clock, however, when he had made up his mind to wait, restless as he was, Dorrington appeared, fresh and complacent.

"Hope you haven't been waiting long?" he asked. "Fact is I got no opportunity for lunch till after four, so I had it then. I think I'd fairly earned it. The case is finished."

"Finished? But there's Kanamaro to be arrested. I've found—"

"No, no—I don't think anybody will be arrested at all; you'll read about it in the evening papers in an hour, I expect. But come into the rooms. I have some things to show you."

"But I assure you," Mr. Colson said, as he entered the door of Deacon's rooms, "I assure you that I got as good as a confession from Kanamaro—he let it slip in ignorance of what I knew. Why do you say that nobody is to be arrested?"

"Because there's nobody alive who is responsible for Mr. Deacon's death. But come—let me show you the whole thing; it's very simple.".

He led the way to the room where the body had been found, and paused before the four-armed idol. "Here's our old friend Hachiman," he said, "whom you half fancied might have had something to do with the tragedy. Well, you were right. Hachiman had a good deal to do with it, and with the various disasters at Copleston's too. I will show you how."

659

The figure, which was larger than life-size, had been set up temporarily on a large packing-case, hidden by a red cloth covering. Hachiman was represented in the familiar Japanese kneeling-sitting position, and the carving of the whole thing was of an intricate and close description. The god was represented as clad in ancient armour, with a large and loose cloak depending from his shoulders and falling behind in a wilderness of marvellously and deeply carved folds.

"See here," Dorrington said, placing his fingers under a projecting part of the base of the figure, and motioning to Mr. Colson to do the same. "Lift. Pretty heavy, eh?"

The idol was, indeed, enormously heavy, and it must have required the exertions of several strong men to place it where it was. "It seems pretty solid, doesn't it?" Dorrington continued. "But look here." He stepped to the back of the image, and, taking a prominent fold of the cloak in one hand, with a quick pull and a simultaneous rap of the other fist two feet above, a great piece of the carved drapery lifted on a hinge near the shoulders, displaying a hollow interior. In a dark corner within a small bottle and a fragment of rag were just visible.

"See there," said Dorrington, "there wouldn't be enough room in there for you or me, but a small man—a Japanese priest of the old time, say—could squat pretty comfortably. And see!"—he pointed to a small metal bolt at the bottom of the swing drapery—" he could bolt himself safely in when he got there. Whether the priest went there to play the oracle, or to blow fire out of Hachiman's mouth and nose I don't know, though no doubt it might be an interesting subject for inquiry; perhaps he did both. You observe the chamber is lined with metal, which does something towards giving the thing its weight, and there are cunning little openings among the armour-joints in front which would transmit air and sound—even permit of a peep out.

"Now Mr. Deacon might or might not have found out this back door after the figure had been a while in his possession, but it is certain he knew nothing of it when he bought it. Copleston knew nothing of it, though the thing has stood in his place for months. You see it's not a thing one would notice at once—I never should have done so if I hadn't been looking for it." He shut the part, and the joints, of irregular outline, fell into the depths of the folds, and vanished as if by magic.

"Now," Dorrington went on, "as I told you, Copleston knew nothing of this, but one of his men found it out. Do you happen to have heard of one Samuel Castro, nicknamed 'Slackjaw,' a hunchback whom Copleston employed on odd jobs?"

"I have seen him here. He called, sometimes with messages, sometimes with parcels. I should probably have forgotten all about him were it not that he was rather an extraordinary creature, even among Copleston's men, who are all remarkable. But did he—"

"He murdered Mr. Deacon, I think," Dorrington replied, "as I fancy I can explain to you. But he won't hang for it, for he was drowned this afternoon before my eyes, in an attempt to escape from the police. He was an extraordinary creature, as you have said. He wasn't English—a half-caste of some sort I think—though his command of language, of the riverside and dock description, was very free; it got him his nickname of Slackjaw among the longshoremen. He was desperately excitable, and he had most of the vices, though I don't think he premeditated murder in this case—nothing but robbery. He was immensely strong, although such a little fellow, and sharp in his wits, and he might have had regular work at Copleston's if he had liked, but that wasn't his game—he was too lazy. He would work long enough to earn a shilling or so, and then he would go off to drink the money. So he was a sort of odd on-and-off man at Copleston's—just to run a message or carry something or what not when the regular men were busy.

"Well, he seems to have been smart enough—or perhaps it was no more than an accident—to find out about Hachiman's back, and he used his knowledge for his own purposes. Copleston couldn't ac-

"SLACKJAW."

count for missing things in the night—because he never guessed that Castro, by shutting himself up in Hachiman about closing time, had the run of the place when everybody had gone, and could pick up any trifle that looked suitable for the pawnshop in the morning. He could sleep comfortably on sacks or among straw, and thus save the rent of lodgings, and he could accept Hachiman's shelter again just before Copleston turned up to start the next day's business. Getting out, too, after the place was opened, was quite easy, for nobody came to the large store-rooms till something was wanted, and in a large place with many doors and gates, like Copleston's, unperceived going and coming was easy to one who knew the ropes. So that Slackjaw would creep quietly out, and in again by the front door to ask for a job. Copleston noticed how regular he had been every morning for the past few months, and thought he was getting steadier!

"As to the things that got smashed, I expect Slackjaw knocked them over, getting out in the dark. One china vase, in particular, had been shifted at the last moment, probably after he was in his hiding-place, and stood behind the image. That was smashed, of course. And these things, coming after the bad voyage of the ship in which he came over, very naturally gave poor Hachiman an unlucky reputation.

"Probably Slackjaw was sorry at first when he heard that Hachiman was bought. But then an idea struck him. He had been to Mr. Deacon's rooms on errands, and must have seen that fine old plate in the sitting-room. He had picked up unconsidered trifles at Copleston's by aid of Hachiman—why not acquire something handsome at Deacon's in the same way? The figure was to be carried to Bedford Mansions as soon as work began on Wednesday morning. Very well. All he had to do was to manage his customary sojourn at Copleston's over Tuesday night, and keep to his hiding-place in the morning. He did it. Perhaps the men swore a bit at the weight of Hachiman, but as the idol weighed several hundredweights by itself, and had not been shifted since it first arrived, they most likely perceived no difference. Hachiman, with Slackjaw comfortably bolted inside him (though even *he* must have found the quarters narrow) jolted away in the waggon, and in course of time was deposited where it now stands.

"Of course all I have told you, and all I am about to tell you, is no more than conjecture—but I think you will say I have reasons. From within the idol Slackjaw could hear Mr. Deacon's movements, and no doubt when he heard him take his hat and stick and shut the outer door behind him, Hachiman's tenant was glad to get out. He had never had so long and trying a sojourn in the idol before, though he *had* provided himself this time with something to keep his spirits up—in that little flat bottle he left behind. Probably, however, he waited some little time before emerging, for safety's sake. I judge this because I found no signs of his having started work, except a single small knife-mark on the plate case. He must have no more than begun when Mr. Deacon came back for his letters. First, however, he went and shut the bedroom window, lest his movements might be heard in some adjacent rooms; the man who was painting said he heard that, you remember.

"Well, hearing Mr. Deacon's key in the lock, of course he made a rush for his hiding-place—but there was no time to get in and close up before Mr. Deacon could hear the noise. Mr. Deacon, as he entered, heard the footsteps in the next room, and went to see. The result you know. Castro, perhaps, crouched behind the idol, and hearing Mr. Deacon approaching, and knowing discovery inevitable, in his mad fear and excitement, snatched the nearest weapon and struck wildly at his pursuer. See! here are half a dozen heavy, short Japanese swords at hand, any one of which might have been used. The thing done, Castro had to think of escape. The door was impossible—the hall-porter was already knocking there. But the man had no key—he could be heard moving about and calling for one.

"There was yet a little time. He wiped the blade of the weapon, put it back in its place, took the keys from the dead man's pocket, and regained his concealment in the idol. Whether or not he took the keys with the idea of again attempting theft when the room was left empty I don't know—most likely he thought they would aid him in escape. Anyway, he didn't attempt theft, but lay in his concealment—and a pretty bad time he must have had of it—till night. Probably his nerve was not good enough for anything more than simple flight. When all was quiet, he left the rooms and shut the door behind him. Then he lurked about corridors and basements till morning, and when the doors were opened, slipped out unobserved. That's all. It's pretty obvious, once you know about Hachiman's interior."

"And how did you find out?"

"When you left me here I considered the thing. I put aside all suspicions of motive, the Japanese and his sword and the rest of it, and addressed myself to the bare facts. Somebody *had* been in these rooms when Mr. Deacon came back, and that somebody had murdered him. The first thing was to find how this person came, and where he came from. At first, of course, one thought of the bedroom window, as the police had done. But reflection proved this unlikely. Mr. Deacon had entered his front door, was inside a few seconds, and then was murdered close by the figure of Hachiman. Now if anybody had entered by the window for purposes of robbery, his impulse on hearing the key in the outer door (and such a thing could be heard all over the rooms, as I tested for myself)—his impulse, I say, would be to retreat by the way he had come, that is by the window. If, then, Mr. Deacon had overtaken him before he could escape, the murder might have taken place just as it had done, but it would have been *in the bedroom,* not in a room in the opposite direction. And any thief's attention would naturally be directed at first to the gold plate—indeed, I detected a fresh knife-mark in the door of the case, which I will show you presently.

"Now, as you see by the arrangement of the rooms, the retreat from the plate case to the bedroom window would be a short one, whereas the murderer must in fact have taken a longer journey in the opposite direction. Why? Because he had *arrived* from that direction, and his natural impulse was to retreat by the way he had come. This might have been by the door to the back stairs, but a careful examination of this door and its lock and key convinced me that it had not been opened. The key was dirty, and to have turned it from the opposite side would have necessitated the forcible use of a pair of thin hollow pliers (a familiar tool to burglars), and these must have left their mark on the dirty key. So I turned back to the idol. *This* was the spot the intruder had made for in his retreat, and the figure had been brought into the place the very morning of the murder. Also, things had disappeared from its vicinity at Copleston's. More—it was a large thing. What if it were hollow? One has heard of such things having been invented by priests anxious for certain effects. Could not a thief smuggle himself in that way?

"The suggestion was a little startling, for if it were the right one the man might be hiding there at that moment. I gave the thing half an hour's examination, and in the end found what I have shown you. It was not the sort of thing one would have found out without looking for it. Look at it even now. Although you have seen it open, you couldn't point to the joints."

Dorrington opened it again. "Once open," he went on, "the thing was pretty plain. Here is the rag—perhaps it was Castro's pocket-handkerchief—used to wipe the weapon. It is stained all over, and cut, as you will observe, by the sharp edge. Also, you may see a crumb or

two—Slack-jaw had brought food with him, in case of a long imprisonment. But chiefly observe the bottle. It is a flat, high-shouldered,
'quartern' bottle, such as publicans sell or lend to their customers in
poor districts, and as usual it bears the publican's name—J. Mills. It's a
most extraordinary thing, but it seems the fate of almost every murderer, no matter how cunning, to leave some such damning piece of
evidence about, foolish as it may seem afterward. I've known it in a
dozen cases. Probably Castro, in the dark and in his excitement, forgot it when he quitted his hiding-place. At any rate it helped me and
made my course plain. Clearly this man, whoever he was, had come
from Copleston's. Moreover, he was a small man, for the space he had
occupied would be too little even for a man of middle height.

"Also he bought drink of J. Mills, a publican; if J. Mills carried on
business near Copleston's so much the easier my task would seem.
Before I left, however, I went to the basement and inspected the ladder, the removal of which had caused the police so much exercise.
Then it was plain why Dowden had cleared out. All his prevarica-
tion and uneasiness were explained at once, as the police might have
seen if they had looked *behind* the ladder as well as at it. For it had
been lying lengthwise against the wooden partition which formed the
back of the compartments put up to serve the tenants as wine-cellars.
Dowden had taken three planks out of this partition, and so arranged
that they could be slipped in their places and out again without attracting attention. "What he had been taking through the holes he
thus made I won't undertake to say, but I will make a small bet that
some of the tenants find their wine short presently! And so Dowden,
never an industrious person, and never at one job long, thought it best
to go away when he found the police asking why the ladder had been
moved."

"Yes, yes—it's very surprising, but no doubt you're right. Still, what
about Kanamaro and that sword?"

"Tell me exactly what he said to you today."

Mr. Colson detailed the conversation at length.

Dorrington smiled. "See here," he said, "I have found out something else in these rooms. What Kanamaro said he meant in another
sense to what you supposed. I wondered a little about that sword, and
made a little search among some drawers in consequence. Look here.
Do you see this box standing out here on a nest of drawers? That is
quite unlike Mr. Deacon's orderly ways. The box contains a piece of
lacquer, and it had been shifted from its drawer to make room for a

more precious piece. See here." Dorrington pulled out a drawer just below where the box stood, and took from it another white wood box. He opened this box and removed a quantity of wadding. A rich brocade *fukusa* was then revealed, and, loosening the cord of this, Dorrington displayed a Japanese writing-case, or *suzuribako,* aged and a little worn at the corners, but all of lacquer of a beautiful violet hue.

"What!" exclaimed Mr. Colson. "Violet lacquer!"

"That is what it is," Dorrington answered, "and when I saw it I judged at once that Deacon had at last consented to part with his Masamune blade in exchange for that even greater rarity, a fine piece of the real old violet lacquer. I should imagine that Kanamaro brought it on Tuesday evening—you will remember that you saw Mr. Deacon for the last time alive in the afternoon of that day. Beard seems not to have noticed him, but in the evening hall-porters are apt to be at supper, you know—perhaps even taking a nap now and then!"

"Then *this* is how Kanamaro 'finished his business'!" Mr. Colson observed. "And the 'very great cost' was probably what he had to pay for this."

"I suppose so. And he would not have believed it possible that he *could* get a piece of violet lacquer in any circumstances."

"But," Mr. Colson objected, "I still don't understand his indifference and lack of surprise when I told him of poor Deacon's death."

"I think that is very natural in such a man as Keigo Kanamaro. I don't profess to know a very great deal about Japan, but I know that a *samurai* of the old school was trained from infancy to look on death, whether his own or another's, with absolute indifference. They regarded it as a mere circumstance. Consider how cold-bloodedly their *hari-kiri,* their legalised suicide, was carried out!"

As they left the rooms and made for the street Mr. Colson said, "But now I know nothing of your pursuit of Castro."

Dorrington shrugged his shoulders. "There is little to say," he said. "I went to Copleston and asked him if any one of his men was missing all day on Wednesday. None of his regular men were, it seemed, but he had seen nothing that day of an odd man named Castro, or Slackjaw, although he had been very regular for some time before; and, indeed, Castro had not yet turned up. I asked if Castro was a tall man. No, he was a little fellow and a hunchback, Copleston told me. I asked what public-house one might find him at, and Copleston mentioned the 'Blue Anchor'—kept, as I had previously ascertained from the directory, by J. Mills. That was enough. With everything standing as it was, a few minutes' talk with the inspector in charge at the nearest police-station was all that was necessary. Two men were sent to make the arrest, and the people at the 'Blue Anchor' directed us to Martin's Wharf, where we found Castro. He had been drinking, but he knew enough to make a bolt the moment he saw the policemen coming on the wharf. He dropped on to a dummy barge and made off from one barge to another in what seemed an aimless direction, though he may have meant to get away at the stairs a little lower down the river. But he never got as far. He muddled one jump and fell between the barges. You know what a suck under there is when a man falls among barges like that. A strong swimmer with all his senses has only an off chance, and a man with bad whisky in his head—well, I left them dragging for Slackjaw when I came away."

As they turned the corner of the street they met a newsboy running. "Paper—speshal!" he cried. "The West-End murder—speshal! Suicide of the murderer!"

Dorrington's conjecture that Kanamaro had called to make his exchange on Tuesday evening proved correct. Mr. Colson saw him once more on the day of his departure, and told him the whole story. And then Keigo Kanamaro sailed for Japan to lay the sword in his father's tomb.

OLD CATER'S MONEY

1

The Firm of Dorrington & Hicks had not been constructed at the time when this case came to Dorrington's hand. Dorrington had barely emerged from the obscurity that veils his life before some ten years ago, and he was at this time a needier adventurer than he had been at the period of any other of the cases I have related. Indeed, his illicit gains on this occasion would seem first to have set him on his feet and enabled him first to cut a fair exterior figure. Whether or not he had developed to the full the scoundrelism that first brought me acquainted with his trade I do not know; but certain it is that he was involved at the time in transactions wretchedly ill paid, on behalf of one Flint, a ship-stores dealer at Deptford; an employer whose record was never a very clean one. This Flint was one of an unpleasant family. He was nephew to old Cater the wharfinger (and private usurer) and cousin to another Cater, whose name was Paul, and who was also a usurer, though he variously described himself as a "commission agent" or "general dealer."

Indeed, he was a general dealer, if the term may be held to include a dealer in whatever would bring him gain, and who made no great *punctilio* in regard to the honesty or otherwise of his transactions. In fact, all three of these pleasant relatives had records of the shadiest, and all three did whatever in the way of money-lending, mortgaging, and blood-sucking came in their way. It is, however, with old Cater—Jerry Cater, he was called—that this narrative is in the first place concerned. I got the story from a certain Mr. Sinclair, who for many years acted as his clerk and debt-collector.

Old Jerry Cater lived in the crooked and decaying old house over his wharf by Bermondsey Wall, where his father had lived before him. It was a grim and strange old house, with long-shut loft-doors in upper floors, and hinged flaps in sundry rooms that, when lifted, gave startling glimpses of muddy water washing among rotten piles below. Not once in six months now did a barge land its load at Cater's Wharf, and no coasting brig ever lay alongside. For, in fact, the day of Cater's Wharf was long past; and it seemed indeed that few more days were left for old Jerry Cater himself. For seventy-eight years old Jerry Cater had led a life useless to himself and to everybody else, though his own belief was that he had profited considerably.

Truly if one counted nothing but the money the old miser had accumulated, then his profit was large indeed; but it had brought nothing worth having, neither for himself nor for others, and he had no wife nor child who might use it more wisely when he should at last leave it behind him; no other relative indeed than his two nephews, each in spirit a fair copy of himself, though in body a quarter of a century younger. Seventy-eight years of every mean and sordid vice and of every virtue that had pecuniary gain for its sole object left Jerry Cater stranded at last in his cheap iron bedstead with its insufficient coverings, with not a sincere friend in the world to sit five minutes by his side. Down below, Sinclair, his unhappy clerk, had the accommodation of a wooden table and a chair; and the clerk's wife performed what meagre cooking and cleaning service old Cater would have. Sinclair was a man of forty-five, rusty, starved, honest, and very cheap. He was very cheap because it had been his foolishness, twenty years ago, when in City employ, to borrow forty pounds off old Cater to get married with, and to buy furniture, together with forty pounds he had of his own.

Sinclair was young then, and knew nothing of the ways of the two hundred *per cent,* money-lender. When he had, by three or four years' pinching, paid about a hundred and fifty pounds on account of interest and fines, and only had another hundred or two still due to clear everything off, he fell sick and lost his place. The payment of interest ceased, and old Jerry Cater took his victim's body, soul, wife, sticks, and chairs together. Jerry Cater discharged his own clerk, and took Sinclair, with a saving of five shillings a week on the nominal salary, and out of the remainder he deducted, on account of the debt and ever-accumulating interest, enough to keep his man thin and broken-spirited, without absolutely incapacitating him from work, which would have been bad finance.

But the rest of the debt, capital and interest, was made into a capital debt, with usury on the whole. So that for sixteen years or more Sinclair had been paying something every week of the eternally increasing sum, and might have kept on for sixteen centuries at the same rate without getting much nearer freedom. If only there had been one more room in the house old Cater might have compulsorily lodged his clerk, and have deducted something more for rent. As it was he might have used the office for the purpose, but he could never have brought himself to charge a small rent for it, and a large one would have swallowed most of the rest of Sinclair's salary, thus bringing him below starvation point, and impairing his working capacity. But Mrs. Sinclair, now gaunt and scraggy, did all the housework, so that that came very cheap. Most of the house was filled with old bales and rotting merchandise which old Jerry Cater had seized in payment for wharfage dues and other debts, and had held to, because his ideas of selling prices were large, though his notion of buying prices were small. Sinclair was out of doors more than in, dunning and threatening debtors as hopeless as himself.

And the household was completed by one Samuel Greer, a squinting man of grease and rags, within ten years of the age of old Jerry Cater himself. Greer was wharf-hand, messenger, and personal attendant on his employer, and, with less opportunity, was thought to be near as bad a scoundrel as Cater. He lived and slept in the house, and was popularly supposed to be paid nothing at all; though his patronage of the "Ship and Anchor," hard by, was as frequent as might be.

Old Jerry Cater was plainly not long for this world. Ailing for months, he at length gave in and took to his bed. Greer watched him anxiously and greedily, for it was his design, when his master went at last, to get what he could for himself. More than once during his illness old Cater had sent Greer to fetch his nephews. Greer had departed on these errands, but never got farther than the next street. He hung about a reasonable time—perhaps in the "Ship and Anchor," if funds permitted—and then returned to say that the nephews could not come just yet. Old Cater had quarrelled with his nephews, as he had with everybody else, sometime before, and Greer was resolved, if he could, to prevent any meeting now, for that would mean that the nephews would take possession of the place, and he would lose his chance of convenient larceny when the end came. So it was that neither nephew knew of old Jerry Cater's shaky condition.

Before long, finding that the old miser could not leave his bed—indeed he could scarcely turn in it—Greer took courage, in Sinclair's absence, to poke about the place in search of concealed sovereigns. He had no great time for this, because Jerry Cater seemed to have taken a great desire for his company, whether for the sake of his attendance or to keep him out of mischief was not clear. At any rate Greer found no concealed sovereigns, nor anything better than might be sold for a few pence at the rag-shop. Until one day, when old Cater was taking alternate fits of restlessness and sleep, Greer ventured to take down a dusty old pickle-jar from the top shelf in the cupboard of his master's bedroom. Cater was dozing at the moment, and Greer, tilting the jar toward the light, saw within a few doubled papers, very dusty. He snatched the papers out, stuffed them into his pocket, replaced the jar, and closed the cupboard door hastily. The door made some little noise, and old Cater turned and woke, and presently he made a shift to sit up in bed, while Greer scratched his head as innocently as he could, and directed his divergent eyes to parts of the room as distant from the cupboard as possible.

"Sam'l Greer," said old Cater in a feeble voice, while his lower jaw waggled and twitched, "Sam'l Greer, I think I'll 'ave some beef-tea." He groped tremulously under his pillow, turning his back to Greer, who tip-toed and glared variously over his master's shoulders. He saw nothing, however, though he heard the chink of money. Old Cater turned, with a shilling in his shaking hand. "Git 'alf a pound o' shin o' beef," he said, "an' go to Green's for it at the other end o' Grange Road, d'ye hear? It's—it's a penny a pound cheaper there than it is anywhere nearer, and—and I ain't in so much of a 'urry for it, so the distance don't matter. Go 'long." And old Jerry Cater subsided in a fit of coughing.

Greer needed no second bidding. He was anxious to take a peep at the papers he had secreted. Sinclair was out collecting, or trying

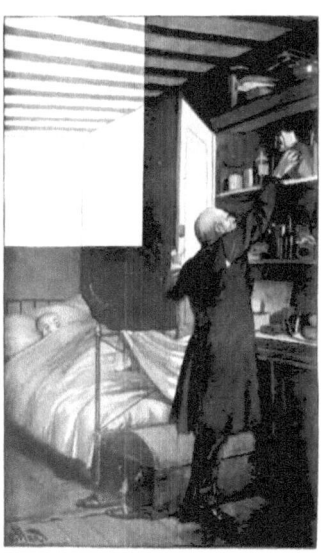

to collect, but Greer did not stop to examine his prize before he had banged the street door behind him, lest Cater, listening above, should wonder what detained him. But in a convenient courtyard a hundred yards away he drew out the papers and inspected them eagerly. First, there was the policy of insurance of the house and premises. Then there was a bundle of receipts for the yearly insurance premiums. And then—there was old Jerry Cater's will.

There were two foolscap sheets, written all in Jerry Cater's own straggling handwriting. Greer hastily scanned the sheets, and his dirty face grew longer and his squint intensified as he turned over the second sheet, found nothing behind it, and stuffed the papers back in his pocket. For it was plain that not a penny of old Jerry Cater's money was for his faithful servant, Samuel Greer.

"Ungrateful ole waga-bone!" mused the faithful servant as he went his way. "Not a blessed 'a'peny; not a 'a'peny! An' them ''as don't want it gets it, o' course. That's always the way—it's like a-greasing' of a fat pig. I shall 'ave to get what I can while I can, that's all." And so ruminating he pursued his way to the butcher's in Grange Road.

Once more on his way there, and twice on his way back, Samuel Greer stepped into retired places to look at those papers again, and at each inspection he grew more thoughtful. There might be money in it yet. Come, he must think it over.

The front door being shut, and Sinclair probably not yet returned, he entered the house by a way familiar to the inmates—a latched door giving on to the wharf. The clock told him that he had been gone nearly an hour, but Sinclair was still absent. When he entered old Cater's room upstairs he found a great change. The old man lay in a state of collapse, choking with a cough that exhausted him; and for this there seemed little wonder, for the window was open, and the room was full of the cold air from the river.

"Wot jer bin openin' the winder for?" asked Greer in astonishment. "It's enough to give ye yer death." He shut it and returned to the bedside. But though he offered his master the change from the shilling the old man seemed not to see it nor to hear his voice.

"Well, if you won't—don't," observed Greer with some alacrity, pocketing the coppers. "But I'll bet he'll remember right enough presently."

"D'y'ear," he added, bending over the bed, "I've got the beef. Shall I bile it now?"

But old Jerry Cater's eyes still saw nothing and he heard not, though his shrunken chest and shoulders heaved with the last shudders of the cough that had exhausted him. So Greer stepped lightly to the cupboard and restored the fire policy and the receipts to the pickle-jar. He kept the will.

Greer made preparations for cooking the beef, and as he did so he encountered another phenomenon. "Well, he have bin a goin' of it!" said Greer. "Blow me if he ain't bin readin' the Bible now!"

A large, ancient, worn old Bible, in a rough calf-skin cover, lay on a chair by old Cater's hand. It had probably been the family Bible of the Caters for generations back, for certainly old Jerry Cater would never have bought such a thing. For many years it had accumulated dust on a distant shelf among certain out-of-date account-books, but Greer had never heard of its being noticed before. "Peels he goin', that's about it," Greer mused as he pitched the Bible back on the shelf to make room for his utensils. "But I shouldn't ha' thought 'e'd take it sentimental like that—readin' the Bible an' lettin' in the free air of 'eaven to make 'im cough 'isself blind."

The beef-tea was set simmering, and still old Cater lay impotent. The fit of prostration was longer than any that had preceded it, and presently Greer thought it might be well to call the doctor. Call him he did accordingly (the surgery was hard by), and the doctor came. Jerry Cater revived a little, sufficiently to recognise the doctor, but it was his last effort. He lived another hour and a half. Greer kept the change and had the beef-tea as well. The doctor gave his opinion that the old man had risen in delirium and had expended his last strength in moving about the room and opening the window.

2

Samuel Greer found somewhere near two pounds in silver in the small canvas bag under the dead man's pillow. No more money, however, rewarded his hasty search about the bedroom, and when Sinclair returned Greer set off to carry the news to Paul Cater, the dead man's nephew.

The respectable Greer had considered well the matter of the will, and saw his way, he fancied, at least to a few pounds by way of compensation for his loss of employment and the ungrateful forgetfulness of his late employer. The two sheets comprised, in fact, not a simple will merely, but a will and a codicil, each on one of the sheets, the codicil being a year or two more recent than the will. Nobody apparently knew anything of these papers, and it struck Greer that it was now in his power to prevent anybody learning, unless an interested party were disposed to pay for the disclosure. That was why he now took his way toward the establishment of Paul Cater, for the will made Paul Cater not only sole executor, but practically sole legatee. Wherefore Greer carefully separated the will from the codicil, intending the will alone for sale to Paul Cater. Because, indeed, the codicil very considerably modified it, and might form the subject of independent commerce.

Paul Cater made a less miserly show than had been the wont of his uncle. His house was in a street in Pimlico, the ground-floor front room of which was made into an office, with a wire blind carrying his name in gilt letters. Perhaps it was that Paul Cater carried his covetousness to a greater refinement than his uncle had done, seeing that a decent appearance is a commercial advantage by itself, bringing a greater profit than miserly habits could save.

The man of general dealings was balancing his books when Greer arrived, but at the announcement of his uncle's death he dropped everything. He was not noticeably stricken with grief, unless a sudden seizure of his hat and a roaring aloud for a cab might be considered as indications of affliction; for in truth Paul Cater knew well that it was a case in which much might depend on being first at Bermondsey Wall. The worthy Greer had scarce got the news out before he found himself standing in the street while Cater was giving directions to a cabman. "Here—you come in too," said Cater, and Greer was bustled

673

into the cab.

It was plainly a situation in which half-crowns should not be too reluctantly parted with. So Paul Cater produced one and presented it. Cater was a strong-faced man of fifty odd, with a tight-drawn mouth that proclaimed everywhere a tight fist; so that the unaccustomed passing over of a tip was a noticeably awkward and unspontaneous performance, and Greer pocketed the money with little more acknowledgment than a growl.

"Do you know where he put the will?" asked Paul Cater with a keen glance.

"Will?" answered Greer, looking him blankly in the face—the gaze of one eye passing over Cater's shoulder and that of the other seeming to seek his boots. "Will? P'raps 'e never made one."

"Didn't he?"

"That 'ud mean, lawfully, as the property would come to you an' Mr. Flint—'arves. Bern' all personal property. So I'd think." And Greer's composite gaze blankly persisted.

"But how do you know whether he made a Will or not?"

"'Ow do I know? Ah, well, p'raps I dunno. It's only fancy like. I jist put it to you—that's all. It 'ud be divided atween the two of you." Then, after a long pause, he added: "But lor! it 'ud be a pretty fine thing for you if he did leave a will, and willed it all to you, wouldn't it? Mighty fine thing! An' it 'ud be a mighty fine thing for Mr. Flint if there was a will leaving it all to him, wouldn't it? Pretty fine thing!"

Cater said nothing, but watched Greer's face sharply. Greer's face, with its greasy features and its irresponsible squint, was as expressive as a brick. They travelled some distance in silence. Then Greer said musingly, "Ah, a will like that 'ud be a mighty fine thing! What 'ud you be disposed to give for it now?"

"Give for it? What do you mean? If there's a will there's an end to it. Why should I give anything for it?"

"Jist so—jist so," replied Greer, with a complacent wave of the hand. "Why should you? No reason at all, unless you couldn't find it without givin' something."

"See here, now," said Cater sharply, "let us understand this. Do you mean that there is a will, and you know that it is hidden, and where it is?"

Greer's squint remained impenetrable. "Hidden? Lor!—'ow should I know if it was hidden? I was a-puttin' of a case to you."

"Because," Cater went on, disregarding the reply, "if that's the case,

674

the sooner you out with the information the better it'll be for you. Because there are ways of making people give up information of that sort for nothing."

"Yes—o' course," replied the imperturbable Greer. "O' course there is. An' quite right too. Ah, it's a fine thing is the lawr—a mighty fine thing!"

The cab rattled over the stones of Bermondsey Wall, and the two alighted at the door through which old Jerry Cater was soon to come feet first. Sinclair was back, much disturbed and anxious. At sight of Paul Cater the poor fellow, weak and broken-spirited, left the house as quietly as he might. For years of grinding habit had inured him to the belief that in reality old Cater had treated him rather well, and now he feared the probable action of the heirs.

"Who was that?" asked Paul Cater of Greer. "Wasn't it the clerk that owed my uncle the money?"

Greer nodded.

"Then he's not to come here again—do you hear? I'll take charge of the books and things. As to the debt—well, I'll see about that after. And now look here." Paul Cater stood before Greer and spoke with decision. "About that will, now. Bring it."

Greer was not to be bluffed. "Where from?" he asked innocently.

"Will you stand there and tell me you don't know where it is?"

"Maybe I'd best stand here and tell you what pays me best."

"Pay you? How much more do you want? Bring me that will, or I'll have you in gaol for stealing it!"

"Lor!" answered Greer composedly, conscious of holding another trump as well as the will. "Why, if there *was* anybody as knowed where the will was, and you talked to him as woilent as that 'ere, why, you'd frighten him so much he'd as likely as not go out and get a price'from your cousin, Mr. Flint. Whatever was in the will it might pay him to get hold of it."

At this moment there came a furious knocking at the front door. "Why," Greer continued, "I bet that's him. It can't be nobody else—I bet the doctor's told him, or summat."

They were on the first-floor landing, and Greer peeped from a broken-shuttered window that looked on the street. "Yes," he said, "that's Mr. Flint sure enough. Now, Mr. Paul Cater, business. Do you want to see that will before I let Mr. Flint in?"

"Yes!" exclaimed Cater furiously, catching at his arm. "Quick—where is it?"

"I want twenty pound."

"Twenty pound! You're mad! What for?"

"All right, if I'm mad, I'll go an' let Mr. Flint in."

The knocking was repeated, louder and longer.

"No," cried Cater, getting in his way. "You know you mustn't conceal a will—that's law. Give it up."

"What's the law that says I must give it up to you, 'stead of yer cousin? *If* there's a will it may say anythin'—in yer favour or out of it. If there ain't, you'll git 'alf. The will might give you more, or it might give you less, or it might give you nothink. Twenty pound for first look at it 'fore Flint comes in, and do what you like with it 'fore he knows anythink about it."

Again the knocking came at the door, this time supplemented by kicks.

"But I don't carry twenty pound about with me!" protested Cater, waving his fists. "Give me the will and come to my office for the money to-morrow!"

"No tick for this sort of job," answered Greer decisively. "Sorry I can't oblige you—I'm goin' down to the front door." And he made as though to go.

"Well, look here!" said Cater desperately, pulling out his pocket-book. "I've got a note or two, I think—"

"'Ow much?" asked Greer, calmly laying hold of the pocket-book. "Two at least. Two fivers. Well, I'll let it go at that. Give us hold." He took the notes, and pulled out the will from his pocket. Flint, outside, battered the door once more.

"Why," exclaimed Cater as he glanced over the sheet, "I'm sole executor and I get the lot! Who are these witnesses?"

"Oh, they're all right. Longshore hands just hereabout. You'll get 'em any day at the 'Ship and Anchor.'"

Cater put the will in his breast-pocket. "You'd best get out o' this, my man," he said. "You've had me for ten pound, and the further you get from me the safer you'll be."

"What?" said Greer with a chuckle. "Not even grateful! Shockin'!" He took his way downstairs, and Cater followed. At the door Flint, a counterpart of Cater, except that his dress was more slovenly, stood ragefully.

"Ah, cousin," said Cater, standing on the threshold and preventing his entrance, "this is a very sad loss!"

"Sad loss!" Flint replied with disgust. "A lot you think of the loss—

as much as I do, I reckon. I want to come in."

"Then you sha'n't!" Cater replied, with a prompt change of manner. "You shan't! I'm sole executor, and I've got the will in my pocket." He pulled it out sufficiently far to show the end of the paper, and then returned it. "As executor I'm in charge of the property, and responsible. It's vested in me till the will's put into effect. That's law. And it's a bad thing for anybody to interfere with an executor. That's law too."

Flint was angry, but cautious. "Well," he said, "you're uncommon high, with your will and your executor's law and your 'sad loss,' I must say. What's your game?"

For answer Cater began to shut the door.

"Just you look out!" cried Flint. "You haven't heard the last of this! You may be executor or it may be a lie. You may have the will or you may not; anyway I know better than to run the risk of putting myself in the wrong now. But I'll watch you, and I'll watch this house, and I'll be about when the will comes to be proved! And if that ain't done quick, I'll apply for administration myself, and see the thing through!"

3

Samuel Greer sheered off as the cousinly interview ended, well satisfied with himself. Ten pounds was a fortune to him, and he meant having a good deal more. He did nothing further till the following morning, when he presented himself at the shop of Jarvis Flint.

"Good mornin', Mr. Flint," said Samuel Greer, grinning and squinting affably. "I couldn't help noticin' as you had a few words yesterday with Mr. Cater after the sad loss."

"Well?"

"It 'appens as I've seen the will as Mr. Cater was talkin' of, an' I thought p'raps it 'ud save you makin' mistakes if I told you of it."

"What about it?" Jarvis Flint was not disposed to accept Greer altogether on trust.

"Well it *do* seem a scandalous thing, certainly, but what Mr. Cater said was right. He *do* take the personal property, subjick to debts, an' he do take the freehold prim'ses. An' he is the 'xecutor."

"Was the will witnessed?"

"Yes—two waterside chaps well know'd thereabouts."

"Was it made by a lawyer?"

"No—all in the lamented corpse's 'and-writin'."

"Umph!" Flint maintained his hard stare in Greer's face. "Anything else?"

"Well, no, Mr. Flint, sir, p'raps not. But I wonder if there might be sich a thing as a codicil?"

"Is there?"

"Oh, I was a-wonderin', that's all. It might make a deal o' difference in the will, mightn't it? And p'raps Mr. Cater mightn't know anythink about the codicil."

"What do you mean? Is there a codicil?"

"Well, reely, Mr. Flint," answered Greer with a deprecatory grin—"reely it ain't business to give information for nothink, is it?"

"Business or not, if you know anything you'll find you'll have to tell it. I'm not going to let Cater have it all his own way, if he *is* executor. My lawyer'll be on the job before you're a day older, my man, and you won't find it pay to keep things too quiet."

"But it can't pay worse than to give information for nothink," persisted Greer. "Come, now, Mr. Flint, s'pose (I don't say there is, mind—I only say; *s'pose*)—s'pose there *was* a codicil, and s'pose that codicil meant a matter of a few thousand pound in your pocket. And s'pose some person could tell you where to put your hand on that codicil, what might you be disposed to pay that person?"

"Bring me the codicil," answered Flint, "and if it's all right I'll give you—well, say five shillings."

Greer grinned again and shook his head. "No, reely, Mr. Flint," he said, "we can't do business on terms like them. Fifty pound down in my hand now, and it's done. Fifty 'ud be dirt cheap. And the longer you are a-considerin'—well, you know, Mr. Cater might get hold of it, and then, why, s'pose it got burnt and never 'eard of agen?"

Flint glared with round eyes. "You get out!" he said. "Go on! Fifty pound, indeed! Fifty pound, without my knowing whether you're telling lies or not! Out you go! I know what to do now, my man!"

Greer grinned once more, and slouched out. He had not expected to bring Flint to terms at once. Of course the man would drive him away at first, and, having got scent of the existence of the codicil, and supposing it to be somewhere concealed about the old house at Bermondsey. "Wall, he would set his lawyer to warn his cousin that the thing was known, and that he, as executor, would be held responsible for it. But the trump card, the codicil itself, was carefully stowed in the lining of Greer's hat, and Cater knew nothing about it. Presently Flint, finding Cater obdurate, would approach the wily Greer again, and then he could be squeezed. Meanwhile the hat-lining was as safe a place as any in which to keep the paper. Perhaps Flint might take a fancy to have him waylaid at night and searched, in which case a pocket would be an unsafe repository.

Flint, on his part, was in good spirits. Plainly there *was* a codicil, favourable to himself. Certainly he meant neither to pay Greer for discovering it—at any rate no such sum as fifty pounds—nor to abate a jot of his rights. Flint had a running contract with a shady solicitor, named Lugg, in accordance with which Lugg received a yearly payment and transacted all his legal business—consisting chiefly of writing threatening letters to unfortunate debtors. Also, as I think I have mentioned, Dorrington was working for him at the time, and working at very cheap rates. Flint resolved, to begin with, to set Dorrington and Lugg to work. But first Dorrington—who, as a matter of fact, was in Flint's back office during the interview with Greer. Thus it was that in an hour or two Dorrington found himself in active pursuit of Samuel Greer, with instructions to watch him closely, to make him drunk if possible, and to get at his knowledge of the codicil by any means conceivable.

4

On the morning of the day after his talk with Flint, Samuel Greer ruminated doubtfully on the advisability of calling on the ship-store dealer again, or waiting in dignified silence till Flint should approach him. As he ruminated he rubbed his chin, and so rubbing it found it very stubbly. He resolved on the luxury of a penny shave, and, as he walked the street, kept his eyes open for a shop where the operation was performed at that price. Mr. Flint, at any rate, could wait till his chin was smooth. Presently, in a turning by Abbey Street, Bermondsey, he came on just such a barber's shop as he wanted. Within, two men were being shaved already, and another waiting; and Greer felt himself especially fortunate in that three more followed at his heels. He was ahead of their turns, anyhow. So he waited patiently.

The man whose turn was immediately before his own did not appear to be altogether sober. A hiccough shook him from time to time; he grinned with a dull glance at a comic paper held upside down in his hand, and when he went to take his turn at a chair his walk was unsteady. The barber had to use his skill to avoid cutting him, and he opened his mouth to make remarks at awkward times. Then Greer's turn came at the other chair, and when his shave was half completed he saw the unsteady customer rise, pay his penny, and go out.

"Beginnin' early in the mornin'!" observed one customer.

The barber laughed. "Yes," he said. "He wants to get a proper bust on before he goes to bed, I s'pose."

Samuel Greer's chin being smooth at last, he rose and turned to where he had hung his hat. His jaw dropped, and his eyes almost sprang out to meet each other as he saw—a bare peg! The unsteady customer had walked off with the wrong hat—his hat, and—the paper concealed inside!

"Lor!" cried the dismayed Greer, "he's took my hat!"

All the shopful of men set up a guffaw at this. "Take 'is then," said one. "It's a blame sight better one than yourn!"

But Greer, without a hat, rushed into the street, and the barber, without his penny, rushed after him. "Stop 'im!" shouted Greer distractedly. "Stop thief!"

Thus it was that Dorrington, at this time of a far less well-groomed appearance than was his later wont, watching outside the barber's, observed the mad bursting forth of Greer, followed by the barber. After the barber came the customers, one grinning furiously beneath a coating of lather.

"Stop 'im!" cried Greer. "'E's got my 'at! Stop 'im!"

"You pay me my money," said the barber, catching his arm. "Never mind yer 'at—you can 'ave 'is. But just you pay me first."

"Leave go! You're responsible for lettin' 'im take it, I tell you! It's a special 'at—valuable; leave go!"

"HIS WALK WAS UNSTEADY."

Dorrington stayed to hear no more. Three minutes before he had observed a slightly elevated navvy emerge from the shop and walk solemnly across the street under a hat manifestly a size or two too small for him. Now Dorrington darted down the turning which the man had taken. The hat was a wretched thing, and there must be some special reason for Greer's wild anxiety to recover it, especially as the navvy must have left another, probably better, behind him. Already Dorrington had conjectured that Greer was carrying the codicil about with him, for he had no place else to hide it, and he would scarcely have offered so confidently to negotiate over it if it had been in the Bermondsey Wall house, well in reach of Paul Cater. So he followed the elevated navvy with all haste. He might never have seen him again were it not that the unconscious bearer of the fortunes of Flint (and, indeed, Dorrington) hesitated for a little while whether or not to enter the door of a public-house near St. Saviour's Dock. In the end he decided to go on, and it was just as he had started that Dorrington sighted him again.

The navvy walked slowly and gravely on, now and again with a swerve to the wall or the curb, but generally with a careful and laboured directness. Presently he arrived at a dock-bridge, with a low iron rail. An incoming barge attracted his eye, and he stopped and solemnly inspected it. He leaned on the low rail for this purpose, and as he did so the hat, all too small, fell off. Had he been standing two yards nearer the centre of the bridge it would have dropped into the water. As it was it fell on the quay, a few feet from the edge, and a dockman, coining toward the steps by the bridge-side, picked it up and brought it with him.

"Here y'are, mate," said the dockman, offering the hat.

The navvy took it in lofty silence, and inspected it narrowly. Then he said, "'Ere—wot's this? This ain't my 'at!" And he glared suspiciously at the dockman.

"Ain't it?" answered the dockman carelessly. "Aw right then, keep it for the bloke it b'longs to. I don't want it."

"No," returned the navvy with rising indignation, "but I want mine, though! Wotcher done with it? Eh? It ain't a rotten old 'un like this 'ere. None o' yer 'alf-larks. Jist you 'and it over, come on!"

"'And wot over?" asked the dockman, growing indignant in his turn. "You drops yer 'at over the bridge like some kid as can't take care of it, and I brings it up for ye. 'Stead o' sayin' 'thank ye,' like a man, y' asks me for another 'at! Go an' bile yer face!" And he turned on his heel.

"No, ye don't!" bawled the navvy, dropping the battered hat and making a complicated rush at the other's retreating form. "Not much! You gimme my 'at!" And he grabbed the dock-man anywhere, with both hands.

The dockman was as big as the navvy, and no more patient. He immediately punched his assailant's nose; and in three seconds a mingled bunch of dockman and navvy was floundering about the street. Dorrington saw no more. He had the despised hat in his hand, and, general attention being directed to the action in progress, he hurried quietly up the nearest court.

5

Samuel Greer, having got clear of the barber by paying his penny, was in much perplexity, and this notwithstanding his acquisition of the navvy's hat, a very decent bowler, which covered his head generously and rested on his ears. What should be the move now? His hat was clean gone, and the codicil with it. To find it again would be a hopeless task, unless by chance the navvy should discover his mistake and return to the barber's to make a rectification of hats. So Samuel Greer returned once more to the barber's, and for the rest of the day called again and again fruitlessly. At first the barber was vastly amused, and told the story to his customers, who laughed. Then the barber got angry at the continual worrying, and at the close of the day's barber-

"A MINGLED BUNCH OF DOCKMAN AND NAVVY WAS FLOUNDERING ABOUT THE STREET."

ing he earned his night's repose by pitching Samuel Greer neck and crop into the gutter. Samuel Greer gathered himself up disconsolately, surrounded his head with the navvy's hat, and shuffled off to the "Ship and Anchor."

At the "Ship and Anchor" he found one Barker, a decayed and sodden lawyer's clerk out of work. Greer's temporary affluence enabling him to stand drinks, he was presently able, by putting artfully hypothetical cases, to extract certain legal information from Barker. Chiefly he learned that if a will or a codicil were missing, it might nevertheless be possible to obtain probate of it by satisfying the court with evidence of its contents and its genuineness. Here, at any rate, was a certain hope. He alone, apparently, of all persons, knew the contents of the codicil and the names of the witnesses; and since it was impossible to sell the codicil, now that it was gone, he might at least sell his evidence. He resolved to offer his evidence for sale to Flint at once, and take what he could get. There must be no delay, for possibly the navvy might find the paper in the hat and carry it to Flint, seeing that his name was beneficially mentioned in it, and his address given. Plainly the hat would not go back to the barber's now. If the drunken navvy had found out his mistake he probably had not the least notion where he had been nor where the hat had come from, else he would have returned it during the day, and recovered his own superior property. So Samuel Greer went at once, late as it was, and knocked up Mr. Flint.

Flint congratulated himself, feeling sure that Greer had thought better of his business and had come to give his information for anything he could get. Greer, on his part, was careful to conceal the fact that the codicil had been in his possession and had been lost. All he said was that he had seen the codicil, that its date was nine months later than that of the will, and that it benefited Jarvis Flint to the extent of some ten thousand pounds; leaving Flint to suppose, if he pleased, that Cater, the executor, had the codicil, but would probably suppress it. Indeed, this was the conclusion that Flint immediately jumped at.

And the result of the interview was this: Flint, with much grudging and reluctance, handed over as a preliminary fee the sum of one pound, the most he could be screwed up to. Then it was settled that Greer should come on the morrow and consult with Flint and his solicitor Lugg, the object of the consultation being the construction of a consistent tale and a satisfactory *soi-disant* copy of the codicil, which Greer was to swear to, if necessary, and armed with which Paul Cater might be confronted and brought to terms.

It may be wondered why, ere this, Flint had not received the genuine codicil itself, recovered by Dorrington from Greer's hat. The fact was that Dorrington, as was his wont, was playing a little game of his own. Having possessed himself of the codicil, he was now in a position to make the most from both sides, and in a far more efficient manner than the clumsy Greer. People of Jarvis Flint's sordid character are apt, with all their sordid keenness, to be wonderfully short-sighted in regard to what might seem fairly obvious to a man of honest judgment. Thus it never occurred to Flint that a man like Dorrington, willing, for a miserable wage, to apply his exceptional subtlety to the furtherance of his employer's rascally designs, would be at least as ready to swindle that master on his own account when the opportunity offered; would be, in fact, the more ready, in proportion to the stinginess wherewith his master had treated him.

Having found the codicil, Dorrington's procedure was not to hand it over forthwith to Flint. It was this: first he made a careful and exact copy of the codicil; then he procured two men of his acquaintance, men of good credit, to read over the copy, word for word, and certify it as being an exact copy of the original by way of a signed declaration written on the back of the copy. Then he was armed at all points.

He packed the copy carefully away in his pocket-book, and with the original in his coat pocket, he called at the house in Bermondsey Wall, where Paul Cater had taken up his quarters to keep guard over everything till the will should be proved. So it happened that while Samuel Greer, Jarvis Flint, and Lugg, the lawyer, were building their scheme, Dorrington was talking to Paul Cater at Cater's Wharf.

On the assurance that he had business of extreme importance, Cater took Dorrington into the room in which the old man had died. Cater was using this room as an office in which to examine and balance his uncle's books, and the corpse had been carried to a room below to await the funeral. Dorrington's clothes at this time, as I have hinted, were not distinguished by the excellence of cut and condition that was afterwards noticeable; in point of fact, he was seedy. But his assurance and his presence of mind were fully developed, and it was this very transaction that was to put the elegant appearance within his reach.

"Mr. Cater," he said, "I believe you are sole executor of the will of your uncle, Mr. Jeremiah Cater, who lived in this house." Cater assented.

"That will is one extremely favourable to yourself. In fact, by it you become not only sole executor, but practically sole legatee."

"Well?"

"I am here as a man of business and as a man of the world to give you certain information. There is a codicil to that will."

Cater started. Then he shrugged his shoulders and shook his head as though he knew better.

"There is a codicil," Dorrington went on, imperturbably, "executed in strict form, all in the handwriting of the testator, and dated nine months later than the will. That codicil benefits your cousin, Mr. Jarvis Flint, to the extent of ten thousand pounds. To put it in another way, it deprives *you* of ten thousand pounds."

Cater felt uneasy, but he did his best to maintain a contemptuous appearance. "You're rushing ahead pretty fast," he said, "talking about the terms of this codicil, as you call it. What I want to know is, where is it?"

"That," replied Dorrington, smilingly, "is a question very easily answered. The codicil is in my pocket." He tapped his coat as he spoke.

Paid Cater started again, and now he was plainly discomposed. "Very well," he said, with some bravado, "if you've got it you can show it to me, I suppose."

"Nothing easier," Dorrington responded affably. He stepped to the fireplace and took the poker. "You won't mind my holding the poker while you inspect the paper, will you?" he asked politely. "The fact is, the codicil is of such a nature that I fear a man of your sharp business instincts might be tempted to destroy it, there being no other witness present, unless you had the assurance (which I now give you) that if you as much as touch it I shall stun you with the poker. There is the codicil, which you may read with your hands behind you." He spread the paper out on the table, and Cater bent eagerly and read it, growing paler as his eye travelled down the sheet.

Before raising his eyes, however, he collected himself, and as he stood up he said, with affected contempt, "I don't care a brass farthing for this thing! It's a forgery on the face of it."

"Dear me!" answered Dorrington placidly, recovering the paper and folding it up; "that's very disappointing to hear. I must take it round to Mr. Flint and see if that is his opinion."

"No, you mustn't!" exclaimed Cater, desperately. "You say that's a genuine document. Very well. I'm still executor, and you are bound to give it to me."

"Precisely," Dorrington replied sweetly. "But in the strict interests of justice I think Mr. Flint, as the person interested, ought to have a look at it first, *in case* any accident should happen to it in your hands. Don't you?"

Cater knew he was in a corner, and his face betrayed it.

"Come," said Dorrington in a more businesslike tone. "Here is the case in a nutshell. It is my business, just as it is yours, to get as much as I can for nothing. In pursuance of that business I quietly got hold of this codicil. Nobody but yourself knows I have it, and as to *how* I got it you needn't ask, for I sha'n't tell you. Here is the document, and it is worth ten thousand pounds to either of two people, yourself and Mr. Flint, your worthy cousin. I am prepared to sell it at a very great sacrifice—to sell it dirt cheap, in fact, and I give you the privilege of first refusal, for which you ought to be grateful. One thousand pounds is the price, and that gives you a profit of nine thousand pounds when you have destroyed the codicil—a noble profit of nine hundred *per cent*, at a stroke! Come, is it a bargain?"

"What?" ejaculated Cater, astounded. "A thousand pounds?"

"One thousand pounds exactly," replied Dorrington complacently, "and a penny for the receipt stamp—if you want a receipt."

"Oh," said Cater, "you're mad. A thousand pounds! Why, it's absurd!"

"Think so?" remarked Dorrington, reaching for his hat. "Then I must see if Mr. Flint agrees with you, that's all. He's a man of business, and I never heard of his refusing a certain nine hundred *per cent, * profit yet. Good-day!"

"No, stop!" yelled the desperate Cater. "Don't go. Don't be unreasonable now—say five hundred and I'll write you a cheque."

"Won't do," answered Dorrington, shaking his head. "A thousand is the price, and not a penny less. And not by cheque, mind. I understand all moves of that sort. Notes or gold. I wonder at a smart man like yourself expecting me to be so green."

"But I haven't the money here."

"Very likely not. Where's your bank? We'll go there and get it.'

Cater, between his avarice and his fears, was at his wits' end. "Don't be so hard on me, Mr. Dorrington," he whined. "I'm not a rich man, I assure you. You'll ruin me!"

"Ruin you? What *do* you mean? I give you ten thousand pounds for one thousand and you say I ruin you! Really, it seems too ridiculously cheap. If you don't settle quickly, Mr. Cater, I shall raise my terms, I warn you!"

So it came about that Dorrington and Cater took cab together for a branch bank in Pimlico, whence Dorrington emerged with one thousand pounds in notes and gold, stowed carefully about his person, and Cater with the codicil to his uncle's will, which half an hour later he had safely burnt.

<h1 style="text-align:center">6</h1>

So much for the first half of Dorrington's operation. For the second half he made no immediate hurry. If he had been aware of Samuel Greer's movements and Lugg's little plot he might have hurried, but as it was he busied himself in setting up on a more respectable scale by help of his newly-acquired money. But he did not long delay. He had the attested copy of the codicil, which would be as good as the original if properly backed with evidence in a court of law. The astute Cater, wise in his own conceit, just as was his equally astute cousin Flint, had clean overlooked the possibility of such a trick as this. And now all Dorrington had to do was to sell the copy for one more thousand pounds to Jarvis Flint.

It was on the morning of old Jerry Cater's funeral that he made his way to Deptford to do this, and he chuckled as he reflected on the probable surprise of Flint, who doubtless wondered what had become of his sweated inquiry agent, when confronted with his offer. But when he arrived at the ship-store shop he found that Flint was out, so he resolved to call again in the evening.

At that moment Jarvis Flint, Samuel Greer, and Lugg the lawyer were at the house in Bermondsey Wall attacking Paul Cater. Greer, foreseeing probable defiance by Cater from a window, had led the party in by the wharf door and so had taken Cater by surprise. Cater was in a suit of decent black, as befitted the occasion, and he received the news of the existence of a copy of the codicil he had destroyed with equal fury and apprehension.

"What do you mean?" he demanded. "What do you mean? I'm not to be bluffed like this! You talk about a codicil—where is it? Where is it, eh?"

"My dear sir," said Lugg peaceably—he was a small, snuffy man— "we are not here to make disturbances or quarrels, or breaches of the peace; we are here on a strictly business errand, and I assure you it will be for your best interests if you listen quietly to what we have to say. Ahem! It seems that Mr. Samuel Greer here has frequently seen the codicil—"

"Greer's a rascal—a thief—a scoundrel!" cried the irate Cater, shaking his fist in the thick of Greer's squint. "He swindled me out of ten pounds! He—"

"Really, Mr. Cater," Lugg interposed, "you do no good by such outbursts, and you prevent my putting the case before you. As I was saying, Mr. Greer has frequently seen the codicil, and saw it, indeed, on the very day of the late Mr. Cater's decease. You may not have come across it, and, indeed, there may be some temporary difficulty in finding the original. But fortunately Mr. Greer took notes of the contents and of the witnesses' names, and from those notes I have been able to draw up this statement, which Mr. Greer is prepared to subscribe to, by affidavit or declaration, if by any chance you may be unable to produce the original codicil."

Cater, seeing his thousand pounds to Dorrington going for nothing, and now confronted with the fear of losing ten thousand pounds more, could scarce speak for rage. "Greer's a liar, I tell you!" he spluttered out. "A liar, a thief, a scoundrel! His word—his affidavit—his oath—anything of his—isn't worth a straw!"

"That, my dear sir," Lugg proceeded equably, "is a thing that may remain for the probate court, and possibly a jury, to decide upon. In the meantime, permit me to suggest that it will be better for all parties—cheaper in fact—if this matter be settled out of court. I think, if you will give the matter a little calm and unbiased thought, you will admit that the balance of strength is altogether with our case. Would you like to look at the statement? Its effect, you will see, is, roughly speaking, to give my client a legacy of say about ten thousand pounds in value. The witnesses are easily produced, and really, I must say, for my part, if Mr. Greer, who has nothing to gain or lose either way, is prepared to take the serious responsibility of swearing a declaration—"

"I don't believe he will!" cried Cater, catching at the straw. "I don't believe he will. Mind, Greer," he went on, "there's penal servitude for perjury!"

"Yes," Greer answered, speaking for the first time, with a squint and a chuckle, "so there is. And for stealin' an' suppressin' dockyments, I'm told. I'm ready to make that 'ere declaration."

"I don't believe he is!" Cater said, with an attempt to affect indifference. "And anyhow, I needn't take any notice of it till he does."

"Well," said Lugg accommodatingly, "there need be no difficulty or delay about that. The declaration's all written out, and I'm a commissioner to administer oaths. I think that's a Bible I see on the shelf there, isn't it?" He stepped across to where the old Bible had lain since Greer flung it there, just before Jerry Cater's death. He took the book down and opened it at the title-page. "Yes," he said, "a Bible; and now—why—what? what?"

Mr. Lugg stood suddenly still and stared at the fly-leaf. Then he said quietly, "Let me see, it was on Monday last that Mr. Cater died, was it not?"

"Yes."

"Late in the afternoon?"

"Yes."

"Then, gentlemen, you must please prepare yourselves for a surprise. Mr. Cater evidently made another will, revoking all previous wills and codicils, on the very day of his death. And here it is!" He extended the Bible before him, and it was plain to see that the fly-leaf was covered with the weak, straggling handwriting of old Jerry Cater—a little weaker and a little more straggling than that in the other will, but unmistakably his.

Flint stared, perplexed and bewildered, Greer scratched his head and squinted blankly at the lawyer. Paul Cater passed his hand across his forehead and seized a tuft of hair over one temple as though he would pull it out. The only book in the house that he had not opened or looked at during his stay was the Bible.

"The thing is very short," Lugg went on, inclining the writing to the light. "'*This is the last will and testament of me, Jeremiah Cater, of Cater's Wharf. I give and bequeath the whole of the estate and property of which I may die possessed, whether real or personal, entirely and absolutely to—to—*' what is the name? Oh yes—'*to Henry Sinclair, my clerk—*'"

"What?" yelled Cater and Flint in chorus, each rising and clutching at the Bible. "Not Sinclair! No! Let me see!"

"I think, gentlemen," said the solicitor, putting their hands aside, "that you will get the information quickest by listening while I read.

'—to Henry Sinclair, my clerk. And I appoint the said Henry Sinclair my sole executor. And I wish it to be known that I do this, not only by way of reward to an honest servant, and to recompense him for his loss in loan transactions with me, but also to mark my sense of the neglect of my two nephews. And I revoke all former wills and codicils.'

Then follows date and signature and the signatures of witnesses— both apparently men of imperfect education."

"But you're mad—it's impossible!" exclaimed Cater, the first to find his tongue. "He *couldn't* have made a will then—he was too weak. Greer knows he couldn't."

Greer, who understood better than anybody else present the allusion in the will to the nephews' neglect, coughed dubiously, and said, "Well, he did get up while I was out. An' when I got back he had the Bible beside him, an' he seemed pretty well knocked up with something. An' the winder was wide open—I expect he opened it to holler out as well as he could to some chaps on the wharf or somewhere to come up by the wharf door and do the witnessing. An' now I think of it I expect he sent me out a-purpose in case—well, in case if I knowed I might get up to summat with the will. He told me not to hurry. An' I expect he about used himself up with the writin' an' the hollerin' an' the cold air an' what not."

Cater and Flint, greatly abashed, exchanged a rapid glance. Then Cater, with a preliminary cough, said hesitatingly, "Well now, Mr. Lugg, let us consider this. It seems quite evident to me—and no doubt it will to you, as my cousin's solicitor—it seems quite evident to me that my poor uncle could not have been in a sound state of mind when he made this very ridiculous will. Quite apart from all questions of genuineness, I've no doubt that a court would set it aside. And in view of that it would be very cruel to allow this poor man Sinclair to suppose himself to be entitled to a great deal of money, only to find himself disappointed and ruined after all. You'll agree with that, I'm sure. So I think it will be best for all parties if we keep this thing to ourselves, and just tear out that fly-leaf and burn it, to save trouble. And on my part I shall be glad to admit the copy of the codicil you have produced, and no doubt my cousin and I will be prepared to pay you a fee which will compensate you for any loss of business in actions—eh?"

Mr. Lugg was tempted, but he was no fool. Here was Samuel Greer at his elbow knowing everything, and without a doubt, no matter how well bribed, always ready to make more money by betraying the arrangement to Sinclair. And that would mean inevitable ruin to Lugg himself, and probably a dose of gaol. So he shook his head virtuously and said, "I couldn't think of anything of the sort, Mr. Cater, not for an instant. I am a solicitor, and I have my strict duties. It is my duty immediately to place this will in the hands of Mr. Henry Sinclair, as sole executor. I wish you a good-day, gentlemen."

And so it was that old Jerry Cater's money came at last to Sinclair. And the result was a joyful one, not only for Sinclair and his wife, but also for a number of poor debtors whose "paper" was part of the